Legend of the Pan

- BOOK ONE OF SEVEN -

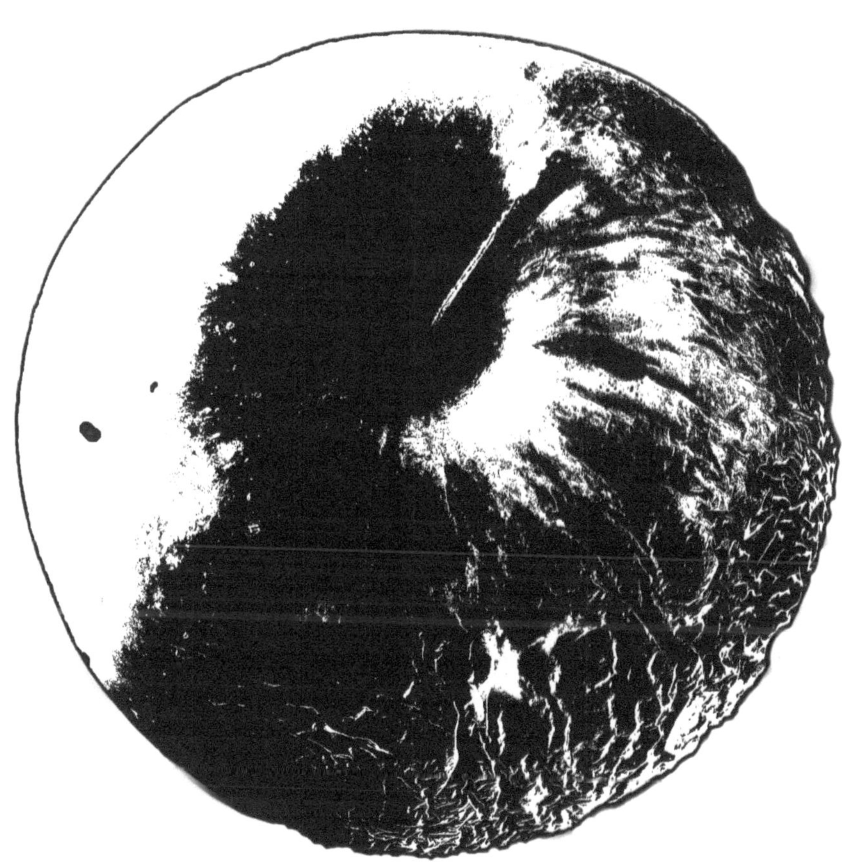

Advent

CHRISTIAN MICHAEL

ADVENT

Legend of the Pan :: Book One
First Edition
By Christian Michael

Legend of the Pan - www.legendofthepan.com
Scroll Media Company - www.scrollmedia.com

Edited by Ellen Sallas, The Author's Mentor LLC
www.TheAuthorsMentor.com

Cover and layout by Christian Michael

ISBN-13: 978-1-7370532-6-2 (Scroll Media)

Printed in the United States of America

Attention Reader

THIS BOOK SERIES IS NOT FOR CHILDREN

The seven-book "Legend of the Pan" series features a variety of adult situations unsuitable for younger readers. This is an adult version of J.M. Barrie's Peter Pan.

THIS SERIES IS ONE CONTINUOUS EPIC

"Legend of the Pan" is one saga into three parts:
Prequel: Advent (1)
Main: Peter (2) to Hook (6)
Sequel: Immortal (7)

Readers can start with Advent or Peter, but should read Advent prior to Tiger Lily.

DO NOT EXPECT REFRESHERS

As an avid long-form fiction reader, I dislike constant plot refreshers at the beginning of every sequel. You will get no more than the barest—if any—in mine.

Thank you and enjoy the journey,

CHRISTIAN MICHAEL

Dedication

This series is dedicated to:

Orson Scott Card
Who taught and inspired me with Ender Wiggin.
Who cemented that children can do great things.
Because the world isn't changed by your age,
Only your mind and mettle.

This book is dedicated to:

Tom Kimball, chief master sergeant and mentor,
Who encouraged me to dive in when I was scared,
A brother in arms and father in faith,
Who sees in me before I see in myself

Acknowledgements

To my pre-readers Hannah and Joshua F., Garrett and Shannon R., Jen and Matt T., Sachiko B., Kerry W., Jen and Matt T., Richard D., Richard M., Ben S., Lori DP, and Evie M. thanks for being my litmus! To Rachel M. and (the late) Bradley M. who have heard this story more times than any human should have to. And to Karen B., for your amazing author photos at The Mill in Greenville, S.C.

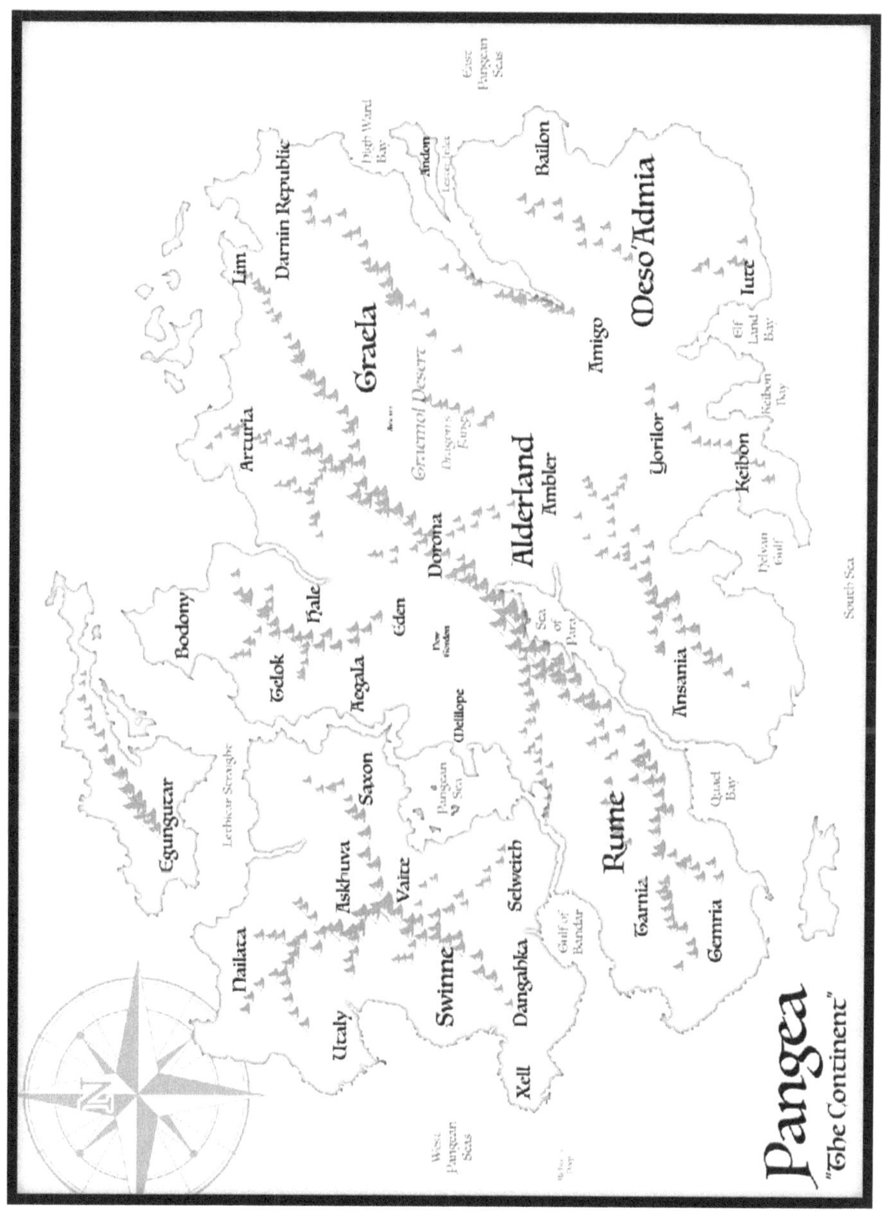
Pangea
"The Continent"
East Pangean Seas
Bailon
Meso'Admia
Darnin Republic
Lim
Graela
Amigo
Iuze
Elf Land Bay
Keibon Bay
Yorilor
Keibon
Alderland
Ambler
Arcturia
Dorona
South Sea
Bodony
Hale
Eden
Ansania
Telok
Aegala
Welllope
Pangean Sea
Saxon
Quad Bay
Egungutar
Askhuva
Vaite
Rume
Selweith
Tarnia
Gemria
Nailata
Swinne
Dangahka
Gulf of Bandar
Utaly
Xell
West Pangean Seas

N
Tri
Horn
Tootles's
Tree
Shadow
City
Pan's
Peak
La'Du
Lira Al'Cular
West Bay
Marooner's
Rock
Swamp
Whirl
pool
Desert
Fjords
never
Never
Land!!!
Grassland
Snowcap
Village
Volcano
Misty
Forest
Sandbar
Algueda
Alterbridge to EARTH
1 mi
SCALE

Contents

Prologue

The inky raven coursed on icy winds crashing over the high snowy peak. The midnight bird crossed the apex and dove along the mountain's jagged northern face before weaving over the western saddle to the volcano billowing black with thick, acrid smoke. He banked across a broad empty waste to a sandy desert broiling in heat.

Northward, the raven crossed a winding river that bisected the small island. He circled an overgrown maze of ruins before climbing a spine of barren ridges westward, north of the island's swamp, to the base of a high, conical peak. Where the ridges ended at the foot of its towering eastern cliffs, the raven landed before a high, mud-caked wall of stone. Cocking his head, the raven cawed.

Moments later, the world shook and falling sheets of mud revealed a carving of a woman whose hair covered her breasts, her legs tucked beneath her, and her arms cradled a pregnant belly. She split in two as great stone doors slid open to reveal a passage. The raven leapt through with a flutter of its inky wings into a narrow hallway, at the end of which rose a tall chamber speared with dusty light from gaps in the rock above. Walls on either side leaned inward to form an A-frame from an outward-leaning base. At the far end of the graduated chamber rose a narrow wall drenched in vinery, upon which rested a larger version of the same carving upon its entry door.

Here, the Mother presided in silence over her cathedral.

Short of where the light rebounded from the stone floor, the raven landed with a few hops and uttered a long, grating caw.

After its echoes danced throughout the chamber and faded, a single point of light appeared in the heart of the room and expanded into the shape of a tall humanoid. Smoky ambience wreathed the figure until his skin opaqued and luminescent robes flowed into place. The light faded over his earthy brown skin, Indigo hair and beard and crystal blue eyes.

He descended to the stone floor of the chamber and, upon touching down, drew air into his lungs. With his toes resting on the sandy surface, he took in the room like an old friend.

"Aiuena," cawed the raven.

Auiena knelt and bowed. "You summoned me."

"It's time for the breaking," said the raven. "Call your fellow high archons. Advent has come."

"And the herald?"

"I anointed him eons ago. He will be ready when the time is nigh."

Auiena rose. "By your will."

The raven leapt into the air and returned to the shadow of the passage. "Indeed."

Auiena gazed again upon the room before touching his heart. Three more beings materialized of varying color and size; voluptuous Suthene of blue skin and black hair, and willowy Nashuan of bronze and blonde, and stocky Helstoy with emerald and ginger. "The exodus has come."

"Finally?" asked Nashuan. "After so long?"

"Alert the races," said Auiena. "Give prophecy to the children, visions to the young, and dreams to the old."

Suthene tugged at the veil draped across her face and looked after the raven. "Praise the Self."

"To the dwarves and the utto-beings, Helstoy," said Auiena.

Helstoy bowed.

"Nashuan," Auiena turned. "To the beastials, the high sentients and partials."

"Honored and eager," said Nashuan with a smile.

"I go to the ancients, the eon-spanners and the magic breathers," said Auiena.

A smile split Suthene's thick-lipped mouth as her eyes gleamed with expectation.

"And you," Auiena turned.

"The humans, the elves and…the vacants," she said as she grinned. "I get to herald him? Truly?"

"Truly," said Auiena.

She grinned and clutched Nashuan's hands.

"Follow the wind," said Auiena. "It is time for change."

"Here we go, general," saluted Nashuan.

Auiena shared a look with his companions before they dissolved into the air and followed the raven through the hall as swirls of glowing dust.

"Yes," Auiena whispered to the great carving of the Mother. "The day of pan has come."

* * *

Misty smoke rolled over the razed midnight terrain. Trees that had burned for two days now stood as haunting gnarled columns of an ancient hellish arcade. Pale moonlight filled the fray and marbled the gray scorched soil. Crows aloft scanned for the now-and-soon-dead in a sky dense with stars visible between wafting clouds of moisture and smoke.

Flashes of colored light fired between long columns of trees before crashing into trunks with concussive explosions. Six robed men and women in a haphazard circle, accompanied by a handful of terrified bleeding soldiers, raced across dark terrain while casting spells and bolts of power into the darkness. Snarling lupine creatures rushed in with unbridled ferocity, jaws open and spittle flying as they lunged inward at the haggard few.

Lycans in their dozens exploded at their violent magic. Bolts of lightning danced between arbors and animals before disintegrating flesh in brilliant blue light. Creatures raced and crashed among cracking dead trees. Fiery bolts of energy pierced and set aflame any who couldn't dodge them. Shards of ice shredded flesh or infected muscle until the beasts crumpled in their loping gaits. Warbling distortions of air crushed them into the ground, brittle trees, or against other beasts until blood burst from over-pressured bodies.

The legions came.

"This way!" cried a short, stocky wizard as he swung his staff. An eruption of light cast a half dozen lycans backward into those racing up behind them and slowed their advance. When the wizard paused at the foot of a haggard tree, the light of his staff revealed a wooden sign. From there, he led them bloody and exhausted inch-by-inch up a rocky incline.

When one woman tripped, a tall, black-skinned wizard stepped over her and fought off the beasts until she clamored to her feet while a frantic young teenager cast spells at anything that moved outside their circle.

"Halt!" cried the leader.

The group stopped at the precipice of a low cliff overlooking a scorched plain, across which rose a white city whose thick, high walls glowed in the evening light. Raising his staff until its upper tip burned brilliant, the wizard rammed it into the ground. A bubble shield expanded from its base, around the group of mages, and snapped into place.

Bestial hordes rushed the shield's outer edge in such mass that those nearest were crushed and scored against its burning event horizon.

The circle of mages knelt or collapsed with exhaustion.

"Bollocks," snarled the lead as the creatures rushed the city. "There's…no way to stop them."

"Great Self," moaned one of the women. "Tuthomere."

A mile distant, a hundred thousand screams erupted from the city.

"The beasts are inside," panted Orzo as he wiped sweat from his midnight skin.

From horizon to horizon, lycans covered the terrain like an insect horde, scaled Tuthomere's high white walls and poured into the burning city.

"We're too late."

Laughter erupted behind them from a single lycan standing at the shield's edge. A field of panting, hungry monsters encircled their bubble. Their haunting yellow eyes shimmered in the shield's ambience. "I told you that before, Elverbane."

Wizard Setherick Elverbane climbed to his feet and trudged past his staff to the tall lycan, signaled by the bejeweled chain around its neck. "Ya fuckin' bastard. CALL 'EM OFF!"

"Even I can't restrain the super pack," sneered the lycan with an inhuman smile. "Not that I would, even if I could."

"This isn't right, Ithnar!" Elverbane barked.

"It's justice," Ithnar clapped his jaws. "Which we are due for centuries of slavery and culling."

"Revisiting crimes of the guilty upon the innocent isn't justice," growled Elverbane. "It's just fuel for the next crime."

"We are due our blood!" Ithnar cried.

"Y'ur spillin' the very blood you aim ta save!" cried Elverbane with his natural brogue. "Fury blinds you to the real way to get whut ya want, ya feeble-minded cunt."

"High minded ideals from a *traitor*!" Ithnar howled with derision, echoed by ten thousand lycans in full-fugue.

"I've tried reasonin' with ya," said Elverbane. "I've tried fightin' ya directly. Ya dunnae call off those fuckin' wolves and I will break the super pack. Right here and now."

Ithnar laughed. "With what? Measly bolts of fire and lightning? Kill me. Kill the rest of my brethren. You don't even scratch the super pack."

"I will *end* them," said the wizard.

"Boast all you like," Ithnar sneered.

"Y'ur a lightblood, right?" asked Elverbane as he raised an upturned palm.

Ithnar's brow flickered.

Tiny flecks of light appeared and drew an intricate sphere above the wizard's hand.

"You know that well enough, *Elverbane*," Ithnar said. "What are you doing?"

"You have one last chance," Elverbane said. "Or else I end everything."

"What is it? You've no more power than me—"

"That's where you're wrong." Elverbane's underlit face intensified with the glow of his spell. "The pack doesn't empower you, Ithnar, it only limits. Only by stepping away from the pack could you learn that the individual can grow far stronger without the group than with it. Tamed power is greater than wild violence."

The mages stood as the light of his construct expanded and complicated.

"The lycan blood feuds aren't the only thing to survive since the Courte Empire," said Elverbane.

Realization dawned upon Ithnar. "No."

"Call em off," said Elverbane. "Last chance."

"Bluff," said Ithnar. "You'd never do that to your own people."

"What is he building?" muttered the teenage wizard.

"It's amazing the skills y'learn from variant disciplines," said Elverbane. Tiny lines of light above his palm formed three inter-rotating bars as secondary spheres of complexity formed a clockwork of violent magic.

Ithnar's hesitation signaled caution in nearby hordes.

"Mining hardened rock required ever more complex tactics to break and fracture increasingly dense subterrain," said Elverbane while fear filled Ithnar. "When I compared the discovery with ancient records, I made connections."

"But…the humans." Ithnar protested. "You wouldn't."

"You mean, leave'em to die under the claws and capers of your breth'ren?" muttered Elverbane. "You mean that kind of mercy?"

He turned toward the city.

"You will see what your mindless fury will bring the race," said Elverbane as he marched to the far side of the bubble nearest the drop-off. Flame erupted from within the city as bronze-lined smoke billowed into the starry night. "Self-control is the only path to peace, you stupid frothing animal."

The young mage approached Elverbane. "You can't! It's forbidden! And—those people!" When magic appeared in his hands, as if to stop

Elverbane, the other mages snatched up the boy with invisible ropes and a gag of air. Mages weary from weeks of desperate battle held no pity for the recent arrival or his pristine civility.

"Take defense," said Elverbane. The construct in his hands brightened with painful intensity.

Orzo took a grip of the teenage wizard and slapped his forehead with a flash of magic. The boy crumpled to the ground unconscious.

Unable to suffer the echoing screams any longer, Elverbane pressed the lightseed with the power necessary to fuel its violence. The growing brilliance of the spell became a handheld sun shining across the southern battlefield. Soon thousands of lycans turned in surprise that morphed into fury. Hordes raced toward him.

"No!" Ithnar cried and his ears pointed forward. The pack surged against the bubble shield with violent desperation. "You can't!"

"I will," said Elverbane, whose eyes glowed in the radiant construct. His voice dropped for his companions. "When I cast, turn away from the city, no matter what."

"Got it," the group muttered as they reinforced the weakening shield. Desperate waves of lycans crushed its outer edge. Spears of light danced between the creatures as Elverbane's spell became so bright even he had to look away. A blood frenzy erupted as those behind crushed those afore, billowing the scent of their dying brethren into the air.

"SETH!" Orzo roared as the shields fluttered, ready to collapse.

Elverbane squatted, shoved his hands into the construct, finalized the energetic connections, and cast the spell into the starry sky in a dwindling streak of light. As it passed through the shield, the bubble popped with a soft concussion that rebuffed the lycan wave enough to halt it. The lightseed became a tiny star among the countless blaze twinkling in the black.

The world fell quiet as Ithnar and the lycans scrambled to their feet and waited in sudden fear. Terrified, panting mages stood vulnerable, ready to fight the hesitant lycans. When silence prevailed, Ithnar smiled. His growing laughter spread across the horde.

"Good try, wizard," Ithnar snarled and licked his chops. "There is no stopping the super pack." When he leaned forward to advance, he and countless lycans locked onto a single streak of light falling from the sky like a tiny meteor that kissed the top of Tuthomere's western wall.

Just before it landed, Elverbane turned from the city. "Now."

The mages spun away before the tiny point exploded across the sky with an eerie quiet. Creatures, trees and scree filled the air. Backlit as he was, Elverbane stood in silhouette to the devastating light spreading across the horizon before he leapt to the ground.

Facing the city, Ithnar and the pack were caught in its scorching brilliance. They shielded themselves as the pressure wave crashed over the cliff and cast them from their feet. The endless horde roared in agony. Nocturnal eyes burned blind that weren't first struck by its concussive power.

Fury ravaged the world and soon faded before Elverbane regained his wits. He rolled over and froze at the sight of the fiery column filling the sky. As his companions struggled to maintain their consciousness, he managed to raise his hand and a shield. Heavy stones once founding the city's walls climbed the sky, fell like volcanic projectiles and exploded a few paces above their heads. Mages and their soldiers cowered until they realized they were safe beneath Elverbane's shield.

When the initial fall subsided and the shield petered out, Elverbane climbed to quivering feet and stumbled again to the precipice.

A mile-wide crater glowed with molten soil and thousands of burning trees as far as they could see. Light spreading across the skies revealed successive layers of the horde caught in the greater blast zone. The immediate area around the column of fire was clear of anything at all—either blasted away or disintegrated. Those further out lay dead and burning. Beyond, hundreds of acres revealed writhing, squirming masses of creatures howling in agony. Their animalistic screams were echoed by the equally struck city populace.

Horror cut through Elverbane.

Mages climbed to their feet and lensed air to magnify their view across the scorched plane. Everywhere, howling half-man creatures lay melted, writhing and twitching. Terrific screams echoed from the city by men, women and children. All voices struggled against the terrible thundering wind whipping over the terrain before the initial cries fell still in shock. Legions of surviving lycans, now blind, wandered in howling terror.

"Bloody hell," moaned Orzo.

Half of Tuthomere was gone, now replaced by the crater. What remained of the city's thick walls and stone towers rained from the sky in house-sized boulders across horde, field, and forest; or lay shattered like fallen porcelain and crumbled with soft thunder after the shockwave dislodged its multi-millennial foundations.

Elverbane killed a quarter of a million living beings in seconds. "Great Self. What have I done?"

Under the hellish light of the mushroom cloud climbing into the sky, conscious remnants of the vicious hordes fled in all directions, unable to see or smell their way home.

Elverbane spotted a lone figure between him and the horde—a petite woman who fearlessly scanned the mushroom cloud. Her hair glowed as bright as the fire climbing the sky, revealing its bone-white purity. He thought he might know her by description, but when he blinked, she was gone.

"You did what you had to do, my friend," said Orzo as he stepped closer and soaked in the aftermath. "The rest will be hunted. We have broken the super pack. We have a chance to end this."

"At what cost, Orzo?" Elverbane asked and scanned the decimated city for signs of survivors, difficult at this distance in the howling winds.

"A heavy one," muttered Orzo as the glowing orange sky bathed the broken city in its light. "But what other choice did we have?"

"What do we do now?" whispered a witch behind Orzo.

"Recover the survivors," Elverbane said. "Slaughter the untamed. Then ahm going ho—" His throat caught. "Back to New Gordon, and the rest of this selfdamn war can go straight to fuckin'ell."

1

The Park

Her silver irises tracked Haephan from halfway across the park. He wouldn't have seen her if he hadn't been scanning for Crimson Guardians. Her red caramel skin, bone-white hair and tan leather outfit contrasted the chocolate skin and pastel dresses of the fine ladies in their bright colors and bronze-suited men wandering New Gordon's grandest city park in the mid-afternoon sunshine. When their gazes met, she didn't recoil from his dark, yellow-coffee skin, wide head and diminutive size like other girls.

Haephan shrank behind the tree. Was she a snitch for the Crimson Guard? Was she new competition? She didn't seem to know how to melt into a crowd. The way her remarkable eyes followed him, he worried he wasn't doing it so well, himself.

Three Crimson Guardians—teenage boys monitoring the crowds for thieves, scammers, and pickpockets—passed between them, one of whom stared at the white-haired girl. When her focus flicked to the smitten boy, Haephan slipped along the trees.

While the park opened to the left at the edge of the copse, Haephan fired across the grass to flank the nearest group of ladies making their daily circuit. Popular among the wealthy, Beltrand Park was a place of gathering, society, business, and politics.

Before the women noticed him, he switched to another ladies group. He walked among men and their teenage sons out on business before backtracking to avoid guardians. Always, he moved outside where people searched.

Men and women cried their wares or causes from atop a variety of stone and wooden boxes and platforms scattered across the park. At its heart, a massive crowd gathered around its largest and finest marble stage occupied by a group of high wizards, witches, and warlocks in formal city uniforms. A ring of martial mages repelled the crowd to form a perimeter while, at the group's fore, a tall, graying administrator raised his hands.

"Everything is being done to keep the packs split." Ilrich Wythe's soft words boomed over more than a thousand attendees. "His Majesty King Myogan has summoned Battle Czars from five Pangean academies to help coordinate between New Gordon and other city states across South Edenia and central Pangea. Even Alderland has donated forces to rein in the rebellious packs."

"We were assured they were broken in Tuthomere!" cried one well-dressed woman with midnight skin and orange sherbet robes in the crowd flanked by attendants. "Tell us, City Administrator...was High Wizard Elverbane not the hero you and magekind made him out to be?"

Before she could finish, hundreds of boos erupted.

Standing next to Wythe, a wizard with windswept hair winged in gray and a trimmed beard raised a hand to quiet the crowd. "Forty years ago, High Wizard Elverbane did more than anyone could have asked of him," said Ornith Dufrain. "Without him, New Gordon would be a broken field and us the meal on a lycan's plate. Despite our best efforts, however, the packs have returned."

Cries and protests climbed from the crowds.

"Just blow 'em up, again!" cried one man, cheered on by others.

Ignoring the exchange, Haephan melted into a crowd. Brushes and gentle nudges with his hands went ignored by adults before their small valuables slipped into his pockets.

"And if the super pack reforms!?" barked a grizzled older veteran. The crowd quieted. "What then? We going to split the atom again? Some of us remember what happened to the survivors. Some of us remember well!"

More protests rose from the group, cheering on the wariness of using 'world enders' again.

Haephan kept his picks small as, unlike adult thieves, larger items stood out on his small frame. After trying to pick an older man, he retreated when the man instinctively padded his pocket. Feeling pressed, Haephan stepped from the crowd.

Encircling him, five Crimson Guardians quietly punched hands.

"Finally," said a boy at the center who boasted the same midnight hair and chalky burnt sienna skin as Haephan, though stood a few inches taller. A knotted rope looped his shoulder and armpit to indicate his status as a Red Captain.

"Dolphus," Haephan sneered.

"I've spent a lot of time looking for— hey!" Dolphus began to say when Haephan dove into the crowd. Dolphus and his buddy Nurmon raced after him while the others fanned out. No other words were spoken or shouts uttered. Crimson Guardians were not to disturb the adults any more than thieves.

Haephan flowed through to avoid Dolphus before reaching the far edge. When one of the guardians passed by, he sprinted across the grass. The guardian noticed too late, but his soft whistle drew the other teenagers in swift pursuit.

Dolphus gave quick chase as Haephan skirted groups of adults the guardians were wary to disturb, but his caution gave precious advantage to Haephan.

Nurmon sprinted with long legs and groped for Haephan but found the boy could turn on his toe. Nurmon looped around to regain speed while the others spread out to flank and slid his feet into Haephan's path.

Haephan spilled headlong over the ground near one of the far edges of the park leading into the warehouse district. He rolled to his feet as the day's pickings flew across the grass while his hands lifted to defend himself.

Nurmon again attempted to sweep out Haephan's feet, but the small boy was a slippery target.

Other guardians fared no better as Haephan twisted and ducked from their best attempts to nab him. When Dolphus managed to finger the necklace flying from Haephan's shirt and yank it free, Haephan panicked.

"Hey!" Haephan cried. He rushed Dolphus, who snapped his fist and cracked Haephan's nose. Haephan dropped to the grass as blood gushed forth.

Moving in, Nurmon swept a hearty kick in Haephan's stomach.

"Red Captain!" barked an adult constable standing near one of white crossed arches lining the edge of the park.

Snapping to attention with a sharp salute, Dolphus directed the others to haul Haephan and his lost pickings out of the park, across the broadway rattling with carriages and wagons, and into a narrow, crate-packed alley.

Haephan twisted out of their grip and disappeared through a tiny gap between stacks of crates.

"Hey!" Dolphus snatched in vain in the tiny gap of crates too heavy to cast aside.

"Gimme back my ring!" Haephan barked at Dolphus while the other guardians searched for a way inside.

Dolphus laughed. "*Your* ring, you fuckin' little picker? I don't care who you think you are, you're still just a thief."

"It's personal!" Haephan said. "It was mine! I saw you grab my picks!"

"You think I wanna keep your pathetic pickings?" asked Dolphus. "Why should I care about your personal shit when all you do is take others' personal shit?" Dolphus shook his head at the awkward statement. "Get a job, you fuckin' rainie."

"Easy for you to say, softwipe!" Haephan said.

"You worthless little bastard," Dolphus snarled at the insult.

Fresh blood drooled from Haephan's smashed nose. "I gotta eat somehow."

Crates rattled as the guardian on Haephan's left found a way to leverage them enough to wiggle along the wall behind him.

"A *third* son, you little shit," Dolphus spat as they worked to flush Haephan out. "You think I'd be in the Crimson Guard if my father was grooming me for his business?"

While Dolphus snarled, Haephan glanced in each direction at the teens, gathered blood drooling from his nose into his mouth and spewed it as far as he could through the narrow gap.

"Fuck!" Dolphus retreated as Nurmon got within arm's reach of Haephan, who wiggled through the gap, planted a kick between Dolphus's legs, and bolted back toward the park. A guardian blocked his path, flanked by another. Clutching his crotch, Dolphus drew his cudgel.

Cornered, Haephan feinted returning to his hiding place but changed directions and kicked at Dolphus's knee. Though he planted his foot well, his short leg did little more than push it back a bit, and stumbled into Dolphus's kill zone.

Fury doubling, the Red Captain swung his weapon.

Haephan spun and rammed his elbow at Dolphus's kidney. He knew he missed when Dolphus took the hit and rebounded with the cudgel across the back of Haephan's head.

Haephan staggered.

Dolphus grabbed him by the scruff of his neck and hauled him down toward his rising knee. Haephan twisted out of the way but couldn't escape Nurmon's well-timed elbow to his face.

Haephan crashed into the side of the unmoving crates. When his crown rang upon the cobblestones, he balled up and cradled his head.

Dolphus reared his foot and kicked Haephan several times in his gut and knees. Had Haephan any food in his stomach, it would have come out.

"Hey!" a man's voice rang out in the narrow alley. "Get away from my crates!"

The guardians stiffened.

"Sorry, sir!" Nurmon locked up.

Glaring, Dolphus spat on Haephan. "Accuse me of being like you, you fuckin' picker." He kicked him again.

"Cap," Nurmon hissed.

His chest heaving, Dolphus squatted, gripped Haephan's hair in his oversized leather gauntlets and growled, "Next time, I'll do what the sweethearts shoulda done and put you in the Vit', myself." He straightened and kicked him again. He pointed his cudgel at someone out of sight. "Oy, you. Get your bitch and go back to the shit hole you dogs crawled out of."

Haephan struggled to think or wonder whom he was talking about until the face of a tiny, almond-skinned boy appeared over him and tugged at his clothes.

"C'mon," said Tilly. "We gotta go!"

Dolphus sneered. "Hurry up, cumstain."

"Shit you!" Tilly shouted.

The teens cackled and mocked his awkward profanity.

"C'mon, Haeph,'" said Tilly. "Before they throw you in the canal."

His vision swimming, Haephan sobbed as the tiny boy strained to help him stagger away.

"I said be off!" the man's voice barked again.

"Leaving now, sir!" Nurmon nearly bowed at the man while the others shuffled back.

"C'mon," Dolphus led the boys away. His voice faded in the soft rain. "Got an appointment over at Goram's."

"Why did'n you h'lp?" asked Haephan as blood drooled down his face.

"Help you? Are you crazy?" Tilly asked. "They're twice my size!"

"Soo?" said Haephan. "Jus' a bunch'o crimsies."

"Dolphus is a cap'n!" Tilly said and stumbled with him down the alley past the glaring man, who double took when he spotted the blood on Haephan's dark skin.

"Just another crimsie," Haephan moaned.

"You alright?" asked the man.

"Shure," Haephan spat blood upon the street.

Turning, they limped away.

"Damn, Haeph," Tilly's scrawny frame strained under his larger friend. "I thought you'd never get caught. You never have been, before. What happened?"

"Yeah, well…" Haephan grimaced. "I…got distracted."

"By what!? I've seen you disappear in the middle of a street."

Haephan recalled the penetrating gaze of the girl with bone-white hair. "Just…something stupid, I guess. They got my ring."

Navigating the narrow alleys to avoid main byways, they headed southwest, away from the affluent districts, through other policed districts, and down devolving streets into Rainhold.

"Wait," said Haephan as he used a small puddle to clear his eyes. He sucked in water, swished and spat out blood.

"I thought for sure Lurli would brain you on the road." Tilly shivered in thin shorts and a ragged shirt too large for his small frame. "Couldn't we have done this when it was drier? And warmer!?"

Haephan climbed to his feet and swayed. "Some things, you can't wait on."

"You're nuts," Tilly took as much of Haephan's weight as he could along the shortest road into Rainhold, which sank to the lowest of its four broad steppes descending to a point where the Vitner and Estamar Canals intersected. Ratty docks jutted out along the Vitner for canal traffic before the water either split southeast into the Estamar or continued southwest and became a river. The Estamar headed southeast as the only major waterway in Pangea to flow across the equator, cut through the Zulta'Mans and empty in the Sea of Para, which eventually led to the south seas.

Northward along the Vitner shore, Haephan strained to make out the Station—a building complex—through the rainy mist while Tilly supported him up the first long switchback climbing to the top terrace. A river of stagnant mud now sat where once stretched pavement of intricate stonework.

At the top, tents and booths covered most of the available space. Vagrants, destitute, and a few hardy vendors managed to survive the awful conditions.

The boys crossed the broad steppe, descended stairs to the next terrace and paused next to the ancient dwarf-carved stone foundations. Haephan knelt in a shallow pool of icy water at its base and leaned in so the runoff would wash his injuries and cool his head.

Once a beautiful ridge carved up for vacation homes called Marina Heights, Rainhold boasted a single home from its wealthier days which now housed the district's richest resident and all his sweethearts busy in beds around the clock. When the climate shifted two hundred years prior, the district disintegrated under the constant runoff from higher in the city. Houses without better foundations crumbled, and those with adequate bases were left vacant as resident quality changed.

Water pooled on each of Rainhold's four steppes and formed four large, shallow and uneven crescent lakes that froze in winter and stagnated in summer.

In this year's temporary number of shanties, residents took every available floorboard above ground to stay dry. Dwarvan drainage had never anticipated the change in rainfall and the city could not afford to hire them for extensive modifications.

"Alright, let's go," Haephan said and stood before the cold water chilled him. Together, they navigated through narrow, well-known alleys for their own safety.

"You said a ring? What kinda ring?" Tilly's bare feet squished in the icy mud.

"It's the only thing I have from my dad," Haephan said. "I think. That's what Querie said. She said my dad left it behind and my mom always kept it."

"Why'd she do that?"

"Maybe she liked it," said Haephan. "Clients leave things behind all the time, says Querie."

"Querie's nice," said Tilly. "At least she still talks to you. My sweet kicked me out and said fug'off."

"Hey." Haephan nudged him with his elbow. "You got me."

"Thanks, Haeph," said Tilly.

Scanning the misty squalor, Haephan sighed. "I'm gettin' outta here, Tilly."

"Do you think you'll make it? To the ocean?"

"One day."

"I still don't get why you wanna go there. What's there ain't here?"

"Anything's better'n here, Till," Haephan said. "Anything."

"But why the ocean?"

"Dunno," said Haephan. "Just always wanted to go. Maybe have a shanty of my own on the edge. Kinda like my spot now."

"It's only water."

Haephan pondered such endlessness. "I-I'm…I dunno. I wanna go."

"I'll probably be here," Tilly looked about. "I mean, what else is there? I'll be lucky to make it to be a man. Maybe somebody will even bury me like those folks with the stones."

"Stones?"

"Yeah," said Tilly as he motioned to the ground as if able to see it. "The dead people with the stones with the letters."

"You mean gravestones?"

"Yeah?" asked Tilly. "I mean, it meant they was somebody, right? To have a stone that doesn't wash away like wood or mud from the canal. It says, 'I was here.' Like, people would want to think about you after you die. It's different from everything here, because it's always changing. That'd be…great."

"In Rainhold?"

"Anywhere," Tilly motioned with his arm.

"You're weird," Haephan said. "Ain't time to die. And if I can get out of here, I'll find a way to get you out, too."

"Really, Haeph?" asked Tilly.

"If I can, I promise you I will," Haephan grunted.

Tilly's hideaway came into view—a tiny, elevated window in a rickety shack barely big enough for himself above a larger room occupied by someone else.

Haephan turned to lift him. "C'mon."

"What're you gonna do now?" Tilly asked.

"I'm going back for my ring."

"What? You're really going to the Station?"

"Not yet," Haephan said. "Dolphus is going to visit a sweetheart. I'll pick his clothes."

"While he's bangin'!?" Tilly asked.

Haephan didn't smirk as he might have. Pain blossomed afresh in his head. "I'm getting my ring back."

"What's wrong?" Tilly asked.

"Sometimes I wish I could burn that place down."

"Goram's House? Why?"

"My mom died there, says Querie," said Haephan. "Like most of the others. It's just…I don't know. But I'd burn it down, with all them inside it."

"Even the sweethearts?" Tilly gasped.

"Of course not!" said Haephan. "I meant all the clients. And Goram and his men."

"Oh," Tilly said.

"C'mon. I ain't got much time." Squatting with laced fingers, Haephan hefted his friend up and through. Tilly pulled the curtain aside to help Haephan up, but the boy disappeared.

"Haeph'!" Tilly yelled and scanned the huts. Pursing his lips, he let the curtain fall before he muttered, "How do you do that?"

Already around the corner and down the alley, Haephan scowled as he veered toward Goram's House, plotting how to reclaim the only thing that had ever mattered to him.

2

Nether

Truly, the first in a millennium? chimed the fairy as she circled several times above a tiny infant elf. She set down upon the pillow next to the child and pulled back her rusty brown hair. Her blue eyes scanned the babe's powder-pale skin and short, pointed ears.

The young male cooed from his well-padded and handcrafted wooden cradle. His silver irises locked onto her glowing aura before widening at the curtains of sparks falling from her circular flights.

Such a cute little child, she chimed. *Hello there, little one. Hi!*

The babe grinned as her sparks settled into his skin.

Sitting next to the babe, the high elven female smiled. "Qaylin and I have always wanted to have a child. Only took two thousand years."

Qaylin sat near the babe's feet while puffing on an ancient, long-stemmed pipe.

As you know, my kind is responsible for pixie birthing, the fairy smiled at the babe's toothless grin. *I love children.*

"I never imagined we would get to meet one such as yourself," said

Qaylin. "It's an honor for you to visit us, Aurora Ven."

Oh, please, call me Ven, the pixie chimed. *I'm just an auroralite. I haven't even had my first blossoming. Aurora Song says it won't be long now…* Her smile faltered. *When that happens, it will signal the final century of Aurora Song's time here in the third realm.*

Sympathetic, the elves nodded.

Meanwhile… Ven chimed and touched the infant's rotund fist, which was wider than her trunk was long. *It's a blessing I can still venture away from the Tree Carlinia while I can. Once I complete my second blossoming, I won't be allowed to leave ever again. My responsibility will be the spiritual care of my flock and the birthing of new pixilarks.*

"Do you fear that?" asked Qaylin.

No, chimed Ven. *When your krys requested an enclave, I jumped at the chance to visit the high elves, especially when I heard there was a baby! Our trip will serve a number of purposes, of course, but I really wanted to see your precious bundle.*

"We are glad you could come," said Havmor.

Such a beautiful child, indeed. How long does will it take for him to reach maturity?

"High Elves usually mature over a period of five hundred years," said Havmor.

Ven smirked. *Middle age by our standards.*

"Pardon, auroralite…" Qaylin pulled the end of his pipe from his mouth. "But as I've been taught, the magnalark lives millions of years in the nether before you are born here as a pixie. Do you not count that against your total age?"

We cannot… Ven approached the infant to touch his chest. *We neither remember anything from our first forms, nor are we allowed to commune with magnas once we cross. And we have no clear idea exactly how long they persist in the nether before they transition.*

"No communication at all?" asked Qaylin.

It could destroy us, Ven chimed. *We're so…thin, here. The mind of a magna, having grown and expanded for eons in the nether? Our tiny corporeal brains couldn't handle such a connection. We must count our lives from the day we're born here. But hey, thanks to your ancestors, we have the chance to pass through the low realm and eventually ascend like all the other corporeals.*

"Have you birthed many pixies?" asked Havmor.

I am not yet allowed, chimed Ven, *but I can't wait! I've looked forward to that from the beginning. To tend the gardens where we germinate? I can't think of a higher calling than to herald our progenitor magnalarks from the nether to here into our second form. It's beginning life anew.*

"Sounds very noble," Qaylin said with a nod.

Ven smiled. *I love pixilites—the little pixies. I've spent lots of time with the feathers as they grow.*

"Feathers?" Havmor asked as she scanned Ven's four golden veined, membranous wings.

Ah, chimed Ven. *We call groups of young pixilarks, 'feathers.'*

Qaylin puffed his pipe. "And your whole group are flocks, correct?"

Yes, chimed Ven.

"What do you call intruders?" asked a small voice.

Did…you speak? Ven asked the child.

"What do you call an intruder, auroralite?" the child asked before his glimmering silver irises disintegrated into endless black circles.

Ven recoiled.

"What do you call the serpent who devours us?" the soft, infantile voice echoed as his form vibrated.

"Auroralite Ven?" Qaylin lowered his pipe as Ven paled.

"Do you hear us?" the child smiled as his voice deepened and slowed. The world around her shuddered. "Do you? Can you hear our cries? Our screams? Our agony?"

What is happening? Ven clutched her ears as the child's voice rattled her.

Havmor scooped the babe away from the pixie. "Are you alright?"

The child cooed in his mother's arms as if nothing had happened.

I-I'm not sure, Ven chimed.

DO YOU HEAR US!? the voice thundered so that the fibers of her flesh shuddered. Falling to her knees, her wings quivered as the voice threatened her ability to focus. Her attendant, Couture Rima, rushed to her side.

"Help!" cried Qaylin.

Several pixies rushed into the hut and Ven's side as she sank to her hip and held her face against the brilliant welling headache.

When Ven looked, a barren island lay before her, ripped in half by a winding river center-pointed by a whirlpool. Dark, heavy clouds formed a low, black ceiling while pale yellow sunlight from the distant horizon provided a faint pall that cast the island's sharp nooks and corners deep into the shadow.

Though she had neither seen nor heard of its characteristics, knowledge of this ancient place flooded her mind.

Algueda, she breathed as violent winds yanked at her hair.

Distant wails and screams wafted on the hot, salty wind. Taking to flight, she crossed the river and headed toward the snowcap mountain on the island's southeast corner. She passed over deep ocean-side canyons layered with frost and mist before braving the open ocean towards the rising wails of fear.

Piercing the heavy mists, she met the end of the world where oceans cast off the horizon and fell into the gray nothingness below. She hovered over its apex in horror as the nether—that thin world between the physical realm and ascendant heaven—was laid bare to her.

I-I can't see this, she shuddered. *I* shouldn't *see this…*

Her fear climbed as the whole of the nether appeared before her.

No thicker than a seam and flowing as liquid smoke, magnalarks wandered far across the horizon. Each existed and failed to exist when she focused on them and the pain in her head burned all the hotter. Across a distance, something bright and pale moved in swift violence.

An outsider had come. As a brilliant three-dimensional violation within the inverted nether, a white, snake-like creature with arms and wings raced through the void taking bites from the magnas. In their slow, passive states, the magnalarks struggled to flee its attacks.

Oh no, chimed Ven.

Predators did not exist in this two-dimensional space. A blasphemer had crossed the boundary. If it devoured the magnas, they would not transition to the low, physical realm and become pixies; if they failed to achieve life in the physical realm, they would never ascend to the High Realm of the Great Self.

They died with no chance of reaching the afterlife.

No! Ven cried.

Had the magnas drawn her to witness their slaughter? Had they learned how to speak without killing her, or might she soon die? Even their whispers left her shaken. They had managed to call for help without taking her mind.

The violator devoured an entire magna by snaking through its smoke-like form and brightened as it consumed the helpless creature. Once complete, the snake-like defiler disappeared in a gentle swirling flash.

"No!" a corporeal voice echoed. "You can't!"

Surprised, she spun toward a world drowned in a similar charcoal darkness as the nether, but this one a physical realm with barren trees under a moonlit waste, and herself lying in the nook of a scorched tree. The landscape swarmed with beasts around a group lit up by nodes of magic and the faint dome of an energy shield.

"Seth!" another voice cried.

Ven followed the voices over an endless horde of lupine beings. Before she reached them, a tiny, intricate sphere of light fired into the sky and set off thousands of secondary spells in the atmosphere. The masses below stilled for a moment before low laughter rippled among them.

Unsure of the exact spell at work, she knew its power would fall with terrible devastation.

The tiny sphere sank from the clouds over a city peeking through heavy smoke. Fluttering to the nearest tree, she landed on a branch and tucked herself behind its trunk before peeking around its edge a moment before the distant spell kissed the gigantic city wall.

For an eternity, the world turned white. Ven clutched the tree as a concussive wave rippled the landscape and crashed over her. She screamed until the roar subsided to a low, thunderous boil. Peeking around the tree's steaming edge, she gaped at a glowing mushroom cloud rolling upwards into the sky.

"The worldender will help." Whispers echoed across the landscape until they rattled in her ears. "The worldender is the way…"

Gasping, Ven screamed. Her world collapsed and she fell into the arms of one of her fellow pixies. Golden blood drooled from the edges of her eyes.

The magnas, she chimed amidst sobs. *Great Self, the magnas!*

The magnalark victim she had seen would never pass to the low realm. The assault had destroyed a helpless creature who now would never become a pixie or have the opportunity to ascend to heaven.

New lights appeared at the door to the home as the rest of the entourage responded to calls for help.

Tyran Han, Eldress Rose and other elders who rushed in stopped at the sight of blood.

Aurora Ven! Eldress Rose rushed to her. *Are you alright!?*

Quivering, Ven moaned and clutched her head. *The magnas.*

The elders shared glances.

I have seen them— chimed Ven.

But you would die, Eldress Rose stammered.

Ven struggled to shake her head. *They cry out. They are under attack!*

Attack? Tyran Han straightened. *By whom!?*

A draco, Ven managed to chime. The group gasped. *A dragon has found a way into the nether.*

3

Uniform

Heavy sheets of rain fell by the time the auburn house rose above a sea of wooden shanties like a lonely island. The house perched at the edge of Rainhold's highest steppe with a rare view of the rest of the district. The deluge obscured anything more than a hundred paces out and soaked his burnt sienna skin to the bone. Clouds reflected a purple-blue mottle into the warm late-afternoon sunlight.

Haephan navigated the maze of nicer shanties around the neighborhood and passed the one where he grew up, raised alongside several other children by three sweethearts. His favorite, Querie, worked wash duty at Goram's House, today.

Haephan crossed the broadway, wiggled through narrow gaps in the ramshackle houses, and emerged through a well-known secret pinch into the rear of the stables. Skipping his usual excuse to interact with a horse, he skirted the animal and used loose boards to move unseen around the muddy stable yard and through a wall blanketed by thick bushes, halfway between the fore and rear of the main property.

Merciless for adults, guards patrolling the house's wrought-iron perimeter would often tolerate small children, but they never spotted Haephan.

Few could.

Haephan crossed the alley between loose bars, pushed between bushes ringing the house, and crawled beneath them to a small hole into a hollow under the grand rear staircase.

Warm, humid moisture filled the alcove from an open low basement window. Heat almost hurt after so much icy rain, but he absorbed as much as possible before wiggling head-first through the tight opening.

A sweetheart hard at work over several large, steaming vats failed to hear his entry.

The room reeked with a mix of human fluids and overpowering soap meant to remove that odor from a mount of soiled sheets. Haephan managed to get his entire body through the window, tiptoe down the upper shelf, step over a large table of folded sheets, and land on the floor. Rising, he crossed his arms with a loud, obvious sniff.

The woman spun with a start. "Bloody hell! You scared the piss outta me, you little spit."

"Oy, Querie," Haephan cocked his smirk.

She scowled before crossing the floor to pull him into a tight hug. "How ya been, Haeph?"

"Not bad," he said.

"What's ya scam?"

"Gimme a lift?" he asked and headed for the dumbwaiter across the room.

"Why?"

"I need something," he said.

"Goram's in a mood today," said Querie from over the vats. "And you're on his shit list after shirking your shift up in Whittle for the fancy dress party."

"I had other stuff to do!" Haephan protested. "'Sides, I told a few sailors about it. Didn't they show up?"

"Sailors, Haephan!" Querie hissed. "You've been tol' before to avoid that lot! They bring their whole crew and get pissed until they bloody riot! You're supposed to be drawing better clientele!"

"For this place?" Haephan asked.

"This place keeps you fed," she snapped.

"I keep me fed." Haephan hobbled over to the dumbwaiter.

"If he catches you, he might take a nut. Eleven years is old enough, you know."

"I'm not here for a sweetheart," he said. "I'm here for a client."

"You know ya can't pick clients! Goram'll take more than a nut for that! You know how'e is when you mess with his business. Don't you forget what happened to that mage who freatened him," Querie scowled.

"Wouldn't let him have the triplets?"

"Not for no measly price," said Querie.

"What'd he do?" Haephan asked.

"Forgot already?" Querie asked. "Freatened to burn Goram out, he did. Goram got him called a low frog round town. You know 'ow the Academy is bout men who like men."

"And?" Haephan asked.

"Then he castrated him in a Whittle alley ten feet from all dem fancy guards. No one ever found. You know Goram."

"I ain't here to threaten Goram's business," said Haephan. "Just a fuggin' crimsie dick who threatened mine."

Querie opened her mouth to speak and shut it. "Who's the mark?"

"Know that one that comes in here on the regular for Cenia?"

Her brow climbed. "Why?"

"This is personal," Haephan said.

"How?"

"Took something from me," said Haephan, afraid to tell her he lost his dad's ring.

"How the 'ell you plan on gettin' your little ass out of here, boy? I ain't waitin' on you and I ain't helping you back down'n'out."

Haephan raised his chin. "Out the front door."

Querie grinned. "You got balls, little one."

"C'mon," Haephan climbed into the dumbwaiter. "Please!"

Querie hesitated when blood drooled from one of his nostrils. "What you been doing?"

He touched his face. "Shit. Hurry!"

"Where?" she asked. Intrigue warmed her pecan-toned skin, soft in a cherubic way that accentuated her diminutive size and attractive curves.

"Top," he said. "You know the younger ones like the quiet."

"I didn't see you," she poked his chest hard enough to draw a faint 'ow' from him before her bright brown gaze softened. "Take care, luv."

He winked before she shut the door. Drowned in darkness, the box ascended with a faint creak of its pulleys. Rubbing his chest, he allowed the dumbwaiter to stop moving and the faint thud of the brake being set in place before he peeked through the doors to scan the carpeted walk. Sliding them open, he emerged onto the third floor.

Dolphus was all brag in the street, but most of the crimson guard who came for bangs—those who could afford it, at least—spent more time wishing for a mother than getting off. Few had better families than orphans like Haephan.

Haephan peered through the railing balusters at the main floor far below. Pretty girls in various states of fanciful dress reclined on couches. Though he could not see most of them, he knew most were like him—dark, pecan or amber skin with various shades of brown or gray eyes. Many were beautiful, as men described it, and dolled themselves with powders, inks and colored hair. Jewelry adorned some, while others shirked metal in favor of the image of purity and girlish qualities.

Men as black as night—many of whom worked the middle and upper classes in New Gordon—came for the variety away from the moralizing of the Academy and its community. Haephan had seen a pale man once, his skin as a cup with all cream but for a drop of coffee. Where did such men come from? It was said New Gordon's people once migrated from the great southern deserts some thousand years ago, but Haephan didn't know or much care about such things. All he wanted was his ring.

Haephan listened at each keyhole. Moans and muffles were the norm until gentle murmuring wafted through. Some clients wanted to feel loved and came to chat as much to bang, but the tones said everything. This had to be Dolphus, or at least another crimsie like him from a wealthy family. Sweethearts didn't bang any random teen who asked—they had to have the money to afford them, and not only once. Dolphus was a fifth son from an upper class family that had more need for a wide network than more heirs apparent.

Though less experienced at locks, Haephan opened the door without more than a faint scuff of wood. Peeking in, he cringed at the unfortunate bottom-up view of the boy atop the woman on the bed. He locked onto Dolphus's uniform draped over a chair on the opposite side of the room near an open dormer window. He shut the door and stalked across the thin carpet to the uniform, where his small, deft hands raced through every pocket, two leather boots and a wide leather belt.

There was no ring.

Haephan wanted back his only prized possession in all the world. While it might be on a chain around Dolphus' neck, he doubted it.

Haephan realized Dolphus might have dropped it off at The Station—a tiny island in the Vitner Canal where northern Rainhold met the southern tip of the middle-class Rose Oak district. Comprised of a small complex of buildings, The Station served as the home of the Crimson Guard. Of course he'd put it where he lived.

The sweetheart on the bed moaned louder, which meant she knew Dolphus was almost finished.

Wrapping up the boots, trousers and shirt, Haephan prepared to cross the room to the hallway when Dolphus climaxed with a squeaky grunt. He took his first step when murmurs and laughter wafted in from the hallway, indicating he would be seen. In a flash, he slipped through the sheer curtains of the window out onto the narrow third-story walk ringing the sloping roof. Holding Dolphus's clothes with one arm, he skirted the edge when one of the boots shifted loose and fell two stories, bounced off the front porch, down the steps, and into the muddy street. He flattened out of sight.

Thick as a bull and well paid as the lead bouncer, Berman descended the front stairs, scanned the house windows and stooped to pluck the boot. Shaking his head, he climbed the stairs.

"What was that?" asked the other guard on duty.

"A fuckin' boot," chuckled Berman. "'e mus'be gettin' his money's werf!" Both guffawed.

Exhaling, Haephan continued until he found and entered an empty room, donned the uniform over his clothes and relished the sudden warmth. The outfit sat loose on him, which was common for new guardians. With only one boot, he cursed, sure he'd get caught. He hoped Dolphus's similar chalky brown skin tone and hair color would distract from their height difference.

With no other choice, he opened the door, hobbled to the stairs and descended past a sweetheart on her way up. She winked, but he kept his blush down as he continued. At the top of the final landing, he combed his thick black hair over his face. This would either work, or he was dead. He couldn't return by dumbwaiter. The front and rear doors—both guarded—were his only way out.

His one-booted limp down the final flight drew the attention of nearby sweethearts, some of whom recognized him with a flutter of their eyelashes. The barkeep across the room leaned on the bar and raised his chin to signal a Meso'Admian man with rich tan skin, thick curly hair and dressed in a fine cranberry velvet suit, who turned from a sheaf of numbers and frowned at Haephan over half-moon spectacles.

"Goram!" belted Berman on his way in, "you won't believe—" He cut off at the sight of Haephan in the one-booted uniform and started laughing.

Haephan reddened, terrified the plan was over. Goram would slice up his goods for sneaking into the house and the guard would probably beat him to death with the boot.

"It fell out a bloody' window!" Berman laughed and tossed the boot at Haephan, who caught it in an awkward hug. "Must'a got his money good!"

Sweethearts giggled.

"No time to linger, Master Lurli?" asked Goram.

Haephan shrugged as he fought to hide the quiver in his hands. "I-I couldn't." The entire room stifled laughter as Goram pulled off his spectacles. Haephan hobbled past clutching the boot to his chest.

"You gonna put it on?" Berman yelled after him.

"Uh huh," said Haephan as he hobbled for the door and held his nose in time to hide more blood. Out on the porch, he descended the stairs and waddled through the mud with one boot on, grateful Goram hadn't noticed who he really was. He defied death once and made it out alive. Now he needed to repeat his luck by walking into a viper's den. As the temporary sprinkling returned to a deluge, Haephan slipped on his boot before hoofing it toward The Station. He hoped against hope he could pull this off without getting his balls cut off.

4
The Station

Haephan had no time to lose.

Dolphus would realize his uniform was gone, the house would realize someone had picked it, and if Goram ever figured out Haephan stole from a client under his roof, he would peel his skin off, one strip at a time; Goram carried grudges only long enough to destroy those who inspired them.

Stopping in an alley, Haephan stooped as blood drooled out of his mouth. Chill thickening the air frosted his breath, but the uniform provided surprising warmth. Lowering the boot, he slid in his muddy foot, tightened and tangled its laces as best he could, like the first. He had no idea how to tie a real knot. Leather boots felt strange around his feet. He had worn shoes before, but rarely, and always with holes in them. While old and worn, they were closed against the icy ground. Haephan unbuttoned the captain's rope looped around Dolphus's shoulder. The Crimson Guard boasted only five captains; he'd be picked out instantly.

Over the next half hour, he navigated the dense vagrant neighborhoods using every trick to hide from a thousand men and boys who would happily attack a guardian found wandering Rainhold. Heavy drizzle soaked and matted his inky hair down his chalky brown forehead. When he drew near enough the island, he slicked his hair like some of guardians. Hiding in plain sight sometimes meant exposing everything to appear to be nothing special.

Reaching the canal, he followed its shore along the docks until the island bridge came into view. He straightened his uniform, calmed his pounding heart, and checked his cuts one more time. He put on his best marching walk, raised his chin with feigned confidence and ambled down the mucky road.

Golden light peeked from under the edge of the storm some miles distant, shimmered across the Vitner, and lit the bridge like a beacon. Approaching its foot, he gulped, mustered himself and climbed it. A pair of guardians headed in the other direction frowned at his tiny size, but Haephan stuck out his chest and ignored them while projecting a sense of comfort and belonging as he reached the other side.

Meanwhile, fear revived the long-held dream of a faceless mother who draped the ring around his neck while whispering about his loving father. Anxiety threatened his facade, but the thought of regaining that ring also inspired him to swagger through the archway along the gravel-packed path into the building complex. He knew the large building in the center was the main barracks and decided to start his search there.

Eons ago, New Gordon city constabulary converted the area into a youth housing and training facility. Twelve- to seventeen-year-old boys spent years as guardians to train and qualify for service as a city constable—a good gig if you could get it. No matter which class the boys came from, they all started at the bottom. Only one or two pickers ever got into the Crimson Guard and were often considered traitors by the rainies.

Haephan didn't care who became guardians; he blamed no one for making it out of Rainhold.

He followed the gravel path around a broad rectangular field at the heart of the complex and stepped through a pair of large warehouse doors left open.

While he had seen this opening from afar, he never knew what lay inside. Most rainies wanted to know, but none who enlisted ever returned.

Inside, a broad foyer stretched a third of the building length and remained open to the third-story rafters. The wall opposite the door filled the rest of the space. Exterior walks lined the second and third stories, while wide, paneled windows revealed constables speaking with each other under bulblight. A staircase climbed the right wall to the second story and led down a dark hallway.

On the main floor, left of the central walk, a senior crimson guard inspected a troop of new recruits. Oversized, stretched and worn-out uniforms hung loose on most of them and made for easy pickings for the "rooster," as rainies called the senior teens, to verbally flay each.

Haephan strutted past, hoping his own ill-fitting uniform didn't make him appear too much like the newbies, despite being shorter than all of them.

A first-floor hallway next to the main stairwell led past doors where rows of guardians sat at strange tables and nosed books while a few inspected sheets of paper pinned to the far wall.

Haephan sniffed at the sight—reading was a waste of time. He walked the length of the building and pretended to read sheets of paper pinned to the hallway wall whenever someone approached so as to hide his face.

Ahead, a short line of listless boys waited their turn at a narrow window with a broad sill. Each boy fished objects from his pockets and set them on the sill for an inspector who sifted through them, passed some and pulled away the rest.

When Haephan realized the guardians kept some of the pickings, he sucked air through his teeth. Would Dolphus have turned in the ring, tossed it, or kept it for himself?

Taking a chance, he got into line. Querie taught him that attempts to hide drew the most attention and being loudest sometimes masked everything. Haephan affected boredom while he scanned the hallway. Time ticked by for his turn at the window. He pictured Dolphus drawing ever closer, probably wrapped in one of Goram's sheets, red with fury.

Haephan grinned at the idea of Dolphus looking so stupid, but his eyes widened at the realization that today he would become a legend—he picked one of Goram's clients *while* in progress.

The two boys behind Haephan frowned his way.

Haephan didn't care if they stared. He'd be a legend, and all because of that motherfucker who stole his ring.

"Next," said the inspector.

Shaken from his reverie, Haephan approached the window. His chin almost reached the sill as he asked, "Cap Dolphus come by earlier?"

"Why would you care?" the boy snapped.

Haephan drooped his lids as if the boy were stupid for asking.

"Oh, Commander Butes lookin' for him?" asked the boy.

"Why do you think I'm here?" Haephan huffed.

"He ain't been by," the boy said. "Not today, anyway."

"He due by?"

"I dunno," the boy frowned. "He don't come tellin' me his where'bouts."

"Alright." Haephan raised a hand. "Ain't trying to pin the blame on you."

"Blame? What happened?"

"Can't say," said Haephan as he walked away. "You don't wanna know!"

The ring wasn't in Dolphus's uniform—which Haephan now wore—so it must be wherever the guardians kept personal things. Now in search of bedrooms, he scanned the hallway and spotted a stairway near the rear building entrance. He ambled closer, climbed the stairs to the end of the second-floor hallway and scanned a wall of nondescript doors. He hesitated, unsure which to open.

"Hey! Greenie!"

Haephan jumped in his skin as a captain advanced on him.

"What're you gawkin' at?" barked the boy with light brown skin, a broad nose and tiny curls in his hair. "You're supposed to be down at the dock."

"Sorry, sir!" cried Haephan as he mimicked standing at attention. "I— uh…"

The captain loomed closer.

"Was looking for Captain Lurli's bunk."

The captain's eyes narrowed and he leaned in. "Why?"

Haephan's death flashed before his eyes as his mouth opened without sound. An idea struck him before he fished Dolphus's rope from his pocket. "Dolphus told me to come bring it here."

The captain slapped Haephan, who staggered into the wall and struggled not to swing back. "You never refer to a captain by his first name, you little shit. That clear?"

"Yes!" Haephan mustered. When the captain raised his hand again, Haephan barked, "Sir!"

The captain lowered his hand and head. "Where do they find brainless crotchfruit like you? Don't you know where captains sleep?"

Haephan shook his head, afraid he'd be slapped again while the first yet stung on his cheek.

The captain glared. "Give it here."

Haephan handed it over.

"Fuck off," said the captain.

Haephan marched halfway down the stairs, turned and peeked as the captain entered a door halfway down the hall. Haephan stalked toward the room but retreated to the nearest door moments before heavy boot falls tipped off the captain's return. Rows of beds stacked atop each other lined each wall of the large room—this must be where common crimsies lived.

As the captain took the far stairs, Haephan returned to the captains' quarters. Compared to the bunk room, this was spacious. Five beds extended from the right wall, separated by heavy footlockers placed longways between them. A stained window at the room's end bathed the dark room in a bevy of colors.

Which bed belonged to Dolphus?

Heavy conversation erupted somewhere downstairs.

Panicking, Haephan passed each bed, scanned for signs of Dolphus, and found the rope on a trunk halfway down the room.

"Yes," Haephan said as he knelt before the locker. When he found no obvious lock, he lifted the lid in surprise when it popped open. None of the trunks had locks on them. Inside, a collection of alcoves held various tools and uniform items, but none were deep enough to explain the heavy trunk. Noting two handles, he lifted free an upper shelf and set it aside to expose a section beneath.

Haephan rifled through clothes, a jar of money, a small leather necklace and other doodads. By the time he was done, the trunk was near empty and Dolphus's stuff lay scattered.

"Where is it?" Haephan struggled not to tear up when the sound of panting drew his attention to the door.

Two captains, four guardians, one adult constable and Dolphus wearing oversized clothes gaped at him kneeling over the trunk.

"What are you doing!?" Dolphus roared.

"I want my ring!" Haephan leapt to his feet.

"Are you *fucking* kidding me. You're going through my shit!? You're goin' in the canal!" Dolphus and the boys raced forward. Haephan bolted for the window, hoping the seams between the colored panels would break under his small weight. He used the final bed on the row to make his leap.

He bounced off and slammed onto the floor with a thud.

Irate guardians descended upon him. With nowhere to run, desperation screamed in his chest for somewhere to go that was safe and warm and easy and had food and a mom and a dad and hope. More than all that, however, Haephan ached to be anywhere but here.

5

Breakdown

Nine students in plain brown uniforms sat scattered among the first two rows of a steep semicircular amphitheater climbing from a half circle floor to an upper walk lined with windows and the hallway beyond. An angled bar of afternoon brilliance fired in from the window next to the professor and reflected off the marble floor to warm the room. Before each student shimmered multicolored, intersecting walls of energy painting them in prismic light while they scribbled notes on parchment.

"Furian's X," said Wizard Elverbane as he scanned the larger version of the spell form hovering above his desk. "One of the best tests for magical continuity by Wizard Victor Furian more than three thousand years ago. Who isn't finished?"

"Almost done, professor," said one young man on the end who struggled to lock his energies in place.

Elverbane scowled through his thick rusty beard at the broad chalkboard covered in notes that stretched across the backside of the room.

"Wizard Elverbane?" A petite blonde raised her hand. "Is it true Furian lost his son in development of the X?"

"No, he did not," said Elverbane. "Therat did, which you would have known if you had actually done your homework." Elverbane motioned to the blackboards behind him. Two slid apart from each other to reveal a third. Once in place, a line of white chalk dust snaked from the small bowl at the board's center and drew bulleted points as he spoke.

"Furian's X displays the quality and stability of dimensional layers that comprise our world, which, if you read last night's assignment, you know what…Marster Wyvel?"

"It's a natural byproduct of the foundational magics coexisting with each other," said Wyvel.

"Good," said Elverbane. He bent over his desk, where lines of white powder crossed over a fine layer of charcoal dust, from which rose the two glowing walls of Furian's X. Within each energetic wall, horizontal layers shimmered and bled over each other. "And how did Furian's X count those dimensions…Marster Blyke?"

"He counted the number of variant energies and their speed of dissolution into prime energy," said Blyke.

"And how did he measure that dissolution? Urman?"

Marster Urman pursed his lips.

"662," said Elverbane.

Urman flipped two pages in the book next to his spell form. "He… stacked their rate of dissolution and compared them, ranking from fastest to slowest."

"And upon ranking and classifying them, how did he display them within the X? Marster Grema?"

A straight-backed brunette raised her chin. "He used the wavelengths of colors on the illumination scale and assigned comparable rates to document each level."

"Thus the segmented rainbow within each wall of the X," said Elverbane. "How did he manage to pierce the veil in order to interact with the dimensions?"

"Hyram's Gate," Grema said.

"Draw out Hyram's Gate," said Elverbane. Groaning students shifted items on their crowded desks to draw out the spell form on paper. "And don't forget to annotate Therat's connecting locks on the event horizon. In the proper elvish."

Students bent over their drawings as Elverbane scanned the undulating walls of his own spell. Small concentric black circles surfed along the edges of each color, warped and shuddered. He cocked his head and leaned in and saw that all of them eventually popped like bubbles.

Elverbane's breath caught. "What in hell?"

Raising his hand, he infused the spell with more energy to get a clearer response on the breakdown.

The construct exploded. Elverbane flew backwards and crashed into the chalkboard, which cracked and fell before shattering on the stone floor with a thunderous crash. The students screamed as the spell form warbled with a few more violent pops before dispersing with a fizzing electric after-flash. Two students scrambled from their chairs to help Elverbane as others doused their own spell forms in terror.

Stunned, Elverbane struggled to breathe while his world closed in. In response to the singing flash, tears overwhelmed his eyes. The shadowy figures rushing toward him drew old, suppressed instincts and he raised glowing hands. He hesitated for a bare second before unleashing bolts of fire.

That brief pause spared the lives of two of his students, giving them the chance to dodge. One bolt struck the corner of his desk, which exploded and cast splinters across the classroom and showered screaming students, while the other exploded in the low front wall of the bottom row. Two students caught in the blasts collapsed to the floor while the others scrambled for safety.

Panicked, Elverbane scrambled to his feet, backed against the wall, and drew deep magic into his hands.

"Out!" cried someone before the panicked students rushed up the stairs on either side of the amphitheater and into the hallway beyond.

To the shocked professor, their fuzzy silhouettes swarmed against the light from warm-lit hallway windows. Raising one hand, he fired a streak of lightning that missed the window by inches; the window spider-cracked instead of exploding. He rubbed an eye with one of his wrists while raising his other glowing hand, ready for the next attack. Screams and footsteps faded before distant doors fell shut.

Sliding along the decimated wall while the shattered slate threatened to slip underfoot, panic filled his breast as he crawled on all fours into the alcove under the high narrow window to his left and out of sight of most of the classroom. He cleared one muddled eye before he worked on the other.

He wasn't sure how much time had passed before a voice called out, "Seth?"

"Who— who's there?" Elverbane barked.

"It's Orzo," said the figure as he descended the main stairs and stepped into view with his hands raised. "It's me, my friend."

"What're you doing here? They're everywhere!"

"Who's that, Seth? The lycans?"

"Aye, the beasts!" Elverbane panted.

"Seth? Look at me, my friend." The wizard took slow, careful steps toward the teaching floor. "Look at me. Look at me."

Raising one glowing fist, Elverbane quivered behind the alcove corner like a terrified animal. His gray-rust hair stood out from the electricity in the explosion as his wild eyes scanned the room.

"Do you recognize me, Seth?" Orzo asked. He motioned at his own warm coffee-colored skin, light brown eyes and thick black beard founded in gray. "Look at me."

Elverbane's eyes darted between Orzo and the classroom.

"You are in New Gordon, at Belfast University, my friend," said Orzo as he scanned the half-destroyed desk, the spell powder bathing most of the floor, faint coals simmering around the room and raised a hand to draw out the heat and kill their flames. Halfway from the desk to Elverbane, he raised his hands to soothe his friend. "You are safe. There are no lycans here."

"They're here! My desk just exploded! Ithnar is here!"

"There are no lycans here, my friend. We hunted and killed Ithnar forty years ago, brother. I assure you. You are safe."

Suspicious, Elverbane inspected the burn marks across his desk and pieces of the chalkboard littering the floor.

"I am your friend," Orzo said. "I will not hurt you. Do you trust me?"

"Yes," muttered Elverbane.

"Breathe slowly, my friend. Take deep, slow breaths. Look at the walls. This is not Tuthomere. This is New Gordon. You are home. You are safe. Look at your surroundings and be present with them."

Elverbane's panting ebbed.

"Where are you?" Orzo asked.

"New Gordon," Elverbane articulated.

"Good," Orzo said. "Can you release your magic? I will protect you. I will stand with you."

"Y'promise?" asked Elverbane.

"I promise."

Panting, Elverbane released the magic from his hands.

Orzo came within a few feet and squatted to the floor. He took slow, deep breaths and drew Elverbane to mimic him. As Elverbane calmed, Orzo motioned for them both to stand upright and continue breathing while Elverbane recentered. When Elverbane pushed from the corner, with a final slow scan of the room before letting out a long exhale, the tension loosened in Orzo's shoulders.

"Are you alright?" Orzo asked.

Elverbane held a quivering hand to his forehead and noted a missing eyebrow. "Hell."

"What happened?" asked Orzo.

Elverbane focused on his memory as worried administrators stared from the hallway windows.

"Something has happened," said Elverbane.

"You mean…other than you attacking students?" asked Orzo.

Elverbane paled.

A woman wearing white and red slipped through the rear doors and descended the stairs.

"Wizard Elverbane?" she asked with her soft, professional voice as she reached the foot of the stairs. "Are we well?"

Elverbane sat upon the stool uprighted by Orzo. "Yes, Medicist Whestle."

"I will perform magic and delve and heal," she said as she approached. "Please remain still."

Elverbane let her set her fingers on each temple. Tiny waves of magic flushed through him and rebounded from different parts of his body to her fingers. She released him.

"Other than your clogged arteries and your mind, wizard, you are well," she said as she stroked her thumb over Elverbane's missing brow. The hair doubled in length under each stroke until it reached a reasonable balance to the other, though its vibrant rust color stood out against its companion's bushy gray.

Orzo smirked.

"Did I hurt anyone?" asked Elverbane.

"Two students received some nasty splinters," said Whestle. "But they're being cared for."

Elverbane cursed.

The medicist harrumphed at his language before finishing her treatment. "Did we have an episode, wizard?"

"Aye," Elverbane whispered.

"Come see me," she said. "We should talk." When Elverbane did not respond, she turned to Orzo.

"You know how often I invite him to Temple?" said Orzo as he raised his hands. "I make him do nothing he doesn't want to do."

She grimaced and pointed at Elverbane. "I will take all your hair away if you don't come see me. Is that clear, wizard?"

Elverbane hesitated and said, "Aye."

She headed for the doors. "And make sure you apologize to your students. They will need to hear it from you, directly."

At the top of the stairs, administrators prepared to rush down when Orzo forestalled them with a raised hand and a slight shake of his head. Frowns in windows judged the mess below.

"Something has happened to the magnalarks," Elverbane said.

"Magnalarks? The nether whales?"

"Yes," Elverbane said. "Something has happened to them."

"How could you possibly know that? And what does that have to do with—"

"The magic," Elverbane said. "The continuity of the nether magics is breaking down."

Orzo leaned closer and asked, "What do you mean?"

"Furian's X," Elverbane said. "You need to see what I have seen."

A half hour later in Orzo's classroom, Orzo wove a containment spell around his desk before even laying out the mat of charcoal dust as the spell's foundation.

Elverbane braced like a soldier preparing for war. His single-minded focus reminded Orzo of their days facing the super pack.

Once assembled, Orzo formed the two glowing walls of Furian's X. From violet upward to red, the walls shimmered as smooth gradient spectrums, which coalesced into distinct colors stacked atop each other as two crisscrossed rainbow walls. He leaned closer to inspect it. "Great Self. When did this happen?"

Elverbane folded thick arms over his heavy belly.

"What does it mean?"

"You've read Hyram's scrolls on concentrics," Elverbane said. "Something must be wrong with the magics."

"Like what?" asked Orzo.

"Hyram theorized the circles were a direct reflection of the health of energetic transduction."

"I remember reading…" Orzo said. "And at what point did this thing explode?"

"I tried a minor infusal to brighten the damn thing." Elverbane's breath cut short. "It was…sensitive."

"Stand over there," said Orzo.

Hesitant, Elverbane retreated from the desk while Orzo wove a second shield spell that diminished even bright flashes or pulses and infused the X with more energy.

Within the containment, Furian's X didn't explode as it had under Elverbane. Violent warps flailed and twisted as the lines between the colored layers broke and mixed. Elverbane looked away.

"Bloody, Immortal," Orzo muttered. "This is—"

"Furian's X is a stable spell form," said Elverbane. "I would never allow a student to weave such a thing without a containment spell unless—"

"I can attest to this, Seth," said Orzo. "Don't worry about the administrators."

"Degreneth will take advantage of this. You know what he tries to do with my time."

"Oh stop worrying about that bloody bureaucrat."

"Then what do we do?" asked Elverbane.

"You still know more about this than me," said Orzo.

"I need to research this. Can you help?"

"I would, but I'm on king's council," said Orzo. "Planning for this new bloody lycan uprising is taking all of my time. If this is truly dangerous in the long-term that won't solve the lycans in the short. For all we know this might be cyclical, like the summer and winter. The current war between the lycans and elfmen, however, could rip apart continental peace, today. We have two packs of lycans living across South Edenia. If they try to support the super pack, we will feel it, too, for all this might be between them and the elfmen."

"Fucking animals," said Elverbane.

"When I am not in council, I will come by and be a voice for you if need it."

"That would be appreciated," Elverbane said.

"I thought it fair to warn you..." Orzo unraveled the X and containment shields and tidied the desk. "An Andonese is on campus."

Elverbane stiffened.

"Might ask for his help," suggested Orzo.

"The *Andonese*?" Elverbane asked.

"They can't all be the same."

"You'll have to prove it," said Elverbane.

"The council will call on you before long. No one has more experience with the lycans than you."

"I made an oath, Orzo," Elverbane said.

"No one will ask you to repeat Tuthomere," Orzo said, "but even things like the spatial shifting techniques you taught a few years ago would go a long way with the young martial mages."

"Killing living creatures wasn't the purpose of the workshop," Elverbane said. "Certainly not more of the lupine or human kinds. And you know those techniques well enough."

"Well enough, sure, but you're the best."

"I cannae go to war again."

"I'm not advocating war," said Orzo. "But I'm not going to let anyone destroy our city, either, because we were unprepared. I don't imagine you would, either."

"No," Elverbane admitted. "I wouldn't. Still, I'd rather not be involved."

"Who would?" Orzo asked.

"There's a list," said Elverbane as his jaw clenched under his thick beard. "What is an Andonese priest doing in New Gordon?"

"Perhaps you should ask him. Nicely."

"Not sure I want to."

"I hear Andonese are well versed on cross dimensional energies," Orzo said. "It might be worth your time to at least seek him out."

With his head buzzed, Elverbane struggled to consider where to begin his research on the magnalark situation. "Where is he quartered?"

"Unsure about where he's staying, but he's apparently visiting the libraries."

Elverbane grunted. "And how do you not spit at even the thought of it?"

"I learned after Tuthomere to forgive," Orzo shrugged. "Lots of time in prayer and reflection helped me forgive the Andonese. The lycans. *Myself.*"

Elverbane scowled at him.

"Good luck," Orzo said. "High Nile tonight. See you there?"

"Sounds good. When?"

"Hour after sunset?" Orzo straightened.

Elverbane gripped his friend's arm and turned to leave.

"Oh," Orzo said. "You said magnalarks were important with the energies. How?"

"If something's wrong with inter-magical continuity," said Elverbane, "something must be wrong with the magnalarks."

"That's a bit of a stretch, innit?" asked Orzo.

"No, Hyram believed magnalarks were foundational to continuity," said Elverbane. "I need to look into it. The X is a base tool, but I've tried refining Hyram's gate to see more across the veil."

"Immortal, alive," Orzo frowned. "Is that what you're doing up at Ashmore?"

"Looking for a way to observe directly where otherwise we cannot."

"Hyram's Gate is dangerous when infused with too much energy."

"I take precautions."

"You think you can do better than *Hyram*?"

"Hyram identified that the magnas somehow possess frequencies of every sub-dimensional layer between us and the nether," said Elverbane. "I've confirmed his original theory, and I've come to believe that they somehow hold a role of vital importance to the health of dimensional stability. If it's true and something is wrong with them, we could be facing something catastrophic."

"A living being necessary for an inorganic ecosystem? Never heard of such a thing," said Orzo. "Who might know more?"

"Only one species in Pangea is the expert on the magnalarks," said Elverbane. "But I seriously doubt the chance of an audience."

"Who?" Orzo asked.

"Like butterflies to their caterpillar progenitors, my friend," Elverbane gripped Orzo's shoulder. "The pixies are the second-stage life form of the magnalarks, and they speak to no one but the elves."

6

Vacants

The blonde beauty stood out as she ambled through Southdown Square. Despite her oversized white blouse vested in ill-fitting blue hemp and the heavy burgundy skirt that dragged the ground, her pale form drew attention. Her haphazard bun accentuated the fine curve of her neck while her crystal blue eyes outshined the vibrant fruit lying in wooden stands lit by golden sunlight spearing through gaps in buildings hugging the square.

Eva scanned vendors' food wares with a mix of yearning and disappointment. Reaching into the pocket of her dress, she fingered her few coins for the day's meal before moving on from the colorful fruit shining in the misty morning's rays to the grains necessary for gruel. Perhaps she could get one pear and make it last a few days to flavor the food? She passed her usual, lecherous grain supplier and approached a former vendor known for too many weevils in her grain, but did so for a lower price. Glancing at the fruit, she sighed.

"Could I have a pound?" she asked and raised a coin.

"Oh, want some now?" asked the brunette woman behind the counter. Her once-beautiful brown eyes hardened at the statuesque blonde with pale skin.

"Do you want my business or not?" asked Eva.

"I see your looks," the brunette growled. "Too good for m—"

Eva lowered the money and turned away.

"Wait," said the brunette. Glaring, she scooped a pound into a worn canvas sack through which bled a few grain flakes, twisted the top, and offered it with one hand with the other one palm up.

Eva took a grip on the small sack before setting the coin into the woman's palm.

The vendor snatched away the coin but made Eva tug at the sack before she grinned and released it.

Eva scowled at her before returning to the fruit vendor. Adamar wouldn't be happy with the weevils. She bought a large pear, stuffed it into her grain sack, and left the square for streets trickling with work traffic.

"Eva!" cried a woman from a yard between tall row houses where a host of women laundered on a commercial scale. On one side of the yard, a long trough of wash water served to clean incoming cloth. A row of women on one side used magic to boil water while a second line directed lengths of cloth into and out of it while stemming water to prevent loss. Steam billowed upward and joined a current of moisture under the control of a single woman at the end of each row, who funneled the cooled water into the vats. At the opposite end, a single woman directed a stream from the end of the trough, through a strainer and into the source bin.

Piles of filthy sheets and clothing, in addition to new hemp and wool bolts, lay at the rear of the yard while fresh, dry folds were moved to palettes lining the street in anticipation of customer pickup.

"Morning, Meara," said Eva with a smile.

"Hello dear," said Meara as she wiped her brow from the remnant moisture. "Would you tell Adamar that Heath wants back that hammer set as soon as he can?"

"I will," said Eva.

Meara offered her a grim smile and returned to work.

Eva scanned the operation and noted that if the collections pool was raised above the trough, a single pipe could funnel the reclaimed water without the need for extra workers to capture lost moisture or to move water from the collection tub back to the source tub. Insert a filter into the pipe, itself, and that would save another worker. Eva, however, kept her mouth shut—the last time she made a suggestion, the women shooed her and left her soaked with an "accidental" splash of water from the trough.

She waved at Meara and continued her way up the street, down a narrow alley and through a squeezed basement door into the small room she shared with Adamar. A thin bar of sunlight lit the room through a narrow basement window on the canal side of the building, interrupted by foot traffic on the sidewalk outside. The room had once been a small basement storehouse to a converted warehouse before they took it as an apartment. Adamar wished to be close to moving water for his experiments. He eventually erected a tented mill a mile away where paved docks gave way to grassy hills.

Mill wheels and other small inventions lined haphazard shelves and the small table that hadn't been used for food since they dissembled and reassembled it in their tiny apartment.

She set the pear in their makeshift sink before pouring the sack of grain into an intake of a handmade mill sitting on a table next to their bed. Ever since Adamar made it as a test to prove water could power work, they used it as a hand-powered engine to grind their food. She took a handle built into the small water wheel and turned it, which through wooden gears and shafts rotated a side-lain stone wheel. The grain vibrated and sank through a funneled hole to a narrow between the top wheel and a similar stone beneath that had no center hole, forcing the grain between the two stones. A tiny spout on the edge allowed grist to fall into a small bucket. She repeated the process to make it finer. She ran her fingers through the tiny grist and noted the weevils unaffected by the process.

Eva knew ways to kill them without Adamar's enginery, but he insisted they use his tools in order to refine them—not everyone living in New Gordon could afford magic to clean their food. Using her breath and several wheel spins, she flushed out any leavings.

Adamar had toyed with a silt sifter for weeks, but it never produced a satisfactory removal of weevils. He told her he wasn't upset with her, but she feared his disappointment every time he picked weevils from their meager meals.

Eva leaned over the sifter before she fished out a rare, pristine stocking from her trunk. She ran her finger over it, having imagined a use greater than removing weevils, but was more tired of their ever-constant grind to produce better machines. More afraid of Adamar's sighs than missing her stocking, she ripped it into a broad square cloth.

In Adamar's sifter, she slipped it between his hemp filters over the rectangular bracing, used twists to lock it into place, flipped it over, and set it into the small engine. Once she emptied the bucket into the intake, she gripped the attached handle and rotated it. The axle turned a wheel from an off-center mount, which lifted and dropped the sifter as if a human shook it. The handle made rotating it easier than a manual attempt.

Fine gristings—including baby weevils and their eggs—dropped through her stocking while the larger weevils lay left behind. While unpleasant, it proved such a surprising success that a grin spread across her face. A desire to share it with Adamar welled within her and she grinned at the idea of his smile when the tiny door to their room burst open.

"Eva!" Adamar stormed in.

"Oh no," Eva's heart sank.

"They tore me apart."

"What?"

"I got to the mill ready with last night's modifications and…" he panted. "I'm done. And we gotta go."

"Gotta go?" Eva's eyes flared. "Not again, Adamar."

"Tell that to the words written in shit across the tent."

"What'd it say?"

"Leave or plan to stay…permanently."

"I told you," said Eva. "This wasn't wise."

"Why? Do the guilds say what normal people can and can't do?"

"They're trying to protect you!"

"From who? Myself?" Adamar protested.

"They—" said Eva as she searched for something to say. "They are trying to help the worker, in general. Maybe not you."

"Couldn't they leave us alone? I wasn't forcing anything on anyone!"

"I don't want to leave." Eva's shoulders sank. "We just got here. For once, I thought we found somewhere to stay. I just—"

"We gotta go!" said Adamar as he stuffed clothes into a sack.

"They just want you."

Adamar froze. "What-what do you mean, just me?"

"They only want *you*," said Eva as she fisted her hands.

Frozen to the floor, Adamar said, "But— we have to go!"

"No," Eva said. "Not anymore."

The door to their room burst open before city constables—marked by their red and white cummerbunds—rushed into the room with hands raised with violent power.

Magic snatched Eva into the air with her arms and hands bound to her sides. "Hey!" she screamed. "Release me!"

Fury welled in Adamar. He kicked one of the soldiers in the chest and sent him flying across the room. Magile constables wielded impotent power against him.

Untouched, Adamar snatched one of them by the throat and rammed the back of his head into the nearest wall. The constable sank limp to the ground. Corded muscles rippled Adamar's forearms from years of manual work.

Two constables unleashed bolts of fire, which disappeared with whiffs of smoke as they touched Adamar. While they gaped, Adamar rammed his fist under the first chin, planted foot and kicked the second into the stone wall of the basement room. Neither rose.

Adamar wrenched the final constable off his wife with the grip of his hand, alone. The constable screamed as his joint popped under Adamar's iron fingers.

Eva fell across their small bed while Adamar smashed in the man's nose. Two more constables coming down the alley stepped into the door. A large mill wheel fell from a high shelf onto their heads, which stunned and knocked them down. Eva rubbed her fingers.

Adamar grabbed what little he had stuffed into a sack and marched her toward the stairs.

"Heath's hammers!" she protested in the doorway. "He needs them, even if you don't."

Scowling, Adamar fished through the mess of their room, grabbed the hammers, pushed her into the alley and out to the broad walk lining the canal and docks.

Once she matched his pace, Eva pulled her arm from his fingers and said, "Not again, Adamar."

"I'm trying to make a living, Eva," Adamar said.

"You were making a living back hom—"

"Don't you say it." Adamar pointed.

"It was fine pay and an easy job!"

Adamar rounded on her. "Nothing is easy when it demands your dignity!"

"Taking care of your wife and children is undignified!?"

"You're pregnant?" Adamar stuttered.

"No!" Eva cried. "But that's not the point!"

"Thank the Self," said Adamar.

"I thought you wanted children!"

"I do!" Adamar marched on. "When we can afford them!"

"Where can we go?" Eva followed. "We've already tried Kuthanel. If we leave Southdown, there's nowhere else to go if we're not heading back—"

"We are not going back there. Maybe we can get to Rainhold for a while. Lay low. Then we can figure something out."

"Do you think this will end here?" Eva asked. "Those are constables! The law's involved now."

"They were involved the moment the guilds took notice of my work," Adamar snapped.

Eva sputtered as they turned the corner and jogged along the broadway past trains of wagons laden with goods, riders and pedestrians on their way across the city into fields of endless row houses and warehouses.

Adamar leaned within the shadow of an alley and motioned Eva out. "Get the key from Meara."

Scowling, Eva returned to the lot where Meara worked.

"Meara," Eva said.

Half-squatting as she was, the stocky woman blinked in surprise at the pretty blonde. "Eva? What's wrong, love?"

"The guilds smashed Adamar's mill. We have to go."

"No…" Meara clutched her brow. "Oh no. Heath will have a fit if you leave without saying goodbye."

"Adamar insists," Eva said.

"Leave his own cousin without saying goodbye," said Meara as she shook her head. "What about the—"

"This will have to be it." Eva revealed the hammers from folds in her skirt. "We fought off constables."

"I can't take 'em here," Meara sputtered. "Can you put them back in the apartment? Heath needs them!"

"We'll put 'em back," said Eva. "Do you have a key?"

Meara motioned at a fellow washwoman before stepping out of the lot to hug Eva and slip her the key. "Hide it in the pocket above the door and get out of here!"

Eva hugged back and rushed away. She and Adamar raced down the street and into a row house. From every open window hung laundry whose drippings left dark striations on the yellow exterior paint. Inside the third-floor apartment, she set the hammers on their bed.

"You couldn't leave well enough alone," said Eva.

"What did you want me to do?" Adamar stood guard at the door. "Every other person like me in this city does little more than gopher work. I want more for us than running errands for other people. I want to build something that means something."

"You could," Eva said. "You have to find a way to do it the way everyone else wants."

"My own way, Eva!" Adamar said. "To hell always trying to do it 'everyone else's way!' I'm my own selfdamn man and I'll do it my own way. I don't need their permission any more than I need their pity. I have a mind and I'll damn well use it."

"Your mind won't let us rest," Eva protested. "It's always your way or a highway—a highway I have to keep walking because your way isn't leading us anywhere!"

"It takes time to build something worthwhile," Adamar said.

"It takes forever with you!"

"I don't have the luxury of a family whose mere presence puckers every ass in the room," said Adamar.

Eva's jaw drooped.

"You got everything you wanted without fighting for it. You don't know what the rest of us have to do to get somewhere we want."

"You think my childhood was free of costs? I paid my own price for growing up where I did."

"What kind of price was too much that you never had to worry about meals or shelter or—"

The pounding of heavy feet echoed up the stairwell and through the open door to the apartment.

Adamar cursed and leaned into the hallway. Below, constables climbed the stairs from the building entrance. He motioned at the window behind him into the narrow courtyard inside the row house block.

Glaring, Eva climbed through onto a flat ledge and down on boxes stacked on the roof of the first story and waited with worry.

Adamar slipped out and pressed away from the window as the constables mounted the third-floor stairway, burst open the door and stormed in.

"No one's here!" cried one of the constables.

"Toss everything," commanded someone.

"I don't sense anyone," the constable repeated as the group searched the apartment.

"You wouldn't, the selfdamn vacants," said the commander. "I worked with 'em before. Can't handle 'em with magic. Gotta use physical force."

"Big problem?"

"Not really. They never survived long where we found 'em. Those who grew up stayed in their place. Didn't think that was a problem here."

"Ain't a problem, necessarily," said the constable. "But there's a number here. And over in Westdowns."

"What do you mean, a number?" asked the commander. "Vacants come from wizards."

"Wizards?" the voice sounded confused. "Not here."

"What do you mean, not here?"

"Whole families."

"Vacants can't reproduce," the commander said.

Adamar frowned and looked to Eva, who frowned back, still unable to hear the exchange.

"These can."

"And their children?"

"Like their parents, as far as we can tell," said the guard.

"Everyone out."

Boots filed down the stairs.

After a moment, Adamar prepared to move when he heard a sniff at the window. He pressed the wall as fingers drummed the windowsill.

"Where's Torlance?" asked the commander.

"Southdown Market," replied the voice.

"Let's go," said the commander. "He needs to hear about this."

Two sets of feet descended.

Unable to hear the exchange, Eva waited in her hiding place below.

Once sure they were gone, Adamar descended the crates, grabbed her hand and pulled her toward the alley exit at the far end of the block.

"Where are we going?" Eva asked.

"Southdown is out," said Adamar. "There's no more place for people like me here. The guilds'll just hunt me down."

"Where are we going?" Eva asked.

"Dunno yet," Adamar gulped. "But we can't stay here."

7

Conclave

They cried out to me, Ven whispered. *It's terrifying. I can— I can still hear echoes of their voices in my mind.*

"You're sure?" Krys Aemon, High Elf King of Wistem, half turned from the bright window of his dark private study. Around him, several advisors reclined and, upon a small table set amongst the cushioned seats, the pixie entourage from Carlinia.

Ven nodded with haggard, sleepless eyes. *Their voices bounce around in there like ripples in my pond...*

If the magnas truly are in danger, chimed Tyran Han, pixie king of Carlinia, *this would be detrimental to the very fabric of magic of the third realm.*

If, in fact, that's what she saw, chimed Eldress Rose who frowned at Ven.

"We have discussed as much," said Aemon. "When the North Andaelans first trans-evolved the magnas, I don't think they fully knew the risk of drawing them from their roles in the nether."

We are grateful to the high elves of North Andaela for doing so, Tyran Han chimed. *Without that, we would never have the opportunity to fulfill the corporeal requirement and enter heaven.*

"Even so," said Aemon. "If a draco is unnaturally accelerating what should be a process of millions of years, drastic measures may be necessary to handle it. I will need to notify the krysdom."

While a possible danger, I would still prefer a second opinion, chimed Tyran Han. *Our very earnest auroralite here should be confirmed by a full aurora. I would not alert the krysdom until we can be sure.*

Ven shrank.

"I think your young aurora-to-be has seen more than any amount of earnestness could fabricate," said Aemon.

Ven perked.

"The rest of your vision?" Aemon asked. "You said a single sphere of light shot into the sky that came and destroyed a city?"

He fired it into the sky where it doubled in power, drew on energy from Pangea and brought it back down, chimed Ven. *After that, it was the whisper to find the "worldender." That the worldender would help. What is a worldender?*

Aemon glanced at his advisors. "A worldender is technically a spell type that has been forbidden since the Courte Empire. Their highly destructive capabilities were prohibited by numerous continental enclaves and parliaments."

We're supposed to find this worldending spell? chimed Rose. *We're not human mages.*

Nor would I support learning any of their juvenile attempts at magic, chimed Han. *Are you saying she saw the destruction of Tuthomere?*

"Those juvenile attempts at magic killed a quarter million sentient beings in seconds," said Aemon. "And yes, Tyran Han. I believe young Ven witnessed exactly that."

Whyever would anyone design such a spell!? asked Ven.

"Lycans have been a continental scourge since they appeared in the Estamilian Period," said Aemon. "Their super packs have destroyed many civilizations."

What's a lycan? Ven asked.

A hybrid of man and wolf who loses its sentient side during full moons and under pack events, chimed Tyran Han.

"Humans call them werewolves." Aemon glanced out the window

at the inner palace courtyard glowing in brilliant morning sunlight. "And are right to fear them. Lycans are the epitome of sentient beings who lose their ability to think individually to the will of a bestial collective. Individuals can be handled and even brought to a semblance of order despite their bestial natures. Once they assemble into packs, midpacks and super packs, all they can do is consume the very resources they need to survive long-term. Their passions overrule their reason until they destroy everything. Once they return to their human forms, they are quick to blame their behavior on those who previously attempted to protect those resources. Reason takes an ever further retreat to such collectivism."

Wait…I saw them, chimed Ven.

Han turned.

They were everywhere, Ven chimed. *They had surrounded a group of mages and were attempting to pierce their shield.*

"You're sure you saw this?" asked Aemon.

Ven rubbed the side of her face. *Aside from the dracos, the sight of them has kept me awake.*

"And the city? Did you see it?"

Yes, chimed Ven.

"Were the lycans climbing into the city?"

Ven focused on the uncomfortable memory. *I didn't know what they were, but they were everywhere,* she chimed. *They slithered up the walls like bugs. The screams from the city were terrifying.*

"Seems to confirm the testimony," said Aemon as he took his seat in the circle.

Testimony? Rose asked.

"Of the survivors," said Aemon.

Beings survived that? Ven asked.

"Half of the city population," Aemon said, "and the casters."

Of the spell? Han asked.

Aemon nodded.

Were they not punished for such a crime? asked Rose.

"The casters testified they were doing all they could to prevent the super pack from entering the city," said Aemon. "After enough testimony and investigations in the ruins, they were released."

Ven scowled.

"And it's possible, your whisper has nothing to do with the spell," said Aemon.

Then why would it have said worldender? asked Ven.

"Because the spell caster has been since labeled as 'worldender,'" said Aemon.

Who? Tyran Han asked.

"Wizard Setherick Elverbane," said Aemon.

Wouldn't he be dead by now? asked Rose.

"It's only been 40 years since Tuthomere fell," said Aemon. "Most wizards live up to several centuries. I would be surprised to find him dead."

So you think we should go find him*?* chimed Ven.

"Perhaps," said Aemon. "You said the whisper told you to find the worldender, not to learn it?"

Find, chimed Ven. *Where is he? This worldender?*

"Last we knew, he resides in New Gordon in the South Edenia region," said Aemon.

How far is that? asked Ven.

Thousands of miles, chimed Rose.

We are not going flying all over the continent, chimed the pixie king. *It was dangerous enough flying the short distance here. And even with your validation of Ven's vision, I would still confer with Song before we act on anything.*

Aemon nodded.

But…it seemed so urgent! Ven chimed. *I-I can't get them out of my head. I need to go find this worldender. I need to go. Soon.*

"There is only one quick way to New Gordon," said Aemon, "and we cannot offer such a path to any pixie."

What way is that? asked Rose.

"The rimsportal," said Aemon. "Pixies are forbidden from using them."

Why? asked Ven.

"Pixie magic dangerously accelerates rimsportals," said Aemon. "If too many beings were using the rimsportal network when pixilark energy was introduced, it could set off a series of explosions that would kill many people. Rimsportals are not to be trifled with."

But the magnas are in danger, we might not have the time to waste flying thousands of miles! Ven chimed. *What if we—*

No, Tyran Han cut her off.

Tyran Han, if Ven is correct and the magnas are truly in danger, chimed Rose, *ought we not explore every opportunity as quickly as we can?*

I won't risk any one life trying to use a rimsportal, chimed Han. *With Ven's condition in mind, however, we will need to cut short this visit, Krys Aemon. I would have Song see to Ven and help clarify the true nature of this issue.*

"Of course." Krys Aemon rose, prompting the rest of the room to climb to their feet before the pixies took to hover. "May I send a mounted escort with your lordship back to Carlinia until you find out the true danger?"

That would be welcome, chimed Tyran Han. *Your support will be appreciated once we identify the true nature of this threat.*

Ven clutched the side of her head as the echoes rebounded inside her skull.

We would retreat until we depart in the morning, chimed Tyran Han. *I believe Ven will need rest before we venture forth.*

"As always, the pixies of Carlinia are welcome to any and all resources here in Wistem," said Krys Aemon. "Call on us for any need."

Thank you, Krys Aemon. Tyran Han bowed before turning to lead the pixies from Aemon's private study.

With her eyes squeezed against the spiking pain in her mind, Ven followed hands through the palace to their private pixilark quarters and laid down on a small mattress surrounded by overgrown roots designed to mimic the energy of their Tree. The incessant whispers grated against her sensitive mind until they consumed her awareness of the outside world.

8

Andonese

War across South Edenia had been on everyone's lips for months. Continental overcrowding, sectarianism, rampant rioting and class warfare, unionism, border disputes, inter-special fighting, genocide and more.

The Battle of Tuthomere forty years ago sometimes felt too fresh for Elverbane. He hadn't had a battle vision in almost a decade, and fear welled at the idea of their return. Sleep was precious to a warrior, even so long after coming home from war.

Scowling, Elverbane recalled the Andonese neutrality; they refused to help, even as the battle-frenzied lycan horde overwhelmed and devoured entire villages. Innocent women and children lay half eaten for endless leagues in the path of the mindless army. Even now, the memory pitted his stomach.

The Andonese had the luxury of retreat on their island nation off the continental east coast, protected from the beasts who would humanize once they submerged in saltwater. Was this new, seemingly tiny discovery, enough to stir them? Though he struggled to understand it, he knew by intuition this was more dangerous even than the lycans ravaging the countryside only weeks' travel away.

As much as he hated to acknowledge it, few compared with the Andonese understanding of magic and its fabric. He heard they worshipped knowledge, itself, though had never confirmed it. If the Andonese refused to help, at least he'd be no more in the dark than he already was. If the lapis-haired bastard did help, so much the better.

Three days of researching produced nothing for Elverbane. Holding off until he had no other course, he left his classroom in a storm and took the great spiral staircase downward past other classrooms and laboratories. Students parted for him. In addition to his gruff reputation, his episode had set terror among some of the students; a few realized how truly dangerous the gruff old veteran could be.

He didn't care much for the young; he worked as a teacher so he could research. Educating young wizards was the price he paid for that freedom.

Only Ian, his long-time manservant who recently passed away from old age, ever grew on him. He had begun working for Elverbane as a teen a few years prior to the war and been with him ever since. His recent passing at the age of seventy five took Elverbane's breath, sometimes. No other servant had been so loyal or attentive as Ian, and Elverbane missed him. Now Elverbane would have to find another vacant replacement for his assistant.

He pressed onward through corridors, across covered bridges and along exterior walkways through the hillside school. Entering the library, he made for the information stand.

"How may I help, wizard?" asked the attendant as she rose in her black uniform.

"Is there an Andonese in the building?"

"One moment." She searched the admittance book. "Yes, wizard. Corran Hall."

He marched from the lobby down the southern hallway to the main library chamber and across the floor. Students at tables on the second and third-story floors glanced from their studies at his entry. Those on the main floor stiffened despite pretending to bury their noses in their books. Murmurs silenced as he passed. He entered the eastern hallway, climbed a half set of stairs, passed an attendant and entered Corran Hall, a private library with sensitive materials reserved for senior students, professors, and special visitors.

A dozen professors loomed around tables stacked with books and maps on king's council imperatives for the lycan problem. None here knew them better, but he wasn't about to step his toe in that mess again.

Lycans weren't prone to open war, despite their individual aggressiveness. Their conflict with the elfmen extended millennia and never resolved itself. If most of the faculty were on call to the king, their free time would be consumed by preparations to advise him. Elverbane refused to participate. His war hero status both protected him and highlighted him—he knew the council would eventually call on him.

Corran Hall rose two stories with walls closer at the bottom along the narrow walk and wide at the top, with cast-iron rails, antique tables, and in-built shelves interspersed on either side. A bright light shone from the uppermost floor overlooking the chamber. Slipping among bookshelves, he climbed the stairs to the upper section and slowed at a long rectangular table where sat a short woman silhouetted by the light hanging low over the long table before her.

"Pardon me," he said as he approached, "but have you seen…" He trailed off as the light highlighted her lapis blue hair and reflective round silver irises. Her breathtaking gaze chilled his blood—*she* was the Andonese.

A smile crossed her beautiful pale blue lips. "Wizard Elverbane."

"Priestess…" His surprise dimmed under caution. "You know who I am?"

She motioned to the seat across from her at the rectangular table. "Please, sit."

Her beauty disturbed him. Dark blue hair swept at an angle across her forehead to the neat bun gathered behind her head and shimmering eyes reflected the lamplight. The powdered quality of her pale skin was natural, he knew. When her soft fleshy lips smiled for the first time, he had to remember to breathe. How could Orzo not have told him the Andonese was a woman!? How could anyone meet her and not make mention of it?

Composing himself, he sat. "I was coming to look for you."

"I'm glad you did."

"Why?" he asked.

"You were to be one of my visits while here at Belfast."

Elverbane eyed her. "Why are you here, priestess?"

Her brow flickered. "You seek me, find me, discover I'm looking for you…but you don't like me."

They watched each other a long moment.

"You were on the Tuthomere Offensive," she said.

"'*We don't involve ourselves in minor conflicts.*'" Elverbane's tone sharpened. "The lycans had secured a stronghold over the Grolan Netherlands—we could not pull them from it. When we asked for your help, your people essentially told us to 'fuck off.' Pardon me if I'm a little displeased at the Andonese apathy to the wolves."

Her eyes softened. "I know what you had to do."

His skin tingled. Elverbane struggled not to choke up before her at the sudden revival of long-clenched feelings. "The entire city. We couldn't let the lycans keep what they had taken. They had already destroyed too much. If we didn't stop them there, there was nowhere else to stop them. If they had reached the marshes beyond the city, we would have lost everything. There would have been no pulling them out."

She waited.

"Your people offered no help. And to top it off…" Elverbane said as he pointed at the table, "Your iron librarian had the gall to say, 'We are here to preserve life.' Truly? After nearly three hundred thousand already dead from a fight that wouldn't stop."

Her eyes lowered as he spoke, but she raised them after he finished and waited a few moments. "Why did you seek me?"

Elverbane rocked his jaw and suppressed his pride. He took a moment to speak. "Something has happened that supersedes my feelings for the Andonese. And now I realize I'm not very good at asking for help."

A smirk tugged at her mouth. To his ire, Elverbane inwardly shrank.

"But before I do that," he asked, "why would you look for me?"

"Your study into dimensional theory has caught the interest of my superiors. Among a number of other tasks on my journey, they suggested I make a visit."

"They want to know what I know?"

"Everyone does."

"No one does," Elverbane said. "Dimensional strata theory is the least studied aspect of prime energy in the world." He eyed her. "At least among the rest of us."

She smiled. "Knowledge is everything to the Andonese."

"Knowledge is power," Elverbane said. "I'd venture that's truly what you're after."

"Perhaps," she said. "And you, wizard? Why do you seek me?"

Elverbane scanned the book she held in her hands—*Archivum of Edenic Enginery*—and kept from scratching his beard. "Have you ever heard of Furian's X?"

She thought for a moment. "Dimensional representation through color variance?"

Elverbane cocked his head. "Close. Do you know of Hyram's indicators in the X? Concentrics?"

"Expanding circles," she said. "They indicate transductional continuity."

"How much do you know of continental hermeneutic cosmology?" he asked.

"Enough," she said.

Elverbane sucked on his tongue. "Then perhaps I could show you something?"

She raised an eyebrow.

Ten minutes later in the lantern-lit depths of his classroom, upon a hastily procured desk from the university warehouse, he recreated Furian's X under three container spells.

She bent close to the spell as he stepped away. He dragged his eyes from her snug white dress trimmed in aqua—her figure drew his attention.

Immediately, she noticed the circles in the spellform and and straightened.

"Great Self," she said. "Do you know what this means?"

"I have a few ideas," said Elverbane.

She pursed her lips. "I have a few of my own. I hesitate to venture them yet. I will need a few hours or a day before I offer you any possibilities."

They shared a look when the sunset bell startled Elverbane. "Och, this day." He patted his robe down, reached into his vest, and pulled out a timepiece. "Andonese eat, right?"

"Sometimes."

Elverbane cocked his head. "Come with me tonight. I'm dining with a friend. Might give us both an opportunity to discuss this. At length."

"Good food?"

"Earnest serves the very best," said Elverbane.

"Earnest?"

"Owns the High Nile. Best place in town."

"Alright, then."

"Oh," he said. "What is your name, priestess?"

She smiled again. "I'm Priestess SonLara Alva Amferadon. But in private you may call me SonLara."

He extended his hand, which she looked at with mild surprise as he spoke, "Thank you."

She took his hand. "A pleasure, Wizard Elverbane."

Her touch thrilled him. "Seth."

Her brow rose.

"In private." His brows drooped.

She nodded gravely with a slight twinkle in her eye.

Over the next half hour, they summoned and took a carriage through the city to The Levy, a six-block area packed with shops, restaurants and luxury lodging. Well-dressed attendants kept immaculate the streets, signs and exteriors; all but pedestrian traffic was prohibited and riffraff were kept out.

As they climbed from the carriage, Elverbane turned when someone bumped into him—a boy with a swollen face covered in dirt and dried blood.

"Pleash, shur!" slurred the boy. "I need hilp! Pleash, I'm 'ungry!"

"Oy! You! Get!" cried a nearby constable, who advanced on the boy. The child bolted under the carriage and moved away. "I'm sorry sir. We try to keep strays away from the nice areas."

The boy slunk away as SonLara asked the guard, "Children are not allowed here?"

"Sorry, mistress, but no," said the guard as he tugged smooth his pristine high-collar coat and slim trousers tucked into high, well-polished black boots. "This area is privately owned and for guests only."

"And children cannot be guests?"

"Not his kind, madam," said the guard. He saluted her and continued his patrol.

"I see," she looked after the boy, who had disappeared.

Elverbane frowned. He never took much time to deal with the streets of New Gordon; they weren't his field. He shook it off. "Come. We're late."

They continued through the Levy among groups of finer city residents out for the night. At its heart sat a well-lit multi-story house converted into a popular restaurant full of smiling patrons visible through the arched bay window and, outside, a lazy gaggle of couples awaiting entry.

Passing their envious glances, Elverbane approached the doorman with the arrogance of a man who got in where and when he pleased. The doorman half-bowed to him with great deference and motioned him through. Elverbane reached into his pocket to offer a tip, paused, and patted himself. "Great Self."

SonLara turned.

"He stole my wallet."

"Then he will eat tonight," she smirked. "And got away with it."

Elverbane frowned in thought before he locked upon a point moving away. "Perhaps."

9

Morning Escape

Ven woke. After an endless barrage of nightmares of the formless nether, the dark room around her lay stable and sane. A faint bleed of blue light through the curtains of a nearby window key-lit edges of room furniture in their spacious guest quarters. Distinct elven cedar scented the cool night air. Whispers faded, as did the pain, and she took a relieved breath at the temporary respite.

She fluttered from her personal pillow to the windowsill to gaze over the starlit city below. Every moment she waited to act increased the urgency from the magnalarks.

While Krys Aemon believed her, Tyran Han only wanted to doubt. Could she trust he would move in time? Fear scored her until she thought of little else. The vision seemed clear enough, and if Aemon was correct, she needed to get to New Gordon as quickly as possible, even if that meant using a rimsportal, the risks be damned.

The sleepers around her could not see the danger. Desperate to try something, she pulled the window lever and cringed when it squeaked.

She feared someone would wake and slipped through the gap to the outer sill. Peering into the shadowy forests below their tower room, she stepped off, and fell free before snapping out her wings to glide. Once her momentum ebbed, she fluttered her four wings and raced from the palace with the distinct pixilark chime.

Crossing Wistem in the heart of midnight reminded her of Carlinia—ancient moon-bathed trees obscured most signs of civilization. All paled, however, to the ancient Bluewood Tree rising a thousand feet high at the city center. The rimsportal sat a mile from the palace in a private grove surrounded by high stone walls. She landed on a rooftop chimney and scanned for the rimsportal through the heavy flora, though wasn't sure how to recognize it.

Nervous but determined, she flew again into the grove canopy as a younger Ven had done with her feather while playing hide and seek. A structure ahead stood in the middle of a grove and drew her to land in a nearby tree. The stonework joined four tall arches in a square. At its center, a long narrow walk between pairs of steps speared through a dais, above which stood three concentric rings.

Ven craned her head to better see what the structure might be when she had the bare warning of a faint chime before Rose snatched her as she landed on the branch next to her.

What are you doing here? demanded Rose. *Get back to the palace.*

Ven cringed at being grabbed. *I have to go.*

We weren't going to stop you, little auroralite, but Han's right! Rose chimed. *We need an experienced aurora to confirm what you think you heard—*

Think *I heard?* Ven stood. *All I hear are their voices, eldress! All they do is whisper for me to 'find the worldender!' I can't stop thinking about it!*

You are young, Ven, chimed Rose. *You haven't even blossomed yet. We need Song's experience to properly interpret what you think you saw.*

I've already interpreted it, Ven gritted her teeth. *I need to find—*

I know what you think you saw or understood, chimed Rose. *But did you hear nothing Krys Aemon told us about the rimsportals? And have you forgotten everything they taught you in your feather?*

My feather learned about the forest and nature and our society, Ven chimed. *They don't teach us about rimsportals they never expect to use! How do we know Aemon isn't just trying to keep us from getting to the worldender?*

How paranoid are you? Rose asked. *Wisteman elves have been our friends for centimillennia!*

You heard what they said, Ven chimed. *They wouldn't have evolved us like the North Andaelans if they knew the danger it would have created.*

The North Andaelans destroyed themselves by not knowing when to quit, chimed Rose. *And the Wistem elves are wise to avoid repeating their mistakes.*

We're a mistake? Ven asked.

Be silent, child! chimed Rose. *Are you not listening to me? Just because I can be grateful the North Andaelans brought the magnas here doesn't mean everything they did was wise, any more than you suddenly thinking you understand what you saw.*

I don't know how much clearer that can get, chimed Ven.

By the rimsportal, a firefly burned bright as it wafted nearer the rings.

The young wouldn't, chimed Rose. *We're going back to the entourage and if you're feeling so awake, we can start toward Carlinia right now.*

I'm going to New Gordon, chimed Ven. *Whether by rimsportal or by air.*

More fireflies appeared near the rimsportal rings. Faint threads of light expanded from them and curled in slow swirls toward the pixies; each thread sank backward toward the fireflies while drawing energy from Ven and Rose.

You have responsibilities to the flock that supersede even your convictions, chimed Rose. *Even if you're right, your job is to anchor our flock with the Tree Carlinia. If Song verifies your vision, Tyran Han and the elderate will commission other pixies to seek out the worldender. That you were allowed on this entourage at all was a gift from Han because he knew this would be your only opportunity ever to leave.*

But we are already out here, Ven chimed. *Out beyond the borders. To return to the Tree before heading for New Gordon would waste precious time we may not have!*

Firefly twinkling harmonized as they danced in flutters. Ven noticed the motion. She straightened as several fireflies melted into the outer ring before it bucked a half turn.

Now, c'mon, chimed Rose. *We're going back to the palace and rest before heading back in the morning.*

But— Ven started.

No, Rose snapped. *We're going back.*

The growing assembly of fireflies fell inward in a conflagration of warbling lights that swirled into the rings. The outer ring spun before the second ring began to counterspin. The third ring rolled in kind and a pop of light shocked the air as their blurring motions became a single sphere.

Several armed elves raced along the pathway.

"What's wrong with it?" cried a guard.

"I don't know," said another. "It wasn't activated from the other side."

What did you do? asked Rose.

Me? Nothing! I just got here!

The ball of bluish white light coughed fits of smoky yellow. The cold air warmed in flashes and singed wafts of air. A tempest of energy swirled outward from the platform. While the thin strands of yellow-blue energy swirled outward ever nearer the pixies.

The lead elf traced the tiny strands of light to Ven and Rose and cried, "Hey!"

We didn't do anything! chimed Ven.

The lead elf scanned the pixies and calculated risk as the wind whipped at his long pale hair and pointed at the portal. "Go!"

What!? Rose chimed. *That's dangerous!*

Unable to hear them, the elf braced against the growing wind. "GO! You've already activated it! Either use it or it will destroy this whole block! Quickly!"

We can't go in there! Ven cried.

Rose snatched Ven's wrist and hauled her toward the violent ball of magic.

I CHANGED MY MIND! Ven screamed as they raced closer.

Too late now, auroralite! Rose darted around the snaking energies and dragged the young pixilark into the fluctuating rimsportal. Moments later, the ball of light reeled, thrashed and exploded.

10

From Southdown

Adamar and Eva marched through the dense dawn fog while huddled against the heavy chill. The icy morning mist hovering over the Estamar Canal washed over the muddy bridge and cut through their thin cloaks. Merchant carriages rumbled past on their way out of Southdown into New Gordon.

Hugging himself, Adamar grimaced when yet another wheel splashed them with mud. He wanted to apologize, to say how much he had wanted to make a good life for her—for them both—but he didn't know how to say it any other way than he already had.

Another splash of mud drew a curse from Eva. "You just had to do it your way, didn't you?"

Adamar's brow drooped.

"Couldn't find a job like everyone else."

"Are we going to hash this again?" Adamar said. "There aren't many jobs for vacants on either side of this damn city."

"There are *great* jobs working for wizards," she protested.

"Self damnit, not this again."

"I say the same damn thing about this," she said. "Again!"

"What did you want me to do, Eva?" Adamar asked. "We've been through this a thousand times…"

"Which is apparently not enough."

"…a *thousand* times that guilds don't let you innovate," continued Adamar. "It threatens their power to control business."

"That is *not* true," Eva said. "Where do you get ideas like that? It's thanks to guilds that we have a stable economy. They ensure workers get proper pay and aren't abused by the kingdom."

"The same kingdom that just sent constables to enforce guild law?"

Eva clenched her jaw. "Noble classes in general."

"You mean protected from people like your father?" he asked.

"My father is a good man. He actively works with the guild to keep the economy going."

"He doesn't have a choice," Adamar said. "The guilds control how the Academy regulates business across New Gordon and Southdown. Why do you think guild masters work so hard to maintain their relationship with him?"

"That's called cooperation."

"That's called cronyism," Adamar said. "We haven't seen major advances in magic, farming or industry in eons. Not since the last age have we seen real development in anything. Stifling innovation looks a great deal like stability to those who fear change."

"Those are exaggerations of the truth. Human wizards leveling mountains? Changing the courses of rivers? Elfmen crossbreeding and high elves force-evolving creatures? Remind me how well all that went."

"I'm trying to make something that doesn't require magic," Adamar said. "Something that could help anyone of any kind or level of magic. A simple mill tool that uses water for power. That means you don't need a wood weaver or a stone weaver. Anyone of any magic could mill grain or sugar or anything they want."

"Listen, I trust you and your engines, but passing that power to anyone who comes along? That sounds like chaos. Who would control it? Who would ensure it was safe?"

"The people who buy from a miller."

"Who would protect them?"

"Who protects them now?" Adamar asked.

"The guilds do," said Eva.

"The guilds protect their own bottom line by preventing change, even change that could improve the lives of the people."

"Change needs to be controlled," said Eva. "Chaos hurts people."

"Life is change," Adamar said. "Breathing is change. Seasons are change. Their idea of stability is like someone randomly declaring that exhaling produces bad air and, thus, must be bad for you. Only *inhaling* is good, so we let people inhale, but then clamp our hands on their mouths to prevent a reality we arbitrarily decided was a bad thing."

"What a stupid metaphor."

"Don't you see?" asked Adamar. "The guilds aren't in it for the people, but they certainly sell their shit like it is. 'We're doing this for your own good.' They keep us from growing."

"And what? Your answer is what we all need?" asked Eva. "Get rid of the guilds and let people do what they want? The people can't be trusted."

"They can't? So…where do these angelic guild-masters come from?" Adamar looked around. "Are these heavenly beings somehow free of greed and selfishness? They come from the very people you claim are incapable of making their own decisions. What makes them better than any average person at figuring out what's good?"

"Their education and experience, for one," she said. "Never mind that they're trying to help the people."

"The people? The ones you've barely spent any time among? Those people? The ones who wish they had more choices and more freedom?"

"Experts study these things," said Eva. "They are wiser than average people about what they need."

"No one knows what they need better than them." Adamar pointed back toward Southdown. "The idea that people who have no skin in the game are better at making decisions than those who do is so arrogant it hurts."

"Arrogance? How about the arrogance of a single common man

who thinks he can change the world while his wife pays all the bills!"

"I'm trying to pay the bills!" Adamar cried when a peal of thunder crashed over them and unleashed torrents of rain.

Adamar cursed and pulled his sopping wife under a nearby bridge pylon. They tucked themselves under a bricked awning and huddled from the downpour.

"We made a deal," Eva raised her voice over the torrent as she ran her fingers through her tangled yellow hair.

Adamar stiffened. "He blacklisted me from the inner city."

"You've always had the option."

"It's a bad option."

"One you promised me to take if Southdown failed," Eva said.

Adamar glared into the heavy sheets of rain.

"You promised me!"

Adamar scowled.

"Why don't we go home!?" she asked. "We won't need to fight for every last thing we have. We can be comfortable and productive again."

"Don't you realize how they control you with family?" asked Adamar. "How they parcel their love so you'll do what they want?"

"It's because my family is wealthy, isn't it?"

"I don't give two shits about their magic or their money," said Adamar. "I am fully opposed to their pride, from which even the poorest man can suffer."

"And is this not pride?"

"My pride is for making my own way. Not being owned by other people's expectations. You shared that when you left with me."

"I didn't think it would take this long," Eva said.

"Doing great things takes time. Perhaps you and your magic don't realize such things."

"How dare you," Eva said. "I married you, didn't I?"

"And you've complained ever since because my work wasn't as good or as quick as your father's natural magic. You have this distorted view of what it takes to build foundations. You look around at all these poor people and wonder why we can't just make them all better. They need time and options. Don't you see that what you're asking me to do is give up my ability to choose my own way in favor of someone else's? I can't be happy living other peoples' lives. Never mind that your mother is the most miserable woman I've ever met!"

"Don't bring my mother into this!" Eva said. "But even she has all she needs."

"I don't live by a philosophy of materialism."

"Does that excuse you from feeding me, too?"

Adamar fumed.

"What would you rather we do?" Eva's voice quieted. "You work in a stable, I go…do what?"

"Maybe my sister would know someone."

"You suggest she could get me a job in *Rainhold*?" Eva stuttered. "There's only one kind of job for a woman in—"

"Not like that!" Adamar said. When Adamar saw hope dwindle in her, his heart seized.

"What would you have me do, if I can't do much more than you in Southdown without being outed to my father?" Eva asked. "We've more than scraped bottom. And I'm *hungry*." Her voice cracked. "I'm starving. I don't care about how it looks or the shame or the gossip. I need to eat, Adamar. I need a warm place to sleep and a safe place to rest. What good is your pride if your wife becomes a whore on the street?"

"We could try Kuthanel."

"Two weeks away!?" Eva exclaimed. "We're already starving!" Eva drew closer. "tIt's time to go home."

Adamar's chest tightened. He didn't want to return or live such a demeaning life again. And yet…she *had* married him, and that came with obligations more important than his pride. When he didn't respond, she turned away.

As she huddled in the frigid morning air, thin and frail, his heart sank. He had failed to achieve his goal and his wife paid the cost. After minutes of fighting, he nodded. "Alright."

"Alright?" she asked.

It took a moment, but Adamar nodded again. "Yeah."

"You're…sure?" she asked.

As if waiting for his surrender, the rain ebbed to a light drizzle to reveal New Gordon's towers rising on hills only a few miles distant.

The relief washing over Eva's shoulders twisted Adamar to the core. Failure cut him deep when only surrender bought for Eva what he hoped his success might afford.

Mists and rain wreathed the old city towers kissed by the distant sunrise. As Eva breathed easier, a tear snaked down the side of Adamar's cheek before he hid it by leaning into the rain.

"Alright…" he said. "Back to the Academy."

11

Gathering the Boy

Haephan's silhouette hobbled in midnight darkness while his ears strained for the faintest warning of a potential attacker, picker or rape gang wandering the dark. His sensitive hearing saved his life countless times. His limp, however, forced him to leave before the sun and return when it was dark. His injuries had increased the pity factor among the wealthy, and though he affected tears when he wished, the actual pain in his swollen face brought them all the quicker and more abundant when he needed them.

The faintest twist of mud caused him to change his path. He slipped around a corner, under one of Rainhold's countless shanty houses, and came out the other side before a pursuer could reach where he had stood in the road.

Disappearing was his best skill. Few could escape unseen as he did. His leg slowed him a bit, but slowness was a way of hiding, at times.

Haephan smirked at his hapless pursuer before he continued with bare feet through ice-crackling mud. He zig-zagged through amorphous neighborhoods of poorly stacked wood and the occasional canvas tent, down Rainhold's four broad terraces and the final drop to the docks. Boathouses lining the docks were often built against the stone walls of the terrace's heavy foundations, forming a solid rear wall that protected them from thieves and weather.

Crossing the merchant's road where morning wagons would wander to gather goods and take them into the city, he approached the roof of a boathouse built over the water. He peeled a few tiles aside far enough to wiggle between two boathouses before resetting to create a seamless roof between the two. After setting his feet on the extended crossbeams twenty feet above the canal, he opened a hole, hidden by a well-placed wooden sheet, and crawled into his nest before shutting the door behind him with care.

If anyone was clever enough to track and witness him sliding under roof tiles, they would not easily find the second entrance to his home.

Haephan winced as his bruised legs brushed over the rough-shod wooden slats on his way into his nest. The guardians had probably broken more than a few bones, though none of those injuries stopped him from being able to go begging or picking. He cried for a moment before wiggling deeper into his nest where the rising roof widened enough for him to sit up.

Finding the pocket was lucky happenstance while hiding from a roving gang. Once discovered, he built a nest with spare boards and filled it with stolen clothes and other scraps. The space was big enough only to lie down or sit up. Before long, he might have to risk discovery by rebuilding it, or by moving elsewhere in Rainhold.

Despite his ache for sleep, Haephan searched his meager belongings for his tin box. He pulled out today's pickings and shoved them inside with his other winnings and savings. Once he closed and returned the tin, he fished around for the last of the spark sticks he scalped from a drunken huntsman. He scraped it across the wood and winced as it sparkled to a brief, piercing brightness.

Holding it to the side while his gaze adjusted, he scanned the old wooden brace where long ago he drew three stick-figures—two large and a smaller one in between. He didn't know who his parents might be. No sweetheart had ever claimed him, and none would likely ever know who the father had been, anyhow. He had nothing more than a wish to have known them.

Haephan curled up and wished to be anywhere else. If only a single thought could carry him far from here; anywhere but Rainhold. He wanted escape, to disappear and reappear in the places he'd heard of around the world. Cities and coasts and all the other places he heard of while stealing from the wealthy and the free.

He wanted to be out there, among the world with new peoples and places.

Anywhere but here.

While he watched, the figures on the wood seemed to move. Father and mother danced in circles with the boy. Haephan didn't seem perturbed by the sight, and smiled as the adults swung the child about with joy.

Light flickered across his makeshift wall as they walked and danced and played. The misty-eyed orphan giggled when the imaginary family tripped and fell together and laughed.

Wiping away tears of weakness, Haephan gasped as they flowed as streams over his body to fill the space to the top. Walls fell away and left behind an infinite darkness interrupted by warbling light shining from far above.

Think and you will move, whispered someone.

He searched for its source before the burn in his lungs drove him upward.

Think and move. SHIFT!

When he thought his lungs would burst, Haephan willed himself to cross the distance. In a blink, the chaotic waves were within reach.

Haephan broke surface with a ripped inhale. Shards of wood rained and splashed into the gentle water around him. Beyond the falling debris, boathouse workers and a stocky wizard with rusty gray hair encircled him from the docks on either side and by the stone wall, lit by the fade of dawn warming the Vitner.

Haephan quivered in the shock of frigid waves and coughed water from his lungs. Beside the wizard, the boathouse owner scowled. Haephan scanned the gaping hole in the bottom of his nest, panicked in search of his tin box and flailed to snatch it.

"What's your name, boy?" asked the wizard in a vested suit and charcoal robe.

Haephan didn't respond, sure he couldn't escape.

"Recognize me, do you?" said the wizard. "You have something that belongs to me. Come here."

Haephan swam closer until two of the workers could haul him onto the dock. He yelped and leaned on his good foot before the workers tightened their grips, afraid he would attempt flight.

When the wizard snatched the tin, Haephan groped for it before the men wrenched his arms away. The boy grunted as he fought tears. The wizard shook the tin and pointed at Haephan. "You have spent some of what you stole from me."

Haephan gulped. How did he know?

The wizard held it up. "I will offer you an opportunity to keep this tin and all that is inside of it. And what you have already expended from it. Either I can sell you to the boat master here and he can use you as a depth marker…"

Haephan gulped.

"…or you will come with me and earn this sum as my manservant."

A cornered animal with nowhere to run and no good legs to carry him there, Haephan's shoulders sank. The funny dreams with the stick figures faded, but the whispering voice telling him to shift rang in his ears the way glancing at the sun too long left an afterimage.

"Master Yonesy…" the wizard addressed the boat master, "does this boy owe you rent or damages?"

"Not sure." Yonesy inspected the hole. "He might be a better anchor."

Haephan shrank.

Yonesy smirked at him. "Two weeks work here, wizard, if you permit. He can pay off his debt."

"Deal. After which, you will return to me to pay off this debt." He hefted the tin.

"How-how long will that take?" the boy asked.

The wizard raised the tin. "I'll let you know."

Haephan clenched his jaw.

"What is your name, boy?" asked the wizard.

"Haephan."

"I am Wizard Setherick Elverbane," he said. "You will refer to me as wizard."

"Yes, wizard."

Elverbane extended the tin, which Haephan took and held at his waist. After speaking with Yonesy, Elverbane led him along the dock.

Haephan struggled to comprehend that his world had been shattered to some unknown and terrifying end. Now bound to a wizard—something everyone knew would lead to torture and death—he followed the old figure up the stairs to meet a beautiful woman in an aqua-trimmed pearl dress with dark blue hair and silver irises. Behind her, a topless, horse-drawn carriage awaited. The boy froze.

They did terrible things to children at the magic school. What would they do to him? Haephan continued to the top of the stairs. At the wizard's motion, the boy climbed into the carriage and perched on the far edge of the forward-facing seat. There was no running from a wizard or a witch. Surely the blue-haired woman was a witch. What had he gotten into?

SonLara made a faint gesture at Haephan, then a second. She leaned toward Elverbane and whispered, "Did you know the child does not respond to magic?"

"Aye," he said. "Only one such as him could ignore a picking ward."

"Such as what?" she asked.

"He's a vacant," Elverbane muttered.

"Fascinating," she said. Her eyes narrowed on the term but said nothing more.

"Come," said Elverbane. "I think we to ought feed the boy before he thinks we intend to eat him." He pointed at the front seat with his thick finger. Haephan bounced to the other side and kept his head down.

SonLara smirked as she climbed into the carriage, followed by Elverbane.

As the carriage moved away, Haephan scanned the shanties on either side. Hundreds of hidden locals locked upon the wealth in their midst. He spotted a pair of eyes he realized he might not again see.

Tilly's head peeked around a tent flap in wonder and terror at Haephan's capture.

Staring into his own fear, Haephan rocked as the carriage returned to dryer land and his doom.

12
Eva's Return

Eva emerged from the grand foyer onto the highest landing of the glittering Hall Eminostra. At the railing, she soaked in the view of dancing couples dressed in their finest, tables of conversation and merriment, circles of elder wizards and tighter circles of their beautiful wives in twitter over the next scandal.

Drawing in and out a slow breath—to taste the sweet cornucopia of exotic perfumes and fine food, as well as the tightness of her silk dress—she descended along the right curved stairwell and two shallow landings to the main floor.

The pit in her stomach danced as she searched for her mother. When she and Adamar returned to her family home only hours prior, she insisted to all staff that no one alert her mother, for fear of ruining the surprise.

Intricate lace adorned the edges of her navy ballgown hugging her slender frame whose colors accentuated the blonde of her newly curled hair. At her appearance, dozens of surprised looks flooded outward across hundreds of shocked faces.

Eva smiled under the first powders she had worn in years. To be under golden magiclight again, wearing her finest, in the aura of her family…Eva sighed. She missed this so much.

Reaching the bottom, she greeted old family friends who struggled to maintain their decorum at her sudden appearance. She didn't care, though the aroma of exquisite food threatened her self-control. Even now, she ached to rush to a nearby table and devour its contents, but instead soaked in the glory of her return.

Hall Eminostra extended as a four-alcoved circle. Her parents table sat in the elevated rear alcove near the center to give them both the best view and ensured they were most likely to be seen by all others. Hoping to avoid their detection, she kept cliques and circles between them as she circumvented the main dance floor.

Her mother sat at the family table while her father stood off to the side with the King's Voice, Ilrich Wythe and another gentleman she didn't recognize.

Eva succeeded in avoiding her mother's gaze and stayed ahead of the rush of shock spreading through the ballroom before she backed toward the table and spun about with a flourish of her long white gloves and blue dress while brandishing her best smile.

First ignored by her mother who did not react at the appearance of ambitious young ladies hoping for her attention, the pale faces of the family members at the table drew her gaze. Shock overcame Seni.

Eva was surprised at how old her mother truly appeared and how caked the makeup had become upon her.

"Eva!" Seni cried with an unceremonious leap to her feet. She opened her arms for Eva to come forward before she gripped her daughter by the shoulders. "By the Self, Eva? What has happened to you?"

"Mother?" Eva asked and fought a nervous laugh. "What do you mean?"

"You appear as if—on death's door," Seni's cry of concern faltered under the whispered fear of scandal.

A strained smile crawled across Eva's face. "I am *here*, mother."

"Of course you are," said Seni with a weak smile. Her attention fluttered to the dress with a brief moment of disdain. "Where did you get this?"

"It's cousin Alda's, mother, left behind from last year's ball, so the maids told me," said Eva. "Is it not lovely?"

"Lovely," Seni said. "We will have to— How long are you here for? Have you returned to us? We will need to get you a fine dress tomorrow." In a moment of abandon, she hugged her daughter.

Eva blinked tears and said, "Thank you, mother."

Her mother retreated. "Please, come." They sat at the large table. A ready attendant uniformed in Venetian blue held a chair, ready to set it for Eva to sit. Eva would have to thank the house mistress, Mistress Donaghan—her watchful eye must have noticed and commissioned the chair.

Eva greeted the panoply of family friends sitting around the table as they welcomed her home—the younger cousins were more enthusiastic, the older more reserved and wary. All, however, gaped.

"Is something wrong?" asked Eva.

"My dear," said her hesitant mother, "you appear as if you haven't eaten months."

Eva was about to reply that such wasn't far from the truth, but instead smiled as if the idea were silly, and reclined.

As questions mounted about her absence, she wielded her smile like a shield. "Please. The journey back has been tiring and I just arrived."

Taking the cue, the women dropped the questions, though Eva knew they would gossip on it without end. Eva let them talk and chatter and admired their finery, dresses and powders, though the amount covering her mother alarmed her. "Are you alright, mother?"

Having never taken her focus from Eva, Seni asked, "What do you mean, my dear?"

"I just—are you well?"

"Of course, my dear," she said and smiled. "You're home!"

The woman to Eva's right tsk'ed loudly enough to draw eyes until everyone realized she was fussing over her own dress.

"What's wrong, Theris?" Eva asked her nearest cousin.

"I have found a scratch," Theris pouted and fingered a tiny hole hidden in the lace of her puffed sleeve.

Eva could not even see the hole.

"I will have the woman fired," Theris growled.

"Fired?" said Eva. "This appears new. Are you sure you didn't make the hole after arriving?"

"What would it matter?" snapped Theris. "I have a hole in my dress."

"In the lace, full of existing holes?" Eva asked.

"That's not the point."

"And you would blame your seamstress?"

"Whom else could I blame?" Theris asked.

"Come here," said Eva as she turned in her chair, used her magic to free a single thread from a hidden fold in her own dress and began weaving it over the hole in Theris's, a skill she had learned working with seamstresses in Kuthanel.

Table conversations came to a halt as Eva anchored the thread and sealed the injury. Once finished, she reclined with a self-satisfied smile.

"How did you do that?" Theris asked with unveiled disgust.

"You made the hole, Theris," said Eva. "You love snuggling up to the senior officers and then are shocked when your paper-thin dresses catch on their medals and buckles. I'm surprised a belt hasn't ripped a new hole in your mouth."

Theris paled and rosied at the same time.

"Don't blame your seamstress because you're careless with your men," said Eva as she locked eyes with her. "I daresay any woman you fire is luckier than those you don't."

The table gasped.

"Seni's daughter has spent entirely too much time among the commoners," muttered one of the older women across the large table. "Going native."

"You don't seem to have a problem with commoners when they let you toss dice with them in the Whittle," said Eva.

The woman paled and her mouth fell open with a squeak while her companion leapt to her feet as if to retort but also failed to speak.

Eva realized holding her tongue for fine society had changed in her short time in Kuthanel and Southdown among women whose banter proved to bond. These women couldn't handle the slightest deviation in their delicacies.

"I shall go look for my father," she said and left the table.

Her father had left behind Wythe and his companion to confer with a city constable, flanked by two Crimson Guardians standing at parade rest.

Wandering among tables, she realized Seni never asked after Adamar.

Adamar hadn't spoken to her since their return. Once at the house, he made for the kitchens. Jealousy tickled her that he probably now slept with a full belly and warm bed.

The scandal of her romance with her father's handsome servant riveted her youth before the two stole away for what Eva hoped would be an adventure from the drag of city nobility, heavy bureaucracy, and her father's constant nagging about her returning to her calling.

The distant scandal seemed silly now as she sought her father's joy, but his last rebuke to her departure gave her pause. Would he accept her return? Would he accept Adamar? Her pressure on Adamar faltered under a sudden fear her father wouldn't allow them to come home.

When Eva pulled herself from her thoughts, she was startled to discover him staring at her through the crowd.

Gulping, she advanced again when he broke from his conversation, rushed toward and scooped her up.

"Eva!" Ornith Dufrain snatched her into a bear hug before setting her on her feet.

"Hi, Daddy!" she cried.

His long fingers cupped her face and drew her forehead against his lips. "Eva, Eva, Eva."

She smiled.

"You're home!" he exclaimed. "When did you get here?"

"Today," she said.

Like her mother, her father appeared much older than last she saw him. Gray filled in what before merely speckled, in addition to heavy bags under his eyes. The well-manicured hair and trimmed beard from a distance hid what nearness could not obscure. "And Adamar?"

She nodded but could not speak.

He pulled her for another tight hug. "Oh, I missed you."

"You, too, Daddy," she said and smiled against his chest. "Who was that? Standing with you and Master Wythe?"

"Oh, the man and the Crimson Guardians?"

"Mhm."

"Sigmund Lurli," said Dufrain. "Head of the merchants guild. Keeps me well-informed on all the goings on around the city."

She hugged him tighter before she checked her makeup. After the gloss in her gaze faded, she noticed people whispering behind gloved hands and wigged curls, glancing at her frame void of its former youthful curves. She hugged her father all the more with gladness as his arms wrapped around her.

"Are you back to stay?" he asked.

"Yes, Daddy," she said, feeling the relief that food and shelter and care would no longer be her problem.

"Wonderful." He kissed the top of her head. "I have missed you so. There is much I'd like to share with you. And I look forward to seeing Adamar again. I have missed him."

Eva smiled against his chest.

"I would have your mind and skills on present city problems," he said. "You will be a welcome addition. I had half a mind to send for you."

"To send for me? You knew where I was?"

"Of course," he said and gripped her arms warmly. "I have never let you long out of my sight. Only now have you surprised me!"

Eva pondered how well her father kept tabs on her while in Southdown but couldn't help but stare. "Daddy, what is wrong? You look so tired."

"The lycans and the wars are drawing ever closer to the city," he said. "It's taking all my time."

"But isn't that Myogan's responsibility? Outside the walls?"

"We're all called up to help. I'm currently studying ways to handle the lycans."

"Are you getting sleep?" she asked.

"There are many long nights," he said. "There is much to be done, but it will be better now that you're home."

"But Daddy, can I not rest first?"

"Of course, of course," he said. "And Adamar. Take time to recover your strength. When he is ready, I would be eager to have him once more in my shop. Surely he's put away all that foolishness of taking care of himself. What could a vacant like him possibly accomplish?" He shook his head. "I'm so glad you're home."

Eva wiped her tears, surprised at the affront his words inspired in her. Adamar had accomplished amazing things—she had never doubted his skill, only his politick in handling the guilds and their interests out in Kuthanel or nearer in Southdown across the Estamar Canal.

"We'll get things back to normal," he said and slipped his arm around her shoulders as they approached Seni. "Even this selfdamn war. We'll get back to life as we knew it." He squeezed her shoulders.

The reason she left in the first place tickled her mind. She put on her smile, ignored it, and searched for food and old friends.

13
Siam's Tree

Elverbane and SonLara stood in the azure ambience of a tall holographic tree rising at the heart of a broad circular amphitheater. A shallow concave ceiling over a three-quarter classroom reflected the blue light downward. Two acute walls met to form the fourth sector of the circular room rising behind the stage and teacher's desk behind the dais.

Elverbane tugged magics to shift color variance across the magical testing construct as SonLara pondered.

"The boy," she said. "He has no magic. Have you ever seen it before?"

"Yes," said Elverbane. "My previous manservant, Ian, was a vacant."

"Vacant?"

"He was studied by the Academy," said Elverbane. "It's a term coined by Dufrain."

"Ah, the city administrator," SonLara said. "He is also the head of the Academy? It's not common for a city to carry two magical schools."

"The Academy is not a school as much as it is a governing body and swinging arm of Myogan's government over all of New Gordon, including Southdown. Dufrain's role is usually a dual-hatted position."

"I thought the guilds ran Southdown?"

"Tenuous partnership," said Elverbane. "Southdown grew because of the Estamar. The monarchy dosnae want to let it go because of all the taxes. The Academy oversees the city constabulary and the Crimson Guard who keep order. If not for the city administrator keeping both sides happy, Southdown would probably secede from New Gordon."

SonLara mused. "I had wondered."

"Have you never encountered vacancy before?" asked Elverbane.

"Not like this," said SonLara. "Not a complete magical voidance. Is Ian the only prior to Haephan?"

"That I've encountered, yes, but I know there are more here in town."

"And its cause?" asked SonLara.

"No answers, yet," said Elverbane, "per what little research we've placed on the subject."

"The Andonese have never had natural vacants. Variable magic, yes, but not this degree of absence. How could such a being survive without a baseline layer of second energy?"

"We're not clear, and other matters have taken priority," said Elverbane.

SonLara scanned the holographic tree. "While the boy is void of second energy, he brims with first."

"I have never studied first energy," said Elverbane. "Most mages don't. It's too ethereal for us. Many think it's farcical."

"You don't believe in spirit?"

"Spirit? Ghosts? Ethereum? Perhaps to believe men have souls. But no method of interacting with first energy has ever been discovered here in the continental core." He raised his brow. "I see the Andonese have."

She met his gaze.

"Interesting."

"How do vacants normally integrate into society?" she asked.

"They don't," said Elverbane. "Without magic, they can't join the guilds, so finding work is very difficult."

"How widespread is the problem?"

"Ahm not sure."

"And how did one previously come to your employ?" she asked.

"Vacants are useful in the lab," said Elverbane. "They cannot be harmed when magical experiments go awry. Also, they can clean up blue objects without fear of being injured or otherwise affected."

"And no one has ever found vacancy's source?"

"Not that I'm aware of," said Elverbane. "To be honest, vacancy has proven only a convenience to me. My interests remain with dimensional studies."

"I've heard of natural vacants nowhere else," SonLara said. "If you've only seen it here in the core, around South Edenia, might it be related to Eden?"

"That occurred to me once," said Elverbane, "but I'm not inclined enough to follow it."

"Curious that you should find so many vacants in your employ."

Elverbane harrumphed. "I'm surprised the Andonese know of Siam's Tree. I imagined you would have come up with your own proprietary test for macroenergetic stability."

"Well, you know, few spells compare to those constructed to mirror the Tree of Life, itself," she smirked. "Eldest spells are often the best."

Elverbane mused after noting how her smirk tugged at her lips. He motioned at the tree. "If I may?"

She motioned for him to proceed.

At his gesture, the outer layers shriveled and disappeared. He deconstructed and added layers that interacted with the dimensional limbs and the thirteen shades of prime energy. "Witch Mira E'Bremiena theorized that vibrating rings were one of the roots of creation, and that their particular acoustical attenuation determined what atomic particle they comprised." As he changed layers and stripped others, the tree thinned and the jagged branches smoothed into curves. He drew out what appeared to be a weak section under the branch into a stark relief and added a color test. Instead of expressing a color usually used for error testing, the section faltered and faded.

"What is that?" SonLara asked.

"Tenth delve, low side."

"The delve of bridging," SonLara muttered.

"The great conductor. Failure at great scale would be catastrophic," said Elverbane. "If this is failing, it would be foundational to not only magic, but the fabric of reality."

"Self in heaven, it does," SonLara whispered. "Does this show up on the primary?"

Elverbane shook his head and said, "I had to relayer it before the fade appeared. No one is likely to notice this unless they're looking for dimensional continuity, and I'm of the very few."

A shiver passed through SonLara. "I need to contact my superiors."

Elverbane nodded.

"Is there any more to this?"

"Unless you know how to push Siam's Tree beyond its known limits? Or other tests?"

"Other delves?" she asked.

"We can try them one by one, but if they don't show up on what we've already seen, they're not likely."

"I will go contact him," she said. "Will you be here?"

"Contact him? Using the rimsportal?"

SonLara did not respond.

Noting yet another mystery, Elverbane plucked his timepiece from his robes. "No, I need to get back to Ashmore. I have chores."

"Isn't the boy supposed to help?"

"The boathouse isn't done with him until late. Come by after?" he asked.

She nodded, glanced again at the construct and left.

Hyram's Concentrics in Furian's X indicated quality degradation. The failure displayed on Siam's Tree might indicate something altogether worse—a complete energetic fault that chilled his blood. He considered all magic vulnerable by such a fault and found no end. Hundreds of magics depended on this continuity, and if it faded, would the others, too?

When he moved to delayer the weave and dissipate the construct, the construct did not respond. Despite a second and third try, the glowing tree remained.

"Hell," he muttered.

From within the depth of the holographic trunk, a light expanded and filled the tree. He retreated and scrambled to raise a shield. He'd never before encountered a violent feedback to Siam's Test, but other forms of magic tests sometimes were dangerous if improperly extinguished. Panic touched his breast as he recalled the explosion by Furian's X, an equally benign magical test that had exploded on him.

When a shield did not appear, terror gripped him when he could not connect with affectational magic.

"Great Self," Elverbane said while he retreated from the growing light and stumbled across the low stage to the floor. When he sat up, the tree was gone, replaced by a towering figure, wreathed in vibrating power, adorned in luminous white robes with a piercing gaze that cut through his heart.

"Fear not, Setherick Tumarel Elverbane," the multi-voice echoed in the white chamber. "I am Auiena, High Archon of the Great Self."

Elverbane quivered in terror. "A subrim?"

"Yes," his voice rippled the dust across the floor. "I bear news which destines all life across your world, a shift in dimensional paradigm sent from the mouth of His Holiness."

"I saw," Elverbane coughed.

"Rise, human, and witness tomorrow."

When Elverbane rose, the room fell away into an empty black, lit alone by the subrim.

"For many millions of years, the whole of your realm has lived together in peace."

"Millions?" Elverbane asked. "Recorded history extends only nine hundred thousand years."

"Your world has fulfilled its purpose, but is now inadequate for the coming age. A new world is dawning for all races across the continent."

A distant sun pierced the horizon of a new, tiny world around them.

Pangea laid out before him as a topographical floor map like one he'd seen in Gumera, only this one had strips and wisps and carpets of clouds and weather, bathed in climbing dawnlight. At the map's edge, only paces away beyond the shore and the broad oceans beyond, the world disappeared into the nether.

Even as horror kissed Elverbane, he marveled at the finitude of the universe while around him the blue of daytime sky met the starlit black of night. Elverbane cursed. “Where have you brought me?”

“Peace.” the subrim’s rumble bathed Elverbane in calm. “And look upon tomorrow.” The subrim motioned toward a lonely speck on the furthest reach of ocean from the continent. In a single moment, the brownish grain of sand blossomed into a green mountain rising from the water. Beyond it, a new second world faded into reality, buttoned to his Pangea by the speck of an island.

More appeared round about the map, each with its own new world stretching outward. One island grew as a great Tree, one formed inside out with its peak at its bottom and shores high in the sky, another of swirled ice and still another of sand and stone. Each stood as a tiny, unique reflection of the shadowy double world beyond, and each more fantastic than the last. Endless sand seas, an undersea city, islands floating in the sky connected by rivers, a ring hovering in the starry black and a ball in space gathering land as it turned.

“What do I see, messenger?”

“The culmination of the Immortal.”

Elverbane blanched.

“The time to come is of breaking.”

“And what role would you have me play in it?” asked Elverbane.

“You have been chosen to shatter the world,” said the subrim.

Falling to a knee, Elverbane’s stomach lifted and ejected its contents into the oceans. He spat it out, wiped his mouth and again found himself somewhere new. Ancient trees climbed around him, a mossy forest floor replaced the map and, out between the trunks of heavy arbors, a crown of peaks encircled the valley in which they stood.

“Where are we?” asked Elverbane.

The subrim motioned behind him.

Elverbane faced the edge of a monstrous crater. At its bottom rose an ancient tree bearing thirteen primary branches and a bevy of green flora. Its root base spread more than seventy yards and its trunk climbed well more than a hundred. “Oh dear self in heaven.” His voice dropped to a whisper. “The La’Du Lira Al’Cular.”

“Within its roots lie the future of humanity,” said the subrim.

“What would you have me do?”

“You will travel to Eden. Using the child you call vacant, you will retrieve its seeds gathered within its bosom.”

“And then?”

“Advent exodus. The boy will herald the coming of new worlds, fresh branches of this realm for the races to migrate. New places will arise that will pave the way to a great peace to last an age.”

“The boy is involved?” he asked.

Auiena stepped close and touched Elverbane’s forehead. A flood of images rushed into his mind like a dam collapsing under the weight of an ocean of knowledge. “The boy is the center point for the soul of the coming creation and representative of life in its entirety. He is the one, the single, the All.”

Sunlight faltered and flickered. A shattered city of marble and stone now filled the valley. The hollow contained remnants of a square mile of a beautiful, abandoned palace of marble and wood. A column of light blazed before him and, within it, a boy with ginger hair floating beneath a pixilark burning with the light of the sun. Above the pixie rotated a sword whose magic dwarfed not only himself, but even Auiena next to him.

More than the boy, thousands more figures hovered all about in a similar trance. A lone figure with bone white hair stood at the base of the column of light and gazed upward at the event.

A catastrophic sound erupted from the child—a crow that reverberated with countless others extending into infinity. Its vibrato rattled the fabric of Elverbane’s sinews. Beneath the ginger child, detritus swirled upward into dust, exploded outward and leveled the crater, the entire valley and all nine mountain peaks around them before traveling outward beyond the horizon. His crow washed away the reality of the world and dimmed to a faintness like all others caught in the air like him.

Adorned in awe, amusement, import and power, the figure standing beneath the ginger boy locked her silver gaze onto Elverbane.

“Because of the dracos, the fabric of this reality is threatened,” said

Auiena. "The boy in your care will pave the way for one who is to come, the reflection of the Great Self's chosen, the herald of salvation." The blazoned image of the floating child remained, even as the rest of the world faded to an empty black. The sky disappeared but for the sword, pixie, boy and the congregation around them. "Through the vacant, you will pave the way for the future."

The congregation now glowed against the new darkness like stars in an endless universe before each fell dark.

"Make haste, Elverbane," said the fading voice. "The Great Self is watching."

14

Dogwood

Drowned in darkness, the throne room flickered in torchlight. Five wizards and ten martial mages stood guard over the king as three tall figures walked in step across the circular throne room. Every curtain was drawn to afford the strange delegation the courtesy requested.

They stopped together ten paces before the king with the same swish of their long robes and drew their hoods to reveal powdered skin, long bone-white hair and silver eyes—high elves.

"Hail to King Myogan of New Gordon," said the leader, a female whose silken voice warmed the stone chamber. "I am Estimia, envoy from Krys Seagol of Kukhel. My lord sends his greetings and thanks you for your hospitality."

"Your presence honors us and New Gordon," said the old man sitting straight on the edge of his throne. Gray filled his close-cropped beard hugging his midnight chin. He dipped his head in their honor. "How may New Gordon serve the high elves of Kukhel?"

"Krys Seagol has well considered the plight of South Edenia and the new uprisings to the west," she said. "After much deliberation, he sends a gift."

One of her companions stepped forward with a wide ornate lead case perched over his upturned hands. Estimia unlatched the lock on the long edge and opened it to reveal a bronze sword with a straight, flared blade and thistled guard.

Myogan frowned, unsure of what a single sword could mean. "Does he—"

Behind him, Administrator Degreneth gasped. At Myogan's gesture, a tall earthy brown man with white hair receding but for three streaks at his ears and along the crown of his head climbed the steps and whispered into his ear. Myogan's brows climbed.

"King Myogan, The Dogwood Sword as a gift to your war effort." Her announcement caused the mages to stiffen.

"The Dogwood Sword?" Myogan leaned forward. "I thought it was lost along with the Courte Empire."

She said nothing.

"As grand a gift as such a thing could possibly be, Estimia…" said Myogan. "Whyever would he part with such a thing?"

"His majesty, Krys Seagol, war master of the Thurmine Conference, wishes peace after centuries of constant conflict," she said. "It encroaches even our lands, and he hopes this will end the conflict sooner than it otherwise might."

Myogan stood and approached the delegation. Eyeing the sword, he bowed his head to her, again, before scanning the blade. "Dufrain?"

From the administrators on Myogan's right, Wizard Dufrain approached with a respectful nod to Estimia before waving his hand over the blade. He snapped his fingers, nodded to Myogan and retreated.

"Your gift honors us beyond reckoning." Myogan motioned for an officer, who approached and accepted the gift. "How may New Gordon honor such a monumental gift?"

"Tell no one." Estimia's soft, silken tone chilled the room. "Ever."

Myogan spoke to the room, "As commanded before the arrival of our guests, this event is sealed to the Throne. Should this word get out, I will exact the ultimate cost on every violator."

Attendees said nothing.

"Is that all—" Myogan discovered the three walking out. Soldiers scrambled to open the doors for them before the trio turned the corner and disappeared from view. Myogan waited for the guardians to shut the throne room doors before speaking. "Bloody hell."

The room relaxed.

"Is that really the Dogwood Sword?" asked Myogan.

"Highly likely, your majesty," said Dufrain as the room gathered to inspect it. "Its magic is ancient."

"Legend has it that its powers are extraordinary," said Myogan. "Do you know how to use it?"

"Your majesty," said Dufrain, "I will have to have my historians consult the scrolls and books for us to have a clear idea on how to use it, but I'm confident I can have it ready soon."

"Can you have it in time for the lycans?" Myogan asked.

"I'm sure we can learn what we need—" Dufrain began.

"Your majesty," Orzo politely interrupted as he stepped into the circle, "I would not use that until I was absolutely sure how it works."

"And why's that?" asked Myogan.

"I know how power can destroy people," Orzo's soft voice echoed in the chamber. "Including those using it. That thing should be studied, tested, and mastered before it is ever drawn on a battlefield, or it will be as dangerous to ourselves as to our enemies. That..." He hesitated. "The Dogwood Sword, sire? This isn't just another magic tool or weapon."

"Coming from the entourage of the worldender—" Degreneth glared at Orzo.

"Which means I know better than anyone," snapped Orzo, who softened his voice when addressing the king. "This is not a power to be trifled with."

Degreneth fumed while Myogan pondered.

"Your majesty," began Dufrain. "The Academy has the necessary facilities and personnel to properly conduct testing. And safely. We would like to take point on this."

"Your lordship," Degreneth said and offered a larger bow, "with all due respect to the Academy, its purpose is not that of an educational or testing institution. Belfast's foundational magile colleges are far better agencies to conduct these tests."

Myogan looked between them. "Dufrain, you may conduct your tests, but take great care." He turned to Degreneth. "When he is complete, you may look at it. Until then, I want it kept in the royal vaults. Is that clear?"

"Of course, your majesty," Dufrain and Degreneth spoke over each other as they bowed.

"Be quick about it," said Myogan. "The front will form soon and I will not have my wizards wasted in bookwork."

"Yes, your majesty." Degreneth bowed to mask his fury.

Dufrain offered another deep bow with a small, self-satisfied smirk.

"Which includes the Hero of Tuthomere," said Myogan. "Speaking of which, where is he? I want him here."

"A thousand apologies, sire." Degreneth half bowed. "But Wizard Elverbane left the city on a task before I received your missive. He is due back soon."

"Once he returns, I want him in the council," Myogan said.

"I will ensure it, sire," Degreneth said.

"A shame," said Myogan as he scanned the weapon. "You don't suppose you could try this on a vacant?"

Orzo stiffened. "My lord?"

"New problems in my city," said Myogan.

"Vacants?" Orzo said. Degreneth gulped at his lack of honorifics.

"I'm hearing new word of a population within New Gordon untamed by magic," said Myogan. "I have to figure what to do with them."

"If this is a magical tool, I'm sure no harm will come to any vacant," said Dufrain. "No magic has ever touched them, before. Why should they now?"

"But…the schools have employed vacants for years," said Orzo. "They've posed no threat. And besides, these are people with value, created by the Self. Can you dispose of life so easily, your majesty?"

Degreneth's eyes threatened to leap from his skull.

"They can be a threat in an instant," Myogan said. "I will not leave a threat within our walls while the wolves approach from without. You have vacants at Belfast?"

"Of course, sire," said Degreneth. "Vacants aren't uncommon assistants."

"Send your vacants to the Academy," said Myogan. "I've already directed Dufrain on the matter. He's in charge of handling them. No one is to discuss the vacant problem with anyone who isn't previously authorized, which starts with Dufrain. I won't have anyone inciting riots or flight in the middle of war preparations."

"Yes, your majesty," Degreneth said.

"You all may go." Myogan waved them off.

As the mages bowed and filed out, Orzo scowled as he slipped from the throne room while a pit formed deep in his gut.

15
Ian's Collection

Haephan scrubbed black metal with steel wool. Grease covered every inch of him as he knelt on all fours halfway into a large cook pot, still warm from being used earlier in the evening. Three weeks of constant labor made him want to pass away into the darkness of sleep and never revive.

He completed his two weeks at the boathouse and was ready to try his hand at an easier life when the wizard caught him picking a student. Ever since, the old man had him working from dawn to dusk in every physical task to be found, to which there was no end.

Haephan would have quit by now and fled if not for the large meals they shoved down his throat. He couldn't leave behind three meals a day after spending most of his life at the meager chance of only a few bites.

His attempt to wipe his sweaty brow smeared more grease and left him feeling dirtier than before. Something thwacked him across his bottom.

"Ow!" Haephan cried, recoiled and banged his head against the inside of the pot. His head rang as the older boy behind him cackled.

Haephan's vision doubled and he dropped the steel wool to press his raw palm to the side of his head as tears welled.

"Richard! You get back to work!" the cook's voice echoed inside the pot as Haephan sat on his bottom and cried as he held his head.

Skinny for a cook in her old dress and clean apron, Sara waited to ensure he was alright before returning to her work.

Dazed, Haephan cried it out while his head ached.

"Back to work, boy," said the cook with a calm but firm voice.

Haephan scanned for Richard and returned to the pot. He scrubbed it down, climbed out to retrieve a bucket of hot water to rinse it out, toweled and rolled it onto its bottom for the older boys to lift onto the hanging arms over the cooled hearth. Most of the other boys were gone when he found the cook flipping through paperwork spread across the main kitchen table.

"Are you alright, young man?" She lowered her glasses from inspecting a ledger.

"Yes, ma'am," he said.

"Get along, then. Tell Elverbane I have no more need of you."

The boy's shoulders dropped with relief. "Yes, ma'am."

"Go along," she said.

"Thank you, ma'am," said Haephan. He left the kitchens for the cool evening air of the open campus, crossed paved paths and stepped courtyards between copses of trees and manicured bushes on his way to Ashmore Hall, a long three-story building lining the highest bluff at Belfast. The ornate building and its paved gardens perched upon a cliff's edge on the north end of Belfast Bluff—the school's namesake—and the city descending from it. North and east, Ashmore overlooked endless miles of farmland and rolling hills beyond.

Haephan wavered with exhaustion at Ashmore's main door before he stepped inside, climbed the circular staircase to the third floor, and followed the hallway to Elverbane's private suite on the building's south side. He gulped at the door, afraid the kitchen's dismissal might bring punishment from Elverbane, or that he might find yet some other chore to occupy him. Mustering, he turned the latch, pushed in the heavy door and stepped inside.

The room rose to a magnificent height with a low-hanging chandelier glowing with magic flame invisible to Haephan, though he saw the ambience it left across the room. A roaring fireplace to his left provided a real light source that warmed the space.

Leaning over the large table in the center, Wizard Elverbane looked up from his papers, as did SonLara from her seat next to the roaring hearth.

Haephan's eyes sank closed as he soaked in its warmth.

"Come here, boy," Elverbane motioned to a chair next to SonLara.

Haephan approached the table. "Cook Emira said I'm done in the kitchen. She doesn't want me back."

"I will never see you steal anything from any teacher or student at this school again. Is that clear?"

"Yes, wizard," said Haephan.

"I won't tolerate theft or lying," said Elverbane. "You will perform your duties here with me and you will do them promptly. You will not complain, you will be grateful. So long as you do, you stay fed and employed. Is that clear?"

"Yes, wizard."

"Look at me," the wizard snapped.

The boy stiffened.

"I have little patience for children or whining. I expect you to do your duty and to live honorably. You serve me until I say otherwise, or you go right back to the streets."

"Yes sir," said Haephan.

Elverbane lifted a thin white box from a nearby chair and handed it to the boy. "Here."

Haephan accepted it with care and waited for instructions.

"Open it," said Elverbane.

Haephan tugged at its soft cardboard corners before the top popped. Inside sat a fine white tunic with black trousers. Haephan's eyes widened as he reached for it.

"Don't touch it," Elverbane snapped. "Not until you've bathed."

"Thank you," said Haephan, who quickly added, "wizard."

"Go on. You look filthy."

"Yes, wizard," Haephan sighed. He hesitated with the box.

"Take it and go," Elverbane motioned.

"Yes, wizard," said Haephan as he followed the hallway into the bathroom, set the box on the sink and took a heavy breath, grateful that he didn't have to return to the kitchens. He was surprised to find the tub steaming hot. Had the wizard known he would return at that moment and ordered the water up from the boil room downstairs, or had he done it himself?

Choosing not to care, he shut the door, stripped off his filthy clothes and sank into the hot water an inch at a time until he soaked his greasy frame. He emerged from the water and slicked his hair before reclining against the curve of the tub to soak in its heat when the sound of Elverbane's and SonLara's voice drifted through the air vents.

"Are you sure they'll fit?" asked Elverbane. "They look big."

"He's a growing child," she said. "You never give tailored clothing to a boy."

Elverbane harrumphed. "I haven't been a child for a very long time."

"Nor I," she said.

"I'm almost done."

"Your trip?"

Silence.

"Does the child yet know?" asked SonLara.

Haephan cracked an eye.

"It's not his place to know," said Elverbane. "Only to obey."

"To walk into the jaws of death?"

Haephan grew pensive.

"The subrim wants it?" asked Elverbane. "He'll get it."

"You don't sound enthused with a mission directly from the Great Self," said SonLara.

"Great Self?" Haephan whispered in disbelief.

"Would you?" asked Elverbane.

"I serve Him every day, in every breath."

"I am not so holy," said Elverbane.

"Who is?" asked SonLara.

"What would you do if a subrim told you that you were going to break the world?" asked Elverbane. "And what does that mean, anyway? Break the world? Are you kidding me? I have things to do."

"Things to do? Something more important than such a mission?"

"If I am to be the one to do such a thing, I'd like to be done with it," said Elverbane. "I have…other, pressing matters to attend."

"Have you considered that what you see in Hyram's Concentrics is in tandem with the subrim's words?"

"What?" asked Elverbane.

"He told you the coming time was of breaking," said SonLara. "Consider your concentrics and ask yourself who better is equipped to guide the coming age amidst such a change."

"Not sure I care to guide anyone," said Elverbane.

"Aren't you a teacher?"

Elverbane fell silent.

Haephan frowned, unable to follow most of their conversation.

"Are you worried about the boy?" she asked.

"Haephan? Of course not," Elverbane said.

Haephan slowed.

"I don't have to think about that one," said Elverbane.

Haephan's shoulders sank.

"The boy is sharp," said SonLara.

Haephan's head came up.

"I've seen him avoid being seen," she continued. "He moves where you don't look. He knows what the people around him are thinking. I think he's as prepared as a boy his age can be for what's ahead."

"He had better be," Elverbane said. "If what the subrim said about him is to come true, it's going to be difficult. I cannae'magine what half he said means. No'for the boy, no'for me, no'for anythin'."

"What do you fear?" she asked.

"Everything," Elverbane admitted. "No. No'knowing. I hate not knowing."

"Uncertainty is no easy thing to face," she said. "You don't stand alone, Setherick."

Haephan climbed from the water and toweled off. The motion of his exit washed away any further echoes of their conversation. He dried as best he could before donning the fine clothes, which hung loose. The trousers did not want to stay on his waist. Holding them in place, he returned to the study.

The two turned at his arrival.

"Where's the belt, boy?" asked Elverbane.

Haephan frowned.

"The belt! Go get it!"

"Oh." Haephan returned to the washroom, found the belt and threaded it through his trousers. He returned to the room with his shirt hanging out, hoping he had done it right, but neither adult seemed to notice his return.

"We will leave early tomorrow for Eden," said Elverbane. "I hope to make good time."

"How long will your trip take you?"

Elverbane rested his elbows on the table and scratched his beard. "Three days to New Eden, two days over the broken Garden Road to get to old Eden. I can't imagine how overgrown it is right now. Not the outer areas. And this," he said as he tapped the 500-year-old map of Eden, "is far too vague to base any real estimate."

Pulling it from the scattering of other maps and notes, he raised it into the light.

"Are we going to Eden?" whispered Haephan.

"The fools brave enough to venture into Eden never reached her heart," he said. "Dragons sense men within ten miles. The cartographers only went far enough to look in between the peaks and scout from a distance." He popped his brows. "I cannae blame them."

"What are the last population counts for Eden?"

"For dragons?" Elverbane asked. "Haven't the slightest. Even if we had the count when this was drawn, who knows how they may have reproduced or killed each other off?"

SonLara rested her hands together in her lap. "Dragon mating cycles differ with species. You can expect a thirteen percent survival rate collectively for the species every cycle, drawn across two millennia is approximately a twelve percent increase in population."

Elverbane calculated. "Barring some growth spike or inter species conflict, they would boast approximately fifteen hundred."

"And conflict is likely, so estimate only a half to two third survival rate of that growth."

"A thousand?"

"At most."

"That's a thousand dragons more than I want to have to face," Elverbane said inside a cough. "Even at my best."

SonLara nodded.

"Are we going to face a *thousand* dragons?" Haephan gulped and this time caught their attention.

Circling the table, Elverbane took Haephan by his waistline, tucked the extra blouse around and stuffed it down the rear of the boy's trousers and yanked him around to inspect. The clothes hung large on the boy. "Alright then. Throw away those ol'rags and go to bed."

Haephan appeared confused.

"Not those, boy! The others. Now get."

"Yes, wizard," said Haephan. "Are we going to Eden?"

"Yes," Elverbane said.

"Tomorrow?"

"Aye."

"And…are we gonna see dragons?"

"Aye, boy," Elverbane said. "Now off ta bed wit'ya."

Haephan started into the hallway.

"Oh, and Haephan," Elverbane said.

Haephan paused.

"So long as you live up to your duties and honor your role, the room and its contents are yours. As is a small stipend."

"What's a stipend?" asked Haephan.

"Money."

"In…addition to the room and food?"

"Aye."

Dumbfounded, Haephan's mouth sank open. Finally, he half-bowed. "Thank you, wizard." The boy retreated to his new quarters.

Once the door shut behind him, Haephan sat on the bed and exhaled with relief. He flipped the gaslight switch for the small bulb to burn to life. For the second time since picking that idiot student who bumped into and shoved him—which devolved into Haephan getting hauled before the headmaster and Elverbane's punishment by sending him to the kitchens—he scanned the room.

By his own standards, the room was luxurious with a tiny window, small wardrobe, a mattress bed tucked into the corner next to the door and, above it, a narrow shelf lined with small objects.

He climbed onto the bed and stood high enough to inspect them in the dim gaslight. Thirty or so objects filled the narrow shelf, including a saber's tooth, a ram's horn sawed off at the base, a twisted marble ring, a crystal carved like a small-flamed torch, a clear piece of coral, a flask in the shape of a knife and more.

Haephan spotted them when he first moved in but had been so overcome with chores that he fell straight to bed each night. After getting caught picking, he had been similarly exhausted by the kitchen.

Glancing at the door, he plucked the flask and laid on the bed. He rolled it over in his fingers and assessed its potential street value. Flasks were common, but one shaped like a sheathed knife would draw a novelty up charge. Most of the shelf could draw a few coins here and there, but this might be a nice sell. He set it down, grabbed the steel feather and spun it in his fingers—this too could draw a coin.

Haephan recalled Elverbane's words—never to steal from a teacher or student. These belonged to neither, and if this was now his room, they were his to do with as he pleased.

Rolling onto his side, he set it on the nightstand and watched it until his eyes drooped and sleep consumed him.

16
Tilly

Dry midday sunlight warmed Tilly's back while he tore into the half-stale loaf of snatched bread. The first meal he'd gotten in two days, he didn't want his stomach to reject it by eating too fast. He bit off a piece of chewy exterior when he heard the whisper of a hand sliding over the sill behind him. Distracted by the bread, he wasn't quick enough before the hand struck through the window, caught his raggedy shirt and yanked him out. His head banged the narrow alley's opposite wall before he slammed into the unforgiving mudpack. Air erupted from his lungs.

"He ain't breathin'," said a teen boy looming over him. Another leaned in and slapped Tilly hard, who inhaled with a ragged screech. "Ah. Pick 'im up."

Four boys lifted and hauled him through narrow alleys.

Panicking, Tilly struggled to gather his wits so he might find a way to flee. Were they the pushers—young gang boys working for the bigger factions—or one of the juicers—older boys who raped the youngers?

"Let me go, you fuckers!" Tilly writhed before they snatched his wrists and bound them behind his back.

When they reached a steppe, Tilly was surprised when they handed him off to boys waiting on the next terrace. No random snatch, this was organized. Why had they grabbed him?

A few minutes later, twelve boys climbed the steps to the only maroon house in Rainhold and handed him off to Berman, who hefted him to the middle of the main room. He dropped Tilly face-first with both wrists bound behind his back to the thinly carpeted floor.

After a loud crack, Tilly screamed as blood gushed from his mouth.

"You're going to ruin the carpet!" Goram snapped.

Berman shrugged, having done as instructed. Saying more would further anger Goram.

Tilly cried for a minute before he blinked through his blood and tears. Clients, thugs and a few sweethearts sitting around the foyer watched him like an uncertain amusement.

"Where's Haephan?" Goram asked from his barstool.

The boy sniffed while blood bubbled from his nose. "Aye dunno!"

"You don't know," Goram said. "Word on the street is you two are mud buddies. If anyone sees one of you, the other isn't far off."

Tilly laid down his head. "No. Haephan lived alone. Always did."

"Did?" Goram canted his head for a better view of the boy bleeding on his carpet. Coagulation formed sticky lines of red between the boy's face and the patterned rug.

"Some fancy people came an' took 'im away," said Tilly. "Dey snatched 'im, they did. Took 'im up the city. I dunno where he is. He didn'do nuffin!"

"He did do something, young man," said Goram. "He did worse than sleep with one of my sweethearts without paying me. He stole from one of my customers. And an important one, at that."

"How?" Tilly asked.

"He stole a uniform from the son of someone who makes my life easier with the city," said Goram. "When you steal from my sweethearts, you steal from me. When you steal from my customers, you do far worse. You threaten me, and I don't take kindly to threats, little boy."

At Goram's gesture, Berman hauled Tilly to his knees by his hair. Tilly braced against the pain as a thin stream of fresh blood wormed past the sludge on his cheeks and down his chin.

"Pay special attention, young man." Goram approached and knelt before the pool of blood. "If you see Haephan reappear anywhere in Rainhold, or hear of where he is outside of Rainhold, you will come and tell me immediately. Is that clear?"

"Uh huh!" Tilly shuddered.

"Or..." Goram pulled out a small knife, "it will be *your* nuts I take, before his." He cut a line down the side of Tilly's face as the child screamed.

17

New Eden

"Original fruits from the tree of life! Grow your own bona fide tree of life!"

"Buy original bones of the first Edenons!"

"Get your soul painted! Our own mage will summon your aura for your life portrait!"

"Holy wizard blessings, two ferni! Only two ferni!"

"High elven hair! The silkiest this side of the Zulta'Mans! Brings long life and longer love!" Hawkers cried their authentically fake wares.

Haephan wondered that such amazing treasures never made it so far south as New Gordon, then suspected forgeries as they did not guard their carts from potential pickers, for things of such value would never be cried out so loud as might draw thieves. Either fools they were or fools they sought, both of which indicated falsehood in their commerce.

Jugglers, criers, hawkers and jokers lined the street. One man with a flaming sword caught Haephan's attention.

Streams of dust flowed along New Eden's broadway. Haephan

sneezed often enough that he huffed his nose every so often in hopes to head them off. He scratched his dark hair with small gloves below the rolled ends of voluminous sleeves. Before now, he had never left New Gordon and the past few days had been exciting.

New Eden was barely a village among the trees. Though Elverbane said little to Haephan beyond instructions, he used last night's meal to educate Haephan on the city's history as the first major center of commerce after "the taking," when dragons conquered and destroyed old Eden two thousand years prior. An attempt by Edenons to recreate their home a hundred miles south of the valley in New Eden proved a bust as New Gordon, where the Vitner and Estamar Canals connected, created a paradigm shift in economic power through cross-continental maritime trade. What once had been a vibrant, growing city now boasted little more than dubious hawkers and a small yet steady tourism industry.

Haephan fought against his horse chopping at nearby grass or bushes. What good was a horse if it did what it wanted?

Elverbane turned onto side streets void of most of the hawkers. Near the end of the road, he veered toward an ancient stone affair with a broad front patio standing a man's height above the street. Visible through its low railing, wealthy tourists ate lunch and sipped drinks at tables draped in white linen shaded by table-speared umbrellas. The wizard guided his horse through broad double wooden doors leading down a narrow alley and emerged into a small circular courtyard, backed by a clean low-built stable.

"Welcome to Dipper's Moon, my lord!" the stableboy took the animals. "Might I ask your lordship's names for the record?"

"I am Seth, this is Haephan," Elverbane dismounted and gave Haephan a specific glare.

Haephan stared back before his brows climbed and he nodded.

Despite Haephan's newfound good fortune in the food and clothing arena, jealousy panged of the stableboy and his job tending horses. He didn't care so much for animals as much as the boy's confidence doing his job.

"Gather my saddlebags," Elverbane told Haephan before he climbed the rear steps and disappeared through the open door into the inn.

"Yessir." Haephan hustled into the barn as the stableboy led each horse into a different stall. After pulling Elverbane's heavy saddlebags from the sand-colored horse, he entered the inn in time to follow Elverbane from the check-in desk to a corner room on the second floor.

"Go get your bags and we'll have lunch," Elverbane motioned for him to set the bags on the bed.

Once deposited, Haephan returned to the stable to gather his own bags before returning to the room as Elverbane bent over a wash bin to clean his face and hands while his cloak hung from a wall peg. Once finished, the wizard motioned for him to follow suit.

Happy to shed the ever-present thick layer of dust, Haephan likewise scrubbed his exposed skin while the wizard waved his hand over the room to layer invisible magic for security.

Downstairs on the large patio, Haephan squinted against the sun-bright tablecloths as a waiter seated him and Elverbane. The wizard ordered for both of them—the light roast turkey, stewed vegetables and fresh bread.

As usual, the meal passed with Elverbane either lost in thought or frowning at Haephan as if the boy were a puzzle. Haephan initially took Elverbane's odd stares as one of the buggerers who would frequent Rainhold seeking boys.

Instead, Elverbane asked him odd questions about his past, where he came from, what he believed about the Great Self and the subrim.

While Haephan wasn't sure what to make of the wizard, he got the distinct feeling the man didn't care about him any more than he might care about his horse or a tool, and was probably no buggerer as he first feared. He knew the old man stole glances at the beautiful priestess before they left; but then, who didn't?

From habit, Haephan scarfed the meal while he scanned and listened for danger. Once the food gorged his stomach from his empty plate, Haephan gulped half the glass of water before noting its pristine taste. A belch erupted from his mouth.

Elverbane's frown made clear that belching was unacceptable before he returned to his thoughts.

"I'll be right back, sir." Haephan stood.

Elverbane grunted as he chewed his food.

Haephan made for the bathrooms on the main floor. Getting into a stall to use a toilet—a concept he discovered since Belfast—he prepared to pee when the door banged open and heavy footfalls stepped in. Instinct drove Haephan to leap upon the toilet seat and squat, ready for anything while he waited.

"It's that ol' fella and the boy," one of them said as the two figures stood at the big water trough at the end of the room. "They're travelin' alone, shouldn't be too much of a problem."

"What ah they here for?"

"Dunno," said the other. "But I bet the ol' one's got money."

Haephan waited as they chuckled, finished their business and left. He waited for the voices to drift away before cracking the door and poking his head out. In an instant, he moved down the dark hallway when a thick hand landed on his shoulder.

"You little shit—" growled a man who snatched him into the hallway. In a twist, Haephan disappeared. The man stood there, stunned.

"Is everything alright, sir?"

The man spun to find a bellhop frowning at him.

"No," he cleared his throat. "I mean, I'm fine." He headed to the rear coat room.

Haephan stuck his head from around the corner.

"Was he looking for you?" asked the bellhop.

Haephan backed around the corner and made his way outside.

"Wiz— Seth?" he whispered.

Elverbane stirred. "Ah. Sit, boy. We need to talk about your mission once we get inside Eden's crown. You have a very important—"

"I think…" Haephan leaned closer. "Some men want to steal from us."

"What? Why?"

"I heard some men talking about you having money. I know thieves when I hear 'em."

Elverbane set down his fork and wiped his mouth, dropped a few coins on the table and returned with Haephan to their room where he checked the lock and his spells. He frowned into thought, but his body tensed like a waking beast at the sound of a threat.

"Did you finish eating?"

"Yes, wizard."

"From here on, refer to me as 'professor.'"

"Yes, professor."

"You're quick on your feet. That's good."

"Thank you, professor," said Haephan.

"Good," said Elverbane. "I will tell you more about your role tonight after we get back." Elverbane rifled through his bags and fished out two coin purses. He moved to the wardrobe, opened it and pressed one purse against its ceiling in plain view. He snapped his fingers at it, shut the doors, and slid the other into his robes. "Come."

Haephan followed him downstairs to the main desk.

"Do you know where I rent some guards?" Elverbane asked the young man behind the desk.

"Guards, sir?" asked the young man. He motioned into the lobby. "Depp, there, is reliable."

Elverbane noted a slender man reclining against the lobby hearth wearing a wide-brimmed hat.

"How reliable?"

"Innkeep uses him all the time, my lord," said the young man. "Trusts him with his kids, he does."

"Are you sure?"

"I'm one of his kids, my lord."

Elverbane snorted. "How long can I rent him for?"

"I dunno, sire," said the attendant. "If he's standing in here, it means he's looking for business."

Elverbane crossed the room.

"Your lordship," Depp offered a small bow. "Tilroy Depp. How may I serve you?"

"I'm looking for a pair of eyes and strong arms for a trip," said Elverbane.

"What kind?" he asked.

"Can you walk?"

The man tipped his head.

They left the Dipper's Moon and followed a side street. Depp gave a sidelong glance at Haephan before scanning the crowd.

"I need to cross the towers and enter Eden," Elverbane kept his voice low. "I believe I might be targeted and I need protection."

"By whom?"

"My attendant overheard a potential thief," said Elverbane. "I don't know much more than that."

"Did he see or know what he looks like?" asked Depp.

When they looked to Haephan, the boy shook his head.

"I have experience soldiering in four wars and three private conflicts."

"You look rather young," said Elverbane.

The man shrugged. "These aren't peaceful times, my lord. It's like the world is about to end."

"You've no idea."

"What timeframe are you thinking?" asked Depp.

"How far is it into Eden?"

"A day's ride to the outer crown, three days afoot to the famous nine towers."

"Four days? I thought only two," said Elverbane.

"Eden is more overgrown than a widow's field, sir," said Depp. "There are easier ways into the proper, but the dragons are never far for foolish wanderers who use roads. If you want in and out alive, you must stay away from them."

Elverbane tugged at his beard. "Are you a guide as well?"

"Sometimes, my lord," said Depp. "Never to the towers. Tourists like to see the dragons, you see, and they can be seen only a day's walk from here near the crown. The dragons like the goats that go up there to feed on the cindergrass."

"Cindergrass?"

"Like ambrosia." Depp kissed his fingertips. "At least to the goats. Might as well call it goatnip."

"What's a crown?" Haephan asked.

"Eden has two rings, you might say," Depp said. "The inner with the nine narrow peaks lining the valley, called 'the towers,' and an outer crown of flatiron foothills we call the 'crown.'"

"What's your rate?" asked Elverbane.

"In local currency, eighty ferni a day. An extra fifty if I require medical attention plus the costs, themselves. But…wouldn't you need more than myself, my lord? I have several profes—"

"I only need someone to watch our backs—I can handle the rest. I'll pay you half upon arriving at Eden, and the rest upon my safe return. Meet me at the Dipper's Moon tomorrow morning before sunrise. My attendant and I will be ready to travel."

"How long will we be staying?"

"Two days at best, four at most, barring worst."

"I will pack dry for two weeks and we'll hunt the rest," said Depp.

"And to hunt for me and my attendant?"

"Three extra ferni a day, I should think."

"Tomorrow before sunrise," said Elverbane.

"Yes, my lord. And your name?"

"Seth," he said. "That's Haephan."

Depp touched his fingers to his brow and offered a soft salute. "Tomorrow morning, then." Depp melted into the crowd with the aplomb of a pickpocket. Haephan frowned after him, especially when Depp's gaze lingered upon him for a brief second before he slipped away.

Elverbane marched through the crowds and wove through small alleys. Unlike New Gordon with tightly packed neighborhoods of stone, most of the houses were mixes of fine wood and waddle and daub with occasional stone foundations, many spaced with trees, bush, and grass. Haephan wasn't sure what to make of so much space for each person.

He followed the wizard by a house with the blue shutters and into a narrow alley. At the second door on a long house to the right, Elverbane scanned the alley and knocked. When it opened, a shadowed face peered from its candlelit dim.

"What do you want?"

Elverbane raised his right arm and offered the man a view of his left hand. He flicked a soft green arc of fire from his palm outward. The door widened and the shadowed figure moved aside to permit him and Haephan, who slipped in without a word before the shadowed figure shut the door. Blooming candles filled the room with a soft, even white light to reveal a straight-backed man with leathery skin and warm eyes.

"Been awhile since one o'you been 'round these parts," smiled the fellow. "I am Sartlam Harbor, my lord. What can I help ya fer?"

"I'm Seth, a professor of dimensional studies at the Belfast School of Wizardry in New Gordon, and I've come looking for a guide into Eden."

Sartlam slowed as he recognized the name. "Into Eden?" The little man cocked his head. "How far?"

"My needs are two-fold," Elverbane said when the little man raised his hand and motioned for him to sit in one of two high-backed, red velvet chairs by the small stove. Though out of place in such a humble home, they appeared well used.

"Have a preference, wizard?" The man approached a small boxed desk, unlatched the center and split the front swings to reveal a broad cabinet. Inside sat a variety of liquors in custom bottles alongside a short row of glasses.

"Yellow hops?"

"Aha!" Sartlam plucked a bottle and set it down on the narrow tabletop before the cabinets. He tapped two glasses along the edge before a thin veneer of frost formed on the outside. He poured Yellow Hops, handed Elverbane the glass, and sat. After a toast, he sipped his and smiled.

Elverbane took a sip. "Two things. I need you to escort me, my attendant, and a bodyguard through the towers to the heart of Eden."

"The heart of Eden? What need have you going there?"

"Can you go further?"

"Further? What do you mean? Into Eden?"

"Aye."

Sartlam's brow dropped. "Pardon me, wizard, I mean no disrespect, but you're fuckin' out of it. No living creature gets into there without them dragons seeing. The real towers, not the measly ones we tell the tourists about, are nigh impenetrable by anything more than the groundlings—the squirrels and groundhogs and such, things dragons don't bother trying to eat."

"Why don't they make it out here? We're surely in flying distance."

"We're not worth the trouble," said Sartlam. "We have a few repellant defenses wizards left a few centuries ago, and even as weak as they are, we fight back enough to not make it worth their while. Contrary to tourist belief, dragons don't destroy for the helluvit. If you anger 'em, sure, they'll wipe out dozens of villages. But leave 'em be? They leave us be. They prefer goats and cows anyhow. More meat on their bones. All those stories about prefferin' us? Some of us are sweet, but mostly taste like whiskey and beer. They don't care too much for us, just hate our interferin' in their affairs."

Elverbane set down his drink. "Can you get us into Eden?"

"I can get you to the edge," said Sartlam. "But no further. I go no further."

"Have you maps of Eden?"

"Aye," said Sartlam.

"Prepare them to travel. We leave at dawn."

"But, sir, I have contracts to fulfil—"

"I don't care about your contracts," Elverbane cut him off. "You're coming with us."

"You can't come in here and destroy my busin—"

Elverbane cut him off when he raised a ring with an octohorned sigil.

"The Pangean Convocation?" Sartlam asked. "You wouldn't. Just to take you to Eden?"

Elverbane waited with his ring raised.

Haephan soaked in the information, having never heard of such a thing.

Sartlam reddened and mumbled something.

"You will report to the Dipper's Moon tomorrow morning before sunrise prepared for a two-week trip."

"Two weeks!" Sartlam exploded. "You're taking me for two weeks!? Not only will that piss off some valuable customers, but I'm not nearly prepared enough to leave for two weeks! That takes planning and money—"

A small bag of coin landed on the floor between them.

"Buy it from someone, steal it, borrow it. Do whatever it takes, but we leave in the morning." Elverbane rose and headed for the door before pausing. "And Sartlam?"

Sartlam scooped and hefted the bag with surprise.

"Tell no one." Elverbane and Haephan slipped through the door, which shut with a silent thunder.

18
Distrust

SonLara leaned over Furian's X as it shimmered atop Elverbane's thick worktable. The fire crackled to her right while dusty afternoon light speared through the narrow corner window across the beaten red rug.

The X flared and fizzled against the thin restrainer she wove over it—a delicate glowing lattice that prevented it from exploding. After stabilizing the spell, she layered it with a dozen addendums that expounded its abilities far beyond what Elverbane or his contemporaries could ever hope to learn. Her silver, reflective eyes noted ultraviolet reactions invisible to wizards without spells. Weaving patterns over and around the X, she increased its layers thirteen-fold to gain unprecedented insight into the interdimensional hermeneutics she hoped to study while Elverbane was away with Haephan.

The X flared and snapped into a circle that wavered near collapse, similar to the breaking circles floating through the spell walls. Surprised, she raised her head. "Seth—"

SonLara shook her head. That was the third time today she had called his name. Despite having been gone three days to Eden, she always expected him to be nearby. The feeling disturbed her, almost as much as her bishop's extended silences.

Using her mirrored journal, she reported new discoveries nightly to the Library of Andon. Questions flooded her pages, but every answer produced longer silences from her leadership. Her communiques had resulted in a massive shift in Library operations once they confirmed the rapid dimensional degradation within controlled environments they could trust. As her fellow librarians dove into the study, their messages dwindled.

SonLara straightened and rubbed her lower back. Bending over the spell for hours wore on her. She scanned the litany of powerful objects mixed among nicknacks from Elverbane's continental travels sitting along his fireplace mantle.

Despite the many blue objects wafting with powers, powerless ones intrigued her. The wizard had seen more of the continent than any of his fellows, most of whom huddled in enclaves rather than experiencing the world.

SonLara thought of Elverbane often and pondered what it meant when someone knocked on the door. Waving her hand, she disempowered the X and its protection spell before opening the door from across the room. "Ah, Dorian. Has there been any word on the energetic event this morning?"

"Not yet, priestess." The sheepish boy half bowed. "I sent your message, but nothing has returned from the Academy. Apparently, there was an incident at the rimsportal last night."

"Rimsportal? I think you answered my query." SonLara tapped her lips. "Thank you for the update, Dorian. You may go."

"Sorry, mum, but Wizard Elverbane has been requested."

"Wizard Elverbane is away," she said. "Who has called upon him?"

"Oh…" the boy frowned. "Special visitors, priestess. What should I tell them?"

"What kind of visitors?"

The boy gulped and said, "Pixies, mum."

SonLara took a slow breath as her heart quickened. "Pixies, you say?" She approached. "Lead on, young man."

"Yes, mum," he said and led her out of Ashmore Hall under a bright mid-afternoon sun, across granite courtyards, and into the main entrance of the administrative building. Students turned at her passing.

The attendant nodded at the main desk as he led her into the council room, empty but for two bolts of light hovering in the middle of the circular chamber.

SonLara paused at the entrance, took a slow breath, and prepared for the worst.

"Priestess?" the attendant realized she had not entered.

Holding her stomach and steeling herself against the inevitable tension, she stepped into the room.

The pixilarks retreated. One of them multiplied in power—her eyes and hands lit up and an aura many times her own size filled the room.

Backing away in terror as all other light dimmed under the sudden aggression, the attendant tripped back over the long, low step at the bottom of the shallow amphitheater.

SonLara remained at the door while eyeing the two pixies. To her shock, she recognized the ruddy color of the younger pixie; SonLara was now the first Andonese in recorded history ever to encounter an aurora.

"Thank you, young man," SonLara dismissed the terrified youth while she struggled to tamp her own fear. He scrambled out while the brunette pixie brightened. Her hair danced like a flame in the undulating fluctuations of her energy.

SonLara laid a hand upon her breast and dipped her head. "Greetings. I am SonLara, Priestess of Andon, Fourth Order, Lower Diclave."

Notable for her paler color, the elder pixie moved between SonLara and the aurora. *Andonese.*

"I mean you no harm," SonLara said. "I assure you."

We requested a specific wizard! chimed the elder pixie. *You are not him!*

We seek the worldender—, chimed the aurora until a glare from her companion cut her off.

"The worldender? I have been the companion of Wizard Elverbane for some time now," said SonLara. She hesitated to say she was his companion, even as the idea surprised her with excitement. "But he is away for a few weeks. How may I help?"

What lie did you use to trick him? the elder pixie chimed.

"None," said SonLara as she pulled out the nearest council chair and sat with knees together and hands on thighs to offer as docile an image of herself as possible. The opportunity to engage pixilarks sent her mind racing. "I was here on a mission to study the fabric of realms."

Lies, chimed Rose.

"I am a librarian second class with specialty in cosmological hermeneutics, specifically al'cularian energy dynamics. Were I to guess, you both are Carlinian, due to the age of your transcendent flux and the al'cularian signature of central heather oak."

How did she know that? asked the aurora.

She's an Andonese, snarled the elder pixie. *She knows a great deal about that which she should not.*

"Of knowledge there ought be no secret," SonLara intoned. "I am happy to share what I know, even if you offer nothing in return."

The pixies waited.

"Or I could choose not to tell you about the recent visit of the wizard whom you seek by a…" SonLara cocked her head, "Subrim."

The elder pixie stuttered before closing half the distance to SonLara and drawing even more power until the room hummed. *More lies!*

A subrim!? asked the aurora. *Eldress. Wait!*

She lies! the eldress cried when the aurora bolted in front of her.

Eldress! the young aurora attempted to block her. The eldress pushed her aside, prepared to unleash power that SonLara could not defend.

In a single moment, as a brilliant red cloud of fire, the aurora drew so much power as to make the eldress seem but a tiny spark before a volcano. SonLara averted her gaze as the light blazed and shut them when it became too intense.

ELDRESS, the aurora's word thundered through the room, ruffled a stack of scrolls left on the table and shattered empty glass decanters on a nearby wall table.

In-power, the eldress recoiled in surprise.

We did not come here to attack Andonese, the aurora's chime echoed down hallways and sent students and wizards, alike, flurrying in surprise.

Calm yourself. We have more important things to worry about.

Though power continued to burn in the eldress's hands, she faltered at the aurora's blazing presence. She took control of herself and offered a reluctant nod.

The aurora dimmed, though her hair continued to float upward as a red flame. Its light, along with her luminous face and hands, filled the space. *Look at me.*

Confident the eldress would have killed her, SonLara obeyed and shuddered.

I don't know why my eldress considers you a threat. Her voice split and tripled into multivoice. *I trust the judgement of my forebears. Whatever cause she may have against you, I will abate. Know, however, that any threat you might pose will be wiped from this world in an instant should I desire it. Am I clear?*

SonLara gripped her skirts and nodded.

The aurora descended until she floated at eyeline with the sitting human and leaned in. *The survival of my kind depends on it, and I will do* whatever *is necessary to see to our survival. I will not force you to help us, but if you deceive us? I know your energy. I will find you before the draco finishes off my kind, and I will suffer you.*

SonLara's jaw quivered as a tear welled in the side of her eye. She had never experienced such fear or helplessness in her entire life. This tiny creature made her feel as a dust mote in a hurricane. She could do nothing but what the aurora demanded, and suddenly wished she had never tempted fate by stepping into this room.

Shutting her brilliant, glowing blue eyes, the aurora's power wafted away before she descended to the long conference table, followed by her eldress. Touching down, the aurora stumbled, sank to her bottom, and held the side of her head. Beneath her, the woodgrains of the table had shifted direction in a spherical pattern eminent from where the aurora had blazed in fury.

SonLara knew she stood no chance against even the weakest aurora.

Hesitant, the eldress fluttered to comfort the aurora. *When did it happen? When did you blossom?*

After the vision and the interrogation, chimed Ven. *Before I headed for the rimsportal.*

Why didn't you tell someone? the eldress pressed. *You're too young! A vision to cause such a thing would have given Han paus—*

Ven forestalled further questions with an upraised hand as she focused on SonLara.

Groping for her comfort zone, SonLara's analytical mind wondered how the staff here even understood the chimal pixie language, whose syllables were in magic instead of sound, and wondered what other secret tomes might be ferreted from even her own queries in the school library. More than that, her mind boiled with questions as to why the pixies would come seeking Elverbane as she had. What might they know? Did they see the degradation, too?

After catching her breath, the aurora looked to SonLara. *I am Ven, an auroralite. This is Eldress Rose. You are right. We come from Carlinia in the southlands.*

Rose's face tightened.

"A pleasure to meet you," SonLara dipped her head. "Pardon me, but it is beyond an honor to meet an aurora—even a young one. I offer blessings upon you and your flock."

Ven took a heavy breath. *May the spring rain shine bright upon your eyes, blue human.*

"Thank you, auroralite," SonLara said. "Wizard Elverbane—the wizard you seek—studies the fabric of realms, but has traveled north on a mission. I, too, study realms, and may speak on his behalf while he is gone."

Holding Ven's arm, Rose leaned in and whispered, *Ven, take care what you tell her.*

We are under threat, chimed Ven.

"All you share," SonLara offered, "will be held in the highest confidence."

Among even your superiors, priestess, chimed Ven. *This may be a threat to your higher nature, but what we face is firm to our complete dissolution and a potential existential threat to the fabric of realms.*

"To only those with direct bearing in your query," said SonLara. "I vow my complete confidence."

Ven raised her hand and it glowed. *Then consider us sealed.*

Unfamiliar magic settling upon SonLara inspired a sense of curiosity and fear.

Ven eyed her for several long moments. *I know not what you know, priestess, but the pixilarks exist in two forms before entering the high realm. We are born and exist in the nether, consuming the interment energies caused by realm conflict.*

SonLara's mind raced.

Those of us who now exist in the low realm were ancient in the second before Thermaya conquered Indehia.

"Indehia…ceased to exist eons ago," SonLara licked her lips. "Aurora, how old are you?"

I am only 150 years this past winter, chimed Ven. *Young by our standards.*

"And you?" SonLara asked the eldress.

I am 720.

"And you spend most of your life in the middle realm?"

They nodded.

But we are threatened, chimed Ven.

"Yes, auroralite. Could you tell me how?"

In our ethereal form, we are… chimed Ven, *completely vulnerable. We have no capability for violence, whatsoever, in offense or defense. And we thus have been sows for slaughter.*

A force has attacked us in the middle realm, chimed Rose. *We are lambs, and as our antecedents are devoured by this entity, our secondary purpose there is destroyed, and thus comes under threat the continuity of our realms.*

Should the magnalarks be removed in such number as to destroy our function, chimed Ven, *all high life here shall be threatened. We consume the dissonant energies caused by conflict and secrete an emollient that fosters a cleaner flow of transrealm continuity.*

"You," SonLara whispered. "You're the leviathans."

The fairies did not deny it.

"Oh…Great Self," said SonLara. "This is why dimensional continuity is breaking down."

Then you know? Ven's asked.

"Wizard Elverbane and I have been studying a significant breakdown in dimensional health and have been baffled as to why. Can you tell us? Something has been devouring your other forms? Do you know what it is?"

The worldender? asked Ven. *He studies the fabric of realms? Does he not practice war?*

"Not since Tuthomere, nearly two score ago," said SonLara. "The war was difficult on him and his compatriots, as I understand. He took to studying how the universe works at its basest energies."

The pixies remained silent a moment.

A draco has found a way to pierce the veil, chimed Ven.

"Great Self," SonLara muttered.

We don't know how, chimed Rose. *Or from where.*

"As we speak," said SonLara, "Wizard Elverbane approaches the single largest dragon's nest in Pangea."

The pixies started.

"He and a companion travel into Eden right now," said SonLara.

Rose leaned closer. *Why?*

"He goes to Eden to retrieve seeds from the La'Du Lira Al'Cular."

Ven leaned in. *To what end?*

"To break the world," said SonLara. "Straight from the mouth of the Great Self by a subrim—"

A subrim, Rose spat.

"Yes," SonLara said. "We have been directed to the heart of Eden."

Rose's eyes flared. *Such a thing is—*

Forbidden? Ven cut her off. *Not if from a subrim.*

We cannot trust an Andonese, chimed Rose.

"I trust the word of my friend," said SonLara.

It seems there is more afoot than a draco devouring our kind, chimed Ven.

"I have not the entirety of this picture, but there is more than merely the restoration of the continuities," said SonLara. "And you are a part of it."

Us? Rose asked.

"In my companion's encounter with the subrim, he witnessed a vision of a pixie floating above a human boy. I think we will need your help to complete our task, and in so doing, save your kind."

To take the seeds from the Tree… asked Ven, *or from the dracos?*

Rose turned.

That would be it, chimed Ven. *A draco is eating the seeds to cross the veil.*

What? asked Rose.

They're eating seeds from the Tree, chimed Ven. *That would empower them to cross the veil.*

How many seeds do they intend to retrieve? asked Rose.

"The subrim said to 'gather its seeds,'" said SonLara. "We assumed that meant as many as were findable."

Ven shared a long look with Rose. *Should your companions manage to steal the entirety of those seeds, it could very well solve our problem. In which case, we would be in your debt.*

Rose's jaw clenched. *Or at least to the wizard and the child.*

SonLara nodded.

"Stealing seeds from dragons is no small feat," said SonLara. "And if those seeds prove as valuable as they seem, and should my companion complete the job, the dragons will turn in kind. Their seer hunters, scouts and martial legions will scour the continent in search of him. Or at least the wizard. They will be vulnerable."

Ven's chin climbed.

If your companions can sneak into the heart of dragon territory, chimed Rose, *and steal the most precious seed from the Tree of Life—*

"I want protection. For them."

You ask much, Rose chimed. *Not since the wars have we fought the dracos. Much has been agreed—*

"They're devouring your progenitors," snapped SonLara without changing her tone. "Have they not already broken any truce you entertain? However lasting that agreement may have been, if what you say is true, then the dracos have started this war anew."

Great Self, Rose cursed.

"I could do little against a dragon," said SonLara. "Perhaps weaken them. Sap strength and cognition, but I am no great martial mage. My companion Elverbane and his decades of battle experience, perhaps, but one high wizard against an entire colony?" She shook her head. "If my companions return and can take every seed, I want their protection."

A big if, Andonese, chimed Ven. *But yes. If you manage to cease the dragon's crossings through the veil, we will owe you a life debt.*

Rose scowled.

And we will fulfill it until your two young humans die of old age, chimed Ven.

But how will you certify the veracity of this boast? asked Rose.

"Ven will know the moment we achieve it," said SonLara. "The dracos will cease their slaughter."

True, Ven admitted. *Or Song should, if she's aware like I am.*

We cannot long keep the auroralite from her Tree, chimed Rose. *And I am not staying alone to wait for their supposed return. If you succeed, you must send someone to us. Only then will we prepare to fulfill our end of the bargain.*

"Understood," said SonLara.

But not you, chimed Rose. *Regardless of the situation, you and your kind are unwelcome.*

SonLara waited.

But someone may come, chimed Ven. *If they can make it.*

"For the safety of my people and yours…" SonLara pursed her lips. "We will send for you, as you have agreed."

So be it, chimed Ven.

"So be it," said SonLara.

Ven offered a bare nod.

We must retire, priestess, Rose chimed. *We are very tired and need rest.* Ven sank against her. *And we can stay no more than a full day. Come sunrise after next, we must return to our companions immediately. Separation from our Trees and our flock is difficult for most pixies, much more for our aurorae.*

"Yes, of course," SonLara rose. "I will send attendants to prepare blue rooms for your rest."

Are you available to speak tomorrow? asked Rose.

"Yes," SonLara said. "I am at your disposal." She rose to her feet and offered a curtsy. "I will leave instructions with the attendant watching over your room. Should you need me, chime three times. I will come immediately."

Good tidings and gentle sleep, human, chimed Ven.

"Until tomorrow," SonLara dipped her head and left. In the hallway, she let out a long exhale and pressed a quivering hand over her breasts as adrenaline drained from her. A circle of nervous wizards stood nearby, gripping wands, staffs and objects of power. Faces inquired with fear and worry.

Straightening, she lifted her chin. "Two pixilarks are inside. Please make arrangements for their lodging and food needs. Leave them otherwise undisturbed and call me if needed." She left with as much dignity as she could muster.

Outside the administration building, she let her mind return to the problem at hand: a dragon ravaged the continuity of the dimensions. Despite such a terrible news, a peace welled from so many disturbing yet simultaneous events. She could not read its design, but a higher fingerprint emerged and served as a strong beacon of hope. However bleak a picture it might paint, there would be a masterpiece waiting in its layers.

At that thought, she headed for the library with a growing list of books to query and spell tests to try that would keep her busy deep into the night, and away from thoughts of Elverbane.

19

Towers of Eden

Haephan was first to spot a tower of Eden. Nine high, narrow peaks encircled Eden Valley. Seeing them meant little, however, as the rest of the trip was spent dancing among a steady rise in the rippling hills climbing toward the ancient birthplace of all living things.

And the next day. And the day after that.

Leaving New Eden had been uneventful. Elverbane tolerated little conversation and no dissension, and his curt mood put everyone on their toes. Though he never raised his voice, he cut off conversations with directions or simple questions.

Haephan had never known Elverbane to smile, and figured his good mood was equivalent to others' neutral moods. He didn't mind. A wizard's gruff was better than scrapping with the Rainhold boys, hiding from Crimson Guardians or the occasional gangs. He enjoyed a warm, dry bed, clean clothes and a stable roof. At least, until they left New Gordon.

Their ill-hewn trail wove through a bramble-thick forest. Haephan relished being the smallest, as he moved through the green with the least difficulty, spied ahead and reported back what he found.

"There's one road into Eden," said Sartlam, "and it's never used by anyone with a brain."

"Wouldn't it be overgrown?" asked Depp.

Sartlam shook his head. "The ancients did something to the road that kept it from growing. Though it's as smooth as glass, a traveler wouldn't get far, no sir. Dragons use it to pick off the unwise stock around here, us included."

"Is that why we came this way?" Haephan asked.

"Aye," Sartlam rubbed his chin. "I take this trip once a year."

"Why?" Haephan whispered as Elverbane mulled over a map by small glowstone light.

"To know it," he said. "Keep it clear. The convocation pays me to keep it clear? I keep it clear."

"And why is that?" Depp asked before lighting his pipe.

"Who knows?" said Sartlam. "Everyone wants to keep their eye on Eden. At least, the powers that be do, I suppose. I've only ever taken one other'un out there—from the Auburn Coven—a cartographer. That was…twenty years ago?" He smirked at Haephan. "Long 'fore you was born."

"What's a cartographer?" asked Haephan.

"Map maker," Sartlam said.

"Oh," said Haephan.

Above them, stars twinkled in evening majesty. Depp sucked his pipe to build a glow in the tamped leaves before puffing it out in thick white smoke that swirled into the air.

"Do you—" Haephan started to ask and paused to formulate his question. "Do you think they've ever made a map of them? The stars?"

Depp and Sartlam looked skyward.

"I dunno," said Sartlam.

"That'd be something," murmured Depp. "They probably do, somewhere men have money and time."

"Maybe…maybe someday we'll go to them," Haephan mused. "Look at 'em hanging there in the black. What do you think they are?"

"Spirits," Sartlam said. "Hanging forever in the sky. The passed ones."

Depp puffed lazy on his pipe.

"Didn't your daddy ever teach you about stars?" asked Sartlam.

Haephan looked down.

"Oh." Sartlam cleared his throat and shared a glance with Depp.

"My friend once told me he thought they were little fires burning in the sky, campfires on another world we could only see when the sun passed away for the day," Haephan whispered.

A warm breeze ruffled the trees and their small fire. After a while, Haephan laid across his roll and winced. He reached back and fished out the monstrous wooden tooth plucked from Ian's shelf. He never knew such an animal could even exist and raised the object to imagine the rest of such a creature.

His eyes drooped as exhaustion settled in with a faint idea that the carved wooden tooth had nothing at all to do with the animal it mimicked.

* * *

"We're near the overlook," said Sartlam. They broke camp two hours before sunrise and now neared the top of the rise of a saddle between two of the Edenic towers.

When a thick wall of green blocked the final approach, Haephan wiggled through while Sartlam and Depp hacked with machetes. Even Haephan had to belly-crawl the final few feet between the interwoven small trees and bushes. Once on the other side, he climbed to his feet, dusted himself off and approached the overlook, where a low ridge had buckled under a large tree, which continued growing out sideways toward sunlight. Its thick canopy blocked the view.

Haephan stepped out onto the horizontal trunk, raised his arms to maintain balance and advanced into the canopy. After navigating most of the tree, he pulled the final "top" branches aside to stare in wonder across the shadowed carpet of Eden.

From their position on the southeastern curve of the valley, the vista sank as a gentle oval flanked by the highest peaks in the north descending on both sides southward around a landscape more verdant than even Haephan could have imagined. The upper third of the valley stretched southward as a high plateau before ending in a series of high cliffs interspersed with waterfalls misting in distant heavy breezes.

"This is it," Sartlam's mutter startled Haephan, who found all three men now behind him. How had he missed their entrance?

For the first time, Elverbane lost his cold gruff as he stared in boyish wonder. Depp, too, stood awestruck.

Lethargic morning mists wandered across the northern plateau, over the lip, thickened from the waterfall mist and pooled across the deep south valley before wandering out through the carved main pass at the south end which they knew never to attempt to use.

Sparrows flit into view and raced along the valley bowl falling away from them. A waking forest sang with a chilling echo across the expanse. Sunrise striking the virgin-white snow of the valley's tallest peak reflected as a brilliant second dawn. Another hour would pass before any other sunlight would even grace the high plateau, much less the rest of the lush valley.

"Boy," Elverbane's tone drew all eyes.

Haephan noted Elverbane gazing upward and followed his line of sight.

A dragon banked high above them through the towers out to the forest beyond and disappeared behind the trees.

"We need waste no more time," he said.

Haephan returned to the men while Sartlam unshouldered his pack, unfastened a wide leather tube and popped the tethered top. Reaching in, he fished out one of the sheafs and unrolled it across the ground.

"Now, like I showed you, use the peaks as your guide." Sartlam pointed out to the peaks as they could see. "Note the distinct features of these three. The tallest peak here," he pointed to the north peak, "and the broken cleft here," he pointed to the southwest-most. "This one," he motioned to the peak to his left, southerly to them, "has a purple tint to the peak tip from all the violet crystals growing up there."

"And the Tree?" Haephan craned his neck to scan the valley, now hidden again by the sideways canopy. "I didn't see anything like you described."

"It's there," said Sartlam. "I've never seen it with my own eyes, but I'm certain it's there."

"Are you sure?" asked Haephan as he swallowed his fear.

"The sooner you get going," Elverbane said, "the sooner you'll get back."

Depp crossed his arms.

Haephan soaked in every map detail before standing. "How many?"

"As many as you can carry without being hindered," Elverbane offered him a small canvas sack. "Put that in your belt."

"How big are they?" Haephan twisted it through his belt with the experience of someone well versed in cutting purses.

Elverbane looked at Sartlam, who shrugged, before answering Haephan. "You're going to have to figure it out, yourself. You're a smart boy. You'll be fine." Elverbane had never praised him before. "Now go."

"Yes, professor," said Haephan as he rose, checked the tooth in his belt, stepped around the root of the fallen tree and disappeared through the lower canopy down the decline.

"Now, I'm not the cleverest goat ever to roam this here world," said Depp, "but I'd love to hear it from you why a boy of his stature and age should be sent into the bosom of death."

Elverbane turned to Depp without expression. Sartlam rolled the map before a fight could break out. Elverbane harrumphed and faced the valley.

"Listen," Depp grabbed Elverbane's shoulder. A brilliant flash of light repelled him and drew a curse as he clutched his face and sank to his knees.

Elverbane leaned in.

"Open your eyes," growled Elverbane.

Depp opened watery eyes and struggled to focus on Elverbane's face.

"Can you see me?"

"Barely," Depp panted.

"Do you know how a dragon sees?"

"No," said Depp. "With his eyes?"

Elverbane straightened. "I didn't hire you to question me, and certainly not to threaten me. Do it again and our contract will be terminated."

"But can I know!?" Depp retorted. The wizard frowned and bent over again into Depp's muddled vision.

"A dragon sees most with his magic," said Elverbane. "The daylight provides us a modicum of distraction, but tonight, we will retreat to one of Sartlam's caves, because outside we would be found without a moment's notice. Our magic is so unique that we might be spotted for miles in the dark.

"But the kid? Why's he special?"

"Because," Elverbane leaned in, "he's a vacant."

"What does that mean?" Depp frowned as his vision cleared.

"It means he has no magic, at all. Not even like the common folk. He has none whatsoever. In the daytime sight of a dragon, he'd be barely more than shadowy movement. In the middle of the night, he's bloody invisible."

"But why does it make a difference for us in the day?"

"They're not blind," said Elverbane. "Their eyes are generally weak, like a bat."

Another dragon crossing the sky descended toward the large green mound at the top of the plateau.

"As blue creatures," said Elverbane, "even as ancient and powerful as they are…their magic is everything, including their blindspot."

Despite his iron voice, he suffered a brief moment of fear that he might be wrong.

20

Testing

Adamar stepped through the high arched doorway into the wizard's private study. Crystal reflectors embedded in the vaulted ceiling spread pale, early morning sunlight in an even glow across the room. Several tables, chalkboards and reconstructed animal skeletons filled the main floor. Shelves along walls held countless books and a wide variety of glass flasks, carboys, droppers, extractors, and tubes. Where a large alcove extended on the opposite end of the main room from the entryway, a great distiller sat upon a heavy wooden table, now inert and bare lit by a smaller skylight.

He took a slow breath. His return with Eva had required biting so much tongue he feared it would shear clean off at some point.

The cold workshop rose around him like a prison cell from which one was lowered through the ceiling. He stood for a moment, unmoving as he faced his new—and old—reality. Morning bells echoed across the complex. Shaking his head, he set about preparing the distiller, turning on the gaslights and warming the space for Eva's father.

Adamar returned to his old role with swift surety but was disappointed that items were misplaced and stacked without care. He returned the shop to proper order. Eight years of morning setup revived in him as if an old friend, one he hoped never to have to meet after leaving with Eva.

He stamped his flaring pride as he recalled her eating full meals and sleeping in a warm, comfortable bed. Even last night's passion was a welcome release of weeks of frustration.

Defeat, however, weighed all too heavy in his gut. His dreams of creating a life without needing magic or those who wielded it appeared broken upon rocky ground. He wondered if there might be another way to revive them. Today, though, it was all he could do to return to his former position with the duty and humility of a husband taking care of his wife.

A haggard Wizard Dufrain appeared through the archway. Clutching a special case, he made for his desk in the alcove to the right and plopped down behind it with a grunt. In the three years Adamar and Eva had been gone, the wizard appeared to have aged. Dufrain was in his 250's and had at least a century left in him, if not more.

"Good morning, wizard," Adamar said as he pulled objects out across the floor in order to return them to their rightful places.

"Where's my coffee?" growled Dufrain.

Adamar lifted his head for a moment but returned to his tasks. He had never before gotten the wizard coffee.

"Where's my coffee!?" he barked.

Scowling, Adamar continued the work he had been hired for—not serving as a personal attendant.

Dufrain grumbled but said nothing more until Adamar finished the task and stood.

"Good morning, wizard," Adamar said.

"Get me some coffee."

Adamar gritted his jaw. "What's our project today, wizard?"

Dufrain stared for a long moment. "Would you call for service, Adamar?"

"Of course, wizard." Adamar hoped he made clear he would only perform previous duties and not take on lesser roles. He pulled on the bell cord by the main door to summon an attendant before he moved to a new shelf to start the reorganization process.

"I'm glad you're here, Adamar," Dufrain admitted. "You are the best assistant I've ever had."

"Thank you, wizard."

An attendant appeared through the door, took Dufrain's order for coffee and left.

Adamar grated at being ordered to do the work of an attendant but embraced a kernel of hope he'd be able to maintain his dignity. He feared it was all he had left.

The morning continued in silence long after Dufrain had his third cup. Adamar placed the finishing touches on the room as the wizard rose and made his way to the main table. "Adamar, prepare a dummy. If you would."

"Yes, wizard," Adamar said. He scanned the room as he recalled where the wooden dummies were stored and headed down the hall to a storage closet to retrieve one. Back in the shop, he set the humanoid frame on a mount and locked its joints to appear standing while Dufrain watched from his desk.

"No, like a lycan," Dufrain said.

"I don't know much about lycans."

"Like an animal."

"What kind of animal?"

"A lycan!" Dufrain snapped. He lifted the case he brought in and approached the main table.

"I don't know what that looks like," said Adamar.

"Like an animal, Adamar," said Dufrain. "Bent forward! Arms up! Crouching, able to run on twos or fours."

Adamar waited a moment before turning and sighing as he made his best approximation. He realized Dufrain might not know any better, unless he had somehow gone to battle in the last three years without Adamar knowing it.

"We could ask that Wizard Elverbane," Adamar suggested. "Up at the scho—"

"Don't suggest such a thing," Dufrain said as he unlocked the case. "I'd rather lose an arm than ask that coward."

"Coward?" asked Adamar.

"Refuses to help with war councils. He knows the situation we're in. The super pack has officially formed north of Alderland! But Elverbane just wants to continue playing with his little transdim studies while people are out there dying under those bloody ravaging animals."

"I thought you once told me he was a hero of—"

"Maybe once," Dufrain frowned. "No more."

Adamar had nothing to say, being neither an expert on magic, war nor lycans.

"And what do you know about Elverbane?" Dufrain muttered with his hands on the case lid.

"Only what I hear 'round here," said Adamar.

Dufrain eyed him for a long moment before scowling at the model. He opened the case to reveal a bronze sword with a thistled guard, crossed blade in the hilt of two intersecting leaves and a flared main blade. "That'll be fine. Go put up the deadboard behind it."

Adamar scanned the main table and the dummy. "Wizard, are you performing directional magic today?"

"What? Yes. Of course," retorted Dufrain. The wizard had not been so caustic last Adamar was here.

"Should we do it in here?" Adamar asked.

"We're doing it here," Dufrain barked.

Adamar schooled his pride as he grabbed a tall vertical deadboard on wheeled feet and moved it behind the dummy. Deadboards served to nullify magic that might go too far during an experiment. He ensured it covered the attack area as best he could before he returned to the main table. Dufrain raised hands over the sword to perform magic Adamar couldn't see.

Adamar realized Dufrain had either gotten drunk last night, had failed to get enough sleep or both. His hands quivered and moved in clumsy fits. Part of Adamar wanted to be kind and ask what was wrong; the other part clamped his mouth shut because he neither wanted to be there nor hear Dufrain's inevitable retort.

"These wars can't keep burning," Dufrain said. "The lycans sign peace treaties and promptly break them. Their animal halves ignore what their human halves decide. We can't trust them."

Adamar inspected the sword.

"There," said Dufrain. "Alright." Raising the weapon, he collected his thoughts. He pointed it at the dummy with a tremor in his posture. A powerful wave of green energy fired across the space and illuminated the deadboard with faint, brief auroral flashes, but the dummy remained otherwise unaffected. Items on nearby shelves rattled as remnant energy dispersed under an unfocused cast.

"What was the goal, wizard?" Adamar noticed the rattling items.

Dufrain scowled at the dummy. "It's supposed to shred the dummy and leave the clothes unaffected."

"Why?" Adamar asked.

"Go adjust it," Dufrain said. "Put it more center."

Adamar frowned but obeyed. He took care to recenter the deadboard behind it, aware of the wizard's careless aim. He stepped behind the wizard and kept his distance, afraid the addled wizard would shoot wide.

Dufrain prepped again, gathered the commands in his mind and cast the spell. This time the deadboard rattled as it struggled to absorb the amount of energy cast across the space. Two glass pipettes and a small stone bowl rattled off their shelves and crashed to the floor. The dummy, again, remained untouched.

"Damnit," he said while Adamar scanned the items across the floor.

"Wizard, are you sure you're…okay?"

"Okay? What do you mean?" Dufrain asked.

"You're…missing."

"Missing? I hit the dummy square!" Dufrain barked. "And how would *you* know!?"

"I-I can't see what you're doing to the dummy, but…" Adamar said and motioned to the items on the floor. "Those are falling. Maybe the deadboard isn't strong enough for—"

"It's powerful magic! Not that would you know enough about it, vacant," Dufrain snarled. "Go clean it up. Won't affect you anyhow."

Gripping his fists and clenching his jaw, Adamar circumvented the table to gather the small hand brush and dustpan. He stooped behind the deadboard to brush glass into the pan when, out of the corner of his eye, he saw a furious Dufrain sweep the sword again with a broad, violent flourish.

Terror struck Adamar, not only because he knew the wizard would wreak havoc with his careless cast, but also that Adamar, himself, could actually see the flare of green light of the sword's spell flushing across the room like emerald fire. He ducked across broken glass as the deadboard crashed over him, unable to absorb the power of the spell.

The entire backside of Dufrain's office exploded and disintegrated. The wall disappeared in a violent flash of magic and thunder. Heavy stonework flew outward across Academy grounds and rained down through rooftops and windows in a monstrous hailstorm. Struck by the deadboard, Adamar had been cast across the room and into the melee, along with dozens of exploding vials of potions stored along the walls. As they exploded, boiling fluids flew across the room. He screamed and writhed as scorching mists and steams bathed his right side.

A shocked Dufrain flinched instead of casting a proper protective shield. The explosion blasted him into the double doors behind him before he bounced back into the room. Broken potion stores set the room aflame in violent green fire that stormed inside the stone chamber. Sections of the ceiling caved in around Adamar in a flush of smoke and dust.

Adamar struggled to remain conscious even as the boiling liquid seared his skin and heavy stones rolled into him from the collapse. Dozens of glass tubes and chemistry equipment exploded while fire started by magic caught on curtains and Dufrain's robes. Unable to see any more magic, Adamar climbed to his feet, untouched by the raging firestorm and clutched his right arm as his skin bubbled under the burns. Though he protected most of his face during the explosion, tiny burn lines steamed along his forehead and lower jaw. He staggered across the floor while glass continued bursting around him under a maelstrom he could not sense.

When he groped at the red emergency cord, it fell away from the upper anchor as ash while real fire devoured Dufrain's clothing. Adamar twisted the door handle, yanked open the heavy wooden portal and stepped into the hallway. Worried attendants from nearby offices raced from the magic storm growing outward from the chaos. Adamar snatched Dufrain by his hood and hauled him from the danger with his good hand.

Wizards and apprentices sprinted down the high arched hallway with raised hands to corral the magic. A wizard tried to heal Adamar, but watched in vain as his power smoked on contact with his skin. The wizard gave Adamar a surprised look, as if he knew what Adamar was and was surprised to find him here, but as others cried for more help, he moved on while Adamar quivered in agony against a nearby wall.

Dufrain stirred from the shock and stared helplessly as others combatted the green inferno he caused. Adamar climbed to his feet and limped away with his one good foot and hand, past gaping assistants, on his way out of the New Gordon Academy.

21
Realm Diving

Tyran Han stood in Aurora Song's dark chambers lit by spears of light piercing the rosebush above. Song lay in her rosebud and writhed deep in tortured sleep. Like Ven, visions and voices infected Song until the aurora struggled to maintain her sanity for lack of quality sleep. *Wake her.*

Hesitant, her attendants tugged open the rosebud and reached in.

Her nude form glistened in sweat. Song jumped at being woken and spun in a panic before locking onto Han. *What? What is it?*

It's time, chimed Han.

Song licked her full lips and tumbled from the bud into the arms of her attendants. They helped her stand before draping her in a robe as she took deep breaths. *The elderate has finally approved of your decision?*

No, chimed Han. *And I'm done waiting on them.*

And if you fail? Or die?

You have proven Ven's claim, chimed Han. *All they do is bicker and posture while the magnas are dying.*

Song flinched as if struck. Crimson irises shimmered as her haunted gaze dashed about the chamber, caught in memory of her constant visions. *All they do is scream at me.*

I thought they whispered? asked Han.

Unceasing whispers soon scream, chimed Song. *They need not be louder or more powerful to drown thoughts even from my own mind. They need only endlessness…* Song gasped and struggled to stay present.

Han approached and knelt before the female and struggled to ignore her sensual curves barely hidden beneath her thin shift. *I cannot wait longer. I must dive.*

Realm diving has always proved disastrous, Han, Song chimed. *It will kill you and we may never learn anything from your sacrifice.*

What choice do we have? Han asked. *Ven and Rose are gone. We haven't heard from them in so long, I have no option but to believe they died in the rimsportal explosion.*

No, chimed Song. *I'm sure she lives.*

Even if you're right, they haven't returned and we must take measures to speak with the magnas, chimed Han. *Or die trying.*

And if the worldender is *her solution? If she has found a way to save the magnas?*

I can't wait for a perfect solution when a viable course of action lays within our grasp right now, chimed Han. *I have to try.*

My tyran, one of Han's guards chimed and saluted. *Please, I would beg you again—*

I said no, Han cut him off. *I will risk myself and no other pixie.*

I know she draws nearer, Song panted. *If you can wait—*

While ever more magnas die under the jaws of this draco? Han asked. *You are a hairsbreadth from losing your sanity. I can't risk the health of our flock by delaying any longer.*

And if I dive? Song asked.

You know you cannot, Han chimed. *A flock without its aurora will die. A flock without its tyran?* Han smirked. *With all these wonderfully bossy elders around, who will notice?*

Song gripped his wrist. *Please. Don't.*

This is the only way to find answers, Han set his large hand over her soft, petite fingers and squeezed them. He leaned in and offered her a small kiss and a wink. *For our youth.*

Han, she chimed.

Standing, he left her chambers and navigated the complex of rooms to emerge from under her rosebush.

Are you sure? asked his attendant, Couture Rima.

It's not too late, chimed Infith, the only elder to support the plan.

Come, chimed Han. Taking off, the small group crossed the hilly terrain to a small shorn stump sitting atop a nearby ridge. He turned around to soak in the sight of Tree Carlinia's braided trunks climbing into her spreading canopy. *I will miss you.*

The elderate will come when you begin, chimed Rima. *They will know the moment you dive.*

Nodding, Han took a deep breath as he worked to recall all details of the necessary spell. *Let's begin.*

Setting the base of his upraised right hand against the base of his down-pointed left hand, Han initiated the energetic surge at the point where they met, allowing his magic to flow through his forearms. He waited until the energy pierced the veils. Closing the fingers of each hand, he separated them—his right hand upward and left down.

A tiny point of blackness appeared between his wrists and split into a vertical rift of nothingness.

The spell fluttered as soft as a leaf in a gentle breeze, yet pixies erupted from the grass across the territory as if a thunderous gong had crashed through the air. A dozen bright pale sparks rushed him from the rosebush, centered by a single crimson light.

As Han tore a separation in the realmic fabric, elements of his form began to evaporate.

WAIT! Song's chime echoed through the air.

Tears snaked down Rima's cheeks as her lord disintegrated and swirled into the growing black rift.

Members of the arriving elderate hesitated at the sight of the realm dive—the first any had ever witnessed.

Rima shook her head. *Too late.*

In microscopic grains of energy, Han's form drifted and danced into the glowing rift. Han's head lolled back and legs folded upward, all followed by his four wings as the gap sucked him through.

Rushing through the gaping elders and eldresses encircling the spell, Aurora Song's curvy frame landed on delicate feet with a furious crash that sent fine cracks through the millennial stump and shoved her glowing hand through the rift. Those on the stump gasped—even among the elders, few had ever seen an angry aurora.

As her forearm sank into the rift, it fluctuated, pulsed and shrank.

Holding her other hand out to balance her reach inside the rift, she closed her fingers into fists. Glowing lines appeared between her hands and the vertical light and arrested its closure.

Can you save him? asked Rima.

Song gritted her teeth as bloodred hair hung down the side of her face. *I'm not even sure he's still alive.*

* * *

From his perch on a tiny tree void of any color, Han scanned a world that resisted observation. A ceiling and floor of void extended across a horizon of faint gray light. He discerned distance neither to sky nor ground. The fluctuating tree beneath him resisted existing.

His essence fluttered as the nether rejected his physical form and his aura attempted to dissipate into the nothing.

When Han took a slow breath, he realized his contracting lungs drew no air. That he had no need of air gave him a moment of panic. He mustered and waited out that fear until realization dawned that good air wasn't necessary.

The nether resisted being seen, felt or heard. What appeared as reality existed because his mind forced its appearance, and only as long as he observed it.

Han first fluttered his wings from habit before flying by willpower, alone. Without a sense of direction, he headed straight. Fast or slow, high or low, he grasped no reality and had to focus through the mind-warping quality of it while searching for a magnalark.

As if called, he sensed a presence off to his "left," if there was a "left" in this place. He "turned," and found a wall—or being—that filled the horizon like liquid smoke. Bare pale light leaked around its distant edges yet displayed no clear definition.

Han hesitated to touch it, as doing so incurred great risk, yet approached and raised his hand.

Though he sensed no moment of contact, an intimate presence engulfed him—more so than any pixie copulation in the wildest of orgies. Neither words nor language-based thoughts held power here; only meanings, which overwhelmed him with fear, worry, fury, love, hatred, compassion, and terror. He struggled to remember who he was under the torrent of its pure essence.

How long had he been here? Years passed under the waterfall of thoughts too high for him to absorb without piecing apart its density, peeling away moments and eons baked together under an oven of millions of years.

Did a year pass by or a mere second? Where was the sun—what was a sun? A vague and distant past tickled at Han's soul while magnalark after magnalark touched him to pass the same, disturbing essence of being that he finally realized served as communication.

Medium didn't exist here. Magnalarks conveyed reality, itself, as language. Reality as it existed here, at least—without clear form, time or space. Even the high ceiling and floor, Han realized, weren't real, only projections of a three-dimensional mind.

Han was born and died in the same moment that had no beginning or ending. He folded inward and outward without conflict. Only when the magnas cried out in fear—the same cry that threatened aurorae sanity—did Han's mind coalesce once more into a sense of self that was unified enough to remember why he had come.

The magnas' memories remained with him and displayed the entirety of the problem: an insatiable draco pierced the veil, filled with the ancient and panrealmic power of the La'Du Lira Al'Cular—The Tree of Life.

Horror drenched Han as he realized the draco had already devoured tens to hundreds of thousands of magnas—if not millions. Numbers were difficult to understand here, save only that pixies who expected their physical race to persist through future ages of Pangean history would be devastated to learn how soon they might finish their time among the living.

Han also knew he might never return to the third realm, for he had no idea how he entered, in the first place.

Screams of the magnalarks drew him back to the problem—Cas'Doren had returned.

Han attempted to draw power into his hands, but the energy fizzled away—he had no hands in which to concentrate such power. Gulping, his mouth fell open as fear welled, knowing a hard truth.

He would not go home.

Tyran Han gritted his "teeth" and "flew" toward where fear had welled most.

In the "distance," a snaking light danced as it struck at magnas. Laughter reverberated through the airless void. Han sped until he encountered Cas'Doren—a white draco head that left an endless streak of winding white light. Pale smoke wisped off the dragon's trail as the three-dimensional horror danced through a two-dimensional nether.

Han remembered himself for a moment—not as a pixie, but as his previous magnalark form. In his previous form, he wandered the nether for four hundred million years, engaging with other larks, letting his mind form and shape under the essences of others, and pondering the enormity of the cosmos while feeding on the dissonant energies of realities-in-friction. Shaken by the memory and its flood of information that threatened his pixie sense of self, his focus returned in time to face a new horror.

Cas'Doren's ghost-white head floated before him with piercing white eyes.

Aahhh...the dragon's voice reverberated in the muted space. *A pixie...here.* His laughter blared into Han's ears. *I see my forays have drawn your attention.*

Han quivered. *Leave the nether!*

I do as I please, little light, Cas'Doren laughed. *And I will have my way here as I always have.*

How do you pierce the veil? HOW!?

To tell you so you might attempt to mount an attack on me? I think not. Cas'Doren turned one eye closer and drew a circle of light around him. *Though I doubt you'll even make it back.* He chuckled.

How do you persist? Tell me! Han cried. *How do you go back!?*

Oh, little lark, Cas'Doren chuckled, *I will eat as much as I desire. I am the top of every food chain. I am a god-in-form. I will take from this tree of life as I please.*

The-the Tree! The La'Du Lira Al'Cular. How? Is that it!? Han asked as the draco drew nearer.

You don't see, Cas'Doren said. *While you are no leviathan, you do look tasty.*

Han would have sunk to his knees if he could, but his essence faded under the intensity of the nether's rejection. The dragon persisted because he had somehow gained access to the basest form of energy—that of the Tree of Life, itself. He knew Cas'Doren was in Eden and pierced the veil from there, but also knew he could never return to his previous life.

His magnalark memories opened something deep within him, knowledge of the fabric of reality inaccessible while in pixie form. His old essence had returned enough to remind him of a single tool he knew he needed.

Tell me, draco, Han gripped his fists. *How do you do it? How do you pierce the veil? How do you access the La'Du Lira Al'Cular?*

Easily, little light. The draco snapped his jaws. *Easily.*

Then let the mighty magnus draco tell his next meal, chimed Han.

The mighty lord of dragons eats his favorite treat, smiled Cas'Doren.

Treat? What of the Tree could you possibly eat? Dragons cannot eat Trees.

Cas'Doren chuckled. *I do not eat Trees.*

Han cocked his "head."

I eat its seeds.

The Al'cular, cried Han. *It bears seed!?*

Yesss, Cas'Doren circled so near that Han could see what little remained of his own form reflecting in the draco's eye—an inversion to his normal glowing aura. *And what delicious, powerful seed it produces, too. Just what I need to grow in form and might. No other dragon before or after me will ever do as I have done. None will be as great as Cas'Doren.*

There is no greatness in destruction, alone, chimed Han. *No nobility in consumption.*

Cas'Doren's echoing laughter threatened Han's thin sanity. *My appetite is the source of my power. It has driven me to rise through a hundred thousand years of life and domination. I, alone, survive the great ancients. Only a few remain from the eons before, and one day, I will devour them, as well.*

Time and truth pierced Han's fear to reveal a future reality— Cas'Doren's chaos would come to an abrupt end one day, all thanks to the work of his own ауroralite. *One day, draco, we will kill you.*

What can a pixilark do against dragonscale? Cas'Doren chuckled. *I was young during the last dracopixie war, but I remember well there is little a speck can accomplish against a mature draco.*

But we did do to you, chimed Han, *or we would not yet remain.*

For now, little pixie. For now.

We did to you. We did. If not dragonscale— if not from the outside… Han said as his voice gave out. *Then we will attack from within.*

A fine summation from one who has no more moment to live, said Cas'Doren.

Han twisted in agony as his power shuddered, but his focus narrowed through time and space to a distant future. He smiled in his pain. *One day, you will die because of the very appetite you believe drives you to victory. And it will not be some great elven or human war who ends your rule, but one of my kind. A lone little pixie will* end *you.*

Turning inward, Cas'Doren laughed all the louder, opened wide his jaws and snapped them closed around Han.

* * *

Aurora Song flinched before the rift collapsed and severed her arm at the elbow. A bloody stump erupted with her golden blood a half second before the seam of the rift shrank, exploded and knocked every nearby pixie from the air. Han's pureed physical form bathed those nearby.

Prostrate over the edge of the stump, half of Song's body burned. Patches of skin swelled dark with scorching.

As the initial pain subsided, elders, guards and attendants climbed to their feet. Rift and Han were gone. Each pixie's essence writhed under the explosive nether energy. Several collapsed to their knees while Infith rose and stood over Song.

Gather her! Infith commanded. Song's attendants rushed to haul her away.

Connected to the aurora as they were, pixies across the territory staggered in their activities under the severity of her injury and its effect on their energetic tethers to her.

Rima struggled to focus with her connection with her Tree halved by the aurora's injury. Guards rushed to help her while Infith climbed upon the stump and scanned the burn mark left behind by the exploding rift.

Great Self, Infith rasped. *What happened?*

22
Losing Seeds

Noonlight caressed the crown of the La'Du Lira Al'Cular rising 900 feet from the sandy floor of the large, sunken chamber. Seven hundred feet wide at its root base and two hundred and eighty feet thick, the canopy spread eight hundred feet at the narrow opening of a hole in the cave ceiling. Brilliant light speared through its massive branches and mottled the cave floor in a perpetual lace of light and shadow. The chamber's concave walls circled the tree up to the opening, through which peeked the Tree's upper canopy to appear like a gentle green hill of bush outside.

In the Tree's western bosom curled the largest black dragon since Umphaedra Dominar—a dragon king dead thirty thousand years at the jaws of the beast slumbering upon the great nest of smaller trees and bushes. Cas'Doren scratched long claws on his narrow chest and huffed in a half-conscious state while his horned tail tapped back and forth between two heavy roots.

From the shadows of the great curved chamber walls, a small green female slithereen emerged to the view of the light-wreathed Tree of Life. Hours of waiting revealed how often guards visited the chamber during their rounds.

A familiar, intoxicating scent caught her attention—the same she identified while wandering near the chamber's apex over the past few weeks. The smell first intrigued her, then aroused her, then kept her awake until it consumed her every waking thought. Known for their sensitive noses, slithereens were prized by draco kings for hunting smaller prey.

Now, she hunted a smell that had ravished her sense of reason until it drew her to enter the rift, navigate the caves, and sneak in undetected.

She crossed the sun-mottled floor, wiggled between the massive roots, and wound her way to the underside of the king's large nest of broken trees and brambles. Holding her breath, she squeezed her head through the narrow underside of the nearest root and waited.

Above her, Cas'Doren shifted and scratched while her nostrils flared with the intoxicant's overwhelming presence. She snaked her neck near the bottom of the nest and nibbled at its tiny branches. The rhythm of tiny seedpods trickled downward as the nest sagged under her effort. When the first pod glanced her snout, she shivered.

The slithereen nuzzled the gap wider until she caught a seed in her lips. She turned her head to set down the seed to discover the ground beneath the roots fell away into darkness. With no alternative, she attempted to retreat from the narrow tangle of Cas'Doren's nest when her back-slanted cranial horns caught on the roots behind her.

She tugged a few times as fear climbed, hoping both to preserve the seed and escape with her life when a heavy breath popped the seed from her mouth and sent it banging into the darkness beneath the Tree.

Desperate for a seed, she leaned again under the nest to nuzzle out another when the dragon above her twisted and erupted with a thunderous roar of discovery. Panicking, the dragaina recoiled and caught against the wood. Through the gaps of the roots behind her, the black dragon's vicious razor teeth chomped and bit at her shoulders. The dragaina screamed as sections of her scales ripped free under his attack.

Unable to retreat or be pulled out by Cas'Doren, she struggled to crawl below his nest to hide from his rage. He managed to sink his fangs around the root of one of her wings and ripped it out. She screamed as blood erupted from the hole left behind.

Thrashing, her wavy horns tangled in the bottom of his sagging nest and ripped open its belly. Panic filled her as the entire trove poured out and banged into the darkness below in a fading musical percussion.

Cas'Doren twisted at the sound, roared, struck, and ripped out the slithereen's midbody. Her head and hind remained tangled in roots he could not get under. He spat out her gory belly upon the sand and roared again.

Guards filled the chamber as he panted in rage and searched the roots' narrow gaps toward the darkness below where he could never fit.

My lord! a red snapper dove in from the entrance above and landed before Cas'Doren with his head low. *What is wrong?*

My seeds, you fool. My seeds! This little sparrow has lost my seeds!

The snapper cowered, having seen Cas'Doren destroy dragons who spoke while he raged.

Get me a slithereen, Cas'Doren barked. *Now!*

Yes, majesty! the red snapper ducked his head and leapt into the air.

Cas'Doren's thundering roar echoed upward into Eden Valley. He waggled his head in rage before searching his nest in vain for a single remaining pod. Ripping out the bramble, he protested that the roots underpinning his nest were too thick and narrow for him to wiggle through. Millennia of searching proved both Tree and its foundation too firm for a draco of his size to pierce.

Get this piece of shit out from under my tree! Cas'Doren roared at his guard.

The smaller guardians snaked their way into the bramble to extricate the pieces of the thief.

Where is my slithereen!? Where? Bring one! ordered Cas'Doren as he paced until the red snapper returned with a slithereen. Cas'Doren pointed at the large roots. *Get in there. Now!*

The slithereen bowed its head. *What am I to do down below, my lord?*

This bloody insect lost me my treepods! Cas'Doren snatched the severed head and ground it into the sand. *You will retrieve every single one and bring them right back here.*

Yes, majesty, the slithereen snaked across the ground, wiggled through the large roots, and disappeared into the black.

Cas'Doren barked angry coughs before he crawled to the red snapper, snatched it by the neck and threw it upon the ground. Rough bites took out chunks of the writhing attendant before he lifted him near his snout. *Explain to me, Percius,* he snarled, *how that little cur got down here.*

I know not, my lord, Percius rasped under Cas'Doren's iron grip. *I shall find out immediately!*

When I set you as my aide de camp, I was assured of your ability to manage my affairs, not the least of which is my personal guard. And you let this interloper within feet of my hide while I was dozing. I should rip out your throat where I stand!

Please, my lord! Mercy! Percius croaked. *I was meeting with Captain Imnavir to discuss the arrival of the Fedra entourage!*

Fedra can burn, said Cas'Doren. *Find out how she got down here.*

I will, my king! I shall make your reckoning!

Cas'Doren squeezed Percius's throat until a single razor claw displaced his scales and sank shallow into his flesh. *My reckoning, you filthy guttersnipe? I am perfectly capable of reckoning my own self, but you will correct this gap in my guard or I will rip off your tail, stuff it down your throat, and eat you while you choke!*

Yes, my lord, Percius croaked.

Go. Gather the wings. Bring every snapper, slithereen and other small draco you can find. You will do everything you can to retrieve my seeds. Day and night, they will stay here until they get them. Now go. Cas'Doren flung the snapper across the ground.

Percius recovered and sprinted away to catch air and lift off. He pumped upwards.

Cas'Doren returned to his perch, inspected his broken nest and roared again. The stupor of eating a seed hung heavy in his mind—as it always did. The energy of a mature magna and that delicious little pixie who dared pierce the veil coursed through his veins. As ever, a warmth burned within him from feeding his desires, but fear threatened it now that every remaining seed lay out of reach.

23

Taken

"Stop. Stop!" Eva cried. Opening the door of her closed carriage, she descended to the muddy street and into the alley. Rain pattered down the high narrow gap between tall stone buildings. "Adamar?"

She leaned over a man huddled in the gutter, who raised a gaunt, bearded face in a mix of drunken stupor and startle to her colorful dress and brilliant blonde hair.

"I'm sorry," she stepped back. "I was looking for a man."

"Ahm uh man," he slurred and failed to sit up.

Grimacing, she headed deeper into the dark streets, determined to find her husband. News from the ministry was grim about Adamar—terrible boil wounds along his body. Despite that, he had saved her father's life before walking out.

No one knew where he had gone, but worry filled her as the air chilled under the approaching thunderstorm. Burn wounds lost heat and could send Adamar into hypothermia in conditions he might otherwise shrug off.

The high heels of her fine shoes wobbled and slipped so much that she hiked her skirt, yanked them off and ran barefoot across cold stone. Aware her bright colors and feminine appearance served as a beacon for the undesirable, she tucked her skirt with one arm to minimize its size while she peeked around corners to avoid coming upon gangs.

Where had Adamar gone? Fury and worry filled her as she searched tiny alleyways, peeked into shanties built on corners and traversed slick stairwells. Every man was Adamar under the heavy gray skies and stark shadows filling these dark corners. She knew crying out his name would not serve her and only draw those she wished to avoid.

Her time in Southdown taught her most people were good and kind, but no amount of policing would eliminate all ruffians and the danger they posed to the unwary.

Eva's hackles rose as occasional boot falls echoed behind her. Was she being followed? Her ears strained to the point of headache to identify every sound as a potential danger.

At a corner, she caught her breath and winced as her feet ached with cold. Her toes lost feeling a while ago and her lower dress was filthy. She retained her heels as hand weapons should the need arise.

Eva wiped soaked hair back over her head. Where might Adamar go? He introduced her to the world without energetic manipulation. Her magic-dominated education biased her toward it, and yet Adamar revealed the world was infinitely more complex than she first thought.

Where might a man go who neither needed nor could use magic?

Pausing to set her hand upon the nearest wall, tears joined the rain. "Great Self...please. Help me. Adamar...is in pain. I need to find him. Help me find him."

Loud boot falls echoed too close for her comfort. She raced as quiet as possible down an alley, doubled back around the block and headed off in a new direction when a pair of feet sticking out from under heavy canvas sheets set her sprawling across the frigid stone.

Eva stifled a moan and clutched her ringing head. A familiar pair of shoes stuck out from under a tarp—the same Adamar wore on his way to work that morning. "Adamar!?" She snatched away canvas sheets to expose Adamar huddling beneath and quivering with a mix of mild shock.

"Adamar!" she pulled at him. "Great Self, Adamar—"

Severe burns scorched the right side of his arm, neck and appeared to have injured his thigh and ankle. Blisters had formed and popped. The infection would follow fast. The wizard who had first attempted to heal Adamar told her that healing magic was useless. Fear welled anew. What was so easy to heal by wizards could kill her husband within a day.

"Come on," she pulled his lethargic figure out from behind the two mats. "Please, help. I can't lift you, Adamar."

Adamar stirred and quivered as he came to. "What? Eva?" He flailed, confused.

"We have to get you back to the Academy, Adamar, quickly," she sniffed wetly. "You're in bad shape."

"Wh-why?" he let her heft him a bit as he staggered. He threw out a steadying hand on a wall before they leaned too far. He hissed and cursed when her grip twisted his injuries.

"I-I'm sorry! C'mon!"

Recoiling twisted his boiled skin. Pain dragged him to his left hip atop the pile of canvas as he flinched his right arm to his side and gritted his teeth to keep from bellowing.

"Adamar," Eva said. She was afraid to touch him and more to leave him. "We have to go! We have to get you somewhere safe!"

"Why?" asked Adamar. "So your dad can kill me this time?"

"That was an accident!"

"Oh, shit," Adamar hissed. "I can't go back."

"But you promised!"

"So he can dismiss me again?" Adamar asked. "To think I'm disposable?"

"He doesn't think that."

"He does!" Adamar snapped and half-raised his quivering arm. "He does enough."

"I'm so sorry, but that's not—"

"I'm not going back."

"Damnit, Adamar," said Eva. "We can't go back to living like this!"

"Then go!" cried Adamar. "*I* will!"

"You're going to die," she said.

"Then I die on my own terms," said Adamar.

"You— stupid— selfdamn arrogant piece of shit!" she screamed.

Adamar sank onto his unburned side.

"You would rather die to maintain your fucking pride than admit when you're wrong!"

"You'd rather I die to maintain yours."

"How *dare* you," she said. "You put words in my mouth. I would never believe such a thing!"

Adamar had nothing left with which to fight her and sank onto his back.

"Are you just going to lie there!?" she screamed over him. Her voice echoed in each direction under pale late afternoon light.

Boot falls interrupted the moment as men rushed around a nearby corner.

"Got her!" cried one of them.

Adamar's head popped up. Eva floated a foot above the ground with her arms and dress pinned to her body as martial mages wrapped her in magic he could not see.

Rage boiled in him as he rolled off the canvas, spun around his wife, planted a foot into the chest of the nearest mage and vaulted him into a wall, slapping his head against the stone before the man sank limp to the alley.

Shocked as their magic failed to grab or halt him, Adamar raised his left hand high and swung the bottom of his fist into the face of a gaping man, whose head twisted before he sank unconscious to the road.

"Release my wife!" said Adamar as he stumbled against the wall into his injured arm. He winced as one of them advanced on him. He ducked under the man's feeble kick and punched between his legs. The mage doubled over with a moan and crumpled.

Without thinking, he raised his right arm to take the final mage. The fragile skin ripped and sent shocks through him that forced him to clench. The final mage, a thick fellow, leaned into the opportunity and planted his heavy fist into Adamar's gut.

Adamar doubled over, slipped and landed on his injured arm. The pain overcame his senses when blackness washed him away.

24

Through the Garden

Haephan stumbled across a forest floor mottled by diffused dusklight. He hissed as he freed his foot from yet another snagging root and rubbed it while itching from dozens of other scrapes.

Eden Valley sank deeper into evening shadow as the sun dipped between a far cleft of two western peaks. Cool breezes turned icy at the loss of its warmth. Haephan huddled against the change, as the breeze carried a familiar dampness common in Rainhold, one that could chill without warning.

Leaving the men at sunrise, he worked east northeast down the slope and skirted the valley wall to avoid descending lower than the northern plateau. Though he had reached the plateau in mid-afternoon, evening's arrival instilled fear that he veered off course. North, to Haephan, was no more than a description of city regions used by Crimson Guardians and Constables until Sartlam taught him direction by the sun and other field tricks. The old man also advised Haephan on how to avoid snakes, bears, and other potential hazards.

Tired and hungry, Haephan decided sleep was his highest priority. Sartlam told him to seek thickets on hillsides without ground holes, which Haephan now realized would be difficult to find in the thickening dim.

Atop a knoll surrounded by trees dancing in the evening wind, he sat and lamented a lack of supper. Weeks ago, going days without food was a regular fact of life, yet now he feared not having as much as three meals a day. Wild fruit he ate at midday did little to fill the growing ache in his belly.

Haephan crawled into a gap between nearby bushes and laid his head on his curled arm. Wind rushed the bush around him in a cacophony he had never before experienced prior to leaving New Gordon.

Haephan's fortunes teased him. Plunged into the service of a wizard who proved more a gruff old man than the monster everyone believed him to be, also brought a near unlimited amount of food, a warm bed and safety from gangs and slavers. Most days, never-ending chores were an easy price to pay for such luxury.

Now the wizard had sent him out into a den of dragons to gather seeds. Was this better or worse than the streets in Rainhold that he knew so well?

Haephan wasn't so sure and now he had no meal, to boot. He clutched his arms round about himself against the growing chill. Tired from his solitary march, he wanted to let the night swallow him into the realm of dreams, many of which had been odd of late—islands in oceans floating in the midst of nothingness, a sea of sand that flowed as far as the eye could see, a city far beneath green ocean waves, a horizon of towering arbors dancing together across a brown ocean...

The memory of those dreams calmed and beckoned him toward sleep when something scrambled over the skin of his belly and chest.

Haephan screamed, yanked off his shirt, and slapped down his skin in a panic to knock away the interloper. Though rare, cockroaches periodically found their way into his Rainhold nest despite its separation from the shore.

Haephan shuddered and calmed, though he was more awake now

than before he laid down. He left the thicket in favor of the crook of a nearby tree to huddle again for warmth. Above, the first blaze of stars emerged from the faint blue sky. Instead of wondering about his dreams, his skin crawled with the fear of a thousand bugs. He tucked his shirt again and hugged his belly, both for warmth and to hide all the slips that could admit further critters.

Now in a gentle gulley, icy mist pooled, flowed around the tree, and bathed him in moisture. Nestling deeper into the crook of the tree did little to shield him from the cold when something bit his bottom.

Haephan screamed again and leapt to his feet. Something tiny snarled from the darkness and sent him running.

Frustrated tears welled as he rubbed his backside and found tiny holes in his trousers where the creature had bitten him. Overwhelmed, he stalked through the forest while rubbing drops of blood from his hands.

Why did he have to be here? Why couldn't he be back in the kitchen cleaning greasy pots, or in Rainhold where he knew how to handle those animals? He stormed into the thickening forest through snagging bushes, thorny vines, and overgrown flora, too afraid to try again to sleep.

He wished to whisk off somewhere—anywhere—he wanted. To leap great distances at a single thought. If only…

Haephan raised his foot to mount a long, broad hillock, when his foot disappeared into the grass and swallowed him whole. He raised his hands as if to catch himself on the hill as it consumed him. He fell through a heavy bramble of arm-thick roots that thrashed him on his way into darkness. He panicked and groped for something to hold onto when the cleft of a branch stopped cold his chest and left his body to whip down.

His mouth gaped like a fish before a ragged gasp ripped from his lungs. Coughing followed as he flailed out with his other hand to grab the branch and alleviate his weight from the biting pinch. He bit through the pain, climbed by his aching wrist, and swung out his feet to nearby springy branches. Little in this midnight underground bramble stood out to him.

Haephan clutched the branches while his feet groped for purchase.

Once secure, he scanned for an escape when a brief bout of light flickered across the underside of nearby branches and drew his focus into the darkness below. He wiped tears with his forearm as he worked to thicker branches on which to stand. Once more secure, he used his sleeve to wipe his face and looked again into the great blackness below, where tiny bonfires came to life and bathed an army of tiny slithering figures. From this distance, the floor appeared to crawl with salamanders, snakes and other lizards.

Realization dawned that they weren't lizards in a tiny sink, but he somehow had landed in an enormous cavern full of dragons. As more fires ignited across a grand, high-walled chamber, he better understood the Tree's true enormity.

The caw of a distant raven sent shivers through his body.

When a dragon's echoing roar startled him, Haephan slipped, crashed onto his nuts and rolled down the incline. He hugged the tree to stop sliding and struggled not to bawl at the pain burning his kidneys, even as fresh tears twinkled in the dim light. Adding insult to injury, his bladder loosed itself and soaked his pants before dribbling around and coursing the underside of the branch.

For a moment, Haephan could do nothing but cling to the tree and sob. Fear consumed him even as his pungent urine cut the air. When the initial panic passed, shame welled in his chest at being so childish as to piss his trousers. The rough bark of the tree brought him back to the present moment. He released his grip, shifted his crotch off the tree, and found a better seat with his feet below his head.

Sulfurous heat wafting upwards dried out his face enough to parch his mouth and cause a nosebleed, which drooled down his chin onto the branch before he stirred enough to sit up and pinch the nasal bridge to stem it.

Though everything ached and reeked, Haephan was grateful he hadn't fallen all the way down. With care, he backed along the thickening branch until he could crawl, turn and walk. Ahead, the monstrous tree twisted from the midnight shadow downward toward a field of flickering bonfires. Haephan wagered the base was larger than Goram's house. Or several of Goram's houses. He never knew trees could be so large, but...

Was this really the Tree of Life? Was he standing upon one of its branches? Its enormity proved evidence enough. He took a moment to soak it in, but awe fizzled under the need to either climb up or down. Curved gaps in the ripples twisting around the Tree offered Haephan the idea of descending inside of one.

Haephan estimated hundreds of creatures filled the vast chamber floor, but none would climb upon the Tree, itself. Should he avoid touching it, as well? He saw no other way to travel but by hand and foot and resigned to descending as best he could.

Before stepping into the narrowing curve, the kiss of cool breeze drew his attention again to the lip of ground hugging the Tree's massive crown. Could he climb the Tree and get to the valley? No branch appeared ready to hold his weight.

Without an alternative, Haephan stepped into one of the massive grooves, found his handholds, and worked his way backwards down its steep decline. Were it not for the angle, the handholds would not hold him. The angled twists in the tree steepened as he continued, hour after hour.

Late into the night, he descended until he neared the root tops. Any further, and the groove would be vertical. Haephan pressed his head to the wood and suppressed his ever-present yearning to flee. Part of him screamed for him to climb back up, jump to the lip of ground and run away, no matter what the wizard told him.

He scanned the chamber. His breath caught when he realized he had descended far enough for the upper curves of the chamber floor to reach eye-level with him, which meant any high-climbed beast might find him.

Elverbane said something about their poor eyesight, but Haephan couldn't remember much from their conversation. When the wizard told him he was to sneak into Eden and steal seeds from dragons, everything else passed in one ear and out the other.

Now, he wished he heard everything. Too tired to reverse his path, he descended with care. The vertical groove fell straight between two massive roots. He took his time to toe for footholds as his tired fingers ached.

When his left shoe slipped, his weight yanked him down. He yelped and snatched at holds only for several splinters to stab his hands. The shoe, whose laces had loosened over the hours descending, slipped free and tumbled into the darkness below. Tears welled from biting his tongue in the shift while maintaining a thin grip with his fingertips.

The sound of an approaching scuffle welled his fear anew before a small dragon approached the branches and fluffed its wings.

Haephan leaned deeper into the shadow of the deep cleft, hoping it would hide him from the creature. The beast turned in his direction and sniffed at the air. The boy cringed, sure the reek of his piss gave him away.

The dragon slithered closer and hesitated, as if afraid of being found out for climbing on the Tree.

Haephan made himself as small as possible, leaned from the groove's opening, and squinted—everything he used to hide in shadows from Rainhold gangs. Would it help?

The yellow dragon climbed closer when a loud bark and roar of another dragon made it retreat. It made obeisance to something out of sight, though it stared in the boy's general direction. After a few minutes of waiting in silence, the dragon ambled off.

Haephan searched for a fresh toehold with his now shoeless, socked foot. Though the sock could slip, it was an improvement over the thick leather sole of the plain black shoe. He secured himself before he braved reaching to untie the other shoe and, holding out, attempted to drop it into the darkness leading underneath the Tree. It banged a part of the root before disappearing below. None of the dragons, at first, seemed to notice.

The boy mustered and continued when fresh scuffling announced the original dragon and a red companion approaching fast.

Both climbed halfway across the roots—one looked his way while the other sniffed into the darkness where his shoe had gone. One of them coughed a small bout of fire and dispelled Haephan's protective shadows. Bestial eyes narrowed in on him with each cough of flame until there was no mistaking their intent.

"Oh no," Haephan muttered.

Neck fins flared as the yellow beast opened its mouth and hissed a stuttering screech.

"No," said Haephan.

The dragon started—as if surprised by his sound. Had it seen him or not?

Desperate, Haephan groped for a handhold to return the way he came when his socked feet slipped out from under him and sent him tumbling between the rough walls of the groove. He twisted and bounced before spinning into an empty black chasm below.

25

The True Tree

Haephan kept falling. Was there a hole beneath the Tree so great as to have no bottom? The air cooled when leaves all around slapped him on his way down. Long, slender shoots gathered beneath him and slowed his drop until he hit the ground above a bed-soft tangle of bushes. Above blazed a night sky of smeared stars burning in a panoply of hues. How had he gotten outside?

The tooth tucked into his belt dug into his back while ebbed all other aches, bangs, and the splinters lodged in his skin. The touch of the grass poking through the bed-like bushes soaked into and warmed his entire body.

Minutes or hours passed before Haephan stirred—he wasn't sure how long he had lain there. He drew deep breaths of the cool, spiced air and accepted an inner rest as sure as if he had slept away his childhood. Rolling over, he rose and pulled open a curtain of flora to discover a starlit jungle and, beyond, a rolling carpet of mottled green under a deep evening blue drifting over the landscape like a curious fog. A bouquet of blues speckled the sky as a starry blaze until he realized a few broke off here and there to drift and flutter through the air. Before him spread gently rolling terrain descending to a hillock, upon which rose a single, sonorous Tree. Around the slender, heavenly arbor, seven angled rays of sunlight speared through cracks in the ceiling that warmed the undergrowth and drifting fog. Was it daytime? But the ceiling, as Haephan could now see, was no doubt larger than the base and rootball of the larger Tree above. From where could golden sunlight come?

The smaller Tree boasted perfect lengths, curves, and twists. He ambled through the high grass into the shallow depression and extended his hands to each side to finger the soft aromatic green freckled by flowers. Peace settled in his flesh while fear evaporated. Chirps, twitters, and gentle calls echoed through the scene. Sleepful rest settled deep in his chest. Ahead, a sourceless blue kissed the top of the Tree as the mist swirled about it.

Haephan reached the base of the gentle hillock and started his climb when his foot slipped on something round and he fell with an oomph. Rolling over, he groped to find a wooden ball as thick as an apple.

A seed!

In a moment, Haephan remembered his mission, even as he desired never to leave this place where his fears died and anxiety ebbed. He even pondered staying when he spotted the long, sinuous snout of a nearby dragon.

Two yellow orbs reflected the golden light through leaves of high grass. Did it see him? He tucked the seed under his armpit, pulled his feet under him, and prepared to flee. The eyes inched closer through the heavy green grass. Haephan took slow steps to the side and saw that they did not track him.

A crash behind Haephan revealed more dragons occupied the chamber. He bolted the way he'd come, down the hill and up the curving ascent toward the root gaps somewhere above. As small as the red and yellow dragons that had scared him into falling, the creatures chased him by sound.

Despite his exhaustion, energy renewed enough for him to sprint. He zig-zagged for cover when a root snagged his foot and tripped him to the dense softness of the floral floor. The seed under his arm disappeared.

A dragon twice his weight landed on him and bit at his head. Though facedown, Haephan twisted and raised his elbow against its neck in time to keep its long jaws away. A foul sulphuric cloud filled the air as it unleashed an ear-piercing shriek.

Haephan screamed and clutched one of his ears while holding off the beast. His world spun as if he had lost his balance and fallen. Its claws gripped and sank against his shoulders, kept out of his skin only by the fine weave of his white blouse. The dragon's next attempt glanced Haephan's face with its rough scales. The newcomer searched for a piece of Haephan and, when finding none, attacked the first creature over the boy.

Using their fight as his chance, he turned to flee when one of them leapt again upon his back and drove him down. His nose slammed against a root and broke. Haephan screamed as the dragon's heavy weight landed on the awkward position of his foot and snapped his ankle.

His pounding ears occluded all sound but the panicked beating of his heart. Certain they were about to eat him, he clutched his head and prepared for the worst when a faint flash of light bled through his eyelids and the weight pinning him disappeared.

Haephan balled up in terror, sure the second dragon had won the fight and would take him, next. When no attack came, he half turned for the beasts and cried out when his ankle twisted. Both dragons had disappeared. The boy quivered in pain and adrenaline when echoing whispers called to him.

Blinking through his muddled vision, he wiped his forearm across the blood drooling over his mouth and left a dark smear across his already chalky brown skin.

Gentle whispers beckoned him closer to the small Tree pulsing in blue light.

He sobbed while he crawled across the grass. Where had the dragons gone?

Haephan stopped several times from the pain, but the Tree beckoned him onward.

Fresh barks and bouts of fiery light revealed the dragons were nearby and fighting. Terrified, he climbed onto his good foot and fell again with a scream. Terror drove him forward through his pain. The thrashing creatures drew nearer but never quite made it to him.

Legions of the tiny motes of floating light gathered to repel the dragons from him. Were they alive!?

In a bout of flame, the dragon burst from the higher bramble behind him and destroyed a squadron of his tiny defenders before it charged the boy.

Scrambling on his hands and good foot, Haephan raced across the terrain and up the gentle hillock. When he set down his broken foot, he screamed and collapsed. With the dragon bearing down on him, he gained two more steps into the nearest column of light. When he passed through, the blue light around the Tree thickened and burst outward.

He fell across the Tree's roots with arms raised to protect himself. The energy passed over him, slammed into both dragons and cast them into the distant jungle with a muffled crash.

"Haephan," a gentle, masculine voice wafted across a warm breeze.

Pain disappeared, as did his fear, before Haephan cracked an eye. To his shock, a brilliant blue sky spread from horizon to horizon across endless miles of forest. The boy sat up and gasped.

"Whoa."

26

Direction

"How long has she been at this?" asked Degreneth. His hands clutched his forearms within large crimson sleeves as his round yellow eyes studied the yard. From a balcony at the end of the international studies building, he and two companions overlooked the spectacle along with a hundred students encircling the Andonese priestess as she terraformed in flora by a magic none had ever seen.

"Since dawn, I've been told," said a shorter but equally dignified older man with a thick mop of white hair and a long mustache hanging thick past his round chin and soft neck.

"Dawn?" murmured Degreneth. "All this since dawn?"

Last night, the yard had been little more than a carpet of trimmed grass.

"She went to see Wizard Verlima before first class and requested a number of things," murmured the third, an old woman with graying midnight hair bound tight behind her head and a broad, flattened nose between narrow eyes.

"Like what?" asked Degreneth.

"Seeds, mostly," said the witch.

"*Seeds!?*" exclaimed Degreneth. "Seeds? These appear to have been cultivated for years!"

"Have neither of you heard of Andonese Gardens?" asked Wizard Orzo as he approached from behind and leaned on the balcony doorframe. "They are wonders beyond wonders."

"I have heard of them," said the short old wizard. "But I have never before laid my eyes upon them."

"And I fear you have yet to do so, High Wizard Rolutzi," lamented Orzo. "Andonese not only cultivate the common with their magic, but also change the very essence of the seeds they breed. There are gardens you could never imagine in their halls and hollows. Not in your wildest dreams."

"And you have seen them?" asked Rolutzi.

"Alas," Orzo replied and straightened. "I have heard but descriptions and seen sketches by those who have been there. Their descriptions…were enough to make me wish I had. And this, I believe, however stunning, still pales."

"Is that her goal here?" asked Degreneth.

"What inspired her?" asked Rolutzi. "Why now?"

"Isn't the groundskeeper visiting his father this week?" intoned Degreneth.

"Think she waited so he wasn't around?" asked Orzo.

"It could stand to reason," said Degreneth.

"Bah," harrumphed Rolutzi. "An Andonese priestess afraid of a salty old groundskeeper? I seriously doubt that, administrator."

"I offer merely the facts," said Degreneth, "not their interpretation."

The triangular plot served as an intersection of three paved walks winding between campus buildings, with a diameter of seventy feet at its longest, separated from the walks by half-buried bricks.

Under SonLara's care, the original yard now split into three, shark fin-shaped plots round about a triangular mound in the center. Common plants that once invaded campus now blossomed into fountain-shaped cups of broadleaves and patterned leaflets of complimentary shades and shapes. Regional ferns climbed into an exotic lacy bulb with a crisscrossing web of straight fronds, with a flat-topped ovary within, covered in clear fur and a circled crown of glow-tipped anthers dancing in the morning breeze.

Brave bystanders leaned in to touch transformed plants, some of which reached back and sent students scurrying and laughing. Most stood in awe.

SonLara worked plants first, but also had terraformed soil to create small pools for rounded rocks, fish and shimmering flora that contributed to the pool's eerie luminescent quality.

Standing atop a tri-spurred hill she formed that morning, SonLara turned to an untouched potted tree sitting next to her. In one motion, she gripped its three-inch thick trunk and lifted with one hand and used the other to smooth its roots into a spearpoint. Onlookers gasped.

Centering atop the hillock, she whispered over the tree in her hands. Her soiled dress and sweaty brow discorded her usual pristine appearance. Strands of her lapis blue hair defied her mane and stuck across her dirt-painted skin.

With imperceptible slowness, her hips swayed and her eyes closed. With the tree clutched to her breasts, she danced around the small tip atop the bulge's outer edge. The courtyard fell still as her song caught the wind, a gentle whispered tune that raised bumps on skin and chilled bone. Memories of happier times in sunshine and breezes filled onlookers as the wind accelerated through the garden.

They gaped as her magical flows emanated outward in watery fractals that danced through air, plants and people. Even as her dance sped, she raised the tree and kept it above the center of the hill. Its short branches danced in waves while its leaves shimmered in a rainbow of colors.

SonLara kicked high soft-booted feet as she spun the tree in the air and, with a twisting whip of her legs to drive power into her arms, unleashed the momentum to drive the speared tree into the hillock until it disappeared entirely. She landed on two feet and flung out a hand to steady herself—her old teacher would have raged at her carelessness.

Panting, she rose, spread her arms and raised her head while a long, breathy note floated from her blue lips for several seconds until, without warning, a long chute fired upward three times higher than she stood. SonLara backed down the hill without unfocusing her attention or lyrics from the tree, which unzipped from the top into four distinct vertical branches. Even as they continued to thicken and lengthen, three of the four fired into the soil and wound outward, braiding together the edges of each of the three plots.

The main trunkt split again from the top halfway and swelled as branches, each of which bifurcated and trifurcated to form a thick canopy of resplendent flora. Leaves and flowers raced along outer edges and twisted about the wood shaded in speckled pastel purples, whites and yellows.

Offshoots threaded across the ground into a woodcomb of lacy humps and twists that danced trisymmetrically down each arm of the garden patch amidst other plants, curled around the bulbs and accentuated the fronds until the entire garden resembled a tree ingrown with flora and stone. As the wood settled in the black soil, trimmings of shortgrass wreathed areas where arbor kissed the ground.

The trunk plateaued and settled upon the triangular hump. The tree's full bloom fattened with a burst of foliage that rained flower petals over gasping witnesses.

Silence reigned.

Exhausted, SonLara prepared herself to deal with the questions and comments. The courtyard was empty. Both Belfast and New Gordon had disappeared, as well. Sparse trees dotted rolling, virginal hills climbing to the bluff beneath her feet and a distant creek where one day a canal would be dug.

Was this New Gordon before being founded?

Returning, she gasped.

Instead of her new tree, a radiant being stood whose presence emanated with power. Awe overwhelmed before her analytical mind pierced the haze.

"Not since the height of the Alperesian Wars have the subrim appeared in the third realm," she said. "What brings the likes of you to the shores of physicality?"

"What makes the Andonese fear the presence of holy purpose?" the subrim's smooth retort rolled off her tongue.

SonLara took a measured breath. "Can I be sure you're a subrim and not a nokburum?"

"I am Suthene, Archon to the Great Self," said the luminous being. She descended the mound and, with a gentle wave of her hand, took every ounce of SonLara's magic. The priestess sank to her knees. "And you are Priestess SonLara Alva Amferadon, Realm Delver and Librarian First Class to the Golden Hall, daughter of Thomthea and Rys, sister of Gilia and Borthoe, and personal attendant to the Silver Librarian Hosnor."

"Come now new war?" asked SonLara.

The subrim bent so that her blue skin and midnight hair shone through her light. She cupped SonLara's chin as her voice softened. "Come now new peace, girl, and your part has come."

"What would you have me do?" asked SonLara.

The world disappeared. As she adjusted to the darkness, she found a dank prison cell bare-lit by a flickering torch through a small door's gaping portal and air fuming of foulest human waste.

Huddled in the corner, yet untouching, two figures lay littered with hay reeking of urine, scat and a hint of blood. SonLara scanned in vain for other cellmates.

"Where are we, subrim?" SonLara asked, able only to sense the subrim nearby.

Keys rang in the heavy lock of the door on her right, which opened and flooded the room with pale light and the hint of fresh air. In stepped a man in a ragged constable's uniform that had seen too little sunlight and rubbed too much sweaty flesh in the course of duties. The door creaked to a stop next to SonLara as the man lurched with a bucket into the cell. "Dinner."

The woman pressed back against the icy stone wall and avoided looking at the man as he took his time to leer.

"Sho pre'y," he said with a grin and wiped his mouth with his forearm. Pale light pouring through the open door revealed narrow, slanted eyes reddened with drink. "Y'know, I could provide better'n'this slop."

The woman hugged her filthy gown beneath the man's lechery.

Hesitant, the man glanced again at the open cell door, as if unused to worry of discovery.

"Touch me and my father will hear of it," she gulped.

The man hesitated. "O'course, miss. Jus'an offer." He dropped two raggedy tin plates on the hay and sloshed stew into each before turning and tromping out with a nervous scowl. The door slammed with a heavy jingle before his boots scuffled away.

The guard appeared uneasy in his own domain. SonLara decided his usual lechery had been prohibited against this woman by a superior—an order the man would resent but obey.

SonLara crossed the room to inspect the two. "Hello?"

Neither of them responded, confirming she was not here in-the-real. The prostrate man struggled to breathe while the woman pained herself not to notice. Burns covered the right side of his body, including a number of broken heat blisters. "He will die soon. In days, if not sooner."

When Suthene said nothing, SonLara squatted and attempted to delve the man. She sensed nothing, and thought it might be because of the vision, but when she delved the woman, the magic within her confirmed SonLara's suspicions. "Great Self…he is vacant. Nothing can save him."

"Eva," the man moaned in a semi-conscious state.

Locked upon the bare light bleeding through the slit in their cell door, Eva's eyes squeezed shut.

"Eva," he breathed.

Eva grimaced between sobbing and screaming with rage before she grabbed one of the plates and attempted to pluck one of the foul vegetables in the reeking stew. Tears welled as the slippery pieces avoided her fingers due to what she guessed was the guard's snot. When she managed to pinch a piece of food, she found the man unconscious with drool sliding down his burned face. She dropped the plate into her lap and cried.

SonLara pressed her hand to her own belly in surprise. She had never before witnessed such abject pain in any human. What tragedy could draw the soul of this poor woman to such depths? The man? Had he been ill so long? Did she cry for him or herself?

Eva took long, deep breaths. "Great Self," she moaned a whisper. "Am I not punished enough?" She held her fist to her mouth and rocked.

SonLara blinked away the first tears she had suffered in decades.

Eva locked once more upon the candlelight flickering through the door's portal as tears dripped upon her filthy silken gown.

After SonLara collected herself, she stood again in her new garden at Belfast under a high moon and twinkling blaze of stars.

"What have I seen, subrim?" she asked.

"The future," said Suthene, "and your responsibility."

"What do you mean?"

"You will collect these two young humans from this very city," Suthene motioned. In the distance, a great three-story stone structure materialized in the northeast region on the empty grassy hills. A stone street flowed along its western side while its southbound end split at a crossroads with two tall lampposts; one bent at a slight angle. Though miles distant, she made out all important details.

"Right now?" she asked. "To what end?"

"Collect yourself, priestess. They will need your wisdom and your wealth. You are to direct them to gather their kind for a coming journey that will secure their liberty from the oppression of fearful peoples. The sin of their fathers will soon cease to haunt their sons."

"Is that all?"

"For the boy to complete his final task, you will gather those brought together and deliver them with the wizard through great and terrible darkness into the bosom of Algueda, and there prepare them for a promised land across an open sea, beyond the edge of the world, to a new land surrounded by stars. They are chosen from among the Great Self's vast living creations to bear the salvation of all living."

"And if they ask, how should I tell them they will accomplish such a feat?"

As Suthene bent over her ear, wordless whispers rushed into her mind like a wild river of thought and meaning, full of instruction, purpose and even the path to healing for the vacant. When SonLara again braved a look at the subrim, lit in relief by the round moon in the distant sky, Suthene exploded into leaves and flora as a blossoming tree beneath sunlit radiance.

When the shaking tree shivered and fell still, the crowd roared with applause.

SonLara jumped, startled to be back where she began. She sank to her hip and took long, slow breaths. The faint foul whiff of the prison cell hung on the air and drew her focus across a real city toward a distant spot where those two now lay, hidden by endless rows of city buildings between them.

Tears streaming down her filthy face left striations. The crowd quieted. After a few moments, she rose to her feet and drew on her pristine calm like a comfortable cloak to the awe of nearby students.

Approaching the stone path, she found the administrators moving to speak with her. Without a word, she followed the walk away. They muttered at her umbrage. She climbed to Ashmore Hall while her mind struggled to understand all she had done and seen.

After yesterday's shock of a full-day's negotiation with the pixies, heavy dreams and sweat-stirring nightmares filled her sleep. The vision of planting a tree had woken her from slumber, drove her from bed to gather supplies, and secure the plot. A desire burned within her as little else ever had, and now she knew it was subrim-inspired. The tree yet lingered in her mind like a sun-burned afterimage; its meaning refused to remain where she had planted it and followed her to her Ashmore apartment and a hot shower.

27
Meeting Eternity

Though the dark chamber had disappeared and the brilliant sun now warmed the space, the sonorous Tree remained upon the same gentle hill, yet a natural garden of resplendent greenery flowed outward across a virginal valley.

The landscape was, without doubt, Eden, though Haephan couldn't say why. The nine peaks of the crown had been replaced by gentle valley walls. Though beautiful when he first set off from his companions, it paled to the native splendor laid out before him.

A man with midnight hair and earthy skin knelt before him in a robe of blues and grays. He smiled. "Hello there."

The boy twisted about in search for the dragons, but like the cavern, they were gone.

"What the—" started Haephan. "What happened?" His smooth, calm voice surprised him. His ankle, splintered hands and broken nose no longer hurt.

The man pulled his feet to sit on his bottom with an arm draped over his raised knee. "Hello, Haephan. How do you feel?"

"Where am I?" asked Haephan. "Who are you!?"

"Peace," the man's deep voice rumbled through Haephan and calmed him. "I am Eternity. You are Haephan."

"Sir," Haephan said. "Where am I?"

"The place of all beginnings, little pan," Eternity smiled.

Haephan inhaled the sweetened wind. "I'm…" he rubbed and tested his ankle. "It feels fine. What happened?"

"Haephan," the man drew Haephan's attention once more. "You have a great purpose."

"What?" Haephan asked.

"You have a purpose, my child."

"A purpose? You mean…but…" Haephan gulped. "I'm a nobody."

The man smiled and cupped Haephan's face. "No. You are everything!"

Haephan's round eyes stared back.

"You are *everything*! You were created with great purpose and with great care."

Haephan stilled. "But, how?"

"Did you think the Great Self did not see you lying in your nest above the boathouse, wishing for a family?"

Tears streamed down Haephan's cheeks as the man cupped the back of his head.

"Haephan, my boy. You are so very, *very* loved."

Unbidden and unstoppable, sobs erupted from Haephan's chest. The man scooped him and clutched him to his breast. His long arms wrapped up Haephan and rocked him as he cried.

Why had the man to say such a terrible, awful, hurtful and deceitful thing that his fears would be so openly exposed? Haephan hated the man for his words and more for his compassion. He needed no such weakness. It would get him killed.

Haephan cried all the more until the world disappeared. When Haephan's eyes opened, sunset gazed back as a golden mottle painted across the breadth of the horizon.

Turning his head, he realized he reclined against the man's chest.

"Why am I?" rolled off Haephan's tongue before he could inhibit it.

The man squeezed the boy's ribs. "The Great Self loves you, boy, and has great purpose in you. You are something new. Something important, and you will set in place a legacy that will serve the world for ages to come."

The sun dipped into the distant horizon.

"Why me?"

"You were made for this very moment, from your mother's womb, your very sinews were prepared for this purpose. You are to stand for everyone on this continent, a protector of powers beyond your reckoning. You are to be of all and for all. You will represent pan peoples. Are you ready to discover it?"

"Pan? Like Pangea?"

"Pan is a word that means 'all,' or everything. Pangea is a singular world comprised of all places in one whole that contains all known peoples. In your case, you do not represent all worlds, like Pangea, but all individuals before the Great Self, regardless of nation, creed or color."

"What am I to do?" asked Haephan.

"Remain quiet before the whispering wind and follow its words."

"The whispering wind?"

"A living force that speaks to all living things in different ways. To you, it will speak more clearly than to some, and in some ways so strongly that you cannot deny its demands, but this will all be for tasks vital to the peace and safety of the coming world."

"I wish…" Haephan soaked in the comfort of the coming cool of evening. "I wish to remain here." The sun disappeared behind the horizon as the man's chest rose and fell under Haephan's back. The boy desired—more than ever in his entire life—that he might have a father. "What am I to do?"

"Follow the wind," said the man.

"Now?"

"Can you hear it?"

Haephan noted a faint whisper echoing across the breeze. "Kinda."

"What does it say?"

"I'm not sure," said Haephan. "I can't understand it. It's strange."

"Rise, boy."

Haephan climbed to his feet as the man knelt before him so they could see eye-to-eye.

"I will translate for you this time only, for hereafter you will understand all peoples of all tongues. The wind says you must gather the seed and travel to the ocean. When next you hear it, you will not understand it by the clarity of words, but the truth of understanding and the weight of need. It will speak to you through instinct and you must follow it to find peace."

"I don't think I can," said Haephan. "How do I get to the ocean? I've never been, and I hear it's a very long ways away."

"I know," the man smiled. "But with the Great Self, there is always a way." He raised his hand and placed it against the boy's sternum. "And never forget, child, He is always with you."

A luminous liquid gold flowed from the man's shoulder down his arm and over Haephan's chest. When the man stood and lifted the boy into the air, Haephan arched backward.

In a swirl of light, the objects Haephan had taken from his new room flew from where they were tucked in his clothing and swirled around him as power flowed from one into the other. The blue of evening deepened into black. When the last of the gold flowed into Haephan, he ascended from the man until he floated above the Tree. His head lolled back as light speared from his eyes, nostrils and opening mouth. The world fell still and silent.

Haephan crowed.

The sound thundered across the expanse.

Light pouring from his orifices spread and coursed over his body while the crow intensified until the ground quaked. As the power overwhelmed him, Haephan listened to the man's still, calm voice complete the universe.

"It is done."

28
The New Pan

When Haephan woke, he recoiled from the cracks of false sunlight spearing from the midnight ceiling. He blinked clear his vision enough to scan the chamber while taking slow breaths.

For the first time in his entire life, peace pervaded him. He slid his hand over his ankle and found it set, though sensitive. The heavy splinters in his hands had disappeared and his nose tingled but felt no longer broken.

Testing his ankle, Haephan pushed to his feet. Chamber light glowed brighter now than in his initial foray. Wherever he focused, shadows retreated. He spotted something lying nearby in the grass, leaned over and plucked it to find one of the objects he'd taken from Ian's old room. Scanning, he searched the grass for them and, to his surprise, found them even when they were covered in lush green, as if he could sense their locations. Once he tucked them away into his clothes, he scanned the lawn.

Six dragons slumbered across the verdant chamber. Had he missed them or were they new? Why were they all here, lazing about?

Haephan struggled to remember everything leading up to that moment. Flashes of a dragon attack and a man with midnight skin faded as fast as they appeared. A faint blue aura wreathed the small Tree of Life while brilliant columns of golden light encircled it. He struggled to recall much else between falling here and waking up.

He plucked a small wooden pod from the grass and held it to the light. The size of a large apple, it weighed little in his hand—his first seed.

"Awww yisss," Haephan smiled, groped his belt line and froze—the sack Elverbane had given him was gone. How was he supposed to carry more than one? How was he even supposed to carry this one?

He unbuttoned his shirt, pushed it inside, and buttoned it once more.

"I'm pregnant," he frowned at its bulbous appearance before searching in vain for more.

He hoped Elverbane could use it. He circumvented the sleeping beasts, crept across the rolling verdant hills, climbed the gentle incline beneath a descending ceiling and into a thick rim of flora. He struggled through the bramble along the rim in search of an escape when he discovered faint light bleeding from beyond. Parting the heavy fronds and thick grass, he climbed into a steep, narrow path that circled along the wall into a bramble of roots larger than most Rainhold shanties. He wove among them until he found a peek at the outer chamber. The one beneath the Tree seemed larger than the one above.

Bars of sunlight piercing the canopy bounced from the sandy floor to underlight the rest of the cave. Hundreds of dragons slumbered across the chamber and up its curved walls. The bonfires which raged last night now smoldered in thin, rising streams.

Climbing the Tree would do him no good, especially without the protection of darkness. He ducked under branches on his way to the outer edge of the roots and scanned the distant walls. A great vertical rift in the distant concave chamber wall caught his eye, sunk back from the narrow cave entrance high above.

At first worried about being caught, it occurred to him that he was not any common pickpocket, but the best in New Gordon and probably even the entire South Edenia region. He disappeared faster and smoother than any other picker he'd ever heard of. Even Lurli thought so the other day with his backhanded compliment. Haephan had picked a crimsie in-progress at Goram's own house!

Haephan could do this.

Scanning the room, he noted how the creatures differed in sizes, colors, shapes, wing styles, leg lengths, snouts and more. He gathered his courage and crossed the sandy floor among the endless field of creatures toward the vertical rift. Every step could lead to disaster by waking a monster. It was like some kind of story.

Haephan was a thief sneaking among dragons with a seed from the Tree of Life. He ought to be in a story!

Suppressing his sudden glee, he pressed onward until faced with a black dragon sixty feet long and thicker than Haephan was tall. The beast lay across a mass of smaller dragons as if he collapsed upon them. Haephan could not continue without crawling over them.

The boy scanned the chamber for an alternate escape when a heavy rumble echoed from the midnight beast. The boy dove between two smaller creatures and waited for the worst.

Percius, rumbled a voice darker than a moonless night.

Haephan peeked over the dragon on each side. "H-hello?"

Percius.

As low as he was, Haephan peeked through the briny plates of the beast on each side in search of someone who might be nearby. The massive black dragon shifted and rolled. The voice did not return.

Gulping, Haephan started his circuit of the massive creature when his foot caught on a wing and he tripped to the ground.

The midnight monster waddled onto his belly. *Percius?*

Haephan hid behind the small dragon.

Percius? Is that you?

The dragon spoke in his mind!

Percius! the dragon's deep voice echoed in his head.

Haephan discovered open buttons on his shirt, scanned the ground in a panic and found the pod wedged under a nearby tail. He jerked it free, stuffed it into his shirt and froze in terror.

The great black dragon loomed over him. *What are you?*

Haephan gasped.

The dragon's eyes narrowed upon the seed in Haephan's shirt. *How did you get that!?* The dragon barked a scorching burst of air.

Haephan raised his hands to shield himself. "I found it!"

What?

"I found it over there!" Haephan pointed.

The dragon twisted his huge head. *Where!?* When he turned back, Haephan was gone. The monster stalked over the smaller, unconscious dragons in search of the boy. *Now now now, little elf. How did you get in here?*

When Haephan realized the dragon already found him, he climbed to his feet. "I fell! I was…just trying to get home. Through Eden."

The dragon looked up. *Such a fall would have killed you, little elf.*

The boy frowned, curious at being called an elf. "I fell into the tree. And I climbed down."

You lie, the dragon's beak-line snout snaked in and pinned Haephan against the side of a smaller slumbering beast. *Give me the seed.*

Haephan struck the snout of the dragon with the seed. "No!"

Then I will take a snack and the seed! the dragon laughed. *Before I eat you, I'll have your name for your boldness.*

Quaking while trying to breathe, Haephan gritted his teeth and cried, "I am Haephan!"

Fire starter?

"No, Haephan!"

You repeat yourself, snack. The great dragon reared and spread his terrible bat-like wings. *I am Magnus Draco Cas'Doren, the Dragon King of Eden.* He grinned. *Say goodbye.*

Closing his eyes, Haephan wished with all his might to reach the rift in the chamber wall. His need stretched out. The air changed. Expecting the final attack to crush him sure, he was surprised when the dragon under him disappeared and he fell across the hard-packed ground. A loud distant thump echoed.

Haephan now stood halfway from the dragon to the rift in the wall.

Where'd you go, fire starter!? Where did you go!? Cas'Doren tore and yanked at the dragons beneath him in search for the boy. *By the winds, where did you go?*

Staggering into a run, Haephan's feet scraped across the hard, rocky terrain.

How'd you get all the way over there? Cas'Doren spun and raced across the field of sleeping dragons.

Haephan vaulted the thinning number of beasts between him and the rift. With a heavy crash behind him, Cas'Doren stumbled and snapped at the boy.

Struck across his back, Haephan flew through the air but by some miracle landed afoot and continued running. Again, the distance between him and rift halved. The cave entrance climbed into the darkness and spread as wide as a Rainhold alleyway. Echoes of creek water trickled from the darkness.

How did you do that!? the dragon roared.

Gripping the seed, Haephan followed the creek ever closer to his escape. Again, Cas'Doren's thundering attack missed by inches and sent Haephan flying into the rift over heavy rocks and splashing along the creek. The seed popped the buttons in his shirt and landed in the water rushing back toward the chamber. He chased it in a panic when Cas'Doren's huffing flame lit the cave. Haephan dove into the creek and snatched it, scrambled to his feet and raced into the darkness. Brilliant firelight and a heavy rumble chased him upward, which died under the dragon's throaty coughs.

29

Losing Haephan

Elverbane reclined against a large tree dancing in the morning breeze while Depp scanned the valley for a sign of Haephan.

Last night, the men woke at the eruption of a tower of light from the small mound atop the northern plateau.

While Depp and Sartlam witnessed the near-blinding light and shining rings of energy firing outward across the sky, Elverbane noted the intricate lacework of auroral magic and its implied importance.

With no real way to further contribute, Sartlam distracted himself by studying maps. "Do you think New Gordon saw it?"

"Anyone this side of the Zulta'mans saw it," said Depp. "It was like somethin' out of a— *there*!"

The men leapt to their feet as a black leviathan burst upward from the mound and ascended with heavy thrusts of its midnight wings.

Depp looked to Elverbane and whispered, "Can't you shield us?"

"Like lighting a match in the black," said Elverbane, "he would be upon us."

Sartlam tucked behind Elverbane and peeked at the valley. The dragon dropped his head and scanned the plateau and forests below across the valley's bosom.

"Shit," said Depp. "He's lookin' for the boy."

"The boy?" Sartlam asked.

"The boy must have succeeded," Depp muttered. "So far."

The flying dragon snaked alongside the cliffs and waterfalls and sometimes dove into the forest. Moments later, after barks of protest that echoed even to their ears, it climbed into the air and resumed its search. Each time, the men exhaled their anxiety.

"What happens if the boy is lost, huh? What then?" asked Depp.

"I am no prophet," said Elverbane. "I have no idea how this will turn out. I know only that this is what must be done."

"Accordin' to who?" stammered Depp.

Elverbane's glare stemmed more questions while Depp paced with a constant eye for Haephan.

The sun climbed near to noon and bathed the valley in heat. Depp scanned for the boy when a small movement caught his eye. "There!"

On the downslope west of them, a tiny speck sprinted from a copse of trees across a clearing and into another thicket. The dragon hadn't yet seen him.

"The boy doesn't see him," said Depp.

"He knows its after him," Elverbane said.

"You said he couldn't see the boy, right?"

"The boy's a vacant. But he might be able to see the seed."

"What?" Depp cried. "You didn't say that!" In the distance, the boy skirted another clearing.

The dragon's scream caught both men in the throat as it banked hard, dove and plowed into the green in front of where the boy was.

"Shit," Depp stepped from the shadows to the edge of their perch, followed by Elverbane. The trees downslope erupted in a small mushroom cloud of fire and smoke. "We gotta do something. He's got the boy trapped!"

"Look at that," said Elverbane when the boy emerged from the other side unhurt.

"How'd he get past that?" asked Depp.

"He used the confusion to his advantage," said Sartlam. "Smart boy!"

The dragon leapt into the air in search of the child.

Where are you ELF!? the dragon's thoughts echoed to Elverbane, who wondered why the dragon chased an elf. Was it not the boy? *You cannot evade me forever. I will have you* and *the seed!*

"He thinks he's an elf," Elverbane muttered in surprise.

Depp noted Elverbane twisting a ring on his finger. "You can understand the dragon?"

Haephan appeared on the other side of the copse sprinting faster than Elverbane would have expected. The dragon caught sight and dove in once more. By the time he could pour fire upon him, the boy was out of view.

"He got him," Depp gritted through his teeth.

Elverbane's brow drooped when the boy, again, emerged on the other side unscathed.

"How—? I'm goin'!" Depp raced down the steep hill into the trees. "C'mon you sack'a shit! We're gonna help him!"

Elverbane launched in pursuit. He shed his outer robe and sprinted as best he could despite his age and weight. They plowed into the thick Edenic forest that tore at clothes and skin.

Lean and tall, Depp outdistanced him. The two men emerged from a copse of trees at the same time Haephan entered the clearing's far side followed fast by a looming black dragon.

"Haephan!" Elverbane cried and waved his thick hand. "LOOK OUT!"

The dragon crashed into the ground behind Haephan and sent him staggering across the grass. Haephan's seed and collection of small objects tumbled from his clothing as the dragon raised his head to the sky and screamed.

Immense magic covered the child. Was Elverbane wrong? Haephan was vacant yesterday morning, yet now glowed with the same translayered magic that had fired into the sky last night. He muttered, "Great Self."

"Fuck, old man!" cried Depp as he drew his sword. "C'mon!"

Elverbane raced again as Haephan scrambled to gather the objects and the seed pod.

GIVE ME THE SEED! cried the dragon while hedging the boy with his long wings.

Huffing for air, Elverbane gathered violent magic into his hands.

Haephan clutched a seed and one of Ian's objects to his gut, faced the beast preparing to strike and screamed.

The dragon's mouth filled with brilliant fire before it struck.

Twenty feet shy of the beast, Elverbane cast a blast of energy and repelled it several feet. The creature stumbled backward in shock. The wizard bellowed, knocked Depp aside and struck with another bout of violent energy that sent the dragon crashing through the trees as it rolled.

Both men stumbled to the small crater where they had last seen Haephan. Ripped strips of his clothes littered the soil along with a scattered collection of objects. Elverbane stumbled to his knees and roared.

Cursing, Depp bent over his sword and panted.

The stunned dragon twitched and flailed in the collapsing tangle of trees.

Depp sprinted for safety.

Elverbane quivered in horror at losing the boy when his eyes latched on familiar objects strewn across the terrain—Ian's prized possessions left behind after his death. As the dragon fought for consciousness, he scrambled over the ground to gather the objects and pursue Depp. "What *now*, ya Great Bastard!?"

30

The First AlterWorld

Haephan hovered in an endless icy darkness of swirling water that threatened to suffocate him. Fear screamed that he had been eaten by the beast, but even Cas'Doren wasn't so large that Haephan wouldn't feel the walls of his stomach or the curve of his ribs.

A distant flash of pale light drew his attention upward. A second flash confirmed a distant watery surface. He climbed as the air in his lungs began to sour. He panicked—wishing to be near that distant light—and a blink later was within arm's reach in time to break out and suck misty air into his lungs. A wave crashed over him before he finished his desperate inhale and drove him under. He wished to be out of the ocean. In a moment, he fell from mid-air into the tumultuous wash.

Lightning interrupted the darkness in fitful strikes across heavy storm clouds unleashing torrents of rain.

Haephan fought to stay above the heavy waves. His grip on the seed in his left hand made swimming difficult and he struggled to get more than a single breath at a time. When the chaotic waves kept him from breathing, Haephan sank.

Something hard plowed into him from underneath and bullied him upward into the air. He clutched at the knobby point of a large, leathery fish. While braced by the animal, he coughed water from his lungs.

We've been waiting for you! The creature chittered words of meaning that flowed into his mind. *Give me the seed! It's time!*

"What?" asked Haephan.

I got it! chittered the animal as it twisted, snatched the seed from his hand, and dove downwards.

"Hey!" Haephan yelled before a wave vaulted him upward and away. He bobbed twenty feet with each rolling swell.

Rapid flashes of lightning captured a heart-stopping scene: on his left rolled endless miles of chaotic sea. Upon his right by less than a mile stretched a line of endless black where the rolling ocean smoothed as if sliding over the edge of a horizon too close to be safe.

Haephan cursed and splashed as best he could toward the open ocean, desperate to flee from what had to be the edge of the world. Each swell carried him ever further nearer the blackness. Had he traveled to the afterlife? Was this death? Perhaps the dragon had killed him and he now crossed over. How had he gotten here from Eden?

New flashes of lightning erupted from the murky darkness below. Curious, he drove his head under the next wave and opened his eyes against its burning saltiness as a boiling mass of light climbed from the depths.

Haephan returned to the surface where lightning danced across the waves in a brilliant web of bursts and arcs. The tumultuous ocean devolved into a boiling froth. Haephan sank too fast to take a full breath. His lungs burned when tiny arms scraped his legs and body. Something snatched his knee and jerked him to a sickening halt.

Inverted in the grip of some dark bug-like monster, Haephan choked on the frothing saltwater instead of clean air. He panicked and wished again to be above the sea. The froth disappeared and he fell with the rain from hundreds of feet in the air. He hacked his lungs while something from beneath the waves exploded.

Little could have prepared Haephan for the pandemonium of a stormy ocean, not to mention the thousand-legged monster climbing from the chaos below.

He screamed as he fell through its first sets of legs, sure there was a mouth somewhere between them. Instead, fresh lightning revealed massive branches sticking out from a heavy trunk.

It was a tree!

Halfway down its height, Haephan wished to be at the top of the tree. Suddenly he fell from above it once more. He could somehow move without moving, and yet retained his speed when he did.

Pondering how to accomplish his goal without dying, he imagined flying upward from a lower point to one higher. A moment later, he flew sideways, crashed into a leafy canopy, tumbled through branches, and crashed to a halt.

Beneath him, the massive arbor continued climbing. He groped his way to a thick branch and hugged it while he panted. Though his hips ached and his head pounded, he was glad to be somewhat stable.

Lightning ebbed as new hills and mountains of trees continued climbing from the ocean. The island shook as it vaulted from the depths and spilled ocean back into the waves.

In a violent quake, the tree's ascent came to an abrupt halt and knocked him from his perch. Falling toward newly formed ground, a blink sent his body skipping across the choppy waves near shore before he rolled into a large splash. He made for shore, set down his feet on tightly packed tendrils of wood and realized the entire island was a tree.

Though the island stopped shaking, he quivered as icy wind chilled the water soaking his clothes while he scaled the wooden shore. Thinking he would seek the first available shelter, an urge drew him toward the island's interior.

The storm above teased a hidden midday sun. Pale light warmed a landscape full of trees climbing hundreds of feet around him. An hour of stubbed toes and scraped heels brought him to the island's heart under a soft, glittering rain. Haephan crested the edge of a small sink where stretched a solid bowl cut by long grooves swirling inward to a tiny hole at its center.

His hand found the only piece of Ian's collection saved from the dragon strike—the saber's tooth. Tucked in his belt, he squeezed it, grateful to have something that belonged to him, and approached the center.

"Hello!?" he stepped into the bowl and followed its shallow curve to the deep chasm at its center. As he stared into its depths, a light appeared within its darkness and an energy welled within him.

Around his feet swirled a vortex of blue and green smoke that lifted him. Above him, a bolt of soft, auroral lightning snaked downward. Power ignited his every nerve and spears of radiance erupted from his eyes, nose and ears. His frame arched as his head fell back. Glowing lines of magic wove around him in complex, shimmering lacework.

Haephan's ascending body rotated into the column of light with the carved tooth raised to the sky and opposite toe stretched to the island. Lightning, smoke and tooth connected in a burst of energy. At the edge of the world, a new ocean materialized and merged with his own, revealing a virgin sky and horizon.

The dark, stormy afternoon crashed into a gentle, faint morning blue that stretched outwards for miles. As the two worlds joined, the sun crested the new horizon and bathed the storm with fresh heat. Moments later, that warmth billowed into the sky and dispersed the cloud cover in a spreading wave.

Haephan was the key and connector of this power, and as it crescendoed, golden energy exploded from his body in a fading sphere that signaled the final connecting lock. Already brimming with radiance, his mouth fell open and its light poured into the sky.

Haephan crowed.

After the roar echoed across the expanses, the link died. Lightning and smoke flashed away and released him to fall from a dizzying height.

Returning to consciousness, Haephan panicked at the sight of the unforgiving ground rushing toward him. He grabbed at that faint memory of magical movement—of shifting distances by thought—and disappeared mere feet from the ground, leaving behind the sound of wind rushing through the congregation of trees and the breathing of a new world.

31
True Home

Haephan slammed into uneven, razor-sharp rock. He screamed and rolled from the fiery ground to face a horrific forest of jagged rock spires climbing into the sky. Sulfur poisoned the scorching air while fits of smoke and steam coughed from the rocky formations and gaping rifts. Glass-sharp stone sliced open his feet and drew blood.

Above it all rose a mountain whose crown spewed skyward a column of midnight smoke dancing with purple and ruby lightning—what Haephan once heard described as a "volcano." Glowing crimson rivers tinged in black wormed from its apex. Thunder rumbled from the ground while the midnight plume stabbed the sky and blanketed out sunlight out to the wan amber horizon.

Rising higher than the volcano, a nearby mountain climbed high beneath a pristine snow cap. From the high saddle between them, endless miles of desert waste stretched northward to a river. Beyond, a low mountain range climbed from right to left like the spine of a sleeping dragon before firing skyward into a high, conical peak.

"Where the hell…?" he hissed and danced to keep his feet from the razor rock. He searched in vain for a better position while blood gushed from his feet, arm and side of his head.

Waves of shattered black volcanic glass extended as far as he could see. He yanked off his shirt, ripped it in two, marveled at his newfound strength, and wrapped each piece around his feet several times. The fabric reddened with blood. The dry, molten air burned his lungs as he started across the hellish field. His lungs shuddered under each foul breath while bouts of steam singed his skin.

Where was he? How had he gotten here? How would he get home? Despite the questions, he had a hesitant belief that he somehow belonged here; like it was his true home. But how could such be?

Haephan moved further from the volcano when the ground shuddered and sent him falling to his hands and feet. Obsidian blades cut deep through his wrists to the bone. Violent red erupted from his hands as he screamed. As he climbed to his feet, the volcano coughed a thunderous wave of smoke down its northern side, which crashed over and sent him rolling across the killer terrain.

Artillerant rocks spewed from the volcano's mouth exploded across the ground. A second wave of boiling air took the hair from his face and half of his head.

Haephan screamed.

Shift, said a voice deep in his mind that interrupted his agony.

In a panic, he staggered over the uneven terrain until a narrow river of boiling rock cut off his escape. He gasped for air when another quake took his footing. Obsidian sliced his back. He screamed again as terror overtook his reason and senses.

SHIFT!

Panting, Haephan turned about in desperation.

"Shift, Haephan," whispered the wind. "Focus…move…be."

"What?" he asked as he struggled to his hands and knees. "Who's there!?"

"Shift to safety…" whispered the wind.

"Who's th—" Haephan attempted to cry before erupting with hacks and gasps.

I am Magnus Draco Cas'Doren, the Dragon King of Eden! the dragon's voice echoed on the wind. Haephan cringed in fear as blood drooled over his face.

Where'd you go, fire starter!? Where did you go!? By the winds, where did you go? Cas'Doren's cry echoed again.

Haephan remembered the dragon trying to kill him and finding himself a great distance away by wishing it.

How'd you get all the way over there? Cas'Doren's voice echoed yet again. *You cannot evade me forever. I will have you and the seed!* The dragon's cry carried on the wind.

Haephan had evaded the dragon; not by running, but by…shifting.

The mountain above him exploded with a violence that cracked the world. A column of brilliant red spewed from its crown as high as the mountain itself and began a slow fall that superheated the air with steam.

He remembered how, when the island of trees climbed from the ocean, he chose how to fall and how to move without moving. He had chosen; had set his will to be elsewhere.

"I gotta…" Haephan trailed off and sucked thin air when the first fiery rivers of rock crashed into the ground and sent fresh molten bits flying. Haephan scrambled away over the next ridge even as it cut through the meager rags wrapping his feet.

One of the falling rocks plowed into the ground and cut off his retreat. Haephan screamed.

"Pain is a teacher," the wind whispered despite the chaos. "Fear no difficulty. Learn."

Haephan gripped his bleeding fingers, searched for escape and willed himself to be there. Nothing happened, even as a falling rock burst close enough to scorch his skin anew. The boy writhed and shrieked as tiny flecks clung and burned.

"SHIFT!" the wind screamed as Haephan sensed a massive boiling rock falling upon his position.

Haephan bellowed, squeezed his eyes and willed himself across the distance.

He flinched at an explosion, but when he turned to its source, found it a distance away.

Looking about, Haephan barked a bitter laugh at his success. He had done it. A fresh explosion nearby cut off his momentary joy as glowing plasma stabbed his skin. He flinched and screamed again.

Pain interrupted thinking. Haephan stumbled to a knee on the unforgiving terrain. He could no longer scream, both from the burned rasp in his throat as well as the severity of the pain. He had to shift again. He had to get out of here.

Oppressive heat dried his tears and gummed his vision. He searched the jagged horizon and picked a spot far from the fiery mountain. Gritting his jaw and his fists, he winced at fresh pain. His head pounded and new agony boiled his blood as the heat overcame him. Blood loss took its toll and his vision doubled.

No, he couldn't shift somewhere on the island. This would take everything he had—he needed to go further, to go somewhere safe where he could get help.

The mountain above exploded again, sending fresh rivers of red falling through the sky. He sensed its approach, knew it would kill him if he could not shift the way he needed. Mustering all he had left, he drew on the only place he knew best—even with its inherent dangers—and shifted.

The change of temperature struck Haephan. He was surprised to find a light Rainhold drizzle falling over him. In the shock of it all, he took a weak step and tilted over as the muddy ground rushed upon him.

32

Finding Haephan

...arrive in Algueda. From there, we are to prepare these vacants for a journey across a vast ocean to a new land void of any sentient life. Last I read about Algueda, it had been barren for millennia. Considering the words and visions from Suthene, I wonder if she intends for us not to travel by ship across the vast oceans to the island-that-cannot-be-found. Might she mean the ebsa—

A knock at the door stilled SonLara's hand. She sheathed the pen into the binding of her private journal and latched it shut before rising from Elverbane's long table. She crossed the room and opened the door. A small, muddy child stood in the column of light pouring from the hallway skylight. He seemed familiar.

"Can I help you, young man?" she asked and noted a long, fresh red scar running from his temple to his jawline.

"You're...the lady who took Haeph'," he said while squirming.

"I'm SonLara," she said with a slight tilt of her head. "And you are...the young man I saw when we procured Haephan."

The boy flinched. "I'm Tilly, mum." He saluted with his knuckles. "He's in trouble."

"Is he?" she asked. "Are you sure? By all accounts, Haephan should be some distance from New Gordon."

"I'm terrible sure, mum," said Tilly. "Goram's got 'im at 'is house. Gonna take a nut for what he did to the councilor's boy, Dolphus."

Noting a desperate sincerity in the boy, SonLara's brow sank. "You're absolutely sure?"

"Yes mum!" Tilly insisted. "Me an' Haeph grew up down in the 'old. I knows 'im anywhere. 'Sides. All the words' 'bout 'im at the 'ouse. I ain't the only one 'round here who knows it, eivah!"

"Come with me," SonLara plucked her hood from the wall knob, swung it around her neck and shut the door in one smooth motion.

Awestruck, Tilly shook himself and followed her.

"How did you find me?" she asked as they descended the stairwell.

"Gots a nose, dun' I?"

At her glance, he shrank.

"Don' mean no lip, mum. Jus' used to findin' what I need, mos' days."

"And gaining access to Belfast?" she asked.

He shrugged.

A smirk tugged the side of her blue lips. "Well done, young man."

He straightened at her praise as they emerged from Ashmore's main entrance under its porte-cochère. She motioned to an attendant, who rang a loud bell. Tilly shuffled to keep SonLara between him and the attendant scowling at his messy appearance.

Tilly's eyes widened as a grand carriage followed the paved path between great lawns of grass and halted beneath the overhang. A footman climbed from the rear of the carriage, lowered the steps, opened the door and bowed with a flourish.

"Inside," SonLara motioned.

The footman and Tilly hesitated.

"They can clean mud away," SonLara said. "Or is Haephan not in as much danger as you say?"

"'e is, mum!" Tilly insisted.

SonLara waited. Tilly climbed inside and sat on the floor before she followed. "On the seat, young man. You are no animal."

Tilly gulped but obeyed by placing as little of himself on the soft velvet as possible.

"To Rainhold," she ordered the footman before the doors shut and several clangs preceded the carriage gliding away over smooth pavestones. "How do you know Haephan?"

"'e'n I grew up togevah in the 'old, mum."

"Rainhold?"

"Yes, mum," he ducked his head.

"And his family?"

"Family, mum? Ain't no one gots family in the 'old. Just the swee'earts."

"Are they not your mothers?" she asked.

"O'course," said Tilly. "But no one knows 'is mum. Not privy to it, you see."

"So, they raise you, but you're not sure which is your mother?"

"Not so much," Tilly frowned, unused to discussing it.

"And you grow up with them?"

"For a bit," Tilly quieted. "I gots outed early. For being small, y'see."

"Why?" she asked.

"Small boys get booted," Tilly admitted. "Big'uns go on to become crimsie dicks— I mean. Crimson Guard, mum."

"Are girls treated the same?" asked SonLara.

"Theta got a new girl right'round when I got outed. Goram prefers the girls. Sells 'em up as maids, he does, ta rich folks. Boys gots to make theah way, you see. Out in the world, n'all'at."

"I see," SonLara said and noted his scar. "And you're making your way."

"Was." Tilly stilled. "Haeph' was a good mate. 'Fore…"

"Before we took him," she said.

Tilly nodded.

Even following this thin possibility of helping a boy who, by all accounts, should be far away, the Silver Librarian's commission echoed in SonLara's mind. Her purpose in coming to Belfast Bluff remained incomplete, but events in play stayed her hand. Her arrival seemed ordained by powers higher than her superiors could ever have imagined.

Even now, the subrim's words pressed upon her—she already had begun her search for the prison from her vision, but finding the right location proved difficult. Inquiries with guard captains produced nothing but apologies—no one admitted to knowing where two such prisoners were being kept. There was no distributed record and offers to help were half-hearted enough to give her reason to believe someone didn't want them found.

The fresh patter of heavy rain rushed the carriage roof as they rocked over uneven cobble. Only the buttoned ceiling of velvet silk dimmed the roar. Hiding his awe, Tilly scanned the interior of the carriage. She wagered he would steal any unsecured element were she not there.

"Who is Goram?" SonLara asked.

"Runs the 'old, mum," Tilly scanned the carriage. "Owns the'ouse where the sweets work. We gets to come in after hours and get some grub before we're out. I ain't been in in a long while. Haeph' got 'isself inside, which is why he's in trouble."

"I see. And Goram sells maids up?"

"Gets 'em jobs with the nice 'ouses n'stuff, he does," said Tilly. "Up in the Whittle and o'vah rich'burbs, he does. Nice of'im."

"But not for boys."

"No, mum," he said.

"Wish he would help you, too?"

Tilly shrugged.

"And you worked with Haephan?"

"He's the best pick in New Gordon!" Tilly declared. "No one gets Haeph…'cept wizards."

SonLara's eyes twinkled. "Yes, well, wizards are very crafty fellows."

Tilly nodded knowingly.

"Why would Goram have Haephan, Tilly? Is Haephan a prisoner or a guest?"

"Well…" Tilly drifted off. "Nuffin', really."

SonLara's shimmering silver irises inspected him until he popped onto his feet.

"Pleez, mum! I don't want ta get Haeph in trouble wif'you none!"

She waited.

Tilly rubbed his arms. "Well, ya see…Haeph got in a fight out at Bert'ran…" The boy rattled off the events leading up to Haephan picking pockets in the Whittle where Tilly assumed he caught the wizard's attention. "I tol'im not to go, you see. Is dang'rous up ovah at the Levy. Dems guards rip you up or frow ya in the'ole. They don'like no picks in'eah."

"Did Haephan frequent it?"

"It's cuz he got ripped up by the crimsie cocksuck— I mean…the guardians, mum," he ducked his head. "He figah'd his pi'iful condition n'all would get him some extra 'tention from'hose wif coin.…S'pose it might'ave."

"How did Goram come to possess Haephan?" asked SonLara.

"Dunno, mum," said Tilly. "Haeph' ain't been seen in the'old for weeks. Suddenly 'ere's a buzz about 'im gettin' dragged to the'ouse. Goram's place. Er'body's yammin' bout it till no one can shut it."

The two sat in silence as the carriage rumbled toward the canal and Rainhold. Reclined in the shadow of her cowl, her mind raced. The carriage stopped. The driver hopped down and opened the door. "Can't go any further, m'lady. Won't get out if we go in. Not in this carriage."

SonLara emerged from the carriage's dark interior and floated to the ground.

"Wait here," she said, handed the driver a small coin for the passage and turned to Tilly. "Lead the way, young man."

Tilly navigated the road with a view of the shabby town and the canal around it. Streets of mud narrowed while pools of standing water soon dominated the walking space.

Those huddling from the rain stared at the pale ghost gliding with barely a footprint across otherwise vacuous muck. Her cloak's imperviousness to rain and filth drew attention. Expanding pools of water dotting the muddy landscape diverted SonLara several times the long way around, being yet unable to walk on water.

She assumed Elverbane and Haephan would return by the Eden Road on the north side of the city and weren't due for another week. Rainhold stretched as the southwest side of the city along the Vitner Canal and its intersection with the Estamar Canal. None of its docks were suitable for passenger transport and instead served as cheaper fare for light, local commerce. Might they have offloaded down-canal and attempted to follow the shoreline back into the city? None of the three eastern bridges would have vectored them into Rainhold.

After leading her along the central broadway and up the incline to the final steppe, Tilly stopped within sight of a three-story maroon house with white trim.

"Sorry, mum," Tilly said. "Would be bes' if I weren't seen back at the'ouse."

SonLara took a long look at him. "What am I walking into, young man?"

Tilly gulped.

"Is this a trap?" her voice steeled.

"No mum!" said Tilly. "Dead serious, it ain't! All I heard is Haeph is in'eah and in'trouble. I can't get'im out. And seein' as he works for you now…"

Confident of his honesty since he appeared at her door, SonLara thumbed several silver coins from her sleeve and shook his hand so he could palm them from her without being seen. "Thank you for bringing me here. If I can procure him from Goram, I'm sure he would like you to come visit."

"'onest, mum?" Tilly piped up.

"Yes."

"Soon's I can!" Tilly beamed and melted into the shadows.

Men lounging on the wrap-around porch piqued at her appearance in the gloomy drizzle. Interest grew as she climbed the porch and stopped before the double doors. The two door guards shared glances before one opened the door on the right. She waited while those inside noticed that no one had entered—half of her bright white dress shone against the overcast afternoon gray outside.

Fidgeting, the other guard leaned around, unlocked the second door and opened it, too.

Gliding into the room, SonLara's holy specter interrupted the finely dressed rabble lounging in the muted lamplight. She scanned the high ceiling, large chandelier, crimson decor and polished bar top to her right. In the foyer on her left, lounging prostitutes stilled at her entrance, as if her presence exposed their shame. Barstool-perched pimps hesitated between shock and lust at the arrival of a fresh, exotic woman.

Beneath the main chandelier hanging low between the bar and the foyer, she drew back her hood to reveal her lapis blue hair. Her reflective silver eyes caught everyone as she scanned the room and latched upon the leading man sitting at the bar's far end wearing a flamboyant crimson shortcoat over a ruffled lace shirt under a peppered beard and shrewd gaze.

"My lady," said the man as he stepped from the stool without taking his attention from her and offered a semblance of a bow. "I am Goram Peddlewaithe. How may my house offer you pleasure?"

"I am SonLara Amferadon, Priestess of Andon. I seek the boy Haephan."

"Haephan? What might the priestess seek with a lowly former resident of Rainhold?"

"Lowly? He is a manservant at the Belfast School. I've been informed he is here. I would see him. Now."

"Informed," Goram muttered and scratched his beard. "And why would a ten-year-old boy be in an adult establishment, my lady? I do not employ children in any function within the house. That would be immoral. I employ only whores and handmaids, here."

"Are you saying he isn't here?"

Goram's eyes narrowed. "Pardon, m'lady, but the boy and I have business that does not concern the school. Or you."

"The child's current business concerns everyone," said SonLara with an unwavering tone. "And I would have him brought up here."

While she spoke, an overwhelming presence of immense magic caught her attention from beneath the floorboards. She struggled to hide her shock that the entire house wasn't yet on fire.

"What you would have does not cancel his debt with me," Goram said. "And his business with you does not satisfy mine."

"What is his debt? I will pay it."

Goram sucked on his tongue. "Money?" he asked and eyed the length of her. "You think I sully my good name with your money?" He avoided calling her a witch—a dirty name in Rainhold—but everyone heard it in his voice. "The boy will pay his own debt, or it will not be him who paid it."

"Then what would suffice his debt, Master Peddlewaithe? Did he steal from you? Cause damages?"

"The boy threatened my livelihood," growled Goram as he raised a finger that struggled to extend past the flamboyant lace sticking out from his sleeve. "I take none too kindly to anyone threatening me." His tone reflected his opinion of her. She sensed men around her checking their knives.

"I've not come to threaten you," said SonLara. "But I will not leave without the child."

"And you believe he is here?"

"He lies there," she motioned toward the energy fount hidden below the floor, taking a gamble she considered necessary, surrounded as she was by dangerous men able to take her at their will. "Surely whatever you have already done to him has brought him enough grief?"

Laugher erupted from Goram. "I saved the boy's life. Some local carried the boy to my porch and got a coin or two from me for doing so. Imagine that. The *Great Self* delivers the indebted to his debtor. Seems fitting, don't you think? Ironic, even, that I saved his life."

A brunette beauty with dark fade caramel skin appeared in the entrance to the back hallway and stilled at the sight of the priestess.

"Show me to him," said SonLara.

"*Please*," said Goram. "I'll not be ordered around my own house like some common manservant, *priestess.* I am not *yours* to command."

"Please," said SonLara with the same, resolute tone.

Goram raised his right hand to the beauty behind him. "Querie, lead the priestess downstairs so we can all look at the boy."

Though only a hunch when she made it, Goram's confirmation the boy was, indeed, downstairs nearly buckled SonLara's knees. Fear, however, screamed at the sheer mountain of energy boiling in the basement.

The brunette standing in the hallway entrance bit her lip and half curtsied. She led SonLara, Goram and a bodyguard down the long stairs into the dim basement, below

33

New Magic

The sweetheart reached the bottom of the stairs and turned back along the hallway. Goram and one of his bodyguards followed them to a thick wooden door beneath the main floor. Querie opened it to reveal three sweetheart beds. Haephan lay shivering upon the far bed, covered in blankets.

SonLara sat next to Haephan, laid her hand upon his forehead, and stifled a cry of alarm at the sheer amount of magic covering him.

"Great Self," she said. "Bring me hot soup, right now." Querie moved to obey, halted by Goram's glare until he motioned for her to continue, and rushed out.

"The boy will die within the day," said SonLara. "Will his death suffice your debt?"

Fuming at the child, Goram fished out a cigar and lit the end with a tiny flare of magic from his thumb. "I have two businesses in this world, priestess—whores and handmaids." He puffed it to life and exhaled pink smoke into the room. "In any other city on this selfdamn continent, comfort work depends on spells to keep women from taking child. We care for men whose wives and work won't, and our ladies stay beautiful and supple, the way we pay them to be."

SonLara watched Haephan.

"But do you know where all these children come from?" Goram motioned with his cigar as he leaned on the doorframe.

SonLara waited.

"The bloody wizards," said Goram. "Don't ask me how, but here their seed sometimes ignores the womb spells. This one. His little friend. The wizards come, spend themselves in my sweethearts and we are left with their unstoppable progeny. What do we do with them? We take them in so they don't die in the cold. My money cares for the young and funds education for the girls. The ones that end up like him?" He nodded at Haephan. "They're sterile. No man will marry a vacant girl who can't bear him children. Cannot bear sons? Can't be touched by magic? They're just…little holes in the world."

"You serve mankind?" SonLara asked.

"Who do you think keeps the little rabbits alive long enough for their own parents to pretend to hire them back?" Goram asked. "You think it's by accident that all these wizards just happen to get vacant assistants? It's their shame, and it's business for the likes of us. All the wizards see it so clinically—they come work out their biological needs and go back to their eminent work. Your fellow wizard…what's his name? Elverbane? Hero of Tuthomere? Even he has graced our fair house. Has a love for those pretty eyes, I see." His gaze locked with hers. "That costs lots of money and I see a fraction of it from those who leave me with their droppings."

She was a rock for all his attempts to rile her. "You wish to extract money from the child?"

"Actually, no," said Goram as streams of smoke billowed from his nose. "I demand an apology."

"From the boy?" she asked.

"From you," he spat.

"For what, Master Peddlewaithe, would you have me apologize for?"

"To me? No, priestess. It is not me who was so offended," said Goram. "He threatened my business sure, but I deal with recalcitrant customers, whores, thieves and competitors every day. No, that little hole in the world insulted my customer, and by him his father, dear customer and…a friend."

SonLara's eyes narrowed.

"I don't suppose the young master told you how he broke into my house, stole the clothes from my customer, and then passed himself as the young man by sneaking into the training barracks to steal from him yet again?" said Goram. "Young Dolphus was well waylaid for the affair, both for the loss of his uniform and its use for infiltration. Do you know what they did to him? I don't suppose a priestess like you would really care, would you?"

Haephan impressed SonLara at almost every turn. Stealing from a wizard in the wealthy quarter was the first sign of his boldness. His resilience and determination were more than any normal human she'd met, including most men. He had never lied, even when confronted about picking a student. She couldn't imagine Haephan doing anything but the least obvious response.

"Set your price, Master Peddlewaithe, and set it now. We will settle it today, or I will not ask again, and Haephan will die too soon for you to extract further from him."

"Apologize to the father and son," said Goram, "and you can take the boy."

"Bring them here," said SonLara. "And I will apologize."

Grinding his jaw, Goram signaled the burly man behind him while taking a long draw from his cigar. "Send a request to Councilor Lurli and his son for them to join us this evening for a…show." Goram leered over SonLara's body. "Would the priestess care to wait upstairs?"

Querie returned with a bowl of soup and hesitated at the tension.

"I will wait here with the child," said SonLara.

"As you wish," said Goram. "You'll be here awhile."

SonLara dismissed him from her mind and took the bowl from Querie's hands. "A stool, young lady."

"Yes, mum," said Querie as she waited for Goram's gesture before retrieving a stool. Goram spared SonLara and the boy a final look before leaving in a swirl of smoke.

"Shut the door," said SonLara. She untied her cloak with one hand, twisted and folded it before pillowing Haephan's head, raised the bowl and blew upon it.

Querie stood nearby and stared at Haephan.

"Sit here," SonLara motioned to the stool.

After sitting, Querie accepted the bowl from the priestess, unaware of SonLara's magical touch upon it.

"Help him sip this very slowly."

"Yes, mum," said Querie. She slid her hand under Haephan's sweat-drenched head. "Come now, luv. Try and sip."

SonLara rounded the bed, sat on its far edge, and peeled away fluid-soaked sheets from Haephan's skin. Bloated, reddened flesh wafted with a stomach-twisting stench. "Great Self."

Querie hurked with the spoon halfway to Haephan's mouth.

"Hold yourself, girl," said SonLara. "Emptying your stomach in here will not serve him."

"Ain't goin' nowhere, mum," Querie's voice steeled.

SonLara noted her commitment.

"You know Haephan?" SonLara asked.

"I do, mum."

"How long?"

"'is 'hole life," Querie whispered.

"Did you know his parents?"

Querie opened her mouth and shut it. "Fings ain't so simple round here, mum."

"Did they work for Goram, too?"

Querie nodded.

"And they didn't think to take their child and flee?"

Querie gazed at Haephan. "Most grow up like this, mum. Don't know no different."

"Yourself?" asked SonLara.

"Rainie, meself," said Querie. "Pretty girls who survive here hope no better than spreadin' their legs."

"And the children?" asked SonLara.

"What about 'em?" Querie's shoulders sank. "Theys gotta make their own way, too."

Soil and semi-dried blood soaked Haephan's shredded fine clothes. SonLara found no scorch marks or melting indicative of an encounter with a dragon, but noted dozens of long, deep cuts around his body. What else might he have faced?

She drew a small knife hidden in her sleeve to cut away the rest of his clothes and peeled fabric which had bonded to his skin.

A tear formed at Querie's eye as she worked soup into Haephan's mouth.

"How do they survive?" SonLara asked.

"The plain girls goes to be maids," Querie said. "Boys he pays to advertise round town."

"And the age they start working Goram's house?"

"No like that, mum," said Querie. "Not till they adults. The hearts would lose it, if he used 'em like sweets."

"Are the sweethearts mothers to most of the children?" asked Son-Lara.

Querie nodded. "And a rare one who survives the Vit'."

"Why does Goram permit children at all? Especially boys he can't sell as handmaids. I doubt any altruism on his part."

Querie took several breaths. "Keeps us alive. We don't get our kids a bit, we would die. That and he uses 'em for ears, he does. They report what they hear, just like the sweets."

SonLara tucked that away. "When do the boys go to the street?"

"Soon as they can," Querie said.

"Why don't the sweethearts keep them?"

"Can't. Not past a certain age. No room, no money, no…nuffin."

Careful not to press too much, SonLara set her hand on Querie's shoulder. "Why don't you go rest?"

Querie wavered and shook herself. "No, mum," she said as resolve anchored her. "I will not leave 'aeph."

SonLara cut away clothes and inspected his injuries, but her mind spun at Haephan's condition.

A vacant before he left, Haephan buzzed with inherent magic. What little power she applied to his soup didn't waft away as it had when she first met him, but disappeared in a tiny flush of energy through his lips as his body absorbed it. Already his skin was less red and the severity of his cuts had lessened.

Haephan healed with the aid of some unknown magic. SonLara set two fingers on Haephan's forehead and two at his bellybutton and pulled them together through the air to draw a single line of pale light.

Haephan's pulse raced outward from the point nearest his heart as dozens of tiny branches spread across his body, along each limb and up over his head—a hovering representation of his central nervous system. Though trained in general emergency medical care, she was no great internist. His magic, however, dumbfounded her.

SonLara marveled at the idea of a vacant somehow manifesting magic, or even being externally imbued with it. In her brief study of Haephan during her time there, magic ignored and dissipated when in contact with him, therefore attaching proved impossible.

As she scanned her construct, faint tinges of gold emboldened on the system's outer edges and crept inward with each pulse of his heart. She had no idea what it meant, as the construct was not designed to possess a color-changing indicator. Rich golden ambience soon possessed the entire strata. After considering it in vain, she untied the construct and let it disappear.

SonLara reviewed a list of options before she pressed the base of her hand against his sternum and applied a minor magnetic resonance test.

Light erupted from his body and sent SonLara stumbling back against the far wall in surprise. Blossoming out from his chest, a golden energy poured into a complex lattice that revealed a spreading vision of amber lace that multiplied with complexity.

Querie cried out and almost spilled the bowl of soup. "Great Self!"

"You can see this?" asked SonLara.

Querie's horror confirmed it.

More power vibrated within Haephan than any living being SonLara had ever heard of. Anything but vacant, the boy burned as a foundational beacon of prime energy.

When SonLara pulled energy away from the resonance test, it resisted and intensified as if fed by his new power. She forced a full null command on the construct before it collapsed. As it ebbed, she wondered where in hell Elverbane was and why the boy had arrived here alone.

She searched her memory for long-lost medical classes in hopes of an explanation for Haephan or his immune system while the faintest veil of new skin formed over his monstrous injuries.

The boy would survive, and possibly avoid scars, but she needed to get him healed. Dismissing the magic problem from her mind, she poured her own energy into his body and sighed in relief as his immune system eagerly responded.

34

Sorry for Nothing

Lanterns blazed when Councilor Sigmund Lurli arrived with Dolphus. Vestiges of a beating peeked through the boy's new uniform as the two entered Goram's main room. Sweethearts and guests packed the lobby willing to delay their hedonism in favor of a spectacle.

Councilor Lurli shed his soaked coat and handed it off to a sweetheart waiting inside the door before he and his son moved to the center of the main room.

Goram in his finest and Berman in his cockiest stood by the packed bar while SonLara waited alone under the sparkling main chandelier. Her aqua-trimmed white cloak draped over a dress of similar cut glowed within the room. Her shimmering gaze, however, instilled fear.

Two nervous attendants from Belfast Bluff stood beside her while Haephan—now bandaged, blanketed and tarpaulined against the downpour outside—lay upon a stretcher across the carpeted floor with his face exposed. The moment the Lurlis arrived and managed to get a look at him, she motioned to the attendants, who covered Haephan with the tarpaulin, lifted the stretcher and walked out the door to a waiting carriage designed for mud.

"Councilor Lurli," Goram crossed the floor to clasp hands with the city prefect, whose dark brown skin exceeded his son's. "I appreciate you coming. I know it's not easy getting into Rainhold in weather like this."

"You said this would be worth it," Sigmund scanned SonLara as if she were to be a sweetheart like the rest of the girls, and thus part of the attendance request. "It better be."

"Oh," said Goram. "It will." He shook the boy's hand, too, though appeared awkward in offering obeisance to such a young man. Stepping back, he motioned to the stretcher. "The young man carried out is Haephan, the cad who stole your uniform."

Dolphus had locked onto Haephan the moment they entered and hadn't stopped glaring at him.

"You let him leave?" said the councilor.

"His charge, it seems, is prepared to pay his debt to you and your boy," Goram smirked. "She is taking it on his behalf. That which you require of the boy, you may require of her."

"Exotic, indeed," Sigmund leered. "A rare find. Yes, Goram, this might settle your account."

SonLara waited as if they were in her court.

"What's your name, young lady?" Sigmund stepped closer.

The corner of her mouth quirked. "I am Andonese Priestess SonLara Alva Amferadon," her smooth voice cut the seedy air. "And I have come to apologize on behalf of the boy."

"Apologize?" the councilor coughed. "Your boy caused the severe humiliation and beating of my son by his own squad at the orders of his instructors. It embarrassed me in court. I won't tolerate anyone doing such a thing to my son or to my reputation, even a child."

SonLara's silver eyes radiated in the low ambient light. "I'm sorry your pimp couldn't protect your underage boy from getting the rash he's probably already burning with," SonLara's voice startled the room. "I'm sorry you have poor taste in entertainment."

Goram's face melted.

"I'm sorry a filthy street picker has more balls than your son, to sneak into a pimp's home, steal his clothes from the same room he's employing one of these young ladies, walk out the front door…" she said as the councilor's widening eyes locked on Goram, who reddened with rage, which caused SonLara to blink with realization, "in front of Master Peddlewaithe who apparently didn't recognize Haephan from your son, and then walk calmly out those doors." She motioned to the entrance. "I'm sorry your son was roughed up for not keeping situational awareness on property for which he was personally responsible, or able to defend himself for his mistake. To be honest, Councilor Lurli, I'm sorry for nothing." SonLara smiled for the first time without guile or patronage.

"You fuckin' worthless cunt!" Goram quivered, ready to kill her there.

Slack-jawed, the councilor and his boy could only gape.

"The next time you wish to blame your failures on others, Master Peddlewaithe, make sure they're fool enough to submit to the lie," said SonLara as she glided toward the door beyond the Lurli's.

"You will answer for your boy and your words," snarled Sigmund as he undid and pulled free his belt.

SonLara calmly raised her left hand and gripped Dolphus's jawline. The room froze. She let them stare for a long moment. "You will move aside, Councilor Lurli."

The councilor paled and retreated.

Her firm grip on the terrified boy's jaw gentled before she patted his round cheek. "Take care you do better than your mentors, young man."

Lifting her hood, she continued to the doors, crossed the porch packed with Goram's thugs, descended the stairs, and climbed into the waiting carriage, which took off the moment her door closed. Goram's main room erupted in yelling and accusations.

Once around the bend in the road, her eyes sank closed and she pressed a hand against her belly to stifle a scream. A moment later, a cough of bile emerged from her mouth onto the carriage floor. Tension sighed through her soft blue lips from the iron pit in her stomach as she spit and dabbed her face with a kerchief.

If Goram had grabbed her or the councilor struck her, there was nothing to prevent them. Her overt strength depended on fear of her exotic nature. Gulping, her inner guard shuddered and ebbed.

As she did, she focused upon the boy lying across from her in the carriage. His eminent and new magic dwarfed any mission commissioned by her own senior Librarians.

How had Haephan come to possess one of the most powerful magics in history?

35

Return to the Hollow

Are you sure? asked Rose. *He said, 'from the inside'?*

Absolutely sure, chimed Ven as they passed terraces of rice paddies. Elfmen toiling in calf-deep water raised hands and pointed at them.

That's it? asked Rose.

I told you; I woke up this morning with his voice pounding in my head, Ven chimed. *There's some other stuff, but I'm not sure what it means.*

How? Rose asked. *I thought only aurorae could do that kind of thing.*

But…it didn't sound right, chimed Ven. *Like his energy wasn't right.*

Are you sure it was him? Rose asked.

Yes, Ven chimed. *It was him. But he sounded wrong. Like Aurora Song sounds when she's in trance.*

And the dracos? You're sure the incursions stopped?

Ven nodded.

Let's get back, chimed Eldress Rose as the two accelerated.

Rice paddies gave way to deep forests climbing into the hills south of Carlinia. A week of travel from New Gordon had come with the challenges of predators and avoiding major cities. Worst of all was the separation from the ancient Trees from which pixies drew strength enough to live out a corporeal life. Without the ancient arbors, pixies could not long survive.

Diving through narrow valleys, the two plunged into an ancient forest full of familiar energy. Eldress Rose climbed above the canopy. In the distance, sunset bathed the distant Tree Carlinia in fiery orange.

Ven's spirit reached out for the Tree to tap its energy and reconnect with the flock when a flood of power crashed into her, so much so she faltered mid-air.

Ven! Rose chimed and grabbed her. *What's wrong?*

Self help us, chimed Ven. *Something's wrong with Aurora Song.*

What? asked Rose.

Tears welled in Ven's eyes. *The tree is void its aurora. I can already feel them; the flock is latching upon me.*

Strings from thousands of pixie lives needled their way into the fabric of her soul. Their presence weighed upon her so that she struggled to breathe.

Ven! Rose hauled her onward. *We're almost there!*

Ven fluttered enough to remain aloft as Rose pulled her the remaining distance to the Tree.

Three great trunks swirled upward from the soil to form a single braided trunk of the Tree Carlinia, and spread out as a canopy. Between their bases sat a hollow now crawling with pixies starving from their aurora-linked connection to the Tree's deepest magic. At their approach, the flock erupted from the hollow, encircled and drew them inside. The congregation energetically chained themselves to Ven to connect with her magic.

Ven fell across the dais while her mind reeled at the invasion of their countless individual lives. Minds, fears, doubts, hopes and desires pressed upon her. Her fingers curled against the glass-smooth floor of the hollow as her flesh quivered with their presence. While the Tree provided her with much-needed energy, the new congregation ripped it away as fast as she could draw it. Pain coursed her nerves as they sucked power through the filter of her body. As their voices screamed for ever more, fury exploded within her chest until her eyes snapped open with a brief flash of red across their normal blue.

ENOUGH! Ven screamed. A pulse of power raced up their connections. Cries echoed across the congregation like starving children ripped from a desperate teat. Ven pushed to her feet but stumbled to the ground as her head spun.

Their lives played in the round before her until she picked out the memory of Han dying. Turning, Ven found Elder Infith quivering among the congregation and climbed to her feet. *Come here.*

Bound by her connection, the beautiful elder male staggered across the floor to her.

How did she die? Ven chimed.

She's not dead yet, chimed Infith.

Take me to her, Ven chimed. *Now!*

Even the elder buckled under the pressure of her command. Back on his feet, he led her through the gaps in the rear of the Tree, along a winding paved walk, and into Song's rosebush rising from a steep incline halfway up the Tree's height. At the bush's entrance, nervous paladin raised glowing hands to bar their passage.

Aside, Ven growled.

They fell away as if pressed. Doors opened of her accord before she descended stone stairs past servants who sank to their knees.

Come, Infith, she motioned.

Hesitant, he followed her.

The path led to a central space where the rosebush hovered above them as a spherical cathedral. Standing in the foyer fed her the reams of energy she needed. Only now could she sense Song's weak life force lying nearby.

Song was about to die.

Ven continued down the ramp to the inner chamber, a round room centered by a fat rosebulb atop a gentle mound. Motes of dying petals wafted as dust into the air. Song's right leg stuck out through two cracked petals, grayed with a dying life.

Attendants knelt round about the dying aurora in stages of shock, terror and grief. Ven's arrival filled them with connection as she loomed over Song in her rosebud.

Bandages wrapped Song's breasts heaving with stuttered breath and around the stump of her arm. Her eyes cracked open and wavered until Ven took her remaining hand.

Take...them, breathed Song.

I already have, chimed Ven.

I...thought...so, Song winced.

You can go, chimed Ven.

Ven, chimed Song. *V-Ven. It's splitting.*

What is?

We must stop...this, stuttered Song. *Draco eats...too fast.*

The dracos are paused for now, and we have found a way forward, chimed Ven. *Han managed to give me a clue.*

Song's face tightened when Ven mentioned Han, but she shook her head. *There is no time.* She gasped. Nearby attendants moaned. *Must stop...now. Or will...go too...far.*

Within a few breaths, the aurora stared into a world only the dead could see.

Attendants erupted with wailing, echoed by the rest of the distant flock. A faint glow spread down Song's form, followed by a wave of disintegration. Specks of her flesh drifted away and disappeared. Several motes swirled, clung to and soaked into Ven's skin. Though Song's weight dissipated, the gaping rosebud sagged and its rosy color sank into charcoal before it, too, avalanched into ash across the stone floor.

Before grief could overcome her, a crimson flame exploded from within and enveloped Ven in a conflagration that repelled the collapsing ash, which flew away and took the bush with it until the aurora's subterranean complex lay bare to the sky. The roiling flame seeped into Ven's flesh and filled her brunette hair with a distinct crimson quality. Irises shed their blue flakes until they glowed red and her skin took on a distinct powdery quality that shimmered with power. As her feet set down on the stone, Infith gaped.

Did you— Elder Infith started. *I thought you had to blossom twice!*

Our time is short, Ven's panted chime cut him off. *And that* was *my second.*

What does that mean? chimed Infith.

What happened to Han? asked Ven. *I saw the memory, but tell me what you know.*

Tyran Han died realm diving, chimed Infith. *We got nothing from it and lost an aurora.*

That would explain much, chimed Ven. *But no, Infith, he did not die in vain. He sent me a message.*

He what? Infith started. *What did he say!?*

Say? Little, Ven chimed. *He sent me visions of our future, though not all of it is clear.*

What is clear? Aurora? Infith realized Ven was no longer an auroralite.

A shift has come to our existence, chimed Ven. *We are be bound to one who will bring about our ultimate end. By seeds will we begin our final war with dragons and,* a smirk tugged on her lips, *by the side of a dragon will we finish our life.*

Alongside a dragon!? Infith asked. *Never! Could we ever be companions? War mates?*

As much more, Elder Infith, she chimed. A full smile opened her new, ruby lips. *As friends.*

36

Earnest

Horseless and hungry, High Wizard Setherick Elverbane rattled between four barrels and two sheep stuffed in an old wagon. He winced as the rain-gutted road rammed his bony bottom despite the unforgiving canvas sack under him. Elverbane snatched the wagon's box railing to lift some of his weight as it rocked over the uneven road. As the rut evened out, he sat again as the cart rolled south along the Vitner Canal flowing dark and fast under the overcast sky.

The faint ghost of a distant tower appeared through the trees—New Gordon. Tears welled before he could squeeze them away.

Twelve days ago, he lost Haephan. The next day, Depp's gang ambushed and robbed him and Sartlam of everything. A day more, Sartlam left him behind as Depp's attack had rang the wizard's head enough that he feared a concussion. A week had passed since getting a ride south with merchants who, while generous enough to give him a lift, offered neither food nor care.

Now in sight of New Gordon with the mounting shame of such loss, despair welled. His week-long headache swelled from every jolt of the wagon and he cringed as it climbed onto the graded hill switch-backing the cliffside of Belfast Bluff. Not long after, he climbed from the carriage, thanked the listless driver, and limped to the gate among other pitiful destitute plying their hopes of generous wizards and guilt-ed wealthy.

"I am High Wizard Seth'rick Elverbane," he grunted to the guards. "You will let me pass."

"Get it," one of them shoved him. "We don't take none took kindly to beggars, sir. Certainly none 'ho lie about sumfin' like that. Be on your way."

Elverbane stumbled and fell across uneven cobble stone. Wavering for a moment like a turtle, he rolled onto his feet and staggered closer. "Wait, just…wait." He held out his upturned hand and tried to summon a simple flame to no avail. "I-I really am a wizard."

"Anuva' one," muttered the other guard. He gripped Elverbane by the neck of his tunic, hauled him aside and shoved him again across the road.

Elverbane's head smacked stone and his vision swam while the pounding in his head blinded him. Wagons and people passed ignorant of his pain.

Pride shattered. Years of dependence on his stature as the 'Hero of Tuthomere," however disdained, crumbled as horses barely avoided him along the rain-slick cobblestone. His mission had failed, his dignity sullied, his victory as smoke. Now, mere steps from safety, he had been denied his place.

Atop his own mounting guilt of loss of boy and pride, fears welled for the loss of esteem with SonLara. He couldn't imagine a woman's opinion holding such sway over him, but she held more than he had imagined they could.

And worse yet, in the meager hours he had between losing Haephan and Depp's betrayal, he failed to penetrate the mysteries of the objects recovered during the dragon attack. He recognized them as belongings of his former manservant, left behind in his room after his death. How had Haephan hid them on their long trip north? Why had he taken them at all? Most important, how had Ian's simple carvings come to bear immense magic? In the few seconds Elverbane saw Haephan, the boy glowed with unprecedented power. Though the objects radiated with similar energy in his brief inspection, they were gone to that bloody thief.

Desperate, he struggled again to approach with hands raised in supplication. "Can-can I send a message? Please? To someone inside? I know their name!"

The guard hefted his cudgel. "We don't take messages from just anyone to people on campus. Now get out of here!"

Eyeing the cudgel as his skull thundered, he dropped his head behind his upraised hands and retreated. Nuclear rage tickled him until he put a firm hand upon it. He would not give into anger that he knew would consume him, as it once had in his youth. He took heavy breaths and centered in the moment, however miserable, until his anger abated. Quivering in cold, hunger and pain, he struggled to think what to do when one small path occurred to him.

He limped away with a knee lame from Depp's surprise attack. Though the man took his purses, he left behind a note blaming Elverbane for the boy's involvement and loss. The thief was smart enough to knock the wizard unconscious before he stole from him and escaped.

Hours of hobbling brought him to The Levy shopping district where he often met Orzo for dinner and drinks, discussed energetic theory deep into the night with SonLara, and even met Haephan. Late overcast afternoon warmed the humid air as he approached the district's outer arches. Limping through, two constables appeared from nearby walls accompanied by two Crimson Guardians.

"Can we help you, old fella?" one asked.

"I—" he started. "I was hoping to reach the High Nile."

"Ooh, that's a fancy place," the guard smiled warmly. "What business have you there?"

"I, uh," stammered Elverbane. "I know Earnest."

"Earnest, huh? Well, Earnest ain't in today, sir. Thanks for coming by."

"Not in, today? He owns the High Nile."

"Then it's closed today. Why don't you go along?"

"What? I can go in, can't I?"

"No, guv," the guard said. "Not today. Get along."

"But—"

"Ge' along before we ge'tyu along," said the other. "Fancy off."

"But—"

Without waiting, the meaner guard gripped his arm and walked him away several paces before giving him a light shove. "Piss off, old man. No rats in 'eah."

Elverbane stumbled away and pressed against the bright outward wall lining the wealthy shopping district while his inner walls crumbled. Even as rage tugged again, he ground it into submission. Alone with his despair, sobs erupted from his chest and he sank to the sidewalk to cry as drizzle fell anew. Despite years of battle with lycans and his own scrappy childhood in Afnia, he had never been lower or more helpless. When his tears ebbed, desperation overwhelmed him again.

Earnest recognized everyone who ever graced his establishment, even if only once, no matter how long had passed. The man was a near savant, in Elverbane's experience.

He had to get inside. Earnest would recognize him, if only he could get inside the district. His tears ebbed and he rose and skirted the wall to a lesser-known gate. He tucked behind a nearby corner until the right group of drunken young wizards staggered into the district from rowdier bars. He rushed in behind them and hobbled along like he belonged. He followed them as far as possible with his head down—his limp mimicked their stupor—before breaking off for the High Nile down wealthy narrow lamplit streets and under tall glass ceilings above.

A block away, the High Nile's unmistakable corner entrance appeared through the finely dressed shoppers and spectacle seekers. His heart raced as he limped faster. He shouldered people aside as his pace quickened. A young Crimson Guardian patrolling the street spotted him and drew a whistle from his uniform.

Panicking, Elverbane ran with his bum leg and knocked people aside as the boy's whistle pierced the air. He scrambled up the marble stairs to the High Nile's glass doors and barreled over the doorman who attempted to block him before falling into those waiting at the hostess station.

"Stop him!" crackled the teenage guardian as Elverbane clawed again to his feet and hobbled into the fine establishment. One of the waiters attempted to block his stocky figure. Elverbane cast him aside as he limped up the second stairs to the bar area on the left before he snatched a table to catch his breath due to weakness and hunger.

Patrons enjoying drinks in the low light at the bar and small tables gasped as he stormed in.

"Earnest!" Elverbane cried as a waitress attempted to pull him out. He yanked his arm from her grip, but accidentally threw her across a nearby table. "Earnest!"

A watchman plowed into him from behind and slammed him to the polished wooden floor as three others raced in to pin him. As a group, they lifted and hauled him away.

"EARNEST!" Elverbane roared from his gut as they carried him out the front doors.

One of the barkeeps yanked the towel from his shoulder, rounded the bar, descended the steps and jogged outside where Elverbane twisted from their grip and fell hard to the stone. The watchmen raised cudgels and laid into him as the barkeep grabbed one of their arms.

"WAIT!" the man yelled. "I am Earnest. Stay your hands."

Elverbane sobbed as he cradled his head, unable to take anymore.

"Who are you?" Earnest bent over the pitiful figure huddling on the street.

Quivering, Elverbane lowered his hands to expose his filthy face and unkempt beard with hopeless eyes. "Earnest."

"Great Self," Earnest set his hand on Elverbane's shoulder and squeezed. "Wizard Elverbane? What happened?"

The crowd bubbled with whispers of 'Hero of Tuthomere' as the dumbfounded guards backed away.

Finally seen for who he was, Elverbane pressed his forehead to Earnest's knuckles and sobbed.

37

Confluence

Ven woke worn but refreshed after three days of orgy. Feasting, drinking, singing, dancing, games and constant fornication consumed the flock as it renewed its energy. She disentangled from others' arms, legs and mouths in the dark of the motionless hollow. Even the more eager of the flock had fallen still, satiated and exhausted as a field of sleeping bodies across the inside of the Tree.

Rising, Ven took to the air and flew outside to the cool morning pools and knelt to clean. She sank into the chilly water and let it shock her body awake—a lesson taught to her by Song.

Ven drew a long, slow inhale and blew it out as the final stars twinkled away under the approaching sunrise. Assuming Song's role as aurora had ignited a pixie fire to replenish flock energy and connection to Tree Carlinia. While this event had been expected, the suddenness of it shocked everyone. She had lost herself to it as a way of dealing with weeks of mental, emotional and physical exhaustion, not to mention a way to avoid weeks of nightmares of the magnalarks. Only when Ven's power returned to full did her satisfaction spread through the entire flock and allow them to get more than a few hours of sleep. She now knew every pixie in the flock—some merely by the connection of her power, others by direct intimacy over the past few days.

Realization dawned on Ven that she had violated one of the few rules of aurorae—to withhold themselves during pixie fires to prevent bonding. While softbonding her own servants and paladin was expected, aurorae served best by remaining aloof of the rest of the flock.

Ven refused to feel guilty for engaging as she had—she smiled at the idea that Carlinia was now hers—at a time when they needed each other most, when energies hovered near a dangerous void that could kill. She recalled faces and lives that she now loved as dearly as only an aurora could.

After bathing, she returned to her dead rosebush, which would soon grow anew with her own energetic signature. On her way, she detoured through the aurora's garden.

Her smile widened as she inspected the field of floral bulbs. The youngest were no larger than her big toe snuggled deep in the dark soil. Middle-grown aimed skyward like common flowers, as if waiting for the sunrise. Nearly ready sprites fattened inverted bulbs hanging from thick, curved stems that reminded her of New Gordon streetlights. This one would be a couture, that a horticul, over there a gaucho and on the other side, a young paladin. With Ven's ascension, a young auroralite shouldn't appear for centuries.

The unborn shifted at her touch. She stroked a bulb of a tinker, the rarest among them. So often, tinkers bore little interest in the social structures and activities of the flock; happy, instead to wander the territory and explore, laze in gaggles and otherwise buck the authority of tyrans and aurorae, alike. And yet…Ven caressed the bulb and smiled. Tinkers often recognized something the rest of them did not—society was brief, changing and too often arbitrary. Might a tinker amount to something important for pixies, one day?

Hello there, Ven smiled. *I'm the mother. How're you this morning?* She leaned to kiss and stroke its soft petalled exterior before continuing on. As the eastern sky hinted the blue of a distant dawn, she checked each bulb, stripped away vines and shifted soil where needed.

Not so long ago, Ven ached to tend the bulb field. Song's untimely death meant Ven would have to learn on her own. Stillborn pixies were not uncommon, but rare was it that it came at the negligence of the aurora. Ven had learned much from Song, but being away from Song at her first blossoming, she never began the century-long apprenticeship common for aurorae.

Ven struggled beneath the weight of learning it all alone. The anxiety deepened as she considered how she softbonded the flock, making them unnaturally amenable to her desires. Even Rose failed to protest as she was caught in the orgy's overwhelming power. That would need to be addressed, and soon, to prevent hardbonding—a form of pixie slavery.

As Ven headed for her subterranean chambers—now roofless for want of a new rosebush—she pondered selecting new attendants and paladin to protect her against unsavory creatures that sometimes wandered pixie territory. She would also soon need to help Song's attendants transition once more into the flock.

As she approached the rear stairwell, Ven slowed as the air changed from a gentle morning breeze to a faint buzz. Her hackles climbed as danger cut the air. She slipped down the rear, secret stairwell to the main chamber and out of a hide in the wall to find four dark figures standing where Song's bulb used to be.

The willowy figure in the center with long, flowing hair interrupted the air with her presence. Ven's suspicions were confirmed—another aurora had come to Carlinia.

Who are you? Ven chimed as warning bells erupted in her head. Aurorae were not to cohabit the same space.

The aurora's face twitched. *Where is Song?*

I am aurora here, chimed Ven. *Song is gone.*

No…Song should not die. She lives.

No, Ven scanned the aurora's personal paladin, drowned in shadow despite the aurora's glow, keylit only in her crimson shading. *I watched her die and transition.*

The aurora drew a stuttered inhale. *What happened?*

Who are you? Ven asked. *And why are you here?*

What. Happened, the aurora repeated, as if unused to others not answering her.

Ven shuddered under her immense power. *She died trying to save our tyran.*

Save him? From what? grated the aurora. *Aurorae do not save tyrans, tyrans save aurorae. Who attacked you?*

Who are you? asked Ven.

I am Chira, of Yenneth.

Yenneth? Ven asked. *Why are you here?*

Where is Song!? demanded Chira.

I just told you.

She must be here, Chira scanned the roofless complex.

As the pale morning blue continued filling the sky, it alarmed Ven that none of it brightened the interlopers. *She's dead.*

Chira's eyes locked upon Ven. *You're an aurora.*

Why are you here? Ven asked.

Chira stepped closer. *Have you heard them?*

Yes.

Then you can tell me how to fix them, Chira chimed.

Fix them? They have already fallen silent, Ven chimed. Anxiety flared—had she failed? Checking herself, she sensed no further cries from the magnas. *No, they're safe. We took care of that.*

No! Chira chimed. *They speak, they speak, they speak... They won't stop speaking. They demand our help, like we can go into the nether! We must stop them.*

We did, Ven chimed. *With the help of the humans.*

Humans? asked Chira. *When did they become a part of this?*

When I went in search of the worldender—

Worldender? Chira gasped. *You sully our race by conferring with a mass murderer!?*

Ven's fists curled. *In the vision, I heard to go—*

I know what you heard, you stupid fucking sprite! Chira screamed. *How DARE you let the magnas dictate your dignity!*

You would let our race die because you didn't want to speak with humans? asked Ven.

Humans... those oversized dwarves deserve to die for the wars they have waged across Pangea, growled Chira. *To involve them is like begging to the worms—*

They were already involved! chimed Ven. *They have seen the breakdown in realmic harmonies and were already acting on word from subrim.*

Subrim? Chira chimed. *They told you these lies? And you believed them!*

They found the dracos responsible, Ven chimed, hoping the silence meant they had, in fact, done so.

Wh-what? Chira stuttered. *Where?*

No.

Chira stilled.

Get out of my bush, Ven's brow darkened. *Go back to Yenneth.*

You dare *to tell me where I can and cannot go?* Chira drew in power.

I said leave, chimed Ven. *This is MY bush.*

A tiny little auroralite thinks to dismiss me— Chira started again.

I said leave! Ven demanded.

The ripples in space emanating from their encounter had woken and drawn many of the Carlinian pixies to peek wide-eyed through nearby bushes with wonder and terror.

What do you know? demanded Chira. *You're hiding information from me.*

I don't trust you, Ven chimed. *And you were not permitted entry to our territory or Tree.*

I have come to save our race! Chira chimed. *You will not bar me—*

You came to save yourself, Ven chimed.

You selfish little bug, Chira stepped closer. *You would deny me information that could save pixilarks so you can take the glory.*

What didn't you hear— Ven began when Chira cast out her hand and unleashed a bolt of golden light that struck Ven in the chest and snatched her into the air.

Ven cried out to the collective gasps of her pixies caught between saving their new aurora and attacking another—something they had been trained never to do.

Wh-hat are yo-u doing!? cried Ven as her body locked up.

I will secure your obedience, chimed Chira.

Ven searched in desperate hope of a rescue. As the magic rippled around her, she recognized a similar pattern in the flesh of the foreign paladin. *Stop—!*

You will tell me what you know, chimed Chira.

Ven's fists curled inward as magic poured over and into her nervous system, wrenching her into excruciating angles. *Leav— me be!*

The spell fluctuated and rebounded, forcing Chira to fight harder to execute it. Unable to use her vision, Ven still traced the energy's invasion of her magic and how it worked to lock others' decision mechanisms to Chira's will.

Chira attempted some kind of control spell.

Hel-p! Ven squealed. *Help me—!*

A hesitant cry preceded Elder Infith leaping from the edge of the complex and igniting a fight with the paladin. Hordes of Carlinians poured into the fray, many struck by unnatural power erupting from the enemy warriors.

Hey! Couture Rima appeared in the chaos and swung at Chira from behind. Her hand struck a barrier hovering above Chira's skin that scorched off her fingers and cast her back into the melee and across the chamber floor.

Rima! Ven cried.

Tell me, Chira panted as her magic struggled against Ven's own powers.

Ven realized Chira's frantic inattention failed to properly execute the strange spell. Despite her agony, Ven seized on those frequent, if short, lapses of focus, and forced her will back down the same veins used by Chira. Bit by bit, Ven repelled Chira's energy.

Desperate to win, Chira snatched Ven by the throat using her own fingers.

Chira was nearly a thousand years old, Ven realized, and replete with untold power and experience.

This is my *Tree,* Ven managed despite the chokehold and focused on Carlinia's spreading canopy. She tapped the Tree's power—something she ought to have done the moment she encountered the intruder.

Power flooded Ven. Noting the spell's pattern and lacework, Ven reversed the entire structure, rammed her fingers into Chira's gaping mouth and snatched it like a handle as her power exploded backward.

As the spell rebounded, Chira screamed and dropped to her knees. Her paladin, likewise, crashed into the stone alongside dozens of injured Carlinians.

Ven screamed as she drove the spell into Chira and completed the execution.

A swirl of violent light and a pop of thunder finalized the energetic lock, affecting all but Ven. As panic flooded through her veins, Ven snatched a rock from the floor nearby, spun and slammed it into the side of Chira's head.

In the eternal seconds between locking onto Chira's face and swinging the rock, submission overcame her prey.

Information flooded Ven from Chira's mind, but before she interpreted it all, she finished her vicious swing and crushed the side of Chira's skull so that the willowy creature snapped to the side in a spray of blood and slapped lifeless to the stones.

Panting over the dead aurora, the memories which had crossed the gap unfolded themselves to Ven.

For centuries, the beautiful Chira had been the kindest of aurorae from the eldest pixie flock in Pangea. Wise and patient, Chira had mothered thousands of sprites to full maturity in Yenneth Grove along the Kardur Montserrat, north of Lubar's Peak, Pangea's tallest mountain. The model aurora, everything changed a little over a year past when Chira was first among the pixilarks to hear the magna's desperate whispers that, over time, burst forth as a tsunami of terror.

At first hopeful for a solution, Chira grew desperate when none appeared. Paranoia crept in so that she suspected her own flock hid the truth from her. She dipped into forbidden magics in her pursuit of an escape from the endless thundering whispers. As Chira lost touch with reality, she enslaved and suffered her entire flock, none of whom suffered anxiety or fear or doubt under their hardbonding.

A wail erupted from Ven's throat when she realized that Chira hadn't needed to die—reversing the attack released Chira's mind from the magnas. A cry ripped from Ven's chest before Chira even hit the floor.

As Ven stood over Chira's dead body, blood oozing from her crushed skull across the floor of her chamber and the stone dripping in Ven's own hand, a spear of agony stabbed her in the heart and sent her to her knees. Thousands of new lives latched upon her, as hardbonded to her as they had been to Chira, all the way from Yenneth, thousands of miles distant.

Ven struggled to cope with the enormity of it all, but suppressed their voices to focus on her own Carlinians moaning with missing hands and limbs. Wails erupted as dead were discovered among them.

Sinking to her bottom, Ven clutched her mouth with her bloody hand and stared in shock at Chira's beautiful face lying crushed in a pool of golden blood.

38
Shadows and Snow

"Father?" asked the young female elf as Nick cast a falcon from his thick crimson leather glove. Her silver irises shimmered the same soft pastel tans, blushes and blue perry painting the evening sky. Orphen gained altitude and circled the tree-dotted grass field bathed in dusty sunlight.

"Yes, Amerela?" Nick asked his twelve-year-old daughter in her blue and red dress.

High Elven white hair looping behind her head bounced as she faced her nine-foot-tall father. "Do you think the Graelans will achieve it? Truly, a flying city such as the ancients had?"

"I don't know," Nick said. "Their krys certainly seems to think so."

"I would like to see such a thing," she said and clutched her hands before her chest. "I dream of riding a brigon."

"I think many might to see such a place," Nick said. "Though riding a brigon sounds a bit scary."

"Father!" she exclaimed. "I cannot imagine you afraid of anything."

"Everyone is afraid of something, my dear," said Nick.

"I will not believe until I witness it, myself," she said and smiled.

"Believe what?" asked her grinning, dirt-painted little brother as he entered their circle.

"Father claims he is afraid of certain things."

"Certainly not father!" cried Iphan.

"Certainly yes father," Nick smirked as Orphen dove through the warm, citron air into the heavy grass.

The children stood side by side wearing the same frown.

"Stop worrying about my fears," said Nick as he ambled nearer the falcon's kill. "Come."

The children took his hands as they crossed the breeze-washed field.

"Father?" asked Iphan as he high stepped through the tall grass. "Has mother said when she would come visit us?"

"Yes, father!" Amarela added. "I have so wanted to meet her."

"I've told you both before," said Nick. "Your mother cannot come. As much as she would love you both, I'm sure."

Both children "awww'd."

"But I love you both very much," he smiled. They hugged his wrists as they reached Orphen.

The bird lay a gory mess under a bogey of shadow and darkness devouring its insides with ragged crunching of bones and wet smacking. Two glowing orbs climbed inside of its semi-opaque blackness and glared at them as a wide, razored grin cut open its face.

The children screamed.

The demon's lengthening yawn released a faint wail that climbed from a whisper to an ear-shattering apex.

When Nick yanked the children backward, their disintegrating forms wafted into the faint afternoon breeze broiling into a tempest. Gorgeous dusklight drenching the field grass and autumn trees twisted with nightmarish necrotic pitch and drowned the world into gothic hell.

When all but its glowing eyes disappeared under the new sunless world, the creature struck.

Cursing, Nick raised hands and formed a metal shield as the demon attacked. The elf tripped back over the rocky soil. He lifted his shield, ready for the next attack, but the bogey had liquified against the metal and flowed around its edge toward his wrist. Crying out, he dematerialized the shield and flung away the burning amorphous demon as he rolled and leapt to his feet. Shield and specter crashed to the ground before it reformed its pseudo-humanoid shape and strafed the landscape without removing its violent gaze.

"ARMOR!" Nick bellowed. Crimson lengths of cloth snaked around his body and solidified as hardened plates to form battle armor.

Heavy, ragged trees speared up all around the field and hissed with the poison of the bogey's essence. Dark, glowing smoke billowed from their branches and swirled as Nick scanned for the creature.

Silver-lined red panels formed over key areas of his body while a snug, bloodred helmet trimmed in pearl hugged his head. His long, pale hair now hung low in bone-white dreadlocks. Intricate holes in the sides of the helmet admitted sound, by which he followed the rush of heavy feet through the obscured battlefield.

Two short silver swords extended from his fists as he navigated the rolling, lifeless terrain. A faint shuffle preceded the creature's attack from the darkness. He dodged and swung with little effect on the disembodied shadow.

Nick flushed blades with fire and swung again. Light struck and repelled its shadowy form.

After retreating, two furious eyes stared from the chaotic foreground and orbited him.

Nick's burning swords lit the smoke and dimmed the demon's horrific bloodred gaze as it circled him in fits. He turned back and forth to keep it in view. When the glowing smoke thickened to the point of blindness, the demon closed its eyes and disappeared.

Despite his own terror, Nick closed his eyes, used his ears and extended his swords to the side.

A faint whisper echoed through the darkness.

As Nick inspected it, the bogey attacked. Its power dimmed the light of his swords until they appeared as little more than glowing outlines in the smoky black. He spun and struck at the creature, which screamed as the swords sliced it open.

Contact with the demon sent pain up Nick's wrists. He clenched his teeth and doubled his effort to reignite the blades as the bogey counterattacked. He swung wild before an ear-piercing scream filled the air, followed by a flush of the same whispers.

Nick flinched under the scream and barely avoided the creature's next attack. The demon rebounded as Nick stumbled to his knees, and missed again as the elf dove aside, rolled, and sprinted into the forest. Cackling laughter followed him as he panted with terror. When he could run no more, Nick stopped and wrangled his fear.

The creature's approach echoed through the trees like the chilling giggle of a thousand psychotic children preparing to feed.

Nick released his swords and their brilliant light. For a moment, total darkness enveloped him and drew the bogey ever closer, so much so that its essence threatened to drown him.

Nick drew both hands before his gut and curled his fingers. A faint light flickered between his facing palms, oppressed by the thickening agony of darkness. As he narrowed his focus upon the light and released his fear of the void, it stabilized and expanded against the inky torrent.

"Identify," Nick's deep voice faltered against the blackness, but he trusted his authority. He repeated with a stronger, smoother voice. "Identify."

The bogey's piercing scream almost made him release the spell and snatch the ear holes in his helmet.

"Identify," said Nick through clenched teeth. "IDENTIFY!"

Struck by his command, thunder cast the demon through several trees, setting them ablaze in red flame before it plowed across distant soil.

Nick twisted his hands and unleashed the spell as a sphere of growing light that disinfected the dark mists with its brilliance. As the sky turned a brittle white and painted the world in a colorless stark, he rushed over the twisting bogey and pointed two fingers at its heart. "Identify."

"Paaannnn," its ragged voice rippled across the ground.

Nick's brow sank. "Identify."

"PPAAAAANNN," the voice screamed, but this time the quality, despite its deep undertone, was distinct—the voice belonged to a child.

"Return to your source," said Nick as he made the spell form with hands streaking light through the air.

The eternal black of its jaws yawned with laughter.

Working faster, Nick unleashed the dispersion spell. The energy passed through the bogey as if it wasn't there.

When Nick hesitated, the creature exploded and knocked him across the ground while it escaped through the forest. The twisted echo of its childlike laughter faded and its souring touch dissipated from the world.

Nick recovered and raised defenses before he realized the bogey was gone. He sank to a knee and panted as his mind raced. He had never before struggled with a demon in a dream— a dream.

His chest stilled. He was in a dream. He filled his blood with oxygen and restfulness by his will.

"Nick," he scolded himself, feeling silly for having been tricked by a nightmare, and tried to will it away. Though it shuddered under his unspoken command, it would not disappear. He frowned. "Reveal."

The dream shuddered again, though this time a wall of pure white reaching into the sky appeared to his left, muted by heavy mists. Surprise overcame him by its presence and his inability to sense beyond it.

His armor smoked away into his traditional crimson robes trimmed in pearl. His dreadlocks unravelled into his long straight white hair down his back and over his shoulders. Inhaling, he pressed through the wall of light.

The swirling mist around him fell away, replaced by the iciest wind. His thin robes thickened until a winter coat covered him, including a red hood lined in white fur to protect his face against icy gusts.

A faint pale thing appeared on the painfully bright milky horizon. At first suspicious of a trick, he scanned for danger. The world behind him had disappeared. Deciding against resuming his armor, he advanced across crunching snow.

When he neared his target, his silver eyes widened.

A redheaded human child lay dying in the snow. Blood drooled from the boy's face onto a hunter-green military longcoat and twisted into shapes of long crossbars down his trunk and a roundel on his chest of the La'Du Lira Al'Cular—Eden's Tree of Life. A dead snake encircled him—a string of blood drooled from one gory eye while the other lay a pale white, blinded from some previous injury. The redheaded child panted in jerks and stared skyward through a blood-pattered face.

Nick stilled at the unprecedented reality of the vision.

The boy muttered as blood-muddled tears froze as fast as they welled. He snatched a breath and said, "I'm sorry."

Kneeling next to the child, Nick hovered his hand above the boy's chest and used magic to identify broken ribs and severe internal hemorrhaging. The boy's mutter drew him back, but as he leaned closer, the child fell still.

"Bye," exhaled the boy. He died with his eyes frosted open.

In a panic, Nick scooped the boy, who disintegrated in a flush of dry crimson snow as the vision washed away. The snow around him drooled into the air until only white remained, which faded to the distant chuckles of the bogey.

39

Reindeer

Nick woke in his favorite velvet chair nestled in a small glass-walled bailey overlooking ancient brownwoods bathed in sunset washing in the evening breeze. A faint thunder rumbled the air, hinting at rain.

He pulled away his long pale hair and pushed away the nightmare when movement nearby made him spin, ready for an attack.

"My krys?" the attendant flinched.

Nick calmed. "Yes?"

"Pardon, m'lord, I did not mean to startle you, but…"

"You did not," Nick said. "What is it?"

"Sire…there is a deer in the stables who…has asked for you."

"What?"

"A stag, sire. A reindeer, to be specific."

Nick verified he had, indeed, woken from his dream. "Did you say a reindeer in the stables asked for me?"

"Yes, sire," the attendant said.

Nick's brows drooped before he rose in his silver-gray tunic and cranberry trousers tucked into soft charcoal boots.

"A white reindeer, to be exact, my lord. A great one."

"Is that so?" Nick asked. He had never before heard of a high sentient stag. "Lead the way."

The attendant half bowed and led Nick from the royal bedchambers through long hallways floored by pearl marble veined in ruby. Intricate wooden halls and arched ceilings framed the path while crystal redirectors spaced along the apex admitted high columns of golden light which bounced from the floor and underlit pristine statues and other artwork lining the path. Large windows to his left revealed the northern edge of the city of Aminrale. The metropolis descended from the Kellan Ridge upon which stood the palace, eastward over rolling hills to the northbound river winding through the range. Shadow drowned the city in the shallow Oman River Valley, yet failed to hide the sparkling river as it wound over sandbars and low rapids before winding out into the farmlands hidden by the high, rippling terrain between them.

The two navigated the palace's ornate hallways wreathed in elvish tapestries. Armored statues of fine-cut pale stone appeared as living guards standing beneath columns of light. Plush carpeting cushioned every step under his soft boots while permaspells maintained air quality. Across the long throne room, tall, thick columns of ruby-veined marble lined each side of the chamber up four stories to ornate arches bracing the ceiling.

Through more doors and descending a winding stairwell, the air filled with music. The two followed a broad, winding staircase until noble-born elves passing its foot came into view. There was no easy alternate route to the stables. "You said a reindeer, right?"

"Yes, sire," said the servant. "We did not wish to disturb her majesty with…this."

Nick motioned him onward. "Carry on."

The servant continued to the bottom. When Nick appeared in the hallway, those within sight stirred at his arrival and offered bows and curtsies.

The hallway lined the exterior wall of the palace's grand ballroom and passed by one of its tallest pairs of open doors. Nick hoped to slip by unseen when the herald standing inside the doors bellowed, "Mine Lord and Ladies! The Krys of Aminrale, Nikal'Odin Kringul!"

Nick halted halfway across the open doors, in full view of the room.

The sea of wealthy and political elves filling the long, ornate ballroom bowed or curtsied with a twitter of shock at his appearance. He cursed under his breath as his wife stood as the lone tree in a field of bowing elves. When she turned with surprise at his announcement, he gave a shake of his head and stepped into the grand ballroom. "Please."

The room straightened as Isheim glided closer in her fine ballgown.

"My krys—" her voice faltered when she saw his outfit. "I feared you would not make it."

"Pardon me, but I have business to attend to," Nick spoke to the room and laid his hand on his chest as if to feign a deep apology. "Please, enjoy yourselves."

"You're not staying?" asked his slender wife. A vision in her snug red dress trimmed in gold, pearl and shimmering gemstones, with her white hair bound above her head in complex swirls, disdain and disappointment flickered across her painted smile.

"No, my queen," he said and offered her a faint bow. "Don't mind me." He passed dozens of staring attendees.

The awkward attendant angled for the grand staircase, which descended to the grand court circle. At its bottom, they followed a walk that led out of sight and descended into the palace stables.

"Make way!" the attendant barked. Servants, stablehands and other attendants packing the entrance to the stable yard scattered and bowed as he passed. Through the high archway, servants and groomsmen filled the space between the arcade's tall columns round about a stable yard empty but for a lone occupant.

A white reindeer stag with tall, intricate antlers stood alone at the yard's heart, backlit by the tan western sky.

"Nikal'Odin Kringul," said the stag.

"Yes?" Nick wasn't sure if he was more surprised that the stag failed to honor his title or that the stag had spoken at all.

"You are summoned," the stag approached and turned to expose its hind.

Nick frowned as the stag snorted. “By whom?”

A long, nasal horn echoed somewhere distant. The servants leaned out from among the ceilinged colonnade, curious. When the stag raised its head, everyone looked to the sky.

To their shock, a cyclone of a hundred reindeer circled high above their heads. Stampeding hooves created the faint thunder he realized he had heard from his bailey.

Nick’s jaw sank.

“Come, Krys Kringul,” the reindeer said. “Climb upon my back.”

Shocked by the display, Nick approached. “Where are we going?”

“An account of purpose,” said the reindeer.

“And my return?”

“You will not sleep else than in your bed,” the reindeer said.

Mustering his courage, Nick crossed the yard while eyeing the intricate and violent antlers before he mounted the beast.

“Grip my mane,” the creature said. “And brace yourself.”

“Why?” Nick asked when the creature spun and raced for the open iron gate. Hesitant guards flinched at the sudden approach when the reindeer leapt high and sprinted into the air and over the tall archway.

Nick’s muscles locked with fear. A nasal horn erupted from the beast while both sides of its heavy antlers danced near Nick. Should the creature twist its head too fast or far, Nick would be impaled, if not cast from his seat.

His long white hair dancing in the wind, Nick scanned the herd sprinting in pairs behind them.

“Look onward, Kringul,” said the beast, “or you’ll miss what is to come.”

The world below flowed with alarming speed as heavy forests wandered over endless miles of farmland and eventually to deserts. Instead of soaking in the impossible swiftness, he pondered the beast beneath him. There was no place upon the continent uncharted, to his knowledge, and such a deerkind would have been annotated, indeed.

Two tall mountain peaks rushed past him on either side as the beast raced through a long, winding mountain canyon. No such high mountains existed for thousands of miles from Aminrale. As they ascended from the winding canyon to expose an endless horizon of snow-capped ranges, Kringul paled as the truth dawned upon him.

Nick and the reindeer had travelled six thousand miles in less than an hour.

How in all creation could any living being move so fast without a rimsportal? The animal rolled and changed direction, dove along a narrow coniferous ravine and rushed toward the base of a high granite wall a half mile high. Nick closed his eyes and clenched the beast, ready to plow into the side of the mountain, when the animal settled, walked a few steps and grunted.

Nick opened his eyes, checked the ground to ensure it was no longer moving, and fell off the creature. In all his five thousand years, he'd never been so unsettled. He scrambled from the stag, climbed to his feet over shaking knees, set his hand on a tree and vomited.

He had to be in some kind of strange dream, one in which he could not identify its inner touch points to manipulate as he could all others.

"This has to be a dream," he said.

"This is no dream," a smooth, feminine multivoice filled the air.

Nick spun.

A feminine figure loomed over him as tall to him as high elves were to humans, wreathed in robes of light hugging a full feminine figure. Luscious hair composed of stars and midnight framed a cherubic blue face and eyes of endless luminescence that sapped his strength with awe. The lingering dusk behind her cast her in silhouette and the long hallway of high mountain peaks on either side of the narrow valley bathed her in a fiery aura.

"Nikal'Odin Kringul," her voice drew him to his knees.

"Great Self," he muttered as he recognized her for who she really was—a magistrate of the creator. A subrim.

"Fear not. His Holiness finds favor with you. I am Suthene, Archon of the Great Self," the wash of musical notes from her lips formed words in his ears. "You are Kringul of Aminrale, noble of the High Krysdom and arbiter of dreams."

Remembering to breathe, he bowed his head and spread open his hands in submission. "Greetings, subrim. How may I serve?"

"Rise, Nikal'Odin," said Suthene. "You have been anointed caretaker for the Great Self's chosen."

"Who am I that the Great Self should send a subrim?" asked Nick.

"You are forged master of dreams," she said.

Images of recent dreams rushed by, most prominent among them that of the boy dying in the snow—so real that Nick again knelt over the child.

"You will move your house to an ancient land beyond Algueda." Her voice cut across the white snow drooling upward while the blood-pattered human child gasped for air. "There, your purpose will be fulfilled."

"Fulfilled? Am I not servant to my people as their krys?" asked Nick as the bitter, icy wind burned his skin.

"Corporeal appointments are tools of His will, not a culmination of your design. Rise and walk."

When Nick stood, the valley around them had returned. She led him toward sunset as streaks of brilliant tangerine light climbed the misty walls of stone on both sides of the valley. After several minutes, they crossed a treeless space down a path which married a bubbling creek winding into the valley bottom.

"You are to seek out the blue-haired woman in the city of magic southeast of Eden," said the subrim. "There you will request conduct for you and your household to a new home in a distant land, a journey you will complete before the green moon rises."

"My household? Do you mean to move Aminrale across Pangea? My entire nation to a new home? Where will we go? There is no corner of Pangea unclaimed by friend or foe who surely will send us elsewhere. Or do you advocate war? Aren't there enough wars upon the continent? Lycan conflicts raging all over again and you're asking Aminrale—"

"No."

Nick blinked.

"All, but only, members of your house, Nikal'Odin."

"What do you mean, 'only members of my house'? We won't have a king!"

The subrim's look stilled his heart. "There is no true king but the Great Self, lowly krys."

Nick's heart stilled.

"Imagine yourself higher than He who designed the universes?" All around the subrim darkened, pierced only by her gaze and an outline of her figure and aura. "He who gave thrones to your forefathers and, thus, to you, now commands your journey into a new world and function."

Nick struggled to inhale as her aura washed away his magic.

"You will not go alone," said Suthene.

Nick inhaled.

"Among the krysdom, two houses will join you," she said, "each with unique purpose."

"And my people? Will they be absorbed into the nine nations?"

"Appoint a steward to conduct the final affairs of you among your people," she said.

"And the people?"

"They will conduct themselves."

His people's safety and continued peace had been his priority for thousands of years. What else might he do? He jumped to feel the subrim's hand upon his shoulder.

"Trust and obey," the subrim's voice softened.

"Yes, subrim."

"Seagol of Kukhel and Hagal of Beersheba journey now to Aminrale," she said. "Together, you will set up new homes in an ancient place to protect His chosen. You and your wife have been barren, but the Great Self has seen all and will bring forth the joy you so desire."

"Isheim will bear a child?"

"She will not."

"But—"

"Keep your eyes open, Kringul."

Nick exhaled.

When a finger tipped his chin, the touch thrilled him until the endless cosmos of her eyes took him to his soul. "The time to come is of breaking, Nikal'Odin Kringul, and you will safeguard the Self's chosen. Take each and every present member of your household to holy purpose."

"For how long?" he asked.

"Until the cycle of Pans is nearly fulfilled."

"What...what is a Pan?" asked Nick.

Her face rushed into a kiss that washed him in a torrent of light and energy. When it subsided, he woke upon the hind of the stag in his stable yard under a sky blazing with a galaxy of stars. Anxious palace guards and groomsmen packed the arcade under flickering torchlight. Dozens of gala attendees surrounded his worried wife near the arcade entrance.

Quivering, Nick dismounted the stag, which snorted, trotted away and climbed into the black of night. A faint thunder of hooves circling above faded away.

"My krys?" Isheim asked.

Nick turned at her approach. Fear and worry painted her face, as it did the dozen young maids flanking her.

"Are you alright?" she asked. "What happened?"

Nick struggled to speak and, instead, shook his head until the words came. "Change, Isheim. Change has come."

"Change? To whom?"

Nick inhaled. "Us."

40

Waking

Elverbane sat up in bed with a cry. Sweat beaded his skin and the taste of the spell that burned Tuthomere seared his tongue as it often did after fugue dreams. He scanned his surroundings.

Brilliance bleeding through a crack in his curtain painted a faint streak across his belly and warmed the room. Calming his breathing, he ran his fingers through his thick gray hair.

Lying in his bed in his room at Belfast Bluff, he coughed at the reek of his unwashed body wafting from beneath hot sheets and reclined to suck in cleaner air. Relief washed over him that he was home.

"Earnest," he muttered with relief.

With reluctant exhaustion, he pulled aside the covers, rolled his feet over the thick, cushy mattress and sat up. He tugged on a small cord hanging along the wall above his bed; a bell rang.

After curling his toes into the plush rug, he climbed to unsteady feet. The filth of soil and unwashed skin painted his sheets and his thin shorts. His head swam at rising so fast and he gripped his headboard to steady himself. He approached the door when SonLara slid sideways into the room.

Elverbane twisted away. "SonLara!"

"You need to sit down," she said. "You're in no condition to be up."

"I will have a bath!" he rasped. "I feel terrible."

"You look terrible," she said. "We were worried when you came back late."

Elverbane shuddered at the memory of the dragon eating the boy. He would have to explain everything to SonLara and wasn't sure he was prepared for that. He hadn't eaten in two days and struggled to stand. "Yeah."

"There is much we need to discuss," she said. "Much has happened since you left."

Why hadn't she asked about Haephan?

After a moment, Runa—Ashmore's keepmaid—waddled into the room with an audible limp.

"Wizard?" Runa frowned.

"I'd like to order breakfast," said the wizard.

"His breakfast has already been ordered," SonLara said from the hallway.

"And when will the wizard stop soiling the sheets, so?" asked Runa.

Elverbane motioned to his bathroom door. "Prepare my bath."

"Yes, wizard," said Runa before she entered the lavatory to prepare hot water in the copper tub.

"Shall I summon Master Quimil?" Runa asked. "Cut that mane o'yours?"

"No, Runa. That will be all."

"Wizard," she nodded and left.

He entered the lavatory, stripped and sank into the hot tub. When he emerged an hour later, his entire mattress and bedding were gone and fresh clothes hung over a chair in the corner. He dressed, combed his hair and inspected himself in the mirror.

Elverbane feared confessing to SonLara more than satisfying his empty stomach. The face in the mirror had lost decades since Tuthomere, and a decade more since losing Haephan. The memory of the dragon striking the child sat low in his stomach. He didn't want to step outside the room, but Elverbane had not gotten here by retreating to his fears or failures.

At his door, his hand hovered over the knob while his heart pounded in his chest. He swallowed the sob hesitating at the base of his throat, opened his door and marched down the hall to his emotional doom.

Sitting by the crackling fireplace, SonLara looked up from her papers as if he had merely stepped out of the room on an errand. She lowered her sheaf to her lap and waited. The woman proved ever ready for anything they had so far experienced. He wished to possess such constitution.

He cleared his throat, ready to explain, when the aroma of breakfast reached his nose. Caught in the moment, he succumbed and sat before the steaming plate. He spared her a nervous glance and frowned at less than half his usual morning portion.

Prepared to dig in, the memory of the boy disappearing beneath the jaws of the ghastly dragon flashed through his mind. He fidgeted the fork while he struggled not to vomit an empty stomach. Quivering with rage and shame, he stabbed the table with the fork and set down his thick hands.

"Elverbane." SonLara's smooth voice startled him. "Elverbane."

Opening his eyes, Elverbane readied for SonLara's inevitable question about Haephan and froze.

Haephan grinned from the empty chair across from him.

Elverbane leapt, kicked out his chair and threw himself against the wall. His eyes widened in terror.

Haephan's grin faded.

Elverbane looked between SonLara and the boy. Did she not see the child? Of course not. The boy was a ghost. He had died and come to haunt him. "What's—" he started, then whispered, "going on?"

"What does it appear to be?" SonLara asked.

Squeezing his eyes, Elverbane couldn't endure her smooth and level voice right now. "The boy is dead. The dragon ate him."

Elverbane opened his eyes and found the boy gone. He sank to the ground and clutched his face.

SonLara rose and rounded the table. "Stand up, wizard."

Terrified, Elverbane stood but couldn't raise his eyes.

"Look at me."

Elverbane obeyed and sputtered, "He-he died because of me."

"Listen very carefully, wizard," SonLara said. "What you have seen is good, not evil, and I will explain. Are you prepared to hear something more fantastic than what you think you saw?"

"I saw— he—" his voice quivered. "I am damned. The boy is dead and haunts me."

"That was no vision," she said. "That was Haephan."

Elverbane coughed as she took his chin in her hand.

"Not only is the boy alive and well, but something fantastic has happened," said SonLara. "I will explain everything we know thus far, but first, pick up your chair, eat your food, and when you are ready to hear the full of it, I will share. Do you understand?"

Hesitant, he nodded. She released his chin and left.

Shaking, Elverbane plucked his chair, sat and devoured his plate. Though he wished for coffee, he downed the sweating decanter of water. He practiced breathing exercises learned after Tuthomere to deal with his battle fugue.

The sun crawled across the floor through the window before SonLara returned to the room and her chair. "Setherick. The world is about to change."

Now calm, Elverbane noted a distinct quality of excitement in her otherwise stalwart voice.

"Everything we know about the structure of space is about to shift, and the sentient continuity along with it," she said. "Your visit by the subrim was only the beginning."

Elverbane sat up. "You were visited, weren't you?"

She nodded.

"And the boy?"

"The Great Self is moving," she said. "And we have been selected to deliver the first step in a plan the depths of which I cannot yet fathom. I have been chosen to prepare a people from out of normal humanity to serve as his chosen, to a new land and place yet constructed, as you have been prepared to break the world."

Elverbane gulped.

"Tell me what happened," said SonLara. "Everything."

Elverbane took a deep breath and explained the trip to Eden, to Haephan's supposed death to Depp's betrayal and his own harrowing journey home. "I got to the gates and no one recognized me. For all my years here and all my infamy…and as little as I look twice at those guards…none of them recognized me."

The sun warmed the window frame until it, too, glowed.

"None of them. They pushed me away as if I were nothing," he stuttered. "I thought…if I could get to Earnest at the High Nile. If I could get there, he'd recognize me. Earnest remembers everyone who walks into his place. I was…lucky." Shame filled him.

"In a moment, Haephan is going to come in here," said SonLara. "Whatever you do, don't be alarmed. It won't be through a door."

"What?" asked Elverbane.

SonLara half turned her head and called, "Haephan?"

With a great crash, Haephan appeared and fell over a table on the wall opposite the fireplace. He rolled across the carpeted floor alongside a shattering vase and other odds and ends before he scrambled to his feet.

Elverbane flinched and recoiled in his chair.

"Hey wizard," said Haephan.

Taking several measured breaths, Elverbane gulped. "Haephan."

"Haephan?" SonLara pointed next to her chair. "Can you shift right here?"

"Yes, mum," Haephan said. The boy disappeared and reappeared in the spot she indicated without a flash of light, change in the air or even the warp of space. She nodded approval.

Fear tickled the wizard that he was going mad.

"What do you think, wizard?" Haephan prompted.

Elverbane stared for several long seconds and exclaimed, "*That's* how you did it! That's how you did it!" He sat forward. "That's how he ate you!"

Haephan's hesitant mouth tugged with a faint smile.

"How'd you do that!?" Elverbane cried.

SonLara forestalled the boy with a hand on his arm. "Pull up a chair, child."

"Yes, mum," Haephan grabbed a stool and sat.

"Tell him your story," she said.

The story erupted from Haephan about his journey through Eden, down the Tree and into a strange cave underneath. He struggled to recall what happened next, but recounted how he found the seeds, escaped the dragons and returned to the surface. After shifting away under Cas'Doren's attack, he discovered he could run faster, jump higher and could now move from one place to another in an instant.

"I had no idea you were coming!" said Haephan. "I had to get away from that dragon, you see! And so when he tried eating me, I *jumped* away! And then I was under the ocean! I'd never been to the ocean, but I'd always heard about it and it was so big and I was about to drown and then I jumped—"

"Shifted," corrected SonLara.

"—shifted and I was way up in the air, and then I was like, in the water again! And this big fish *talked* to me! It talked to me! Said, uh, said it had been waiting on me! And then it grabbed the seed and went like, way down. Oh, and I was at the edge of the *world*! I was gonna fall off into the nothing and die and…" The story bubbled from the dramatic boy while ringing with incontrovertible truth.

Elverbane sat stunned as Haephan finished with a dopey grin. He knew he should congratulate the boy, hug him or somehow celebrate him, but did none of them. Instead, he stood, rounded the table and left.

"I'm going to the library," Elverbane croaked on his way out.

Upon seeing Haephan's sinking shoulders and the disappointment that Elverbane didn't seem to care about Haephan's journey, SonLara set her hand upon his shoulder. "Steady, young man," she said. "The road ahead will require tougher stuff than tonight demands of your heart. Take strength in your new ability. You have done well. Wizard Elverbane is struggling with himself, not with you. Go on to bed."

Tears welled before Elverbane pushed open the door to the stairwell and hustled from his quarters and their moment of madness.

41

Algodemere

Algodemere, Dragon King of Fedra, snaked through higher crosscurrents of frigid morning wind. The drake serpentia's long spinal fins rippled as he raced over thick cloud cover glowing in morning sunlight. Long tendrils whipping from either side of his snout piqued at the familiar scent of the La'Du Lira Al'Cular, an aroma absent for two millennia.

A squadron of similar dragons followed him through the thick cloud ceiling into an overcast valley drowned in slate and heavy billows of fog wandering rolling hills of heavy canopy.

Below the nimbostratal layer, rivers of moisture coursed between the low Crowns of Eden, merged deep in the valley and flowed out its southern end toward the human settlements. Dozens of the local dragon guard nestled in the scrubby flora shy of the tree line as the newcomers breached the ceiling.

Algodemere fired between two high peaks into the valley proper and banked north in order to begin a wide circle. A clear horn call burst from his nose and vibrated across the space to announce his arrival.

Moments later, Cas'Doren's midnight silhouette climbed from the gray soup below. A train of dragons followed him into an upward swirl to match Algodemere's circuit. The two narrowed their flight paths and altitudes until within a wingspan of each other.

With several bursts of the nasal horn natural to his long black snout, Algodemere entreated to Cas'Doren, who returned a long, sharp blast and veered into Algodemere, who twisted and blocked the coming blow and retaliated with his hind claws.

The two fell into a diving tornado of slashing, hitting and clawing. They broke, banked and climbed again for a second round. This continued for several minutes before Algodemere cried his horn three times and Cas'Doren cried his twice, the first to show his loss, the second to show his respect.

Algodemere flew on Cas'Doren's wing for several minutes as a display of unity before the magnus draco led him and his entourage to a small clearing north of the La'Du Lira Al'Cular in a gap between inflowing mists.

All but the kings landed first and created a circle for Algodemere to land, who offered a regal bow to Cas'Doren as he alighted and touched down with thunder.

All hail Magnus Draco Cas'Doren! Algodemere tipped his head, *Lord of Eden!*

And welcome and honor to Drake Serpentia Algodemere, Cas'Doren motioned his own display of honor to his lesser, *King of Fedra.*

We are honored to pay homage to the magnus draco who defeated Umphaedra Dominar, Algodemere bowed his head as fitting a fellow king. *All praise to Cas'Doren!*

The Fedrans blew their horns in unison, but Algodemere hesitated.

What is it, Algodemere? Cas'Doren asked.

Pardon, Lord Cas'Doren, Algodemere scanned the dragons behind him and noticed a heavy tension. *But what preys upon you and your dracos?*

Cas'Doren huffed and said, *An interloper has transgressed Eden and stolen something precious to me.*

Something precious? Has he stolen treasure?

Treasure most valuable.

Algodemere cocked his head. *And how much gold could he take, my lord?*

Gold? It wasn't gold.

Then what could he steal? asked Algodemere.

Seeds from the La'Du Lira Al'Cular.

It bears seeds?

Yes, very powerful seeds, said Cas'Doren, *which I have gathered over many long years as my horde.*

How long has it been seeding?

It began shortly after we took Eden, said Cas'Doren, *but I only recently discovered how powerful they are.*

Pardon my lord, but how powerful can they be?

Worth more than anything in all the world, said Cas'Doren. *I first thought them mere novelty—the holiest seeds fallen into this vast chamber, barely one a century, and untouched by any living creature until gathered in the dozens. When I discovered what they could do, I would wage eternal war to return them.*

For seeds? asked Algodemere.

Powerful seeds which have given me unique sight and powers beyond reckoning, said Cas'Doren, tiring of his questions but keen on Algodemere's prejudices from years past. *A cunning elfchild has stolen into my inner sanctum and taken them.*

An elfchild!? Algodemere reared his head. *Do they* dare *incite new war?*

Yes, Cas'Doren tipped forward his head. *They will bring down our wrath.*

Does my lord know from where this elfchild came?

We have prepared to venture there before you arrived, said Cas'Doren as he nodded southeast. *Those who came with the elfchild have returned to the human city of New Eden, where the apes fled after we reclaimed the valley.*

Humans, as well! They are involved? Algodemere asked. *This will be a mistake they will not soon forget.*

It will be a mistake they will not survive! Cas'Doren barked. His colony joined in the din. *Join us, Algodemere. We hunt elves again.*

A vicious smile spread across Algodemere's snout. *At last.*

42

Practice and Preparation

"Everything seems inverted," SonLara pursed her lips.

"Water flowing up instead of down?" Orzo asked.

"It's true!" Haephan scowled. "I saw the vision *after* I woke up. Just like I told you. It's a new world waiting for me."

"We believe you, boy," Elverbane said and took a slow breath. "Doesn't make it any less difficult to comprehend."

In a circle of four chairs, Haephan, SonLara, Elverbane and Orzo sat under whitish, hazy early afternoon sunlight bathing the third story courtyard of Ashmore Hall.

"How are we supposed to find it?" asked Elverbane. "And why does it exist?"

"I don't know," Haephan said. "But…I feel. Something. I have to do it again."

Orzo frowned. "Again?"

"Yeah..." Haephan said. "It's like...you know when you have to piss? And that it's to piss?"

Orzo nodded.

"It's like that. It will be another new place. But...I don't even remember how I did it! I had the seed and light appeared and suddenly I woke up in that...water stuff. Been feeling it since I got back."

SonLara exchanged glances with Elverbane.

"Perhaps you need to take another seed and go where this feeling directs you?" Orzo said.

"Is...is that okay?" Haephan asked Elverbane.

"Yes, boy," he said. "We don't know what's happening...but you should do as Orzo suggests. The subrim said you would herald new worlds. This sounds like it might be what you're doing. When you're done, you should return here. Do you understand?"

"Yes, wizard," said Haephan. "But how do I get there?"

"How did you get where you needed to go last time?" asked Orzo.

"I just...kinda thought about what I needed," said Haephan. "Then I *shifted* there." He smiled at SonLara's tiny nod of approval.

"Then gather everything you saw in your vision and when it's fully in your mind, shift," said Elverbane.

"Yes sir," said Haephan.

"Alright, are you ready?" SonLara asked. "This will be our final test."

Haephan fidgeted to psych himself. Each of his forearms lay in Elverbane's thick hands. Orzo leaned in as SonLara lifted a scalpel.

"You might want to look away, child," she said.

Haephan exhaled. "Just do it."

"As you wish," she said, pressed the curved blade to the skin on the inside of his forearm and made a three-inch cut a quarter inch deep. Blood bubbled out, streamed between Elverbane's hands and dripped upon a small towel laid across the stone at Haephan's feet.

Though the cut was clean and quick, Haephan hissed and squirmed. The cut bled for ten seconds, stemmed and ceased. While coagulating crimson clung to the wound and the drip line, the flow was gone.

SonLara exchanged her scalpel for a small wet cloth and dabbed at the cut, which sealed in the same direction it had been made and disappeared without scar or scratch.

"Great Self," Orzo breathed. "Is he an immortal now?"

In SonLara's eyes, the mantle's intricate structure sealed his injury before it returned to its natural place over his body and faded away. The expended energy replenished itself, though from where she did not yet know.

"Immortal?" asked Haephan.

"I thought there was only one immortal," Orzo winked.

"Who can say if he is?" Elverbane said as SonLara wiped clean the smooth skin. "But he heals quickly."

"He healed from massive burns and malnutrition in a fortnight," said SonLara. "I showed you the mantle earlier today in the study."

"Shouldn't we have an artist diagram what we saw?" asked Orzo. "This is amazing and worth further study. Who knows how we could use it to help people."

"Or hurt others," said Elverbane. "Make an army of men who heal from wounds in seconds and you'll conquer the continent without losing a soldier."

"Are you saying this is too dangerous to even try?"

"I'm saying I don't trust enough people here at Belfast to put it down in writing," said Elverbane.

"Even me?"

"You're *here*, aren't you?"

"We can't trust anyone more than as we have already," said SonLara. "We told you everything that's happened, professor, to use you as our control. Elverbane trusts you and I will trust you, but outside of this circle, no one else knows the true magnitude of the past month. Visits by the subrim? Directions to collect seeds from the La'Du Lira Al'Cular? And now this, the boy carrying the most powerful abrucari in recorded history? No, Professor Orzo. I think discretion is our most important course of action right now."

Elverbane turned to Orzo. "And you've never seemed surprised by our revelations about the subrim."

Orzo shrugged. "The things you and I have been through. You think a visit by some ancient spirit lord's going to phase me?"

Elverbane's brow drooped.

"What's an abucari?" asked Haephan.

"It's a mantle," said Orzo.

"What's happening to me?" asked Haephan.

"We don't know," Elverbane released Haephan's forearms. "We know it's for your mission, whatever that may be."

"Collecting seeds?"

"Yes, that," said Elverbane. "And whatever else may come."

"Like shifting?"

"Shifting is part of it."

"I like shifting," Haephan said.

"We're glad you do, boy," Elverbane said. "We need you to practice it, and in a place where no one can see you."

"Why?"

"You have a very special ability," said SonLara. "One that could draw the dangerous eye of people who would abuse you to gain it."

"But I can escape now!" Haephan smiled. "Right?"

"We're not sure," said Elverbane. "We don't know the limits of this ability, or even what side effects you may experience."

"Side effects? What's that?"

"Unintended experiences that come through an increase of power in one particular area of chemistry and energy," said Elverbane.

"Things that could hurt you for shifting," said SonLara.

"I can take it," Haephan puffed his chest. "Can't stop just cuz what could happen."

Orzo's smile was grim as he patted the boy on the back. "That's a good attitude."

Haephan beamed.

Elverbane scratched his beard. "Practice and be careful where you do it. Don't hurt yourself." He eyed the boy. "Don't be seen."

"Yes, wizard," said Haephan.

"Go on," Elverbane shooed him. "We have things to discuss."

"Yes, wizard," Haephan said, smiled and was gone.

43

Learning to Shift

Standing in the center of his room, Haephan scanned the shelf that once held Ian's collection and lamented that he had no idea where to find them. Once his disappointment ebbed, he let yesterday's vision fill his mind, full of water flowing uphill, trees growing sideways from angled terrain and a great hole in the world. He soaked in the details. As he shifted, an old desire interrupted the vision in his mind.

Icy wind plowed into Haephan and sent him staggering to the sparse yellow grass across a rocky landscape under an angry gray sky. He spun about, wondering if he made it to the strange place of inversions or if he had gone where he wished most to go.

His shoulders sank. A roughly hilled field covered in the yellow scrub and slate rock as far as the horizon. He feared he had gone to neither location when the rumble of thunder drew him to his feet. Climbing a nearby high hill, he crested its crown.

Heavy charcoal water rolled for endless miles under a ceiling of thick clouds that occluded the afternoon sun but for sparse, distant rays spearing from heaven. The knoll upon which he stood jutted out further into the ocean than the rest of the coastline and gave him an unprecedented view of the endless waters.

Heavy sheets of frigid rain razed him in sparse waves but did little to steal his wonder. He laughed as mountains of water thundered against the cliff base below and cast high its salty spray and added to the moisture soon soaking Haephan in his fine clothes.

"Heat," he chattered through teeth. As he shifted, he first recalled the lava world, panicked and thought of somewhere not so hot.

He must have shifted into an oven. A vast, gusty wasteland stretched away under a blinding, cloudy day. He gasped air that did little to satisfy his lungs. Abrasive gusts snatched at his soaked clothes and scored grit across his cold skin. He raised a protective arm and squinted against the relentless sand to search the horizon; at least there wasn't an exploding volcano above him.

He shifted to the first mound he saw. Despite being free of most of the violent grit, the wind here was yet more violent and dragged him across the ground. Haephan squat and scanned the world. Another mound stood across the wasteland in the thick desert haze.

Haephan shifted and fell through the air—it was no mound, but a mountain, one he overshot and now fell on its far side. He shifted again to the tip and continued to fall at the same speed. He neared the ground until, seconds from impact, he shifted higher into the air and fell even faster.

Panic filled his chest that he wouldn't be able to slow when he remembered the first night on the tree island—he had shifted from falling to flying sideways. He focused on "upward" and shifted again.

When Haephan ascended and slowed, he shifted again to the peak, appeared above its apex and plowed into the rocky ground. The boy curled up to clutch his head from the rough fall and his body slid downward on a steepening incline. He scrambled for a handhold when the slope disappeared and he soared into open space. He shifted again, but this time appeared next to a vertical rock face with nowhere to grab or land and continued to fall.

Panicking, Haephan searched for a destination without falling into a mountain and replaced the ground with distant ocean. He hit it so hard he wondered if he missed the water. Chaos sucked him across heavy boulders. Without a sense of up from down, Haephan reshifted to the yellow-grass outcrop he first found after leaving the school.

Haephan collapsed onto the wind-washed scrub, coughed water and dragged inhales.

Shifting proved more difficult than he had hoped. He rolled onto his side and lay for a while to rest his aching leg and hip. He huddled until warmth suddenly filled him as if he had gulped hot tea. He relaxed and relished the occasional gusts as clouds wandered above him.

Haephan lounged for hours to soak in the clash of stable coastline and wild ocean. Pale haze wafted from a yellow horizon until the air brimmed with its reflections. Shimmering herds of light wandered across the churning ocean beneath luminescent columns of afternoon sun that raked from the steely clouds over miles of roiling ocean and jagged coastal cliffs.

Hugging himself, he struggled with fear and doubt. Wet black hair clung to his skin while his big brown eyes soaked in every wave and wash. Mustering his courage and his focus, he shifted to the furthest tip of the jagged cliff before him and stood, fisted both hands, and hesitated as the waves thundered below. Beams of light lit the auburn-washed sea.

Haephan drew in the icy air, remembered that he needn't take one moment more than he could handle, and stepped off the edge.

Seconds stretched into minutes into hours before he crashed into the water far below. Torrents tossed, rolled, spun and sucked him about. He shifted into the sky to gather breath and fall again. The chaos soaked every crevice and enveloped every inch while it bathed, cleansed, anointed and baptized him in its violence.

Over and over, he shifted upward to fall again. He relished each crash and thrust. A calm overcame him as he loosed himself so completely, secure with the knowledge that he could escape at-will. Rapture filled him as he fell back and forth between the peaceful air and tempestuous water.

Suddenly Haephan wept. Unable to hold it any longer, fear disintegrated under his soul's desperate need to be free of the hopelessness that so long had held him in its grasp. His deepest heart realized he had found freedom—true freedom—from any bad place or bad person he might ever encounter.

Haephan sobbed as he let the waves snatch and attack him with concussive power. Safe from prying eyes, his tears lost themselves in the ocean's noise, his screams beneath its froth. He fell over and over again until he expended himself. When drained of the tightness he never knew had burdened him, he reshifted to the stony ledge and lay across the rock as the wind and spray reached for him in vain.

Haephan drew long, deep lungfuls of wet, salty air and rubbed his hands on the pocked stone beneath him. Patches of blue peeked through the slate ceiling of thick clouds racing across the sky.

Worn and exhausted, the boy nestled in his deepest peace. He climbed to his feet as wind whipped at his clothes. Prepared, baptized and ready, Haephan felt commissioned for the task before him.

"C'mon," he whispered under the roaring wind. In a blink, he was gone.

From the tips of arid mountain giants in Harbad to the depths of desert canyons in Son Defdon, to the jungles of Thema Carta and the mirror cliffs of Irie Sana, Haephan leapt great distances and followed his imagination across dozens of continental locations until his mind drowned in endless wonder.

When he could go no further, he discovered fields of high grass washing in gentle breezes filled with glowing flies that danced like the coastal waves of his baptism. A galaxy of bright, colorful stars painted the sky. When he verified the flies were harmless, he danced and played among them. They swirled about him as he ran and swayed to a natural music until he fell laughing. Their swirls brightened as they neared and tickled his magic.

Soaking in the stars in fades of colors he never knew existed, Haephan first wondered what had drawn it all together. New Gordonites said someone called the "Great Self" created the world and planted the Tree of Life. The Wrefthai, a cult living outside the city who sometimes visited the parks and cried from the boxes, claimed a creature of multidimensional mind drew the continent from a hole in his belly. A Rainhold man once told him an evil creature had attempted to steal the continent from heaven but had been shot with an arrow running away and dropped it here, a place suspended between the nether and the world above. Unsure what to believe, Haephan accepted its wondrous beauty until sleep tugged him away.

He knew not how long he slept before a rocking thunder jolted him awake under a dawn-kissed pink sky. He scrambled to his feet and rubbed his eyes. The fiery flies were gone, replaced by other insects hopping across the high grass.

Haephan swallowed a dry throat and coughed a few times as he collected his thoughts when the ground thundered again. A faint pumpkin haze built on the near horizon as the hill fell away. Thunder developed into a rolling cacophony that shook the ground and shivered the grass.

Curious, Haephan advanced on the sound when, from the far side of the hill climbed a cow with crescent horns on each side. Were they making the ground thunder? These, however, continued to grow until they towered thirty feet tall.

Sunrise struck and cast in silhouette the entire herd as it approached him through the clinging morning mists.

Ignorant of his puny size, the first few plodded by with hooves as high as his waist. Aware they could crush him without noticing him at all, he shifted between two running past.

Though he had little experience with livestock, he recognized them as oxen from herdsmen who sold them at Southdown market, though of monstrously different size. In the growing light, their color revealed a dull blue sheen on their fur. Soon, too many approached for him to navigate afoot.

Instead of fleeing, he grinned and shifted to the head of the nearest bull. Several tries and falls landed him upon its back. He gripped its thin mane and half-squat to take the animal's wild bouncing motion.

Though excited, the bouncing soon got to him. He shifted to another beast, and another, and another. He tripped a few times before he shifted across empty ground beside the herd and rolled to a stop with a stupid grin. He sat up as the herd thundered past, leaving deep grooves in the ground. He coughed at the clouds of dust billowing upward and froze at two figures staring down at him.

"HO THERE," a sky-filling figure loomed over him with hands on hips. "WHAT HAVE WE HERE?"

Haephan gaped.

"DOES IT SPEAK?" approached a second.

"I-I do!" said Haephan. He raised his voice and cried, "I DO!"

The first giant knelt closer. "HE DOES. AND YOU SPEAK BUNISH, TOO?"

"WHAT A STRANGE CREATURE," said the second as he bent over.

"I don't know what Bunish is!" yelled Haephan, "But I understand you! Do you speak Low Edenic?"

"LOW EDENIC? ARE YOU FROM EDEN, LITTLE BEING?" asked the first.

"No! But I have been there," said Haephan. "I am from New Gordon."

"WHAT KIND OF SENTIENT ARE YOU?" asked the second.

"Human!" Haephan cried.

"HUMAN? I THOUGHT HUMANS WERE BIGGER," frowned the first.

"I WOULD HAVE GUESSED DWARF," said the second.

"I'm a boy!" said Haephan. "And I'm small!"

"I SEE," rumbled the first. "AND WHY ARE YOU IN BUNLAND?"

"I'm…" started Haephan. "I'm passing through!"

"ON YOUR WAY TO WHERE?" asked the second. "MEN DO NOT ENTER BUNLAND."

"Am I not allowed?"

"NO," said the first. "IT IS NOT SAFE FOR MEN HERE. EVEN OUR SMALLEST OF CREATURES COULD EAT YOU."

Haephan puffed his chest up. "I can escape!"

"CAN YOU NOW?" asked the first. "IT IS EASY FOR THE YOUNG TO THINK THEMSELVES INVINCIBLE."

"HUMANS, I HEAR, DOUBLY SO," said the second.

"Whatever you heard, I'm not afraid to be here!" cried Haephan. "I just rode on the oxen!"

"THEY ARE NOT OXEN, LITTLE ONE," thundered the first

with a smile. "THEY ARE BAYBS."

"They're what!?"

"THEY ARE OUR BREED. YOU CALL THEM OXEN," said the first. "WE CALL THEM BAYBS."

"I see," said Haephan. "I thought they were giant cows!"

The two laughed as low, echoing thunder.

"WELL, LITTLE HUMAN," said the first. "WE MUST CATCH THE HERD. CAN WE CARRY YOU ANYWHERE? IT WOULD BE SAFER WITH US."

Haephan smiled. "Thank you! But I will make my own way! I have more places to go, still!"

"BUT HOW WILL YOU TRAVEL?" asked the second one.

Haephan grinned and cried, "Close your eyes and count to three, and you will know that I have moved on safely!"

The two giants traded smirks.

"If you find me, then you may carry me!" laughed Haephan.

"ALRIGHT, THEN," the first one stood to get a better view of Haephan and the ground round about. "GO AHEAD AND TRY TO HIDE."

"Hide!?" laughed Haephan. "Goodbye, giants! I may come back to visit!"

The two smiled.

"Now close your eyes!"

Smiling as they obeyed, the two waited in silence to the sound of the morning crickets buzzing and the gentle wafting breeze. The first cracked an eye a few seconds later, thinking the child would attempt to hide behind his heels, before he scanned the ground with intrigue. He nudged the second, who also looked around. Both turned with care, stepped aside and checked their feet in case the small human attempted to hide close by. In short time, both stood dumbstruck.

Where had he gone?

44
Dragon Tears

Depp rolled a metal disc over his fingers while he reclined in a wooden chair and propped his feet on the corner of a table. The disc's intricate metalwork caught his attention from among the litany of items taken from the child-murdering professor. Those items now littered a white cloth overlaying the center of the table.

Guilt tickled Depp's conscience about the affair, but he remembered that Haephan was the professor's responsibility. Depp attempted to save the boy while the professor seemed content to watch.

Morning sunlight dimmed as a petite, balding man, climbed the steps from the muddy street outside, shuffled past his guard and bowed. "Master Depp!" When his focus found the table, he rushed over and sat.

"Hey!" Depp dropped and kicked under the table at the man's stool. "I didn't tell you to sit at my table." One of his guards peeked inside.

Hashnoy retreated and cowered. "I'm sorry, Master Depp, so very sorry." He clutched his hands while he lusted for the table. "I was just excited, you see. Very excited. I could feel these things when I got into town."

Depp stilled. "You could?"

"Oh yes," smiled Hashnoy. "Very powerful objects, these things. Very, very powerful. Unlike any I've seen in years, I'll say. Years."

"Then take more care when you charge into my presen— house," Depp started and cut off. He didn't like sounding too arrogant.

"Yes, Depp, sir," groveled the man. "So very sorry. Please forgive me."

"Tell me about them."

The man uprighted and sat upon the stool before he bent over the items. His fingers waggled at each object. He licked his lips and rubbed them dry over and over, a nervous habit that annoyed and gave Depp reason to think better of his loot.

"Oh, well," Hashnoy smiled. "This here is a gauntlet." He pointed to a small concave disc with a fist carved in bas relief. "This would allow any magic user powerful telekinesis—the ability to move or hit objects much heavier than with normal magic. These are rather hard to come by in recent decades. The Winsterharven are buying these up something fierce."

"Really?"

"And this!" Hashnoy moved on. "This is the magical equivalent of a magnifying glass! Sort of. It lets you separate layers of magic for study. This one, here, you can rub and it will taste in your mouth like you're sucking a piece of strawberry candy. And this one here…well, that's interesting." He pointed at a ring of a snake eating its own tail. "Ah! This allows you to speak with dragons!" Confusion flickered across his face. "Are-are these all you have?"

Depp frowned. "I got these off a selfdamn professor of wizardry. They aren't powerful enough for you?"

"Oh. I mean, it's…" Hashnoy frowned. "These are very rare and powerful. A professor of wizardry you say? Makes sense." He frowned at the objects. "These aren't what I felt when you returned."

"They're not?"

"No, Master Depp."

Eyeing Hashnoy, Depp grabbed the corners to the cloth under the objects and bagged them. While Hashnoy frowned, Depp set a second, smaller sack upon the table.

As Depp had taken great patience to learn, Hashnoy only twitched like this when near very powerful objects. The man's bare-bottled excitement raised Depp's brows. Depp dropped his feet, sat up to ensure Hashnoy pilfered nothing, and undid the sack to reveal more objects.

Hashnoy's eyes widened with awe.

"What is it?" Depp asked.

"Oh, interesting indeed. Indeed! Where did you say you acquired these?"

"A professor who didn't need them anymore," Depp darkened. "Why? What is it?" Depp waited.

"Well now…" Hashnoy frowned. "I'm not quite sure what these are…"

Depp frowned. "But isn't that your trick? You can figure out blue items just by being near them?"

"Yes, of course," said Hashnoy, "but I have to have some idea of what magic can do for my mind to translate a particular thing. I don't think I can quite translate these. I—" His mouth opened as if hoping that speaking out loud would help him understand them, but it fished open and closed.

"Well?" Depp demanded. "What are they?"

Hashnoy's mouth opened for a moment before he spoke. "I-I don't know, but…they are immensely powerful. Unlike anything I've ever seen before. Anything."

Depp inspected the carvings—well-made but mundane in nature—and asked, "What do they do?"

"I can't imagine," said Hashnoy.

Depp realized someone might come for these objects when the light by the door blinked out for a brief second.

Curious, both turned to the doorway when screams erupted in the street.

"It's a dragon!" yelled Depp's guard.

"What?" Depp leapt to his feet, followed by Hashnoy.

"Fuckin' dragons!" he cried before an explosion of fire cast him through the door and across the floor with an acrid cloud of yellow and black smoke reeking of sulfur. Dragon's liquid flame spattered and ignited parts of the room while the man's brief screams of agony ended with a sickening gurgle from his melting throat.

Despite his terror, Hashnoy snatched for one of the carvings.

Depp swung out his fist over the table and waylaid Hashnoy, who staggered over the dead guard and crashed headfirst into the corner. Depp made sure Hashnoy hadn't grabbed anything before snatching the four corners of the cloth to sack the items. He prepared to flee through the back door when Hashnoy moaned. Grimacing, he stormed over the floor while the walls raged in flame, took Hashnoy by the collar, hauled him around the dead guard and out the back. He dropped him in the middle of the alley.

"TO ME!" Depp roared. His men who hadn't fled in terror converged from nearby alleyways as another dragon swooped low over the alley. Billows of black smoke erupted beyond the rooftops across the street.

Depp groped inside his makeshift sack, fished out Elverbane's small ring of a snake eating its own tail and pushed it onto his finger. He flinched as dark and terrible voices crashed into his mind with demands "for the elfchild."

"What's wrong?" asked one of his men named Breck.

"Scatter," said Depp to the group. "Take care of your families and your women. Gather at the cave tonight if you can. Go!"

All but Breck fled into the panicked town. More fires billowed into the air and screams echoed. "I'm with you."

"Good, man," Depp struggled to handle the crash of voices in his mind.

"Can you understand them?" Breck noticed Depp fingering the ring.

"Yeah," Depp frowned. "But I'll be damn—"

Where is the elfchild!? Where are my seeds, you filthy apes!

Depp coughed. "They want the boy."

"The one you said died? In Eden?"

A dragon banked low above several houses in the distance to their left.

"Yeah. I don't get it," said Depp.

"Well, maybe he ain't dead?" said Breck.

"This is why I keep you around."

"You are obviously in love with me," panned Breck, "but that's okay. Sara will understand." His dry humor and blank expression belied the danger of a town under attack.

"Hardly," said Depp as he slapped Breck's back, wondering if the professor had indeed caused the boy's death. How could a boy survive a dragon's attack? And if he somehow survived those jaws, why wasn't Haephan found after the professor struck the beast? What really happened out there? "Let's go."

Swinging wide of burning houses, they jogged along the street northward into the city's ruins. Weaving through buildings, they avoided wide roads and scanned the sky as they escaped the populated area. After emerging from one alley, Depp snatched a handhold and stopped.

"They're following."

A line of fire erupted in a copse of trees a hundred paces ahead.

It's moving north! cried a dragon.

Depp cursed and pressed against a wall with Breck close behind. "They're following us."

"How?" asked Breck.

Depp hefted the bag. "That selfdamn professor! Getting me in trouble even now."

"Get rid of it."

"I got a better idea." Depp squatted to undo the bag. "Let's split up. Take half and run through the ruins. Drop one item at every cross street. Make sure you don't chuck 'em randomly."

"Why do you care?" Breck asked.

"Cuz I want to know which of these things is drawing him to us," said Depp. "This is too valuable to just throw away cuz we're afraid."

Breck nodded.

"Go west and circle north. I'll head east, first, then circle around. We'll meet…" He thumbed out half the number of pieces to Breck. "By the half-moon ruin with the old oak."

Breck noted the second sack on Depp's belt. "What about those?"

"I'll take the risk," Depp said. "Go."

Splitting up, Depp parsed out the pieces across the ancient city and scrambled into a sink behind the large oak tree, backed by a round stone wall. Most of the tree covered him from the sky while he peeked over the wall at the rest of the burning city.

Breck slipped in not long after Depp arrived and asked, "You still have the ring?"

"I have to be able to hear them," said Depp. "Or we won't have a chance to avoid them."

Two distant dragons banked and dove through distant canopy. Two more joined them while fire continued erupting across the area.

Breck sank against the low wall near the tree while he panted for breath. Depp squeezed the snake ring on his finger while listening to the dragons scream about "living objects" and "no elves."

Depp realized the ring might be what drew them; his only hope to stay ahead of the dragons could kill him.

"What do they say?" Breck asked.

Depp listened. "They're arguing over whether what they've found is what they were looking for."

"The boy?"

"But all they've found is some object…One of those the professor had. Sounds like they were tracking him through whatever it is they're arguing over."

"What do thi—" Breck stopped as Depp grabbed his shoulder.

A deep flap of heavy wings rattled the air before a great shadow passed over them.

What have you found? a deep, terrible voice pierced Depp's mind.

My lord! answered a voice. *He is not here. We cannot find him!*

LOOK HARDER!

My lord, there are no elves here! Just a bunch of living stones!

It ran from the villages, you stupid sparrows! said the terrible voice. *If we have followed stones, then their carrier cannot be far. USE YOUR NOSES!*

"Self damnit," cursed Depp. "Let's head out. See you at the cave."

"Can we outrun them?" Breck peeked again at the dragons.

"No. Sneak, don't run," Depp knuckled Breck's arm. "Go."

As Breck tiptoed away, Depp stalked further into the city's outer ruins, discovered an abandoned, roofless home with two thick trees growing from its heart, and scanned for anyone following him. Inside, he hid behind the close-growing trunks and fingered the snake ring.

Growing restless as time passed, he reclined against the tree while he wondered what really happened in Eden, as well as the safety of his men. Breck had been with him since the beginning and had shared in troubles and spoils, alike.

Sighing, Depp reclined his head into the crook of the bifurcated trunks when his heart seized. Seconds stretched into hours as a great black comet crashed from the sky. Both trunks ripped apart under the dragon's terrifying force. Only by flaring his wings at the last possible second did the dragon keep from crushing Depp, too.

Pinned under the dragon's left paw, Depp's world spun under the dragon's ear-shattering roar.

Youuu… the dragon's long, beak-like snout drew near while broiling heat from its nostrils raked Depp's skin, *are not whom I seek.* The dragon turned his eye nearer the human. *Where is the wizard and the elfchild?*

Depp struggled to breathe under the shock of the dragon's attack and weight of his paw.

Speak, human, or die in my teeth, the dragon's thoughts pierced Depp's haze.

Depp attempted to reply before the dragon thrashed him and released pressure from his lungs. He cried in pain as the dragon's fingers viced his wrists to his waist.

I know you can understand me, human…but you are no wizard, the dragon said. *Where are your blue companions?*

"I don't know!" Depp coughed with a bloated red face. His temple veins bulged. "Great self, I don't know!"

You lie! the dragon's voice struck him again as the great claws contracted on already broken fingers. Depp feared his hips would break under the agonizing pressure. *Where is the wizard? Where is the bloody elfchild!?*

"No wizard! Just a professor!" Depp rasped in terror. "No elfchild. A boy!"

"*A human child!? How!? Where are they!?*"

"New Gordon!" coughed Depp. "New Gordon. He's down there!"

Where is this New Gordon? Describe how to get there.

"South to the Vitner Canal!" Depp groaned. "Follow it to New Gordon. Big city. Wizards! A full conclave!"

And the child! Where is the child!?

Depp despaired. "I saw you eat him!"

Eat him? NOO! the dragon thrashed Depp. Something popped in his back. *That little morsel can fold space. If he came with the wizard, he will have returned to him.*

Fold space? Depp grimaced. "I don't know what that is! That's all I know!"

And the seeds! Give them to me, said the dragon.

"I—" Depp managed. "I don't have no seeds!"

Open the sack you little worm, said the dragon as he relaxed his top fingers.

Depp's strained arms flopped out as blood burned again into his muscles. He made every effort to move them, to reach for the sack lying next to him to avoid his head being bitten off by the dragon. The dragon waited as his limp hands grasped at the sack and untied its top. Upending it, the carvings spilled out across the roots. Cas'Doren leaned over a nearby carving and licked at it before thunder rumbled in his throat. *These are not the seeds.*

"That's all I have!" Depp moaned. "I swe'r!"

Then you, too, have been deceived, Cas'Doren tilted his head to eye the carving for several long seconds before he flicked Depp into the stone wall of the house. The beast leapt into the air and flapped his massive wings to gain altitude.

The stone wall filled Depp's vision before going black.

45

Isheim

"No no no," said Isheim. Long white hair swept in curls over her painted face. Shadowed eyes blinked at the mirror as she turned left and right to inspect the multicolored dress that lifted her bust but did less than she liked for her hips. Isheim's red lips pouted. "This will just not do. Take it off."

Dressed in the crimson livery of her household, Isheim's three female attendants took their time to unfasten and remove the delicate dress from their mistress. After stripping her to a thin shift, they set the dress aside and raised the next in cue, a deep-necked sleeveless affair of bloodred trimmed in lacy black that showed most of the interior of her petite bust almost to the base of her abs.

Once inside of it, she raised her chin, cast back her shoulders, lifted her chest and slender arms, and pointed out her delicate fingers. She whipped her hair for effect and smoothed her furrowed brow. Wrinkles wouldn't do—especially from worrying about the whole debacle with Nick the night before last.

For the first time in centuries, Isheim worried about her husband. Feelings long smothered now simmered in her chest.

"Mmm…I'm missing something," she said. She raised her chin to try and shake away the tightness in her stomach. "Ah, yes. Put my hair up."

Two of the three put up her hair in a sprawl that hung about her head, accentuated her long, slender neck and dove into her attempted cleavage.

Isheim readjusted her small breasts for maximum curve.

"Three hours," she huffed. "This is all I have for next week's ball. This will not do."

She wanted to stamp her foot.

"And this hair is less than acceptable. It's rancid," she said and scowled at the attendant in charge of her hair. "You're dismissed from service."

The attendant paled, curtsied and left, now dismissed entirely from palace service.

"Summon another one of your kind. And also the tailor," she spat. "Great Self, this is awful." She put her hands under her breasts and pushed them up again. "Self-damnit."

"My queen?" her door attendant approached with a curtsy.

"What is it?"

"The krys is at the door."

"He can't see me in these dresses," Isheim said. "Tell him I'll be out directly. Hurry, grab my sephan and wrap it around me."

Her remaining attendants rushed to shed the red dress, wrapped a long white sephan about her and tied it off around her waist. She combed out her curls with her fingers while she stepped into her slippers.

Fear pitted her stomach that Nick had come about the reindeer incident, which she had forbidden discussion of throughout the palace. She would not have rumors that the krys might somehow be losing his mind, especially as she worried about it, herself.

Isheim glided from her dressing room, through her bedroom and out into her parlor wreathed in expensive paintings and intricate vases. Thick, exotic rugs padded the ancient wooden floor. Bathed in the light pouring through a tall narrow window next to her grand fireplace, the krys stood in his crimson shirt over black trousers tucked into auburn boots. Why did he always wear such common clothing, especially when she bought him so many other wonderful outfits that made him handsome?

"My krys," she offered a curtsy, hoping he might take notice of her paints and figure.

"Dismiss your attendants, Isheim," Nick said and stared out the window.

"Is this about the reindeer?"

Nick waited. At her nod, the attendants curtsied and left.

Her stomach pitted at his mere presence, and further at his somber face.

"Isheim," he started. He took a good look at her and marveled at her beauty. "We must talk."

"Of course," she smiled while her stomach sank. "Would you care to sit?"

Nick paced among her chairs, past the cold fireplace and into the light of the window on the far side. "Something has happened."

Worry filled Isheim's mind. Despite her prohibition on discussing the incident, drama among palace staff pitted her insides to near breaking. Each new failure felt like one too many. She wet her lips. "What is it?"

Nick peered through the far narrow window as if it hadn't the same view as the one nearer Isheim.

Had he wanted to stand apart from her? Isheim held her belly.

"I know everyone is talking about the other night," he said.

"Yes," she said. "I do worry."

"Worry?" he asked. "I was perfectly safe."

"I have never seen such a beast," Isheim struggled with how to respond.

"It was a fine one," he said. "But it's where it took me that I've come to talk to you."

"Took you? I watched you," she said. "You just…sat there."

At first silent, Nick asked, "What do you mean, 'sat there?'"

Isheim's brow twitched. "My krys, you climbed upon the stag." She waited. "And sat there. For hours."

"I—" Nick started. "What do you mean, sat there for hours? It took me away."

"Away, my krys? To where? You sat upon that stag and did not move for many hours. We were very worried."

"No. That's not true. It took me. It *flew* me thousands of miles!"

"I'm sorry," she said as terror welled in Isheim that Nick was losing his mind— had *lost* his mind.

"I spoke with a *subrim*!" he said.

Isheim gasped.

"The reindeer asked for me. An attendant came and escorted me to the stables where it told me to climb upon its back, where it took to the air and flew beyond Lubar's Peak!"

"My krys, it is true a white stag appeared in the stable and that you emerged shortly thereafter, but none of the servants I have queried spoke of it…speaking to you or anyone. You merely climbed upon its back and sat. When finished, it turned and— well, yes, it did fly away."

"Isheim," Nick crossed the room. "I spoke with Suthene, Archon of the Great Self, within the bosom of the Kardur Montserrat."

Isheim stared.

"She has commissioned me— us, to a new mission."

"The Kardur Montserrat? In the Zulta'Mans? That's thousands of miles, Nick. How could you have travelled so far so fast without a rimsportal? No creature can reach such speeds!"

"Aren't you listening?" he asked. "A subrim has commanded our household."

"What? This is mad. My lord. A subrim? Subrim haven't been seen in this realm for ages."

"A subrim came and spoke with me."

"Are you sure? My krys, you sat upon that stag for many hours. How it even got into the stable, I don't know, but it never spoke and it could not have—"

"Do you call me a liar?" snapped Nick.

Isheim could not respond.

Nick turned away to cool.

Clearing her tight throat, Isheim asked, "What did she tell you, my krys?"

"We are leaving," he said.

It took a few moments for his words to register. "Leave? What do you mean? Are we going on a trip?"

Sadness tempered Nick. "We're leaving Aminrale. For good."

"I don't understand," she said. "What do you mean, leaving Aminrale?" Her brain struggled to grasp his statement. "Who is?"

"Our household."

"Our household?" she asked. "Why would we do such a thing? I don't— what are you saying?"

Nick approached and took her arms. "The royal household is stepping down from the throne. We are leaving Aminrale and its people for a new land and a new purpose."

Isheim remembered to breathe as her mind attempted to grasp the meaning of this mad idea—that a royal line would leave its own people. Had Nick truly gone mad? "This doesn't make sense! Leave Aminrale? How could we do such a thing? We have laws. And duty! We have a duty to—"

"To the Great Self, above all," Nick's deep voice cut her off. "And he has commanded this."

"But *how!?* The Great Self doesn't meddle in common affairs! And what possible reason could he have to pick us!?"

"Because of my gift," Nick said.

"Walking dreams?" asked Isheim. "Why would he need you? Or us? This is crazy, Nick."

"This is the way it is!" Nick yelled and cut off. "We're leaving. Seagol and Hagal are already on their way here."

"Krys Seagol? Of Kukhel?" Isheim's eyelashes fluttered. "And Sgaar? Why?"

"They are coming, too."

Isheim lost her words.

"We have until the Green Moon," Nick's voice softened.

"Are you…*absolutely* sure, my krys?" she begged.

"I…can only speak to what I experienced," muttered Nick. "Prepare for the arrival of our fellow krys." At the lost look on her face, he raised his hand, as if to touch her cheek, but she flinched. He retreated and, thinking better of it, made for the door.

Isheim didn't want him to go away, or fail to touch and help her understand, but also couldn't absorb the enormity of it all. "The what? The green moon? That's barely a month away! And where are we going!?"

Nick opened the door as the attendants waiting outside rushed from the keyhole. "I don't actually know." He left.

Her tight-lipped attendants filed in before Isheim sank to the floor and clutched her skirt.

"My lady!" her attendants circled her. "Are you alright?"

"He's…" she whispered. "He's lost his mind."

46
The School

Haephan emerged from a small bush on the Belfast campus under a cold midmorning drizzle which cut through the fine clothes Elverbane had bought for him, now that they had been bedraggled and soiled like attire from his Rainhold days. Students and faculty scowled but otherwise ignored him until one wizened professor approached with a scowl.

Haephan's toes sank into lush grass held sacred at the school—only teachers were allowed to cross it. Students circumvented them by long gravel paths. He smiled at his toes when the professor approached.

"Hear!" the professor raised his finger. "Who are you and who allowed you on these grounds?"

Haephan furrowed his brow. "I allowed myself."

"You impertinent little vagabond," the professor reached for him.

"That's not nice," Haephan said from behind him, having shifted.

The professor jumped and spun. "How did you do that?"

"Do what?" Haephan asked before he shifted again, this time to the

Belfast Dining Hall. He stepped out from between two potted plants in the foyer to the surprise of students on their way out. Grinning, he padded barefoot over the stone floor along the forward wall of the grand dining hall as students rushed out late for classes. Haephan entered the serving hall and grabbed a tray as the ladies behind the glass pulled food away.

"Excuse me?" Haephan raised his hand. "Can I get some? Please!"

"Boy, what did you get yourself into!?" Cook Emira appeared from a storage room and set her bowl on a nearby table.

"Good morning, cook," Haephan said.

"Wizard Elverbane won't like you running around like that," said Emira. "Especially in here!"

"Told me to go out for some chores and come back," said Haephan. "I'm back."

"You're gonna eat in the rear," she sighed. "I won't have you looking like a tramp in the dining room. Come on." She summoned him around the tray line with a tilt of her head. He left his tray behind, rounded the row and passed a score of white-frocked attendants wiping the serving stations, through a pair of doors into the main kitchen. She handed her bowl to a younger server, dusted her hands, motioned for Haephan to follow into the back locker and pointed at a barrel. "Sit."

Haephan obeyed and waited as she left. Dry stores of flour, salt and sugar, canned jars of vegetables and fruits and several boxes of eggs surrounded him from parallel rows of shelves. If what he'd learned was correct, agricultural studies students spelled many of the foodstuffs for long storage until removed from the shelves.

Returning, she set a plate of food and a glass of juice on the adjacent barrel, pulled silverware from her apron and handed them over. "Eat and go." Despite her stern tone, she set her hand on his head as she left, found grease on her palm and veered toward the nearest sink.

"Thank you!" Haephan said, bent over the barrel and shoveled it into his mouth. He barely took time to wash it down when he sensed someone standing in the doorway. Looking up, he grinned. "Hey, Son-Lara!"

"Hello, Haephan," she smiled. "My, what have you been into?"

The boy's stupid grin stretched from ear to ear. "I saw giants! Great big giants with hyuge cows! They had these great big horns and were, like, as big as this building!"

SonLara's brow climbed. "You saw the men of Bunland? You have traveled a great distance. How did you find them?"

Haephan chewed on a forkful of hashbrowns. "Dunno. Danced with light flies last night. When I woke up, they kinda came up out of nowhere and I-I jumped on them! I shifted on them! It was so amazing!" His voice climbed so that the ladies in the kitchen slowed to listen to his rather strange but vivid imagination.

"I see," SonLara said. "Sounds like you had a very interesting day yesterday." She noticed his filthy state.

Haephan beamed and asked, "Did you know I was here?"

"We have business, young man," said SonLara. "It's time we sat down with Wizard Elverbane for your next task."

"Yeah, I gotta get another seed."

"Come," she said. "You need to wash before we meet with Wizard Elverbane. He will not be pleased with your current disposition."

"Yes, ma'am," he pushed off the barrel and followed her through the kitchen where all the cooks curtsied to her. Cook Emira snuck Haephan a wing and gained a smile breaking across his dark face.

Haephan held open the door for SonLara before they followed the paths toward Ashmore Hall.

"Priestess?" asked a man standing off to the side of the path who removed his hat.

"Yes?" she slowed.

"A message from Mayhouse," he ducked his head and offered her an envelope.

"Thank you," she handed him a coin and motioned for Haephan to continue.

Glancing at her envelope as they advanced, Haephan chattered about the desert and ocean, omitting his more emotional moments, and everything else he encountered across Pangea. He finished with the "baybs" and Bunyans—as SonLara corrected him.

Entering Ashmore, they climbed to Elverbane's suite where, at SonLara's direction, Runa prepared a hot bath. Haephan scrubbed between his toes while soaking in the steaming hot water with a splash. While he continued scrubbing—a complete luxury—he pondered what the coming days might bring.

Anxiety and fear were inescapable elements of life in Rainhold. Yet since coming to Belfast Bluff to serve the wizard, he had begun to adjust to life without constant fear of knifing, slavery, starvation or rape. Since receiving his "mantle," as SonLara called it, he said a warm emotional blanket had wrapped around him that fended off the worst fear and doubt. While still uncertain, his unbearable misery was gone. He was almost happy, and in its own strange way, it made him uncomfortable.

He climbed out and toweled off before dressing in a second set of clothes which Elverbane had commissioned for him—a fortune, for sure. He combed out his thick black hair when a knock on the door preceded Elverbane's brogue.

"Haephan, do you have any filthy clothes you can wear?" he opened the door and blinked at the bright light shining through the window. "You're about to go out again."

Standing over the clothes hamper with his arms extended to drop his filthy rags, Haephan exhaled. "Yes, wizard."

"Hurry up now," Elverbane motioned with mail in his hand and shut the door behind him.

Haephan grimaced and changed once more into his dirty rags. Scratching his chest, he returned to the main room where SonLara sat in her usual chair by the empty fireplace.

"Ah, SonLara," Elverbane followed Haephan from the hallway. "I'm about to send Haephan out again. Did you need to talk to him before he left?"

"He already knows his next task," she said as she tucked a letter into an open envelope. "Instinct appears to be driving him."

Elverbane took a seat at the table to check his papers. "Good. We can conjecture all we like how this is supposed to happen, but sometimes I feel as unprepared as the youngest student."

"The Great Self will see this through to the end."

"I hope so," said Elverbane. "I'd not like to see a subrim again any time soon."

SonLara smirked and noted Haephan back in his rags. "Dirty clothes?"

"He's about to head out again," said Elverbane. "Better not to keep ruining them."

"I think it might be in our best interest to have several ruddy outfits made for his travels," she said.

Surprised at the appropriate and logical conclusion, Elverbane said, "When you return, boy, you'll go to a tailor."

"I can't afford that," said Haephan.

"I'm paying for it," Elverbane said.

"Yes, wizard," said Haephan.

"Now, do you know what you need to do? We need more seeds from Eden. Now that you can..." Elverbane looked to SonLara. "Shift?"

She nodded.

"Go get as many as you can. In and out. And be safe. Bring them back here." He pointed at a lidded wooden box at the end of his large table.

"Yes, wizard."

"I'm...I'm very glad you made it through Eden, boy," said Elverbane. "I thought we lost you." His sudden kindness surprised Haephan. "I-I'm sorry for putting you in danger. When the dragon attacked...I was afraid I'd have to live with that. I've had to live with too much. I'm glad you're here with us."

Haephan gulped. "Thanks, wizard."

"A'right, be off with you," said Elverbane. "Remember, we'll get you better clothes for next time. Oh, and don't forget the sack."

Haephan nodded, grabbed the sack and smiled before he disappeared.

* * *

After the exchange, SonLara tapped her hand with the envelope. "I will be gone for most of this week on my own errand."

"Oh?" Elverbane asked. "Will I see you at all?"

Noting the obvious disappointment in his voice, SonLara hadn't quite figured out what she liked so much about him. "I expect to be unavailable," she tapped the letter in her hand. "But the weekend would be a welcome respite."

"I know I've been spending a lot of time down at the Blue Nile lately—"

"Your bond with the owner is quite understandable," she said.

"Earnest saved me," said Elverbane.

"A friend, indeed."

"Oh, I suppose Earnest is friend to all his customers, but he saw me at my darkest," he said. "A bit like Orzo."

"Your companion professor?"

"Aye," said Elverbane. "Was there for me after Tuthomere. Don't know how I would have survived without him."

SonLara waited.

"Anyway," said Elverbane as he emerged from his thoughts. "Are you…?"

"I must leave," she said and rose. "But I will see you this weekend."

"As you will," he raised a hand.

SonLara nodded in kind, pondered a moment, glanced at the empty lidded box and left. Though Elverbane occupied a space in her thoughts, the lidded box invaded. Ever since the seeds became a goal, her mind had raced—to acquire one for study would achieve long-sought plans the Andonese would not soon forget. She wondered if and how she might gain one for her people. Would it violate the subrim's commission?

One way or another, she would do all she could to send one home to Andon. For now, she hefted the envelope and headed back to her quarters to prepare to head into the city.

The man and wife in prison had been located.

47

More Seeds

Haephan appeared among the tall grass of the dark, starry space beneath the La'Du Lira Al'Cular.

Shifting felt instant; he was in one place, then the other without wind or flash. Its simplicity could be a great advantage when picking. He could pickpocket wizards and nobles and anyone else. They could never catch him!

"HA-!" he erupted, then shut his mouth.

A dragon across the cavern raised its head. A moment later, it licked its snout, ruffled itself and returned to sleep. Nearby, another tiny dragon snored gentle purrs of glowing light.

Haephan searched for more seeds, now unafraid of the beasts who might attempt to attack him. No shadow could hide seeds from his powerful gaze, and nothing resembling a seed lay among the grass.

He shifted into the branches of the massive Tree above him. Drizzle wafted downward through its canopy and chilled the air. He scanned the branches for seed-sign when the sound of a congregation drew his attention. He shifted closer to the north side of the Tree and found a great vertical cave many times larger than the rift through which he escaped during his first, harrowing adventure.

Inside, hundreds of dragons crawled and settled. Despite its darkness, he could have counted every creature within sight and identified its color.

At its heart, Cas'Doren posed upon a great mound while a long, snake-like dragon wove back and forth before him at its base.

Haephan walked along the branch in the soft mottle of misty sunlight to draw nearer and get a better view. Beneath Cas'Doren, a panoply of seeds shimmered from his new nest.

You do not understand, Algodemere, said Cas'Doren. *Seeds are borne only once every century and score. We must follow this evidence to New Gordon at once. Do you know what kind of effort I've gone through to gather and keep so many?*

You are mad, my lord, said Algodemere. *We searched New Eden and found no evidence of elves, human armies or seeds. Now, you wish us to attack a city with more wizards than Al'Infria ever boasted at the height of Aman'Kur? For seeds!?*

Cas'Doren snapped at Algodemere but would not stray from his nest, giving Algodemere easy room for retreat.

Witness the mighty king upon his nest! Algodemere erupted to the congregation. *He is thus so mighty as to be the first king to have one like a dragaina! With no gold or treasures of worth!* He barked bursts of fire as laughter poured from his mind.

I sacrificed a dozen slithereens to get these back from beneath the Tree, Cas'Doren's curling lips exposed long fangs backlit with a huffing fire as he tracked Algodemere's snaking. *Speak no ill of their sacrifice to return my horde.*

Sacrificed, you say! cried Algodemere. *They ate many of the seeds themselves, did they not!? You ate them for dwindling your worthless horde. They lay down there for days, sucking up countless little pods. Did my serpentals not find them laying about drunk and high with but a bare handful left from their feasting?*

THEY TOOK MY TREASURE! Cas'Doren roared. *Dracos of Eden should know better.*

What a dragaina he's become! Algodemere cried to the colony. *He can't leave his precious little trinkets like eggs unhatched!*

SILENCE! Cas'Doren roared with a spout of mushrooming fire that flashed the chamber with its light.

Algodemere clapped his jaws over the billow and swallowed it in a clear and audacious challenge. *Silence me, yourself.* Algodemere snaked backwards while facing Cas'Doren in a mock retreat, daring the magnus draco to leave his nest.

You overstep yourself, Algodemere, growled Cas'Doren. *What I have done is to increase the feeding grounds of our kind—*

You've stuppored yourself! Addicted your mind to these seeds! You have chased phantoms and now seek to take us to start a new war with the wizards over podseed. You claimed an elfchild stole from you and yet we have found no evidence! There was no scent of young elf in any city we burned!

Cas'Doren charged a few steps, hesitated and retreated to his nest.

Haephan gained a better view of the seeds and tried to count them before Cas'Doren covered them again.

Fools! Algodemere laughed. *He is caught upon a snare. I will call upon the council and have you declared unfit!*

You will do no such thing! Cas'Doren reared upon his hind legs and spread his midnight wings. *Or I will kill you, myself!*

Kill me!? Ha! Algodemere barked. *The rules stand for you as us all! You cannot kill me without violation of our laws, laws written long before even Umphaedra!*

Our laws be damned to question my authority!

As is appropriate by our laws! Algodemere said. *Try and stop me and see if you don't lose every one of those precious seeds.* He coughed fire several times while eyeing the nest.

Cas'Doren charged Algodemere, whose loose, open coil took the strike and snaked around him. Both rolled into a melee of flames and claws that cast dust and debris into the air.

Cas'Doren's colony and Algodemere's entourage retreated while the two clashed with razors and flame. The two groups eyed each other but would not engage in combat while their leaders fought, themselves.

Algodemere surprised Cas'Doren again and again. In a few short twists, Cas'Doren lay flailing and gasping in Algodemere's doubled coil.

I claim victory! Algodemere spit blue fire in a long high arc that lit the chamber. Dragons recoiled at the sight of Cas'Doren so quickly bested. A litany of their voices filled the air before the blast of a warning horn stilled the congregation.

Everyone gaped at the small biped who crouched in Cas'Doren's nest stuffing seeds into a sack. He didn't notice their attention until he struggled to stuff the final seed into the overpacked bag.

Tendrils of smoke swirled up from the shocked horde.

Algodemere's powerful eyes saw far more than a sentient being, but a blue human of immense magical power.

Hefting the final pod, Haephan grinned at them and disappeared.

With Algodemere's shocked coil loosened enough for Cas'Doren to draw breath, the magnus draco whipped his powerful tail around Algodemere's neck and yanked the dumbfounded drake serpentia into the ground with a bone-crunching thud.

Rolling over, Cas'Doren vaulted atop Algodemere, snatched his head in his fore talons and pounded it several times into the unforgiving rock peeking above the sea of sand. Yanking his barbed tail from around Algodemere's neck cut through one of the drake serpentia's eyes, leaving a stream of blood and fluid that Cas'Doren flicked over the cringing onlookers.

Algodemere's roar echoed far beyond the cavern and out across the hills of Eden before he fell limp.

Cas'Doren restrained himself by the very laws Algodemere had warned him of violating. The drake serpentia had been right: should Cas'Doren have killed him, the dragon kings would have come for his head, and however mighty, he could not best the convergerate even with the fourteen hundred dragons of Eden, as weak and sloth as they had become.

Instead, he straightened his bleeding shoulders and neck to return to his nest and assume his most regal pose. His head swam and vision doubled from the fight, fury raged at yet a second and more thorough burglary of his treasure, but he roared a horned note that reverberated and echoed long after he had dropped his head. Liquid black smoke poured from his snout over the unconscious foe.

I…am Magnus Draco Cas'Doren, he faced the dragons. *Who else dare challenge me?*

No one spoke.

Cas'Doren mustered his sanity. In his weakened state, flying to New Gordon would be the suicide Algodemere claimed. But how could he get his seeds?

My lord draco, an Amberdine Slipperant named Kaurust crawled forward into a grovel.

What!? Cas'Doren reared, ready to strike.

I have seen the child. I can now sense his flow, Kaurust bowed his head. *He moves across the continent.*

He does? asked Cas'Doren. *To where?*

He travels across Pangea with the stolen hoard, he waggled his neck. *He moves great distances. He is traveling out and away from New Gordon.*

Cas'Doren sank to his fore claws and drew nearer. *Aaah, my dear sight-hunter. What else can you see?*

Kaurust calmed with a growing certainty he would not die for speaking. *I see him alone and vulnerable.*

Fresh black smoke billowed from the fires raging in Cas'Doren's chest and out through his mouth. *Who is your finest?*

I am, my lord, Kaurust ducked his head.

Then go and meet the child before he can waste my precious seeds. Capture the boy or kill him. Whatever you do, bring me back what he has stolen.

Yes, sire, Kaurust ducked his head and took the air.

As he left, fear tickled at the edges of Cas'Doren's soul.

48

The Household

Nick and Isheim sat on opposite sides of the same seat as the carriage rolled down the shallow switchbacks from the palace. A crimson velvet longcoat trimmed in white fur hugged Nick's broad shoulders over a cross-wrapped white blouse beneath and dark trousers tucked into high red boots. Adorned likewise in a dress of red and pearl white, Isheim hugged the opposite window.

A gulf greater than the arm's reach extended between them as the carriage swayed over a stone road smoothed by millennia of traffic.

Isheim held her breath before forcing an exhale with obvious anxiety.

Shame and anger washed over Nick, first for believing the vision without question, and second that he would be asked to step down from his role as krys.

Why was he turning over so quickly to some supposed heavenly command? Was he certain he spoke with the subrim? Everyone in Aminrale believed he was mad. He heard the whispers of servants in the halls and prefects in their meetings. He knew they questioned his sanity. Ought he not as well?

Perhaps he was mad. How could the Great Self demand he surrender his life's purpose? Didn't his people need him? He certainly needed his people.

"Speak to me, wife."

Isheim clenched her jaw.

Nick scowled. "Have you nothing to say?"

"What would you have me say, my krys, that the servants haven't already spouted?"

"I don't care what they have to say, I care what you have to say."

"What *I* have to say?" she asked.

"Yes."

"Where was this same query before you decided to hand off your crown to the council?"

Riled, he clung to his decision even as he questioned it. "I don't need your opinion on an order I receive from higher authority."

"Am I nothing in your decisions, my *liege*?"

"Watch your tone," he snapped as his anger climbed. "I am still krys."

"I know," her voice flattened.

"Have you no mind for the journey ahead?" asked Nick.

"I have no heart for it."

Nick wondered if he had such heart, either. Over the past week, amidst constant whispers questioning his sanity, he, too, questioned the validity of the fast-fading memory.

Hesitant, Isheim gulped. "I fear."

Nick half turned his head.

"I fear you are mad and we cast aside our purpose because of it."

"I'm not," Nick insisted to himself.

"Are you not so sure?" she asked.

"Do you think I am happy to do this?" asked Nick.

"You seem so."

"I am not."

"Then why do it?"

"Because I cannot cast aside so easily the magnitude of my experience," Nick said even as he questioned himself.

"My krys," she said. "You sat upon that reindeer, but you went nowhere. Nowhere! You responded to no one. How might you have gone as far as you say you did? That is not possible without a rimsportal! This must be madness! Or dreamsickness, even! Surely, we can call healers to come and—"

"No."

"But Nick—"

"No!" said Nick. Uncertainty and fear threatened to overwhelm him. What if she was right? What if he was mad? With so many witnessing the same thing, how could he be more certain than them that he hadn't dreamt the whole thing? Though rare, dream walkers had fallen to dreamsickness before, where the dream state mixed with reality in ways the walker could no longer discern. Might Isheim be right? Though he was young, it was a remote possibility.

"What would you have me do, then? Walk openly into this madness? Support you—"

"Yes!" Nick cried.

"Like you have me?" she retorted.

Nick faltered as tears welled in her furious round eyes.

"Like you have me, Nick? While you go away into your dreams and…" she drifted off and looked away.

"I will do what I must do."

She dashed tears with delicate fingers to keep them from smearing her makeup. Her voice whispered, "No, you retreat to do what you want."

Nick's hands fisted the fabric of his coat.

The carriage continued to the Court Therendroy, a tree-lined plaza at the city's heart that served as a park, venue of celebrations and markets, and even hosted the decadal Trials of Henrif.

Beautiful buildings hugged either side of the road, packed with ancient trees keylit by approaching sunset. Warm, earthy reds dominated the city in a panoply of shades and styles, contrasted by occasional deviations in navy blue, charcoal black and various whites. Faded light refracted by low sheer clouds bathed everything in a gentle wheat ambience.

A tear threatened Nick's eye; he grew up near the city and had come often with his father on business. When his dreamwalking manifested, he apprenticed to the krys and had since lived at the palace.

Leaving Aminrale and his mission—however long unused—terrified him. How would he handle living so far from his people? Where was he going? Why should he?

Fury welled, again, within Nick.

He didn't want to leave. He didn't want to go on some holy mission to serve the Great Self's chosen. Were not his own people chosen by the Great Self? Why should others be special above his own? What elvish kingdom might he go serve? And why should he, a krys, serve anyone but his own people?

Nick struggled not to explode.

Like each time before, the visceral memory of Suthene brought him up short. He wished to say it was nothing more than a dream, but it felt too real.

His fury and fear did not ebb this time, but doubled as the whispers of his potential madness pounded in his ears. Wouldn't losing his mind make him feel as such an encounter were true?

When the carriage stopped, the door opened. An attendant put a stool into place beneath the step and moved aside.

A battle raged within Nick.

Isheim turned when he didn't follow her out.

Nick questioned himself. Could it really have been an archon of the Great Self? A holy subrim? Isheim and the others said he only sat upon that reindeer. Might he truly be losing his mind? Either way, he ought to pass the crown, but at least he might be able to retreat to a home near the city to live away from anyone he might hurt.

Surely, he could stay in Aminrale.

Yes. That's what he ought to do. He should surrender the crown—for the sake of his people—but he could remain here near his people and trust those around him. A subrim? Visiting him? A krys? To leave his people? That would make Isheim happy, especially after what he had done.

Gathering his courage, he climbed from the carriage to the council of prefects. An intricate wall of stone rose behind them—the backside of a stage built on the north end of the court. Most often used for public performances, the stage now served as a platform for his ultimate humiliation.

Nick greeted each prefect as their eyes questioned his sanity. He accepted them, even as he struggled to formulate what he would tell his people. He would admit that he ought to step down for his health and their safety, not some supposed holy mission from the Great Self.

The mere idea now made him want to laugh out loud, though doing so would only cement their certainty of his madness. Or ought he not, since it had to be true?

He planted his feet and mustered his courage. "Council of Elders, I have come to step down from my royal appointment."

"Are you sure, my krys?" braved one of the prefects. Hesitancy hung heavy over the group, caught between the desire to fight change and an equal need not to be ruled by a krys who could not discern reality.

"Nick," Isheim's pained, panicked whisper reached his long, pointed ears.

Nick took a slow breath. "I fear my wife is correct."

She stiffened.

"And I will surrender myself to the wisdom of this council," Nick's stomach lurched. "I— I cannot—"

Heavy hoofbeats interrupted him as Nick's personal attendant, Ephterehn, reined in so near to the council that they recoiled in panic. He leapt from the horse and offered a bow before saluting with his fist to his chest. "My krys."

"What is it?" asked Nick.

"They've come," panted Ephterehn.

"Who?" Isheim asked after a moment.

"Kryses Seagol and Hagal," he said. "Two entourages have arrived at the palace, together, just now, and asked of you."

Nick and Isheim stiffened.

"What? Why now?" asked one of the prefects before he locked onto Nick. "What does that mean?"

"Great Self," Isheim's pale face lost what little color had gathered.

Shame filled Nick at having retreated from his conviction, and the sinking awareness that Suthene had, in no way, been a fabrication of his mind.

"It means that by the green moon, I must surrender my crown and my home…and I will bid farewell to my people," said Nick. He turned to the prefect. "We are leaving."

49

Rescue

SonLara's carriage rumbled to a stop on the rough cobblestone street before the driver hopped down, hinged the steps and opened her door.

Her gleaming, hooded figure emerged from its shadow and glided to the street while two hulks descended from the rear of the carriage. Guards at the gate came to attention at their approach and raised hesitant weapons.

She stopped before them. "I am Priestess SonLara Alva Amferadon. Summon your captain."

One licked his lips at the sight of her, shared a look with his fellow, and backed through the gate to ring a small bell. Through the gate and the courtyard it guarded, a captain emerged from a windowed guard station built alongside two massive wooden doors leading into Stonebridge Prison.

SonLara noted the nearby bent light post she had seen in her vision. Her heart fluttered with reassurance she had reached the proper location as the captain crossed the yard, slowed at the sight of her, and approached.

"I'm Captain Consello," he said. "Why do you call?"

"This is Priestess Amfradon," said one of the constables. "She called for you."

"Amferadon," corrected one of her guards with arms thicker than the man's thigh.

"Amferadon," the constable ducked his head.

"Me?" asked the captain.

"I am here," she said. "I would see them now."

"Them? You mean the couple?" he asked. "Did Wizard Dufrain send you?"

She waited, as if it should be obvious.

"This way, priestess," he said and led her across the courtyard.

She stepped off, but when her two attendants made to follow, the other constables raised their hands. She stopped and refused to look back, even as the captain realized she hadn't followed him across the courtyard.

"You need them?" he asked.

"One woman and two men will hardly overcome your entire prison guard, captain," SonLara's voice clipped.

At his nod, his men stepped aside with wary gazes at her guards. They resumed their journey across the courtyard, past the hangman's gallows built along the right-side wall, beyond the watch station and through a small port door built inside the larger ones. They crossed a smaller inner courtyard full of doors and stairs leading to the first and second floor. He led them through an archway and down a long set of stairs that passed two-landings deep beneath Stonebridge into a musty reeking hallway full of rotting wooden doors with metal portholes.

SonLara had never encountered such a foul reek in her entire life, yet hid her discomfort. They wound among cells open and closed. In the distance, someone's agonizing scream echoed along the moist corridors and sent chills up her spine.

They came to a stop before a small door that opened to reveal a constable buckling his belt and freezing in mid step. His eyes widened in horror and his filthy face paled. He stood motionless, unable to reconcile their presence.

Without turning from the disgusting guard, SonLara said to the captain, "A shame what Wizard Dufrain will think of you when—"

Enraged, the captain drew out his sword and rammed it through the constable's heavy gullet. The fat man screamed most femininely before he collapsed. Death came slow as he spasmed around the sword sticking him through.

Terrified, the captain bowed his head and said, "Oh priestess, I did not know. What can I do to allay the—"

Her upraised hand cut him off as the sound of heavy footsteps announced fresh constables with short swords drawn. The captain raised his gauntlet to halt them.

"She has been here weeks, no?" asked SonLara.

"Yes, mistress," his voice quivered.

"Prison is a dangerous place, is it not?"

"Yes, mistress," he said.

"Then I will take the two with me and you will be remembered for how well you facilitated my visit."

"Of course," he ducked and bowed.

"Clear the cell," she said with a dismissive flick of her hand. The captain motioned constables inside to check the cell while others grabbed the dying guard and dragged him aside; he moaned in agony as the sword shifted his insides.

"Clear, captain," said one of the constables inside.

SonLara stepped over the pool of blood into the room and a palpable wall of stench within laced with the recent aroma of the constable's stinking cum. In the corner huddled a woman in a soiled dress who gaped at the exchange and the appearance of a pale glowing angel in her midst.

"Is it time?" moaned the woman in fear of death. In her fingers, she clutched fresh bread and a bowl of hot, thick stew lay nearby untouched, steaming with heat.

SonLara noted the dying man outside hadn't forcibly raped the woman—her desperation for real food had broken her into submitting to his lechery. How many prisoners the constable may have forced himself upon over the years could have warranted his death, but Son-

Lara hadn't enough evidence to convict him. Instead, she focused on the woman's obvious frailness and the motionless body lying next to her. "The man?"

"Is he dead, yet?" asked the captain.

His expectant tone revealed he had been waiting for the man to die.

One guard leaned over the man and said, "I think so."

"He—" Eva muttered as she stared at SonLara. "He is. Alive."

"Take him," SonLara motioned to one of the hulks standing behind her, who gently pushed constables aside to stoop over the body. SonLara motioned to the other. "Gather her."

While one guard lifted Eva from her corner, the other lifted the man so SonLara could draw near and lay a hand on his forehead. Her attempts to delve him with normal magic wafted away. She touched his filthy throat and waited until the faintest pulse of blood proved his survival. At her gesture, the two men carried them into the hallway.

"Thank you, mistress," he ducked his head again. "So much."

SonLara strode from the cell and led her men back the way they had come as if intimate with Stonebridge. Again, her exotic nature suspended mens' suspicions. She battled eagerness to race up the stairs and escape the foul stench oozing from the walls. She emerged in the inner courtyard with a guarded sigh of relief and waited on the captain, aware that appearing without him might raise suspicions, before letting him lead her out through the courtyard to the carriage.

Oncc there, a grating caw drew her to a large raven perched upon a nearby streetlight.

"Wizard Dufrain will remain unwise to what has happened here so long as you and your men are clear on how one of your dangerous prisoners took a careless constable's own blade and ran him through," she said.

The captain nodded slowly as his eyes darted back and forth. "Of course, priestess. And the couple?"

"They escaped in the chaos, did they not?"

He nodded.

"Good," she said. "Then this will be the last I hear or speak of it."

He saluted and half bowed again as she climbed into the carriage to sit beside the horrified woman huddled across from the guard still cradling her husband.

"To Mayhouse," she said after the door was shut.

When her second guard knocked on the ceiling from his perch on the rear of the carriage, it started forward.

"Hello, young lady," SonLara said. "I think it's time you told me who you are and why your husband is nearly dead."

Clutching her bread, a sob erupted from the woman's throat, followed by more, until all she could do was lean against the window and weep. Her energy spent, she sank against the wall and passed out with the small loaf still curled in her fingers.

50

Closure

Haephan smirked. Moments ago, he shifted into Elverbane's study, dropped all but one seed behind the wizard sitting at his large table, and shifted away before they could hit the floor. He giggled at the thought of the wizard leaping in shock or crying out in fear.

Instead of rolling ocean, he stood on solid ground drowned in thick, wafting smoke. He covered his mouth. The need that drove him to collect seeds and move him across space had brought him here, but this wasn't where he needed to plant a seed.

Haephan followed a low wall of stones, behind which smoldered a large pile of ash, a lone point that added to the endless river of smoke around him. Remnant boards and charred nails indicated a house had been burnt down, though it was hardly the only one, as he could tell. He wove between the walls and alleys until the smoke thinned to reveal a city of hasty tents strung out between trees growing in the ruins of stone buildings.

Haephan scanned the residents as they walked about with manic eagerness—a quality he witnessed in New Gordon among those who lost their homes to fire.

The trees seemed vaguely familiar, as did the terrain.

Why was he here? He had been thinking about planting a new world. He had the seed. What else did he need? Why had he appeared again in a place for which he hadn't aimed?

He prepared to shift again when something nearby called to him like the sound of his own voice, like a piece of himself was nearby.

Frowning, he followed the deep-rutted road between the heavy-stoned ruins and avoided carts and pedestrians. Pickers who drew too near found his hand on their fingers before they could slip into his pockets. He realized his fine shirt and trousers made him the mark he often sought while out in New Gordon and kept his head on a swivel. With his enhanced senses, he could smell the unclean children, hear their whispers and move faster than their fingers. He almost laughed at how easy it would make his own future picks—no one would ever see or stop him.

When he caught the fourth picker, he yanked too hard and sent the child screaming with dislocated fingers. The boy fell to his knees and clutched his hand.

"Just stay away," said Haephan. He grabbed the two fingers and wrenched them back into place to further screams. Shaken, Haephan moved on while the boy's cries faded along with the ebbing pain of dislocation. He warded future pickers by locking gazes before they could sneak up on him while he narrowed in on a small hut surrounded by dangerous, lounging men.

Like thugs common to Southdown, they appeared disaffected until time to thieve or fight. Something within the hut called him. He passed the building and its guards as if he were headed elsewhere before circling round to use trees to hide his approach. Peeking around a thick bush, he was surprised how well he could see across the distance, between other trees and through the filthy window into the hut as if he stood at the windowpane.

Within it, a sitting woman spooned food into the mouth of a man lying under blankets. Frowning, Haephan focused on the corner of the small room opposite the couple and shifted.

Now inside, Haephan scanned without moving and noted a man sitting behind him hidden from the window. First reading a sheaf of paper, the man's head popped up and locked onto Haephan. His gaze darted to the door, noted its latch and returned to the boy.

"How did you get in here!?" the man threw the sheafs to a nearby wooden chest, stood from his seat and yanked a blade from his belt.

Haephan spun, snatched his wrist and pulled it down. To his surprise, the man slapped on the wooden floor of the hut with a thunder and heavy oomph.

Startled, the woman fled the fight as the man on the bed gaped at the boy.

"Oh Self," the man moaned.

Haephan retreated from the man on the floor. "Depp?"

"You're dead!" Depp moaned. His half-crushed face drained of color.

"Nope," said Haephan as he cringed at the sight.

"But I saw you die!" Depp slurred and raised his left arm as if to protect himself. The door thumped with his guards outside attempting to get in.

Haephan raised his hands. "I didn't. I'm here. I'm alive."

Depp quivered.

"I didn't die," Haephan said.

"I saw it," said Depp. "The dragon ate you."

"No. He didn't."

The woman pressed to the window next to Depp's head as the man on the floor stirred.

"Breck? You okay?" she asked.

Breck noted the blood and the cut on the side of his hand. He snatched the knife and planted it in the floor. "Just a cut."

"You can see him?" Depp begged the woman.

"He ain't dead, Depp," the woman said. "I see him. He took Breck to the floor."

Depp paled. "How?"

"Let's just say I have a knack for getting out of trouble," said Haephan.

Depp nodded.

"But I came here for something," Haephan scanned the room.

"The stuff," said Depp.

"Yeah. Sure. Stuff."

Depp motioned to a sack sitting in the corner next to where Breck had been sitting.

Haephan ensured no one was behind him as the guards outside resorted to kicking at the door. He stepped to the corner and opened the bag. "My stuff!"

"You made 'em?" Depp asked.

"No," Haephan said as he pocketed the objects as fast as a pick. "But they're mine."

"What are they?" Depp begged. "They drew the dragons right down on top of us."

Haephan raised the last object from the sack—a steel feather—and enjoyed a relaxation of the inner drive ever pushing him forward. He tucked it into his belt. "Dunno. But I'm taking 'em. How'd you get them?"

Depp gulped. "I'm-I'm sorry. I thought the dragon ate you. I…took 'em from the professor."

"From Wizard Elverbane?" said Haephan. "That makes sense, now."

"Great Self," Depp moaned. "The Hero of Tuthomere? He said his name was Seth!"

Breck climbed to his feet and groped again for his knife. "How'd you get in here?"

"Same way I escaped the dragon," said Haephan as the door burst open and armed men pressed inside.

"Wait!" Depp moaned. The men hesitated.

"Those are ours," Breck snapped. "Get him!"

As they rushed him, Haephan disappeared. The men scanned the empty corner while Depp flinched beneath Haephan crouching over his bed.

"Glad the dragons didn't kill you," said Haephan. The men spun toward his voice. "Hope you feel better." He disappeared.

No one moved.

"Depp?" asked the woman.

"As soon as we can," Depp gulped, "we're outta here."

"Out," the woman pointed at the men, who nodded and left. When the door shut and Breck tended to his bleeding wrist, she asked, "What're we gonna do?"

"Prolly go straight. Dunno," he gulped. "But no more wizards. And no more Eden."

51
First Conference

"What do you think will happen, father?" asked Amerela standing opposite her father. Brilliant sunrise speared into the dusty library through broad windows to paint the eastern wall of Nick's private collection. Its brilliance bathed and outlined the girl's pale hair, bounced off the open books blanketing the long table, underlit her face and silver eyes. Her pale skin warmed in shadowed radiance.

Iphan sat at the far end of the table scrawling images with charcoal.

"I'm not sure," said Nick.

"Have you not spoken with them yet?"

"I sent a messenger for them to forgo the formalities and settle in for the night. We will breakfast shortly."

"Did you find anything?" asked Amarela.

Nick scanned his private collection. "No. Not sure I even read much of it, honestly. There's so much to read and so little time to do it."

"What were you looking for?" she asked.

Nick grimaced. "Some kind of precedent, I suppose."

"Pre-ce-dent…pre-ce-dent…" Iphan sing-songed while he drew on a sheet of paper nearby.

"For what?" Amarela asked.

"Subrim visiting the world, passing commandments, issuing dictates…" Nick said.

"Do you still question if this is real?"

"Heilbin and Sgaarsbad prove it's real enough," said Nick. "But I've never heard of something like this before. Even our most ancient records don't mention such things."

Amarela's silver irises shimmered as she scanned the books glowing in sunlight. "Surely there's something."

"Oral tradition tells us that in eons past, the subrim were much more involved in Pangean affairs, but we have no detailed accounts, just lore going back centimillennia and further. There's nothing concrete to…I don't know. I can't get a grasp on what's happening."

Amarela mused. "Perhaps you're not supposed to?"

Something shuffled off to Nick's left.

"My krys?"

Nick's eyes opened to the same table and sunrise, but both children were gone. An attendant waited on his left in a partial bow. "Yes?"

"Pardon me if I have woken you, my krys, but a guest has asked to speak with you."

A well-dressed young male stood in the archway leading to the greater library, where multiple stories surrounded a high chamber. He motioned for him to approach.

"My krys," said the young, dark-haired figure wearing Graelan cut and colors as he bowed with piercing gray eyes.

"Come, sit," Nick motioned across the table where, in his dream, Amarela had stood.

"I apologize," the elf obeyed. "I didn't realize you were dozing."

Nick raised his hand to placate. "Did you sleep well?"

"Very, my lord," said the elf.

"What is your name?"

"I am Uron, of Graela," the elf ducked his head.

"Welcome to Aminrale," said Nick.

"Thank you, my lord," Uron said. "I hadn't expected to be here."

"Why are you here?"

"I was on a limited apprenticeship with Krys Seagol when the subrim came to him. The krys invited me along."

"Are you in line for Graela?" asked Nick.

"I am among a few," Uron admitted.

"But not eager for it?"

"To be a krys?" Uron blushed. "And lead a nation as old as elven nations can be in our present age? It is a responsibility I am unsure I could live up to." Uron scanned the books across the table, noted Nick's tomes, and lowered his head, embarrassed. "I apologize, I should not intrude."

"You are well, Uron," Nick said. "Just because you become krys doesn't mean you have all the answers, nor should you try. There is too much in our grand world to capture in the mind of a single elf, however old or wise we might someday become. We ought to lean on the wisdom of others so long as we live."

"Wise. And whom do you lean on, my Krys?"

Nick struggled to hide his seizing heart and pulled on a grim smile. "Even I need reminding of that, sometimes."

Uron nodded.

Nick stood. Uron leapt to his feet. "Come, before we are late for breakfast."

Uron took a position on Nick's left as he followed him through the large library. "What do you think will happen, my lord? Where do you think the subrim is sending the three of you?"

"I do not know," said Nick. "She mentioned the Great Self's chosen, but are not all chosen by the Self?"

Uron pondered that.

"Whatever it is…" Nick said and offered a good-natured wink at Uron. "At least I'm not going alone."

Uron nodded as the two continued through the palace and entered the royal dining suite where the others waited. Isheim and Krys Heilbin Seagol of Kuhkel stood in the bright windows chatting to each other while Krys Sgaarsbad Hagal of Beersheba adored bowls of steaming food.

When an attendant announced Nick's arrival, Isheim and Heilbin turned from conversation while Sgaarsbad rose. Heilbin noted Uron, who remained a step behind Nick.

"Forgive my tardiness," Nick said.

"Nick!" Sgaarsbad ignored formalities as he lumbered over for an embrace. "As skinny as ever!"

"And Sgaarsbad…as you, as ever," Nick motioned at Sgaarsbad's heavy belly before both laughed. Sgaarsbad's curly hair was as combed as it might ever get.

Heilbin bowed from Isheim before approaching Nick with a more formal slight bow—appropriate for one krys visiting the kingdom of another—before clasping arms with him. A krys of battle, with broad shoulders and tight with muscle, Heilbin's grip tightened on Nick's forearm. His midnight hair lay snug upon his crown, bound behind in a thick black braid.

"Welcome, both of you," said Nick. "Though I can't say these are circumstances any of us expected."

"This is real, isn't it?" Sgaarsbad asked. "Heilbin and I have spoken at length of our experiences. And surely you experienced similar? The all-powerful being calling us to some vague and indeterminate future?"

His words confirmed the truth in Nick's heart and his shoulders lightened. "Yes."

"Such a strange thing, this," Sgaarsbad muttered. "The first in ages, so I can find."

"Not since Eilevor was called to conquer," Heilbin said. "I've wasted many nights searching my library for understanding."

"As have I," said Sgaarsbad. "But can we not discuss this over breakfast?"

Heilbin frowned.

"Let's," said Nick. They took their seats—Isheim on Nick's left and Heilbin beyond her, with Sgaarsbad on Nick's right and Uron beyond. "For now, let us free our formalities."

Servants poured coffee and juice and averted their attention when Sgaarsbad served himself without waiting.

"How is Kukhel?" asked Nick.

"Very well," said Heilbin. "Outside of our current situation. Trade remains strong and steady. We have less conflict with the yeti in the north. My wife has taken lead in arbitrating with them. I admit, I hadn't much hope, but it seems to placate the beasts without requiring their slaughter."

"And how is your lovely Ymenia?" Sgaarsbad asked with a full mouth.

"She is well," said Heilbin, who frowned at Sgaarsbad's lack of decorum. "She arranges our departure, even now."

Nick glanced at Isheim. "We have not yet begun ours."

"That so?" Sgaarsbad asked. "When did the subrim come to you?"

"Only a week past," Nick said. "How long have you had?"

"Three months," Heilbin said.

"Two," Sgaarsbad said. "I imagined we all had more lead time."

"Perhaps for the travel requirements?" Isheim offered.

"But why Nick last?" asked Sgaarsbad. "Why bring us here now?"

"How did it happen for you?" Isheim asked Heilbin.

"I was on holiday with Ymenia at House Pavda when I was woken," he said. "I followed a specter through the house and down to the lake where she disappeared beneath the waves and beckoned me follow. I felt…compelled. I walked beneath to find breath, to the very bottom where the world vanished and I stood in a round room, in the center of which glowed a blue and green sphere covered in earth and water, rotating very slowly. From out the sphere stepped the subrim.

"He said I had a new duty," Heilbin recalled. "That we all did. New purpose. My family has served as war master for elvenkind since before the Thurmine Conference."

"And suddenly all gone," Sgaarsbad muttered.

"Furthermore…" said Heilbin with a tone that drew every eye at the table. "I was commanded to send away my kingdom's most prized possession, in complete secrecy."

Sgaarsbad sat up. "Truly?"

Heilbin gulped.

"What is it?" Isheim asked.

"The Dogwood Sword?" Nick asked. "He sent it away?"

Uron's face flinched, as if unaware of this.

"Truly!" Isheim asked. "Where did you send it?"

Heilbin could not speak for several moments. "The subrim commanded me to send it to…New Gordon, of all places. To the human king for his war with the lycans."

"To waste the power of the ages on a spat with wolves!" Sgaarsbad growled.

"I wanted to deny the subrim," admitted Heilbin. "I tried to say I would never do such a thing. But the command felt like Pangea, herself, crashed over my heart. I could not say no. I could not disobey."

"It's already gone?" asked Nick.

Heilbin grimaced. "None of my people yet know. I would be slaughtered should they discover it before my departure."

"Why?" asked Isheim. "Why would the subrim demand such a thing?"

Heilbin struggled to muster its meaning. "And now I'm going to protect some petty gaggle of *humans*?" He took a heavy breath. "I don't understand."

"Humans?" Isheim asked. "This is about humans?"

"He mentioned humans to you?" asked Nick.

"Did he not to you?" Heilbin asked.

"No," Nick said. "She referred to a group known as the 'Great Self's chosen.'"

"Oh, this mystery grows deep, indeed," said Sgaarsbad as he raised meat dangling from his fork. "The subrim took me to this new world. I have seen the fabric of its realm. It is older than Pangea."

"Older?" asked Isheim. "What could be older than Pangea?"

"It was the most incredible and baffling experience of my life," said Sgaarsbad, "and I am still working to make sense of it all. Contrary to common knowledge, Pangea is several billion years old, and yet this place is older than that, by a little. Its weight in spacetime is heavier, despite having the same volume. Also, it appears to be almost seventy percent covered in water."

"What else?" asked Nick.

"Not much, honestly," said Sgaarsbad. "I am to be its transrealm engineer. I am to shelter it in contrast to the other worlds and hide its transrealmic signature."

"More worlds?" asked Heilbin.

"Yes," said Sgaarsbad. "I saw them clearly as I studied the new one. They are parallel to it and to Pangea. I couldn't help but feel as if they were waiting for something."

"They're already there?" asked Heilbin.

"Oh yes," said Sgaarsbad. "Pristine…virginal…untouched by sentient terraformation. I didn't know such places could even exist. Is there a single spot upon our fair continent we have not seen or explored? Some place untouched by sentients? I think it no uncommon account that the constant fires of Pangean war wage because we have nowhere else to retreat."

"I am its warden," said Heilbin. "But against what, the subrim would not say. Only that I was to preserve the integrity of the races after the coming shift. Those who go are to stay, those who do not are to remain. And that was all."

"Seems vague, my lord," said Uron.

"Indeed," said Heilbin, "but it may fit with Sgaarsbad and Nick that we are escorting a protected group to a divine safety."

"And I, its dream lord," said Nick. "We are apparent for the preservation of its integrity; for its person." The others nodded.

"Your words sound true," said Sgaarsbad. "Heilbin its body, I its soul, you its spirit."

"How can we do it?" asked Isheim.

"To leave my people is already proving difficult, indeed," said Heilbin. "The looks of my beloved warriors wrenches my heart. They appear abandoned for something contrite."

"Pardon my asking, Heilbin," said Isheim, "but are not the warriors of Kukhel sensitive to the spirits of war?"

"Yes," he said. "Quite. The dead are honored as they rise. But there appears no foe to fight with sword or shield and thus is beyond their approach. Without a physical enemy with which to pursue, they find it difficult to believe we are sent to fight no one."

"But we know not whom yet you will fight," said Nick. "None of us know what dangers lie ahead."

"Or what pleasures," Sgaarsbad offered a half smile. "Serving the Great Self will not be without its pleasures, I'm sure."

"We might hope," Isheim's words were cool. "Best we prepare with all haste."

Nick nodded.

"How was your experience?" Sgaarsbad asked Nick.

"I rode upon a white stag from here to the Zulta'mans in a mere hour. There, I walked with a subrim who told me I was to serve as a dream warrior for the chosen."

"What humans are these?" muttered Isheim. "That we should sacrifice so much. Are we so mad? Punishment?"

Nick laid his long fingers upon her hand and squeezed it. She did not return in kind. He held onto it but moved no more.

"Our Houses have been chosen," said Sgaarsbad, his usual smirk gone under clear vision. "We serve vulnerable humans, so this isn't for our glory. And this isn't for our holiness, else I would never have been chosen. As for the rest of you, we were chosen for our skills, skills we reasonably may assume were bestowed upon us for this very purpose. What comes next for us might well define our very existence, alone, together, as Houses. It matters not. None of are here for ourselves. We are here to serve the Almighty, and the Almighty we will serve, in whatever capacity he may ultimately choose. I, for one, will worry little about my coming fate."

All soaked in his words.

"And we leave our peoples to forge ahead without us," Heilbin's words were bitter.

"Do we hate it because we cannot go with them? Because it feels like a betrayal? Or because we lose such power?" Nick whispered. "We cannot escape the difficult questions as to our reticence in leaping."

"There is no single reason this is difficult," Heilbin said.

"Of that, I offer no question," Nick said. "As for my house, we've had no easy time severing our ties. We love our people. We come from our people. They are our everything." Tears rimmed his eyes. "I don't want to leave."

Isheim stared.

"Will we even be yet krys?" asked Sgaarsbad.

"I, for one, will always be krys," said Heilbin as his fist tightened round his butterknife like a sword. "Even if only over myself and my decisions."

Nick pondered that.

"How can the Great Self ask us to leave our responsibilities like this!" Heilbin stammered. "I might as well end my life as to protect humans. *Humans*!"

Sgaarsbad reached for a goblet of coffee to take a long draught. "My beauties aren't looking forward to leaving Beersheba." Everyone knew he had a wife and several women on the side. Thus far, everyone lived contentedly with the arrangement; even his wife. The group realized that would likely change and gave more weight to his earlier words. He was less the jolly, happy-go-lucky elf he seemed a moment ago.

"I am to seek out a blue-haired woman in the hills southeast of Eden," Nick said.

"Hills or cities?" asked Sgaarsbad.

"Hills, but possibly cities."

"New Gordon?" Sgaarsbad asked.

"Of the three moderate sized cities southeast of Eden, I think New Gordon is the only one known for its hills," said Nick.

"It is New Gordon," Heilbin declared with an intensity reminding them of his own story, of sending his nation's most prized object to the same destination.

"Very curious," asked Sgaarsbad. "Did the subrim say why?

"She's supposed to conduct my house to this new place, and possibly for yours."

"How?" asked Heilbin.

"I have wondered, myself, how we will move our houses," said Sgaarsbad.

"I will leave soon for New Gordon in the South Edenia region," said Nick. "Once I find this woman, I will keep you both updated as possible. Do you intend to stay until our planning is complete?"

"I do not know," said Heilbin. "The subrim said only that I was to gather Sgaarsbad to come here. After that, I suppose it's up to us to determine."

"The same."

"Then stay. In a few days, I will travel to New Gordon and, when

I find this blue-haired woman, I will return so we can finalize and prepare."

"I agree," said Heilbin.

"Truly," Sgaarsbad said with a full mouth and toasted with his coffee. "However. Let us commit, here and now." They waited as he finished chewing and swallowing his food. "Let us commit, together. If we are truly traveling to a new—if ancient—world, to do a bidding beyond any one of us, let us commit to this partnership. Not as lords and ladies, but as elves of honor." He raised his goblet.

"This ought be done with wine," Heilbin said and raised his own goblet. Uron joined him.

Nick raised his own. "Then so be it. Whatever we do, so much as is appropriate to this mission, may it be as one."

They turned to Isheim, who stared into space. Realizing they waited upon her, too, she raised her own glass. "Indeed, my lords." She lowered the glass and her voice. "Together."

52
Waking up

Eva braved opening her eyes after a long debate as to whether or not she lived. Memories from last night wormed their way to the forefront of her fledgling consciousness with strange visions of glowing subrim, hulking monsters and her prison guard run through with a sword and squealing to death on the cell floor.

Blinking clear her muddled vision, she scanned the room.

Her weak body lay beneath a plump comforter pinning her to a warm, cloud-like mattress. Above her hung a ceiling gilded in navy blue trimmed in ornate silver patterns. To her left, an open doorway revealed a fine water closet illuminated from a curtained window on her left. Opposite stood an expensive wardrobe of cherrywood warm-lit by a second window.

Within the ray of light bleeding through the thick white curtains, steam danced into the dusty air and drew her to a small loaf of bread, saucer of butter and a cup of broth atop a delicate, gold-lined plate.

She struggled against the heavy blanket to free her arm, rub clear her vision, roll to her right and snatch the loaf. She bit into its brilliant warmth. Sensitive teeth cried in pain while tears welled. She ignored both as she bit it through and gulped before gnashing away another. Her shriveled stomach flared in protest and stopped her after only a few bites. She lay across the pillow with the half-eaten loaf and took slow, calming breaths.

One of a set of double doors beyond the foot of her bed admitted a young maid in a simple charcoal dress with a white ribbon sash around her waist and blonde hair bound in a neat bun behind her head.

"Oh miss, you're awake," she said as she approached. "Please, take it slowly. She said you couldn't eat much very fast."

Eva clutched her fork in defense.

"Watch yer eyes," said the maid as she opened the curtains on each side to admit bright white light into the room, whose late-morning radiance enriched the hues painting the ceiling and walls. "Come now, let's get you up so we can put some food in ya."

Eva mustered herself.

"Aww, there now," said the maid before helping Eva sit up. She fluffed her pillows, scooted Eva back and had her recline into their softness before she pulled up a stool, plucked the bowl of soup and set it with care into Eva's hands. "Now, cup this and take care. It's a bit warm."

Eva reveled in its heat.

"Take your time, love," said the maid. "The priestess says you shouldn't eat fast or you won't be able to keep it down. I'll feed it to you, myself, if I have to."

Eva plucked the ornate cutlery and lifted the spoonful to her lips. Despite its heat, she gulped it. The maid mentioned a priestess, but Eva was overcome with clear notes of potato, bacon and chicken in the thin broth. The maid tore off and offered small pieces of bread and sips of fruit juice at intervals while Eva finished the soup.

"Very good," said the maid before she gathered the dishes. "I'll be back in a moment."

Eva cleared her throat. "Thank you."

"You're welcome, darling!" said the maid as she lifted the tray and headed for the door.

Once she was gone, Eva wiggled out of the snug comforter, climbed on shaky knees and rounded the bed to empty her bladder in comfortable privacy.

Outside the window stretched a lush garden where two children played among brick-lined flower beds round about a small pond splashing with goldfish. Their exuberant play cried antithesis to the hollow exhaustion deep in her bones.

"How do you feel?"

Eva twisted to find an angel standing in one of the open double doors, clad in a smooth dress of white trimmed in aqua. Lapis blue hair capped a pale face with the same haunting silver eyes she remembered from last night. She nodded.

"Better, then? Good. Would you like to sit?"

Eva moved with care to the near side of the bed and sank upon its edge.

"Please, take your time if you'd like to return to your spot," said the angel.

Eva gulped, made her way, hand over hand, to her spot and sat.

The maid returned with a formal chair and set it behind the angel. "There you go, mum. Will you be needing anything else?"

With a bare shake of her head, the priestess sat with such regality that Eva wondered if she ought not to try and curtsy, as well.

"How do you feel?" asked the woman.

"Much…better, thank you." Eva rested both hands on her lap. "I'm…" Tears threatened to return and she blinked them away. "Why did you bring me here? Why am I here? And…where is here?"

"You are at Mayhouse, the home of Theras Bennett, esquire," the angel's crystalline voice winnowed the chill air. "For the moment, you and your husband are his guests."

"Adamar?" Eva inhaled. "Is he still…?"

"Adamar lives," the woman said. "He is in need of a great deal of rest, which you both can find here."

Grief overwhelmed Eva for a moment. Faint sobs bubbled from her before exhaustion sapped her.

The angel made no move to offer comfort or a tissue, but Eva was happy to use her own sleeve, however unladylike that might appear.

"Why would you help us?" asked Eva. "I'm—" Guilt welled at how she dragged Adamar back to a society she realized was not as wonderful as she remembered. She loved and hated Adamar for dragging her down and revealing a world full of hardworking people who didn't constantly backbite or scheme. "I'm nothing."

A tiny smirk quirked the angel's mouth for a moment. "You are certainly something, young lady, but not due to what you have done to this point."

"What do you mean?" asked Eva.

"You have a purpose; one I am here to facilitate," said the priestess. "I will explain after you and your husband regain some strength."

"My husband..." she said. Guilt flared as, for a brief moment, she felt grateful to be free of his pride. "He survived last night?"

"You have slept two days," said the angel. "I kept you under to address your early pneumonia and severe nutritional deficiency. Your weakness is a side effect."

"Two days?" Eva stammered. "Why am I here?"

"First to rest," the angel said. "And reconnect with your husband."

Eva's cheeks burned.

"Or perhaps also to convince yourself you still love him?"

How did she know? thought Eva.

"I—" Eva lowered her head. "I don't know about a great many things right now. Most especially about Adamar."

"You will need each other, now more than ever, I should think," said the priestess. "Whatever the past has brought you through, know that you both are here for a reason, one I will explore with you in the coming days. Take this time to think on yourselves. You have come so far. Do not think it has been in vain."

"But," Eva grimaced, "I just..." She squeezed a weak fist. "I can't keep going on."

"The end of our course is never set," said the woman. "It is not for us to decide when our journey is complete, only how we will face each day."

"My days have been nothing but misery!" Eva cried and was shocked by her own bitterness.

"Nothing?" asked the priestess. "Including the days of youthful luxury with your family? A rescue to this fine home? A life raised in comfort?"

Eva's glare faltered.

"It's time you came with me," the priestess stood.

"Wait," Eva said. "What do I call— Who are you?"

"I am SonLara Alva Amferadon," said the angel, "Realm Delver and Librarian First Class to the Golden Hall." She motioned to the maid. "And this is Orthni."

The maid offered a faint curtsy and a wink from the corner.

Eva gulped.

"But you may refer to me merely as SonLara," SonLara said and motioned to Orthni, who helped Eva from her bed and into a house robe. "Come."

The three left the room into a glass-topped courtyard where pale dawnlight illuminated a small jungle of flora. Eva had never seen anything of its like outside a greenhouse. They followed the arcade's outer walk to the next room while Eva grappled with the enormity of it all.

"Wait here," said SonLara before she entered alone.

Eva stood with Orthni's help as waves of memories overcame her. Moments later, a soft bell within the room prompted Orthni to lead Eva inside, where Adamar lay tucked beneath a similar comforter as her own. SonLara stood next to him holding one of his thin, bony hands and spoke with him in tones too low for Eva to discern. His frailty alarmed Eva. When SonLara set her hand upon his forehead, he fell from consciousness.

SonLara motioned to the bed. "Please, lie next to your husband."

Eva recoiled. "But…why?"

SonLara waited.

Eva shrank beneath the passionless gaze, powerful in its changeless focus. Despite her shame, she shuffled to the other side of the bed and sat. With Orthni's help, she shed the robe and climbed under the blanket. SonLara appeared around the corner of her bed, set down a stool, sat and took Eva's hand as she had Adamar's.

"Why did you save us?" Eva asked. "What purpose do we have?"

"For now, rest," SonLara said. "Further, I will tell you both in a few days."

"What is this all about? Why am I sleeping here? This won't help me. I don't know how to love Adamar right now. I don't *want* to."

"I know," said SonLara.

"Then, what? Why?"

"Because he needs your warmth."

"Warmth? Couldn't you put a pan of coals beneath the bed or something?"

"A beating heart offers metronomic support to a body in need," said SonLara. "Your presence will act as a biological timer to help his, which is now struggling to find a stability by which to set all its other processes."

"I don't understand," said Eva.

"Your body will help the rhythm of his so he can heal faster."

"I've never heard of such a thing."

"There are many things I'm sure you've never heard of," said SonLara. "It makes them no less effective."

"What were you talking to Adamar about?" Eva asked. "And, is he asleep?"

"He's deep in sleep. He will not wake until I summon him."

"But he's a vacant. Magic doesn't work on him!"

SonLara waited.

"And me? Are you going to put me to sleep?"

"Yes."

"Right now?" asked Eva.

"Why did you marry your husband?"

"What?" Eva asked.

SonLara waited.

"I was young and in love, once," Eva admitted. "Adamar was different from the rest. He didn't…bow to me as everyone else had. I fell in love with him. Or…at least the idea of him." Eva wasn't sure which was truer.

A slight tilt cocked SonLara's head.

"Have you never been in love?" Eva asked.

"I'm not yet sure," admitted SonLara.

Eva cocked her head.

"Remember Adamar's quality and character," said SonLara. "It will be vital for you."

"Vital for what?" Eva asked as SonLara set her hand on her forehead. "No-! Vital for wh…?" Consciousness ebbed until darkness consumed her.

53
Talking Fish

Haephan treaded water near the edge of the world. Without shifting, the inescapable current would cast him from its edge into the nether below. As the steel feather dug under his belt line, he was curious what lay beyond the rim of existence .

We have heard of you! a voice floated to him in a series of "eh-eh-eh's."

Startled, Haephan found a long, leather-skinned fish with a hole atop its head swimming next to him.

Hi, the creature's voice filled his mind. *Can you understand me?*

"You can talk?" Haephan asked. "You're like the other one!"

Yes! And you can understand me! Wonderful! Now, we keep heading to the edge and I'd like not to go over. Would you like to hold on?

"Yeah," said Haephan. The animal wiggled into his arms and swam away from the edge.

Try holding onto my dorsal with your hands!

Haephan hugged the fish tightly behind the top hole. "What's a dorsal?"

My top fin! the fish slowed so Haephan could readjust. *There you go! Just hold on!*

When they had traveled a distance away, the fish wiggled out of his grip and twisted about.

"What kind of fish are you!?" asked Haephan.

A fish! The nerve! I am no fish! I am a porpoise!

"What is that?"

What is that? Know you nothing about the sea?

"Not really," said Haephan.

I see. Well, the sea is vast and boasts an endless variety of animals of all kinds, sizes, shapes and colors! I am a porpoise, and I am a warm body like you!

Haephan spat salty water from his mouth.

We like humans, for the most part. A shame some of you don't release us when we get caught in your nets, but we have yet to find a good way to communicate with those of you who can't manipulate magic. You must be very powerful indeed. I can sense it in you, though I didn't know wizards could be so young.

"Wizard?" asked Haephan. "I'm not a wizard! I'm…well, I'm not really sure what I am. But I'm not a wizard. I'm only eleven!"

Eleven! That's a wonderful age! I'm five, myself. Sure sure, I know what you'd say if you knew better. Gee, that Rikki looks so mature for his age. But you don't, so I won't hold it against you. But all my other friends say that all the time, especially the females. Females are wonderful. Do you have a female?

"A female?" asked Haephan. "Like, a mom? No, I don't have a mom."

You don't have a mum! Was she eaten?

"Eaten?" Haephan stammered. "No. I-I don't think."

Oh. Well, that's a shame. My mum was eaten last year. Got caught by a blackwhale. The porpoise trailed off. *Ohp! We're getting close again. Hold on!*

Haephan again let the porpoise carry him away.

"Hey, was that you at the other island? With the other seed?" Haephan asked.

Me? Not me! I live about two hundred leagues north of here in the crystal shallows by the great western reef. What did he look like?

"Like…you? Except maybe a longer snout?"

HA! Longer snout, indeed! That was a dolphin. They have long, ungainly snouts. They also have smaller heads—and smaller brains if you ask the likes of me.

“Can all fish talk?” Haephan asked.

All fish talk!? The idea! Of course not! Fish talking. Who ever heard of such a thing!?

“But you can talk!”

And I’m no fish, little human! No fish at all!

“But you both live in the ocean and have fins! And things.”

You live out of the ocean with other animals with fur all over ya, don’t ya? Can they talk, too?

“Well, no.”

There you have it, then! Seriously, little human. Fish talking. Anyway, while I love chatting, pulling you back and forth in all this downsuck is getting a bit tiring. Let’s do this, shall we?

“Right,” said Haephan. “So…what do we do?”

Rikki wiggled free and came about. *Put it in my mouth. This is goodbye!*

“Goodbye? Are you going to die?”

Die! I sure hope not. That would ruin my day. I have other things to do. Fish to eat. Females to mate. The porpoise erupted with eh-eh-eh-eh-eh kind of laughter.

“Why would I give you this seed?” Haephan asked.

Do you *plan to take it to the bottom and plant it?*

Haephan shook his head. “Is that what the dolphin did?”

Can’t speak for that ungainly fellow, but I woke from a dream telling me to come take your seed and plant it. Never happened before, but it’s certainly been an adventure—don’t get me started on the orgy I *interrupted yesterday. Now hurry up before we reach the edge again!*

Hesitant, Haephan set the seed in the porpoise’s long rows of teeth.

Right then! he said. *This should be it. See ya!*

Disappearing for a moment, the porpoise shocked Haephan moments later by leaping several lengths of its own body out of the water with a forward flip before diving back in.

Haephan shifted away from the edge but remained in the ocean, waiting for the animal to return, when violent flashes boiled from the depths and arcs of lightning danced across waves. This time, when the froth threatened to sink him, he shifted high into the sky and fell.

He shifted nearer to the water and misjudged by almost slamming into it. He shifted again to repeat the fall but not from so high. He seesawed by shifting in directions so that before hitting the surface he "fell" upward until he slowed and sank. He fell ever closer to the water before shifting. He laughed and shifted sideways, then "through" a wave before going up again.

Nearby, a spear of barren rock fired upward from the waves high into the air. He shifted to it and landed on a flat along a ridge and rolled under its ledge as waves of seawater continued sloughing from its sides like heavy rain. The island continued to climb.

Tired of the water, he shifted toward the island's highest point, thinking he would land normally. The ascending peak slammed into him and knocked out his breath. Before he recovered, the mountain halted so abruptly that he ascended several feet before falling against across the rocky ground. He waited out a pounding head before he inspected the new island.

On rising, the familiar urge overcame him. To his surprise, the metal feather slid from its hiding place and swirled into the air. Curtains of light snaked from distant horizons as colored smoke billowed and climbed his legs toward the down-snaking aurora. Smoke and light met at the object in a gentle waft that drew every bolt of lightning crawling across the new island. Every strand of Haephan's hair flared.

Below, the peak fell from his feet as the island turned itself inside out so the peak sat at its bottom and its shoreline climbed upward into an inverted cone. As the peak reached its base, the tip disintegrated and a pillar of warbling sunlight burst from the new hole to warm him from below. Unlike the previous islands, the new world connected within the inverted peak beneath him, instead of out to the side.

Haephan plucked the stem of the glowing metal feather as the magic locked into place. A chorus of galactic notes harmonized into a single tone, answered by a sound reverberating from the new world. Where the peak disappeared, a lake formed and billowed outward to worm its way up the inverted cone as creeks and rivers.

Haephan threw back his head and roared while light poured from his eyes, nostrils and mouth. Another, narrower strand of auroral light fired downward from the sky, pierced him and stabbed through the inverted "peak." The world rang like a gong to seal the connection. The chaos of waves and wind faded away.

Rotating upward, Haephan crowed.

His hand loosed the feather, the pillar of power disappeared and the boy fell. He gained his bearings in time to plow into the shimmering lake with a bone-jarring crash.

54

Emergency

"Eva?"

Standing with her friends, Eva turned to her mother in the middle of the Elysian Court, a long rectangular arcade preceding the New Gordon Academy where her father worked alongside the wizard conventicle. "Yes, mother?"

Seni's gloved gesture drew her across the courtyard through the early afternoon dapple of cloudy sunlight wafting over it. Slender trees growing between the heavy marble columns washed in the fluted breeze.

"Your aunt has requested your assistance with her Inishan guests this weekend."

Eva stiffened. "But mother, I had plans to see the circus in the east—"

"Circuses come and go, my dear," said Seni. "Every year, in fact. Entertaining the Inishans is very important to Ethne."

"But mother," Eva pouted. "I promised my friends weeks ago that we would—"

"Eva," Seni cut her off. "Family comes before pleasure."

Eva's cheeks reddened with indignation. "I'm eighteen, mother. I'll do as—"

"HOO!" a faint cry turned heads among those wandering the courtyard. The heavy rumble of an approaching caravan raged over the cobblestone climbing to the arcade. Groups scattered as they barreled through the tall archway into the courtyard. Covered in blood, the driver of the lead carriage bellowed, "MEDICAL!"

Gasps erupted as people recognized Academy carriages. Constables and attendants rushed to open the carriage doors and fish out a host of bloodied wizards and assistants.

While her mother locked up, Eva rushed forward to those spilling out. Despite blood everywhere, she leaned in and helped those who would walk to move into the Academy as warning bells belched across the square.

One servant from the cavalcade collapsed while trying to make it on his own. Eva dropped next to him and found blood pouring from a wound on his back. Ripping at her dress, she pressed cloth to the flesh to stem bleeding. "MEDIC!"

"Make way!" a young commoner roared from the top of an inbound carriage to the scattering curses of others rushing to help, heading right for her.

Eva faced him. Snatching the reins, he hauled so much that the horses almost reared, stopping an arm's reach from her. His fearless command to an arcade full of New Gordon's wealthiest surprised her—commoners did not command magile. After breaking the look, he turned, dropped to the ground and, to her horror, dragged her father's limp body out of the carriage.

Hefting the wizard like a sack, the commoner marched toward the academy as a host of attendants and wizards emerged from its main entrance down several landings to the arcade.

"Here! Gather him!" an older wizard belted and pointed at Wizard Dufrain.

"I've got him," said the commoner. "Tell me where to go."

"Aven, take him," the old man pointed at a young wizard, who led the commoner and Wizard Dufrain to the main entrance.

Eva waved over a young wizard incoming from the Academy to the victim under her hands and raced for her mother, who hadn't noticed her husband among the wounded. "This way, mother!"

Together, they rushed through the chaos and up the landings in pursuit of Wizard Dufrain. They passed through the high academy doors and kept straight.

"To the infirmary," said Seni. Gripping Eva's hand, they navigated the thinning current of young wizards, wove through long, high halls filled with pale afternoon light to the infirmary entrance boiling with medics and assistants.

The thin commoner held Wizard Dufrain with ease and set him on a wheeled bed before medicists rushed him away.

Eva stared at the blood painting his body as incoming injured forced the two women aside.

"Get this man out of here," one doctor pointed at the commoner.

"He saved Wizard Dufrain's life," cried the carriage driver while he helped carry in another wizard.

"Then save another and get out of the way," the doctor barked.

After handing off the wizard, the driver stepped aside along with them.

"What happened?" Seni asked as she and Eva followed the two from the entrance.

The driver gasped for breath.

"Are you hurt?" the commoner asked the driver, who noticed the blood crusting his clothes and shook his head.

"No," he coughed. "I don't think so."

"What happened?" Eva demanded.

The commoner hesitated at the sight of her but shook it off and turned to the driver.

"We were just through Delvin when we were set upon by men," the driver said as a train of others brought more injured inside. "They were ripping us apart."

Eva clutched her mouth.

The driver gripped the commoner's shoulder. "This man…" He pointed. "You saved us. Great Self, you saved us."

The commoner helped the driver to a stone bench along the broad hallway under a portrait of Eden larger than most hallway windows.

"You saved us," the driver said. "How did you do that?"

"Do what?" Eva begged.

"Wizard Dufrain tried to counterattack, but they were better professional martial mages. *He* walked right through their magic," said the driver. "He waylaid them. He scattered 'em. If it weren't for him…" Shock overcame the man, who reclined against the wall and fell over, leaving a streak of blood from his shoulder.

"DOCTOR!" the commoner bellowed. Medical personnel rushed into the hallway to gather the driver.

"Who are you, sir?" asked Seni.

The commoner waved his hand. "No one."

"No," she gripped his arm. "You are everything."

55
Winter Storm

Haephan had never before gone into one of the new worlds, but as he floated in the pool at the bottom of the inverted cone, the light pouring from the lake below him was brighter than the blue sky above.

Flipping over, he sank through several feet of water until he "surfaced" on the far side, now upside down to his entry. He climbed the shore and gaped at the world, shaped like a ball, but on the inside with a sun shining in the center.

All around the pool, new trees sprouted and matured until a forest blocked most of his view.

Throughout the day, Haephan shifted across the innerglobe. He explored inside-out mountains, convex riverbeds and other things he never knew could exist. The sun appeared as a great eye whose light poured from a single foremost side that bathed the nearest terrain in brilliance. He picked berries and watched with curiosity as the half-burning sun "rotated" with painful lethargy to create a common day cycle.

Reclining under a tree, his hand fell along his belt. Where was the metal feather? Bolting upright, he realized he couldn't remember having it since waking. Haephan scowled—losing valuable objects wasn't a habit.

Realization hit him that he hadn't recovered his father's ring, either. Even as he pondered how to return and search Dolphus's belongings, the urge welled within him to plant another seed. He had an equal need of sleep. Every planting exhausted him.

From his perch along a high-pointed ridge, trickling upward with creek water before it pooled at the ridge's crest, he watched the sun "set" to little more than a bare orange tint against an otherwise black night. The exhaustion of his work tempered his awe until it disappeared under his need to press on.

Fear kissed him that he could not stop. He shook it off and suppressed it until the urge became too great to deny.

Haephan shifted to Elverbane's empty study in the last, dusty light of late afternoon. After taking a seed from the wooden box and stuffing it into his shirt, he lamented again the loss of the feather. Where had it gone? Haephan hated losing pickings and fought again the shame of losing his father's ring. Eager to flee the pain, he shifted to the university kitchen storage room.

Haephan plucked and bit into an apple from one of the cloth-covered boxes, tore into jerky and made his way through a loaf of bread when entered one of the scullery maids.

"'Ow did you get in 'eah!?" she snarled and screamed when boy and jar disappeared.

To Haephan, a wall of icy water replaced the warm room with a deluge of terror. He spun and flailed upward until he gasped air. A razor-sharp wall slammed into and drove him under. Panicking, he shifted to the surface and snatched ahold of a massive block of ice bobbing in the heavy waves as blood oozed down the side of his head.

"Heeeyy!" he yelled. "Come and get it!" The cold seeped in so fast he struggled to inhale. Desperate to get out of the water, he shifted to the top of the block to scan across an endless forest of towering ice.

"C'mon!" he yelled with a cracking voice drowned by wind.

"C'mon!" His focus ebbed. He formed in his mind a vague idea of where he might go—somewhere warm. As it coalesced, a thunderous groan rippled up the ice beneath him and cast him through the air.

Horror filled him as he fell over the edge of the world.

Panicking, his desperation caused him to shift to his most recent safety, but to his dismay traveled only a mile inward and fell once more into the mind-biting icy water.

Haephan struggled against the cold to focus on shifting, but his mind failed to form the necessary images to forge a destination and he sank beneath the waves, which ascended from him. His vision dimmed when his final breath escaped too soon and bubbled upward.

Something slammed into and lifted him from the icy grave. Gasping, he twisted atop a massive leathery creature before an eruption of water from a tiny hole bathed him in shocking warmth. Grateful for its brief heat, he cared little for how much it reeked.

Human! You are dying! the animal cried with a feminine lilt.

"Y-y-y-yyeah!" Haephan balled up in the frigid wind.

You must give me the seed! Quickly!

"I-i-i c-c-c-an't can't! Aaaa-a-a-aa!"

Oh dear, I can't leave you like this, cried the voice. *Wait! I will call for another!* Before the voice was finished, the creature erupted a long audible wail.

"P-p-p-orpp-ois-se?"

Heavens, no! Annoying little creatures, the animal said. *I'm an orca.*

"Or-ru-ru-ru-rc-ca?" Hacphan chattered as his body struggled to handle the cold.

Close enough, she carried him from the world's edge as a magical warmth spread through Haephan's extremities. *Why are you dying, little human? You seem a bit unprepared to me.*

"I di-d-n't know it was so-so-s-so cold!"

Likely excuse, she said. *Listen, when the narwhal shows up, you hold onto it. She can't speak but she'll do as I tell her. Now gimme the seed so we can get moving. I have things to do.*

"What?"

Get off! she said. *She'll be along in a moment.*

"What? Wait!" Haephan cried as the orca sank and left him again to tread water. Cold stabbed him while the waves dragged him ever nearer the world's edge. He fought to maintain his focus and expand the warmth when a long-spiraled horn fired up from the surface before him, followed by a large pale fish-thing.

Haephan clung to it as it distanced him from the edge. He could not climb upon it as he had the orca. He shivered so much he feared he would lose his grip when the orca returned in a fluster.

What's wrong? What didn't you do? she demanded.

"What d-d-d'you me-ean?" chittered Haephan.

Nothing's happening, you little sea monkey! retorted the orca. *I'm here! I dove downward with the seed! What didn't you do!?*

"I d-d-uno!"

The orca burst her hole, blew nasal horn and calmed. *Patience, Myar. Patience. Listen, man calf. I am here and my own calves are huddling in a small cove very far away waiting for my return. If I am not with them, they remain in danger.*

"B-b-ring them here!" Haephan stuttered.

To the edge of the world? the orca cried and thrashed water over him. *Finish this. Do it! I don't know what you need, but this isn't working and I cannot leave them there!*

"I dunno!" Haephan moaned in terror as he struggled to think.

Think, human! Think! cried the orca. *What didn't you do? What happened before that isn't happening now?*

The image formed in his mind of the metal feather glowing above him during the last planting. The magic demanded one from his collection. Where could he find more— Ian's collection!

"Ian!" Haephan muttered.

What?

"I kn-n-ow! I g-gotta go!"

Then go!

Desperate to wake his mind, Haephan drove his fingernails into his palms but he couldn't feel his hands. Instead, he bit his tongue.

In a flash of pain, he shifted and fell from the air upon the large wooden box in Elverbane's study. The box overturned and spilled its contents with him across the carpeted study floor.

Haephan moaned as the warmth burned him. He lay in shock with fingers as blue as ice until the pink crawled up his skin and into his hands. He cried as his nerves revived with electric agony.

The orca's pounding words drove him to roll over, plant a fist and climb to his knees. He crawled on prickling hands into the hallway to Ian's room. The first object on the shelf was a wooden talisman. He snatched it, rolled onto his back and relished the heat for one final moment before he braced for his return.

Haephan appeared a hundred feet above the icy waves in the slate gray clouds and began his long fall. He hoped to find the whale before he had to return to the mind-numbing water. Haephan shift-fell across the sky in search of the beast while a violent wall of snow and wind raced closer.

The tiny white spot on the horizon proved to be the narwhal. Haephan see-sawed in mid-air as he searched for the orca. "HAVE YOU SEEN THE ORCA!?"

The narwhal moaned and thrashed to point with its long horn.

"Got it—!" Haephan cried when a wailing, agonizing scream erupted from the approaching storm. Afraid to shift directly into the wall of snow, he see-sawed closer when a guttural roar echoed across the water.

Haephan twisted around at the unmistakable thunder of a dragon.

As if announced, the beast materialized through the milk-white storm with a bloody snout agape as fire huffed behind its fangs.

"Shit!" Haephan screamed, shifted away and crashed across the top of the waves before sinking into the roil.

There you are! the dragon cried. *Where are the seeds, little elfchild!? Surrender them and I will make your death quick.*

Haephan did not know how the dragon knew, but he feared being trapped once more in this icy grave. It was then he bumped into something slippery. Myar's limp, desiccated corpse bobbed in the waves rushing closer to the edge of the world barely a half mile distant.

I'm not an elfchild! Haephan struggled to cry.

Gallons of her blood erupted from the massive hole in her body, ripped open by the dragon's fangs.

Collecting himself, Haephan climbed from the water onto her slippery body behind the gaping dragon's bite and shivered as heavy gales iced the seawater clinging to his skin. Myar had the seed when he left, but where would it be now?

Tucking the wooden talisman into his belt line, he inspected the gory hole and slipped into the water to crawl along to Myar's jaws. He found the seed wedged between two of her teeth and pried at it. His fingers were slow to respond due to the deep cold while the storm's front rolled over them.

The dragon's roar drew a fresh curse from Haephan as it banked toward him. *Surrender the seeds!*

Haephan ducked behind the orca and kept his head low. The dragon descended and accelerated before slamming its feet into Myar, which crashed into Haephan and drove him into the ocean. Haephan kicked above the fray. Fresh claw marks on Myar's nearby body revealed the dragon couldn't pick her up.

Haephan tried shifting away—the world shuddered and refused to change. Desperate to complete his mission, Haephan swam for Myar as the roar of the edge of the world filled the air. He paddled hard and grabbed her half-open jaws. He planted his feet on her lips and gum line and pulled at the seed as the water below them disappeared. They fell over the gray nether below.

With all his might, Haephan yanked the seed free and kicked away the dead orca.

The dragon's scream drew Haephan's attention as the beast dove toward him into the expanding spray of the ocean fall. Unsure if he might fall forever, Haephan was caught in the moment.

Come back here! the dragon's voice sounded afraid.

Fire flashed him before the dragon slammed into and sent him spinning.

Haephan gripped the seed and shifted by the demand of need to somewhere deep underwater. Immense, midnight pressure crushed him from all sides so that he could not keep air in his lungs. Bubbles burst from his mouth and he knew if he inhaled, he would take half the ocean into his chest.

As the darkness closed in, a burst of light exploded from the seed in his hand and engulfed him. A glowing disc spread below his feet in expanding concentric circles. Instead of ground rising like other islands, his body raced upward through endless ocean, exploded from the water and cast him into the sky in seconds before coming to a stop. He coughed the ocean, rain and snow in violent fits.

Searching for the boy, the dragon saw his ascension, beat his wings to crest the world's rippled edge and raced for Haephan. The beast failed to notice the aurora bursting across the sky or a thick tendril of glowing water snaking upward from the ocean below.

Light filled Haephan and arched his back until his eyes and mouth faced skyward and appendages splayed outward.

So close to the child, the dragon opened his mouth, determined not to miss again, and took one final leap.

Aurora, luminescent water, and boy converged a moment before the dragon could snap his jaws closed. The construct exploded outward in a thunder of air and sound that consumed the beast.

The auroral flow overwhelmed Haephan's senses as the wooden talisman fired from his belt line into the ocean below and froze it all in a downward wave that congealed an island of ice down to the bedrock.

The light disappeared and Haephan sank, his body numb from the cold water, shock of the fight and the inky depths. He hit the sharp inclines of the island and landed on an outcrop without hurting himself too much.

Steam rose from his warm body. Entwined with the old world, a fresh ocean appeared and overlapped the old. Across that new horizon stretched away as a world of endless icebergs. Haephan scanned the new world and stared at the shadowed silhouette of the dragon's body frozen within the island, itself.

"Wha..." he started to say when vertigo washed over him. Much of the flesh of his right arm was gone. Freezing in shock, he fell and shifted away to a place of safety.

56
Eva's Work

Adamar tugged on the collar to his snug, tailored uniform as Wizard Dufrain inspected his new sanctum, a large room centered by a heavy wooden table with alcoves on all sides and a set of tall double doors. Crystal reflectors spread a wide beam of light upon the wizard and his workspace.

"This isn't how I wanted a promotion," Dufrain said. "People ought not to have to die just for others to move up in this world."

"Isn't that all of life?" Adamar mused. "The young become the old and pave the way for the next wave?"

Dufrain pursed his lips. "I hope this role is acceptable to you. You saved my life," he said. "I cannot forget what you have done for me. There's not much more than an assistant role for a vacant, in an academy such as this, though."

"Being a vacant isn't the insult to me that it might be to you."

"I…suppose not," Dufrain said. "Anyway. Let's get going. I have work to get to and I'd rather not delay."

Adamar followed him into the hallway.

Dufrain slowed as Adamar came alongside him. "Forgive me, Adamar, but vacant assistants must follow behind their masters. I cannot make an exception for you, but know that I hold you in much higher regard than our typical assistants."

Frowning, Adamar nodded. Around them, vacant assistants bustled along the hallway, many of whom appeared small and shriveled.

"Why are they like that?" asked Adamar as they set off again.

"Hm?" Dufrain asked.

"The other vacants?"

"What about them?" he asked, as if unused to answering an assistant.

Adamar waited for an answer.

"They are…" said Dufrain. "They come from the city's poor."

"Are all the city's poor vacant?" asked Adamar.

"No," said Dufrain.

"But…" Adamar began, "how many are there?"

"To be honest…Adamar," said Dufrain, "I'm not sure. We source vacants from the poor to give them an opportunity to better themselves, give them a home, help them out of the rain, so to speak."

Adamar's face tightened as they continued into the Academy complex. "Sounds nice."

"Ah," Dufrain led him into a smaller office with a single alcove to the right, packed with bookshelves and books, lit by a crystal reflector in the ceiling. Impressed, Adamar scanned the room and its contents before latching onto a chalkboard full of diagrams.

"What are those?" Adamar asked.

A shadow passed over Dufrain as he scanned the drawings on his way to the desk in the corner. "Magigrams."

"Magigrams?" Adamar asked.

"Diagrams of magical structures," said Dufrain. "You need not concern yourself with them. As a vacant, you won't be able to see them in-power."

Adamar scanned the structures and noted arrows and marks indicating direction and movement. "Power direction."

Dufrain paused.

"It flows up and then counterarcs here and here," he tapped the chalk. "Did you make such a thing?"

"My daughter drew that," said Dufrain.

"Really?" Adamar rolled his jaw.

"She's one of the finest at magigrammy in South Edenia," Dufrain said.

"I've never seen such a thing drawn like this," said Adamar.

"I don't imagine you have," Dufrain said and resumed searching his desk. "It's magic."

"Oh, no," Adamar said. "I've seen mechanical diagrams before."

Dufrain eyed him.

"She's very good," said Adamar. "I've never seen it laid out quite like this, but it's brilliant."

"What have you seen before?" Dufrain asked.

Adamar scanned the diagram and said, "I've dabbled in creating engines."

"Can you see magic?" asked Dufrain.

"I'm sorry, wizard. I haven't. I mean, I can't."

Pausing, Dufrain raised an upturned hand. Adamar frowned at it until Dufrain dropped it. "Then let's focus our attention on the work I have for you." Dufrain motioned to the rear alcove. "Let's pack and move to the new office."

"Yes, wizard," said Adamar. He spared one final glance at the board before following Dufrain into the rear alcove.

57

Working Days

"You did what, exactly?" Elverbane asked with his pipe halfway to his mouth. The fireplace crackled and popped as he propped his feet on the hearth to warm them. A lone pale lantern hanging above him lit the list in his other hand.

SonLara sat next to him in her own rocking chair with a large tome sitting in her lap. "I used something unconventional from Belfast's select storage rooms."

Distracted by the flicker of firelight on her powder-white skin, Elverbane clomped and puffed on his pipe. "*Archivum of Edenic Enginery*?"

"You remembered," a smirk tugged the corner of her mouth. "The archivum references The Rose Thread, a tool I thought useful for those two."

"Rose thread?" Elverbane asked. "Never heard of it."

"It's a diplomatic tool most useful to help highly variant cultures discover bridges of experience," said SonLara. "When both parties contact the rope, they share memories through more than words."

"How is that supposed to help a married couple?"

"Two parties unable to communicate their most deep-seated needs because they don't know how to properly communicate them?" SonLara asked. "I needed them to remember why they fell in love and attempt to rekindle cooperation. Our time is short."

Smoke swirled from Elverbane's protruded lips. "Very clever. But they're vacant. Are you sure it worked?"

"I have learned that vacants remain inert against second energy, but not first."

"Spirit?"

SonLara nodded.

Elverbane pulled the pipe from his lips. "You created a cohabitational interactive hallucination using spirit?"

SonLara smirked.

"How?" Elverbane struggled not to be distracted.

"Spirit is more powerful than magic, Seth," she said. "This the Andonese have known for millennia."

Elverbane held her gaze for as long as he dared and looked away. "I'm…impressed."

SonLara's smirk deepened into a smile.

"So, what is your plan?" he asked.

"Those two will spend the next few of our days rediscovering their pasts."

"Will that work?"

"I know many things in this world," SonLara said as she scowled into thought. "But I'm no psychologist. I don't know how to fix their problems. I just remember what a mentor of mine often used to do with visiting dignitaries who could not agree."

"Which was?"

"Lock them in a room together until they learnt to get along."

Elverbane clomped on his pipe and read his list. "Fine idea."

"I've been thinking," SonLara said.

Elverbane paused.

"I have reason to believe Haephan is using khordecs."

"Magical anchors? For what?"

"For the islands," said SonLara.

"Wouldn't the islands be anchor enough?" he asked.

"I'm not sure. It appears the magics need something more defined to anchor against."

Elverbane scowled.

"And Haephan's mantle? Does it have a khordec?" asked SonLara.

"I can't figure that out. If there is a khordec, I'm not sure what it is."

"What about the La'Du Lira Al'Cular?" asked Elverbane.

"The Tree?"

"You said the mantle's properties were intrinsic to creation. Might it be connected?"

"Quite a fair chance," said SonLara. "If that's true, that's a khordec that can never be destroyed."

"But if a tree is a khordec for Haephan's mantle, what are the other khordecs for?"

"Only one tree lives forever," she said. "If it does, so does its status as a khordec."

"No one lives forever."

"Even the Immortal?"

Elverbane harrumphed. "Still not sure what to think about him."

SonLara mused. "What makes you think it's a him?"

"What do you know?"

A smile tugged her face. "Nothing, but I would hate to assume."

"I've always heard him referenced as a *him.*"

"Don't always believe everything you hear."

"I suppose not," Elverbane said. "Can't imagine a woman as the Immortal, though."

"Maybe I'm the Immortal."

Elverbane's brow drooped. "You're no Immortal."

When SonLara giggled, Elverbane forgot to puff his pipe.

58

Fight

"C'mon, Ev'," said the brunette as they scanned each way at the T intersection. "He's gotta be back here somewhere."

"This isn't a good idea, Helni," said Eva.

"You said he was really cute," said Helni. "I want to see." She turned left.

"No, I said he messed with one of my magigrams," said Eva.

"You said he made it better," said Helni.

"That's beside the point," said Eva. "He had no right."

"So, he does what he wants?" Helni said with a mischievous grin and looked her up and down. "Do you wish to be something he wants to do?"

Eva's eyes flared.

"Ha!" said Helni as she pressed onward.

"You've already seen him," said Eva as she followed.

"In his uniform," said the mischievous brunette. "Maybe he wears only tights in his quarters or something."

"Helni!" Eva hissed as her cheeks blushed. "He's boring. I mean… all he does is work and take walks."

"Wow," Helni smirked. "You pay a lot of attention to this vacant."

"It— it doesn't matter that he's a vacant," Eva scowled. "But he's my father's servant. This is stupid."

"Then why are you following me?"

"Someone's gotta get you out of trouble."

"What if I'm trying to get you *into* trouble?"

"Helni," Eva growled.

"What? You said he was cute. I wanna see."

"He's all throughout the academy every day!"

"I don't look at servants."

"Obviously," said Eva.

The two reached the end of a long hallway. The door on the right wall stood ajar. On it hung a wooden nameplate of "Harel" below a closed viewport.

"I don't see Adamar," Helni pouted.

"That's it."

"What?"

"That's his last name—Harel."

"Silly name," Helni pushed his door open to peer inside.

"It's an old term for 'man,'" Eva peered curiously into the room. "We shouldn't be in here!"

"I don't see you averting your eyes, you angel, you."

"Hush," Eva said. Shcafs of paper sat upon a tiny desk against the near wall next to the door, lined with unlit candles. On the desktop sat several strange objects.

"Why does he have candles?" Helni leaned inside.

"Because he's a vacant."

"So?"

"The touch plates don't work because he has no magic to spark them," Eva said.

"Really?" asked Helni as she scanned his desk. "I mean…I knew vacants had no magic. But I never thought about that. Is this one of his thingys?" She plucked one of the objects—a paddled wheel axled by a long metal pole. "Such a strange boy."

"Be careful with that," said Eva. She took it from her and inspected it.

"I wasn't gonna break it, sheesh," said Helni as she stepped into the room.

"Where are you going!?" asked Eva.

"Fine!" Helni feigned scandal as she stepped outside the room, gripped the doorframe and leaned inside to get a clear view of everything.

Eva scanned the construct's paddles, wheel structure, spoke supports and octagonal metal axle. "This reminds me of Denum's Intercogs… He saw my Turnum's Axle magigram. That's my modification!"

"Your drawings?" asked Helni.

"Yes…" said Eva as she inspected it. "I never imagined you would make something physical like this…Did he plan on using this on water? It would transfer third energy along the axle to a second machine…This is amazing."

"What're you talking about?" Helni leaned out to frown at the wheel before leaning back through the door. "He looks like he sleeps lonely." She smirked.

"How would you know if someone sleeps lonely or not?" Eva asked.

The door at the end of the hallway opened to reveal Adamar—covered in mud and holding a new mill wheel—barely a pace away.

Wide-eyed, Eva popped straight while Helni's rump remained the only thing in his view as she bent into his room.

"Helni," squeaked Eva.

Adamar fished out the metal axle from the mill wheel in his hand and smacked Helni on the bottom.

Spinning out of the door, Helni's face flickered between shame and indignation before she screamed, "How DARE you!"

"I'm not standing in *your* bedroom without your permission," said Adamar.

"The idea of a servant *spanking* a lady!"

"You mean a man getting the attention of an interloper?" Adamar set the pole's end upon the floor like a cane.

"It's not decent to touch a lady!"

"You keep using that word like you know what a lady is," Adamar cocked his head to the side.

"The nerve of some low-life little fucking vacant—"

In two strides, Adamar snatched her collar, hauled her back, hipped open the door leading outside and sent her sailing down two steps across a thin veneer of rich brown mud. After the initial slap to the ground, a scream erupted from her that made even Adamar wince before he stepped inside and let the heavy door slam shut.

"What did you do!?" Eva cried.

Adamar turned to her with an anger that surprised her. "How dare you come into my room for your amusement."

"Wh— But— I can go where I can do what I want!"

"Can you now?" Adamar stepped close enough to force her back. "So, following that idiot sop is good enough for you, now, is it?"

Red filled Eva's face. "I defended you to her!"

"That allows you into my room? I don't need your defense," Adamar said before he stepped into his room and kicked the door shut.

Eva gaped before snatching the door open. "You bloody well do before she sic's her father on you for touching her inappropriately!"

"I didn't touch her," Adamar said.

"You bloody well did!" Eva cried and grabbed the metal pole from the small table.

"Hey!" Adamar spun and reached for it as Eva retreated into the hallway. "That's mine!"

"You got it from this academy!"

"I earned it!" Adamar advanced as she retreated with it behind her back.

"What is that even worth?" she scoffed.

Scowling, Adamar snatched her by the front of her dress.

"Unhand me!" she twisted and held the rod out of his reach as he pulled her closer.

"Release the rod," he said.

"Make me," she retorted.

Cracked doors revealed servants aghast at the drama.

Adamar slowed his breathing and released her. They glared at each other from inches away.

"What's this even worth, anyway?" she asked.

"I'm working on something."

"On what? A new wheel?"

"Something like that," he said.

"Tell me."

"No."

"Aww, Adamar upset he can't get his— Hey!"

In one smooth motion, Adamar snatched her dress, hauled her past him and yanked the rod from her hand. Ensuring she didn't stumble to the ground, he released her.

"How dare you!" she cried.

"There's that word again."

She reached for the rod and he let her grip it. She tugged in vain as he waited.

"Why?" he asked.

She frowned.

"Why do you hang out with them?"

"Who?" Eva asked.

"These brainless little know-nothings who sit around vomiting bullshit about a world they refuse to understand."

"What're you talking about?"

"These little fops on daddy's money who chitter and laugh at everyone different from them but never achieve anything."

"Those are my friends!" Eva said.

"They're a waste of air. And a waste of your time."

"What would a stupid homeless man know of it!?"

"Homeless? You just broke into my home."

"You were homeless before— this isn't the point! What would you know about friends? You don't have any. All you do is walk around the academy and play in your stupid creek with your mill wheel."

"I know I would choose better friends if I had the world to pick from."

"Pick of the world? Have you actually met any of the people I grew up with? All they know is about this gilded life that controls every last thing about who they can or cannot be. You think our society forgives difference?"

"You do."

"What?"

"I saw you the day I brought your father back," Adamar said. "Unlike all the other ladies in their fine dresses retreating from the chaos, you alone helped a servant bleeding out on the ground. You refused to move even as my panicked horses aimed straight for you. Servant or wizard mattered little to you until your father came in. Even then you returned to helping others."

"You know nothing," she said. "I did what was necessary."

"But then go back to all your fancy parties and vapid friends?"

"You've been *watching* me?" she asked.

"If you hate society so much, why don't you leave it behind?"

"To do what? Be a lowly servant like you?"

Adamar's shoulders sank. "What is it with the childish insults? You pretend you're happy in society but I've seen you light up when you're helping a teacher or talking magic with your father. Why don't you work with him instead?"

"You have no right to demand such an answer!" said Eva. "I made decisions for my own good."

"By choosing an option you hate?"

"I don't hate society."

"You sure as shit do," Adamar said. "Go back to your father. He obviously wants you to work with him."

"My father and I cannot work together," Eva gripped her fists.

"So, you choose your mom?"

"I had to choose between my mother and my father," said Eva. "My father would have me alongside him working magic in politics and…I can't follow into such a two-faced world."

"Instead, you chose your mother and her suitors and her society?"

"At least I don't have to fight my father anymore," she said.

"You surrendered one master for another," said Adamar.

"I can *choose* in my society!" cried Eva.

"Two? That's all you got?" Adamar said.

"What kind of options do you think someone like me has?"

"The world, Eva. The world!"

"What is out there but chaos and disorder? At least here I can choose between a life of bureaucratic service or social prominence."

"Filled with idiots you obviously can't stand to be around," Adamar pointed after Helni.

"She's my friend."

"She's an idiot that keeps getting you into trouble," said Adamar.

"Who else do you think I have, Adamar? They are all I got."

"If you would look past their thin veneer and be brave enough to step outside your bubble, you could find someone of real value whose love actually meant something to you."

"What, someone like you!?" Eva cried.

Adamar hesitated.

Eva moved to speak and faltered before her eyes widened. "You…"

Their hearts thundered when the heavy door behind Eva swung open to reveal a livid, mud-covered woman heaving with fury, who opened her white-toothed mouth and bellowed.

59

Honesty

Adamar knew it was a dream. This couldn't be real—he remembered it before it happened. He struggled against the flow of time and inevitability of events. While he couldn't remember how he got here, he knew it wasn't the present day, but somehow a living memory of his past with Eva.

Eva lay next to him in bed, tangled from last night's passion, yet another in a string of encounters months after their fight in the hallway.

He would ask her to marry him shortly after she woke and she would hesitate—not because she loved him less but because of obligations she believed were hers since birth.

Any moment, he would reach over and touch her face. She would stir and roll her head. He would slide his hand down her opposite cheek impressed by ripples from his pillowcase.

Instead, Adamar fought the dream, reared his arm and pulled the sheet away. He crawled off the tiny bed and dressed. The dream pressed harder and harder until, suddenly, it stopped.

Eva woke and sat up. "Adamar."

He turned.

Her eyes were too old for the nineteen-year-old that once lay in his bed.

"What's happening?" she asked.

"I don't know."

She pulled away the sheets, rose and dressed alongside him as she stared into thought.

"Where are we?" he asked. "Is this magic? You can't use magic on me."

She searched her memories and said, "The priestess."

"Who?"

"An Andonese priestess came and rescued us," she gulped.

"Rescued? The…prison? Right?"

Eva nodded.

"I vaguely remember. Why? And why are we here? I remember her talking to me, but not about what."

Eva opened her mouth to speak, shook her head and said, "I don't know."

Adamar cupped her face and drew her attention. They shared a long look mixed with hesitant affection until she turned away.

"Are we still in?" she asked.

"I didn't think this was possible for me."

Eva opened his door and stepped into the hallway where her father and several constables stood outside, ready to bang on the door. The men offered listless stares.

Adamar stopped behind her. "What's wrong with them?"

Eva pressed her hand to her stomach and said, "We've interrupted the memory." After a long moment, Eva turned to the door at the end of the hallway.

Adamar scanned the lifeless memory of her enraged father and took Eva's arm. "I'm sorry, Eva."

She spun.

"I resented your father. I resented his success. How he managed you. And I didn't want the way he raised you to be the way you treated me as your husband, especially one who hadn't come from a life like yours." He approached the wizard. "I never resented his wealth. I wanted to provide for myself and you and, our children, the way he could."

Eva hesitated at his sudden honesty.

"And for me to go back to your father to ask for a job was to say… that I couldn't do it myself," he said. "I couldn't do that. I feared that if I locked myself into always depending on someone else for a living instead of making my own, that I'd always have to depend on being hired. You know what my father was like. I couldn't turn into him, always begging for work because he was a vacant."

Eva hugged herself.

Adamar gripped her arm. "I'm so very, very sorry you went hungry. It hurt so much to see it. I was afraid of that, but I was more afraid that you'd leave me and run away sooner if I turned into my father. Or worse, once we had some kind of income, you would never let me leave working for someone else. Turned into a man who could never do for himself, never do for his own family."

Eva's eyes glassed.

"I was wrong," said Adamar. "I didn't think it through. I let my fear prevent me from getting on my feet long enough to start fresh. I should have. I should have listened instead of cutting you out. I should have trusted you."

Eva walked out of the heavy door at the end of the hallway and held it open for him to follow into pale daylight. Outside, only a flat plain of grass under a blue sky stretched into oblivion—neither people nor buildings existed in the memory.

"I thought you were afraid of having to work for someone else because you hated being told what to do," Eva said. "Or that you hated my father because he was a wizard. Or that your pride…I was afraid of your pride. I've always been afraid of your pride. That…I couldn't live up to it. Your…" she searched for the word. "Sense of honor, maybe. Always, you and your honor. I was the one who fell in love with a man I thought was below my station." She sighed. "I think I spent the rest of my time trying to wonder if it was the other way around."

They ambled across a nearby grass quad.

"Adamar," she said, "I don't know if we can continue."

Adamar stiffened.

"I still love you," she whispered. "But—"

A soft ring filled the air.

"What was that?" Eva spun.

The distant horizon shrank in a wave flowing closer as wind picked up.

Adamar pulled Eva to him, aware of her body against his.

Hesitant at first, she feared this belied her previous statement. She also feared he would let her go. She laid her head on his chest as his arm slipped around her.

The world rippled away and brightened into a soft, enveloping white before turning to darkness.

60

Loyalty

"And so the bloody dyad turns to me with this massive drumstick in his hand and green yeti meat falling out of his mouth and he says, 'This is WHO!?'" Sgaarsbad guffawed.

As always, Sgaarsbad's wild stories made Nick laugh. Sitting in a window-lit corner of The Dundel's Fuss in southern Aminrale, Nick and his aide de camp sipped mugs of ale and laughed at the froth sticking to Sgaarsbad's thick copper beard.

"Aahhh..." Sgaarsbad moaned his exhale. He reclined and scanned the ancient curved supports and their seamless joints of the 8,000-year-old pub.

"I know there's a dream in that head, old friend."

"Oh yes," smiled Sgaarsbad.

"When's the last you built anything?"

"Too long," Sgaarsbad said. "Been so busy with transrealmic studies the past millennia that I've let my first love go untouched."

"Never a wise thing," said Nick and hid thoughts of Isheim by drinking again from his mug.

"No, it's not," said Sgaarsbad. He showed more desire for the wood above them than Nick had for Isheim in longer than he could recall. "She will be beautiful. Something elegant, I think. Long curves with thick buttresses. I will use ansmeric crystal, I think, for her windows."

"Ansmeric? That's incredibly expensive," Nick piped.

"Oh, I know that, but I've been hoarding some for a few centuries. I found a stash and immediately knew I needed to keep it for something special. Never knew it would be for an entirely new home!"

Nick shook his head.

"Ah, but a lovely winding home. And a grand stable! The finest!" he said. "Ah, but I am a lone engineer." He took a draught on his ale.

"A lone engineer? You are the finest north of the desert."

"No, my friend," Sgaarsbad said. "I am amazing, that is true, but what I wouldn't give to hire but a single Corduron."

"Cor—" Nick choked on his ale. "What about Cordurons?"

"The brilliance of those wee elves! The buggers are better builders of wood and stone than any sentient in ages. And I mean in *ages.*"

"Well," said Nick, "I don't think many elves would agree with you."

"I wouldn't fault them for it, either," Sgaarsbad said. "Thantil's Rebellion isn't something many of us would soon forget."

"Then why hope for them?"

"I think it's important to separate people from their skills—people are more than what they can do and less than whom they project themselves to be."

"Waxing poetic over ale?"

Sgaarsbad harrumphed. "I *am* a poet, brother." He frowned into his ale. "But until that might cover my debts, I should plan to build a house like none ever seen. I will only have to do my best, in spite of my deformities." He scowled at the fingers of his free hand in the faint light by the window behind him. "But yes. A stable. Entirely indoors, I should think."

"An indoor stable?" asked Nick. "Why would you build that?"

A twinkle kissed Sgaarsbad's eye. "It will be necessary."

"For what? Bestabled don't thrive in closed conditions."

"Certain ones do."

"Certain—" Nick scanned his thoughts. "Only in extreme conditions. Like the desert heat or the icy fringes where the sun is thin and wind ever-present."

Sgaarsbad's twinkle intensified.

"Where are you building this home, Sgaar?"

"Our destination is round, my friend. Round like a sphere."

"Heilbin mentioned that. How? Did you see it, too?"

"Oh yes, I have seen it." Awe filled Sgaarsbad. "A magnificent corporeality in a universe of infinite definition that makes our world seem simple and ham-fisted. There, space is an endless construct in which the physical rests, weighted by mass and connected by gravity."

"The force which keeps us down from up?"

"Oh, so much more," Sgaarsbad said. "While the force is the same, it exerts itself differently in a grander three-dimensional space than our bilateral marriage of terraspace."

"Why would it be different?"

Sgaarsbad leaned over the table until the rays pouring from the nearby window reflected off of the wood and underlit his face. "They *all* are."

"These new worlds?"

"Oh yes," Sgaarsbad said. "Each possesses its own unique set of physical laws. I never knew such a thing was possible until the subrim walked me through them. I saw each and every one with the sight only a transrealmic engineer can possess. And to think, I thought it a silly pursuit when you and I were lads!"

"How much has changed."

"Indeed. But for the good," said Sgaarsbad. "And yes, this house will be such a beauty."

"You mentioned in a hostile environment," Nick said. "Where are you building this house? Have you already seen where we're going in that level of detail?"

"Us? No, not quite yet."

Nick frowned.

"The first house I build will be yours."

Nick blinked twice and asked, "Why?"

"I don't know the details, my friend, but the subrim said yours was to be first, for it will also be last."

"What does that mean?"

"It means that, however long we three are to serve this commission, your house must endure the ages."

"Times as these," said Nick. "Why should I protect the dreams of humans? I've never even tried. Is it possible?"

Sgaarsbad set down his mug so a pretty hostess could refill it. She blushed under his wink but left with a scowl for Nick, her transitioning krys.

Though their arrival had silenced the pub, Hagal's rowdy tales provided enough noise for other patrons to return to their drinks and low conversations.

"I don't know," Sgaarsbad said. "But as I am a transrealm engineer experienced in Pangean energetic terrography, I am best suited to learn this new world better than any other. While Heilbin might be a fine warrior here, what challenges might he have in protecting such people, and from what kinds of dangers? Certainly not by magical dangers of which he is accustomed to fight. So what, then? He is chosen to act as the Great Self first designed him to act before he was born, just like us."

"I miss simpler times," said Nick.

"We're still in simpler times," Sgaarsbad said. "The complicated stuff isn't even here yet."

"When did you get so wise?"

"Oh, I dunno bout that," Sgaarsbad muttered into his ale. "Keeping up with all my females is starting to wear on me."

"All your females? I thought you loved having a wife who didn't seem to mind your sides."

"You know…I thought so, too," said Sgaarsbad. "Now I ask myself how much she loves me. Is she with me only because I am krys? To have it all means to have nothing. I envy you and Isheim."

Nick's stomach pitted. "I wish it were so."

"Is it not?" Sgaarsbad asked.

"We have grown apart," Nick admitted.

Sgaarsbad frowned.

"But if your wife doesn't love you, you have the others," Nick said.

"No, my friend. For all their fun, I distrust their love, as well," Sgaarsbad muttered. "Your father once told me something I long dismissed."

Nick paused.

"Valuable women cost, and their love even more," said Sgaarsbad. "Free love is worth its price."

"What does that mean to you now?" Nick asked.

"It means I would trade a thousand of my lovers for a wife who saw me to my depths and still said 'yes,'" Sgaarsbad said. "The longer I live, the more I think our holy Self intended the challenge of single union. To collide, both in sex and, more importantly, in the heart and soul until we become one. Sounds more and more like the calls of Holy Writ, the more I think on it. You and Isheim had that once."

Nick sighed.

"What happened?"

"I'm not sure," admitted Nick.

"Not sure? Or don't wish to admit?" Sgaarsbad asked.

Nick said nothing.

"Do not fret, brother," said Sgaarsbad. "We are immortal. There is time to fix and correct."

"Is there? Are we to mix with these humans? I think not. I feel we are to stand separate, even as we watch over them. One day we might become legends and fables, of magic and elves and dwarves and wizards…Their generations will forget our presence by the potentially sheer number of them to grow. What could we possibly do for them? Isheim goes, but her heart left me a long time ago."

Sgaarsbad half lifted his mug and took a heavy gulp. "At least we can visit and get in trouble!"

Nick chuckled.

"We're being foolish, worrying like two washwomen," Sgaarsbad barked. "Come. Let's be off."

"Yes, I think it's time to return."

Sgaarsbad narrowed an eye. "Indeed."

Paying their tab, they left the pub and climbed towards the palace.

Nick gripped his friend's shoulder. "I've missed you, my friend."

"It's been many a year since we were young among the hills of Avondere, stupid and daring beyond reason!"

"We did many unwise things."

"Like hunting Wendigo in the dead of Kerbecktigan winter!" Sgaarsbad laughed. "Or that time we chased down that group of nymphs in the Jeruvian Marshlands!"

"That wasn't me," said Nick.

"Oh," Sgaarsbad said. "I guess that was just me then!" He guffawed. "But you were on the trip with me when we went to the Angodils to retrieve the wayward son of…" Sgaarsbad began snapping his fingers, "what's-his-name?"

"Krys Baidol."

"Krys Baidol!" Sgaarsbad laughed. "That bloody sop of a worthless— That youngling deserved the thrashing his father gave him for runnin' off as he did. I'd have done the same with any of my sons. Of course, they grew up hearing that story."

"You don't appear to have changed too much," Nick smiled, changing the subject from children.

When Sgaarsbad slapped his round belly, the large thing jiggled. "Bully! I have changed quite a bit, you skinny waif."

Nick's demeanor darkened as they reached the palace gate and entered the complex maze of long, tapestry-lined hallways.

"Does it worry you to travel to a new land with Isheim as you are?" Sgaarsbad asked.

"Of course," Nick admitted. "How will we weather a broken home without socicty to occupy us as it has? How easily we have fallen to our distractions instead of facing ourselves."

Sgaarsbad put his hand on Nick's back. "My friend, we all have our desires and our hopes. It is never easy to leave that which we love. If we must, let it be under all commitment to each other to bear through these difficult times. Reach out to her. Build this bridge as you transition to what will surely challenge us all."

"I'd like to be there for her," said Nick. "You're right. She shouldn't be alone. I'll try and do what I can to allay her fears and comfort her."

"Humility, my friend," said Sgaarsbad. "She probably wants gentle humility. Come. Let's get to the library. I'll show you a few ideas I have for your house." They entered the guest wing on their way to the library when Isheim emerged from one of the guest suites wearing nothing more than a thin silk robe.

Nick and Sgaarsbad slowed. Nick noted whose door it belonged to while a disheveled Isheim tugged on mussy hair. She scanned the hallway and stilled at the sight of them staring.

As the air chilled, she blushed, lifted her chin, and marched off.

"That's—" Nick's eyes widened. "Seagol."

Sgaarsbad cursed.

Isheim disappeared around the bend in the hallway.

"That bloody son of a dwarf—" said Nick as he started toward Seagol's doors.

"Whoa there!" said Sgaarsbad. His thick fingers clamped Nick's wrist and hauled him away.

"What are you doing!?" Nick yanked at the iron grip.

"It's not his fault," Sgaarsbad's joviality disappeared.

"Not his fault? What in hell are you talking about! He— with Isheim!"

"He is not to blame, brother," Sgaarsbad's gravelly words remained calm.

"He just—"

"Unless he took her against her will, Heilbin did not violate your marriage oath."

Nick gulped.

Sgaarsbad eyed his panting friend. "Heilbin has been a cheater for as long as you and I have known him, but never a rapist."

Nick pressed for Heilbin's door. "But he—"

"But he did not VOW HIS LOYALTY!" Sgaarsbad barked loud enough to shock Nick. "He did not break your marital vow."

Nick sank.

"Now…" Sgaarsbad slipped his thick arm around the shoulders of his taller friend and tugged him away, sure that if Nick attempted to harm Heilbin, the warrior could maim him or worse. "I think it's best if we retreat until we can clear your head."

"But—" Nick attempted again to advance on Heilbin's door. Sgaarsbad's resolute grip dragged him to the stairs.

"It might be time for you to stop sipping that bloody watered wine for a night. Guardsman!"

A guardsman approached.

"Go get my guard and tell them to grab my silver ale and bring it into town and find us," said Sgaarsbad. "We will need it tonight." Sgaarsbad knew he would need help ensuring Nick did not slip away while drunk.

The worried attendant half bowed and headed into the palace.

Kringul stood there dumbly before Hagal pulled him away. "Come. I think it's past time more than me got drunk."

"But a clear head?"

"Certainly not a priority at the moment," muttered Sgaarsbad as he hauled his friend out of the castle. "S'gonna be a long night."

61
A New Mission

"Oh dear! I'm sorry, Priestess SonLara," the old man staggered across the manicured lawn. "I wasn't thinking when I let Cappy out for a run."

"It's alright, Master Bennett," said SonLara as she loomed over the prostrate mop of a small dog deep in sleep with the end of a short rope in its mouth. "I was about to remove the rope, anyway."

He hobbled closer and stooped to pull at the rope when SonLara's hand forestalled him.

"Lest you, too, fall into memory," she said as she pulled away and coiled the rope.

"Oh, I don't know," he chuckled. "I might like to visit some of my old days. When I was a bit more of a troublemaker."

"I almost struggle to believe it," she said.

He chuckled with a mischievous grin. "I might have been bold enough to ask such a pretty young lady like yourself out to dance."

She smirked. "I believe you would."

He grinned as the dog stirred, spotted him and climbed to its feet as if from a heavy sleep. It looked about as if surprised to be here.

"Priestess," he knuckled his brow and led the dog away.

Flanked by maids, SonLara approached Adamar and Eva laying on a futon spread across the grass under cloudy afternoon sunlight. She had them moved outside to take in sunlight for health but had not anticipated the dog taking the rope—pets were uncommon in Andon.

First to wake, Adamar rolled over Eva in a protective gesture as he struggled to clear his filmy eyes. He locked upon the blue-haired woman standing at their feet. "Priestess?" He took a slow breath. "What… happened?"

Eva woke, shielded her eyes from the brilliant sun and asked, "Where…Great Self. Where are we?"

"At the house," Adamar answered her and asked SonLara. "What was all that?"

"Come," SonLara said and motioned to the house. "It is time both of you ate."

Approaching maids helped the two onto their feet.

"I'm so hungry," said Eva.

Holding much of their frail weight, the maids led them across the grass and up two steps to the broad rear patio.

Capped by an umbrella, a table hosted a bowl of fruit, two empty plates, two glasses and a pitcher of water. After taking turns in the water closet, they sat in the cushioned chairs and soaked in the warm sun and cool breeze.

As Eva tore into a pear, Adamar bit into an apple and almost cried. He hadn't had fresh fruit in a long while. After downing two pieces, both sat panting as their stomachs gurgled to life.

"Where are we?" asked Eva.

"Sorry miss," said the maid. "Not for me to say. The lady will answer any questions you have."

"And if she doesn't want to?"

"That's up to the lady," said the maid.

Eva noted that Adamar's gaunt frame had lost the beauty that had taken her to bed, and yet, within him burned the same spark that first captured her—a fire even prison could not kill.

He extended his hand. "Let's go find out what this is all about."

Hesitating, she set her thin hand in his before they struggled to their feet. The maid led them into the kitchen, along a hallway and into a grand high room filled with flora and frosted glass. At its heart, the priestess sat in a circle of three chairs round about a small table.

After they sat, SonLara took a teapot and poured three cups of tea. Raising her cup, she prompted them to do the same. She sniffed, sipped her tea and set her cup in the small saucer. "This will help with your stomachs."

Relaxing, they sipped.

"I am Priestess of Andon SonLara Alva Amferadon, Realm Delver and Librarian First Class to the Golden Hall," she said. "You may refer to me as SonLara."

"I am Adamar Harel. This is my wife, Eva. We would like to know why we're here. Not that we aren't grateful. I'm sure I would be dead if you hadn't taken us. But…why? Why did you save us?"

"Yes," said Eva. "Why?"

"And why that thing?" Adamar motioned to the yard. "The memories?"

SonLara lifted a short, tasseled rope from her lap. "This is a Rose Thread, used to renew and re-experience memory for contracts, negotiations and investigations, among other uses."

"But I'm a vacant," said Adamar. "Magic doesn't affect me. At all."

"There are more energies in this world than common magic," SonLara said. "There are three forms—magic as you've always heard of is merely second energy. You, Adamar, are quite familiar with third energy, I would wager."

"Third energy?" he asked.

"The energy of physics," said SonLara.

"And the rope? Is that third energy?" asked Adamar.

"You speak of spirit. Of first energy," said Eva. "No one can manipulate that. That's *lifestream.* And vacants have never responded to first-energy tests any more than second energy."

"You have spent two days asleep under this cord," said SonLara, "and within it you experienced much more time, time I did not have here in the real world."

"Two days!?" Eva cried. "We had weeks of experience!"

"I hope you learned well," said SonLara. "There is much to do."

"What were we in there for?" Eva stammered.

"Your lives were not dying, alone," SonLara said. "Much within you has broken in recent days. It was important to give you time to rest together, away from distractions."

Eva shook her head.

"The road ahead will require much of both of you," said SonLara.

"And if we don't want anything to do with your mission?" Eva said. "Priestess. We are, indeed, grateful for your rescue, but…what if we're not ready for a mission or can't do it or…" She trailed off.

"There is an opportunity for restoration," said SonLara, "for both of you. Not merely in flesh but in soul. Do you want only to live, or would you like to believe again? There is life on the road ahead."

Their hearts churned.

"I don't think I can, anymore," Eva's voice faltered. "I think I'm done fighting. I'm…"

"There is more in both of you than you think, and a purpose greater than either of you could be alone," said SonLara. "I have been assured of it."

"By who?" asked Adamar.

"It is up to both of you to choose freedom for your own kind," said SonLara. "And start a life of clean opportunity, away from the land of magic."

"Away from magic?" asked Eva. "What kind of life is that? Magic is life."

"Spirit is life," said SonLara. "Magic is another energy entirely, and weaker. Spirit is much more powerful, and Adamar is positively brimming with it."

Eva glanced at her dumbfounded husband.

"So…what does that mean, exactly?" asked Adamar. "I can do stuff, but with spirit instead of magic?"

"Consider less that you are the maker and think more yourself the conduit, a glove, of sorts, for the Maker of all things."

"What?" asked Adamar.

"Largely, this is irrelevant to you," said SonLara. "First energy is not so easily manipulated as second, and therefore not as useful in daily life."

"First energy?" Adamar looked between them.

"What matters more at this moment is how you became vacant," said SonLara.

"Why would that matter?" asked Eva. "He comes from the south side. Lots of vacants live down there in Rainhold."

"But Adamar isn't from Rainhold," SonLara said.

"No," Adamar said. "I was born in Chiffen. How did you know that?"

"I know as much as one can from a disparate line wandering central Pangea," said SonLara. "Your father is from one of the cities north of here."

"My father died years ago," said Adamar.

"One of your family line has been to Eden."

When Adamar stiffened, Eva noticed.

"Which one was it? Your father? His father?"

"One of my dad's tall tales," said Adamar slowly.

"It's true?" Eva asked. "And how do you know that?"

"Tell me the rumor," SonLara said.

"Old story about great-great-grandad sneaking into Eden. I didn't think it was real."

"Tell me all of it, please," said SonLara.

Adamar's brow drooped. "He was obsessed with the Tree. Had been a businessman in Meliliope and started collecting everything he could find about the LaDu Larca."

"The Tree of Life?" asked Eva.

"Yeah, that," Adamar said. "Dragged the family all the way up to New Eden looking for artifacts. Went poor chasing dreams. That's how we ended up in Rainhold. I barely managed to escape it when I discovered some of my cousins in Southdown."

"But he found something real," SonLara said.

"That's the story."

"How did he get the seed?"

"The seed? What seed?" Adamar asked.

"From the Tree."

"A seed from the Tree of life?" Eva sat up. "The Tree doesn't seed."

"It does, indeed, Mrs. Harel."

Eva stiffened.

"Dad mentioned something about…some pod or something," Adamar said. "Just a detail, really."

"The most important one," SonLara said.

"Said he fell into a big hole in the ground with a Tree taller than the Academy bell tower. Claimed he saw dragons. He was stuck a couple days. Started starving when he saw a dragon eat what looked like a rock. Found something similar growing from a branch, broke it open and ate what he could. He supposedly regained all this strength in one bite, and in a few more, found the strength to leap from the hole and run out of Eden." He shook his head. "Came back trying to convince everyone he'd found the Tree of Life. Thought he was immortal. Got run over by a wagon shortly after." Adamar shrugged. "Great-great-grandma moved to Chiffen, rarely ever spoke of him."

"No," Eva said. "The Tree cannot possibly seed. Everyone would know it. Everyone would kill for that."

SonLara reached into a small pouch and fished out a pod the size of an apple. "You're right. Everyone would." She pressed magic against its edge. A golden lattice of auroral lace burst to life and dimmed all other light in the room.

Eva gasped.

"What the hell?" Adamar muttered.

"You can see that?" asked Eva.

He nodded.

"This is such a seed," said SonLara. Her silver eyes shimmered as vibrant gold, green and blue danced around the pod.

"How did you get that?" Eva sat forward.

Each shivered in SonLara's reflective inspection. "Your ancestor ate one of these, and thus lost his ability to touch or sense second energy completely."

Neither spoke.

"Honestly, if a magile creature ate one of these—or enough of these, they would likely lose all magic and die," said SonLara as something connected in her mind. "Though I have queried, few know your most recent history." SonLara put away the seed, casting the room into candlelit warmth, again. "Tell me why you came back from Southdown."

Still in shock at seeing magic, Adamar swallowed. "We—" He drifted off as shame filled him.

"Business did not work out as we intended," said Eva.

"What business did Adamar attempt to work without his magic?" SonLara asked.

"For years, I've been attempting to harness the power of nature."

"Third energy," said Eva. "He has been working on a tool that could transfer the energy of moving water into kinetic work. It's brilli—" She gulped.

"Is that so?" SonLara asked.

"I call it a waterwheel," said Adamar. "Water moves paddles along the wheel, which turns the axle which moves other toothed circles that can perform work like milling."

"That sounds intriguing, and under any other circumstance, I would ask you to show me," said SonLara. "Where did it fail?"

"It didn't," Eva said.

"No," said Adamar. "It was the guilds."

"The guilds destroyed every attempt to put it to use," said Eva. "They threatened us, got the constables to chase us..." She drifted off.

"Like all government, guilds are agents of stability," said SonLara. "People do not like change, unless change founds their philosophy, and rare is that the case. In all my travels across Pangea, few have learned to embrace change with the regard it requires. Threats to a philosophy against change endangers life's continuity and can inspire great evil in men."

"They claimed it would destroy the water workers' jobs," said Adamar.

"They were right," said SonLara, "but they forget that prior to the emergence of second energy, men farmed by hand. The advent of powerful tools gave rise to better work."

"By hand?" Eva asked. "Sounds awful."

"Back breaking," SonLara said.

"How do you know that?" Eva asked. "Second has been around since before the agecross."

"Compared to now, the Courte Empire is barely a whisper of time since second energy was shaped by the ancients, and yet there are records. But again, Adamar is different from common vacants."

"Why?" Eva asked.

"Adamar was sired by a vacant."

"Right…" said Eva.

"Have you not considered that fact?"

"Why is that important?" asked Eva.

"Has your father not explained vacancy to you in detail?" SonLara asked.

"Few speak of vacancy beyond its benefits in study," said Eva.

"He told you vacancy was unique to Rainhold," SonLara said.

"Yes," Eva waited.

"There are two traditional forms of vacancy, both are common to New Gordon and other cities with heavy magic industry."

"What do you mean?" asked Eva.

"Vacancy is a common result of the coupling of highly powerful mages, a practice long forgone across the continent since the DracoElven Wars and the abrucari period."

"But my father was a wizard and my mother a witch. I'm no vacant."

"Not universal, but more common," said SonLara.

"What does that have to do with Rainhold?"

"How many vacant-born are there among the mages of the Academy?"

"None," said Eva.

"None?" asked SonLara. "Or none reported?"

Eva shook her head, confused.

"You know your people," said SonLara.

"They go to Rainhold?" Eva asked.

SonLara lifted an eyebrow.

"Are you saying the orphans of Rainhold are vacant children of Academy mages?" asked Adamar.

"Great Self, no," Eva breathed. "They dump them in the 'hold."

"But there were a number of vacants at the Academy," Adamar said.

"They come from Rainhold," Eva whispered.

"Really?" asked Adamar.

"As assistants," said Eva. "Fucking Self, those bastards toss them into the 'hold. If they survive, they hire their own children to assuage their guilt."

"All the vacants in Rainhold are abandoned by wizards?" Adamar asked.

"Not all," said SonLara. "While multi-mage progenesis can produce vacancy, a second, though more rare form, comes when a tiered mage copulates with a common human."

"The Academy boasts the highest concentration of tiered wizards for ten thousand miles in any direction," said Eva. "Is vacancy possible among nonmages?"

"Not as far as my recent research suggests," SonLara said. "The power of the mage faults periodically in procreation. Usually offspring are as or more powerful than their parents, but the balance is found by producing sterile vacancy."

"But that would mean the sweethearts in Rainhold are either made up of powerful mages—" began Adamar.

"There are easily hundreds of such vacants in Rainhold." Eva scowled. "Those lecherous bastards across the city are letting themselves out in the sweethearts down there."

"I have met at least one such vacant," said SonLara. "He reminds me a bit of you, Adamar. He is resilient despite what many would consider a handicap."

"I am not handicapped," said Adamar.

"I think he would say the same, at least, prior to more recent events…" said SonLara. "But you don't come from a coupling of powerful mages, Adamar. Your vacancy and that of your blood is new and will ignite a fire across Pangea."

"Why?" asked Adamar.

"Is anyone in your direct family line not vacant?"

"Sure," Adamar said. "Mom's not a vacant. Grandad on dad's side wasn't, either. I have vacant cousins across the Estamar in Southdown. And a vacant sister. Closer."

"Has any coupling between a vacant and nonvacant produced anything but vacant children?" asked SonLara.

"No," said Adamar.

"How do they make a living?"

"Menial work," Adamar said. "It's the only thing most of us can do, especially in places run by guilds. Or as assistants or what-have-you."

"Remember what I said about changeless philosophy?"

Adamar nodded.

"Up to your family, vacancy was a self-solving problem for people who rule by magic," said SonLara. "The first two types of vacants are sterile; no children to propagate the problem. As the third and new type, capable of having *more* vacant children, regardless of whom you couple with, what do you think will happen if permitted through an entire population?"

"I don't understand," said Adamar.

"Great Self," said Eva. "They will slaughter them."

"What?" said Adamar.

"The guilds are hardly the only powers that would feel threatened by an expanding populace free of magic. The Academy would feel even more threatened by your vacancy than the guilds."

"Law enforcement across Pangea is second energy-based," said SonLara. "Entire populations impervious to martial magic are populations that change dynasties."

Reality dawned on Adamar.

"Your entire bloodline is a threat to humanity's dependence on magic," said SonLara. "And those who wield the greatest magic will do anything necessary to maintain their power."

"But how would they attack or kill us?" asked Adamar. "If second energy magic can't affect vacants?"

SonLara raised her hand. Her teacup darted from her palm and stopped an inch shy of Adamar's face. He recoiled against the chair from the now-motionless cup.

"I wouldn't need to use magic to actually touch you," said SonLara. "All I need to do is employ second energy to generate third energy through the momentum of this cup, or an arrow, or a rock." She shook her head. "Anyone can throw a stone by hand, and enough people throwing stones will kill you as surely as anything else."

Adamar gulped. "Then why worry about us if they can hurt us?"

"It's not nearly as efficient as the ability to actually use magic against you, directly. This problem is new and small but virulent enough to draw attention. They will not wait for you to become the problem you could be."

"So, what do you want from us?" Eva asked.

"I have been commissioned by high authority to gather all possible vacants before the Green Moon and conduct you safely to a new refuge."

"As many as possible by the Green Moon?" asked Eva. "And by what authority?"

"A subrim," SonLara said.

"An angel of heaven?" asked Adamar.

"What kind of bullshit is that!?" Eva said.

"Do you think I would have given two thoughts about a penniless vacant and his wife in prison without such foreknowledge and direction?"

Eva gulped.

"And so you two have a choice," said SonLara. "Work with me to save your entire bloodline of vacants before the central governments discover their danger. Help deliver them to a new world created for them by the Great Self."

Adamar exhaled while Eva squirmed with indecision.

"Or run away and die as you were," SonLara's tone never changed, yet weighed with import that chilled both.

"I—" Eva's breath stuttered. "I can't."

"Eva," said Adamar.

Eva climbed to her feet as her knees wobbled.

"Eva!"

"No!" she cried. "I appreciate you saving me, priestess, but I would rather die than be thrust into some Self-forsaken mission to populate some fantasy land! This is madness and I don't want any part of it!"

"Eva!" Adamar groped for her arm with his weak fingers.

"No. You stay the hell away from me!" Eva kicked back her chair as she ripped her arm from his hand. "I'm done!" Tears formed in her eyes. "To hell with this."

She marched to the front door, slammed it open and disappeared.

"Eva!" cried Adamar as he struggled onto his weak legs. "Eva!" Out of breath, he sank onto the arm of his chair before sliding into the seat.

"You must get your rest before you return to Southdown to collect as many vacants as you can."

"I didn't say I would go," Adamar protested.

"You didn't ask her to wait for you," SonLara rose to her feet. "Use this time wisely. We will feed you and I will strengthen you as I can, and then you must press to save your people." She turned to leave.

"I don't want this!" Adamar said and pounded the chair's arm with the bottom of his fist. "Why me!? Of all vacants, why me!?"

"Because you are the only one I know of to see more potential in your vacancy than others in their magic."

"What does that matter?" he asked.

SonLara leaned closer and said, "Because more than you or any second energy mage knows, this universe is the product of observers. How the observer, through first-energy direction, chooses to see and interpret this universe most affects how it responds."

"What does that mean?" asked Adamar.

"It means, young man, that you are among the few I've ever met—mage, commoner or vacant—to know a core truth of this universe."

"Which is?"

"That you are not a product of this universe," said SonLara. "It is a product of you."

62

Commission

Elverbane eyed the Dogwood Sword lying inside its red velvet case while his mind raced—he had seen this sword before. Staring at it gave him chills of import. "Duffie did what?"

"The fool tested it in a closed environment," said Degreneth. He frowned from behind his large wooden desk, backed by a towering window revealing an unprecedented view from the high bluff of the agricultural fields northeast of the city and the twinkling Vitner Canal as it traveled north and east into the foothills leading to Eden. "Nearly killed three wizards, seven administrators, eighteen attendants and his own vacant assistant."

"We know almost nothing about this bloody thing and he points it at a human being?" asked Elverbane. "Fookin' wankstain."

"What matters is that it has come to us now," Degreneth said. "And I expect you to *safely* figure it out."

"Me?" Elverbane's brow drooped.

"I've given you enough leeway as it is," said Degreneth. "Weeks of free leave to pursue this mystical mission you say you're on and I need you in the saddle on this war council! Packs have been spotted moving in our direction from the east."

Elverbane frowned.

Degreneth leaned on his fists, underlit by sunlight bouncing off the piles of sheafs littering his broad desk. "I can't offer you anymore time unless you want to take sabbatical, and before you even offer to do such a thing, I need you! Your experience is why the king asked specifically for you. The Hero of Tuthomere."

Elverbane scowled. "Surely you can send Al'Sun or Rolutzi to this… commission. Didn't Rolutzi just return from helping with the Utalian trade agreements?"

"Trade agreements are hardly adequate for war councils," said Degreneth.

"You might be surprised," said Orzo from behind Elverbane.

Degreneth glared.

"Orzo has a point," said Elverbane. "Trade agreements are all about finding what each side wants and negotia—"

"I already saw your point," said Degreneth, "and you're ignoring that lycans can't be reasoned with, merely cowed!"

"Why commission *me*?" Elverbane asked.

"I have no freedom in this matter," said Degreneth. "I already offered what you're thinking and the king won't allow me out of the city."

"What? Why?" Orzo asked.

"The king is jealous of his counselors," said Degreneth. "He won't risk us."

"There is a great deal at stake right now," said Elverbane.

"More than yet another lycan war in Pangea?"

"Wars, half wars, rumors of wars," said Orzo. "When are we not at war?"

"You both well know the threat we face should the lycans recommit open warfare," Degreneth leaned over his desk. "It doesn't just affect one nation. It affects nearly all of them!"

"What we're doing might affect a little more than that," said Elverbane.

"Pardon me if I'm having a little trouble believing that," said Degreneth. "Unless you're prepared to tell me what you're doing?"

Elverbane swallowed.

"Tomorrow morning, you will attend the king and his council with Wizard Orzo and be prepared to offer him what service you can," said Degreneth. "I don't get you, Elverbane. What could be so important to keep you from helping the king and that you can't tell me about it!?"

"I'm sorry, administrator," said Elverbane. "I don't think I can say."

"Then you will attend the king after breakfast tomorrow," Degreneth straightened.

"On one condition," Elverbane said.

Degreneth paused.

"Under no circumstance—even by order of the king—will I teach anyone how to use a worldender or this sword in the same way."

Degreneth hesitated a second too long. "Of course not. I remember your stance from years ago."

"Good," said Elverbane.

"Don't be late," Degreneth said. "The king will be expecting you."

The two wizards left.

"Tha' bloody white-livered feartie," muttered Elverbane as they left the administration building. "That fuckin' roaster." Turning, he marched onward, scattering students in his wake.

Elverbane glowered as they marched along the paved walk.

"What will you tell your lady?"

"What?" asked Elverbane.

"SonLara."

"What are you talking about?"

"I've seen how you look at her," Orzo said. "And how she—"

"What do you know?" Elverbane asked.

"I know you're a puppy," said Orzo. "As much as Setherick Elverbane could be a puppy."

"I don't want to hear it."

Orzo chuckled. "How many seeds did you say he left?"

"Eight," said Elverbane.

"And the pixies?"

"Supposedly will help," Elverbane said.

"Tell her," said Orzo.

"Baah. Why are you following me?"

"I thought you could use a refresher on the wars for tomorrow," Orzo shoved his hands in his robe. "You only have a few hours before Myogan might want something remotely wise to come out of your mouth."

"To hell with that," Elverbane said.

"Can we help the vacants?"

"From what you heard during the secret enclave?" asked Elverbane. "I dannae have the capacity to save more than I'm already fighting for."

"And Haephan?"

"Yeah?" asked Elverbane.

"What will you do about him?" Orzo asked.

"Not a self damned thing," Elverbane said. "He's staying with me."

"And if they come for him?"

Elverbane's countenance darkened. "I keep me and mine."

"Good to hear."

"Doubted me?"

"Not for a second," Orzo said. "Still want to know if you have a plan if things turn south."

"If those bastards haven't already figured out by now," Elverbane rounded on him with a raised finger. "I am the fuckin' south."

They continued into Ashmore Hall. Inside Elverbane's study, they found seeds everywhere. The wooden box and a chair lay overturned under the thin angles of pale light from the windows on the left. Elverbane's breath quickened as he scanned the room. Orzo retreated as Elverbane's presence found brief menace. After a moment, Elverbane relaxed. "It's a'right."

"What happened?"

"I think the boy got carried away," Elverbane stepped inside and stooped to gather seeds.

Orzo helped reorder the room. "Are you sure? Was anything taken?"

"A few seeds are gone, but the boy has been busy."

Orzo nodded.

"I'm not really going to help them," Elverbane said.
"I didn't think you would," said Orzo.
Elverbane gripped Orzo's arm with thanks.
"We need to spin you up so you look prepared," Orzo said. "Grab a seat. I'll put on some coffee. Let's get started."

63

Cordurons

"Are you sure you wouldn't rather wait a day or two?" asked Sgaarsbad. Nick's haggard face winced as the carriage bounced over rolling, grassy terrain. After leaving Aminrale before sunrise, they approached a high wall of rock at the base of a low mountain range under an overcast morning sky.

"I can't— I can't be in the palace right now," said Nick as he blinked his dry, bloodshot eyes. "I'll…either I'll try and kill Heilbin, or I'll…I dunno."

Sitting across from him in the open carriage, Sgaarsbad grimaced. "I'm sorry, my friend. Still, we could put off whatever it is you want to show me."

"No," said Nick. "We don't have much time and it would be good to try and think on something else. Besides," a bump brought another wince, "bloody hell, Sgaar." Nick cradled his head as the carriage bounced down the rocky road. "What was in that damned drink?"

"That," Sgaarsbad raised a finger, "is my special concoction. A secret, and one not to be shared with you again until you have a better stomach and less of a reason for inhaling it."

"What? Why?" asked Nick.

Sgaarsbad shook his head.

The carriage rolled to a stop. Sgaarsbad, Nick and Ephterehn climbed out and untied three horses tethered to the rear. Mounting, Nick led them into a narrow canyon hidden from the plain by its shallow angle of entry. Once inside, the walls climbed and drowned them in shadow as drips of water fell from the sky above, forcing the three to raise their hoods against the sudden damp chill.

"Ephterehn," said Nick as he pinched the bridge of his nose.

"Yes, my krys?" Ephterehn asked.

"You and I will be traveling to…um," Nick drifted off.

"New Gordon," Sgaarsbad said.

"Yes, there."

"Of course, my krys," Ephterehn said. "How many will be coming?"

"Just us."

"My krys?"

"Just us, Ephterehn," Nick said. "Small and short, no formality, and the Prince of Klaus will be joining us."

"Ah, yes, my krys. When will we be going?"

"Three days," Nick said. "By rimsportal, so pack light. One pack for each of us."

"No other attendants, sire?"

"No," Nick held his forehead.

Ephterehn nodded.

"Prince of Klaus?" Sgaarsbad asked. "Weren't those the old—"

"Yes, the original dream walkers," said Nick.

"Krys Kringul travels under the name when he wishes to remain otherwise anonymous," said Ephterehn.

"Ah," Sgaarsbad mused. "Fine idea. I don't know if there's an original name for drunkard king, though…"

Ephterehn suppressed a smirk.

An hour later, the winding canyon widened before splitting into three, narrower rifts. The elves dismounted under gentle rain between high walls of pale rock, tied their horses and continued afoot. Scrub climbed across the rippled walls to the high edges where it met low bush and trees.

Sgaarsbad tilted his hood. "I did not know you had such territory in Aminrale."

"It's a small, usually arid pocket along the Ifnan Ridges," Nick scanned the upper edges of the canyon rim as thick gray clouds drifted by overhead, drowning the canyon deep in shadow while wet air painted everything with a cold sheen.

"What's up here you wanted to show me so badly that you risked the worst hangover of your life?"

Nick cringed as his head pounded. "Our time is short and you need to know of a very important asset I have for our move."

Curious, Sgaarsbad looked to Ephterehn, who offered nothing. His intrigue deepened as the two followed Nick into a rift filled by a deep creek. The tall high elves half ducked as the rock walls narrowed and dipped. Ten minutes of twisting back and forth, briefly marching through frigid water and one squeeze where Nick and Ephterehn had to push through Sgaarsbad's thick belly, they reached a cul-de-sac where a rushing waterfall fed a pool. Scrub lathered the chamber's interior around the waterfall, which fell into a large pool covering most of the base, snaked across and disappeared into a thin crack in the terrain to their left.

"Wow," Sgaarsbad panned. "I never knew you owned such a thing. I've never moved a waterfall before."

Shaking his head, Nick rounded the churning pool along the narrow beach and walked sideways up the wall. Sgaarsbad hustled behind him to the base. His mouth fell open to discover a secret set of narrow stairs climbing the cul-de-sac's walls in a long spiral.

"Ha!" Sgaarsbad laughed. "Clever!" Leaning on the wall to balance his bulk, he followed. Ephterehn brought up the rear with a free hand ready to steady Sgaarsbad, should he lose his balance on the rain-slick steps.

The stairs looped around the high chamber three times before they slipped behind the waterfall beneath its apex. Sgaarsbad climbed the final stairs. He caught his breath and pulled back his hood where, in the recess of a narrow hallway of rock deep in the shadow of the waterfall, he picked out a hidden doorway.

Nick felt chagrined as the natural engineer picked out in seconds what had taken him a week to find.

"Great Self in a hand basket…" Sgaarsbad gulped. "What do you have back here?"

Nick nodded for him to proceed.

Sgaarsbad slid his hands over the rock wall like a man feeling out a new lover. His fingers caressed its curves and nooks before sliding into a hidden divot. He squeezed with his right and pushed at the center with the left.

The door didn't push in as he expected, but rotated inward and faded from reality to reveal brilliant sunlight pouring through.

Sgaarsbad retreated.

Nick stooped through the small door into the ambience. Raising his hand to block the glare reflecting off a polished floor, Sgaarsbad wiggled through the doorway and onto a balcony overlooking a high-walled valley bathed in noonlight—not due for another four hours on the previous side of the door—thick with moisture and covered in greenery.

Following them in, Ephterehn twisted a stone in the wall. The door reappeared and rotated back into place.

"Where have you brought me?" asked Sgaarsbad.

Shielding himself from the painful light, Nick said, "Where you wanted most to be."

"What?" Sgaarsbad gulped.

A horn erupted from the valley in sets of three bursts.

Tiny pedestrians visible across the pocket valley rushed out of sight while others raced into sight with weapons in hand.

Nick tapped his mouth with a look at Ephterehn, who nodded. Nick covered his tall, pointed ears as Ephterehn produced a high warbling whistle that echoed across the valley.

Most of the advancing figures slowed to a walk while a few continued to the base of the switchback stairs far below them.

"Come, Sgaar," said Nick as he started his descent.

Sgaarsbad rubbernecked as he followed. Ephterehn gripped his shoulder more than once to keep him focused on a safe descent until they reached the high base platform rising above the rolling terrain where a group of elves awaited—none of whom stood taller than a human child.

Once Nick came into clear view, a leader waved at his guards, who lowered their crossbows and shields, which appeared to vibrate until set down.

Sgaarsbad's mouth fell open.

"Master Sandark," Nick greeted the leader, an elf shorter than a dwarf but taller than a gnome with short-cropped midnight hair and cherrywood eyes. Sandark raised his hand in greeting, wearing a snug cobalt blouse beneath a navy vest tucked into a broad belt over trousers bloused into high black boots.

His sleeves were rolled into smoothed flats ending above his elbows. His two breast pockets were sewn in long half-circles downward at angles from his neckline. A long crescent with the two sharp points connecting at the tiny hinge formed his belt's ornate buckle, with a square clasp slid through his belt hole and connected to the far side of the crescent.

"Krys Kringul," Sandark's deep, clear voice belied his small stature. "You are welcome in Helmsland. What brings you here today?" *Without warning*, his tone made clear.

"Pardon my unannounced arrival, Master Sandark," said Nick, "but..." He searched for the words, "great change has come to Aminrale, and I have come to discuss a paradigm shift for us both."

Sandark stiffened. "What kind of change?"

"The big kind."

Sandark pursed his lips. "And my lord's guest?"

"Ah, yes. This is Krys Sgaarsbad Hagal," Nick said and motioned to Sgaarsbad, who gulped and offered a half bow.

Surprised, Sandark raised a hand in greeting. "Krys Kringul, this does not abide our agreement."

"Our agreement will have to change, Master Sandark. May we speak?"

Sandark raised a hand in greeting to Ephterehn as he had to the two kryses before motioning to a companion who rushed off. "Of course.

Please, this way." He descended the stairs and led them along valley paths.

The entourage wound among small fields and thickets. Narrow rifts in the canyon walls led to other small pockets of fields. Carved from rock and adorned in refined wood, foreign stone and metal, windows and balconies peppered the vertical sheets of red stone wreathed in verdant green. Some even boasted planes of glass with a clarity Sgaarsbad struggled to believe could be done without the telltale rippling of magic.

Small bridges crossed the expanse at narrows and even formed landings with second bridges. They entered a new canyon the size and beauty of the first and wound toward a tall building carved into its end. Thousands of locals leaned out of windows and balconies.

"They're bloody Cordurons!" blurted Sgaarsbad.

Sandark scowled at Nick.

"I don't know about 'bloody,' but they are Cordurons," he said. "Does this bother you?"

"Hell no," said Sgaarsbad.

Sandark pondered as they passed through an ornate marble archway into the canyon wall, climbed sets of stairs and entered a high marble hall braced with ribs of rich yellow wood lit with dispersed white light.

"We fabricate the light without magic, Krys Hagal," said Sandark.

"How?" asked Sgaarsbad.

"Diodic bulbs."

"Impossible," said Sgaarsbad.

Sandark waited.

"Impossible without magic! It has been tried!"

"And achieved," Sandark said.

Sgaarsbad stared. "Amazing."

"Can we offer refreshment?" Sandark asked.

"Water, please," said Nick.

Sandark noted Nick's condition and whispered to a nearby attendant who stepped away.

"How—?" asked Sgaarsbad. "No, no." He raised his hands. "How are they here?"

"Would you like to or me?" Nick asked Sandark, who offered a bare shake of his head. "The Cordurons were hunted after Thantil's Rebellion, and by more than wizards. Apparently the Corduron penchant for high-functioning creativity makes their minds easy pickings for a certain magical psychic."

"Daleens?" Sgaarsbad's brow drooped.

"They did most of the damage during the early years after the rebellion failed. A few Corduron hiding here in the buttes paid a wizard willing to help for a protection spell. They were here 800 years before the spell began to wear off."

"And you found them?"

"When I was a bit more active, I would husband the dreams of my people and go wandering my territory for travelers and the like," Nick accepted a glass of iced water from the attendant. "One day, Corduron dreams began to trickle into my own."

"Do you serve him?" Sgaarsbad asked Sandark.

"We…not exactly," said Sandark. "Family doesn't serve family."

Sgaarsbad frowned.

"He's right," said Nick. "We are family."

"What?" asked Sgaarsbad.

"In order to extend my protection over them, permanently, without a spell, I accepted them into my household," said Nick. "Formally."

"Through…marriage?" Sgaarsbad asked.

"Through a kinsbond," said Nick.

"You *adopted* them?"

"Yes," Nick said.

"Why!?" Sgaarsbad blurted at Sandark. "I thought you hated the krysdom and were committed to destroying the old order and all that?"

"We were committed to destroying divine right," said Sandark. "As Aminrale operates more upon functional pragmatism than divine selection, we found Krys Kringul an acceptable compromise, both for his kindness and his ability to protect us from Daleens and the tyrant who sent them after us."

"Tingal the Great," said Sgaarsbad. "No elf could fail to know the name, regardless of den or country."

"My…great granduncle," said Nick. "I never met him."

"Poisoned!" Sgaarsbad extended a finger before turning to Sandark. "You agreed to let him be your krys?"

"Krys Kringul was kind enough not to associate us with our progenitors," said Sandark. "And in exchange, we would improve Aminrale's agricultural machinery."

Sgaarsbad spun. "*That's* why!"

Nick nodded his thanks when the attendant returned with another glass of water floating with green particulates. He gulped it down.

"Aminrale's agricultural efficiency grew tenfold! No one knew why," said Sgaarsbad. "Do the people know, too? This would be a big secre—"

"It was an arrangement made in private, as much to preserve their dignity as their security," Nick raised his hand. "No one knows but me, Ephterehn and now you."

"And why have you violated that agreement?" Sandark asked. "You made an oath on your responsibility as krys—"

"I am no longer krys of Aminrale," Nick said. "Or…am closing that chapter, at least."

Sandark paused his upraised gesture. "What?"

Nick took a slow breath and set the glass down as an attendant refilled it. "I have been visited by a subrim, who has commissioned me to travel to a new land and protect a people chosen from among Pangean humans."

Dumbstruck, Sandark asked Sgaarsbad, "You, too?"

Sgaarsbad nodded.

"Nick, you of all people know what we think about your elven religions," said Sandark.

"You and my wife might get along," Nick muttered and raised his voice. "Like it or not, Sandark, something supernatural visited me, Sgaarsbad, and Heilbin Seagol—" He hesitated at Seagol's name. "Both suffered similar visits by a being of profound power."

"Just because a more powerful magical being visited you doesn't mean heaven somehow sent some kind of angel to the mortals," Sandark's eyes narrowed.

"You have no idea," said Sgaarsbad.

"That could very well be true," said Nick. "However, my experience with the subrim shook me to my core. I've met dragons who were ancient before even the Courte Empire had its first thatch settlement on the Tuney. I even met an aurora, once, when I was young." He shook his head. "I've never been exposed to such power as the being who summoned me to the Zulta'mans upon the back of a reindeer in a single hour."

Sandark looked to Sgaarsbad, who shrugged.

"I'm not asking you to believe as I believe, Master Sandark, but my convictions have set things in motion which will take me and my household to a new land to protect humans."

"Humans?" asked Sandark. "I've never before heard of a high elf serving humans."

"It's a first for us, too," said Sgaarsbad.

"Why would a powerful being ask you to do such a thing?" asked Sandark. "And what are you to do?"

"I'm to protect their dreams," Nick said. "And I'm not even sure how I can do that. I've never interfaced with a human before."

"Then why would you be chosen by this supposed general of heaven?"

"I don't know," Nick said. "Much of this is new to me, but I am willing to obey my commission."

"And your part?" Sandark asked Sgaarsbad.

"I am a transrealmic engineer," said Sgaarsbad.

"You don't say…"

Nick smirked at the Corduron's growing intrigue, gulped more water, and sat up. "Master Sandark, I have come to tell you I can no longer function to my oath, now that I am leaving Aminrale."

Sandark's curiosity evaporated.

"However," said Nick, "I have a new arrangement to propose to you and your people."

Sandark raised his chin.

"Come," he said. "Join me. If we are taking these humans to a place of their own, away from the magical conflicts and rulers here in Pangea, it might be the perfect place for you. Come and build your homes in a place of safety, so that no matter what happens to me, you might have a place for your future generations to enjoy the same security.

And according to Sgaar, a fine place of wonder."

Sandark cocked his head. "Away from Pangea? Where could that be?"

"To a new place," Sgaarsbad smiled. "A new realm beside Pangea in spacetime. It's a new dimension, so-to-speak."

"What do you mean?" Sandark asked.

"A new world!" Sgaarsbad's voice hovered with awe. "To the very fabric of its physics! This new world is a wonder. It's a ball in space, hovering with other—"

Sandark leapt to his feet, cutting him off.

"…what?" Sgaarsbad sat up.

"Worlds of matter suspended in gravitational spacetime in an endless vacuum of expanding binary energies?"

"Great Self…" muttered Sgaarsbad. "That's what I saw."

"By my mind," Sandark spun to Nick. "When do we leave?"

64
Saving Haephan

When SonLara's carriage stopped outside Ashmore Hall in the early morning dim, she found a worried, waiting attendant.

"Priestess SonLara!" he cried as soon as the driver opened the carriage door. "Haephan was found wounded in the kitchen. He is at the infirmary. Please, hurry. He is dying!"

"I can drive you there!" the driver said.

Without a word, she descended the steps and headed for the infirmary across the sacred quads of grass. The attendant followed at a light jog while she glided. Glowlights warmed the walkways under the evening mists wafting up and over the edge of the northeastern bluffs upon which the school sat. Her white cloak glowed as slow heartbeats of a specter beneath each lamp under the deepening evening darkness and thickening fog.

She flew across the ground to the main administration building whose bright windows blazed against the night. Attendants yanked open the heavy front doors to admit her to the brilliant lobby where a nurse turned at her arrival.

"Priestess!" she cried. "We've been looking all over for you, mum! Please, come with me." She turned on her heel, led the way down the hall and turned the corner by the intensive care rooms. Nurses waiting by a door perked at her approach and moved aside as she led SonLara into a room spilling warm light across the hall.

SonLara set in her first foot and identified the scene before her second foot followed: table, doctor, wizard, wizard, doctor, nurse, boy on table with rent back oozing blood, two wizards behind that, doctor on near side and four wizards at the end.

Freezing inside the doorway, her gaze chilled them.

"Out," her voice snapped the air. "Now."

"Priestess SonLara—" said Degreneth as he turned from the group.

"Get out of this room before you kill the child," she cut him off and stepped out of the doorway. "Now."

"We don't know why he has magic," Degreneth said. "How did that happen? But if he's not vacant, our magic should work. We tried healing him but something won't let us. What can you tell—"

"He is more important than all of you combined, now get out of this room."

One nurse moved to obey and slowed when no one else did.

For the first time, SonLara scowled. "NOW!" Every glass pane in the room splintered. Those inside snatched their ears. Her gaze dared them to disobey.

Cradling their heads, the nurses left, followed by the doctors and all of the wizards but a hesitant, indignant Degreneth. Hesitant to look her in the eye, he left. Once gone, she stepped into the door and pointed at one of the waiting nurses.

"Gather five water-sealed canvas sheets no less than ten by fifteen feet," she said. "You can retrieve them from the services administration and you will get them here immediately with forty feet of rope."

From another, she ordered four quarters of alcohol and general disinfectant. The boy already had an intravenous fluid line in him. Turning, she shut the door and raised her hands to warm the air temperature to body-normal.

It appeared the doctors and nurses debated how much bandaging would help or hurt the boy. Though a wise question, none had given a second thought to the threat of infection while the boy remained open as he was; they were too accustomed to sterilizing magic.

The professionals they were, they subsisted entirely on common magile medicine; the wizards among them had probably never seen a magic such as Haephan's. Did the mantle protect Haephan from their attempts to heal him? Perhaps their methods were too aggressive.

SonLara had so little to go on, but she had to try anything that might work to save the boy. His survival thus far testified to his mantle, but she did not believe it would inoculate fully against death. The weakening magic struggled to preserve the boy. If she couldn't restart the functions the child would die.

While Haephan's first heat-based injury was of unknown origin, this carried the distinct indicators of dragon's fire. How had the boy encountered a draco at the edge of the world?

Haephan stole seeds from the dragons of Eden. Likely enraged, the magnus draco would have deployed hunter seekers to find him.

"Self in Heaven," she muttered at having missed that potentiality.

She traced the massive burn that ran from the back right of Haephan's right cranial occiput down to his right buttock and halfway across his left posterior rib cage around to his right anterior breast. His right arm lay ripped open missing most of his bicep and the rest of it melted with skin hanging and dripping with grease. His injuries at Goram's were severe but survivable. Haephan now lay well past death's door by any reasonable assessment, but she could not let him die.

She pressed her left hand on the good flesh of his lower left posterior and crown of his head.

Delving herself, she loosed the gates that protected her soul from his and let the information flow. Great Andonese internists had restored lost fingers and severe cranial impacts. What could she do with Haephan's mantle? Her efforts had to be passive or it might activate the same defenses that blocked the wizards.

The thread of energy left within him poised for connection yet evaded for completion. Securing that first filament took minutes she hated to spare. Anxiety deepened within her as the mantle fought her control.

SonLara gritted her jaw and loosed more barriers in order to passively meld her immune system with Haephan's to serve as a consulting surrogate for sections of his body whose immunity no longer functioned.

Pain raced up the tiny thread of connection and raked over her own nerves. At first moaning in shock, she diverted and hid the pain in a corner of her mind so she might press onward.

She feared he would die before she could make this work when the first whispers of response followed the pain through her connection.

The distant echo of the knocking door returned her to consciousness.

Her eyes opened and flinched when the light in the room now burned her sensitive eyes. "Come."

"We have your materials, priestess," said one of the nurses.

"Seal them to the ceiling and close in around this bed," SonLara kept her fingers on his body to maintain her tenuous connection. "Make sure both ends remain tight against each other. Use the alcohol and wipe down the table, inside of the canvas sheets, floor and, finally, the exterior of the boy without dribbling into his body. When finished, have one nurse remain behind in the room and outside the curtain. Do not disturb me again."

Closing her eyes, she loosed herself once more to the work. She released her outer senses and gave over. The link enveloped her more than she had dared let happen in her entire life—a skill few Andonese ever mastered.

Instead of trying to imagine how experts did it, she drew upon her own experience from dimensional layering.

All conscious beings were little more than layers of energy, beginning with the observer spirit—the hallmark of Andonese study. Next came the vernacular soul abridging spirit to incarnation. Ego served as a mental structure to coordinate incarnation—what sentients identified as self. Above ego and its compositional layers spread the finest energetic lace she ever knew to exist—the new bencari Haephan acquired in Eden.

Haephan's mantle tingled her fingers as she delved the fine layers.

She dismissed it as she focused on his immune system and its responsive nervous cilia. As she reached for them, however, they shrank from her caress. Time passed as she groped on his thin synaptic pathways; the harder she pressed, the more they evaded.

SonLara recalled her original intent—to use what she knew, not what she didn't. Haephan's bencari tickled her fingers again, as if inviting her attention.

Focusing on the mantle, a view of it spread in the endless darkness of her mind's eye like a shimmering solar lattice. Letting her psychic fingers caress its infinity, seams of it curled about her.

She dismissed the nervous filaments and focused on the bencari. Intuitive like no other mantle she before had studied, its complexities behaved less as constructs and more as if alive.

With care, she disconnected from the boy's immune system and noted its immediate withdrawal and falter. The flame of life within Haephan stalled. Instead, she offered herself to the bencari.

The mantle *recognized* her. Her mind's aperture widened in shock before the bencari exploded with countless threads into her own nervous system. Though disconnected from her, she knew Haephan's body glowed like a small sun and hoped the nurses had finished her orders by now.

She marveled as the mantle drew from and allocated what she could spare into each area the boy needed most—a symbiote dedicated to save and empower its host. The bencari moved with surgical precision to restart vital healing processes and restore areas of his central nervous system.

Most of Haephan's spinal column, several organs and large sections of bone lay open to the air. She ignored the visible problem—as her Librarian had often instructed her—and focused instead on what was to be achieved and how.

That in mind, she dismissed how close he lay to death, how gruesome it appeared, or even that he was a brave boy who deserved more in life. Task was all.

The bencari responded to her intelligent input and directed her steps, led her energy and siphoned what it needed without putting her in danger. Over time, the boy's breathing changed and warmth bolstered.

Like an exhale held too long and finally released, the life within the child sustained itself. Reluctant to sever the connection, she knew that once done, she might be too depleted to return.

After several minutes of a steady heartbeat independent of her own autonomic nervous rhythm, she withdrew the connection, let her mental aperture dissolve and returned to present consciousness. Her body revived with signals she'd long ignored, including aching feet, stinging back, full bladder and exhaustion.

Once returned to presence, her knees faltered and she sank to the floor. Blinking under blinding light, she took heavy breaths and worked to clear her vision.

Coughing a dry mouth and swollen tongue, she climbed to her feet, pulled her fingers from Haephan's back and discovered part of his skin had grown into hers. Shock overcame her.

His arm had fully regrown. Warm brown skin covered what once had been rent torso and a decimated appendage.

She battled growing exhaustion to continue her inspection of the boy. She recognized the curtains in place as she swooned on her feet under a wave of dizziness.

SonLara stumbled through a fold in the canvas tent into pale morning blue bleeding through the window on her right—she had been at this an entire night.

"How is he?"

Surprised, she spun into Elverbane's nearness and gulped.

"Seth," she said.

"How are you?" Elverbane asked.

"Long day…" she crumpled as exhaustion consumed her.

The last she sensed was Elverbane scooping her against his barrel chest and carrying her into darkness.

65

Kringul Come

At the center of a thirty-foot-long walk surrounded by an arcade of columns, three concentric rings counterspun to form a fuzzy ball of glowing light. From the orb stepped two high elves clad in crimson longcoats and leather packs.

Dawnlight bathed the courtyard before they dismounted the far end of the platform to a scribe hunched over a monstrous book atop a short, fat column. Next to him, a guard saluted as they approached.

"Welcome to New Gordon," the guard half bowed. "May I have the names of m'lords?"

"Presenting the Prince of Klaus," Ephterehn motioned to Nick with a half bow. "And I am his attendant, Ephterehn."

The scribe's pen never changed cadence as the nearby lamp cast a fitful shadow of his quill across the parchment.

"M'lord's purpose in New Gordon?" asked the guard.

"Consult at the Academy," said Ephterehn.

Still, the scribe's pen danced heedless of the new information.

"Compensation is available for high elves who visit New Gordon," said the guard, "which includes lodging on Academy grounds, should m'lords wish it."

"We will be staying at the Majestery," said Ephterehn.

"Of course, m'lord," the guard bowed his head and straightened. "My lords are welcome anywhere in the city. According to city law, peacebinds are mandatory for full armaments and informal dueling is prohibited, to include street fights. Might I recommend avoiding the southwest quarter, known as Rainhold, lest my lords wish to lose their hair or break the law by killing the vagrants living there. All other needs may be submitted to the Academy at my lords' leisure."

"Understood," said Ephterehn.

"Lastly, your lordships, know an army is marching in our direction," said the guard with a flicker of worry on his face. "The king hasn't yet ordered it, but visitors might be ordered out soon. Especially ones as… regarded as yourselves."

Ephterehn nodded.

The guard bowed and extended his hand aside to indicate the exit.

Scowling, Ephterehn led Nick away, through a small archway and down a wide staircase into a broad plaza crossed by gaping pedestrians. "We're going to draw attention."

"Unavoidable," Nick continued through the crowd.

"I wish we had brought a few guards, m'lord," Ephterehn eyed the passersby.

"That would have drawn even more attention," Nick said as he headed east along Broadway, the widest east-west corridor in New Gordon. "Word of us will reach the deafest ears by lunch."

Ephterehn scowled and followed Nick into the throng of morning commuters.

A third higher than the tallest human, everyone watched their every step. Nick ignored them as he searched for brilliant blue hair. While he doubted finding her by chance, he would not dismiss the possibility.

As the two wandered the city, Ephterehn realized his plan to pay for information would fail; they were too aberrant to the social structure—no one could speak with them privately and most openly gaped. High elves did not mingle among commoners; they came in grand entourages and only engaged with nobles and wealthy merchants.

"Are you here for the wolves?" cried a teenager on the street before being yanked away by his mother with an apologetic half-curtsy.

The evening sun kissed the opposite horizon before the two made it to Bertrand Park. On its south end rose the Majestery, a vast lodging complex peaking above the sparse trees. The two cut across the grass. At this late hour, hundreds of men made their way home from work while gaggles of youth lounged.

"I look forward to returning home, sire," Ephterehn murmured.

"Hm?" Nick asked. "Home."

Ephterehn gulped. "Sire, I did not—"

Nick forestalled him with his hand. "Let us focus."

"Yes, sire," said Ephterehn. "If no one will speak with us privately, how are we to avoid the Academy or Belfast for information? I know you wished a low profile, sire, but…"

They passed uncontested through the Majestery's entry arch and climbed the long sets of stairs to the building entrance. Copper domes capped the grand marble structure. Multiple wings glowed in the deepening dusklight. All told, the estate sprawled larger than the royal palace in Aminrale.

"You wonder why, if we're keeping a low profile, we stay here?" asked Nick.

Ephterehn turned.

"High elves traveling the continent unguarded can draw unscrupulous figures," said Nick. "I would not endanger even the kindest innkeep with our presence. In daylight, we're untouchable. Asleep in bed? No. We will stay where the guards are sufficient to keep those kind at bay. We will pay the price for our inconsistency in other ways."

Ephterehn nodded as drizzle fell.

"Though to be clear," said Nick, "there is danger enough inside of other kinds. Come."

At the top of several grand flights of stairs, a white-gloved man in an ornate uniform met them with an expectant smile and a small entourage. "Welcome, my lords." He bowed deep. "Your presence honors us. Per your instructions, your rooms are ready. If you will follow me?" The manager motioned for them to follow to a lift up to the top floor, along a plush, red-carpeted hallway of white stone lit above by flower-shaped skylights and amber lanterns.

At a grand pair of doors, two guards opened the way and offered bows.

Inside, the manager led them through the grand foyer, presented the royal bedroom and motioned to attendant bedrooms nearby.

"All is prepared as you requested, Lord Prince," the manager stood in the middle of the suite. "Is there anything we might provide for your comfort or pleasure this evening?"

"Peace, sir," said Ephterehn.

The manager bowed his head. "To alert your graces, we received word this morning from the king that all visitors are to leave the city by week's end, due to the impending siege."

"We have heard and will be gone," said Ephterehn.

The manager bowed and led his small entourage away before the guards shut the door behind them.

"Finally, no eyes," Ephterehn sighed.

Nick stared at the doors to the bedroom.

"Shall I prepare our dinner, my lord?" Ephterehn inspected the room.

"No," Nick said. "No. Thank you, Ephterehn. I'm not sure I'm hungry. Please, rest. We will rise early tomorrow to begin our search. That will be all."

"Sire," said Ephterehn. "I'm available as you need."

"Yes, good night," said Nick.

Ephterehn retreated to his room as Nick struggled to step into the royal suite alone. Though he and Isheim had lived in separate suites, she had been his faithful wife. Her presence had been a comfort for so long that to be here alone with the weight of her betrayal was unbearable.

Atop the burden of following this damned subriminal commission to protect humans, it was more than he could stand.

Thinking of the bar downstairs, he left the room, descended the broad spiral staircases and navigated to the main lobby. He passed through the tall double-door arch into the Majestery bar. Along the far wall to his right, tall windows revealed the extensive gardens lit by small amber lanterns and underlit fountains.

Doors angled into the far corner joined the two walls of windows. Between him and the exit, a field of white tablecloths glowed in the light of tiny candles set upon the center of each.

A massive underlit bar and bar back stretched longways along the wall to his left with only one occupant near the far end nursing a brown liquor.

Nick ambled along the wall of windows with nervous energy coursing through him. He saw through the dark despite the tinted window reflections.

He didn't want to be around people and couldn't stand the idea of being alone. However close, Ephterehn was a reminder of Isheim. He served them their entire marriage, and memories of Isheim were short without Ephterehn near at hand. A flicker of worry crossed his mind of the two coupling in secret, one he fast dismissed for his trust in Ephterehn's character.

Nick made his way among the tables to the bar and took a stool halfway down from the lone customer.

"Sire," said the approaching barkeep, who offered a respectful nod of his head while avoiding any undue appearance of awe—a welcome respite from a day of open gaping. "What can I get for you?"

Nick pointed. "Brandy."

The barkeep set about pouring a large glass for his tall customer.

Nick could smell the brandy before the barkeep could uncap the bottle. The cherrywood liquid swirled for a moment in the glass before he lifted it and took a sip. As it tickled his tongue, he soaked in the moment of quiet.

The days since witnessing Isheim's emergence from Heilbin's room had been the most difficult of his life. He wanted to rage against the betrayal by blaming his fellow krys, but Sgaar was right—Heilbin wasn't the violator of an oath of fealty. Isheim had broken that faith.

"It's not right," said a feminine voice.

Nick turned in surprise. A woman sat next to him whose short stature gave an unfair view down the curves of a fine coat thick with dust fit snug over an ample figure.

"Pardon?"

"It's not right," she repeated as she motioned for the barkeep.

"What isn't right?" he dragged his attention toward her face. Rich mahogany punctuated bright eyes that gazed back with a seriousness about them in a caramel face that seemed to glow in the dim ambience.

"The way they mix their drinks in this town," she sighed from full, thick lips in a way that revealed how high her breasts had risen with breath.

Nick questioned how to speak with the woman who probably stood barely higher than his waist. Raising a gloved hand, she pointed at the backbar behind the bartender.

"Rom Ale, please, dear," she said.

Dressed in a prim vest and white blouse, the man gathered her bottle and a glass.

She raised her big brown eyes to Nick and finally posed a plush smile with a hint of porcelain teeth behind them. "It's rare I encounter high elves in my travels."

"How far do you travel?" asked Nick.

"Too far, my dear," she said and shook her mane of thick brown curls. "And too often for my care."

"Then why do it?"

"The money, I suppose," she said. "The adventure is nice, too, except when I keep coming back here."

"Don't like it here?"

"Too much rain," she said.

"Where do you come from?"

"Admia," she said. "And please, don't confuse me with the Meso side."

Nick struggled to focus on his lonely sulk and ignore the vixen beside him.

"What're you having?"

"Not enough."

Her throaty giggle interrupted his thoughts. "I usually say that."

"What is it you do?" he asked.

"Relationships."

His brow furrowed.

"Not like that," she nudged him with her elbow. "I'm a market networker."

Nick paused.

"I travel between cities getting to know available industries and then broker cross-continental partnerships."

"That actually sounds interesting," Nick admitted.

Though she had opened the front of her coat and revealed a partially unbuttoned top and a view deep into her bosom, her luscious smile swallowed him. "Doesn't it?"

Nick focused on his drink as his mind swam. This was not a place for him to be.

"What brings you to New Gordon?" she asked.

"Holiday," he lied. His mind played through images of his wife emerging from Seagol's quarters. Indignation welled within him—he ought to have the same right as Isheim to chase his pleasures. He should be able to play into the presence of such a beautiful young lady, too. Didn't he have the right?

Right. Nick's left fist flexed and loosened. It wasn't Isheim who upheld Nick's honor, but Nick. Were he to surrender to his own carnality, it wouldn't right the imbalance of his wife's betrayal, only dishonor himself.

"Oh? How long are you staying for?" her soft voice pressed against him as firmly as if she had hugged her breasts on his arm.

"If you will excuse me," he stood and pushed the remnants of his drink across the bar and fished out a coin. "I'm very tired. I think it's best if I try and get some sleep."

"Of course, my dear," she set her hand upon his forearm. "I know the troubles of long roads and cold sheets." She squeezed before he politely peeled away.

Nick forced himself out into the lobby and up the stairs to his hallway and room. She was only being nice, of course. Two travelers in a big empty bar, of course she would sit next to someone. Probably an extrovert who might love small talk with a man who sat alone at a bar and might be lonely.

Her curves played over in his mind until he envisioned his hands roaming over her body, pulling apart her coat and—

Clearing his throat, Nick returned to his room and started a shower.

This was going to be a long night.

66

Threats and Deals

Algodemere woke to pain. A dull sear burned an unresponsive eye while the other struggled to clear from heavy sleep. Thoughts and recollection danced from his grasp.

With care, he mustered from the ground and curled up. His slow exhale warmed the horn of his snout before he could focus. Shapes of several dragons drew nearer.

Where is the Lord Draco? asked Algodemere.

He hunts, said a dragon. *He will return shortly.*

By the winds, what happened to me? Algodemere asked.

Does my…Lord Algodemere not remember? asked the attendant.

No, I do not, Algodemere exhaled.

It would be best for the…Lord Draco to tell you, said the dragon. *We will tell him you're awake.* At his nod, an attendant took to the air, gained altitude and disappeared through the boughs of the Tree.

Good, said Algodemere. *Where are my Fedrans?*

The dragon glanced at his companion. *They're…out hunting for you, your majesty.*

The ache swelled in Algodemere's head which he laid down.

Sometime later, the distinctive snap of Cas'Doren's wings preceded his arrival before he and the attendant banked and alighted before Algodemere.

Cas'Doren loomed for a moment. *How fares the Dragon King of Fedra?*

Algodemere raised his head and winced. *My lord. What has happened to me?*

What do you remember, Algodemere? asked Cas'Doren.

Not much, said the dragon. *We came for our…visit. We…burned a village or something. And then a boy with…with a magic, of some kind. I could see it… it was…*

Cas'Doren cocked his head, ducking it as he waited for what Algodemere would say.

It's a bencari.

What? Cas'Doren asked. *A bencari? I saw no such thing.*

I am certain, Cas'Doren, said Algodemere. *The boy wore a mantle, and further, it was as the magic of the La'Du Lira Al'Cular, the Tree of Life. It is immortal magic, magic that could empower him beyond anything we faced during Aman'Kur.*

Like the Tree? Cas'Doren ruffled his head. *A bencari of the same magic? One of those mantles the wizards used to wear?*

Yes, my lord, said Algodemere. *Were you not there to see it? It shone like the sun. I've never seen such power upon a human, never in all our battles together. Had we faced such a thing during the war, we might not have won.*

The child wears…is that how he finds me!? Cas'Doren begged his thoughts. *Is that how he moves without moving?*

Tell me, please, said Algodemere. *Why can't I see from my eye?*

Cas'Doren's mind raced. He wouldn't need the time-bending sight hunters to track the child. The scent of the La'Du Lira Al'Cular could draw him anywhere on the continent in search of the child. Why hadn't he seen that before!? *The child attacked you. He appeared from nowhere, using his…magic, and struck you in the eye. Surely with the same bencari you saw. We got tangled trying to…fight him off.*

The boy? The boy made me feel as if I'd been rolled by the Lord of Fire?

Yes, said Cas'Doren. *The child is powerful and has…stolen from us. Do you remember the seeds?*

Seeds? Algodemere asked. *Perhaps. I can't think clearly, Lord Cas'Doren. Seeds of what? The La'Du Lira Al'Cular? The Tree! It fruits?*

He has stolen my small collection of seeds as a sign of dishonor to us, said Cas'Doren, surprised at Algodemere's lost memory. *They goad us to prove they can. To incite us. He and his wizard—*

Wizard? Algodemere's good eye narrowed as a snarl rattled deep from his throat.

Yeesss, said Cas'Doren. *A wizard who helped the child steal into the heart of Eden. They wish to prove we are weak and vulnerable. I will, myself, go to prove them wrong.*

Alone, my lord!? growled Algodemere. *My lord shall not go alone. Fedra awaits your call.* He flinched as his eye drooled fresh blood anew. *And I...I will have my revenge.* He cracked open his good eye and locked upon Cas'Doren. *My lord, where are my Fedrans? I did not come alone.*

No, they are seeking out game to feed you in your weakened state, said Cas'Doren. *I will retrieve them myself. Remain and rest. We have a long fight before us.*

Yes, said Algodemere.

At a nod, Cas'Doren led two of the attendants into the air and above the cavern. Once above the surface, he turned north.

We will convince our guests of the importance of getting the story straight, he said. He banked over a sink hole a few miles north of the Towers of Eden and descended over of his dragons guarding the Fedran entourage. Landing with a thunder, he whipped around to cow them.

Listen and listen well, growled Cas'Doren. *Your lordship has woken to hesitant memories. I've come to make sure all of you remember it as you should, and if any of you get the idea to correct the Lord of Eden, let me remind you why magnus draci are well known for eating enemies—dragon or not.*

The Fedrans recoiled.

While Cas'Doren told them the *correct* story, he thought about what Algodemere had said: The boy wore a bencari? A mantle of power like that from Aman'Kur? How could Algodemere see such a thing and he could not?

Even the weakest of bencaris shone to dragonkind. Wizard magic was in-born, however powerful they may become, and they could hide it if they wanted to. But mantles were another magic entirely, a structure formed of artificially laced power that clung to its bearer like a human cloak with roots in the being's soul. To the eyes of the magic'd, it shone as a tiny sun.

Cas'Doren didn't even know the boy had one!

His breast constricted with fear. Was his vision blocked? Might the child have thrown a spell upon and blinded him to his presence? Algodemere first saw the child upon the nest, but why hadn't Cas'Doren sensed such powerful magic only a few paces away?

Cas'Doren considered the wizard who had attacked and kept him from eating the child. He had been so dazed; the wizard must have cast some kind of spell upon him to allow the child to escape.

His sudden roar of fury at the realization cowed the Fedrans against the wall.

AM I CLEAR!? he bellowed.

None spoke for several seconds until one whispered a *yes*.

Good, he said when a shadow passed overhead. A sighthunter circled above.

Huffing, Cas'Doren clapped his jaws at them one last time, smiled at their flinch, cast himself above the sink and gained altitude.

My lord draco! cried the sighthunter.

What is it, Zicthang? asked Cas'Doren as he circled. *Do you have news from Kaurust?*

I'm afraid, sire, Zicthang said. *Kaurust has gone silent. We fear the worst.*

Cas'Doren rumbled deep in his throat.

And the boy! The other sight-hunters and I have seen him as Kaurust did. He plants new worlds in spacetime. Entire new realms have appeared in our minds! He uses your seeds to do this.

He steals and wastes my precious treasure? asked Cas'Doren. *Go, take half with you and do better than that proud fool Kaurust to ensure the child is dead. Capture every seed and return them to me.*

Half, sire?

Yes, half! Of the colony!

Zicthang hesitated, then banked south. *Yes, sire!*

Cas'Doren's only consolation was the pending new seed of the La'Du Lira Al'Cular. Intimate with the Tree's patterns, the seed would emerge within weeks. He would not leave until it emerged and would protect it like he hadn't before. With that seed, he would finish off the leviathans in the nether and return with their power. This time for good.

Cas'Doren admitted he had grown lazy and fat upon their energies, wasted for its own pleasure. When finished, he would no longer retreat to his Edenic den, but venture forth as he had in his youth.

The humans had brought this upon themselves. It was time to reclaim his power. With his draco population four times its size since first coming to Eden two thousand years ago, it was time to restore the birthright of the dragons.

It was time to rule Pangea, once more.

67

Fear and Doubt

Elverbane sat for hours while she slept in his sheets. For all his years without a companion, he hoped more to inspire her attention by his presence than through the passion of youth. The curve of her body beneath his covers, however, did not go unnoticed.

When Orzo came knocking on his door to check on her, he led his friend to Ashmore's rooftop deck to get fresh air. Elverbane faced the wane light of the setting sun, whose dusklight bathed the city as it fell away beneath him.

"…like I said, I tried her suite downstairs, first, but her door was spelled and I wasn't about to try navigating that with a woman in my arms," Elverbane tapped the railing.

"I didn't think you did anything vulgar," said Orzo while leaning on the corner rail.

"Some might have," Elverbane's brow sank.

"What's wrong?" asked Orzo.

"She's leaving."

"What? Why?"

"No," said Elverbane as his shoulders sank. "When we're done, she's going home."

"Did she say that?"

"Did she say that? Of course not. She doesn't have to! She doesn't belong here!" said Elverbane. His voice intensified until it echoed. "She's Andonese! We're not!"

"So, you're saying you don't want her around?" asked Orzo.

"I don't want her here!" Elverbane barked. Gripping the railing, his voice gentled. "I ne'er want her to leave."

"My friend," Orzo gripped Elverbane's shoulder. "You are in love."

"I feel like a fool," Elverbane admitted. "Is it love, Orzo? I haven't felt like this since I was forty-five, I think. I don't remember those years very well."

"I'm only 213," said Orzo. "I think those are foolish years for every wizard. We think we know and we don't really have any idea."

Elverbane searched the golden, setting sun. "Great Self. I thought this was supposed to be for fools. And easy!"

"Love is never easy."

"And what makes you so versed?"

"I had a wife," said Orzo. "Left me for a Tenician after the war, before I found faith and could give grace to myself as much as I needed to give to others." He leaned against the railing and crossed his arms. "Expert? No. But versed, yes."

"It's a fool's errand?"

"I would not say that," said Orzo. "If anything, it is a wise man's game. For the making and the keeping."

Seth's fingers clenched the railing. "What am I doing, Orzo? I have…things, to do. This is not the time to deal with this…bullshit!"

"You fell in love with that woman the moment you saw her," said Orzo. "And why are you so riled up about it? If you love her, talk to her. Tell her how you feel."

"I don't want this!" Elverbane erupted, slapping the railing. "I don't want her! I don't want these stupid distractions!"

Orzo dropped his arms as he moved from the column. "What are you, five years old? Get ahold of yourself! You can't go on forever living like some bloody hermit. You're human. Live, damnit! Love her. Come what may, she might love you in return. Who are you to decide her behavior before she does?"

Elverbane slumped. "I don't know how to do that."

"What?"

"Love her," Elverbane admitted. "I don't know how. I don't—" He clenched his fists. "I don't know how to do anything but what I've been doing for two hundred years. And you know what I really am, Orz—"

"Time to man up, Seth," said Orzo. "You can live the rest of your life in fear, always wondering what might have been or thinking your insides should dictate your outsides, or you can step out and tell the possibly best woman in the world for you how you feel."

"But, if she knew—"

"Are you not *the* Setherick Elverbane who has for our entire friendship taught that it is your mind that dictates who you are?" Orzo asked. "That fear is the surest path to unleashing the very animal you wish to keep hidden? One that all of us have and all must tame?"

Elverbane clenched his jaw, wiped tears of frustration from his cheeks and sniffed. "Maybe you're right."

"Maybe?" Orzo slipped his arm around Elverbane's shoulders. "By the Immortal, of course I'm right, you silly old galah."

"What now? Go tell her?"

"Yes, go tell your feelings to an unconscious woman," Orzo panned. "I'm sure that will go over wonderfully."

Elverbane's hesitant chuckle became relieved laughter.

"Come," said Orzo. "I'm hungry."

"Why do I always find you eating?" Elverbane muttered. "And how are you so skinny?"

"Because I don't stop eating!" Orzo laughed as they headed for the stairs. "And I have a good metabolism. I get it from my father."

68
Overheard

SonLara woke in increments. Each sense came alive in turn before her eyes fluttered open. Slivers of brilliant mid-afternoon sunlight cut between thick curtains and lit dust motes. Elverbane's scent hung heavy in her nose.

Suppressing her alarm, she scanned the room. Though she did not fear Elverbane, she was surprised to wake in his bed and grateful she was fully clothed.

Blue rosebuds floated in a bowl of water on the nightstand. Letting her head sink to the pillow, she smiled, drew in his scent and marveled that of all times, places and situations for a man to capture her mind and heart, this husky, gruff, bearded common human forged more heat in her belly than any pretty Andonese man ever had.

The lover she enjoyed in her sixties spent all his time climbing mountains and boating the great rivers. Though fun, it was brief and he was left behind in her role at the Library. Even the handsome older bookkeeper who took a brief interest did little more than scratch her surface.

SonLara married her career as she became a full Realm Delver, attained Librarian First Class to the Golden Hall and was chosen as the personal attendant to the Silver Librarian. Since then, she wasn't still enough to feel lonely.

While she studied transrealm digressive mechanics, the Silver Librarian sent her on his decadal walkabout. Though an exciting prospect in her youth, she would have rather cloistered in her dark rooms to study and catalog.

Lying alone in Seth's bed, she wondered what it would be like to share a life with someone, with all its accompaniments.

What was love?

How did it fit in the life of a Librarian First Class?

The life of a priestess of Andon?

What did it mean to SonLara Alva Amferadon?

What did it mean to her?

SonLara watched the connection between them form and grow with an excitement she thought long dead, and was amused that a man her junior who appeared her senior was the man of whom she became fond.

What it would be like to touch him and be touched in return?

Shivering, she wasn't sure how to deal with such resurgent yearnings.

Though secondary ramifications tickled the reaches of her mind, they didn't enter her conscious thought. She would deal with one thought at a time, letting each coalesce before weighing further considerations.

Were her feelings real? Did he think the same of her, or was his affection fraternal or paternal?

SonLara dismissed that idea. The way he looked at her said he felt something more that. But was he prepared to explore it any more than she was? Or less? Or was she being a complete and utter fool?

SonLara admired the roses and for a moment dismissed her questions. He liked her, of that much she was sure. She considered all she liked about him—his mind, intelligence, demeanor, eyes. She even liked his graying beard and stocky frame. A younger SonLara and her friends favored the young, narrow, hairless types, with easy smiles and flirtatious cheeks.

Today she couldn't imagine living with such an empty husk and pondered going home.

Home. She'd been here for many weeks and had begun already to think of Belfast as home. No, Seth felt like home. He was why she sought to return from her side trips, and for whom she yearned every night for their fireside chats. But home was also Andon.

Sighing, she never imagined she would return from this trip with anything more than reams of notes to study. However this trip ended, a great cost would incur, and she knew not how she would pay.

Unsettled by her sudden fear, she pulled away the sheet and climbed to her feet. She touched the petals, which quivered and floated away from her touch.

After a lingering glance at the bed and its roominess, she suppressed a sudden visual of two bodies lying there, shook her head and left. Out of the suite, down the hall and stairs to her own quarters, through the spelled lock and into her room, she started to disrobe in anticipation of a nice hot shower and meal.

Muffled voices bled through her window. She stepped closer, sure she could hear Elverbane's brogue.

"… doesn't have to! She doesn't belong here!" said Elverbane. "She's Andonese! We're not!"

SonLara's breath caught as the voice lowered, before rising again.

"I don't want her here!" Elverbane barked.

She stood, shocked as the voice dropped again. She pressed her loose fists to her breast over her shift, paling.

Perhaps she was wrong. She was definitely wrong.

SonLara took a step back and sat on the side of her bed facing the window. Her heart sank. How could she have been so wrong? Not only was he not in love with her, she was a distraction! Maybe that's why he was always looking, wondering when she would leave. Thinking she was mad or a nuisance or nag.

Tears welled as her heart flipped. How had she mistaken this for love? All the hope and chance she might explore a feeling she thought out of her reach, a chance at love.

Not only was she wrong, she was blind to his distaste for her even being here. She dropped her hands to her lap as tears snaked down her cheeks. It was as much from the shock of feeling anything as for realizing she was wrong.

She blinked at her flowing tears.

"I don't want this!" Elverbane erupted. "I don't want her! I don't want these stupid distractions!"

Instead of stemming her tears, she cried softly and held her face with both hands. How could she respond to being called a distraction? How could he call her such a thing? She came with good reason. And that silly man called her a distraction!

The priestess wept to the sound of Elverbane's soft laughter echoing through the window.

69
Looking for Tilly

Haephan woke beneath a blinding light. Blinking several times clarified recessed gaslights shining from a flat ceiling filling a space walled by canvas sheets. He scanned them, pushed up onto his elbow and rubbed his face. Collecting his thoughts, all that came to mind was the memory of losing his dad's ring.

Haephan cursed. He would go to the barracks and hunt down that son of a bitch next. The wizard didn't need to know.

Nearby, a chair scraped before canvas sheets parted next to him to reveal a startled nurse.

"You…" she started. "How're you sitting up!?"

Haephan's brow drooped. "Like a person?"

She pulled away his bedsheet to reveal new flesh a paler shade of brown than his normal dark coffee skin.

"Hey!" Haephan yelled and yanked the sheet back, when the nurse's eyes rolled up inside her head and she collapsed against the curtain and thumped across the floor. Her brunette hair caught in one of the clips binding the curtain sheets and dragged them from their tenuous ceiling mounts to the floor with a crash. "Gah!" Haephan started to climb off the bed when he realized he was nude. "What the hell?" He yanked the bedsheet with him, slid off the table and wrapped himself before checking on the unconscious nurse.

The door slammed open to reveal a hallway full of nurses and a few worried doctors, who gaped at him standing over the nurse in a haphazard toga.

"You-you should be dead!" cried one of the doctors while those in the hallway jostled their way in to inspect him.

Startled, Haephan shifted away, fell through the air and crashed into icy water. He disentangled from the sheets, surfaced and inspected the familiar roof of his nest in the old boathouse. To his surprise, "home" meant a nest that no longer existed. He splashed to the dock and climbed out shivering. A shirt and trousers hung to dry on the edge of a nearby boat. He shifted to grab them and appeared in a private dead-end alley to don them. He used an old Rainie technique to cinch the oversized pants around his waist. The empty alley was familiar—this nook was used to corner victims for theft or assault. Often empty, he figured it was a safe place to put himself together.

Once clothed, Haephan set both hands on either side of the narrow as exhaustion washed over him. Dolphus. He needed to find Dolphus. He thought of a few ways to scare him into handing over the ring.

Haephan could shift Dolphus into the air, drop and catch him before he hit. That would certainly scare him!

The echo of yelling preceded the panting of a desperate boy who rounded the corner and flinched at the sight of Haephan. He backed against the corner wall leading into the narrow.

As the gaggle of snickering boys approached, their leader cocked his head. "Haephan?"

"Kilgy," Haephan glanced between the wolves and their sheep. "Fresh meat?"

Kilgy snickered.

Haephan frowned at the panting young boy—some middle-classer thinking he was tough enough to venture into Rainhold. "Leave him be."

When Kilgy laughed, his gang echoed. "You want in on the action, too? Or were you hoping to end up like your little bitch, Tilly?" Unhooking a chain tied to his belt behind his back, Kilgy whipped it into a spin.

"Tilly?" asked Haephan. "What's happened to him!?"

"Wouldn't you like to know?" Kilgy laughed. "How about we take you over to him when we get first go!"

"...in a place where no one can see you," Elverbane had told him.

The wizard's words echoed in his mind. Haephan had been careful, done his work and for once would do something *he* considered important, and he was alone enough to do it.

Kilgy lunged with an over-arm swing, but despite being within arm's reach, missed Haephan and struck himself in the legs. He yelped, hopped in surprise and bumped into someone standing close behind him. His gang flinched as he half-turned and found Haephan behind him. How had he—

Haephan rammed his knee upward into Kilgy's ass and sent him flopping in a backward flip into the far stone wall next to the startled young target. Kilgy slumped into the mud. Caught in the narrow, the gang didn't see how far Haephan kicked their leader before two rushed him.

He shifted before their shoulders could get him, snatched and shifted the target aside as the two rammed into the corner wall. Haephan shifted to the final two as they advanced, confused how three of their small gang lay stunned at the foot of the wall.

Appearing before them, Haephan snatched them by their hair, yanked hard enough to pull them off their feet and shifted both of them high over the canal before returning. Terrified, the target pissed his shorts.

The two who ran into the wall recovered without seeing their cohorts disappear. As one advanced, Haephan spun, drove his fist across his jaw with a satisfying crack and sent him flopping and screaming to the ground. The second ducked under, planted his shoulder in Haephan's gut and prepared to drive him into the mud.

Haephan shifted them so that the boy drove him into the open ocean. The thug released him and flailed for the surface while Haephan reshifted to the alley with a small burst of water.

The terrified middle-classer screamed at his reappearance. Haephan marched to Kilgy now regaining his wits and hauled him up by his shirt.

"Where the fuck is Tilly, you piece of shit!?" Haephan roared.

Startled from his shock, Kilgy burst out sobbing.

Haephan thrashed him until Kilgy raised his hands in fear. "Where is he!?"

"Goram's!" Kilgy sobbed. "He's one of Goram's sweet boys!"

"Goram doesn't use sweet boys. Querie told me they outlawed it when Goram was getting started."

"He does now!" Kilgy sobbed. "He does since that trouble back when that woman came and took you away!"

Haephan paled.

"Even the sweethearts couldn't stop him," Kilgy quivered. "He killed one who tried, right in the main room. Cut her open."

"Who?" Haephan asked.

Kilgy's voice failed.

"WHO!?" Haephan roared.

Kilgy coughed a sob. "Ginnie." Ginnie had raised Kilgy.

Haephan stilled.

"He let sailors gang the others till…" Kilgy sobbed. "No one stops him, now."

"What about the city guard? It's illegal!"

"I dunno," Kilgy sobbed. "I seen constables still coming. Even councilors! Ain't nobody stoppin' him!"

Haephan released Kilgy as drizzle fell from the dark, overcast sky.

Rain came here to die. Whether it fell from above or drained from across the city, it pooled here and stagnated into a reeking cesspit of mud and people like Goram who forced others to serve him in the vilest of ways.

Boiling with fury and with Goram in his mind's eye, Haephan shifted away.

70

Purpose and Passion

Ephterehn returned to the royal suite, ready to wake Nick, whose silhouette stood at the large arched window facing northward over Beltrand Park.

"My lord," said Ephterehn in surprise.

"Morning, Ephterehn," said Nick as the rising sun painted the western city in gold.

"Wasting no time, sir?"

"Wasting no time," said Nick.

"Then you'll be pleased with what I've already learned."

Nick turned.

"Word has been buzzing for weeks around the city about an Andonese priestess," said Ephterehn as he joined his krys at the window.

"An Andonese priestess? The blue-haired woman?" asked Nick. "That would mean a great deal."

"The Andonese, my lord," said Ephterehn. "Crafty. Isolationists. Untrustworthy in intercontinental affairs. They sometimes make elves feel over involved. Will she help us?"

Nick scanned the city. "We must hope."

"Have faith, sire?"

"Yes," said Nick. "I think very much so right now. Any idea where she might be?"

"Rumors range from the council's palace on the south side of the city—they call it the 'academy'—to the wizard school on the northeast bluff. I might be inclined toward the wizard's school."

"There's as much poor history between the Andonese and most human wielders as it is for us," said Nick. "They seem to make enemies with many. Let's save that for a later option."

Ephterehn nodded.

"Let's get some breakfast."

"The restaurant downstairs?"

"Let's..." Nick gulped at the memory of the stunning Admian woman from last night, "go out." Leaving the room, he feared they would encounter the woman whose mere five-minute conversation kept him awake half the night.

Outside, they headed east along the Majestery Road and south onto the split-lane Orden Avenue. Merchants and carters, guards and farmers, bankers and scribes bustled in the misty morning chill. Fewer stared than yesterday, though Nick guessed most were struggling to wake fully enough to notice.

Once past the Majestery grounds, expensive townhomes and shops woke from their slumber. They purchased meat pies from a street vendor and ate on the go while they searched every crowd for the Andonese priestess. Each hour compelled Nick to walk faster and ask more random passersby—anyone who seemed remotely knowledgable about city affairs. Many mentioned hearing of the Andonese but none knew more.

Standing on a busy street corner, Nick crossed his arms as endless rivers of people flowed around them. "I didn't imagine how many people would be here."

Ephterehn frowned.

"Looking for someone?" asked a wood elf outside a leatherman's shop wiping his hands with a rag.

"Yes," said Nick. "A woman of deep blue hair."

The elf raised his chin. "The priestess. Yes, I know of her. SonLara Amferadon."

"Are you sure?" Ephterehn asked.

"Quite," said the wood elf, who stood at-height with the common humans walking past.

"And where she is?"

The elf raised an eyebrow. "Maybe."

"And we can trust you how?"

"Because I'm obviously the first elf to offer you a name."

"Doesn't mean it's true," said Ephterehn.

"Doesn't mean I'm wrong, either."

"You're rather sure of yourself."

"Myself? Eh. As sure as one can be of the weather. But of this? I am sure."

"And your price?"

The wood elf admired Nick's pale hair. "A lock of your lordship's hair."

"Hair?" Ephterehn stared. "You want a lock of his hair?"

"I want a lock of his hair."

"Whatever for?"

"Pardon your lordships," the elf raised his hands. "Where you come from, your hair might just be hair. Out here with the rest of the uncivilized folk," he mused, "your hair is gold."

"That's preposterous," Ephterehn stuttered when Nick pulled a dagger, cut half a long lock of his pristine white hair and handed it to the elf, whose eyes widened.

"That will do," Nick's voice ended the haggle.

"Yes, your lordship," the elf tucked it away and scanned for anyone who might have seen the exchange.

"Where is she?" Ephterehn asked.

"The Belfast School for Wizardry," said the elf. "She's been consorting with a High Wizard Elverbane, I believe."

Nick's eyes flickered, recognizing the name.

"Anything else we ought to know?" Ephterehn asked.

The elf patted the breast of his vest, where he had stowed his prize.

"She has been seen near the Whittle. A large yellow house with a walled garden and two iron horses on the entry gate."

"How far?"

"If you aim for the school, I'd hire a taxi," said the elf with a nod the other way. "The Whittle, though, is a five-minute walk that way."

Nick and Ephterehn headed for the Whittle. As the street descended, the two and three-story houses fell away to larger estates and small, gated mansions. Passersby wore fine attire and maintained more subtility in their gawk.

"I think it's time we ate something, sire," said Ephterehn.

Nick didn't want to waste time eating, yet his stomach protested walking without fuel.

Noon approached when both stepped into an open-wall cafe and took seats in the street-facing archway.

Ephterehn scanned houses visible from their table. "I believe the house we're looking for might be smaller than many of these mansions."

"Why do you say that?"

"A mansion stands out. People remember its symbols. But here? No one seems to have heard of the two horses on a gate as the elf described. Though, perhaps we were fooled." He sighed. "I wish you had let me cut my own hair."

"No," said Nick. "This is my mission to complete. It will be my cost to pay.

"I sometimes wonder what life will be like away from Aminrale," said Ephterehn. "I've only ever traveled with you, and then on business."

"Wish you could have gotten away more?"

"Not really," Ephterehn said. "I love Aminrale. My cabin up in the Thespens is all I could ask for."

"Ephterehn…" Nick frowned. "When this is over, I want you to think about what you want from your life."

Ephterehn raised his head.

Nick hesitated. "Which, before we are done, may include leaving my service."

"But— sire," Ephterehn tried to speak.

A crash erupted at the intersection nearby. Horses screamed at each other in a tangle between carriages. Ephterehn turned as Nick leaned. Two drivers yelled at each other as they backed and disentangled their animals. Both entered the same street without yielding.

"Humans," Ephterehn muttered and returned to his menu while Nick's powerful sight narrowed in on one of the carriage windows. Through a pane of glass reflecting a bright street and well-dressed pedestrians, he caught sight of intense blue hair and pale skin.

"There," Nick said.

"What?" asked Ephterehn.

"Her!" Nick bounded over an occupied table and sprinted for the intersection. Ephterehn followed fast as they dodged carriages and carts while their long legs carried them faster than even horses at full speed.

The target carriage, though, coursed down the decline among tall, painted townhomes, slowed and turned out of sight as Nick reached the first intersection.

"Sire!" Ephterehn's voice echoed behind Nick as he sprinted along the road with his crimson cloak and white hair flowing behind him. At the next intersection, he scanned empty streets. The carriage was gone. Ephterehn caught up. "You saw her?"

"Yes," Nick jogged past dumbstruck pedestrians while he scanned over black iron fences, down side streets and narrow alleys. He turned into one alley and stepped closer while craning his neck.

A hint of yellow peeked through tight alley corners and thick trees. The two followed the narrow street to a beautiful, light-mustard home tucked from the main road in a tree-filled property surrounded by taller homes and townhouses. The narrow street passed the estate's wrought iron gate with two horses with a brick wall extending to either side.

"We are blessed," Nick smiled and motioned to a long brass handle. When Ephterehn pulled on it, a faint bell chimed on the property.

Fifty paces from the gate, the house rose with a wrap-around porch with inviting swings and tall glass-lined wooden doors. From one emerged a manservant who crossed the porch, descended the stairs and followed the cobbled driveway to the gate.

He hid his surprise behind a mask of professionalism. "Welcome to Mayhouse, home of Theras Bennett, esquire. May I help you?"

"We have come to call upon the Priestess SonLara Amferadon," said Ephterehn.

"And who may I say is calling?"

"The prince of Klaus."

Nodding, the man disappeared behind the nearby brick wall. A moment later one gate slid open with the sound of a rolling chain.

"If it please your lordships, you may come with me," he ushered them in before the gate shut itself.

Returning to the house, he led them inside to a small courtyard within the home where all three floors were open, capped with a glass ceiling.

"Please, sit and relax," he bowed. "I will return directly."

He shuffled off while they remained on their feet, gazing about at the arboretum. The creak of a nearby door revealed a woman with stark blue hair and a pristine white dress trimmed in aqua and a maid following her inside.

When she stepped into the midday light falling through the frosted glass, her dress glowed and eyes shimmered. The woman curtsied low before rising. "Good afternoon," she said. "I am Priestess of Andon SonLara Alva Amferadon, Realm Delver and Librarian First Class to the Golden Hall, and am honored to stand in the presence of two high elves. You called upon me."

"I am pleased to introduce the prince of Klaus," said Ephterehn. "Thank you for allowing us to speak with you."

"Please, sit," SonLara motioned before she took a seat of her own while a maid waited nearby. "How may I assist you?"

"I will offer no lie to you, priestess," said Nick. "I am—"

"Krys Nikal'Odin Kringul of Aminrale," SonLara said.

Nick cocked his head before answering, "Yes."

"Lord of Dreams," she said. "Why have you sought me?"

"To speak truly…I fear to tell you," said Nick. "Not because of my uncertainty of its truth, but how you will perceive it."

"Such a judgment cannot be made until you offer the evidence."

"The only evidence is my word."

"Then speak and let me judge."

Ephterehn scowled, unused to anyone speaking to his krys so frankly.

"Some time ago, I was visited by a subrim," said Nick, "who sent me to the hills southwest of Eden to seek a blue-haired woman. To gain her help with a very important task. And I believe it's possible you are that woman."

"Tea and sandwiches, Orthni," said SonLara.

"Yes, mistress," Orthni curtsied and slipped away.

"And what is it the subrim said I was to help you with?" asked SonLara.

"This might sound mad," said Nick, "but I was instructed to abdicate my throne, move my household to a fabled world beyond Algueda and protect the dreams of a group known as the Great Self's *chosen*." He waited for her reaction. "I'm sure you think it's mad."

SonLara inhaled. "You might be very surprised, Krys Kringul, what might or might not seem mad to me. I think it's time you told me everything the subrim said to you before we continue."

Nick shared a look with Ephterehn before leaning forward. "Before I share. I must ask, given the fantastic nature of what I just said, why might you so quickly believe?"

"Because, my dear krys," her eyes glowed in the light, "you were not the only to be visited by the generals of heaven."

71

The Fall of Goram

Haephan stood on the roof of a two-story ramshackle house across the broadway from a spectacle. Goram's large red house swarmed with customers and more pressing to get inside.

Somewhere in there, his best and only friend lay under one of those sick buggerers. Tonight, whoever touched his friend would die horrifically.

Haephan had, at first, wanted to barge into Goram's home and lay waste, but he pondered something altogether more frightening for the man. Instead of merely destroying Goram's business, he would tear down his home with not only Goram inside, but his customers—all those who preyed on the women, men and children, and so spent the day sending whispers all over Rainhold: *Come to Goram's for Twice the Delight!*

He made every inference that tonight would be special. He spent the past 24 hours shifting all over New Gordon, making every rumor he knew to make in every corner he knew to make it in about Goram's party tonight.

They came in droves.

Stupefied, Goram emerged throughout the night to welcome hordes of eager customers. Part-timers and satellite workers poured in to service them.

Stragglers made off with less-expensive whores to the nearest alleyways and alcoves, some with great violence free from the watchful eye of Goram's bouncers. The whores accepted it, otherwise they would lose customers—either the bouncers would slap them around for losing business, or they could get paid and allow the customers to do it.

Haephan cried with quiet fury at the laughter and echoing moans, cries of pain and delight, and the occasional scream from some little boy or girl surrendered to those monsters.

For years Goram prided on only offering adult pleasures. Now, because of Haephan, Goram began using the orphans.

That would end tonight.

As a light rain cut the frigid air, steam wafted from Haephan's hot skin. On the outside, he stood as a motionless stanchion and would be visible to Goram's bouncers only if they looked toward him during a lightning flash. Otherwise, his coffee-dark skin veiled him. When Goram's house bulged to bursting and the first-wave quickies stumbled their way out, Haephan's rage reached its limit. He closed his eyes, drew in the sounds bleeding through the rain and locked onto the stragglers in dark alleys.

Haephan started with them.

In the nearest alley, the sound of an exerting man echoed between the narrow walls. Above him hovered Haephan's dark silhouette against the cloudy sky flashing with distant lightning. Stepping off the ledge, the boy tucked his ankles and aimed.

Seconds became minutes before Haephan landed on the man's shoulders, which collapsed under his weight. The man's head crashed into the whore's face, knocking her unconscious as he slammed into the mud and gaped like a beached fish. Collapsed lungs wouldn't inflate and he suffocated.

The boy shifted to the next alley where he found the silhouette of a woman kneeling before a man. She gurgled for air, unable to pull back for his insistent fingers in her hair. Unable to breathe, she panicked and choked.

Darkness took Haephan. He shifted twice as high as the three-story rooftop, aimed his fall by microshifting and raised his feet. With great momentum, he veered toward the man's shoulders and kicked with all his might. Thinking he would knock the man aside, as he had the first, he was shocked when the man sank straight into the mud until he was half as tall as the woman.

Her mouth open, the woman recoiled against the fence in terror. Panting for air, she flinched from the boy standing on the man's shoulders. She screamed as the man's face erupted with blood pressured from his own legs being driven up into his body.

Panicking, Haephan slapped her unconscious with a single hit before he stumbled off the corpse. His ability to see in the dark burned every gory detail into his mind. He scrambled away in search of another target while his rage buffered the first kill. He embraced his anger and picked off every client he could find—male or female, gentle or rough. Those he found with children, he sent to the volcano, and the children to Bertrand Park.

After dozens of kills, Haephan emptied his stomach while blood drooled down his body. Fear welled that far more death awaited him, but thinking of Tilly silenced it. Steeling himself, Haephan stalked onto the broadway before Goram's house as the rain picked up. The blood and gore lathering him thinned and washed as he passed patrons stumbling out and others waiting to get in, when two of the bouncers barred his way.

"And whea do you think you're— hey, it's the littul shit that bitch walked out of heah wif!"

"Yeah!"

"C'mon!" the first snatched him by the collar and both hauled him in through the front door to the thick smell of flavored smoke, liquor, various weeds and sex. "Hey boss! Lookey who jus' trumbled in!"

Customers and prostitutes crowding the front room craned their necks as the bouncers dragged the newcomer across the ornate carpet. A small gap expanded around the exchange and a few stood for a better view.

Sitting at the end of the long bar that ran from near the front door to a left-turning L, Goram turned from conversations with high end customers at the intrusion. A vicious smile spread across his face.

"Well if it isn't the master, himself?" Goram smiled.

Haephan glared through a wet shaggy mane clinging to his chalky burnt sienna face as he planted his feet.

"Where's Tilly?" Haephan growled.

"Where's Tilly?" Goram mused. "Where's Tilly? That sweet little fucksnot you were consorting with before you drew the high and mighty favor of an Andonese fuckin' princess? Why, he's making me money in the same filthy bed where I saved your selfdamn life."

"Let him go. Right now. Or I will kill every last one of you. I will rip out your eyes and burn this whole selfdamn place to the ground."

The room erupted in laughter, mocking and murmurs.

"I've killed enough tonight," Haephan's voice cracked. Furious tears snaked down his cheeks. "I've killed. And I will kill again. Let him go, and I will try to have mercy on you." The room laughed.

"Mercy? Mercy!?" Goram stood up. "You've cost me so much selfdamn business you worthless littul cunt that I have every mind to put you on your face and let any customer have his way at your ass as likes. Without charging a single coin."

Grimacing with cold fury, Haephan set his fingers on the hands of each bouncer gripping his shoulders. His small fingers viced until each man moaned. He rolled his hands forward and away, forcing both men to drop to a kneeling position. Onlookers stared.

He extended his hands out to the side until both men bowed forward and yelped.

"You think I can't?" Haephan asked. "You think I'm weak."

Goram's certainty faltered.

"You think I'm anything close to that little boy who stole from you? You think I'm here because I'm afraid of you?" Haephan's voice quivered. His hands twisted the men's arms until each screamed in a now silent room. "I'm not here asking for salvation."

He raised his foot and pressed it into the shoulder of the man on the right.

"I'm here because you have my friend!" Haephan kicked until the only thing keeping the man's arm attached was his skin.

The man howled and writhed in agony.

"I'm here because you hurt people," he raised his opposite foot and put it on the other man's shoulder. "I'm here because you're evil!"

Sobbing, Haephan kicked until the other man bellowed as his arm ripped off but for his shirt now bubbling with blood.

Patrons retreated. Haephan dropped the wrists so that both arms thumped into the soaked carpet before he approached Goram. He wiped tears with his arm, raised his eyes and whispered, "I'm here because you need to die."

Terrified, Goram lunged forward with a brass-knuckled swing through empty air and stumbled into the growing pool of his men's blood.

No one moved, unable to reconcile that the boy had disappeared.

Goram stumbled over one of his men and spun about in terror. In the following silence, the sound of a basement door banging open startled everyone.

Haephan kicked open the door into a dark room and revealed a man midway through fastening his belt who paused in surprise.

"Do you know what the worst thing you can do to a boy, mister?" Haephan's silhouette stepped in from the dim-lit hallway. "What you just did. And for what you've done…" Haephan kicked the broken door shut, his voice muffled behind it, "there is punishment."

The hesitant patrons upstairs flinched as a gut-wrenching scream erupted from beneath the floorboards. Bloodcurdling cries for mercy and help lasted the better part of a minute before cutting off.

En masse, customers left their drinks, settees and whores in pursuit of the double front doors which both shut. Men pushed on them to the rising alarm of those behind.

"You wanna know what all your revenge upon me is worth!?" Haephan's scream echoed down the stairs from somewhere above. "DO YOU!?"

Cries from upstairs patrons preceded screams of those waiting outside as a mixture of half-dressed and fully nude customers rained from the sky to their death. Guards posted on the porch fell from inside the great room open to the floors above, crashing into screaming patrons and sweethearts.

Too much for Goram's guests, they shrieked for another way out.

Goram's leap into the first-floor hallway drew the mob behind him as they trampled his armless bouncers and the lake of blood soaking the carpet.

Haephan blocked the way, bathed in bloody death from his head to his knees.

Goram stumbled to a halt, desperate not to touch him as others pressed him from behind until they, too, saw the demon barring their escape.

"What the fuck are you!?" Goram moaned as he fought those behind him.

"I am death," Haephan's whisper echoed along the hallway as lanterns flickered and dimmed.

Goram pissed his pants as he fought the panicked crowd pressing him forward.

"Goram," Haephan's whisper whipped the man around as the boy shifted forward in a series of flutters. He stopped face-to-face with the man, whose gaze sank to Haephan's hand sticking inside his chest.

Small arcs of electricity danced across the wet tips of Haephan's blood-soaked hairs. He bared his teeth and bellowed before squeezing Goram's heart until it burst in his fingers.

Goram sank, dead, until his weight hung on Haephan's hand. The crowd behind him screamed in terror before Haephan planted his foot on Goram's chest and ripped free his hand with the crunch and spray of his exploding chest.

Haephan eyed the bits of crushed heart clinging to his bloody fingers before they fell closed. Through gritted teeth, he whispered, "I want you to burn."

From his feet, a wave of flame raced outward across the rug. As it chased away those at the end of the hallway, Haephan shifted to Tilly's room, gathered him in the filthy bedsheet and shifted to the street outside where the rain had ebbed.

Patrons inside screamed for help and banged on the doors, unaware of the chains Haephan had used to secure them.

Squatting, he set Tilly in the muddy street, surrounded by bodies of dead men, and tugged on the sheet to ensure he was covered. Tilly stirred.

"It's okay, Tilly," said Haephan. "No one is gonna hurt you ever again."

The windows shattered as those inside struggled to flee. Goram's new bars—erected because of Haephan—blocked their way to safety. Their screams climbed as fire engulfed the first floor on its way upward.

Tilly stirred under the cool, growing drizzle.

"Tilly? Tilly?" asked Haephan. "Are you okay?"

Tilly muttered something.

Haephan placed his ear by Tilly's mouth. "What?"

"Querie…" the boy muttered.

Haephan froze. "Oh no."

Setting Tilly down, Haephan reshifted inside to the second floor as flames licked at its fine carpets and tapestries. He shifted from room to room and, upon finding sweethearts, shifted them outside in a quickening rush. When he could find no more, he shifted into Goram's suite to find Querie strapped nude to the wall, suspended in chains and covered in whip marks.

"Querie?" managed Haephan.

Blinking through a drugged stupor, a smile drawled across her face. "Hayphun."

"Querie!" Haephan stumbled forward. "We gotta get you outta here! We gotta get you out!"

He jerked at chains too thick for his enhanced strength. Though his pulls cracked the wood round about the anchors, they would not come free. The roar of fire in the hallway climbed, as did the screams of customers who raced upstairs to search for an escape. Those unable to climb higher wailed as fire took them.

"We gotta get you out!" Haephan cried.

"Haephan," she moaned with a sad, half-smile. "Haephan, Haephan."

Frantic, he yanked to break the chains or pull them from their iron moorings—anything to free her.

"Haaaephaan…" Querie managed as she grew cognizant enough to recognize the danger but too stuppored to fear it. "Haephan, luk at me, honey. Look at me my little boy. My shun."

Haephan froze in a torrent of his tears. Fire caught the rug behind him and spread through the room.

"You did!" she said and blinked slowly. "You got outta here. I'm sho proud of you. You did so good!"

"No!" Haephan wheened. "No! NO! C'mon!" He railed at the chains as the fire filled the room.

"Baby! Baby!" she cooed. "Go. Go! I want to go. I want to be done! I want to die. But save yourself! Go live better than I could offer you. Pleesh?"

"No!" Haephan climbed onto the construct and sobbed against her breast. "NO!"

"Haephan, Haephan," she said.

His torrential eyes locked upon her.

"That is my wish for my little boy," she cried as fire tickled her toes. "Go. Live. I will love you alwaysh."

"No," he moaned. "I-I lost dad's ring. M-mom. I lost the ring. I'm so sorry!"

"Go," she said. "It's my time. Go before it reaches me. You can't see that." She squeezed tears down her cheeks. "I love you."

In the silence between them, despite the flames, Haephan looked upon his mother for the first time. And the last time.

"Go, baby," she said. "Go now." She surrendered as the room burned too hot even for him. Haephan climbed and kissed his mom on the cheek, even as fire drew closer, and shifted out to the street.

He sank next to Tilly, wrapped in sheets, as Goram's house blazed as a beacon visible throughout the low city.

"Haephan?" Tilly stuttered. "Haephan?"

"Yeah!? Yeah, Tilly?" asked Haephan as he wiped his tears with his arm.

"I'm not feeling so good," Tilly said.

"It's okay," said Haephan as he bent over him.

"No, I mean…" said Tilly. His quivers faded. "I can't feel anything."

"What?" asked Haephan. Blood stained Tilly's sheet that hadn't been there before. Haephan noted the ripe scar down the side of Tilly's face.

Tilly's serenity startled Haephan before he said, "They hurt me, Haeph. They…hurt me, bad. I'm gonna go. Now."

"What? No. No! Who!"

"Bye Haeph. Thanks," he said. "Thanks for being my friend. Thanks for…loving me."

Tilly's chest sank and stilled.

Life drained from Haephan. He broke. A scream ripped from his throat as he gripped his hair and rocked to the bonfire of his life raging before him in the black of Rainhold night.

72

Details

Atop the center wing of the Majestery perched a cafe rung by an ornate metal rail, forested by furled table umbrellas and patronized by a half dozen early risers sipping on their coffee as dawn mists rolled by, as if the building were an island in the midst of a vast river descending from Belfast Bluff toward the canal. Key-lit in the first vestiges of a peach sunrise, Nick and Ephterehn breakfasted in the northeast corner of the cafe facing northward where other tall buildings rose above the thick fog.

"While I'm in Carlinia and making preparations with Master Sandark for moving the house, I have tasks for you," Nick sipped his nutmeg coffee. "Let's review the details."

"Sire? The..." Ephterehn lowered his voice. "If I may ask, why are you involving the Cordurons?"

"The Cordurons must come with me," said Nick. "After I've protected them for so long, I would hope they would continue to trust me."

Ephterehn hid his scowl.

"Do you distrust them so much?"

"I'm sorry, sire," said Ephterehn. "But…"

"Speak your mind, elf," Nick said.

"What elf could trust them, sire?" asked Ephterehn. "You are kind beyond measure, but I have struggled to understand why you extended them parley."

"Their rebellion was wrong, but their protests against divine right weren't without merit," Nick said.

Ephterehn gulped. "But sire, the krysdom was first crowned by subrim, themselves."

"And it doesn't excuse any of their abuses of their elves," said Nick. "The Cordurons may have been misguided in how they rebelled, but I can't blame them for lashing out after millennia of ill treatment for their tiny size and amazing innovation."

"Their mastery of tactile magic makes one think they have bound their souls to the nokburum," said Ephterehn.

"I would advise caution in blaming a supposedly inferior species for seemingly supernatural abilities," said Nick. "I understand why you don't trust them. The war they waged was brutal and shocking. But if you or I were in their position, we might do the same to protect those we love."

Ephterehn pursed his lips.

"I gave them parley because I found them doing their best to live away from the rest of us."

"Hiding for their crimes, sire," Ephterehn said with care.

"Never blame an entire race for the crimes of a few," said Nick. "As well the pixies should be willing to work with an Andonese for the chance of saving their race."

"When the priestess said the pixies had agreed to help her, I was sure she was lying."

"She was not," said Nick. "Her heartbeat spoke true."

"She also seemed distracted," said Ephterehn.

"I noticed," said Nick. "When she mentioned the worldender, her heart skipped."

"Worldender, sire? You mean the wizard?"

"Do you not know? Her Wizard Elverbane used the worldender at Tuthomere."

"Truly?" asked Ephterehn. "And he went unpunished?"

"Hearings by a continental trial absolved him," said Nick. "But humans don't live with their past very well. Perhaps he might see this as a redemption?"

"Or he felt perfectly justified before," said Ephterehn.

"Perhaps," said Nick.

"As you said, the trial seemed to think so," said Ephterehn.

"I hope only he is no wild stag rutting about for conflict or glory," said Nick, "and that our fair priestess from an isolationist, immortality-obsessed sect remains true to her espoused purpose."

"Querious indeed, sire," said Ephterehn.

"Still," Nick said and lowered his cup. "There's a design to all of this."

"I admit I have not seen as much of the world or time as you," Ephterehn said. "Or the likes of Emastus or Ilphenia. To have lived during the draco-pixie wars, and still be here, today. What are hundreds of millennia like?"

"I don't know," Nick said. "Not sure I care to, either. Too much time can wear heavy on the soul."

"The priestess seemed sure with unsure information," said Ephterehn.

"Unsure?" asked Nick.

"Transporting vacants to Algueda, of all places, by the green moon, and then on into…some new world?" Ephterehn asked.

"This seemed uncertain to you?"

"I don't think she understands the vacants nearly as well as she sounded."

Nick waited.

"She lied about nothing, but something about the vacants means more to her than the subrim's commission. Especially the boy she intends to send to us."

"What did you notice?" asked Nick.

"She's very interested in what has become of the boy," said Ephterehn. "I daresay she's more interested in him than the vacants.

For all her calculated control, she cannot meter her heartbeat."

"I sensed the same, but your interpretation is worth considering."

"Thank you, my lord," said Ephterehn. "Sire, I wish I could go with you to Carlinia."

"Stay here to iron out the schedule with the priestess," said Nick. "When we return, I want to know more specifically the dates they expect to reach Algueda, estimations on resources and travel periods for the vacants."

"Are we sure they can't use the rimsportals?"

"If vacants have no magic, no rimsportal will work for them," Nick mused. "The boy, however, she said could travel thousands of miles instantly. That would imply immense magic."

"Might explain her interest in the boy," said Ephterehn.

"If he can, truly, travel as she says, I could employ him to carry me, Master Sandark and our supplies all the way to our destination," said Nick. "We can build the first rimsportal in decamillennia and complete the rest of the transition."

"My lord," Ephterehn said. "If they are vacant, can your magic truly help them?"

"We have the subrim's command. I must assume my skills will somehow be used for their protection."

"What if your magic doesn't work and the subrim has sent you in vain?" asked Ephterehn.

"I don't know," Nick admitted. "But once the rimsportal is built, we will move into tents while Sgaarsbad starts on my home. I will enter a period of retrain while we await their arrival by sea from Algueda."

"Sire? By sea?"

"Algueda is an island, in our world and the one to which it bridges," said Nick. "They will not be walking to their new homes. They will need to build ships once they arrive on Algueda. That should be easy. The last scouting to the island reported heavy flora."

"That was almost three thousand years ago, sire," Ephterehn said.

"I know, but we can hope it remains lush for their arrival."

"I see," said Ephterehn, who finished his coffee and held it out for a white-coated waiter to refill it. He nodded his thanks before glancing at Nick. "And the pixies?"

"Their oath binds them to these humans," said Nick. "They will fulfill it no matter the cost."

"Sire, what is the end of all this? What's the point?"

"I don't know, Ephterehn," Nick pursed his lips. "We do have a direction. We will pursue it and trust that what answers are relevant will be revealed in their due time. Between now and then? We are here." He toasted Ephterehn with his coffee.

Ephterehn pursed his lips as he toasted back, sipped it and soaked in the beautiful view.

73

Buried

At the foot of the northeast bluffs in a scattered settlement of farmers, dirt erupted from a small rectangular hole and fell onto a large pile.

Within the recess, shadowed from the early morning light lacing the fade-blue sky in pale mauve, Haephan strained against the hard-set wet-pack with a dull shovel blade. His tears had dried, but he struggled to remember hope under the deadening weight of loss and guilt.

His fury ripped chunks from the ground as he dug the grave of his friend.

Tilly lay next to the grave, wrapped in a velvet curtain taken from Degreneth's office.

Haephan dug until dirt fell back in from the steep pile outside. The grave was almost twice as deep as he was tall.

The shovel sank to the bottom as he leaned into the wall with his elbow. Dripping sweat served as his tears before he hugged himself and sobbed again. Having cried so much, this time didn't last more than a few moments before he climbed to his feet, grabbed his shovel and raised his face to the rectangular doorway to life and light above him. It retreated from his reach, an illusion he wished true for the weight of shame on his heart.

He shifted to the surface where golden sunrise burned from the horizon, defiant of the self-hatred growing in his chest. He retreated from it and gathered his friend. He reshifted to the bottom of the tight grave and set him down with care. With his feet on either side of Tilly's body, Haephan quivered.

"I'm sorry, Tilly," he whispered. He snatched both sides of the grave walls and bellowed, "I'M SORRY!" He sank to a knee by Tilly's side and set his hand on his chest. Drawing his hand away, the mud-stained handprint left behind welled anew his guilt.

He disrespected his friend, even in death.

Rising, he stood over Tilly's body.

"I'm…" he started to stay. He stood there for several minutes, afraid to move, to know what came next. When the silence became too great, Haephan shifted up, took his shovel, scooped dirt and loomed over the shadowed hole. He was afraid to say goodbye, but to bury a rat from Rainhold like Tilly in a full grave was to bury him like a man. Haephan braced against his own shame and heaved the dirt into the hole as light morning rain betwinkled the sunrise.

Water drooling through his hair left long rivulets of mud and dirt down his face and body.

Tilly disappeared one shovelful at a time until the last throw that would cover him forever.

Haephan peered into the hole with a despair that halted his breath. He let the shovel roll in his hands to release the final dirt that covered Tilly's face.

Once his friend was no longer visible, Haephan filled the grave until the ground lay flat and bare with nothing to indicate its importance. Recalling a graveyard near the bluff, he shifted there, found a small marker in a corner weathered under years of rain and wind, and, with great effort, he pulled it from the ground. Returning to Tilly's grave, he raised the stone above his head and drove it hard into the unpacked dirt. After wiggling and tamping, it remained upright and firm.

In Haephan's blind rage, he killed his best friend and mother. Guilt demanded he leave, but Haephan waited on the shallow grassy hill at the foot of the bluff under the morning sun rising into a heavy ceiling of clouds.

High on the cliffs above, the wizard school sat ignorant of his shame and sorrow. There, that damned wizard and priestess wanted him only for their holy fucking mission—now the only family he had. He didn't want to return, but he had nowhere else to go.

With a burst of anger, he broke the shovel handle over his knee and threw each piece in a different direction. He scanned the horizon as sunlight disappeared behind the heavy ceiling and drowned him in dim wet shadow.

Turning, Haephan headed west toward the switchbacks climbing to the Eden Road. While he could shift at-will, he could think of nowhere he wanted to be. He trudged into a long line of people making their way into the city and disappeared among them. He fantasized for a short while that he walked with a family, a real family, that loved him, that wanted to spend time with him. Who could hold him.

He wanted nothing more than to feel someone's arms around him, and feared he might never experience such a thing in his life; not after what he had done. Maybe he wasn't meant to have a family. To have love.

At the top, the road turned due south and merged with the Eden Road through the North Gate between high-walled apartments. From here, the city descended across slopes and terraces and, ultimately, into Rainhold.

Haephan headed east past shops, workhouses, restaurants and stores, through intersections of commuters and carriages, wagons and horsemen. When Belfast came into view, he hesitated to return.

What might he do in there better than lying down here and dying?

Why did he take so long to rescue his friend? Why couldn't he have grabbed him and escaped? And Querie? Why did he have to kill Goram and his customers? Why didn't he know? Why?

With his smallest hope that SonLara might be kind, he continued into the West Gate of the school.

"Hey, Haephan!" one of the guards smiled before noticing the rivulets of mud layering the boy. "Where you been?"

Haephan passed in silence.

"What's eating him?" the other guard asked.

Haephan stayed on the north walk between buildings and cliffside gardens rising high upon the bluff looming over Tilly's fresh grave. He plodded into the north side of Ashmore Hall, climbed stairs to the third floor and, instead of entering Elverbane's quarters, continued to the top-floor courtyard and approached the railing overlooking the territory north of town. The bluff's edge hid any view of Tilly's grave, yet his buried friend was all he considered, even now when he was too exhausted to shed tears.

"Haephan?" SonLara startled him.

He spun, stared for several moments and asked, "Why am I here, SonLara? What is this for?"

Her face flickered with concern. "The Great Self has chosen you to make a new world, young man. That's an important task. One that affects all of us. In a way, that makes you a representative, an ambassador. Perhaps even a herald, of sorts."

"A pan?" asked Haephan.

"What did you say?" asked SonLara. "A pan?"

"I don't want to be," said Haephan. "I don't want to be anything."

"Haephan," she stepped closer. "Are…you, alright?"

Haephan broke inside, trying not to sob as tears slid down his filthy cheeks. "No."

She raised her hand to touch his head.

"SonLara!" Elverbane climbed the steps to the patio.

Stiffening, SonLara withdrew her hand.

"Wizard Elverbane," she gulped. "Is there something you need?"

Elverbane glanced between them before focusing on Haephan. "Boy?"

"What is it you need, wizard?" she asked coldly.

"I, well," stuttered Elverbane. "I wanted to talk with you."

"Haephan and I have business before he leaves with the next seed," she said. "Is it important?"

"It— kind of," said Elverbane as his shoulders sank. "I mean…it can wait."

"Do you know where the Majestery is?" she asked Haephan.

Haephan inhaled and nodded.

"You need to clean yourself and report there immediately to speak with the prince of Klaus in the royal suite, top floor," said SonLara. "He will instruct you on what he needs. You are to help him until he says otherwise. Understand?"

"Yes, ma'am," he whispered.

"His new clothes are done," Elverbane injected.

"Thank you, wizard," she said with an icy tone. She softened her voice for Haephan. "Go on, young man. The sooner you're gone, the sooner you can return. And rest."

Haephan blinked away his tears and disappeared.

Elverbane's brow sank. "Is everything alright, SonLara?"

SonLara turned, passed him and descended the stairs.

Worried, Elverbane stared after them.

74
Truth

"Eva? Eva!" Seni stepped into the room. Upon seeing her daughter standing in the window, she rushed across the carpets and embraced her. Leaning back, horror crept over Seni. "Great Self, what happened to you?"

A small blue dress hung loose on Eva's emaciated body. Though healthy from SonLara's aid, her skin hugged her frame until her cheekbones and knobby wrists stood out. What weight she gained since her brief return from Southdown was gone. Her crystal blue eyes lacked their luster and glared for the sunken quality of her face.

"It's been a rough couple weeks," said Eva.

"With all the prep for the siege…" said Seni. "I-I was worried."

Eva's brow flickered. "Was father worried?"

Seni hesitated. "Of course. He always worries about you."

"Was he?" Eva stood at the arched window of her family apartment overlooking the Academy grounds while outside the city prepared for war. "How well does father monitor city activities?"

"As senior councilor, he hears of all sorts of…goings on," Seni said.

"Does he?" Eva whispered. "Remember when Helni got picked up with that older wizard?"

"Of course," said Seni. "Everyone knew about it."

"But he wasn't arrested."

"As scandalous as that little girl could be, she was 18," Seni shuddered, "even if Wizard Urmai was nearly 400."

"And the entire city knew?"

"Anyone who matters," said Seni.

Eva's jaw clenched. "And when Esman was arrested selling bluelites?"

"The shame," Seni said. "But that boy was always trouble. Didn't surprise me a bit he was selling psychedelics. Never figured him for—"

"And everyone knew about it," said Eva. "Even though he was arrested in private. Across the canal in Southdown, wasn't it?"

"Yes," said Seni. "Someone of his import arrested? The guards can't keep their mouths closed. Awful lot, they are. Why…are you asking?"

Eva drew a slow breath and whispered, "Where is he now?"

"He's holding a war council for his majesty over in Thistlewaite."

Eva glared. "I didn't think it of him."

"Think what of him?" Seni gulped.

Eva marched for the doors.

"Where are you going!? You need to eat! Let's summon Wither for some—"

Eva spun. "You're coming with me." Turning, she pushed open the heavy door and stormed into the hallway as her mother's timid footsteps pattered in pursuit.

Passersby scrambled aside from her fury. From Herean Hall across the grounds into Thistlewaite Hall, her mother struggled to say something that would stop Eva. They crossed the grand lobby to the double doors leading into the Academy's main hall.

"I'm disappointed in you," said Eva as she turned on her mother. "But sadly, I am not surprised."

Shame filled Seni.

The guards moved to block her when they were cast aside and both doors slammed open with a thunderous bang. Hundreds of attendees spun from rows of wooden seats round about a massive table. Seven men and women looked up from the table backed by a high wall with maps and markings.

Her father's lack of surprise confirmed her fears.

"You son of a bitch!" Eva stormed across the room as guards rushed in from side doors.

"Young lady," said the king, "this is not the place—"

"With respect, King Myogan," Eva interrupted him, "I'm here for that *bastard* who let me sit in prison for WEEKS!"

Attendees gaped.

"Wait," said the king. Guards slowed at his command.

"You fucking bastard," Eva glared at her father. "Did you really hate him that much?"

"It wasn't about hate."

"He saved your life from an explosion *you* caused," Eva's voice echoed across the chamber. "And you send men after him? They don't bring him back here, but they throw him—and *me*—into a prison!"

The king mused at the revelation.

"Nothing in this town slips through your fingers," Eva quivered. "You let them take us and let us rot in that—" Her voice cracked. "That fucking cesspit."

"I couldn't help him," Dufrain stammered. "He's a vacant. Nothing we could have done would save him from the sword."

"YOU DIDN'T EVEN TRY!" Eva bellowed. "What do you hate about Adamar so much that you'd just let him die? And swor—?"

"Did he?" asked Dufrain.

"You *wanted* him to die? How dare you. He was my husband—"

"Whom you've been at odds with—"

"He's *my* husband to be at odds with!" Eva said. "The man I chose to love and to fight. Not yours. What could you hold against him so?"

"He's a fucking vacant!" Dufrain erupted. "All he's done is distract you from your appropriate studies. And now I find out he could nullify your ability to bear children with magic? You could be here at this table helping us prepare for war and you're out there chasing that *mule* of a man!"

"Do you hate them so much?" Eva's voice softened as she asked the group.

"He's one man," Dufrain protested. "And your powers would be better served here, with us, not chasing after someone who has nothing to contribute to our society."

"Other than the value of his mind," Eva said. "Or do you only see his value based on his magical usefulness? Or mine? And what *sword?*"

The table stiffened.

"Did you test a weapon on him?" Eva whispered. "A human being?"

"There are more important matters than just one man or woman," Dufrain gulped.

"No, the point is you're willing to toss aside a man's life because of how it costs *you*."

"Or maybe it was a lesser of options," said a reddening Dufrain.

"Like what? Cut him open, yourself!?" Eva stammered.

"Like arresting and sending him to the quarry with the rest of his kind," Dufrain said.

"What?" asked Eva.

"King Myogan has ordered all vacants transported outside the city," said Degreneth from his place down the war council. "For the safety of our people."

"The safety—?" Eva asked. "Whatever have vacants done?"

"They cannot be ruled," Myogan's voice stilled the room.

"They live here peacefully, every day."

"Adamar waylaid a dozen constables," Dufrain said. "That's one man. Imagine if they all turned on us!"

"They're just trying to get by!" Eva said. "But you don't believe that about Adamar. I see it. You *hate him*."

"He was taking you away from us!" Dufrain planted his fist into the table.

"Did you forget I stopped working with you before I ever left with Adamar?"

"I didn't want to lose you like I lost your mother," Dufrain said.

Eva motioned to her mother standing in the door backed by a dozen guards. "She left work to raise me! That's abandoning you? Magic isn't everything, father. I could have lived a happy life with Adamar if you hadn't blacklisted him from working in New Gordon."

"I wanted him to work for me."

"He worked for you, but he's not a slave!" Eva said. "Or is that now legal, your majesty?"

"Slavery hasn't been legal in South Edenia in six thousand years," said Myogan.

"You couldn't force him to work for you, so you prevented him from working anywhere else."

"His stupid projects were a waste of your time! A wheel that captures the power of water to mill…bloody grain!? You are a first-tier mage, Eva! We couldn't lose you to that stupid vacant—"

"He's my husband!" Eva erupted. "And now you would cast aside hundreds of vacants because you fear they can't be governed by your selfdamn magic!?"

"They are a threat to our very survival," Myogan said.

"So, you imprison innocent men and women 'for your safety,' but working them in the mines is in no way slavery. *Is it,* your majesty?" she asked Myogan. "You self-absorbed monstrosities. Casting aside those who don't carry the spark of power necessary to be subject your rule. Who don't maintain your idea of the right way to live?" Eva stepped back. "Great Self."

"Bite your impudent tone, young Dufrain," said the king. "The wolves besiege this very city. This is not the place to have this conversation."

"I don't know to whom you speak, your lordship," Eva's soft voice carried. "I am no Dufrain. I am a Harel. And I would rather spend a life among vacants who believe in the beauty of life than the audacious who would go to public war with monsters while committing equal evil in private. At least the lycans suffer from bicognition. You have no fucking excuses, you selfdamned bastards."

She locked upon her paled father.

"Never look for me again," Eva whispered. "Never speak to me again. Your idea of love is worthless."

"Eva—" Dufrain raised his hand.

"Remove her from this chamber," the king commanded.

Eva advanced to the entrance. Guards who moved to restrain her were cast aside in a successive wave out into the walls. Attendees leapt to their feet and kicked chairs aside as her power shielded and ejected anyone who approached her. Powerful martial mages were buffeted as they moved to bar her.

"Stop her!" the king cried.

Eva stopped next to her mother, who clutched the doorframe and silently wept. "I love you, mother. Goodbye."

Sobs erupted from Seni's clutched mouth as Eva marched into the foyer.

Gathering their wits, wizards rushed for the front doors.

Eva spun and raised her hands. Her mother was knocked into the room before both doors slammed shut between them. Their edges flared with orange light as they melted into place.

Eva blocked dozens of incoming martial mages and stormed out of Thistlewaite on her way off Academy grounds and into the chaos of New Gordon preparing for the siege.

75
The Majestery

Haephan appeared on the rooftop of the Majestery wearing a new sturdy outfit. Adorned in a hunter green shirt vested in black leather, he wore heavy-woven black wool trousers bloused into new leather boots.

A bath and meal had helped, but Haephan struggled not to curl up and die. His hand rested on the oversized pocket in his belt now carrying an apple-sized seed as he let his mission distract him from guilt heavier than the world.

Mustering, he scanned the rooftop of its small cafe and two breakfasters deep in conversation who hadn't noticed him. He slipped past the tables to an awned stairwell and descended to the seventh-floor doorway. He walked under gothic arches supporting the hallway, lit within by a glowing amber ceiling painted in long expanding lines and colors.

In the formal suites area, where SonLara had instructed him to be, Haephan found the tall wooden door with the symbols as she indicated. Upon it, two carved trees faced inward with mirrored pieces inlaid between the swirling branches. When he raised his hand to knock, the door swung open to reveal a pale figure taller than any person he'd ever seen.

"Master Haephan?" the elf asked.

Haephan withdrew his knuckles. "Yes."

"Please, come in," the elf stepped aside for him to enter.

Inside, another elf scrawled on paper over a table in the center of the room. The elf set down his pen, smiled and moved around the table as Haephan entered, though the boy's short stature barely came to the elf's mid-thigh.

Haephan bowed. "Your…majesty."

"I am soon to leave behind my throne," the elf's deep voice filled the room. "I insist you call me Nick."

Haephan eyed him. "Really?"

"Yes, please," Nick's warm smile surprised and cautioned him. It was another adult and another ploy.

"Okay," Haephan said. "What kind of name is Nick?"

"It's short for Nikal'Odin."

"Is that an elvish name?" asked Haephan.

"A very old family name."

"I didn't know kings— I mean, krys's had first names."

Nick smiled. "Most of us do. Come in. Have you had anything to eat?"

"A little," said Haephan.

Nick motioned to a chair on the near side of the large table. "Still hungry?"

Haephan shrugged and sat.

"Well, did Priestess Amferadon tell you what we'd be doing?" asked Nick.

"Who?" Haephan asked.

"Priestess SonLara Amferadon?"

"Oh, SonLara."

"Yes," said Nick.

"I didn't know that was her last name."

"It is. And we spoke at length about what you would help us accomplish. Did you get to speak with her?"

"No," said Haephan. "She just said to come out here."

"I see," Nick said. "Would you like to know what we're doing?"

"…sure."

Nick noted the boy's hesitation. "First, we're going to visit an ancient magical creature known as a pixilark."

"Pixies?"

"Indeed."

"Really?" Haephan asked. "Huh. Why?"

"Well, SonLara has made a deal with them—a seed from the Tree of Life in exchange for their help in protecting you from dragons."

"Their protection? How can pixies protect me from dragons? Aren't they tiny?"

"Have you never heard of the DracoPixie Wars?"

"No, it's DracoElven," Haephan said.

"Actually, those are different. The DracoPixie Wars didn't last long, but it was a brutal conflict."

"What could pixies do to a dragon?" Haephan asked.

"Every pixie has more magic in their tiny body than any other living being in Pangea."

"Really?"

"Really," said Nick.

"Who won?"

"No one is sure," Nick said. "Neither race keeps records and most of the fighting was away from civilization. We do know the pixies took the fight to the heart of dracodom."

"Eden?"

"Only one colony of dragons lives in Eden and they moved in relatively recently. The heart of the dragon society resides in the Graemol Desert thousands of miles from here, in a massive vertical cave known as the Dragon's Fangs."

"I had no idea."

"So, we're going to meet them, first."

"First?"

"SonLara really didn't tell you anything?"

"She tells me where to go and…I go."

"Ah," said Nick. "Well, she said you have a fantastic ability to move without moving."

"Yeah."

"I must admit, if it came from anyone other than an Andonese priestess, I'd struggle to believe it."

"Do you need to see me do it?" Haephan asked.

"No," Nick said. "I trust you both. But it would greatly help a mission I've been given to—"

"By the subrim?" Haephan asked.

"Yes," said Nick.

"Everyone keeps seeing them except me."

"You never met one?"

Haephan shook his head.

"Well, it was very scary."

Disbelief creased Haephan's mouth.

"It's true," said Nick. "A being with enough power as to dim the sun commanded me and…Two other kryses to travel to the world where you will help the vacants go for safety."

"You're not coming with them?"

"No," Nick said. "You're taking us there so we can build a rimsportal."

"How? I didn't know people built those."

"They haven't for a very long time. We're going to build the first new one in a decamillennia."

Haephan scowled.

"Ten thousand years."

"Oh," said Haephan. "Is that how the vacants are traveling?"

"They can't," said Nick. "They cannot use magic. They will travel first to Algueda, and from there to a new world. At least, that's how we understand it."

"They can't use the rimsportal?"

"No," said Nick.

"That's stupid," Haephan scowled.

"Stupid or not, that's how it is."

Haephan frowned.

"Are you ready to help?"

"Yes. Sir," Haephan said. "The sooner we get out, the sooner we get back."

"That's true," Nick pursed his lips at the lackluster child. "Would you like any sweets or snacks while I tell you the plan? I have a few here in the room."

"No, sir," said Haephan. "I'm good."

"Alright then," said Nick. "Let's get started."

76

Brave

Adamar returned to Southdown in better shape than when he left it. Dressed in fine clothes and riding a beautiful chestnut mare, he descended the south end of the long bridge crossing the Estamar Canal.

When he started his mission a few days ago, he worried at the lack of vacants in the Old City, Belfast quarter or the Whittle. Those he asked about vacants became nervous and drove him away. No one would speak to him, confirming his fear that Dufrain had done his best to prevent him from finding success in anything, despite the fact that Eva had left him.

Adamar scowled, but he had committed to the mission.

After Southdown, he would head to Rainhold and try to convince anyone there. He was fairly confident he'd find a few, but he didn't know what SonLara would say if he returned empty-handed.

He owed her a great debt, but worried about the mission. It seemed too fantastic to be true, regardless of her ability to use some kind of magic on him. And to find "a people" by the Green moon, due in only a few weeks?

Adamar thought of his wife living somewhere in the Old City without him, unwilling to see him. It broke his heart, even now. He wanted to speak with her, talk to her, convince her, but even after their time in "Eden," he was so tired of her shit he found loneliness restful.

Yet he hungered for the presence of his wife.

To the left, the glow of sunrise speared across the sky to bathe the low Southdown buildings in burnished gold. The Southdown gate was unguarded at this hour, though Adamar had learned the hard way not to assume he went unnoticed, even dressed in simple clothes and riding a common horse. He passed through its high arch into a bustling throng of people. Though many wealthy lived in the district, common low brick buildings dominated the city's architecture with a pragmatic approach to lifestyle and design.

He turned east along the perimeter road, south on Roth Haven Lane and wove among the morning cartiers on their way to Forn Market to sell their wares. Through a forest of short, fat columns used each day to set up tents, awnings and stands, Adamar navigated through a city from his boyhood. He rode into Oriole Heights where buildings pressed together in narrow streets and tight corners. Adamar was soon the only rider amidst a sea of workers plodding their way across or out of the city for work.

He crossed a bridge rising over one of the offshoot canals, entered Hevel, and aimed for a four-story row house squeezed among countless others. He began to pass an empty lot full of women laundering with streams of water when voices rose.

"Adamar!" one of the women cried.

"Hey Meara," he said. "Have you seen Heath?"

"Heath went to market early this morning," she said. "What are you doing here?"

"It's important I talk to him," said Adamar as his horse shifted on the uneven cobble.

"You need to get your face off the street," she said.

"What? Why? Think a constable will recognize me?"

"Get off that thing and get inside," she said. "Urin, get that damned thing tied off in the warehouse. Come on, now!"

Adamar handed it off to Urin, who appeared wary of the animal but pulled it along like a cart donkey. Adamar followed Meara up to their rowhouse, entered and climbed to their apartment where her children ate breakfast.

"Finish," she pointed at one playing with his porridge before she led Adamar into a room and pushed the door to.

"What's wrong, Meara?" he asked.

"You don't need to be here," she whispered.

"Why?"

"After the trouble you and Eva caused? Why did you come back?"

"Trouble we caused? What are you talking about?"

"You don't know?"

"Don't know what? Last I remember, the only trouble we caused was to ourselves, and we got out of here quick and fast."

"You caused a lot more than just getting yourselves kicked out of Southdown," she said. "And why are you back?"

"I need to talk to Heath," said Adamar. "It's very important."

"You know what will happen if they recognize you!"

"I don't, actually," said Adamar. "What's going on?"

"They're rounding up vacants," she said.

"What?" he asked. "Why?"

"Danger to the public, they say," said Meara. "Now Heath has to sneak to work every day and we have to pray he comes home!"

"Momma?" asked the little girl with pigtails as she approached the cracked doorway. "Are we going to be late?"

Meara huffed as she ushered the girl out. "Stay here! I gotta get these on to class. Do not leave, Adamar! Great Self help me, I will throttle you."

The girl stared with big blue eyes framed by a chocolate face, alarmed at her mother's scolding of him.

"Go," Meara shooed the girl. "And get your brother so we can get on."

"Meara!" Adamar called along the hallway.

"Stay!" she cried, ushered out her children and shut the door.

Adamar was shocked SonLara's predictions had come true—and

so soon. Walking to the room's window, he watched Meara and the children leave the building and disappear into the flow of traffic. On the opposite side of the street, a man pointed at his window alongside three martial mages. Had Meara outed him, or was she merely lucky enough to escape? He'd never believe she would betray him, but he had to move.

Cursing, Adamar slipped from the room and the apartment. The door below slammed open before heavy boot falls climbed the stairs. Like last time, he slipped out the hallway window into the building courtyard and clung to a nearby drainpipe. The thin metal tube buckled, fell away from the wall and cast him across several clotheslines draped across the causeway. He flipped and landed sideways on the roof of the first floor, stunned as he rolled over and clutched his knee.

"There he is!" a man's head emerged from the third-story window. "Get downstairs!"

Clutching his knee, Adamar scrambled to his feet and along a narrow alley to the broadway. A nearby quad of constables turned at his emergence, one of whom locked onto Adamar as he ambled away. Foot falls announced their chase.

Despite his knee, Adamar sprinted across the street and into another alley until he reached a canal offshoot of the Estamar, turned along the railed walk toward the bridge and slowed when he spotted a patrol. He stopped to plan his escape.

How could building waterwheels have resulted in vacants being rounded up like cattle?

"Psst!" hissed a voice. One of the small doors from a nearby narrow alley gate cracked open to reveal a young girl peeking out. "C'mon!"

Adamar squeezed past her. She closed and locked the old wooden door behind him.

"Go! Go!" she pointed down the alley as narrow as his shoulders. Halfway along stood another, wider door. It was open and he followed a tight staircase into the basement. He waited there for the girl to slip in behind him and shut the door. "You're one o'them vacants, aren't you?"

"What? Yeah, I am," said Adamar.

"What are you doing in Southdown?" she hissed.

"Looking for my— a friend," he said. "Why are you helping me?"

"I don't think it's right, and—"

"Burnie!" a woman's muffled voice called from somewhere upstairs. "You're late!"

"Yes mum!" the girl yelled, then whispered to him, "when they're gone, you're gone, or my mum will kill me!" She took her skirt and ran upstairs. "Coming!"

"Thank you!" Adamar called after her under his breath. Once the door shut behind her, he approached the narrow windows at the top of the basement to scan the alley walk and ducked into the shadow to stay out of sight. Constables tromped past the gate, peered over it to search the alley and pressed onward.

Adamar laid his head on the wall.

"Start checkin' da basements!" yelled a voice.

Adamar cursed, climbed the inside stairs and peeked through the cracked door as Burnie and her mother left for the day. Once the front door was shut, he peeked out, crossed to the exit and spotted heavy cloaks hanging by the door. Pulling one on, he slipped out, shut the door, descended the steps to the sidewalk and hunched over with an unfeigned limp.

He needed to find his cousin, Heath.

Wondering how he would do that, he realized those passing him on the sidewalk veered aside—he was being followed. Casting aside the cloak, he bolted from a troop of wizards and soldiers. How did they find him so quickly?

He raced down the nearest alleyway to the next street and headed for the market another block west and south, past carts driving the opposite direction and commuters weaving amongst each other, as men in pursuit shouted and scattered pedestrians. Passing another cart at the next road to the left, he turned about and ducked behind the wheel on the opposite side. He ambled while quivering with adrenaline. Once his pursuers ran past, he bolted eastward, turned south at the next alley and leaned on the wall to rub his knee.

The need to locate Heath dwindled under a desire to run. He couldn't help Heath or any other vacants in the city. If they were already actively rounding up any vacant they could find, Adamar had no chance of bringing any with him.

He didn't know what he would tell SonLara, but being captured in Southdown posed great risk to himself and her mission.

A crowd of laborers trudged by on their way to a worksite. Adamar shuffled out and joined them by the rear.

He didn't need to die chasing after some stupid mission. If the Great Self had really commissioned all this, he wouldn't need one man, especially not someone who couldn't even manage his own wife or household. Why was he even out here running around gathering vacants? Didn't he have enough trouble being a vacant and a vagrant than to seek out more like himself?

Adamar followed them with his head lowered when the Estamar Bridge came into view. His heart fluttered when a troop of soldiers crossed one of the three intersections between him and the bridge gate, almost a half mile away. Every step closer pounded harder in his heart. Fear filled every nerve. He hugged himself, cupped both elbows and feigned a chill while he struggled not to piss his trousers.

As he followed the workers to the Estamar Bridge, shame welled within him. The vacants were being rounded up and he ran like a coward. But what SonLara asked for was impossible. If the government was arresting vacants, how could he hope to find any and get them out? Even the Great Self wouldn't get those vacants, now.

His group crossed the wide plaza toward the bridge gate as if walking through wet sand. Adamar struggled to suppress his terror. He shuffled out with the rest of them as tears rimmed his eyes and skin flushed. Through the high shadowed arch, they entered streaming morning sunlight onto the foot of the bridge.

What should have been glorious relief weighed him so that he stopped walking. Truth nailed his feet to the cobblestones.

He couldn't leave.

Torn inside, Adamar's heart seized at the strange but undeniable certainty that more than his fear and pride were at stake. A knowledge of uncertain origin anchored his feet to the ground as tears streamed down his cheeks.

Memories of regret, failures with his wife, fears about his own validity, his thorny pride about Eva's father and the ache to be more than his upbringing wafted past his mind. His entire life, summed so quickly, cut him to the core. He had absolutely nothing to flee to.

With sudden, terrifying clarity, he realized the trouble that drove him from the city might have instigated the government locking up his kind. Time stopped.

"What do I do?" he breathed. "Great Self, what do I do? Please help me."

Around and inside him, the world stilled. The sound of breath filled his ears as morning wind washed across the bridge before him.

Something shifted inside, as if someone new stepped into the room of his heart. The new presence stilled the screams of his fears until only a single whisper remained.

Go back inside.

So soft he barely heard it, the inaudible whisper wasn't magical or insistent, but it was undeniable. He didn't doubt its gentle clarity.

He squeezed his eyes and exhaled.

Go back inside.

Something fresh and long untasted grew inside of him as he surrendered to the simple instruction. Unsure how to react, Adamar almost buckled under its foreign touch. Its presence required no effort from him as it seeped into the cracks of his soul, the gaps in his confidence and into the hole in his heart as a warm flood that surpassed comprehension or understanding.

With a faint smile, his body calmed, breath slowed and he squeezed remaining tears over his cheeks.

Though lighter and freer, Adamar had to turn around. He had to obey. It wasn't enough to feel the possibility. He had to choose. He had to commit.

He had to surrender.

Turning around, the first step took a minute. The next step moved on its own and led to another until he split the crowd leaving Southdown.

Despite fear of his doom, freedom filled his heart. He approached the middle of the plaza, unsure what to do next, when a horn blew several sharp blasts. Soldiers racing across the plaza scattered pedestrians as they converged on him. He raised his hands before bulky men tackled him to the cobblestone.

77
Carlinia

Atop the murder of a standing aurora, you…you made a deal with an Andonese*?* asked Morna. As Carlinia's newest tyraness and Han's replacement, selected from the elderate, Morna's glare bored holes into the young aurora. *We lost a foolhardy tyran while you made deals with evil, itself? And then you bound us to protect a* human wizard*?*

Aurora Ven gulped as she hovered in the center of a dozen concentric wooden platforms rising around her to form an amphitheater packed with the Carlinian flock. Around them, the three primary branches of the Tree Carlinia flared upward from a tight braid climbing hundreds of feet from the soil into a thick-leafed canopy as broad as the Tree was tall that extended outward like an inverted floral bowl. She hovered above the gap between the braided trunks as she faced Tyraness Morna and the elderate, who loomed from their places on the lowest ring. Round about them swarmed thousands of pixies eager for the spectacle of the young aurora formally summoned before the tyran, an event rare in pixilark history. *When I reversed her spell…I was already trying to stop her. I didn't realize I had control of her until after it was over.*

Any death of one pixie by another is murder, Morna chimed.

Then you would have stopped Chira? Ven asked as she hugged herself. *You had the ability? The eldest and most powerful aurora in Pangea on a murderous rampage? You could have merely restrained the single-most magical being on the continent?*

Morna didn't answer.

And that spell? You saw it, Ven chimed to Infith. *Would someone* please *tell me what that was?*

The elderate exchanged glances.

Please! begged Ven. *All any of you have done all week is avoid my question. I want to know what Chira was trying to do to me.*

Morna raised her hand. *It's forbidden even to speak of—*

She used it on her entire flock, Ven's voice echoed. *And then, while I'm soft-bonded to all of you, she tried it on me. Do you know what would have happened if she had succeeded? She would have spread her spell upon each and every one of you.*

You should have considered that before you soft-bonded us, chimed Morna.

You said nothing, chimed Ven. *None of you, the entire fire.*

Someone must be held accountable for that mistake—

And it's going to be me!? Ven stammered.

You were supposed to be here when this all began, chimed Morna.

Well, I wasn't, Ven chimed. *We can say* should *all we like around here, but no matter what tradition has demanded, I wasn't here. And the aurora was fine when I left. What happened cannot be thrown on my shoulders because I was elsewhere.*

But that's your role as an aurora! cried Morna.

That also means protecting the flock from powers unseen, chimed Ven. *And as Song was in good health, I was pursuing that course.*

There must be a reckoning, chimed Morna.

Then reckon me, Ven chimed. *But please, tell me what that spell is.*

Rite of Aikina, Infith chimed to the muttered protests of the elderate.

That was the Rite of Aikina? Ven unfolded her arms. *Why would she use such a thing on me?*

For the same reason you already knew her thoughts, chimed Morna. *It was abused by the ancients to enslave creatures of lesser magic for a variety of unspeak-*

able reasons.

Such as reading someone's memories? Ven asked to silence. *You think avoiding telling me its name somehow avoided the fact that Chira was using it liberally to get her way? You accuse* me *of murder while actively hiding the fact that Chira wielded forbidden magic?*

The elderate said nothing.

The deal is sound, chimed Ven. *However unlikely I thought they might actually succeed.*

You're sure they succeeded? asked Elder Infith.

The incursions have stopped, chimed Ven.

Chira didn't think so, chimed Morna.

Chira was an elder aurora, chimed Ven. *Which means she saw more of time than I yet do. I am more present than she could be. She was still hearing the screams from before they stopped. The deal worked.*

You said you weren't sure they would succeed, chimed Morna. *Why did you make the deal?*

I didn't think we had another choice, so I chose to trust her.

By your own words, you failed to deal with the worldender, chimed Infith as he crossed his arms and cupped his chin. *You didn't pursue?*

It seemed best not to interfere with his mission just to get probably the same answer, chimed Ven. *So, we spoke with the Andonese at length about the details as she knew them. With Rose's counsel, I was satisfied.*

The Andonese are prohibited from all pixilark lands, Morna chimed. *And cohorting with them in any way is strictly forbidden.*

Even when it provides a way to our survival? Ven protested.

You have no evidence she had anything to do with ending the threat from the dracos, chimed Morna. *Luck of timing—or more likely, a deceitful Andonese taking advantage of someone else's victory—doesn't give her leave to call upon our flock for a single bloody thing.*

I say it does, Ven softly protested. *The dracos stopped as she described they should. This puts us into a debt with them.*

This is in violation of some of our most foundational laws, Morna's tone quieted the din of attending pixies. *Aurora, or no, what you have done could put our entire flock to the threat.*

Ven waited.

They were truly going to procure seeds from the Tree of Life? asked Brye. *An aurora should have killed her on the spot and gone after the interlopers.*

Where were you when the dracos took Eden? Ven's quiet question chilled the congregation. *You judge me for acting when you have never tried anything.*

Starting a new war with the dracos must be a last resort, Morna chimed.

I-I would hate a war, Ven chimed and hugged herself, again. *The last thing I wanted to do,* her voice cracked, *was kill another pixie, much less another aurora. I don't want to kill more. But what was I to do?*

Return and speak with us, chimed Brye.

I wasn't going to wait for you to deliberate us to death, Ven whispered. The congregation fluttered as they repeated her soft words outward.

You think so little of our elderate for being such a young aurora, chimed Brye. *You weren't summoned to lecture us.*

Summoning an aurora for performing her duty was the least of your mistakes, Ven chimed.

Morna leaned forward. *You were summoned for violating ancient pixie law—*

I acted where I believed you wouldn't, Ven chimed. *I made a deal to preserve our people and would do so again. I will do anything to save my pixies.*

You had no right, Morna chimed.

When they arrive to call us on our debt, Ven cut her off, *we will all support their efforts to plant these seeds and connect new worlds. Tyrans, elders, the class-es…all of us.*

What are you saying? asked Brye. *You're leaving the Tree? You're a full aurora now. Leaving Tree Carlinia is forbidden.*

None of you are listening, Ven drew a hesitant breath. *We are blood-bound to these humans for saving our very species. We have a life debt—every one of us. When they come, they will have two flocks to respond.*

Two? Morna's stern face faltered. *You intend to involve the Yennethens in this madness?*

Thanks to Chira's insanity, I am now their aurora, chimed Ven. The truth settled on the elderate. *As I am yours.*

You overstep your authority, chimed Brye. *You have neither role nor right to deliver up entire flocks to the blasphemy of bloody humans.*

When it comes to the spiritual health and survival of our flock, I have every right, Ven chimed. *And when they get here—*

If anyone attempts to pierce our border, they will die, chimed Morna. The pixie din, again, quieted.

What have you done? Ven asked. *You're going to kill even more beings?*

A standing order has gone forth that all but pixies and high elves should be destroyed on sight, chimed Morna. *More likely that a draco should save our souls than any of those conditions be met any time soon.*

Ven searched the faces of the elderate and held out her hands. *We can't keep killing!* She realized the eldress had revealed the deal to Morna and locked eyes with Rose. *You already knew the deal I made with the Andonese.*

When a senior eldress and the flock's holy aurora disappear for several weeks, not to mention the loss of our tyran to realm diving, Morna spat, *I will demand answers every way I can. That you waited this long to tell us only shows I had every responsibility to find out the truth.*

I would have told you everything, chimed Ven. *Did you think I would hide something?*

You never shared this deal to me, chimed Morna. *You had an entire week before now to volunteer this knowledge.*

Ven fell silent.

I never thought we would have a flightfallen aurora, Morna chimed low, but the mutter spread on lips as fast as the wind.

Ven gulped. *I am not unfit.*

You are too young for this, regardless of your blossomings, Morna leaned forward. *And I will call the aurorate for a conclave if I must.*

Ven shrank.

Don't think that will go unpunished, either, chimed Brye as the multitude hummed with scandalous conversation.

SILENCE! Morna roared. The hollow fell quiet. Panting, Morna raised her hand to speak when her attention climbed above Ven's head.

"Whoa," a voice muttered.

Thousands of dumbfounded pixies stared at a small human sitting in the canopy above the debacle who hadn't been there a moment before.

Ven spun and her eyes widened. *The boy.*

The what? Brye asked.

"We're looking for Auralven?" said the human boy, who narrowed in on Ven. "Is that you?"

Yes, Ven chimed.

PALADIN! Morna cried.

In an explosion of activity, guards rushed inward from around the outer canopy with eyes and hands glowing with violent energy.

"Not again," muttered Haephan. "Hey! I'm here to see Ven! Are you her?"

Yes, chimed Ven as she faced Morna. *Leave him be!*

How did he get up here!? Brye asked.

As the guards advanced on him, the boy pointed at Ven and the ground before he disappeared.

The paladin rushing inward slowed to a slack-jawed stop.

Where did he go!? Morna stuttered. *Spread out and find him!*

Ven's attention sank low. As the platform roiled with shock, her wings stilled and she fell straight through the gap between the braided trunks until she reached the empty hollow at the bottom. Her wings snapped out and she fired through the openings toward the boy standing at the tree base. Her face melted to find a high elf standing next to him.

Are you the boy? Ven alighted before them. *From the Andonese?*

"Priestess SonLara?" Haephan asked. "Yeah."

Who are you? she asked the elf.

Haephan nudged Nick's thigh with his elbow. "Ain't you gonna answer?"

"Did she speak?" Nick asked.

"Do you not understand?"

"I never learned pixilark," said Nick.

You brought a high elf with you? How? Ven asked. From the canopy above, a flood of sparks exploded from the Tree and bolted for them. *Morna has ordered your death.*

"My death?" Haephan asked.

Except... chimed Ven as she turned to Nick. *Who are you to travel with an Andonese and a human boy?* She looked at Haephan. *I thought you were with a wizard.*

"Yeah, he's back home," scowled Haephan. "This is Nick."

"Krys Kringul of Aminrale," Nick took the cue and half bowed.

"Yeah, Krys Kringul," said Haephan as the pixies raced for them.

A krys!? Ven stuttered. She faced the closing paladin and raised her hands. *Don't!*

Out of the way! Morna cried as she summoned her own powers.

He's a krys! Ven cried.

Morna faltered and floated to a stop. *Impossible.*

Speak to him! Ven pleaded and pointed at Nick.

This is another deception! Morna fisted her hands.

Then verify the spell sign, chimed Ven.

Did you? Morna asked.

Just...do it! Ven cried.

The paladin following Morna surrounded the interlopers with powers ready to attack. She advanced on the boy and the elf with glowing eyes.

"It's okay," Nick set his hand on Haephan's shoulder. "Don't shift us away yet. Let's see what she does."

"I don't like it," Haephan scanned the flock. "It's like the border guards."

"Remember what I said," Nick sounded patient with the boy. "If we don't face the danger, we'll never get through this. The only way is *through*."

Haephan didn't appear comforted.

Morna scanned the two before locking onto the high elf. Full of doubt, she raised her hands and drew the tyran spellsign that glowed as a mark of her place and position. If Nick were truly a krys, he would know easily how to do so.

Before Morna could finish, Nick raised his hands and drew out the spellsign for Aminrale.

"I am— *was,* Krys Kringul of Aminrale," said Nick. "I come with the boy on behalf of a mission from the Great Self."

Haephan translated before Morna's hands dropped in shock. Her violent power fell dark.

Was? Morna chimed.

Ven flew to face her tyraness. *This is bigger than us, Morna.*

Morna struggled to cope with the reality before her. *Wait, how did you get here? There's no way you could have pierced our borders.*

"We already faced your border guards," said Haephan. "They

wouldn't let us through, so we came in."

You attacked our gu—

"I didn't attack no one!" Haephan protested. "They came at us. Wouldn't believe Nick. So we came in."

How!? Explain yourself! Morna chimed.

"Like this," Haephan said inches away from Morna. He hadn't been there a moment before.

Morna leapt backward and her paladin flinched.

"I can move without moving," said Haephan with a scowl. "And I didn't come here to be attacked. Got it, lady?"

Morna gulped.

"Are you really Ven?" asked Haephan. "No one said anything about fighting."

How did you do that? asked Ven.

"Are you Ven or not?" Haephan demanded.

"Haephan," Nick raised a hand. "Yes, that's their aurora."

"Are you sure?" Haephan asked.

I am Aurora Ven, chimed Ven. *And I was expecting you.*

Haephan returned to Nick's side to further gasps of the congregation. "We didn't come to fight. SonLara told us you would help with the dragons."

We promised, chimed Ven. *And we will. All of us. We live up to our debts.*

You said you were going to the La'Du Lira Al'Cular! Morna stammered. *How do we know you truly stopped the dracos from—*

Haephan fished out a pod the size of his fist from his leather belt. "I don't lie."

Morna and the elderate flinched as its magic sprang forth like a midnight sun to their magical eyes. *Great Self, that's…*

Ven alone noted Haephan's light mantle bore the same magic inherent to the seed.

"Yeah, a seed from the tree," Haephan said. "Now, let's talk. I got, like, four worlds to plant with the seeds I got." He stuffed it once more into his special belt pocket.

Morna's mouth moved without sound.

How did you do that? Ven asked. *How far can you go?*

"I was in New Gordon before we came to the border," said Haephan.

"It's instant, I think."

Truly...Ven asked. *Where can you go?*

"Anywhere I want," said Haephan.

And you brought the elf with you? Or he met you here?

"As long as he's touching me, he comes with me," Haephan said.

You're planting four worlds with that one seed?

"What? No!" Haephan scowled as if the question were stupid. "I'll go back and get more when I need them."

Instantly?

"Instantly."

Ven spun to Morna. *We don't need to wait to summon Yenneth. We can all go in a single moment. We will fulfill our debt. This is our part.*

Morna floated, dumbfounded.

Ven faced the congregation. *Gather yourselves, Carlinia. Starting now, we go with the boy and make good on our oath.*

And what will it take to fulfill that debt? asked Morna. *How far are we to go?*

However far it takes, Ven chimed. *Do you hear me?*

Soft-bonded as she was to the entire flock, every pixie heard her gentle chimal words. Each of them raised their right palms and shined the light of agreement until they became a shimmering star field.

We are ready to fulfill our oaths...human child, chimed Ven. *What is your name? And what kind of mage are you?*

"Mage?" Haephan asked. "Dunno about that. I'm Haephan. But you can call me..." The word floated into his mind. "Pan."

Alright, pan, Ven lowered her hand. *Let's begin.*

78

Rimsportal

Haephan and Nick shifted to an endless sea of grass under a mid-afternoon sun. The two took in the scene as a heavy breeze washed over them.

"Where?" Haephan asked.

Nick noted life seeping from the boy. "I'm sure we can move everything here for now and then the Cordurons can move it to a better place. Alright?" He half tilted his head to try and catch the boy's eye.

Haephan hesitated, met his gaze for a brief moment and disappeared.

Worry grew within Nick that more than shy or listless, the boy was deeply hurt. His heart became heavy as he wondered what might have befallen him. There was a spark within Haephan, but it flickered on the tip of a wick beneath a heavy wind.

Haephan shifted in a single pale stone, then another, and another in stacks that expanded upward and outward. Over the next few minutes, Haephan shifted so fast that all Nick could make out of him was the faint blur of his appearance to put a stone in place and head back.

The stones transitioned in shape and size as Haephan moved through the predesigned elements for the coming rimsportal. Trapezoidal blocks with curved tops and sharp-edged bottoms filled one end while heavier foundation stones comprised the other.

When twelve quarter sections, mid and heavy-tier foundation stones finished their journey, secondary metallic elements appeared across the grounds in the same pattern as they were laid out in Aminrale. Three final capped cylinders finished the materiel transition.

A few seconds passed before Cordurons appeared across the grass. Haephan moved faster, shifting them up to three a second. How he achieved it boggled Nick's mind. Forty finished the journey before Haephan reappeared. He bent over panting and set his hands upon his knees. Once the moment passed, he straightened.

"Are you alright?" Nick asked.

Haephan jumped and said, "Yeah, yeah. I'm, fine. What next?"

"After we left Carlinia, how many worlds did you plant before you joined us in Aminrale?" Nick asked.

Haephan took several heavy breaths. "I'm not sure. Three?"

"You must be very tired. Do the pixies help?"

"Not really," said Haephan. "They kinda spread out and look for dragons while I do the work."

"It must be nice to have companionship, at least," said Nick.

Haephan shrugged. "Ven tries to talk to me, but sometimes she really babbles on." His shoulders sank.

"Why don't you take a walk? Get some rest. We'll get this done."

After staring into nothing, Haephan plodded off. "Okay." He shoved his hands in his pockets.

"We've double checked all the materials," said Sandark as he approached. "Everything is here."

Haephan disappeared around a bend in the terrain.

"What do you suppose has happened to that child?" asked Sandark.

"I fear something terrible," said Nick. "He's tired from planting these worlds, but…something terrible happened to him. That such evil could be committed upon this world as the destruction of the innocent. It stills my heart."

Sandark nodded.

"Come, Master Sandark," said Nick. "We have much to do and little time to do it."

"Yes, of course," said Master Sandark as he opened a scroll in his hand so both could scan it.

Over the next few hours, Nick and the Cordurons located a small cave sunk into low, rigid hills peppering the terrain. The Cordurons cut open an entrance large enough for Nick to stoop through before carrying the materials inside and beginning their construction of the rimsportal. The small elves dug and set foundation stones, into which three metal cylinders were set. Master Sandark performed the magical connections that would charge using terrestrial energy that would last as long as the world beneath them lived under the sun. They capped the matrix and began final interlays to convey the stored energy into the rings being assembled by five experts.

Once the stone foundations, capping and interlay were set, Nick helped Sandark perform the interconnection spell that would open it to the Pangean network, a feat Sandark worried wouldn't work given their unknown distance. His doubts were founded as it required hours of tweaking the spell and shifting power structures to complete a connection. Once performed and inlaid, the ring assembly team lifted the first metal ring—comprised of six seamlessly connected pieces—and mounted it to the center. They set in the second and third concentric rings and locked their gearings into place before performing the final energetic locks.

"Nonessential personnel, out," Sandark's voice echoed in the small cave.

Unworried Cordurons filed out while chatting amongst themselves. Two remained behind who crossed their arms and frowned at the new creation.

"I'm staying," said Nick.

Sandark approached the address panel facing the rings on a lectern-shaped stand. He rotated three dials laid in a three-point arrangement, each with symbols along the outer edges. When he matched three appropriate symbols in the center, he set his fingers upon a gentle bulge between them and inlaid the appropriate magical cypher.

On the platform, outer edges of all three rings popped with a thin line of sharp white light before the inner ring spun until it blurred with a glowing ambient cloud. The second counterspun until it, too, intensified the existing light. When the third finished its spin, only a pale glowing sphere remained.

"Test one," Sandark said.

One Corduron clasped arms with his companion, nodded at Sandark, and mounted the leftmost end of the low platform. He ambled proudly into the ball of light. The second leaned out from side to side while eyeing the portal's functionality.

"Powering down," Sandark said and executed the null action. The light dissipated and the rings slowed before clicking to a stop in three concentric circles.

"This hasn't been accomplished in at least sixty thousand years, Master Sandark," Nick said.

"I wish it could have been longer," said Sandark.

"You don't trust instant travel?" Nick asked.

"We consider it dangerous when those with power can so easily access those they wish to rule," Sandark said. "Especially when those ruled have no wish to be so."

"I would imagine your ancestors would disagree with you," said Nick.

"My ancestors failed because they fought the past instead of outsmarting it," Sandark said. "Innovation has been our salvation…Master Kringul." He frowned at the words in his mouth. "Not war."

"Nick, please," Nick said. "I own no title by those that belong in history books, Master Sandark."

"Then it's as well you don't call me otherwise," said Sandark. "Nick."

"Is your only name Sandark?"

"It's Rufus."

Nick raised an eyebrow.

"But I almost miss calling you 'krys,'" said Sandark.

"The egalitarian in you must be rolling over."

"And yet…you are taking us to a land long sought, Nick," said Sandark. "I think I would honor you with the title, sometimes, even if I don't think of you as my monarch."

Unsure how to respond, Nick dipped his head.

Sandark faced the rings as they glowed to life and spun. "Incoming."

Nick wondered after the boy. A few moments later, the traveler reappeared carrying a small stone token, which he carried to Sandark.

Taking it, Sandark nodded at the second traveler and began a spin-up for the next destination. Over the next 30 minutes, they tested ten rimsportal locations across the continent, all predetermined to pose the least risk at their appearance.

"Rimsportal is complete," said Sandark. "We're ready to return to Aminrale for the night."

Nick nodded.

"Everything alright?"

"Haephan has not returned," Nick said.

"Perhaps he returned to New Gordon," said Rufus. "He knows we can go home."

"He is here, and not far away," said Nick. "I will seek him out." He headed out. "I'll send in your workers. Go on through. I'll return when I'm done."

"As you say," Rufus said.

Nick climbed from the dark cave and squinted against the blazing sunset. He motioned to the workers chatting outside before heading across the terrain in search of Haephan.

Nick headed west over the gentle grassy hills and narrowed in on Haephan sitting on a rock bathed in sunlight. Approaching, he stopped shy of the weeping child.

"I couldn't save them," Haephan stuttered. "I couldn't. I-I didn't!" He coughed a sob. "I could have. I could have made it! I could have just gone in! Saved them. But I didn't. I didn't!" His lungs shuddered. "I didn't! And now they're dead!" Anguished eyes climbed to Nick. "I didn't. They died because— because I wanted revenge. They died because I had to do it my way!" Wracked with sobs, the boy swayed.

Nick waited while his own tears slid down his cheeks.

"My mom died because I waited! My best friend—" inhale "-died because I—" inhale "didn't go! I didn't go, Nick! I didn't go! Why didn't I go!? Why did I wait!?" Haephan sobbed. "And I'll never find my dad!"

Nick crossed the distance, scooped Haephan and sat with him curled in his lap. His long arms closed around Haephan as the boy erupted with wailing. He wracked with hidden sorrow as Nick hugged him to his chest.

The child sobbed with torment as he clung to Nick's shirt. He coughed, sobbed and sucked for air as his emotions shattered the numbness damming up his heart.

Struggling to help the boy find release, Nick snaked a tendril of his spirt inward to the boy's and, in a rush, took upon as much pain as possible. Though unable to see Haephan's memories or thoughts, the boy's mounting guilt and shame overwhelmed Nick until he struggled to cut off his own sob.

Loosed of the internal pressure, Haephan's sobs subsided until he hiccuped with exhaustion. He sniffed wetly as his head sank upon Nick's chest.

"I-I just…" he breathed.

Nick rocked him. "It's alright, Haephan. You're safe. Rest now. You can rest now."

"But…" Haephan protested as his eyes drooped.

"You never have to fear me," whispered Nick. "Rest. You are safe here."

"But they're dead," the boy whispered.

Nick kissed the top of Haephan's head. "I forgive you, Haephan. I forgive you of this sin."

Terror, fury and guilt washed over the boy before he fell limp.

Nick clung to the child as his own tears freely flowed. "You're forgiven, child," Nick whispered. "No matter what you've done or what we may yet face…You're forgiven."

79

Thoughts and Feelings

Hot watert rained in soft droplets from the holed silver dome above SonLara's head and flowed over her wet, navy-blue hair and pale white skin into the drain while its heat rebounded off the low tile ceiling and narrow walls and wafted with heavy moisture into her lungs. A single, dim light fell across the back of her shower and cast her as a silhouette in its amber glow.

SonLara pressed her head against the cool diamond-shaped tiles. Despite a brief cry, her inner walls had returned. Why she had let her defenses thin and crumble after only a few weeks in New Gordon, she could not fathom.

A younger SonLara wondered why the genders lost their minds over emotions. She opened her fist and planted it on the cool tile. She ached for solitude; the subrim commission could go to hell.

In a single moment, her feelings ebbed. She cut off the shower as the weight of the water drained from her hair and followed the rest down her body. She snatched a towel, dried her skin and wrapped herself. With another, she bound up her hair and entered her room.

After shaping her nails and cleaning her face, she used her own ancient technique to smooth her hair, close the ends and bring in the shine. Strict Andonese upbringing demanded she maintain an appearance of self-control.

Across Pangea, Andonese were considered beautiful for their fair skin, elven silver eyes, blue manes and delicate features. The selfdamn old man living down the hall was an unkempt, fuzzy, graying asshole. Her attraction to him over anyone from her homeland infuriated her.

SonLara calmed her mind by focusing on her task. Her hands stroked her hair before she sifted it out, flattened sections in knuckle-lengths and wrapped them around her head until they formed ribbon-like layers in an oval coil.

From there, she donned her dress and overcloak, checked herself in the mirror and calmed her heart. While smoothing the fabric, she dismissed her emotional concerns and readied her mind. She had a mission to perform, a study to continue and a bastard to leave behind. She needed to focus on her original purpose in coming here. She needed to get a seed.

How might that affect the subrim's commission? Would it violate her oath? Would it put Belfast or Haephan in jeopardy?

Her hands pressed over her fluttering stomach. What should she do? Adamar. She needed to check on Adamar and be away from Ashmore and its temptations. Elverbane was consumed in his war council. No one would be around his study or the box. She could…

SonLara left her apartment and descended the building to an awaiting carriage. Once inside, it started off along university streets, through the main gate and rocked over the cobbled New Gordon roads. Schooling her vagrant thoughts, she planned for the coming deadline. How might accomplish what the subrim had asked of her?

Despite her struggle to focus on her mission, she wondered how she misread Elverbane's feelings. Again, she tamped her anger.

Haephan had planted five new worlds—the last two with the protection of two full pixie flocks. Now working with Haephan, the pixies refused another audience with her. Their involvement dumbfounded her, but it could not last much longer now that three seeds remained.

Adamar missed last night's deadline. Where was he? They could not afford more time. She would have to send a scout to Southdown immediately—

The door opened to reveal the carriage driver. "We're here, priestess."

The loss of time surprised her. Rising from her seat, she descended the carriage steps onto the Mayhouse driveway. Her nerves frayed with every small interruption to her usual habits. Shaking her head, she mounted the steps when the front door opened to reveal Butler Donovan.

"Welcome back, Priestess SonLara," he intoned.

"I've come to see Adamar," she said. "Could you call upon him?"

"Lord Adamar?" the butler asked. "He has not returned, m'lady."

"No word at all?" asked SonLara.

"No, mistress," he said.

She sighed.

"Shall I summon Master Bennett?"

"No," she said. "I have someone else to call upon to help with this matter."

"Yes, priestess," he bowed as she returned to the carriage. If only the boy could be summoned as easily as he could travel. As soon as he returned from his next seeding, she'd send him to Southdown.

While the driver held open the door, she hesitated at the carriage steps and peered into its dark interior as her heart pounded at the idea of returning to the school and seeing Elverbane again. She loathed her desire for him and raged at his callous disdain. That stupid man had no idea what he chose by rejecting her.

Ice flushed her veins. She would do whatever was necessary to serve her mission and go home—where she belonged. SonLara pictured the wooden box lying on Elverbane's table. "Take me back to Ashmore."

80

Acceptable

Bare lit by gray predawn, a jagged spire of twisted rock speared up from the heavy waves advancing on the world's edge. Inside a narrow cave bisecting the granite formation, Haephan lay sleeping along its cold stone floor not far from one of the ends.

Sitting side-by-side on the cave's curved wall, Aurora Ven and Eldress Rose watched the boy sleep.

Aurora, I owe you an apology, Rose chimed.

Ven turned.

I was worried about everything we had done, chimed Rose. *Morna. Morna…*

She pressured you, Ven chimed.

That's not good enough, aurora, chimed Rose. *I've withstood far greater pressure than that dirtlick of a tyraness. No. I didn't trust you or the priestess.*

No you didn't.

I'm still right not to trust the priestess, chimed Rose. *But I should have trusted you.* She set her hand on Ven's arm.

Thank you, chimed Ven.

I still don't get this arrangement, chimed Rose. *Or why you're convinced it's the best path…but you were right. It feels like where we need to be. All of us.*

So many worlds, chimed Ven. *I never imagined something like this was possible. Not since creation.*

Did the boy say this was the sixth world he's created so far? How many more will there be? asked Rose. *When will we be done with this?*

I'm not sure, but I can tell you there is more to this than these islands, Ven chimed. *Much more. We are beginning something that will last to the next age.*

The islands? asked Rose.

A bond, chimed Ven.

With humans? asked Rose.

Just one, Ven chimed.

This one?

And those who come after.

How many islands will there be? Rose straightened.

Ven smirked. *Only nine.*

Then what could come after this? asked Rose.

So much more, chimed Ven. *This is the beginning of a unique symbiosis. Even the power that courses through this human is unlike any power I've ever seen.*

How so? asked Rose.

I can't yet say, Ven chimed. *But it's something new to time, I would wager.*

Really? Rose asked. *A human?*

Ven nodded.

Rose scowled.

He saved our people and does not know it or what it truly means, Ven smiled.

Will this really stop the dracos? asked Rose. *They might be stopped for now, but won't the La'Du Lira Al'Cular merely produce more? How far is this child willing to go to save us? Will he fight the dracos alongside us or leave us to die should they appear? If he is as powerful as you say, why does he even need us?*

I can sense the import of this boy, chimed Ven, *but I cannot see what next we will do with him or how I will one day ascend. Because of that, I've been thinking about the rite.*

The rite? The one Chira used on you and Yenneth? asked Rose. *Why?*

What if he won't help us keep the seeds away from the dracos when we're finished with his current supply? chimed Ven. *I have no intention of abusing the child. I can't imagine ever wanting to hurt any youth. I would protect him while he protects us.*

You ought to forget such a blasphemy, chimed Rose.

You forget I already possess the rite over an entire flock, Ven chimed. *This power isn't dangerous if we intend to use it wisely.*

Wisely? chimed Rose. *What wisdom is there in slavery?*

What if it's our only option? asked Ven. *And we have the best of intentions!*

Could enslaving a living being ever be an acceptable price for survival? asked Rose. *We do not subjugate our enemies more than necessary, much less our allies.*

I am willing to explore every option and pay the price, myself, if necessary.

Before you forget about Chira, chimed Rose, *don't think being an aurora gives you unlimited sway with the honor of our flock.*

Ven pressed her mouth to her arms.

I respect your heart, aurora, but...if we stoop to slavery, then do we deserve to survive? While every creature must fight for its survival, and every being must consume another being to persist, we do so within the framework designed by the Self. This is the nature of all living beings, each to see to its own survival by competing in the great chain. She shook her head. *Enslaving another creature is not the same as eating it.*

I do not want to die by tradition.

An aurora you might be, and flows you might see, Rose chimed, *but you are missing something vital to who we are as sentient beings, Aurora Ven.*

Ven turned, surprised.

We exist to participate in this world, not control it, chimed Rose. *The entirety of our existence, like all sentients, is to partake in what the Great Self has created and, in so doing, learn more about the Self. Such is the point of every intelligent being—draw nearer to its creator through the medium of creation. Every act we commit ought reflect who we are with and to the Great Self. If we cannot live but by committing an act that would separate us from Him, then it's better to thank His Holiness for our time here and prepare to move on.*

Ven waited.

Survival isn't our highest ideal, Ven. Holiness is.

How can committing a rite on a single being suddenly sully our entire race? Ven asked. *Won't he return to do what he did before and leave us alone to this task?*

It is not for others to do for us what we can and should do for ourselves, chimed Rose, *especially while we yet have the ability to act and options yet to explore.*

What are those options, eldress? asked Ven. *Are we going to go to Eden to confront the draco?*

If we must, chimed Rose. *We are a proud flock. And we will do all we can before even thinking of lowering ourselves to trollish depths such as performing the rite on others. We do not enslave sentient beings!*

It's not slavery if it's for our survival! stammered Ven.

Should slavery by any other name be as acceptable? asked Rose. *We will not commit any such atrocity, on any sentient being, as we have breath in our lungs to save ourselves. It's what Chira did. Are you validating her decisions?*

She was mad! chimed Ven.

We are not, chimed Rose.

And this alliance? chimed Ven.

If this voluntary exchange didn't benefit us all, we wouldn't have agreed to it, chimed Rose. *And as it was before the boy, we are responsible for our survival, not him.*

Ven pondered. *When it comes to the survival of our flock—our species—I do not feel we can set any boundaries to what is required to achieve that survival.*

You are an intelligent fairy, Aurora Ven, chimed Rose, *but do not let your fear get the better of you. Pixilarks do not rush. Now that the boy has the seeds, our magnalarks are safe, for the moment. That affords us options, not the least of which is using time wisely to find out how to undo the rite over the Yennethens. They deserve their freedom and their own aurora.*

Ven rubbed her face. *Yeah. They…they are so heavy.*

Rose slid her hand across Ven's back and let the aurora lean against her for a few moments before an echoing chime drew her attention into the cave.

I will go see how the flocks fare, chimed Rose. *I know of no two flocks to spend as much time together as we have and I'm hoping against too much conflict… or too much fucking. Especially not three thousand of them. Stay with the boy.*

The boy shivered for a moment as a fresh icy breeze rushed through the narrow cave. Outside, the sky pinked with approaching sunrise.

Try to keep him warm, chimed Rose.

How?

You're all-powerful, chimed Rose as she hovered above the cave floor. *Be creative.* She flew away.

Ven scowled after her. Even as an aurora of two flocks with a clear direction, she didn't like the idea of being so helpless before potential threats. Rising to her feet, she approached the boy and touched his forehead.

A brilliant golden lacework flashed outward in ripples from her contact with his skin. Ven recoiled. Reaching again, her touch repeated the effect. Why hadn't it happened before? Nearly three thousand pixies came into contact with the boy over and over again over the past few days.

Ven realized she had never touched him during any of their previous shifts. Always, other pixies surrounded her and kept her from him in a protective cocoon. Stepping closer, she inspected the lacework with growing wonder at its immense complexity and intimate familiarity. Though she had only heard of abrucaris in tales of the Draco Elven Wars, never were they described as so powerful or intricate.

For all her bluff and bravado, Ven considered herself inadequate for the task ahead. Rose's words echoed in her mind and spoke of a pixilark identity that would require centuries of experience to appreciate.

Still, an aurora's role was to retain knowledge useful for her flock's survival and prosperity. Whether or not she would abide Rose's noble morality or remain more pragmatic, she would do as only an aurora could in this moment.

Running her fingers through the shimmering lacework hovering above Haephan's skin, she would learn. Over the next hour, she tangled and untangled her mental fingers through the web of energy clinging to the boy's very soul before he stirred.

Ven withdrew when his eyes fluttered open. Though she had little experience with humans, she noticed his disappointment in waking, as if he dreamt of somewhere wonderful and woke somewhere less.

Welcome back, she chimed.

He disappeared.

Ven turned about, terrified he'd abandoned them, when he reappeared with a monstrous meat pie in his hands.

Ven studied him until he noticed.

He broke off a tiny bite of the breading and offered her a piece.

Ven raised her hand to waive off.

Shrugging, he ate it and the rest of his pie, licked his fingers and rubbed the rest on his clothes, drawing a frown from her. "Arvin?"

Aurora Ven, she corrected him.

"Ah. Sorry," Haephan said before a yawn erupted. He stretched high his hands with a gaping mouth before sinking against the concave stone wall. "Where are we?"

We're still at the new island you created.

He moaned again. "I'm losing track."

You've channeled immense power several times in a row. I don't know how you're even awake.

"Heh," Haephan half-chuckled. "Me either. Great Self, I'm hungry."

You shouldn't use the Great Self's name in vain.

"What're you, a temple ward?"

Don't be daft.

"Don't be a nag."

They scowled at each other.

So...where now? asked Ven. *Are you ready?*

"Maybe?"

And...what will you do after? she asked.

"I dunno," said Haephan. "Go back to New Gordon? Maybe... somewhere, else. I'm not really sure. Maybe just go away where no one can find me."

Aurora Ven frowned.

Haephan! Eldress Rose circled the spire. *Are we off to our next destination?* A rough wave hit the spire below and sprayed them in salty mist.

"Yeah, soon," said Haephan.

How do you feel?

The sun peeked above the horizon of the new world of endless ocean he planted last night.

"I'm tired," said Haephan.

Will you be able to continue?

"I don't really have a choice."

Ven frowned.

"C'mon," said Haephan. "Let's get it done."

Nodding, Rose fluttered away to collect the flocks.

What do you mean when you say you have no choice? Ven asked.

"I don't have a choice," said Haephan. "This mantle makes me do this. And once I'm done? I'm fuckin' gone...I'm going somewhere far away and never coming back." Eyes too experienced for his age narrowed in on her. "Ever."

81

Light and Fire

An enormous sphere of pixies appeared over open ocean and exploded in all directions before Haephan fell as a silhouette for a sun much larger on this end of the continent. Taking deep, measured breaths, Haephan crossed his arms, pointed his toes, straightened his head, and speared the rolling waves. The water's intense warmth surprised him as he searched for the animal helper who always had appeared.

The fairy swarm swirled above him in heavy morning gusts.

"Hello!" Haephan cried. "Hello!?"

Haephan! Ven swooped low.

The boy looked up.

Look! she chimed and pointed opposite the immense sunrise.

Barely a mile away, a sky-high wall of heavy tropical rains bore down on them.

Haephan scanned in vain for a helper. The minutes ticked by before he grimaced. "I'm going to the bottom to get this started!"

What!? Ven cried. *No! That's incredibly dangerous! What if you drown!?*

"I'm not sure I care…" Haephan trailed off as he remembered Tilly and Querie while the approaching storm excited the waves.

What? Ven struggled to hear.

Haephan shook his head and disappeared.

No—! Good Self in heaven.

Rose drew close. *Where'd he go!?*

The bloody bottom! chimed Ven. *That infuriating child.*

What!? cried Rose.

The violent wind surged before the gray wall crashed over them.

How long do we wait before we decide he's dead!? Rose cried. *Morna and the elders will demand we leave if he doesn't surface!*

They can wait! Ven yelled, twisted with alarm and slammed into Rose, knocking her aside in time to avoid a streak of liquid fire erupting across the waters.

DRACO! Ven roared.

Collecting herself, Rose squeezed Ven's arm in thanks before she raced to gather the flocks.

Pixies screamed as a second draco crashed through a swarm and caught several in his mouth. Thousands of new stars blazed to life in the vicious rainstorm.

BATTLEFEATHERS! Rose bellowed. Pixies formed several cross-rotating defensive rings.

Ven sensed the initial pulses of magic indicating the boy's success below. Magic swirling high above the storm snaked toward the blossoming well of energy below the waves and lit the murky torrent in a blue-green light.

Dozens of dragons struck and swooped, taking a hundred pixies in moments. As the initial storm wall ebbed, Ven scanned the swarm and estimated almost seven hundred dragons—the first dragonswarm seen since the wars.

A boiling sound drew her attention to the world's watery edge where a froth billowed from the depths. When the snaking aurora speared it from above, the waves exploded with a light that forced early morning into a midday sun and winked out as fast. An island burst from the waves, only a few hundred feet wide, and stuck out over the edge of the world half as much as it remained in the ocean.

Ven raced for the edge while scanning for attacking dracos. Beneath her, a bulge of seawater crashed into and over the island, broke several sections of stone, coursed inland and fired out into the empty air where it wound like a common terrestrial river.

What the…? she muttered.

On high! screamed a nearby pixie.

Pixies split in time to avoid a billow of fire across the water followed by a thunderous snap of angry jaws and a wash of its wings that cast Ven into the froth. She struggled so stay above the water as the ocean dragged her closer to the island.

WHERE IS THE BOY! a dragon bellowed. *Where is boy with the light mantle!? Where's the boy with the seeds from Eden!?*

Fuck you! Rose screamed against the chaotic storm and unleashed powerful bolts of energy that illuminated the rain clouds. The swarm scattered until the energy dissipated and reformed with laughter.

A cursing pixie? cried a dragon. *I will have stories to tell my king when I return home with the boy's body! Now where is he?*

Stop fleeing, you cowards! Rose cried at her fellow pixies. *And fight back!*

Again, the dragons laughed.

PIXIES! Rose cried. *FIGHT!* She unleashed another pair of bolts before a hesitant few tried to fire power from their hands.

Ven scrambled ashore, knelt to gasp and discovered Haephan lying nearby coughing water and quivering in obvious pain. While he hacked, crimson splotches expanded on exposed skin.

Where is he!? the dragon roared again. *Or has he run like a coward eggling? Back to his mother? Tell him Zicthang has come to send him to his ancestors.*

Dracos and pixilarks danced around each other in a melee of violence. Darting pixies unleashed bolts of energy and space warping while heavy dragons ignited the air with liquid flame. Where pixie bolts and dragon's fire contacted, spherical eruptions exploded across the sky in a staggered and repetitive cacophony of thunder, roaring and chimal shrieking. The dragons struck at and even caught some of the pixies, crunching and swallowing them. The pixies blinded, flashed, burned and even halted dragons in mid-flight, forcing several into the waves where they failed to return.

Haephan! Ven coughed. *Are you okay?*

Haephan coughed blood across the stone.

Ven drew nearer as the mantle struggled to restructure the boy's energies and increase healing. Watching his magic work through him, she considered how she might secure her pixies' future by ensuring his survival. The rite would be such a quick, simple thing and could enable her energy to flow into his, make him more powerful and heal faster. Her touch to the boy's forehead again rippled the mantle.

The Rite of Aikina could save countless pixie lives. She could control— no, *secure* their only chance to survive. It didn't have to be slavery if she only asked him to save her people? That was one thing. And for a good cause!

Before temptation overcame her, the splotches on his pale skin shrank, his color returned and his breathing evened.

Haephan coughed and spat out remnant crimson before he pulled his legs from the icy river and moaned. "What happened?"

Ven blushed. *Are you better?*

"Yeah," Haephan coughed. "What's going on?" He turned at the explosive thunder erupting in the nearby storm. His jaw sank.

A dragon chased a pixie from the storm and banked when it spotted Haephan. *There he is! The island!*

Dozens of dragons emerged from the torrent.

Haephan snatched Ven and rolled into the river that carried them away into open air. Surfacing, he set Ven on his head while she sputtered in a rough, coughing chime.

The dragons formed a snaking line and accelerated.

Haephan couldn't leave the pixies behind and the dragons would never allow them to converge enough for him to shift them all away as they had arrived.

Haephan, Ven chimed. *Look.*

At the tone of her voice, Haephan searched the vast sky ahead. A line of inverted stars shimmered across the horizon of the pale blue sky. Ahead of the snaking river, the midnight dots swelled from nothingness and thickened into tumbling islands as large as homesteads, villages and cities before more appeared in a rolling wave that preceded the river.

Each new land rolled as it accumulated, slowed and stopped with a faint thunder.

The river's head banked for the nearest new floating island, carved a path across its top, fired again into open air and veered to the next.

By the Self... Ven muttered.

The slight flutter of leathery wings was Haephan's only warning.

"Hold on!" Haephan shifted to the new island ahead before the dragon crashed into the flying river, flailed and fell out the river's bottom before it recovered and struggled to gain altitude. More dragons banked in pursuit.

Haephan scanned for the next forming island and shifted too soon; he tripped as the rolling landmass leveled itself. Scrambling for a handhold to avoid sliding off, he waited to stand until the island came to a stop. When he did, he was shocked to find himself covered in soil.

Pixies emerging from the storm struggled to pace the dragons.

Flush formation! Zicthang cried. The dragon chain spread outward with varying altitudes.

Brushing away heavy soil, Haephan noted the newest island wasn't growing, but gathering from the air. Each black dot that appeared in the sky waited like an anchor. When one flared and began to gather material, he recognized its shimmer as a kind of magic.

Haephan! Ven chimed. *They're coming.*

"We need to get your pixies outta here."

We can't, Ven chimed. *We must face the dragons.*

"But I can shift really fast—"

That's not the point, Ven chimed. *They will merely come for us again. Again and again until there is new war and my people dead in the thousands.*

"Fine," Haephan scowled. "What do we do?"

I-I don't know, Ven admitted.

Haephan scanned the cascade of forming islands as the river danced and split to reach each one. As another rock gathered into existence, Haephan remembered the dragon getting caught in the island of ice. "The islands."

What? Ven asked as two dragons approached.

"The islands!" Haephan pointed. "If we can get the dragons into those things, they'll be trapped!"

Well alright, then, Ven gulped. *What do we do?*

"What do we do? We gotta…get them! Great Self," said Haephan. "Get off."

What?

"Fine," Haephan said and shifted before Zicthang's face, who flinched in surprise before snapping at him. The boy fluttered backward in stages to lead the monster, who accelerated in hope of the kill.

By Sen'ria Al'Cular! Ven cried. *Cease, boy! CEASE!*

Dozens of islands now hovered across the sky at a variety of altitudes, connected by the river and its tributaries. Some dwarfed Rainhold while a few outsized New Gordon.

"Go!" said Haephan. "Get them ready!" He shifted to the battlefeathers, released Ven, and reshifted to Zicthang.

"You want me!?" Haephan cried. "You want me!?" He wove back and forth while, in his peripheral vision, he searched for the sign of a new island ready to form and shifted onto Zicthang's snout. "Come and get me."

Zicthang twisted and snapped for the boy with a mad clap of his jaws. Enraged at missing, he bolted for the child, who fell limp through the air. The draco grinned, sure he must have knocked him senseless. He tucked his wings to accelerate and narrowed the gap between them.

With his jaws open, about to strike the human, Zicthang slammed into something small and unmoving. He thrashed as tons of ground buried him. Soon even his long tail disappeared as rock and soil swelled into a sizable island, all without a single horn blown in protest.

Having branched out, the dragonswarm appeared unaware of Zicthang's demise.

"This can work," Haephan said. "This can work!" He shifted to Ven, snatched her from the jaws of a diving dragon, and reshifted to safety.

He won't leave the pixies! one of the dragons cried.

Oh no, Ven spat.

Rose's distant chimal battlecry seemed small until both flocks echoed their crystalline fiercest and shattered the air.

"I can still get you out of here," panted Haephan. "I think I can shift fast enough to get you out in smaller groups!"

I told you. We cannot run.

"What? Yes we can! That's what I do!" Haephan said. "That's what I do..."

Haephan, Ven chimed. *We cannot run. They might be ripping us apart, but if we want to survive, we have to fight right now.*

Haephan clenched his jaw as Tilly flashed in his mind's eye.

We can't wait, Ven chimed. *Whatever it takes, right here. Right now.*

Her words thundered into Haephan's shame over waiting to save Tilly. For running away and never taking his best friend or his mom with him. After his breath stuttered, he gulped. "Okay. What do I do?"

Help, chimed Ven before she fired into the air to join the battle-feathers. She rang out a single warbling chime that drew close nearby pixies. *We have to use the islands to trap them.*

That's right, pixies, chimed Rose. *We fight 'em off, we go home—*

No, Ven cut her off. *This isn't the time for half measures so we might make it back. We must trap them inside. Even if that means stopping them in place, ourselves.*

Rose and the rest of the pixies gasped.

This is easily half an entire colony, if not a full one, chimed Ven. *They'll chase us down if we don't stop them here. We don't have the power, by ourselves, but if these islands can wrap them up and lock them away, we have to risk everything. We have to keep them from the boy, and that boy has to stop Cas'Doren from getting more seeds, no matter what the cost. Are we clear!?*

The pixies nodded with the sad reality of their situation.

But Cas'Doren isn't even here, chimed Rose. *We can drive them away—*

We stop them here! Ven cried. *Or they'll just follow us.*

Rose stared until she couldn't deny the truth. *She's right.*

The flocks nodded.

We know where we go if we die! chimed Rose. *But without our help, the magnas will never have a chance to ascend! We stop them, then whoever survives can go on to stop Cas'Doren. We gather the flocks; we take this fight to Eden. Whatever it takes!*

Ven clenched her fists.

How can we stop them? asked a terrified fairy.

The warping, chimed Rose. *When we attack intruders with disruptions, it ripples space to hurt. If we use it to slow a dragon instead of trying to pierce its armor, it could allow the islands to gather. Spread out the energy not to destroy, but arrest.*

But they dodge us! protested another pixie.

Spread out your warps, chimed Rose. *So broad they can't easily see it. And when they do, it's so weak that they won't even fear it, but it will slow them down. Maybe enough to trap them!*

The pixies nodded.

Spread the word, Rose commanded her feather. *Disperse to other feathers and tell them the plan. Go!*

Ven clutched her arms. *I don't want to lose my flocks.*

Don't be afraid, Ven, Rose chimed. *We pixies lead boring lives, and we're happy with it. But you're right. This is a time for action, even if it comes at great cost.*

Ven leaned in and kissed her with all the respect she could muster as she wept. *Let's fight.*

Rose cupped Ven's face and kissed her forehead. *No, my dear aurora. Stay with the boy. Whatever you do, you must survive to carry on our knowledge. It is your highest duty to carry forward who we are so others might learn and our species might survive.*

Tears welled in Ven's eyes.

See you on the far side, Rose chimed. Offering a grim smile, she bolted into the battle as the messengers spread the word and the feathers changed formation.

Ready yourselves! roared a dragon who noticed the tactical change.

In rapid succession, battlefeathers fled into the new world.

The dragons split into groups of five that converged on the pixies, who accelerated while the dracos closed the gap.

WHATEVER IT TAKES! Rose cried. The pixies attacked the dracos in concussive thunder, light and smoke. Startled, the dracos scattered. The spherical battlefeathers shattered into small teams racing in different directions and the dragon formations exploded in pursuit.

As the dracos gained, the fairies aimed for the tiny points of inverted light indicating incoming islands.

Get ready, chimed Rose as she led three other pixies. Close at their heels huffed a dragon.

Grim determination painted her companions as they drew nearer the point, even as the heat from the dragon's snout warmed their feet.

Together, Rose chimed and pulled energy into her hands. *NOW!*

The four halted as the light disappeared and unleashed broad warps against the advancing draco.

Rose launched into the dragon's open gullet, loosed her power and froze the beast in place next to the tiny dot. Tons of soil manifesting from the nether washed over him and the pixies. He thrashed in a panic as it formed faster than he could fight. The melee of soil and rock buried them all.

Obsessed in individual pursuits, and distracted by the smoke, flashes of light and thunder erupting from the fairies, the dragons were blind to the traps as pairs and quads of pixies tricked or pounded them into the choke points to be caught and buried.

At first overjoyed at the fool dragons for disregarding the swarm to their own destruction, the deaths of her pixies crescendoed until she quivered in horror. In a few minutes, pixies sacrificed themselves to trap hundreds of dragons. She found no joy at the speedy cost of their success. Fleeing a yellow snapper, Ven coughed a sob as each pixie death stabbed her heart.

"Hey!" Haephan shifted to Ven, kicked the snapper's head down and braced as the creature's body slammed into and sent them both flying. He shifted to a nearby island before rolling to a stop. He pushed onto his knees as blood drooled from his nose and facial lacerations to scan for Ven, who lay panting nearby on the ground. "Ven, you okay?"

Half conscious, Ven clutched her head and moaned at each pixilark death. *So few remain!*

Scanning the skies, Haephan plucked her with care. Barely two dozen dragons remained by the time reality dawned on them. Terror overcame and sent them fleeing. Equally fearful the dragons would escape, the remaining pixies summoned magic they did not know existed and managed to kill dragons directly, blowing holes in heads and tails until most of them rained from the sky in drizzles of flaming blood. Exhausted pixies, too, followed them into the heavy cloud cover wafting below and disappeared. Only two dragons escaped, the smaller of which raced for the horizon.

The remaining battlefeather first prepared to chase him until they realized the larger draco had locked onto Haephan and Ven. Racing, they unleashed their powers on him until he barely stayed aloft. Together, the pixilarks pummeled him until their fury decimated his body into a gory mess that flew in pieces through the air. Spent to their end, motionless fairies followed the corpse out of sight.

Clutching her mouth, Ven locked onto the remaining draco through her tears. *We have to stop him.*

Haephan climbed to unsteady feet.

We have to, chimed Ven. *So many…* She struggled to say it. *They died, Haephan. Finish it.*

Sharing a long look, Haephan nodded. He approached the edge of the island, hugged Ven to his chest and stepped off.

What're you doing!? she cried.

"Trust me!" Haephan yelled over the rising roar of the wind and pointed his toes to gain speed. Somewhere far below, Haephan made out tiny waves of a vast, dark ocean.

Ven clung to his shirt in the whipping wind as she sensed the final few pixies slam into the sea with their draco prey and slip into the depths.

"Aim for the neck…aim for the neck," Haephan muttered, pulled his feet up under his bottom and shifted.

The fleeing dragon had no time to register Haephan's appearance above his head before the boy's powerful two-heeled kick broke its neck. The crack echoed off nearby islands. Advancing by momentum, the dragon's heavy body and dense spinal plates crashed into Haephan and knocked him unconscious as both fell and tumbled miles above dark ocean.

Boy! Ven screamed as she tucked her wings and dove in pursuit. The spinning, flailing mass of dragon and boy slowed enough for her to veer in, snatch Haephan's bloody hair, and climb to his face. *Haephan! HAEPHAN!*

Desperate not to lose another companion—especially not the boy—she groped for any idea to revive the child.

The rite.

With all so lost, her friend and eldress gone, entire flocks dead and hope dwindling, control evaded her. If she could tap the child's mind through slaving his magic, she might wake him enough so they could escape.

Gripping the bridge of the boy's nose, she laid the foundational anchor of the simple rite and followed it with the capstone. The light mantle struck and burned her hand, but rippled with the change. The dark, rolling ocean appeared violent and hungry as they fell ever closer.

When Haephan's bencari shifted, the world around her slowed until wisps of moisture piquing from their fall formed over several seconds. The rushing air quieted, replaced by a rhythmic double thunder. Ven was shocked to hear the boy's heartbeat. Information flooded her mind as the rite took effect.

Perhaps over lesser or equal creatures, the Rite of Aikina was control, but to her horror, the light mantle inverted the rite. Fear climbed as she realized that as her life linked to him, his will had more authority than her own.

She had enslaved herself to the human.

WHY!? she screamed.

Haephan jumped awake. "What happened!? Ven!?"

Get us out of here!

As the ocean rushed closer, mere seconds from impact, he snatched Ven and shifted away. The dragon smashed into the waves in a mushroom cloud of spray that disappeared into the violence of howling wind.

82
Rejected

SonLara slipped into Elverbane's study, wary of his presence. War planning kept him away longer hours, but he would need sleep. Pushing open the door to admit a servant with a silver tray of food, she reignited the hearth with a flick of her hand and motioned to the table.

While the servant set it down, SonLara glanced at the box, followed the hall to Haephan's room and opened the door. To her surprise, a pixie lay asleep on the pillow next to Haephan's midnight mop of hair.

SonLara frowned—he always returned the pixies to their home Trees before returning. She bent closer for a second inspection and noted a faint magical thread linking the two—their magics were entangled. She wasn't sure what to make of it, but she would investigate later.

"Haephan?" she asked and rocked his shoulder with her hand.

Facedown, the boy took a moment to stir before he flinched from the pillow. Calming, he rubbed sleep from his eyes. "SonLara?"

"Time to wake, Haephan," she said.
"Why?" he asked.
"I have food for you back in the study. I'll speak with you there."
"Okay," he groaned and sank to his pillow next to the waking fairy.
"I'll give you a few minutes," she said. "Bring your friend."
"Huh?" he asked.
"A few minutes, Haephan."
He grunted.
Leaving his door open, she returned to the study as heat built. She dismissed the servant with a motion of her hand and hesitated over her usual seat. Instead, she sat at the head of Elverbane's worktable moments before the door opened to reveal the wizard. At the sight of SonLara, his frown faltered.
"SonLara," he said. "How're you?"
"Wizard Elverbane."
A moment of silence hung between them before he shut the door. "How're plans coming for your vacants?" He approached the table and noted her empty chair.
"I'm managing them as per the subrim's direction," she said.
"I see," he said. "SonLara—"
"Priestess, wizard," she corrected him. "Amferadon."
His jaw clenched. "What happened?"
SonLara's icy gaze turned. "Pardon, wizard?"
"What happened?" he set his hands on the table. "What changed?"
"Do you have a complaint as to our working relationship, Wizard Elverbane?"
"I thought…We were getting along."
"As soon as my mission with the vacants is complete, Wizard Elverbane, I will return to Andon. I request you keep me informed on all matters related to the mission."
"SonLara," he mustered. "I can't let it go by withou—"
When Haephan appeared from the inner hallway, Elverbane scowled. The boy approached the chair before the covered food and plopped down. The fairy chimed in protest. Staring at the plate for several long moments, he pulled away its cover, plucked a fork and dug in.

Awkward in the new silence, Elverbane glanced between the two.

When the fairy chimed, Haephan cut a piece of fruit and handed it to her.

Noting the connection, SonLara felt that the sight of them together seemed appropriate.

"How do you feel, Haephan?" she asked.

"I'm okay," said the boy. His black hair stuck out at angles as he chewed on the late afternoon meal. "Tired."

"And how're you, aurora?" SonLara asked.

The aurora raised a face so haunted that SonLara struggled not to press her hand over her stomach. The pixie said nothing and resumed eating.

"She's hungry and tired, too," Haephan answered.

"I see," said SonLara. "I have a new task for you, one that should be rather simple."

"Yeah?" Haephan asked listlessly.

"I need you to travel to Southdown. There's a man there named Adamar. He's overdue to return, and I need you to find and bring him back."

"Track him?" asked Haephan. "I don't know how to track people."

"I think you've done a finer job of finding what's needed better than anyone," SonLara said. "I have faith you'll find him."

"Whatever you say, priestess," Haephan harrumphed with mouth full of food. "And if I find him?"

"Bring him here," she said and frowned at his tone.

"And then?"

"Then you can go back to your mission," she said.

"I'm getting tired of that," sighed Haephan.

"We all have things we must do that we may not want to do," said Elverbane. "Focus on completing it and it will be over before you know it."

Haephan poked at the few remaining bites on his plate.

The boy was different to SonLara. He'd lost something. A luster of youth was gone. The fairy shared whatever weight sat upon his shoulders, and SonLara wanted to weep for it. She had no innate love for children, but she could not imagine what injured the boy in so short a time.

"Do you need time to rest before you go?" SonLara asked, afraid he'd say yes.

Haephan twisted his mouth and set down the fork. "No. I'll go after I get a bath. This is itchy."

"That will be fine," she said with stilted kindness.

Haephan stood and left.

Elverbane looked to SonLara as she stared after the boy. Frowning, he turned from the table, paused at the door and left.

SonLara wished the door would open once more, Elverbane would deny everything she heard him say and relieve her broken heart.

He did not.

83
Finding Vacants

Bathed and clean, Haephan donned his fresh uniform, plucked another object from Ian's shelf and tucked it into his belt. "Where's the seed?"

What? Ven sat on his pillow as he readied himself.

"Where is it?" Haephan searched the old, soiled uniform. "Where's the seed?"

Ven scanned the room. *I don't think it's here. I would see it.*

"Great," Haephan spat. "That was my last seed!" He lifted the belt to show what remained of his seed pocket. "Shit."

What?

"Selfdamnit! That dragon. I bet he bit it off me when I put him in that island. Damnit! I need that seed. I'm not done!"

What about the thing the priestess needs you to do today? Do you need it for that?

"No," said Haephan.

Then let's head over to…wherever she said for us to go and then we'll worry about the seed.

"Okay," he said. He doublechecked himself and held out his hand. She popped into the air and sat on his shoulder. "Why are you coming with me? Don't you have a home to go back to? I can take you there."

I'm…hara, now, she chimed.

"Flockless?" Haephan translated.

Ven nodded. *And I need to help you see this through. My flocks? They're gone.*

Haephan shared a look with her. "So is mine."

She set her hand on his cheek and took several heavy breaths before swallowing her pain. *After that, we'll see.*

"I'm glad," said Haephan as he wiped tears. "Glad we can do this together."

She took a quivering breath.

Haephan straightened. "Southdown…Adamar." He closed his eyes. "I need to find Adamar. I need to find someone who knows Adamar."

He relaxed and shifted.

Haephan opened his eyes in a small bedroom with a quilt over the single, wall-bound bed, a window to the side and rudimentary shelves. An open doorway behind him revealed a short hallway, in the center of which stood a small girl who stared with wide blue eyes framed by mussy black hair.

"Hey," he whispered and half-turned with the fairy hidden on his left shoulder. "Do you know who Adamar is?"

She blinked at him.

Somewhere along the hallway, someone bustled around a large room.

"M-mama?" the little girl said as her brow furrowed.

"Sh! Sh!" Haephan squat with his finger to his lips. Turning, the fairy came into view.

Falling still, the girl's eyes rounded.

Haephan looked from the fairy to the little awestruck girl and asked, "You want to meet my fairy?" He raised his right hand to his shoulder for Ven to step onto it. "Let her look at you. C'mon."

Frowning, Ven sat upon the palm so he could present her to the nervous little girl, who clutched her chocolate hands together and stepped closer.

"Would you like to touch her?"

What is she? Ven asked.

"She's a little girl," Haephan said.

Is she going to hurt me? asked Ven.

"No, no," Haephan said. "Stick out your hand. Let her touch you. C'mon. It won't hurt."

Are you sure? Ven asked.

Haephan winced at the chimes' volume and scanned the hall.

"Larie?" a woman's voice called. The little girl spun and clutched her mouth. When she turned around, boy and fairy were gone.

The woman stuck her head around the corner. "Larie, what are you doing?"

Larie stepped into and searched the bedroom as her mother approached and wiped her hands on her apron.

"Larie? Were you playing with mommy's music box?"

"No, momma!" said Larie. "I saw a boy and a little doll!"

The woman scanned the room. "Okay, Larie." Shaking her head, she returned to the living room where sounds of a loom began to rock.

After her mom left, Larie returned to the room.

Haephan climbed from under the bed and the pixie appeared from a nook above the door to land on his shoulder. "Do you know anyone named Adamar?"

Staring at the fairy, she nodded.

"You do? Can you tell me where he is?"

She shook her head.

"Do you know someone who does?"

She nodded again.

"Who?"

"Momma."

"Larie, who are you—" her mother reappeared to discover Haephan kneeling before her daughter.

"What are you doing in my home!?" the woman stomped along the hallway.

"Please, please," Haephan stood and raised his hands. "I'm just looking for someone!"

"How did you get in!? Get out! Now!" she faltered as a fairy rose from Haephan's shoulder with a glow and faint whisper of chimes.

"What is that?" her voice faltered. "Is that a— fairy?"

"Yes, it is," he said.

"Larie, come here," she said as fear filled her voice.

Larie obeyed before her mother snatched her and retreated.

"Please! I need your help." Haephan protested.

They're going to leave, chimed Ven.

The mother turned to leave and found Haephan now between her and the front door. The fairy floated alone at the end of the hallway.

"What are you?" fear crept into the woman's voice as she pressed against the wall.

At a loss, Haephan sat on the floor.

What are you doing? Ven asked.

"I'm not going to scare them anymore, and I can't leave without finding out where Adamar went!"

"Adamar?" the woman asked. "You're looking for Adamar?"

"Yeah," said Haephan. "Adamar the vacant."

The woman gulped. "Great Self, not again."

"What do you mean, 'not again?'" asked Haephan.

"What are you!?" she stammered.

"I'm…the Pan," Haephan said, afraid to say his name and trying to sound soothing. "I can move without moving. Believe me, I'm not here to hurt you. The fairy ain't, either. She's a friend. We just want to find out where Adamar is and we'll be gone."

"You need to get out of here!" she cried out with a hushed breath. "Any talk of vacants will get me thrown into jail. My husband was already taken and they've taken down my kids' names in a big book, said they'd be watching."

"Tell me where they are," Haephan said. "We'll leave right now. All we want is Adamar."

"What are you?" she asked. "What's a pan? Are you some kinda midget wizard?"

"Midget wizard? No. I'm…something new," said Haephan.

Ven snorted to avoid laughing, drawing a frown from Haephan.

"And you can go, places, without moving," said the woman.

"Yeah," said Haephan.

"Can you carry things?" she asked. "People?"

"Yes, I can," Haephan said.

"How far can you go?" asked the woman.

"I was in New Gordon a moment ago," said Haephan.

"New Gordon? Really?" she asked. She hefted Larie. "I'll make you a deal, Pan. You promise to bring me my husband and I'll tell you where Adamar is. But I want your word."

"I'll bring your husband," said Haephan. "That's easy. I promise."

Clutching Larie, she gulped. "His name is Heath. Heath Kiro."

"And your name?" asked Haephan.

"I'm Meara," she said. "And-and is that really a fairy?"

"Yes."

Meara stiffened. "Please tell me what to do. I don't want to anger it."

"Anger it?" asked Haephan. "Why would you anger it?"

Did she call me an 'it?' chimed Ven, able to hear Haephan, alone.

"You don't have to be afraid," said Haephan. "She's my friend. She isn't into hurting anybody. 'Cept dragons."

"Alright, alright," said Meara as she pressed her hand to her chest. "You promise?"

"I promise."

"Heath and Adamar are both being held at the quarry outside Southdown," said Meara. "Them and hundreds of other vacants all working the quarry."

"Really? The quarry?"

"The vacants have all been rounded up, from here and other districts, too," she said. "Called menaces to society."

Haephan pushed to his feet. "For what? They can't use magic like wizards and hurt people."

"No, that's the problem, you see. Guilds here can't stop 'em with magic. They can't see them or control them with magic. They're calling 'em evil because if the wizards can't control them, then it's too dangerous to let 'em live among the populace."

Haephan scowled.

Meara's voice dropped. "Could you imagine? A world where wizards could no longer control the people? It frightens the guilds. It frightens all the power wielders. Vacants keep having vacant children…a world without magic."

Haephan had never thought about what having no magic might mean. But now, according to Ven, he had more magic than even great wizards.

Not that he knew how to use it.

"Well, I promise you I'll get Heath and bring him back to you. But, if he got arrested, you're gonna wanna run."

"I know," said Meara, "but I can't run until he's safely here with me."

"I understand," said Haephan. "I promise you I'll get him back. And soon."

She watched him for a long moment. "I'll hold you to it, Pan."

He held out his hand for Ven. When the pixie passed her, Meara cringed. Ven landed on Haephan's shoulder, instead, and gripped a lock of his black hair.

"I'll be back with your husband as soon as I can," he said. "You should start packing."

"I will," she said, but did not finish speaking before he was gone.

84
Dark Thoughts

The carriage stopped in the grand arcade of the New Gordon Academy before a waiting attendant opened the door. From out the dark interior, Elverbane's haggard face appeared in the light of magic bulbs glowing around the entrance. Woken from sleep, he noted an hour after midnight by the stars.

"This way, high wizard," the magile prefect followed him out of the carriage and led him up the steps through the tall entrance of the academy into the broad gilded foyer. Guards saluted Elverbane as he passed. Grumpy from being woken, he ignored them.

"Where are we going, boy?" asked Elverbane.

The young prefect scowled. "I'm eighty-two, wiz—"

"I don't give the first fuck what you are," Elverbane cut him off. "Why did you get me up?"

"As I said earlier, high wizard. King's orders," the prefect gulped. "This way." The presence of day guards among the night watchmen raised Elverbane's attention and stirred him to wakefulness. He flexed his fingers and assessed himself, wondering if a fight awaited him around the corner. After a small maze of corridors and a lone narrow stairwell to the first basement, they walked among bureaucratic offices to a guarded briefing room.

The guards saluted before one double-rapped twice on the door, which opened and Elverbane was motioned to enter. Inside, a large in-fugue lycan struggled against a small web of ropes binding it to the floor with magical anchors. Martial mages circled the room as the beast scanned them. A third larger than a typical human while in-fugue, the creature filled the space in which it was bound with outspread paws. Its mouth was forced open and gagged with a hard rubber ball around which its slobber drooled and dribbled to soak the carpet.

The beast's snarl deepened at the arrival of the stocky newcomer.

When Elverbane stepped into the pale light falling from the hole in the ceiling, the lycan's ears fell back and growl died. It recoiled against the tight ropes. Bloody areas of the creature and its muscles quivered from what Elverbane identified as torture. A few guards chuckled at its newfound terror of the Hero of Tuthomere.

On the outside, Elverbane scanned the room for blood spatter. Obvious torture was the sign of an amateur magile practitioner. The beast was in middle-age and at its most dangerous. Several of her teeth had been yanked, and blood oozed down her face, in addition to several wounds hidden in the darkness. He took it all in within seconds.

Inside, Elverbane struggled not to flee the room. The sound of her growl, low lights and distinct odor revived countless terrible memories. He fought to keep his hands from quivering as the scent of the lycan female flooded his nostrils. "What is this?"

"We hoped for your help, wizard," said Wizard Dufrain as he stepped from the shadows.

Elverbane locked onto him. "What kind of help, Duffie?"

Dufrain scowled as he motioned to the creature. "We have questioned this beast for several hours. What little we've gotten from it, we'd like to get more."

The beast was more terrified than he thought lycans could be of a human. Cold shivers washed over him, even as his heart screamed for release from this dark chamber.

"Why is she still in fugue?" Elverbane asked.

"She?" asked Dufrain. "We caught a large one."

"Lycan females are sometimes larger than the males," said Elverbane. "The fugue?"

"Simple spell in the ropes," said Dufrain. "How do you know she's a female? Males don't bear genitalia in-fugue."

Elverbane locked eyes with her. "Bring up the lights."

Dufrain motioned to the guard standing by the door, who used the light plate to adjust the recessed bulbs to clear brightness. The creature thrashed and whined though refused to take her sensitive gaze from Elverbane.

Motioning to the nearest magical anchor, Elverbane released it. The rope flew free. Martial mages tried to wrangle it before the end whipped into Elverbane's hand. At a flush of power, the entire web's magical structure faltered and fell limp.

Violent magic filled the room as mages prepared to attack but halted at Elverbane's upraised hand.

Free of the painful ropes and their magic, the lycan reverted. Over the next minute, her body shrank, hair receded and structure smoothed to reveal a beautiful woman of long, dark brunette hair and brown eyes huddling on the carpet with blood drooling from her mouth and exposed wounds on her smooth white skin. Uncomfortable, the men shuffled at the sight of the damage they caused to such a beauty.

When Elverbane stepped closer, she clutched her head in terror.

Kneeling over her, Elverbane motioned to the nearest martial mage. "Go get me a blanket of some kind."

Hesitant, the mage looked to Dufrain.

"Boy, test me," said Elverbane.

The mage saluted and rushed from the room.

"Avert your eyes," said Elverbane.

"Seth, this—" Dufrain began.

"Avert yur FUCKIN' EYES!" Elverbane bellowed.

Reluctant, Dufrain motioned to the room. Men turned their faces.

Elverbane regarded the woman quaking in fear. "What's your name, woman?"

She did not respond.

"You know who I am," Elverbane said.

She bared her human teeth.

"If I want to end you, or anyone here, I can," he said. "Look at me."

Gulping, she raised her beautiful gaze to him through her wild brown hair.

"I've not come here to harm you," Elverbane said. "Since you know who I am, what I can do and what I have done, do you trust me when I say that?"

She nodded.

"Tell me your name," he said.

"Larath," she said.

"Where did these men find you?" asked Elverbane.

"Bridge of the smaller canal."

The reek of lycan filled the air. Elverbane's own heavy sweat soaked his robes so much he had to wipe his brow.

The mage returned with a large tablecloth and offered it to Elverbane, who covered the woman's body.

Suspicion filled her.

"What did you want from her?" Elverbane asked Dufrain.

"We want their plans, their purpose," said Dufrain. "You know how difficult it is to actually catch a lycan. We want to know as much as we can about their strategy."

Elverbane watched Larath's eyes. "You don't have the first clue, do you?"

"Death is our goal," she bared her gapped teeth. "Justice our aim."

"You build nothing," Elverbane said. "Only a mind to destroy."

"We destroy what has been denied us!" she protested.

"Your kind deserve what you get!" Dufrain loomed behind Elverbane. "You've killed countless people in your packs!"

"Be quiet," said Elverbane.

"You deserve to be collared," said Dufrain. "And treated as the beasts you ar—"

"I said SHUT IT!" Elverbane barked.

Dufrain ground his teeth.

Elverbane scanned the men around the room, knowing that with her beauty, several now saw her as prey. Whether the lycans in their bestial fugue or the humans ready to submit to baser pleasures, there was little grand difference between the two.

Elverbane leaned his elbow upon his upright knee. "My dear…The real danger isn't that you have an animal inside, but that the side of reason refuses to grow strong enough to rein it in."

She appeared dumbfounded. "You know what I am—"

"I know what you are," Elverbane said. "And I know you've always been taught your bestial side was inconquerable. It's that kind of belief, compounded by the pack, that kept Larath weak and her beast stronger."

"Are you saying lycans could master their animal side?" Dufrain asked.

"All of us has a bloody animal side, Duffie," Elverbane noted the men leering the shape of her body beneath the tablecloth. When they saw his glare, they blanched and averted their eyes. "Every one of us."

She snarled. "I'm a lycan—"

"Which makes it harder, no'impossible, woman," Elverbane cut her off. "The strength of your wolf could have fueled your work. Like all of us, you needed self-discipline. Instead, the pack demands obedience to its every whim and reinforces that your strength comes only from being a member of the pack."

"I think you don't understand us, wizard," she said.

"No, Larath," Elverbane said. "I fear it's you who have been held ignorant for the benefit of those who control your group."

"No one controls the race or the super pack!" she barked. "And thus, we are free from corruption!"

"No act performed without the clarity of truth, embraceable only by an intelligent mind and voluntary thought, can claim the morality or wisdom of its decision," said Elverbane. "While you justify the acts of your inner animal, instead of taming it, you do little more than rile up the worst in your own inner nature and then explain it away after-the-fact. So long as your inner beast reigns, then no act you perform, however good or bad, bears you a lick of moral credit or absolution."

Her jaw clenched.

"What you've done is kill countless innocents, all because you're afraid to tame yourself. If you had truly stepped into your own agency," Elverbane's hard brown eyes flashed lycan yellow, visible only to her from her low angle, before fading again to brown, "then you could have controlled what no one else in your pack could."

Her body stilled.

"I'm no'here to save you, dear," he said. "But I'll offer you a choice. Do you want your chance to fight as the beast by which you were caught, or do you want to go with dignity and honor as a human being with a mind?"

Dufrain looked between them, unable to see what Larath saw, or what made her drain of color.

The quaking of her body softened. Watching him for a long moment, she sat erect and nodded.

Elverbane touched her ear.

"What are—" Dufrain asked when a muffled flash of light and smoke bolted from Elverbane's fingers into her ear canal. Her beautiful brown eyes flashed and faded. A scorched, ashy gaze spaced out as smoke drooled upward from around him before her body fell to the side and slapped dead to the ground. "What did you do!?"

Elverbane pushed to his feet and turned to find Dufrain's finger sticking in his face. Elverbane snatched and wrenched it, forcing Dufrain to cry out and leap onto his tiptoes.

"You're truly dense," Elverbane said. "The super pack doesn't respond to logic. Never has. The bigger the group, the bigger the group*think.*" He scanned the men in the room. "Your mistake is believing that there's logic behind their animalism. The same bureaucratic bastards who run this kingdom suffer the same sin as the beasts—everyone believes their power comes from their packs and, thus, follow whoever's in charge. They claim pack decisions are group decisions so they get to pretend they had a hand in it, but the truth is, it's all mob rule at its bloody worst."

"I never knew lycans could overcome their worser natures!" Dufrain whined as he fought to stay upright.

"Everyone can make better decisions every day to overcome their inner beasts," said Elverbane. "Including you. Unfortunately, it's no shock that you're dumb enough to let one in here. They've come to destroy the city and eat everyone they can because they refuse to tame themselves. And you find and drag one in with the potential to escape and give weak points to her fellows?"

With his elbow and heels in the air, Dufrain hissed as he struggled against Elverbane's iron grip on his fingers.

Using his grip, Elverbane forced the old man to stagger backwards into the wall as mages scattered aside.

"I told you before," said Elverbane. "There's only one way to deal with the super pack, and none of you fuckers are ballsy enough to do it."

"You're a human and a citizen of New Gordon! Why don't you do— ahahAH!" Dufrain cried out and leapt onto his toes as Elverbane wrenched his finger.

"I've long disciplined meself against groupthink, Duffie," Elverbane said. "And I have a greater mission in my life than letting a fuckin' group dictate my identity or my purpose. Why am I wasting words on you?" He released Dufrain's finger.

The man slid down the wall and clutched his hand.

"And now knowing she was a female, and a lovely one at that, some'o'you bastards would have taken your turns at her, yeh? The rest o'you would have felt guilty enough to leave before the worst of it," Elverbane scanned the blue-painted room gilded in gold etchings and the mages dressed in black and red. "As long as you think like a pack, you will only draw the ire of other packs of humans much better at reveling in their worser natures than you. It's a race to the fuckin' bottom, one I'aven't participated in since before I spent my youth killing others like me."

"But you're on king's council!" Dufrain barked. "He will know of this."

Elverbane eyed the man kneeling in his shadow. "The beasts already did their work." He motioned to the woman lying dead under the tablecloth. "I know fear. Even now I don't know if I'll ever be free of it. But you don't yet truly know what that is." Leaning in so his face fell into the same shadow covering Dufrain, his eyes darkened and flashed a distinct bestial yellow.

"You're— but how?" Dufrain paled and his jaw drooped. "This *whole* time?"

"Aye," Elverbane's feral tone bottomed into gravel. "And if you do anything to color the king's impression of me, or anyone else's, I will be sure you understand it better than you thought possible. Am I clear?"

Dufrain stilled and his mouth clamped shut as he realized Setherick Elverbane was the most dangerous man in history.

"Ahm going back to bed," Elverbane said and turned to the room. "And you will wrap her in the cloth and burn her *in-shield* until every ounce of her death scent is vaporized, or the reek of it will fill the air and incite a pack frenzy before you're ready for it. Or did you not realize why a female was sent in here? Are we clear?"

Men paled at how close they came to setting off a trap.

Turning from Dufrain, Elverbane marched out of the room headed for the carriage with a growing realization that his next stop was not bed, but the king's armory.

85

Prison Camp

From the branches of a tree taller than the quarry fence, Haephan scanned a yard of stones piled by size and onward to a cliff's edge. The yard at the top teemed with vacants moving stones from one of the great wooden elevators hauling larger stones up from the quarry floor.

A road winding through a small campsite turned at the edge and descended along the quarry wall into the great pit. He scanned for guards along the walk, shifted among the piles and snuck to the quarry edge.

Below, workers hauled rocks from piles to one of the three cranes on the quarry wall to his left.

What are you going to do? Ven chimed.

"I gotta get down in there," he said. "I think it'll be best if you stay here."

Ven bit her lip and asked, *What are they doing to them?*

"Treating them as slaves."

A terrible practice, Ven chimed and blushed.

"Don't worry," said Haephan. "We have plenty more to do later. Stay here for now. I'll come back and get you before I return to New Gordon."

Okay, she chimed and took to the air.

"Just, don't get eaten or anything," he said. "Or caught!"

I'm not the one you need to worry about, she chimed. *Be careful.*

"I will," he offered a grim smile. "Be right back. Wish me luck."

Like luck is enough to keep you out of trouble, she muttered. When a smirk appeared on his face, she smiled as he disappeared.

Haephan stepped out of a nook below and joined a line of workmen trudging from a drop pile across the broad quarry ground. Hundreds of men worked walls with hammers and picks. The line passed a dozen men tied to wooden poles anchored in the ground. Once past the poles, Haephan tapped the man in front of him. "Hey, you know Adamar?"

The man glared.

"Hey, do you know Adamar?"

"Of course I know'im," said the man. "He's why we're all here!"

"Where is he?"

The man rounded on Haephan and lifted his fist. "Why the fuck you want to know!?"

"I can't exactly throw a rock at him if I can't find him," said Haephan.

The man glared at him as the line behind Haephan stacked up. "How don't you know where he is?"

"Do I look like a magician?"

"I will fuckin' rip you—"

"Oh get on, Tom!" yelled a woman behind Haephan. "Get the line moving before we get in trouble!"

"You stop asking stupid fucking questions, you little shit," the man reached out to smack Haephan, who ducked fast enough to avoid it. The man reddened and stormed off.

Haephan turned to the older woman behind him and asked, "Hey, do you know—?"

"Shush!" said the woman. "Or do you want to get beaten?"

"Listen, I'm just trying to find two guys. Do you know anyone named Heath or Adamar?"

"Don't talk to me about him," she said. "Get back to work or I'll haul you to Ruftan, myself."

"Who's Ruftan?" Haephan asked and ducked when she raised a hand. He shuffled to another line and avoided further questions about Ruftan.

Ten more questions in different lines produced the same answer before whistles announced the end of the day. Exhausted vacants finished hauling their loads to the piles before they climbed the quarry road to the campsite at the top, where they passed through a large archway into a second enclosure full of large tents.

When a commotion erupted ahead, he wiggled closer to witness people fighting along large troughs over food. Angry at the sight, he left the group and searched among the tents to find prostrate workers too tired to fight for dinner. Along the north wall of the compound, under the watch of a guard walk, he encountered small wooden cages where prisoners were kept off the ground in boxes too small for them even to sit up. He ducked behind a tent when several guards hauled a large man to one of the cages and stuffed him inside.

When they left, Haephan shifted beneath the cages and tapped the legs of prisoners. "Hey, are any of you named Adamar or Heath?"

Defeated men and women refused to respond.

"Heath?" he asked along the line until a whispered call bought him back to the man just forced into the cage. Haephan noted his injuries, receding hairline and strong nose. "Are you Heath?"

"Yeah," said the man. "Who are you?"

Haephan ducked lower as one of the constables walking the wall scanned the cages below. "I'm Haephan. Is your wife's name Meara?"

Heath snatched the bars. "You know my wife? Is she okay? Where is she?"

"She's okay," said Haephan. "She sent me to get you."

"What?"

"I'm to bring you home," said Haephan.

"I won't try escaping again," Heath said. "Not right now."

Haephan realized why he'd been beaten. "I'll get you out of here."

"No," Heath gulped. "You won't."

"Listen," Haephan touched Heath's shoulder through the bars. "I need to find Adamar. I came to get him."

"Adamar?"

"Yeah, where is he?"

"He's—" Heath said, "He's down in the pit with the others."

"One of those on the poles?"

"Yeah," Heath said.

"I'll be right back. Wait, what does he look like?"

"He's got black hair and is on the post closest to the bottom of the road."

"Okay, I'll be right back," Haephan ducked under the cages and reshifted to the poles in the quarry. He found a man fitting the description.

The man hung from both wrists bound high with his ankles tied to either side of the roughhewn log.

Haephan touched him. "Hey, are you Adamar?"

The man's blood-shot eyes cracked open and struggled to lock onto Haephan in the dim.

"Are you Adamar?"

"Leave me be," the man groaned.

"Are you Adamar?"

"Go away."

"You're Adamar, aren't you?" Haephan asked.

"What of it?" asked a man without hope.

"I've come to get you out of here," said Haephan. He tugged on the rope binding Adamar's feet and drew a groan of protest.

"What the hell are you doing?" Adamar rasped. "Leave me!"

"No," Haephan said. He shifted into and searched the camp, found a knife in a guard's tent and returned to discover Adamar struggling to breathe.

With several stabs, he severed the rope at Adamar's feet, shifted to the top of the pole and stabbed through the ropes suspending him.

Adamar fell without enough strength to stop from slapping the stony ground.

Haephan cursed and cringed at how it echoed. He shifted closer and rolled him over, whispering now. "I'm sorry, man! Are you okay?"

Adamar moaned as blood bubbled from his nose over a haggard face in the dim evening blue.

"C'mon, let's get you out of here." Haephan rolled him over, looped Adamar's arm around his neck and tried to shift.

The next slow moments hurt Haephan. Part of him slid to his destination, but every contact point to Adamar stopped cold, yanked him back and ignited nerves across his body. He buckled under the shock, dropped Adamar and collapsed to the ground while clutching his head.

Haephan groaned.

"Leave me," Adamar sputtered, ignorant of the boy's attempt to shift him.

"What the hell?" Haephan muttered as the pain subsided. Rolling to Adamar, he helped him recline against the pole. Haephan shifted to Rainhold and back to ensure nothing was wrong with his ability. Gulping, he put his hand on Adamar's chest and tried again. When it failed, Haephan cried out and clutched his hand.

"What is wrong with you?" Adamar asked, unaware of the attempt.

Cursing, Haephan wiped his tears and flapped his burning hand.

"What are you doing?"

"Look," Haephan said. When Adamar complied, Haephan disappeared and reappeared.

"What are you?" asked Adamar.

"SonLara sent me," said Haephan. "I'm here to get you out."

"I can't," Adamar said. "These are my people. I belong here with them."

"No, no one deserves to be here," said Haephan. "I won't let people be treated like this." He thought of Tilly and Querie. "Not anymore."

"And what are you going to do?"

"Get you all out of here."

"How do you do…that?"

"Shift? It's a gift, kind of," Haephan said. "But I can't do that when I'm touching you. I can't shift you out."

"It's just as well," Adamar exhaled.

"No, it's not," said Haephan. "I can still get you out of here."

"If you can get us all, I'll go with you," said Adamar. "But you're better off telling the priestess that I tried, but I couldn't leave."

"You won't have to. Not without your people."

"What are you going to do?"

Haephan scanned the top of the quarry. "Do the constables come down here?"

"I don't know," said Adamar. "No?"

"Listen, you stay here and stay quiet. I'm gonna go get your friend, Heath and I'll be back tonight."

"If you don't return and they find me here, they'll kill me," Adamar moaned.

"I'll be back. Stay quiet."

"Okay," muttered Adamar.

Haephan shifted to Heath's cage and whispered, "Are you a vacant?"

"What?" Heath jumped. "Yes. Where'd you go?"

"What if I got you and your family out to somewhere they could never find you or the other vacants?"

"What? Where is that?" Heath asked.

"A new home where vacants are perfectly safe," Haephan said.

"You speak in stupid dreams."

"I speak truth," Haephan noted the guard on the raised walk. When the guard turned away, Haephan shifted into the cage next to Heath, who jumped in terror. "You can trust me. I'll be back tonight, and you, your family, and every vacant in here is coming with me."

"What the hell are you?"

"A boy," said Haephan. "Do you want to get these people out of here or not? And your family?"

"Okay," Heath gulped. "What can I do?"

"Would the constables notice if you weren't in the cage?"

"I mean, probably," said Heath. "When the guards come down."

"You leave that to me," said Haephan. "Can you walk?"

"I think so," said Heath.

"Then you'll be my herald. I need you to tell everyone that we're coming to get them tonight."

"How're you gonna do that?"

Haephan fished his hand between the wooden bars, gripped the lock slide and ripped it out.

"How did you do that?" asked Heath.

"It doesn't matter," Haephan said. "You wait for the right opportunity to sneak out and tell everyone."

"And what are you doing to do?"

"First, I'm going to go visit one of your guards," Haephan said. "And then I'm going to get some help." He leaned in close, his voice dropping. "Be ready."

"I will," said Heath. "What now?"

"Right now," said Haephan. "I need a uniform."

86

Letter to Andon

Greetings Bishop Darenel,

Austus 23, 15,221 Wylemthea Age

This will complete my reports for the month from New Gordon. Haephan, now also known as a Pan, has returned from New Gordon's Southdown district with positive news about the status of the vacants.

Something has changed in the local politic I fear will soon explode across the continent, especially with our forthcoming plans. Vacants have moved from being a magical anomaly into a political subclass the humans consider dangerous to the maintenance of power. Their impervision to second-energy surveillance, warding, manipulation or assault has led local guilds to mark them uniquely dangerous. Should the vacants unify, no use of magic will prevent their will save only by use of third-energy weapons such as blades and projectiles. While the powers across New Gordon possess both, they rely on second-energy tactics to maintain power.

The vacants have been gathered in a camp outside of the city, numbering up to near a thousand, according to Haephan. The boy has discovered that the vacants' anti-magical nature prevents him from using his shifting ability while in physical contact with them. He can neither extract Adamar nor anyone else from the camp but a small group of caged non-vacant citizens detained for supporting or otherwise hiding vacants from the local authority.

From what Haephan has shared, I venture fear of vacancy will take on a religious fervor—as does so much else coming out of this region of Pangea—and spread. I fear for the vacants whom we cannot gather with us—they will be slaughtered if they cannot remain hidden.

Haephan's news also brings an urgency to our plans, setting them into motion earlier than scheduled. Wizard Elverbane and I will convene here and Haephan will transport us both to the camp where we will effort to free the vacants. The Estamar Canal crosses the Zulta'Mans to the Sea of Para, where we will travel south to Ansania, land in Paradorn City on Quael Bay and proceed to the Ebsa Cauv'Nau Duran, the only passageway afoot to Origin. It will take all we have to make it to Origin by the Green Moon in less than a month, but I will claim faith we will make it.

Elverbane makes preparations to support this mission in full defiance of his own king. I do not know his motivation in this matter, but I will employ his experience until this is complete.

As I wrote previously, our involvement with the Pan is vital to the continued preservation of what the Great Self has commissioned. I do not know what to expect in the coming years, but the Andonese cannot afford to ignore what will become of the Pan.

So goes the Pan, so goes Pangea, so goes the future of the third realm.

I will update as I am able. With luck, the boy will be in my custody at that time, an opportunity to study this incredible light mantle upon my return.

Until then, may the light of the Great Self shine upon you.

Priestess SonLara Alva Amferadon
Librarian First Class to the Golden Hall

87

Assembled

SonLara fastened the binding on her mirrored leather journal when someone knocked on her door. Crossing her small suite, she opened it to a surprise.

"Hello, priestess," Eva gulped.

"Mistress Harel," SonLara raised her chin. "Do come in."

"Thank you, priestess," Eva said as she entered.

"Is there something I can help you with?" SonLara asked.

"I-I've come to see Adamar. I was hoping you could connect us. Before he left, that is."

"He's gone," SonLara said. "He's in Southdown, and from there we're traveling south. You will not meet him again."

Tears welled from Eva's eyes before she sank on the foot of SonLara's bed. "No. No no no. Please, no. I have to see him. I have to see him!"

SonLara frowned at the display of emotion, infuriated that it inspired her own ire at Elverbane.

"I thought..." Eva sniffed wetly. "I thought I could go away. I thought I couldn't suffer any more than I already had. I thought...I thought Adamar had brought me nothing but suffering. I thought I'd be better off without him. I didn't think I could put up with anymore. I-I couldn't put up with anymore. Only now," she half sobbed, "I realized I can only put up— I mean, I— Adamar is and has always been my best friend. I'd rather suffer a life of hardship and pain and confusion with him by my side than an easy life without him."

SonLara wrestled her own boiling emotions. "So, you wish to join us?"

Eva nodded.

"Did you bring any supplies?"

"I have nothing," Eva blanched. "I've had nothing."

"Come," SonLara said. "We're meeting at the bluff before we leave."

"We're leaving tonight?" Eva wiped her cheeks.

SonLara took one final, cursory glance around the room, pocketed the journal from her desk and opened the door.

Haephan stood there with his hand raised to knock.

"Hey, priestess. You got— ah," he said and took the bag she offered. "See you upstairs." He disappeared.

Eva squeaked. "Did he?"

"Yes, he did," said SonLara. "Come."

Eva followed the priestess to the top floor where they stepped into a large study busy with Orzo and Elverbane as they packed items using the large table. Haephan stood as the two men argued.

"Wait—" said Orzo. "Where did you get these?" He plucked an alabaster fishhook and held it to the light. "I saw these at the king's armory walkthrough last week."

"I know," Elverbane plucked it from his hand and fished it into a pocket sewed into the interior of his pack before cinching the opening.

"How did you manage to sneak it out past the watchman?"

"Sneak it?" Elverbane continued packing items. "I told him I was taking it."

"All of these are from the university's secure storehouse."

"What's your point?"

"These are for the war effort!"

"I *am* going to war," said Elverbane as he tightened his pack straps.

"What if the administrator finds out? Or the king!"

"Ah don't fuckin' care," Elverbane muttered. "They're going with me to protect the vacants."

"Who would attack the vacants?" asked Orzo.

"Other'n half the city? Nothing about this mission has been…" Elverbane drifted off when he spotted SonLara standing in the doorway, "expected." He cleared his throat. "Priestess Amferadon."

SonLara led Eva into the room and shut the door. "This is Eva, wife of Adamar, whom we are going to collect and escort to the new land."

Elverbane proffered his thick hand. "How do you do?"

She shook his hand and offered a weak smile. Her eyes widened to saucers and she recoiled when a bolt of light flew from the hallway and landed on the boy's shoulder. "What is that?"

"Come in! Have a seat if you like," Orzo motioned to the chairs as he continued packing. He plucked a long object wrapped in blue canvas tied with leather thongs and held it up to Elverbane. "And what is this!?"

"That's a pixie!" Haephan answered Eva's question as he carried items.

"Great Self," Eva muttered.

Elverbane took the bundle from Orzo and stuffed it into his pack. "Worst-case scenario."

Orzo leaned in and said, "You can't even *think* of such a—"

"Can you imagine the devastation Degreneth would wreak with this thing?" Elverbane's voice dropped to a whisper that brought Orzo to a moment of stillness. "You heard what Dufrain did to the academy and that vacant assistant of his. He destroyed half the selfdamn wing and injured dozens in his first tests."

"Which is why—"

"I aim to keep it away from other mangled fuds!" said Elverbane. "The moment it's out of my hands, Dufrain or some other eejit will try to swing this thing at the wolves, and might destroy South Edenia in the process."

Orzo gulped.

"Safest place is with me," said Elverbane, "away from this whole bloody mess."

Orzo struggled to form a protest. "By the immortal."

"I told you," Elverbane said, "he's a bloody fairytale."

Orzo's mouth twitched, causing Elverbane to frown deeper. He raised his mouth to speak when Orzo cut him off.

"Before you go, I want to pray for you," said Orzo.

"What?" barked Elverbane. "Not that bloody—"

"What if you don't come back, you ugly bastard?" Orzo's tone cut the room.

Elverbane stilled.

"I want to pray for my friends," Orzo looked across the room. "All of them. For a safe journey. For success. For peace. Can I do that before you all go off gallivanting across the continent?"

Sheepish, the group circled up for Orzo to put one arm around Elverbane and the other on Haephan's shoulder. When all stopped shuffling, he began to pray.

Standing in the circle, SonLara glanced at the fireplace where she and Elverbane had spent so many nights talking about magic, goals and points of view. So much connected them beyond the physical, beyond what she saw so many humans fall for—mere carnality, as such that only led to lifelong bickering.

And yet, she wanted to love him. Struggling with the admission, SonLara fisted her hands. Was it weakness to want love?

"Priestess Amferadon?"

Ever stoic, SonLara discovered the room watched her, waiting. Orzo had apparently finished praying. "Yes, Wizard Elverbane?"

"Are you ready to go?" he asked with a tone that denoted he had asked before.

"Yes, I am," she said. "How shall we do this?"

Elverbane shared a long look with his oldest friend as the weight of their journey settled in on him. "First, the life of a man in need of medical care. We rescue Adamar and the rest of the vacants. Then we take the Estamar south for the Ebsa Cauv'Nau Duran with all haste before the Academy finds out what's happening."

The group shook itself from the moment.

"Grab your bags," said Elverbane. "We're gone."

88

Breaking Free

Covered in fading bruises and healing cuts, Dolphus Lurli scanned the isolation cages. He noted another crimsie in an oversized uniform making his rounds along the guard walk and wondered when he arrived. He prepared to go ask when Sergeant Trower approached.

"What you staring at, crimsie?" the sergeant snarled.

"Sergeant Trower," Dolphus gulped and came to attention. "Constable Ruftan went to check the cages awhile back, but he hasn't returned."

Trower's ever-angry gaze lingered on the boy before scanning the cages. "Ruftan!?"

The crackle of nearby torches lingered in the misty air.

"What is it?" a constable approached from behind the sergeant.

"Selfdamn Ruftan gone missing," Trower said and snatched Dolphus by the front of his uniform. "What'd you see?"

"Thought I saw a kid near 'em earlier," Dolphus gulped. "Was talking to one of the prisoners. Th-thought I recognized him."

"Who?"

Dolphus shook his head. "Some rainie who—"

"The rainie at Goram's?" Trower half-laughed. "The one who got you sent here?"

Dolphus gulped.

"Think he left Belfast to come down here?" Trower coughed and shoved him. "Idiot crimsie. Go check it."

"Yes, sergeant." Dolphus plucked a torch, descended the nearby stairs and approached the shadowed isolation cages. Prisoners recoiled as he searched.

"Which one was it?" Trower asked from above.

Dolphus reached the end and returned to the one cage with a man lying motionless inside with his back to him. "This one." He raised the torch and leaned in. "Hey! Wake up." He knocked his leather glove on the wooden bars. The man failed to move. Dolphus inspected for the cage lock—it had been mangled. "Shit."

"What?" the sergeant straightened.

Dolphus snatched open the cage door and rolled the man to reveal his face. "Ruftan? It's Ruftan!"

"It's Ruftan?"

"Yes sergeant!" Dolphus cried.

"We're missing a—? Sound it!" Trower roared. The guard at the main gate heard him yell, grabbed his horn and blew it in repeating blasts which were repeated across the lodging compound.

"Who is it?" Trower rushed down the stairs and glanced along the walk, noting curiously how empty the far side appeared in the dim torchlight but for the Crimson Guard rounding the guardwalk.

"It's…the one they brought in last night," said Dolphus. "He got carried in here a few hours ago."

"And you saw the Rainie talking with him? You sure?"

The nearby horn blasts disappeared, but more erupted across camp.

"I'm not sure, sergeant," admitted Dolphus, "but the boy up and disappeared."

"You weren't watching?" asked Trower as he snatched his uniform again.

"I was!" said Dolphus. "No way the boy could have unbarred the cage, drag out a man who couldn't walk, close it, rebar it and then drag the man away! Specially not that fuggin' rainie!"

Trower thrashed him and roared, "He's still gone!"

"What's wrong?" a captain appeared on the main beaten path along the inner wall while adjusting his armor as the Crimson Guardian walked down the stairs behind Trower.

"We're missing a prisoner, sir!" said Trower.

"Which one?"

"Dunno his name," Dolphus said, "but they just dragged him in here."

"Heath Kiro," the captain said. "Tried escaping again."

"What's the order?" asked Trower.

"Bring 'em out, line 'em up and search the tents," said the captain, who rounded on Dolphus. "Are you sure he's not in another cube?"

"I'll check immediately."

"You didn't check?" asked the half-woken captain.

Dolphus locked up.

"Check 'em! Now!" ordered the captain. "They're to be working tomorrow, not dragging ass because you failed to be thorough."

Once Dolphus verified Heath was gone, he joined the others as they lined the vacants along the wall north of the tents for accountability. Trower scanned the vacants and noticed a dearth of guards.

"So he's gone," said the captain. "And how did you miss him putting in a two-hundred-pound guard into the cube?"

"I do not know, captain," Dolphus said. "I saw a boy talkin' with the prisoner. When I looked back, the boy was gone. I never strayed far, so how that happened…I can't say."

The captain glared and cried, "Trower!"

"Yes, captain?"

"Wake Wizard Fetras. Quickly!"

"Why?" asked a young voice where Trower had stood. The man was nowhere to be seen, nor the other guards who had hemmed the vacants; a boy in an oversized guard uniform replaced him.

"It's him," Dolphus declared with a mix of fear and fury. "Haephan!"

"You think magic's afoot!?" Haephan asked. "Magic! I thought you rather liked it. Don't you love magic? You hate the people you can't control with it. Did I get that right?"

The captain approached the boy. "And who might you be?"

"I'm the Pan," Haephan smirked. "And people ain't animals."

"Where is the prisoner?" the captain snatched Haephan's hair with his gauntlet.

"Ow!" Haephan cried. He gripped the captain's wrist, flung back his foot to build momentum and slammed the captain face-first into the ground. He grabbed the captain's armor, hauled him upward and slammed again. "STOP HURTING ME!"

Nearby, the sleepy line of vacants gaped at the violent display.

Dolphus flinched when such a tiny boy yanked such a large man like a rag doll.

"Rounding up people cuz you fear them?" Haephan turned on Dolphus. "Well fear them! Fear 'em all! They ought to be feared, because they cannot be hurt by your magic anymore! They are free of your power!"

Dolphus tripped and fell in a cower.

Haephan snatched Dolphus by the front of his uniform. "And so am I." He took Dolphus by the throat. "VEN!" He cut off as Dolphus paled and buckled.

"Don't kill me," Dolphus sobbed.

Quivering with fury, Haephan loomed over the pitiful boy who could be mistaken as his own older brother. He realized Dolphus was no longer a captain. He was merely another crimsie on shit duty, thinking he was about to die.

Haephan entertained the temptation to crush his windpipe with his thumb when the flash of Tilly dying in the street drew him up short. He could try to blame Dolphus for this whole debacle, for his father's ring and uniform, the clout of Dolphus's father and Goram's reaction and...But all he saw was another boy dying, and his heart shuddered. Inhaling, he drew the terrified guardian close and whispered, "Run."

Dolphus nodded as tears flowed when he flinched under a sudden sunrise.

In the black sky above, a single star exploded in a blossom of silent light as a blinding midnight sun. An eruption rocked the main gate and flooded the compound with a concussive wave of air and smoke. Vacants screamed.

Appearing through the thick haze, Elverbane stormed into the guard's camp holding a long staff whose head glowed with a bright yellow orb. Sleeping guards scrambled from their cots, grabbed bows and arrows and rushed into camp ready for a vacant uprising. Instead, they encountered a worldender. They loosed their arrows while martial mages unleashed bolts of fire and lightning, all of which diverted within feet of the wizard's body and exploded elsewhere.

A swipe of Elverbane's staff sent nearby tents swirling in a whirlwind and exposed constables waking from a stupor. He picked them off with lightning before handling the wizard now climbing from his ornate tent.

"Where are the other guards!?" cried the wizard when so few constables responded to the ruckus.

Elverbane raised his staff and swung it at the wizard, who only now raised shield before he and a dozen guards were struck backwards into the night along with their tents. As constables fled, he picked them off.

Turning, a flash of light caught him, but he raised a half-bubble shield and blocked an attack from a second wizard. After the spread of fire bolts crashed over his shield, he replied with lightning and took the young man through the head.

Raising a passive shield, Elverbane rubbed his eyes.

SonLara appeared in the vacant camp like an angel materializing in the mists. Haephan shifted her so fast she didn't even sense his presence. She walked among the tents of the terrified, emaciated vacants, approached a group and asked, "Where is Master Kiro?"

"Here, mum," a muffled voice emerged from a nearby fallen tent. At her motion, those nearby raced to pull it aside to reveal a bloody, bruised man clutching his head.

"Master Kiro," said SonLara as others helped him stand. "Good to see you still alive into our endeavor. Please come with me."

"Who are you!?" Heath stammered.

"A friend of Adamar and of the young boy who is about to save your life. Now, we need to collect Adamar. He is currently in the quarry, is that correct?"

"Yes, m'lady," Heath ducked his head.

"Did you do as you told the boy you would do?"

"Yes, m'lady," he said. "They knew you'd be coming."

"Then send several men down to gather those on the poles."

"Yes, mum," he knuckled his brow and set off to gather men.

SonLara made her way to the gate where Elverbane stood alone under a shield.

"Wizard Elverbane?"

"Got flashed," he growled. "I'll be fine."

"By the pixie?"

"Nooo…" he said. "One of their bloody wizards."

"How long before you can walk?"

"I can walk right now," he said. "Just can't see. Where's Haephan?"

"He's nearby," she said as Haephan flickered along the guard walk and shifted away the constables. Raising her hand to her mouth, SonLara concentrated the air in an invisible bell. "Haephan."

Haephan "disappeared" the final guard, shifted in front of her and dusted off his outfit.

"Where are the constables?" she asked.

Haephan shivered as he remembered Goram's. "The Vit'."

"We need to secure a ship at the waterfront," she said. "Can—"

"I'll get it," he said. "But you're gonna have to go get Adamar."

"We're already taking care of that," she said. "It's time to get the ship from Southdown. As we planned."

"I'll get it."

"Be quick," she said. "The city will be on high alert after hearing our ruckus."

Haephan nodded, held out his hand for Hara Ven to land and together disappeared.

"Lady!" Heath's voice called from the fallen gate as vacants gathered around him. "What now?"

"Heath? Heath!" a woman ran from the tree line through the decimated camp with two children in tow, followed by a stream of other family members related to those inside, including Eva carrying several packs.

"Meara? Great Self, Meara!" Heath stumbled to and clutched his wife and children.

At SonLara's approach, a hush fell. She lifted a cupped hand before her breast. A small ball of blue fire appeared above it, illuminating her pale white face.

"When the men return from the quarry, we will take you somewhere safe. This will be your exodus to a new land far away from here."

"Exodus?" Meara asked. "Where are you taking us?"

"Where you will be safe," said SonLara as Elverbane approached from behind. "Where you can start again. Where you belong."

"Where could that be?" asked Heath. "Won't they follow us?"

"A new world," said SonLara, "where they cannot follow."

89
Chilled

Deep in darkness of his royal cavern, Cas'Doren quivered upon a new nest with cold settled deep in his bones.

Weeks ago, the first icy shiver formed in a chest that hadn't ceased to burn hot since the wars of Aman'Kur pitted elf and dragon in a fifteen-hundred-year long conflict more than forty millennia ago. A young draco, he was eager to grow and prove himself in the hellish battles.

Now he lay curled and shivering with weakness, cold and hunger.

With a barking start, Cas'Doren jumped from his half-dozed nightmare. Branded upon his mind, he dreamt himself as a tiny, broken sparrow staring upward as a seal of earth closed like an iris above him and denied him the sky.

Cas'Doren struggled to separate fear from reality. Huffing his chest-fire against the chill and the remnant terror, the image lingered on his consciousness and tickled his doubt. A few moments passed before he confirmed he was awake and not in another stage of the dream. He gathered his wits and rubbed heavy sleep from his eyes.

Midday sunlight bled through the branches of the great Tree. Visible through his vertical cave entrance, forty dragons lay about the chamber—a few of those who hadn't gone in pursuit of the boy with Zicthang. He awaited their return, eager for news the boy was dead and his horde rescued. He feared they would lose seeds in the melee, that the boy had spent too many or that he wouldn't have them all with him, but killing him would be enough. Cas'Doren could rebuild his trove and his colony. He had ages to do so.

At Cas'Doren's order, Zicthang took more than half the colony to deal with the child; overkill by any standard, but the human worm proved difficult to handle. And if he could recover no seed, at least he could prevent the boy from taking any more.

Despite waking, the chill in his bones would not ebb. The world now whispered, and the reach of his mind cozied only to itself, an unfamiliar feeling. Cas'Doren had ruled Eden for two thousand years but had ruled the Eastern Graemol Desert for thirty thousand since defeating Umphaedra Dominar.

Since succeeding Umphaedra as Pangea's draco dominar, a status of ancient and ultimate power among the continent's sentiental serpents, Cas'Doren had assumed Umphaedra's daleenal network—psychic connections to his colony powered by magic. Always, he sensed their state and location, empowering him to deploy forces where they were most needed during battle or spreading them out to maintain his power. With each enemy colony defeated, his daleenal network expanded.

When Zicthang succeeded, he would know by the sense of victory he and the others would bear as they began their journey home. Their determination was the last thing he remembered from them as they departed to hunt the human child.

Today, however, never had he suffered such quiet in his mind. Whatever chilled him must be separating him from his network. He needed another seed, another taste of the Tree of Life that had given him such wings as the physical world had never provided, such a flight into nether skies separating his kind from Charis, the city of the Great Self.

The thought of devouring another delectable seed sent shivers through him and amplified the deepening cold. Alarm welled so that he decided to stand, leave his chamber, climb the Tree and launch into the warmth of sunlit Edenic skies.

Cas'Doren collapsed and tumbled from his nest while gasping and wheezing.

Burgir! Cas'Doren called out. *Bring me Burgir!*

Chamber guards raced inward from the rift.

Lord Cas'Doren! one cried. *You're awake!*

Where is my physician? Cas'Doren clutched his pounding head.

Burgir! cried the guard. *Come now!*

Moments later, an old yellow dragon lumbered through the chamber entrance with his heavy belly swinging between short, stubby legs.

My lord, Burgir waddled in. *You are awake. We were worried.*

Awake? How long have I been slumbering?

Days, my lord.

Days? Cas'Doren exclaimed. *I've been out for days!?*

Yes, my lord, said Burgir. *I've been monitoring you. You are severely depleted of energies and need to eat to rebuild your strength.*

Why am I ill, Burgir!?

I do not know, my lord, said Burgir.

Cas'Doren rocked his head as pain flared. *Bloody hell.*

How do you feel?

Like shit, said Cas'Doren while dozens of dragons crowded his chamber entrance, all with a high sense of alarm and anxiety.

Has my illness caused such sorrow in my dragons? Cas'Doren asked.

Your illness? It has caused concern, said Burgir, *but it's the loss that affects us so.*

Loss? Of what do you speak, Burgir?

My lord, do you not know of Zicthang's defeat? We all felt it. Did you not sense it? The single greatest loss in our colony in a score of millennia! We heard Zicthang's cry, Lord Draco. Did you not hear it? We assumed that's why…

No matter how great an illness struck him, Cas'Doren would sense such a loss. Never had he lost a single dragon in his colony whom he did not hear across the expanses. Fear blossomed.

What is happening to me? muttered Cas'Doren.

My lord, you have lost power to ranges I have never before thought possible short of death, Burgir's words dropped to a whisper. *You are isolated, unconnected and diminished from us. I am surprised you live.*

How much?

My king?

How much have I lost? How long until I can recover to my full strength?

I do not know how you have lost your innate power, my king, but if we compared growth to natural levels of development, it would take millennia for you to regain what you once were. Tens, even.

Millennia!? Cas'Doren leapt to his feet, stumbled to the side and collapsed into a coughing fit. *Curse that bloody child! The Great Self! All be damned!*

Dozens more dragons crowded the chamber's entrance.

The seeds, he muttered. *I need my seeds.* His nose caught the sweet, signature drift scent common in days leading up to a new seed. Waiting for it captured his attention; he wouldn't leave even if he could. He needed more seeds to drift in the nether. That would restore his magic. To consume more magnalarks would replenish his lost energy. He needed that seed. Once ingested, he could muster and retake the continent as he had planned.

Then he could rally all Pangean colonies. He would, once again, rule the continent.

Lord Cas'Doren, Algodemere's voice was faint before the snaking draco flew through the cave entrance with a younger draco serpentia in tow. *News!*

News? Cas'Doren raised his heavy head.

You are awake! Praise the lord of serpents! Algodemere and his attendant landed next to Burgir. *My sighthunter, Uthel'rah, has seen the boy!*

My lord, Uthel'rah ducked his head. *I have seen a vision of the boy! He will plant his final seed on Origin.*

Origin? he asked. *Origin? He is going there? But the other sight-hunters said he creates new islands. Why go there?*

He will plant it, my king, said Uthel'Rah. *He goes to have it planted, at least. I cannot see the details, but that is why he goes. I see…a Tree of Life there.*

Did he plant them before? Cas'Doren demanded.

I don't know, my lord, but that's why he goes now.

Origin is so far— another Tree of Life? That is not possible. There can be only one! Cas'Doren growled, frightening the young one. *When? When will this happen!?*

A week, two. No more. Wait, Uthel'rah gathered more in his mind. *The Green Moon. By the green moon. And fire! There will be fire! From the sky!*

Cas'Doren purred. *Yes. Yess yesss yess! Yes youngling! There will be fire from the sky! Ha ha! This is finally good news! Gather! GATHER!*

He sat up despite his quivering forearms and clenched them to stillness as the remnants of his colony gathered. He fluttered his wings and maintained his regal pose despite fear he would again collapse before them.

I am sending each and every one of you to secure the future of this kingdom, Cas'Doren said. *You will all fly to the birthplace of the third realm, to Origin, itself.*

His colony gasped.

But my lord, Burgir started, *there is only one way to Origin. It is the island that does not want to be found! Must we go…by the cave? The ebsa?*

Yes it is by the ebsa! said Cas'Doren. *Our colony, our future, our lives are at stake! There is nothing you should fear more than that! No amount of history or superstition will keep us from striking the boy where he seeks to seal our fate! You will pass through the Ebsa Cauv'Nau Duran. You will fly beneath the earth to reach the island that cannot be found. You will kill that cursed child who stole my seeds and eat that bloody wizard who dared strike me, and you will do so with anger and death and the THUNDER OF OUR TERRIBLE MIGHT!*

The dragons straightened their backs as resolve built in their hearts.

It's time to grind your fears like sparrows—the image flashed through his mind as a sparrow yearning upward while jaws closed above him and extinguished the light—*and be the dragons you were meant to be. Rise, dracos of Eden. For in a fortnight, we will devour this remnant of Aman'Kur that threatens us. We will reclaim this continent. We will revive our victory and reclaim Pangea. Rise dracos! TO ORIGIN!*

90
The Maw

A little more than a week after escaping Southdown, the small caravan wound into rocky hills a few miles from the south seas. Rain fell over the terrain in a gentle but ceaseless blanket that soaked them to the bone. They trod into the narrowing limestone hills and green forests, weaving among the narrow cuts and gorges of the territory east of Paradorn City, an agricultural hub on the Gulf of Quael.

That morning, they broke camp on the eastern edge of the city and wound into hills the townsfolk avoided, save for the goat farmers who let their stock roam about to eat from its limestone nooks and perches. Hills climbed and gorges narrowed, forcing them at times to walk single file.

Anxiety drained from the vacants since their escape, but walking into haunted hills wore their nerves while the icy, torrential winds made going miserable.

At their head walked SonLara in her white dress trimmed in aqua, ever dry and pristine despite the weather, while Elverbane followed in his earth and charcoal travel robes. They spoke to plan their path, secure supplies and handle surprises, but otherwise worked in silence.

Twice a day, SonLara called Haephan and sent him with money to markets to buy food and supplies. Otherwise, boy and pixie remained among the vacants. The adults were so wrapped in their own thoughts they had little time for him.

Haephan ached for a kind word or moment of interest from the wizard. From SonLara he remembered that time she almost comforted him after Tilly's death. And yet, they denied him, time and again, for themselves.

Elverbane had the life he wished for—purpose, power, money, someone to share life with. SonLara possessed every room she entered. Why couldn't either of them find room for Haephan?

Once this was over, where would Haephan have to go? To what purpose would he venture? Was he free? Haephan's uncertainty kept him awake at night until he remembered that once he was done, he could go anywhere he wanted, anytime, forever.

After SonLara came Elverbane. Behind him, Adamar and Eva walked hand-in-hand through the narrow gorge. Despite the obvious scorn for Adamar after their initial escape, his story and the reality of their situation drew the vacants to him so that he soon served as a leader of the caravan. He admitted to kicking off the storm that evicted them from their homes, but SonLara made it clear he was merely a feather upon the pile that would inevitably have fallen.

"Do you know how much further, Wizard Elverbane?" asked Adamar.

Elverbane turned to ask SonLara when he stopped in surprise at a dead-end gorge. The priestess was gone. The three scanned the empty space. "SonLara?"

When came no response, the wizard raised his staff and approached the end, thinking of a possible hidden doorway or bandits who might have gotten the drop upon SonLara, when he noticed a hidden nook in the wall to their right, invisible until standing within feet of the end of the path, filled by a tall, narrow bush. He pulled it aside to discover a tight twist and squeezed through. Adamar pulled open the bush and motioned for the train to file in. A few minutes passed as they wiggled through the s-shaped space before he followed the last into a box gorge shorter and narrower than it was tall. He made his way through the group and stared at a great vertical maw—a hungry monster of jagged limestone waiting to devour them.

Silence reigned over them as a distant caw echoed between the high rock walls while drizzle danced in the swirling breeze and shimmered in a faint ray of sunshine.

Eyeing the vacants, SonLara motioned Adamar over.

"I can stir them with words or scare them with magic," SonLara said. "I am leading you through the ebsa, but I am not their leader. These people appear as sheep before a wolf. They will run if they are not inspired to go on their own accord."

Adamar shared a look with Eva before he faced those who had kept together since their escape.

"It's time," he said. His voice echoed up the narrow canyon. Eight hundred terrified souls faced the seventy-foot cave that narrowed into an A-frame cathedral under the flat-topped butte. "We've come this far. We can make it through."

Heath clutched Meara and their two children closer.

"We can't stop now," Adamar released Eva's hands and approached the group. "We've come so far. We've lost and gained, but we can't stop now. C'mon, let's go."

"I'm not going in there," said a tall man in the back. "In there is death."

"So is out here," said Adamar. "We just came from death! There is life on the other side."

"There is life down here!" exclaimed another from the group. "We've already escaped the reach of the guilds or the Academy. We're thousands of miles away. That's already a miracle!

"A miracle, indeed," said another man. "I worked the canals and river me entire life. Never seen wind so steady or a boat so fast to get us all the way down here as it did. But I don't see why we need go any further."

"We aren't finished," said Heath as his anxious wife clutched his hand. He raised his voice. "We aren't finished."

"We can be!" said one of the non-vacants rescued from the cubes. "I don't have to go back to New Gordon. My family and I could just stay in Paradorn."

"Listen," said Adamar. "Listen! I told you all before, none of you have to stay with us. You can go your way. You could always go your way."

The crowd murmured.

"But there is death there for people like us," said Adamar. "We told you that before!"

"I'm not people like you!" exclaimed the same man.

"Then go," Adamar stepped forward, his voice growing bolder. "No one is keeping you."

The man fidgeted, glancing sidelong around him. "Doesn't anyone want to go back?"

"I do," said one woman as she eyed the cave.

Others piped up.

"Then go and go now," said Adamar. "But we will not be joining you."

"But we could start our own community! Away from everyone else," declared one woman.

"Yes we can, and we will," agreed Adamar. "On the other side, where no one can reach us!"

"But do we need to go?" asked one of the men. "Why must we go through here? What's on the other side!?"

"Go where you will," said Adamar. "If you don't want to come, then leave! But we want you to come with us. To the opportunity on the other side."

"Why must you go?" asked the woman. "We want you to take us away from here, but not through *there*."

"Don't you get it!?" Adamar's cry silenced the murmurs. "Don't you remember our nights aboard the boat? Have you already forgotten what the priestess shared with us? Things have changed. Our kind won't merely be left alone or rounded up in the city where it's convenient. They're going to start hunting us all over the region. From here to the Zulta'Mans, we're nothing more than a disease to the wizard class. Without their control over us like they have with everybody else, we'll be nothing more than a threat."

"Maybe we should be!" retorted the large man. "I mean, I'm not a vacant, but we should start a revolution or something. No more magic!"

"No more magic?" moaned one of the other nonvacants. "I can't imagine a world without it! My grandfather's a wizard! He ain't hurt nobody!"

"And I'm just a seamstress," moaned a woman. "I use magic every day. Are you saying I'd have to use my *hands*?"

Arguments erupted among them, debates on the value of magic and magicians. When SonLara offered Adamar no help, he clenched his fists and struggled to yell over the crowd.

"LISTEN!" the sound of Eva's voice erupted from the walls. Birds took to flight as it reverberated in the high, narrow canyon.

Above her upraised fist, a small ball of fire hovered over her knuckles. She lowered and hugged the arm to her chest while the light illuminated her face. Misty ambience falling from the great opening in the canyon walls high above bathed her from behind.

"Magic is a tool," she said. "It can help. But it can hinder, too." Her approach split the throng. Once in their midst, she let the fire dissipate from her fingers. "As the daughter of High Wizard Ornith Dufrain and First Tier Witch Seni Dufrain, I am among the most powerful mages in South Edenia." Onlookers twittered at the names. "And according to the New Gordon Academy, the Council of Guder and countless other magical sects, I am superior to you all." Vacants scowled. "My magic means I am more capable than anyone else—certainly vacants with no magic—and therefore I have a moral responsibility to exercise authority over you. Because, after all, if you can't do everything I can, you must be oppressed, lesser beings in need of my wisdom and power. It sounds noble, at least to people with lots of magic.

"When your vacancy threatens my moral responsibility, I have every right to cull you for the *greater* good, right? You think they're somehow inherently evil people afraid of you. And they are, but on a conscious level, they think they're doing the right thing because the people, in general, are sheep to be shepherded, not individuals to be respected. Power, however, does not beget responsibility. Power is just a tool. Your supposed lack of magical power hasn't made my husband a lesser man by a single ounce." She adored her husband. "I wouldn't trade him for anything. His character is his greatest asset, and in him and many of you, I have seen greater power and worth than ever I encountered growing up at the Academy." She offered him a bittersweet smile. "And his mind, one capable of conjuring amazing inventions and tools to do the same work we all have been taught is impossible without magic.

"Magic sure makes things easier, but it can also hamper us when we forget the power of minds and hands."

Rain falling into the narrow box canyon shimmered in the light.

"You have the opportunity to build something new and amazing without magic, far from those who believe your death is the moral high ground," Eva said as she pointed the way they had come. "You can go back to hide somewhere in Pangea, but know that such a decision will come with a slow but certain death sentence; if not for you, then for the generations who come after you who must face what your form of vacancy brings. At best, slavery and isolation until you die, and certainly not the opportunity to enjoy the family you have or might have had."

The vacants gulped.

"Or," she said, "gather your resolve. Think of your future, and follow us to freedom. There is a dark road ahead of us. For all of us. But the darkness is no excuse to hide. There is a light at the end, brighter than that which shines above us, but only if you're willing to walk through the black. As the Immortal once said, 'Only through the darkest night can you hope to see the brightest dawn.'"

She turned to SonLara.

"I didn't trust you," she said. "I'm not sure how much I can." She returned to Adamar and took his hand. "But I trust my husband. And if he feels this is what we need to do, I'm with him, all the way."

Adamar squeezed her hand.

"Do what you want," she said to the group. "I'm going."

Adamar kissed her cheek and said to the crowd, "You can go back to the world as you knew it. But there is life ahead. Life without fear of being hunted for who we are. Dying because of other men's fear.

I've lived with fear long enough. With, or without you, we will walk through this cave. We will make it through to the other side, whatever may be there, and we will live on. Will you walk with us?"

Meara's daughter Larie moved first. She approached Haephan and took his hand. Taking the hand of Heath and her son, Meara crossed the gap to stand next to Adamar and Eva. One by one, more formed a new group.

Only a few retreated through the narrow pass behind them and disappeared. Elverbane thought of them as deserting soldiers but said nothing—no one would ever follow their group into the darkness.

Without ado, SonLara resumed walking as if the speeches had never occurred. As one, the group followed into the gaping maw of the Ebsa Cauv'Nau Duran.

91
Settling In

Three weeks wandering through narrow, winding rifts made emerging into a vast new cave a wondrous experience. Haephan peered into a blackness untouched by Ven's glow. The chamber was so large, neither ceiling nor walls were visible from its entrance, even to Haephan's powerful gaze.

Holding a staff with a glowing tip whose ambience reflected from her white dress, SonLara scanned the vast chamber and said, "A little space might be nice for a change."

"How much farther?" Haephan asked. "To the surface?"

"A day or two," SonLara said. "Almost there."

Haephan nodded.

"Great Self," Elverbane muttered as he came up behind them leading a train of vacants dotted with oil lanterns. "Let's set camp."

"Yes," SonLara said before her voice softened. "Long day."

Haephan tensed, hearing the words they refused to say to each other as he and Ven headed into the chamber.

"Haephan," Elverbane called. "Scan the chamber before we bed down."

Haephan raised his hand for Ven to land and shifted all around the chamber, which proved to be a mile long and a quarter mile wide by estimating distances from the bright yellow point of Elverbane's staff. He returned after small fires had been lit and rations were being distributed. "Fires?"

"I told them to go ahead and use some wood," Elverbane said. "We're so close and everyone's tired. A little boost will help the last few days."

"Is that why you had me get extra food today?" Haephan scowled—he was the one who went for the supplies, so burning wood meant more work for him. He plodded among the small camps and found a fire to warm up. Despite his ability to escape the terrible darkness, invisible chains of the heart bound him close. Two weeks of walking through the ebsa wore on him. SonLara denied his request to show up only at mealtimes and Elverbane scolded him for not dropping the subject, saying if he was willing to walk, the boy should be, too.

"Yes," Elverbane said. "So eat well, tonight."

Ven did her best to cheer Haephan, but she too fell silent under the constant darkness. Once he fished out his blanket, she ventured for her nightly visit to all the children—a task she took to with zeal once she knew her presence could bring them even a small joy. Though she couldn't speak to or understand any of them, she enjoyed their smiles when she visited, flew in circles and drew curtains of sparks to light for their grins and laughter.

Haephan curled up by the fire while SonLara and Elverbane avoided each other by tending to the vacants. As they neared the end of the ebsa, her tension increased; a fact he knew because he could hear her heartbeat. Elverbane awkwardly broke into conversations and muttered when the cave fell too quiet. Their pride infuriated Haephan, who knew that waiting to speak to loved ones could cost everything.

Elverbane took his place by the fire to Haephan's left and thumbed through the objects of power tucked throughout his cloak. Haephan had seen him go through each three to four times every night. When asked, Elverbane said that in a time of war one should always know your weapons as intimately as one knew himself. When asked about the blue bundle in his satchel, Elverbane said it wasn't for anything at all and instead muttered about the idiots of New Gordon.

Lulled by the crackle of the low flame, exhaustion tugged Haephan to lie down. Ven found her spot on his chest with a tiny blanket and prepared for sleep as his body sank from consciousness. Before the fire melted away to the blackness of sleep, it surprised him by reforming into a single hovering flame two-hands wide. Its bulbous body and flickering head floated above a concave stone dish atop a teardrop column.

Looking around, Haephan gasped.

92

Rejecting Fantasy

Orphen flapped his wings from his perch on Nick's forearm as beige sunlight bathed the construction site of his future home. Amerela and Iphan explored the empty columns and rafters on blank foundations.

Rolling grassland stretched in all directions in silence but for the endless polar wind.

"How long has it been, Father?" asked Amerela as she climbed upon the unfinished stair-step blocks of the outer wall of his future home.

"Weeks, here," Nick said.

"Then why do you worry? Isn't he with the wizard and priestess?" asked Amarela.

"Are the vacants at the island yet, father?" asked Iphan.

"I don't know," said Nick. "I was hoping when he was finished, he would return."

"Surely he's found some better place and some path to happiness," piped Amarela. "He already would have returned. He can shift anywhere he likes. I could never wait so long to see you, Fath—"

"Time passes differently here," Nick scowled as their ever-hopeful words grated on him. "We learned that when Sgaar began construction. It might only be hours since Haephan finished his mission, or perhaps he hasn't yet done so. I had hoped he would come visit."

"I wanna meet him!" Iphan cried while hopping from a foundation to the packed mud below.

The pit of worry in Nick's stomach burned since he last saw the boy on the day of the rimsportal construction. Haephan had woken in his arms long after sunset and moonrise. The boy clung to him for a while, then raised his walls as he prepared to return to the mantle-driven mission.

Nick encouraged Haephan to come find him when finished, and for a moment, hope touched Haephan. The boy stared at Nick a long moment and disappeared.

Weeks later, Nick couldn't get Haephan out of his mind. Sgaarsbad would soon finish construction and Nick's household would move in. Far from closer, Isheim and Heilbin avoided each other—as if whatever happened between them cooled faster than it burned. With Sgaarsbad's help, Nick communicated with Heilbin. He even sensed a faint attitude of regret on Heilbin's part, though the warrior krys would never admit wrongdoing.

Nick admitted that he hadn't done so, yet, either.

"You'll fix everything with Heilbin, father," Amerela stood before him with her hands behind her back in her perfect white dress and looped hair.

"I never said anything about him," said Nick.

"But you thought it," she said.

"Get out of my head!" Nick snapped.

Amerela froze.

Iphan turned.

"I'm sorry, father," Amerela paled further. "I-I would never try to hurt you—"

"Then be silent!" Nick demanded.

Tears welled as Amarela retreated and clutched her hands before her.

Iphan followed his sister with the same contrition.

"What're you doing?" asked Nick.

"We have angered you, father," Iphan gulped.

"I wasn't talking to—" Nick cut off. "Bloody hell. You're…too self-damn perfect."

"What's wrong, father?" Iphan asked.

"Why don't you fidget?" asked Nick. "Why don't you find a way to go do something else. You're a child. You should be bored."

"What would you like us to do?" asked Amarela.

"You should be troublesome," Nick cried. "Be a child!"

"Would you like for us to disobey, father?" Amarela lit up. "We'll disobey if you want us to—"

"You're not real," Nick muttered.

Amerela fell still.

"You're not real children!"

Iphan's round eyes locked onto Nick who, for the first time in his memory, was unmoved by these images of false progeny.

"You…you were never real," Nick breathed.

"P-please, father," Iphan's voice quivered. "Don't say that."

Nick recalled the abject torture in Haephan's chest. Shame welled over the constructs of children his wife could never bear. "Great Self, what have I done?"

"You wanted love! Love, father!" Amerela stepped closer and raised her hands to him. "We can love you—"

"YOU AREN'T REAL!" Nick bellowed.

Amerela staggered in fear. Iphan panted like Haephan when last Nick saw him.

Rage filled Nick. "Stop. Stop that!"

"I-I can't help it, father! You're scaring me—" Iphan sobbed when his voice died and his face fell slack.

Nick gulped as he willed the construct to cease thinking.

"What did you do to Iphan!?" Amerela cried.

"I don't…" muttered Nick. "I don't want you anymore."

"But father!" she cried as tears ran freely. "Without us, how will you experience the love of children!?"

"I would rather live…with a single moment of love from a real child, than an eternity of the false love of this empty fantasy. You're not real," said Nick as he loomed over her. "You never were. You were just pale reflections of what I thought I needed. Validation from the false love of an image. Self help me, never once did I truly ask what Isheim needed."

"But she didn't give you what you wanted!" Amerela screamed. "She can't have us. She can't have any children!"

"Since when did what I want begin to trump everything she could be?" Nick's heart sank. He clutched his chest and stepped back. "Self in Heaven, what have I done? I fled to fantasies of my desires instead of living in the present with my realities. With…" He shook his head. "I could have fed Isheim instead of starving her of my love. Instead, I gave it to you. And you aren't even real."

"Daddy…" Amerela panted. "DADDY!…" Her face slackened and arms sank. The children drained of life as mindless automatons before each began to disintegrate.

Nick's hands fisted, torn between reviving and destroying them with impudence. Instead, he let them drift into the breeze and disappear.

"Goodbye," his voice stuttered. "Great Self, please forgive me…"

Nick stopped, unable to ask for help in seeking Isheim's forgiveness. Under the warm sunset, he did not know what he would do next or how he would handle his loneliness. All he knew is he couldn't do it with fantasy, anymore. Opening his real eyes, he watched the Cordurons finish for the night and head for their temporary lodgings on the far side of the compound.

Setting his hand upon a nearby wooden beam, he realized the real fear that isolation could get the best of him, yet could only wonder how he might restore his relationship with his wife.

She refused to speak with him, even as she continued managing the household. He sensed pride and shame in her and knew he could not press her with anything yet. Nick prayed time would soften a heart he was responsible for hardening. He would have to carry that weight until the day came he could ask her forgiveness and seek a bridge between them. Until then, he would have to wait on her, and upon Haephan, should the child ever make it through.

"Wherever you are, boy," his voice quivered. "I hope you make it back."

93

Dreams of Pan 1

Haephan bolted upright. The hard stone of the cave was gone, replaced by plush grass under stars blazing through multicolored clouds. He turned to a broad, rippled valley bisected by a shimmering river winding towards the distant sliver of moon peeking above the horizon. Warm yellow lights of distant cottages bespeckled the terrain as thin trails of smoke faded into the midnight air.

Backed by copses of flowers, ornate bricks hemmed the tiny patch of grass and the bulb of blue flame hovering above a dish sitting atop a stand. Faint, shadowy figures stood beyond the ring. His powerful sight could not penetrate the darkness between them as a warm breeze buffered the cool of evening.

How had he gotten here?

"Who are you?" asked a boy.

Haephan spun to a ginger teenager floating a foot above the grass. "Who are you?"

"I asked you first," said the teen wearing ruffled clothing. His green eyes flickered in the firelight. "Where am I?"

"I don't know," Haephan said and double checked the boy was, indeed, floating above the ground. "I just got here."

"Where from?" asked the teen.

"How do you do that?" Haephan asked.

"What?"

"Fly?"

"I CAN FLY!" the teen laughed as he regarded his feet and bolted around the fire in celebration. He paused and gaped when Haephan shifted out of reach.

"How did you do that!?" the teen asked and slowed.

"I asked you first," Haephan said.

"Who are you?" demanded the teenager. "And where have you brought me?"

"Bring you? I didn't bring you anywhere," Haephan protested.

"Then how did you get here?"

"How did *you* get here?"

"Don't play games with me."

"I don't play games!" protested Haephan. "I have more important things to do than playing games.

"You don't know who you're talking to!" said the floating ginger.

"And you don't know who I am!" said Haephan as fisted his hands.

"I AM THE PAN!" both yelled.

The teen sank to the grass. "No, I am the Pan. There can only be one Pan."

"If that's true, then you are a liar," Haephan approached. "I am the pan."

"Actually, no," a girl's voice startled them both; the teen leapt into the air, Haephan shifted to a spot equidistant to the boy and the newcomer.

A beautiful girl stepped into the light wearing a simple leather dress that ended above her knees. Against her yellow brown skin and high cheekbones, her bone-white braid and reflective silver irises glowed in the fiery blue light. She looked familiar, but more than that, she was the most beautiful girl Haephan had ever seen.

"But I'm the Pan," said the boys before they glared at each other.

"*We* are Pan," said the girl. "We represent the centerpoint of creation."

"How can we all be Pan?" asked the teen.

"Because we all exist at very different times from each other," she said as she focused on the teen. She ambled around the circle nearer Haephan. "For the most part."

"What do you mean?" asked Haephan. "I still don't really know what all this means."

"In one way, your journey is nearly at an end," said the girl as she squeezed his arm. "What comes next will be difficult, but trust that what you accomplish will endure the ages. And while many will never know your name, you will never be forgotten."

Haephan's chest tightened.

"I must prepare you, though, for a difficult time to come, beyond this part of your journey," she whispered. Her eyes glassed over. "And in that, too, I can offer you a small hope. It is a sure hope, it will take its time in coming, and *I* hope that it will make the time of difficulty to come…" she took a breath and gulped, "worth it."

"And Peter," she said as she continued circling the lawn and drew Haephan along. "Your journey is going to change soon, but it will not be over for some time."

"What journey?" Peter asked.

"And you—?" Haephan asked. "Are you a pan, too?"

"I am," she said with a smile that broke across her face like an unfamiliar dawn.

"How can you be the Pan?" asked the teen. "How can either of you be the Pan?"

"We are the ghosts of Christmas," she drew them in close. "Haephan, here, is the boy who can move without moving. He is the ghost of Christmas past." She motioned to Peter. "And you, Peter," said as her voice caught, "are the ghost of Christmas present."

"And you're of the future?" asked Peter.

She smiled. "Yes, I am."

"Where are we?" asked Haephan.

"This is a secret place," she said. "One reserved for those like us."

"What is it?"

"I can't say," she said. "Not yet. None of us have come to stay."

"Then why are we here? And what's your name?"

"I am Wind," she said. "And I am not here to stay, either. All I can say is that we are here to meet, to close the loop. And to prepare us for what is yet to come."

"Yet to come?" asked Peter. "But you are the future. Do you not know?"

"I am not everlasting," she said. "Only Eternity and death last the ages. Death, I believe, you both know well?"

Both boys fell still.

"There is so much more," her voice grew distant, "so very much more than we now can know before the end of our realm. For my part, I will herald its finality, as both of you have heralded your own time of breaking."

"Breaking?" asked Haephan. "You mean the islands? All the seeds from the Tree?"

"You mean the AlterWorlds?" Peter asked.

"I mean the phases of maturation," said Wind. "Our entire universe, the land of physical, has a definite beginning, middle and end, and though it began many ages before Haephan was born, we three represent its inception, culmination and conclusion."

"And what happens then?" asked Haephan.

She smiled. "We go home."

They scanned the scene.

"This is our home, a night a very long time from now, and already for some of us." Pained, she scanned them in the pale blue light.

"I cannot stay here," said Peter. "I'm in the middle of battle in Graela."

"I know," Wind said. She paused as if listening to something only she could hear. "But this is a chance for us to meet. A simple moment for all of us before what is about to be the most difficult time in all our lives."

Haephan's eyes grew round as Peter's narrowed.

She clutched Peter in a fierce hug. "I don't want you to go." Her voice cracked. "I miss you so much."

At first alarmed, Peter couldn't help but hug her in kind. She whispered something to him.

Jealousy crushed Haephan—for the first time, he wanted a girl to like him.

When she stepped from Peter, she approached Haephan and embraced him as fiercely, though she stood much taller than him. "And you," she whispered, "I will come to miss you, terribly. In ways you're only beginning to now know."

Haephan hugged her back.

"I need you to remember something, Haeph," she whispered into his ear. "When the coming darkness lifts and you are free? Remember. Remember the Hollow. Can you remember that?"

He gulped a tight throat. "I promise, I won't forget."

"When things are at their bleakest, when you can't go any further, don't stop, don't stop, don't stop," she pulled away. "If you do, you can't come back to me."

When she kissed his cheek, Haephan blushed.

"I love you both," she cried with a half-smile. "And I will see you both in due time."

"But—" Haephan stammered. "What do we do now!?"

"Wake up, Peter," she said. "Your Wendy needs you."

Yanked away, Peter disappeared upward into the starry blaze.

"And you, my beloved Haeph," she said. "Wake." Her tone sharpened. "Dragons are coming!"

94

Ebsa Cauv'Nau Duran

"Wake up, boy!" Elverbane roared in his ears. "UP! UP! UP!"

Haephan flailed in his thin blanket, stumbled to his feet and staggered. "What! What?"

"Listen!" Elverbane hauled him to face the vertical entrance to the massive chamber.

Despite the pounding of his heart and the growing murmur of waking vacants, Haephan picked out the distant flap of heavy, leathery wings, and asked, "How did you hear that?"

"I didn't," Elverbane said. "SonLara sensed it. She's been setting wards our entire journey throughout the ebsa."

"What?" Haephan fought to clear his vision. "I haven't noticed."

"You don't need to, boy! Just ready yourself!"

"Ready myself? What am I supposed to do?"

"Fight!" Elverbane snatched him by the arm. "Do whatever you can. We must protect the vacants."

As the wizard stalked away, Haephan's senses woke. From her position a hundred paces from the entrance, half-sphere blossoms of light erupted outward and thinned to translucence from SonLara's outstretched hands.

Haephan's skin tingled as they passed over him. He watched them expand when the outermost popped like a bubble. SonLara, Elverbane and Haephan searched for the cause when they saw the next layer encounter a vacant and disintegrate.

"Shit. Run!" SonLara cried. "RUN NOW!"

Haephan stared, having never heard her raise her voice.

"Pick them up, Haephan!" Elverbane barked. "Carry the weak. Only you have the strength. We will hold them at bay!"

Nodding, Haephan shifted to an older woman limping behind the rest. He picked her up, balanced her weight and ran with Ven close behind. Once he had his stride, he outdistanced the rest of them, many of whom tripped over uneven terrain the further they ran from the fires. "Ven! Light our way!"

Got it! Ven flew high ahead and blazed as a torch. Her light glared so that she appeared a vertical column of steady fire leading the way.

At the far end of the chamber, Haephan set down the old woman and reshifted for another while yelling at the others. "Pick up the weak! Pick them up!"

Though several men had already done so, more turned to help.

"Where's Eva?" Adamar asked as Haephan reached the far end with a third vacant.

Haephan spun and spotted Eva standing with the wizard and priestess at the opposite end of the chamber. "She's there. You keep going! I'll bring her, myself! Don't stop!" He shifted to Eva. "Eva! You gotta go!"

"No, I can help," she said as her hands glowed bright with power.

On Eva's left, Elverbane whirled his staff and drew lines of light in the air that expanded and intensified.

"Go, girl," said Elverbane. "This is our fight. You have your own people to look after now."

"And that's what I'm doing," said Eva.

SonLara focused on the expanding half spheres of light as they blossomed outward, slowed and settled into place.

Elverbane thrust up his staff through a swirled wreath of light. With a heavy swing, he cast the construct to a point forward where it fizzled, reignited, expanded and split into a long horizon across the tall chamber entrance.

Beyond the dark entrance flicked a pale orange light interrupted by the shadows of a multitude of dragons.

Haephan shifted to the group of terrified vacants and bellowed, "Here they come. RUN!"

"But my wife!" Adamar roared.

"I'll bring her! I can shift her! She's not a vacant! Just run!"

Adamar snatched Haephan's vest. "You bring her to me, Haephan. You bring her to me!"

"I will, Adamar," said Haephan. "You get these people out of here!"

"Go!" cried Adamar.

Haephan! Ven called. *They need light!*

"What about you?" Haephan asked.

I'm with you, boy, Ven chimed. *All the way.*

Sharing a meaningful look, Haephan shifted and reappeared so fast that three lanterns seemed to appear in his hand. He handed it to Adamar. "Go, and don't look back!"

"But what about—"

"Go!" Haephan cried as Ven landed on his shoulder and both disappeared.

Adamar saw him reappear next to the wizard, but could not see the complex, growing lacework of magic designed to unleash hell. Turning, Adamar led the group away as fast as he dared.

Haephan fisted his hands as Ven gripped his hair. "Our turn." He shifted beyond the cave entrance beneath the host dragons racing for the chamber. His heart pounded as he listened to their heavy wing beats. In the darkness, hundreds of dragons huffed fire to illuminate their way through the midnight cave, which produced that distant flickering light they saw from the chamber.

Scowling, Haephan shifted above them, fell and bellowed, "I'M HERE YOU UGLY BASTARDS! COME AND GET ME!"

When dozens of dragons spewed fire, their knee-jerk reactions bathed dozens more in flame and incited fights. Several pairs of dragons were caught in the brief melee and discovered they had too little room to bank away before they crashed to the cave floor. Most broke wings or legs.

"Come on!" Haephan roared as he shifted again and fell. The swarm boiled in search of him. This time, dragons took more care and attempted to snap at him while avoiding each other. The light of their huffing created a shimmering glow throughout the chamber that revealed their numbers.

As Haephan's mantle blazed as a bright sun to their magical eyesight, many dragons forgot to huff for light and shot for him before hitting a stone wall their magic could not see before falling in a daze.

Seeing their shortcomings in the tight vertical cave, Haephan stirred them to a frenzy by shifting back and forth, letting them draw ever closer and using their desperation to force them into fighting each other.

"You want me!" Haephan rasped. "You can't have me! None of you can have me! You worthless sparrows! You earthworms! You pigeon sucking hummingbirds!"

Who is it that taunts us!? Algodemere cried. *You will die for your insolence to the gods of Pangea.*

"You again!" Haephan laughed. "Cas'Doren didn't beat you badly enough!?"

You stole from the La'Du Lira Al'Cular! It belongs to us! You will return what you have stolen! Algodemere snaked, twisted and snapped at the boy.

Haephan allowed the dragons ever nearer. "C'MON!"

I am Algodemere, King of Fedra! he roared. *You are a morsel!*

The boy shifted to Algodemere's snout and snatched his long tendrils. "And you're a FUCKING GARDEN SNAKE!" With a vicious twist, he nearly ripped off the tendril. Algodemere flinched with an ear-piercing shriek that threw Haephan into the nearest rock wall. Ven managed to avoid being thrown along with him and raced toward him as he fell. He shifted to safety and rolled into Elverbane's feet with Ven fluttering aloft. He clutched his head as blood drooled from his ears.

"Haephan!" Eva cried and approached the boy.

"HOLD yourself!" Elverbane roared. "Here they come." From his effort, an iris of glowing liquid rock two hundred feet high and ninety feet across had inched inward from its tall outer edges to seal the cave entrance. Elverbane poured magic in to close it in time.

The first dragon speared through the narrowing hole. The second crashed into the molten rock, thrashed and screamed before falling along the wall and ripping open a huge gash.

Elverbane cursed as dragons poured into the chamber above them and spread out into a descending vortex of death.

SonLara untied and tossed aside her cloak before she fished out a small alabaster object from Elverbane's collection. With a graceful twist, she swung it toward a dragon high above her.

The beast crashed into an invisible wall, fell from the air and landed head-first with a sickening crunch.

Eva drew her gathered power and fired bolts at the beasts, who scattered and twisted to draw in on her. Ven joined her in firing bolts of power.

"Damnit!" Elverbane stepped between the two women and thrust his staff upward as several dragons spat heavy fire that crashed against a rippling half bubble shield.

SonLara focused on her spells designed to sap the beasts' energy and reduce their ability to attack.

"Boy, get up," said Elverbane. "We need you!"

Eva launched attack after attack when the pain of overuse seared through her skull.

Elverbane kicked the boy. "Get up!"

Haephan struggled to think clearly as his mantle fought to heal his cracked skull.

"Boy!" Elverbane yelled.

Haephan turned.

"My pack! The blue bundle! Take it! Use it!" Elverbane used his free hand to send lightning at nearby dragons.

Haephan shifted to and dug through the pack while his balance swam.

EVA! Ven screamed as dragons rushed in from the side.

Eva lowered her hands from her head and screamed while unleashing waves of power at an incoming dragon and rammed it to the ground. She advanced out of Elverbane's shield to decimate the beast, who screamed as its scales disintegrated under her fury.

The swarm dove in on her. In a panic, Eva stuck out her fist at a draco swooping in low. Exploding rock struck it in the jaw but the momentum carried the dazed animal onward. It crashed over Eva, knocked Elverbane and SonLara across the ground and extinguished their lights. Eva screamed as her ankle broke.

Haephan spun as another small dragon swooped in for the kill. He shifted to it, shifted it into the depths of the ocean, and returned alone. He collapsed at the violent pressure change, grateful it lasted a half second, and marveled at having moved an entire dragon. He realized he could not easily do that again.

Haephan! Ven chimed and swooped in. *Are you okay?*

The first beast's left wing erupted in fire before Elverbane rose through it. He knocked another low-swooping beast from the air into the unforgiving rock before reforming the shield with his staff in time for a lake of fire to wash over it from several dragons banking nearby.

SonLara climbed out from under the wing and raced beyond Elverbane's shield towards the boundary of one of her invisible wards.

"Watch it!" Haephan yelled.

She ducked in time to avoid a diving dragon and again from a second.

"SonLara!" Elverbane sprinted for her and used a spacial shifting technique to knock a third dragon aside in an explosion of scales.

"Wizard!" Haephan cried as two dragons dove for Elverbane. The boy shifted to the snout of one of them and kicked its left eye while Ven unleashed powerful bolts that pierced the dragon's snout into its head. The beasts twisted, crashed into each other, slammed to the floor and slid toward Elverbane.

Haephan shifted, snatched the wizard and dropped him off out of reach. The dragons came to a stop before they could reach SonLara, who faced another dragon diving in on her. Once avoided, she returned her attention to a new spell on the edge of the bubble ward she created at the onset of the fight. A green fire exploded outward in a ring from which electric arcs erupted and struck at all nearby creatures. Roil lighting mushroomed upward with a brilliant web that exposed how many dragons surrounded them—easily more than five hundred.

Elverbane struck another dragon and barely avoided a second.

Haephan, we have to get Eva out of here! Ven chimed.

Nodding, Haephan shifted under the dead dragon lying over the main camp, grabbed Eva and shifted her to their destination.

They fell two feet onto hard-packed ground. Around him lay a dead, barren island awash in sporadic waves of snow.

"What the hell?" he muttered. Why had he shifted here instead of to Adamar?

"I can help!" Eva screamed while clutching her broken ankle. "Take me back!"

"Where are we?" asked the boy.

"Don't leave them!" pleaded Eva.

Haephan took a final scan across the familiar landscape and returned to the cave. More dragon bodies littered the floor while the blood-spattered mages fought back-to-back.

Give me the seed, said Algodemere as he dove in for the wizard. *Give me the seed and I'll only kill the boy!*

Knowing neither Elverbane nor SonLara could understand Algodemere, Haephan shifted in time to move them out of Algodemere's way. "I can get you two out of here."

"Not till they're out!" Elverbane cried.

Deep into the darkness, vacants chased the flicker of Adamar's lantern toward the end of the vast chamber.

YOU! You will die quickly! Algodemere snaked for the mages and unleashed a billow of fire. Elverbane knocked the fire aside while Haephan had to shift him again to safety.

"The bundle!" Elverbane cried. "Get the bundle!"

Haephan reshifted to the burning camp, snatched the blue bundle, and ripped open its bottom to reveal a bronze handle with a thistled guard. Yanking it out, he held the sword in the flickering firelight. When his fist compressed its handle, the flared blade burst into blinding flame as Ven returned to hover next to him.

Elverbane and SonLara gaped.

"The…*Dogwood Sword*!?" stuttered SonLara as her face melted.

"That should be in Kukhel! How did you—"

"Use it!" Elverbane roared over her question.

Baring his teeth, Haephan shifted into the fray and cut into tendrils, eyes and wings. He was a stuttering blink that moved all around the dragons and drew their attention to him instead of Elverbane or SonLara. The sword cut through thick scales and spikes with little effort, but they moved too fast for him to get a deep swing.

At the far end of the chamber, Adamar and the group looked back from the high narrow rift leading to safety and scanned the battle one last time. At this distance, the fiery sword swung back and forth in blips and wild swings against a flying swarm of serpents. In his heart he knew he would never return to the land of his forefathers. Turning, he herded the group past the corner and into the unknown with lanterns they feared would not last.

Algodemere blew his horn to direct the swarm into groups for coordinated attacks.

Haephan reshifted to the wizard. "I can't get them up there!"

"Then bring them down here!" Elverbane said with SonLara at his back. They conjoined their shields and traps to cast bolts of fire and lightning, sap oxygen from the dragons and weaken their nerve systems. While singles and pairs fell from the sky, it did little to reduce their numbers.

"Got it," said Haephan as he shifted upward and lopped off one of Algodemere's tendrils. The beast screamed as the boy fell.

The dragons raced for him while huffing fire. Before two could snatch him at ground level, he shifted in reverse and flew back up the same path he had fallen, forcing many to bank above the mages and their dangerous magic. Two dragons chasing Haephan crashed into and twisted around each other. He shifted to their heads and spun the blade, drove it through a neck and sliced half of it as blood erupted from the injury. He twisted and drove the blade through the other as it recovered. It shrieked and leapt for him. He released the blade, shifted away and returned to yank it out, severing a quarter of the neck with a deep gash from which blood poured.

Chasing after him, Ven used his taunts to strike enraged dragons at their weak spots, burning holes in wings and sending them tumbling.

Haephan returned to the adults to find a host of dragons writhing in mind-numbing pain around the priestess.

"It's not working, Seth!" SonLara cried as dragons formed in packs and shifted tactics. "We need to leave!"

"I love you!" he blurted.

"What?" SonLara sputtered.

Elverbane panicked as a dragon bore down on them, shouldered SonLara aside and used his staff's power to slam the beast's head into the rock.

Behind him, Algodemere used the distraction to swoop in on Son-Lara, who tripped across the rock and barely avoided the bite, but the draco serpentia's long body raked them both across the ground.

As another dragon followed Algodemere to finish off SonLara, Haephan shifted to the ceiling above her and kicked off to gain fast momentum. Before the dragon's gaping jaws reached her, Haephan shifted his targeted momentum directly into the gullet of the beast with this sword sticking upwards from his narrow frame. He cut the beast down the center anterior and was caught in its weight as it rolled over SonLara.

"SonLara!" Elverbane cried as he struggled from the ground and struck another dragon racing in on him.

Haephan reappeared covered in blood and dragon's saliva that scorched his skin. He hissed as he used his fingers to shuck steaming fluid from his body.

Elverbane planted his feet over SonLara, spun and drove his staff into the ground. The yellow tip became a pulsing red coal from which a warping crimson shield expanded around the three of them. He crouched over the blue-haired woman lying limp in his arms as she gasped in shock.

"No," Elverbane coughed. "No. Please no."

Haephan ripped off his exterior clothes and used the rags to wipe free what he could as Ven circled him with worry.

"Get her out of here," Elverbane begged him as he clutched Son-Lara to his chest. "Whatever you do, get her out of here."

Standing in a ripped pair of shorts while smoke wafted upward from his skin, Haephan loomed with terrible fury. "Why should I?"

Elverbane's shield crashed as a dragon attempted to pierce it.

"What?" Elverbane asked.

"Why?" Haephan huffed. "Tell me why. Why should I help you when you treat me like a servant? All you have for me are missions. All the Self has for me is more missions. I'm tired of being bossed around like I don't mean anything!"

"Please, boy. I know I haven't done right by many things in my life. I never wanted a litter. I never wanted any of this. But I have nothing, nothing without her! I'm sorry if you wanted more of us, but please, save her. If not for me, then for her!"

"I—!" the boy roared as tears snaked down his cheeks. "I just…" His voice faltered. "Why doesn't anyone wanna save *me*?"

Ven landed on his shoulder and touched his neck with sympathy.

Drenched with sweat from the adrenaline and heat, Elverbane closed his eyes as waves of fire roiled over the weakening shield. Dragons encircled them to attack with tooth and flame. Clutching her to his chin, Elverbane shook his head. "I'm sorry."

Quivering, Haephan bellowed, broken by a sob. He stormed forward and pulled SonLara from his arms. "I'll be back for you."

As the boy gathered her, Elverbane grabbed his arm. "Don't! If we don't stop them here, we won't stop them. You take her somewhere safe. You take her out and don't come back!"

"I'm coming back!" the boy yelled, now angrier for being told what to do again.

"GO!" Elverbane roared.

"No!" Haephan hefted SonLara in one arm while he plucked his sword.

Elverbane rose, planted his foot in SonLara's hip and thrust both of them through the shield. As he expected, Haephan's instincts kicked in; the two of them disappeared.

Elverbane mustered as dragon strikes warped the shrinking shield. He coughed his only sob before grabbing the staff. The pulsing red orb exploded outward and repelled the beasts. He raised the staff once more and reignited the yellow light he first used.

The ripped stone wall that had once drooled down the entrance to the chamber flared back to life and began to seal itself again. He poured power into it while the dragons recovered. In seconds, the jagged hole closed.

Once done, by however thin a layer, he spun and pointed the staff at the far end of the chamber through which the vacants had disappeared. He poured energy from every blue object strapped to his person and every ounce of personal reserve. Energy loss climbed to dangerous levels whose momentum would break all natural failsafes and drained his own life force to fuel the spell.

With a blossom of light at the far end, the wall edges melted, tinged in a fiery blue outline as the different magics collided in spells they weren't designed to accomplish. A glowing tornado of molten stone filled the vertical gap.

Algodemere's nightmarish eyes and gaping jaws emerged from the darkness into the light of Elverbane's staff. *Do you think to prevent us from getting to the child? There is nowhere we can't fly and no place our hunter seekers cannot find.*

Panting with sweat, Elverbane tightened the grip on his staff. "My name is Setherick Tumarel Elverbane, you fucking worm, and you will go *nowhere at all.*"

Algodemere's eyes locked onto the far closing portal. The swirling vortex licked at the edges of the rift and sucked the melting stone inward as a vertical iris. The dragon's head turned. *He's closing us in here! To the exit! To the exit!*

The dragons aground raced into the air. Those who braved crashing into it first found the new stone wall too strong to pierce. Others raced for the vortex at the far end.

Desperate, Elverbane released all safeties in his magic. His own life force yanked from his heart, through the staff, across the expanse and into the spell. With the final, potent element of his beating heart poured into the construct, the glowing iris cinched closed in seconds before the vortex swirled into the new wall, drawing in tons more liquid rock.

The lead dragon plowed into it and found itself tangled in its cooling molten surface. The beast screamed before being swallowed.

With a pulse of blue light on both ends of the chamber, all dragons who braved diving into the wall were thrown back before touching its liquid-marred structure, barring their passage. Coming about, the swarm raced for the wizard.

Wavering, Elverbane's blank sweaty face sagged and his fingers released his staff. Now a mere shell without a soul, the body took a step forward before collapsing to the stone floor and disintegrating as glowing ash and smoke that faded away in a gentle pulse of blue light.

Twisting away from the door just as the light flashed from the floor, Algodemere landed with a thundering crash. *Where did you go!?* He clawed at the air, as if he could re-tear the hole in space he believed allowed Elverbane to shift away like the boy. *COME BACK HERE!!*

95
Rushing About

When they appeared on the island, SonLara fell on Haephan's skull and rolled off. Haephan flailed and clutched his head as her weight caused more blood to flow from his ears while Ven fluttered above the boy.

"Haephan! Priestess! What happened!?" Eva exclaimed.

Blood-spattered, SonLara scanned a barren island under an overcast sky before she crumbled to the ground and clutched own head against the blossoming pain of spell overuse.

An urge overwhelmed Haephan—the same as every island before him. A vision of life erupted across the landscape with countless types of flora and fauna under warm golden sunlight. A new La'Du Lira Al'Cular bloomed on a jut of the northwest mountain. Hunger to return the seed burned every fiber of his flesh.

"Priestess?" Eva asked. "Where's Adamar? What happened!?"

Haephan! Ven cried, aware of the severity of his injuries.

"I gotta," Haephan rolled onto his hands and knees as blood drained down the side of his face. "I gotta go."

"What? Where are we! What's wrong with the priestess!?" Eva asked as she noticed the blood. "What happened!? Are you alright?"

The world flickered as Haephan fought between escaping the melee and obeying the overwhelming urge to plant. In surrender, he pointed at SonLara and said, "Wake her! Whatever you do, wake her!"

Wait! Ven cried and missed the boy by a blink.

Haephan appeared in Elverbane's study, collapsed against the table, dropped his sword and knocked aside chairs. He staggered across the room for the seed box and found it fallen and empty. He searched in vain for a seed before tripping and collapsing to a bookshelf and fell as several books rained.

"Where is it?" Haephan moaned, clutched his pounding skull and wavered. "I can't do it. I can't do it." His desire to fight ebbed. He could die and be all the happier for it.

Then he remembered the beautiful girl from the lawn, Wind. His breath caught as he realized he had seen her before—months ago in the park, when he lost his father's ring. She had been there watching him.

When things are at their bleakest, when you can't go any further, she had said. *Don't stop, don't stop. If you do, you can't come back to me.*

Haephan didn't know much about girls or adults. He didn't get a lot. But there was something in that girl's eyes, something he'd felt only once before. Like Nick, she looked at him like no one ever had—with real love.

He wanted to finish.

Haephan knew he wouldn't find what he needed here. He couldn't. There was only one place he could find it, and there, he knew, was the hardest fight. He sank to his knee, grabbed the sword he'd dropped and shifted.

96
The Final Seed

The La'Du Lira Al'Cular bloomed. Flowers opened to brilliant sunlight raining from a cloudless Edenic sky. The world round about the Tree of Life slowed in abeyance to the coming birth of a new seed, which happened in a single instant from some unknown point in the Tree's great canopy. Creatures of all kinds ceased their constant battle for mating and mauling to lay in peace. Predators and prey shared shade as the air swooned with spices, flavors and feelings. Even the sunlight softened and filled the valley and cavern with a warm ambience.

Eden breathed life anew every century or so as it had since time's distant and unknown beginning—all for and by the Tree.

Cas'Doren lay upon his empty nest and gazed through the vertical rift alive with light and sound in wait for that special moment when the air stilled and the Tree would produce its golden podseed. He had done little more than lay there in anticipation of its arrival, of news that his colony had captured or killed the boy, and that they had recovered at least a few of his original treasure horde. He struggled to tamp the fear they had failed. Once he returned to full strength, he would lead his colony—and Algodemere's—into this New Gordon and decimate the wizard populations there.

Humans would again learn to dread Pangea's apex predator as they had done for most of history. All he needed was a seed or two to feel normal and lead his dragons to a much-needed victory. He saw defeat in them before he sent them off in pursuit of the boy. They questioned his ability to lead, which is why he didn't hesitate to send them away. Fear anew tickled that their return might draw challenges to his power, as he once had done to Umphaedra Dominar.

The old monster was a battle, indeed, that nearly killed Cas'Doren, but he won by ripping out the codger's throat before a thousand witnesses.

Cas'Doren salivated at the chance of wolfing a seed and disappearing once more into the nether to consume the bovinesque creatures who wandered there. Helpless yet omnipotent, their rapturous energy filled his dreams and obsessions. Even now he could taste one upon his tongue.

A tiny voice screamed from the deep recess of his mind that he ought to ignore the seeds and recover his strength as he had prior to Umphaedra; to build himself with war and battle, with conquest and flagrancy. Doing thus had proved him the greatest draco of an age—perhaps an eon—and he would best be served by returning to his predator ways—

No. His mind and body cried out for the seed.

Having made his decision, the tiny voice fell silent. Free of its buzzing, a question revived that had plagued him since he cast away Eden's ancient peoples and settled in the great chamber.

Why was the La'Du Lira Al'Cular sunken into the earth instead of standing upon the surface? Had the ground, itself, risen to protect it? Had some past calamity allowed the Tree to sink, an arbor whose deepest roots stretched thousands of miles across both the continent and into Uttogea, beneath?

Though a proud and long-lived race for millions of years, dracos were no more primordial than the high elves or the diamondic dwarves.

Cas'Doren had once met a true Primordial whose mere presence bespoke traces of the La'Du Lira Al'Cular's own energyfabrik. Like all creatures from time's beginning, she breathed magic, not air, and feared him no more than the tiniest mouse who might grace her nest. Neither dragon nor other great beast, she existed in tune with and remained as immovable as Pangea's deepest foundations.

He wondered if she yet remained in this realm, or if she might have followed her countless brethren who had ascended beyond to coexist with the Self.

Cas'Doren clapped his jaws. It mattered not. Such beings hid to sleep away the silence of their age while he would prepare a second draco renaissance.

Despite the exciting idea, focusing his anger and ambition were always difficult when the Tree prepared to seed.

In a single moment, the dusty air stopped moving. Gentle cooing notes echoed from the walls of the fore chamber and reverberated into his inner cave. The breeze sharpened with the faint aroma of cinnamon.

The Tree had seeded.

The Dragon King of Eden lifted his head as reality itself slowed like water. Blossoms upon the Tree changed color from dogwood white to crimson red and blue. Gathering his strength, Cas'Doren rose upon quivering paws, stalked to the entrance and out into the ethereal light.

Crossing the sandy floor to roots thicker even than himself, he drove long talons into the soft treeflesh and dragged his heavy body upward in search of his prize. His nostrils groped for a trail to follow or sign of disturbed boughs. Tucking his wings, he snaked up the swirling trunk amidst monstrous branches, aware his magical senses had dulled his ability to narrow in on his goal. He struggled even to sense the Tree beneath him. Had he grown so numb to magic that even the Tree appeared little more alive than rock?

Rising fear disappeared under blossoming desperation to reach his salvation—his escape from his lethargy and pointless existence.

Cas'Doren hesitated. No. That was not why he ate the seeds. That couldn't be. He was Cas'Doren, draco dominar of Pangea. He needed escape from nothing. He ate the seed because he was the lord of serpents and could do as he pleased.

Unable to find it on thicker boughs, he expanded his search onto thinner out-branches that sagged under his weight. The seed appeared neither to his bluesight nor his eyesight.

Damn, he coughed as he scraped at the bark beneath him. *Where is it! Where!?*

No other dragons were available to command; all had gone in pursuit of the boy, who would surely be dead. The human could not destroy them all. They would devour the little worm and—

The boy appeared low and to his right.

Cas'Doren struggled under the undeniable certainty that his entire colony had failed. The boy stood before him, alive and in search of yet more seeds. Rising fury and fear obscured his ability to think.

The human child leaned toward Cas'Doren's cave and disappeared. He reappeared in the nest. The child sought even more seeds! Had he used them all? They were gone? And he wanted more!?

Rage welled anew as Cas'Doren hugged the branch and ducked his head to match its sinuous profile. Surely the child could not know the Tree would produce seed today.

The boy searched the nest. Did he see Cas'Doren? When the child blinked away, the dragon searched the canopy and found him high in the boughs.

Recalling his days as a young draco in hunt of larger prey, Cas'Doren stalked up the opposite side of the trunk with an eye for the boy's movements.

The boy moved as if narrowing in on something.

Cas'Doren climbed to his natural place of attack—the high ground—and snaked out on a branch. He sensed the seed nearby and searched for it while approaching the boy from behind.

The child held his arms out to each side—a sword in one hand—as he balanced out on narrower branches. He extended the sword out to one side and leaned opposite with an outstretched hand.

Finally, Cas'Doren spotted the seed dangling from a nearby branch and in desperation, leapt onto the limb behind the human.

The boy's fingers brushed the seed when he noticed movement

behind him. The limb fell out from under his feet, whipped up and slapped him through the air—boy one way and sword another.

Cas'Doren raced for the seed when the same limb sank and broke under his weight, forcing him to scramble to safety. He spun and whipped the seed with his tail, knocked it from its root, through the air and along the concave chamber wall. Cas'Doren leapt into the air, snapped out his wings and banked trying to catch it in his teeth.

The boy blinked into his path to snatch the seed. With Cas'Doren so close, he glanced it aside before disappearing. As it landed and rolled across the sandy ground, Cas'Doren banked and dove. Haephan again reappeared and disappeared; he was clumsy where before he was nimble and audacious.

Distracted by the boy's appearance, Cas'Doren bottomed out atop of the seed. Despite his dulled senses, he relished how it pushed against his scaly underbelly. He backed until he centered over it when the boy appeared several paces away scanning the ground around the dragon.

Each panted with exhaustion.

Why have you come, boy? asked Cas'Doren. *To strip me of my final joy?*

"I need it," said the boy. "I need the seed."

Why? You've been planting islands. Connecting us to new worlds? For what reason!? Who are you? How do you fold space?

"I'm...," the boy pressed his hand to his eye, "Haephan. Fold space? You mean shifting? I don't even know."

Then why have you stolen my seeds? Why!?

"Because..." Haephan shrugged. "I'm the Pan."

Is that what you are? Cas'Doren asked. *What is that, human? Tell me.*

"I don't know!" Haephan laughed with exhaustion. "I don't know. I'm serious."

Leave! said Cas'Doren. *I am Cas'Doren, Dragon King of Eden! These seeds are mine. Mine! You hear me?*

"I can't," the boy wiped away tears. "Ugh, shit. I'm tired."

Leave! Cas'Doren roared.

"I've come for one final seed, dragon," the boy's pained mirth faded. "I don't need any more. I just need that one."

You can't have it, said Cas'Doren.

"I will have it!" Haephan retorted. "You think I've come this far, faced everything you've thrown at me to turn back now, you slithering serpent? I've lost everything! I will have that seed!"

When Haephan stepped forward, Cas'Doren reared and snarled.

Haephan's brow drooped. "I will have it."

You will have nothing but my flame! Cas'Doren spewed fire.

Haephan shifted out of reach, scanned through the shimmering heat rising from the dragonsfire and shifted to a new vantage point. "How do you know you're on the seed?" He then shifted all around the dragon while yelling questions. "How do you know?" "Are you sure it's not a rock!?" "I think the seed's in the rocks nearby!" He stopped between beast and Tree, paced and raised his hands. "How do you know, Cas'Doren? Oh mighty dragon king?"

Cas'Doren coughed fire in several directions. *Oh, to taunt me, little human. To think you could goad me into moving for you to grab the seed.*

Haephan searched his hands, disappeared and reappeared upslope where the concave earthen wall crumbled into rocky scree to search the floor. The sword stuck up from rocks near the dragon's spiky tail, which snaked over and curled around it.

"Fine," Haephan said and disappeared.

From atop the seed, Cas'Doren waited for an attack. When his tail cinched around the sword, he yelped when the blade sank through his scales. He flinched from it. What human-made blade could cut a dragon? It had to be high elven or dwarvan to be so sharp.

The child had to be waiting nearby. Each hoped for the other to misstep and expose themselves to attack. A strange sense of life tickled Cas'Doren under the slow yet vital battle—a sense long forgotten under his fattened rule of Eden.

An instant shadow above him was his sole warning before a heavy boulder slammed into his head. Dazed, he barely spotted the second before it drove his head again into the sandy floor. Cas'Doren barked in shock before another landed on his neck. Instinctively, his tail constricted around the sword and flinched again from another cut.

Haephan appeared over the sword and yanked at it.

You filthy ape! Cas'Doren roared and attacked.

Haephan shifted away before he could free the weapon, but Cas'Doren's lips caught the guard, yanked it free when he retreated and sent it spinning across nearby rocky ground.

Cas'Doren backed again over the seed to ensure its safety under his belly.

Haephan appeared over the sword's new location, plucked and whipped it about.

Know how to use that, human? Cas'Doren huffed flame in his mouth.

"I know how to kill you."

Then do it and be done with it, you worthless little mouse!

"I'm not worthless!" Haephan roared.

Then kill me!

"Shut up!" Haephan shifted forward with a wild swing at the dragon's head.

Cas'Doren dodged the unfocused attack and rammed his snout into the boy, who flew backward.

The child shifted before slamming into the ground and reappeared a few paces further, rolling over the sand instead of pounding into it.

Cas'Doren huffed. *Die you worthless sparrow!* Rearing, he spewed flame.

Scrambling to his feet, Haephan panicked and swung his sword at the fire. With a blue pulse of power, he knocked aside the burst of fire and swung wild with the second. On the third, he swung upward and screamed as dragon's fire washed over his left arm.

Seeing his opportunity, Cas'Doren vaulted forward. As he did, he lifted off the seed.

Haephan's need overpowered the torture of his melting bicep and he shifted for it.

Panicked, Cas'Doren snaked his head under his belly to catch the boy reaching with his free hand. The dragon clamped over hand, arm and pod, yanked him out and thrashed him until he flew free and rolled across the ground.

Cas'Doren snapped and swallowed arm and seed. Time slowed as the first tingle of its power inspired quivers of narcotic euphoria.

Haephan tumbled across the ground and slid to a stop with the sword's flared guard caught in the fabric of his trousers. He groped for the sword's handle despite his thundering head and lay there quivering while the stump of his left arm poured blood across the sand.

You lose, little groundling, said Cas'Doren as he approached.

Waiting until the dragon loomed over him, Haephan swung and cleaved a curve of the dragon's midnight beak.

Howling, Cas'Doren recoiled.

Muscles in Haephan's stump seized to stem the blood flow. Neither the scorching of dragonsfire nor the loss of his arm compared with a new agony burning deep within. His gaze climbed chamber wall and ceiling to its source.

Fire he knocked away with his sword now spread across the Tree of Life.

Soul-searing terror gripped him while Cas'Doren staggered under the drug-like pod flooding his veins.

Where shock first insulated him from so much pain, the sensory load now overwhelmed him. The mantle flared about him as it fought to keep him alive while he ached for death. Even his sanity wavered under the enormity of it all. Reality warped as he tried in vain to shift to safety.

As the fire danced its way up and around the Tree and its illumination filled the chamber's near side, his shadow slowed and stretched away, irreverent to flame or boy.

When a scream erupted from Haephan's gaping mouth, it split into a second, fifth and twelfth voice that clawed the air. When the shadow ripped itself away, two red eyes opened within its face.

Cas'Doren's wavering head turned to the new creature.

Relieved of his shadow, Haephan squeezed away tears and focused. "Algueda!"

Crossing the distance faster than the stuppored dragon, the demon shadow clutched on the boy like a second form as Haephan and sword shifted away.

Cas'Doren barked a pitiful protest at Haephan's escape when drifting sparks caught his attention. When he turned, he froze.

The Tree of Life blazed in a slow vortex that climbed beyond its scorched, lifeless trunk into a whirlpooling bloodred sky above. Swirling flames from its broad canopy bathed the cave's highest molten edges now sinking inward and drew the heavy weight of soil and stone behind it.

Bleeding, exhausted, drunk and defeated, Cas'Doren knew he could not fly free as he always had before. He stumbled over scree as he ran the length of the chamber into his private cave while behind him pieces of the dying Tree rained and the air itself wailed in terror.

Never had he fathomed setting the Tree afire. Every nerve in his body quivered. Despite the dulling of his magic, he sensed, as one, the entirety of the known universe clench in terror. Could they see it? Did skies everywhere boil with the Tree's fire? Was it so bright? Was her death so undeniable?

The cave's crest sagged over the collapsing Tree canopy until it irised closed in a sinking point above the trunk's apex.

Gripped as he was, he did nothing but stare as the swirling fire doubled on itself and expanded to fill the entire chamber. The tempestuous conflagration roared and rushed the space until he feared it would advance into his cave. The fire flushed out in a burst of acrid smoke. Silence thundered like a gong while the molten ceiling lit the smoke with its brilliant orange ambience.

Terrified of staying a moment longer, he struggled onto shaky feet as stone liquified by the fire drooled into an impassable drape over his small cave.

Shuddering in terror, the Dragon King of Eden raised his head, roared his loudest and disappeared from history.

97
A New Tree

Dark purple bruises climbed SonLara's pale sweat-soaked skin under the dim evening slate. Vibrant red painted most of her right eye and the side of her face swelled. Her body throbbed with the shock of the dragon rolling over her. She wove healing into Eva's swollen ankle while the woman struggled not to moan. Sitting on SonLara's shoulder, Ven struggled to handle the enormity of it all.

The lifeless island's whistling, ceaseless wind roared, but Elverbane's desperate words, alone, echoed in her ears.

"I love you."

Had he meant it? Was he merely afraid of dying? SonLara shook her head, knowing he spoke true.

"I'm sorry if you wanted more of us, but please, save her. If not for me, then for her!"

She would shed tears if possible, knowing Elverbane had given his life for her and the others. She knew it without doubt, despite being nearly unconscious when Haephan deposited her here. In the fog of her shocked mind, Elverbane's words, alone, remained clear.

Scanning the island from her perch on SonLara's shoulder, Ven croaked, *Bloody hell...I've seen this place.*

SonLara frowned and for the first time took in their surroundings. She spun about and scanned the ridges, the looming snowy peak, the volcano and a high conical peak. "Great Self. We're here."

"What?" Eva asked as she winced.

"Algueda," said SonLara as she pressed her hand to her brow and hugged herself as she began to cry. Haephan could have safely taken her or Elverbane or Eva here in an instant, but someone had to stay behind and hold off the dragons. Knowing what Elverbane attempted to accomplish to keep the dragons out of the chamber, she guessed he would have done the same before allowing himself to die, the stubborn bastard.

SonLara snuffed her grief to focus on Eva's ankle, a mission to narrow her attention. She tried to calculate how long it would take the vacants to finish the journey here from their progress through the Ebsa and knew they would be waiting another day or two. Haephan should be able to bring them food as they waited, once he returned. He had recovered from debilitating injury—even brain trauma.

Thoughts of the boy threatened her with yet more grief. With her guard shattered and emotional reserves bottomed out, the tragedy of his journey made her want to weep all the more. He deserved so much better—

"SonLara," said Eva. "What is that?"

SonLara looked up and froze.

Great Self, Ven chimed.

Upon the distant horizon, a line of electric orange raced across the sky with alarming speed. She seized the ankle in terror, causing Eva to scream as the dark evening sky caught afire.

Horror filled them both as the world roiled in successive outward waves of flame. She followed the tsunami of death across the sky as the light around them burned crimson.

Already terrified, a popping sound nearby made her scream. Haephan appeared across the ground a few feet away.

"Haephan!" SonLara and Ven cried together.

When SonLara rolled out from under her, Eva's ankle slapped the ground and drew a scream.

SonLara scrambled for the boy as a pool of blood gushed from his stump of a left arm. The Dogwood Sword lay tangled in his trousers. "Haephan! Haephan! What happened!"

Ven swirled about Haephan as he sucked a ragged inhale when his chest thrusted upward and a multivoice scream erupted from his dark mouth.

SonLara clutched her ears as the sound rattled her bones. To her horror, the boy's shadow ripped itself from his body.

In a panic, Ven unleashed bolts of fire at it, driving it down the incline along the mountain behind her.

Haephan fell limp.

"Haephan! What's going on!?" SonLara set her hand on his chest. "What happened!?"

Haephan stuttered. "She burns." His strained, unfocused eyes turned upwards.

"Who burns, boy!? Who!?"

"Tree," the boy whispered.

Chills washed over SonLara's skin.

Oh no, chimed Ven.

"There's no hope," Haephan moaned as his stump sputtered blood. "The dragon. He took the seed…I have no pod."

SonLara clutched her belly. The seed she stole was to be a prize for her people. The seed had one final purpose. "I have one."

Haephan stared hopelessly at the sky.

"I have one!" SonLara yanked it from her tiny pouch and held it before him. "I have one! What do I do!?"

"There—" he snatched a strand of her blue hair with a finger extended from around the seed and pulled her closer as his consciousness ebbed. "I have to take you there."

"What? Where?"

"There," he gasped. His veins pulsed red and gold through his dark skin. His voice strained through a clenched jaw. "To the ledge! To the mother!" He wheened. "Please! Now!"

As Ven rushed in to touch them both, SonLara pressed her weight atop him. "Go!"

They shifted and fell a few inches with a *whomph*.

Haephan writhed. "Plant it! It's the only way! Plant it before we burn!"

Now on the low jut of the conical peak, SonLara climbed to her feet under a burning sky.

"Plant…" Haephan's voice faded. "Plan—"

An image flashed in her mind of planting the tree on Belfast Bluff. She snatched the seed from his hand, covered in his blood, and searched for the right place to plant.

Multicolored pulses of light emanating from the La'Du Lira Al'Cular washed across the sky, followed by lightning. In those moments where fear consumed and death loomed, time slowed. Instants became seconds became minutes of her slow breath, the brushing of her disheveled blue hair and her lethargic blinks.

Judging the space such a tree might one day need, she judged a third of the distance from the jut's outer edge to where the flat met the steep mountain wall, raced for the spot and poured her magic into the seed to wake its dormancy.

SonLara had no experience summoning lightning as Elverbane had, but in the long seconds, she sensed an energetic buildup in the sky above her and reached out to take control. She noted her target in the broad depression near the jut's outer edge and raised her free hand to initiate an electric anchor to summon the bolt there. Ultraviolet light flared as electricity welled from the ground upward to create a channel. Opening it wide, the first strike was followed by dozens. Startled, she recoiled and loosed control.

The island exploded with lightning as a thousand bolts struck across the terrain, shattering the rock into fine dust.

Somewhere distant, Eva screamed and huddled in terror.

A too-near strike cast SonLara across the stone and took her attention enough for the lightning to cease and the seed rolled for the jut's outer edge.

Scrambling to her feet, she sprinted and leapt. Thunder crashed above as the sudden heat of so many lightning bolts billowed through the atmosphere. She fell hard across the ground and grabbed the seed as it bounced out over the edge.

Ignoring the blood and sweat drooling over her face, she scrambled across the now-dust layered terrain, slid across the ground and drove the seed into the hole.

"GROW!" she screamed and unleashed her energy. Tendrils fired outward from the seed between her fingers, dove into the rock and expanded. She yanked her hand free and climbed to unsteady feet.

The next few moments were the most tenuous. Breaking contact severed the energy poured into it, but she couldn't grow a garden by clutching a seed. In long, drawn seconds, she shifted her inner energy and wove a lacework for the new growth. Having never seen the La'Du Lira Al'Cular in person, she didn't know what latticework already existed, but if it was a Tree, it would operate on the same basics. If it was the Tree of Life, it could handle details for itself. If Haephan had gotten his magic from it, she knew where to start.

She yanked off her outer dress and squeezed every ounce of blood and sweat from it over the hole and impressed the magical lace onto the seed. She pulled from that seed a single physical tendril that fired upward, and from there she danced.

Weaving and washing, pulling and pushing, she created the core of life for the Tree in a lifeless place, pushing it unnaturally to grow faster than it otherwise could. Desperate, she split the primary tendril as it climbed as high as her head and then pulled from the bottom to extend the trunk while the main body thickened and grew.

The Tree soon became too large for her to manually grow as she had at Belfast. She focused on layering the latticework over the arbor to coax it to continue on its own. Minutes passed until a gentle blue aura that had been growing around the tree burst from its base and knocked her toward the cliff's edge. She snatched a hold before too much of her weight slipped off, and climbed to safety.

The fire in the sky was gone. From an endless field of thick smoke covering the sky snaked an auroral thread that dove into the tree and rippled across the barren landscape.

Haephan and Ven hovered above the Tree with eyes and mouths glowing.

The buildup of magic was SonLara's only warning. She twisted away in time to avoid the Tree flashing into a noonday sun with a shattering pulse that raced outward across the island, crushing additional barren top rock into a fine dust.

The world fell still before a thunderous crow rattled her bones, spread across the island and echoed over the seas. Huddling in terror, she screamed as the sound shook her to her core.

As quickly as it came, the chaos disappeared.

Braving a look, the blood-spattered priestess climbed on shaky knees and pushed to her feet as Ven, alone, fluttered toward the ground. Despite the agony in her leg, SonLara raced, leapt and slammed into the rock in time to catch the pixie. When a whistling *thunk* kissed the sides of her fingers, she found the quivering Dogwood Sword sunk halfway into the ground a hairsbreadth from her skin. After a few moments to let the pain pass and the shock of having barely avoided losing half of her right hand, SonLara rolled over.

The Tree had changed—now three times higher than a moment before with a trunk as thick as her body. To her surprise, a brilliant streak of sunrise appeared from her left. A new world merged with her own. Holding the unconscious fairy, she approached the curve of the jut with the best view while the edge of existence sewed itself outward into a new world and sea bathed in dawnlight.

Tiny spots of black appeared next to her as ash-filled rain began to fall shimmering with auroric energy that dissipated into the new dust covering the island. A lone caw pierced the sudden quiet with alarming portent.

After SonLara sank to her knees and vomited, relief washed over her. She wiped her mouth with her wrist, climbed on shaky feet and approached the jut's edge to scan the island as the disintegrating sky revealed a full green moon from the Pangean side. Bathed in green moonlight and yellow sunrise while Ven stirred in her hands, she coughed.

"Haephan?" she called out. "Haephan?"

98
Haephan Sleeps

Haephan's eyes cracked open to a muddled vision of faint gray light. He blinked several slow times. Swallowing the thick gunk in his throat, he sighed against the soft cushion of the pillow.

Sunlight fell through a nearby window. The bed beneath him was so comfortable he barely felt it.

A friend materialized through his clearing vision.

Nick loomed close as he knelt next to the bed.

Haephan's heart slowed with relief. Not only was the never-ending urge to plant seeds now gone, Nick was near.

"Hello, boy," Nick smiled grimly. "Glad you returned to us."

The energy Haephan should have expected after sleep did not appear. Instead, weakness and exhaustion clung to his waking mind. Memories of the past hours, days, weeks and months weighed upon him, all the way back to the girl with bone-white hair from Bertrand Park and his strange vision.

He remembered the boy who had stolen his father's ring, the mother he didn't know he had—now dead—and his best and most faithful friend he had ever known, also gone.

He remembered the wizard to whom he looked at like a father, and the bedraggled priestess whom he left to plant the final seed on Algueda. The dragon, and the islands and the giants and the great blue oxen and the fireflies and the fairy—whom he sensed lived somewhere very far away…

Haephan remembered the fight with the dragon and the stump of an arm left behind. The pain of breaking his head on the stone walls during his battle. The sheer agony of the burning Tree of Life, and yet all of it paled to the shame and loneliness staked in his heart.

Turning to Nick, tears welled in Haephan's eyes.

"Oh boy," Nick set one of his massive hands on the side of Haephan's face. "You have gone through so much. You can rest now. You're safe here."

Haephan's breath stuttered. "I'm tired, Nick."

Beyond Nick stood a tall female elf in the doorway. Though Haephan noticed her, he returned to Nick and his love. He soaked in every ounce as his heart sagged.

"I'm tired," Haephan cried. "I don't want it anymore! I don't want it! Please, don't make me stay! Don't make me stay!" His weak sobs struggled above whispers.

"You don't have to," said Nick as he pressed his forehead to the boy's. Though Haephan's stump of an arm had been healed over with elven magic, the boy's health had not returned. "You don't have to. I'm here for you. You can do whatever you want. You are safe here. No one will ask you for more."

"I just want to sleep," Haephan's eyes drooped. "I don't want it anymore."

Nick struggled to keep his voice calm. "You're safe, boy. Sleep. No one will ask anything more of you. You have done so very, very well. Rest now."

Haephan took heavy breaths.

Nick drew close. "Go to sleep, child. Go to sleep."

Drawing several long, labored breaths while staring at Nick,

Haephan fell still and breathed no more.

Nick lowered his head to the boy's chest and cried.

When he fell silent, he remained alongside the child for some time.

Eventually, he pulled aside the blanket, lifted the boy and carried him to the stables. There, they wrapped his body in linen.

As the sun set, Nick carried Haephan out of the house, through the construction yard, dug the grave and laid Haephan's body with care. He sat on the hole's edge to take a final look at the boy before he climbed to his feet, grabbed the shovel and filled it in.

Having gathered round him and the grave, the Cordurons trickled away after saying their own goodbyes, leaving Nick to sit at its foot as the sun kissed the horizon. Isheim stood nearby while the wind tugged her pale hair.

"Who was this?" Isheim finally asked. "The boy? The one you mentioned?"

Nick gritted his jaw as he struggled with the pain of her betrayal and the shame of his own.

"How did he die?" she asked.

Nick turned from the grave to the sunset, afraid to answer, and suppressed a sob. "The same way we might."

She shook her head.

"Following this self-forsaken mission," he said. A tear slid down his cheek.

"And our mission?" she asked. "For these humans?"

"A heavy price was paid for them, today." He set his hand upon the bare mound. "A very heavy price. I think that whatever the Great Self intended, they had better live up to it."

"And what is it they're supposed to live up to?"

"I'm not sure," said Nick. "But whatever it is…it had better be grand."

Epilogue

Rysa raced through the forest in her small brown dress fluttering in the wind. She wove through thick jungle fronds across moist detritus into a thicket of white birch and covered in crunchy dead leaves. Ahead, her two brothers outpaced her as they often did. "Wait up!"

Birch gave way to a grove of oak stumps recently felled. Her bare feet padded over sharp wood chips and deep soil ruts where trunks had been dragged away. She raced north along the road to the edge of the plateau to where the road descended, offering her an unprecedented view of the island's northern coast. In a small cove sparkling with evening light reflected from low pink clouds, three ocean ships prepared to sail.

When the road turned, she kept straight into the bush descending the steep terrain. She crossed the zig-zagging road several times before she headed east along the coast and sprinted across a small grassy field toward a house.

Comprised of a circle of trees grown together, the arboreal home sat as a sunset silhouette between a gentle grassy ridge and the northern beach. Cookfire smoke snaked from the branches of the hut's roof of interwoven branches and the windows glowed with its light.

Climbing the stone steps into the house's shadow, Rysa pushed through the hut's only door. "Laaraa! Lara!" She closed the door behind her. "Lara!"

Sitting in a rocking chair between the fireplace and a broad stump filling the main room, atop which sat a humble bed, a woman turned to the little girl. Adorned in a simple white dress with a blue shawl with blue-gray hair bound in a haphazard bun, SonLara opened her arms and smiled as the girl ran to her.

"Ohh, so big!" SonLara pulled her close. "So big! You have gotten too big, my little bunny." She leaned back. "We have fed you too much!"

The girl giggled. "Uh huh!"

"Oh yes, I do believe we have," SonLara brushed hair from Rysa's face. "You are a mess."

Rysa giggled before the pixie appeared from a basket hanging above the bed. "Ven!"

Ven emerged from her tiny house and encircled the girl several times before hovering near with a smile.

"It's time!" said the girl.

Two boys barreled through the door and slowed at the sight of Rysa. "How'd you get here first!?"

Rysa stuck out her tongue.

"Hey Lara!" panted the elder boy, Qayin, with his black hair and narrow, slanted eyes. "We're leaving. Mom and Dad are on their way."

"I know, I know," SonLara smiled sadly before sitting on the stump's edge with Rysa in her lap.

Ven raced between the two boys, who grinned, before she alighted on Havel's shoulder, drawing a brief frown from Qayin before they drew near.

"I will miss you all so very much," said SonLara. "You have such great lives before you. I wish I could be there for them."

"Why don't you come with us, Lara?" asked Qayin. "There's plenty of room! You could stay with us!"

"Yeah, Lara!" said Havel. "Please come! You and Ven!"

Ven shook her head as she patted Havel's neck.

SonLara squeezed Qayin's hand. "I wish I could, young ones."

"Why can't you?" asked Havel.

SonLara kissed the side of Rysa's head. "My place is here. I cannot leave."

"But we want you to come!" grimaced Havel.

"I love you all very much," said SonLara. "But I cannot. One day I hope you will understand. Your parents will teach you why, I hope."

The children sighed.

"Alright now, enough moping," she set down Rysa and stood. "I have gifts for you."

All three of them lit up as she led them into her greenhouse on the cabin's north side. Small triangles of crude, semi-opaque glass lined the walls on the north, east and west walls of the nook. Rounding a table in its center, circled by plant boxes, she motioned for the children to approach the table's opposite side while Ven hovered over them.

"Now, for your long journey across an icy ocean to untold adventure, I've made each of you a special tool I hope you will take care of."

The trio brightened with anticipation.

"For Rysa, I made you a doll," SonLara lifted a doll woven of plant strands colored and shaped like a small child. A turnip formed its head with a delicate face carved with the quality of porcelain.

"She will grow with you until you become a woman," SonLara smiled. "And when you are a woman, she will fade." SonLara patted the doll. "But I hope she never fades from here." She put her hand over Rysa's heart.

"Thank you, Lara!" Rysa hugged the doll.

"You're welcome," SonLara touched Rysa's face and addressed the boys. "And first, Havel, my little animal keeper."

Qayin frowned at his younger siblings being mentioned first as SonLara set a wooden disc into Havel's hands.

"Wherever you roam, you will always have fire," said SonLara. "So, as you wander far from home with your flocks, you will always be able to stay warm and cook your food."

Havel lit up. "But I thought we couldn't use magic!"

"You cannot," she said, "but set the disc down and command it by voice and it will produce a small amount of fire. When you are done, command it to cool and it will stop, and then you can pull it out and carry it on with you."

"How does it work?"

"It works by spirit," said SonLara. "By energies that existed before magic and will continue to exist long after magic is gone. By the same energy that the Great Self lives and by which all realms exist. All you must remember to do is believe in it. So long as you remember the testimony of your parents and believe in the Self, this will work for you."

Humbled, Havel bowed his head with gratitude. "Thank you."

"And you, my little green thumb," she ruffled Qayin's wild hair until he smiled. "You've spent so many afternoons here with me learning to draw life from the soil. For you, I have this." She produced a long, cylindrical rock the length of Qayin's forearm and half the diameter of his wrist. "Let this rock reside in the field you want to grow most full. It will never break and your crop will always grow with even the slightest rainfall. Like your brother, so long as you believe in the Self, the power of spirit will flow through you and this will obey your commands."

"Thank you, Lara," Quayin said, though his smile hesitated as he accepted it.

"And to all of you," SonLara leaned over to brush Rysa's bright hair. "Remember each other, remember love, remember family. And most of all!" She leaned in. "Remember the Great Self, who sent you here, who protected your parents from the evils of the past, the war over their survival, the elves and dwarves and magic of your homeland, the dragons who came to stop us from delivering them here, about the Tree of Life. He is your highest father, one who loved you all enough to give you a whole new world so you could live in peace."

"Yes, Lara," they said.

Tell them I will miss them, Ven chimed.

SonLara translated when a voice called from outside the hut. Sunlight warming the greenhouse dimmed.

"Go out to your parents!" SonLara pointed. "I'll follow you in a moment."

Rysa latched upon her with a hug.

"I'll be along in a moment, my dear," SonLara hugged in kind. "Go on."

"Yes, ma'am!" Rysa chased her brothers out the door.

Is it time? Ven fluttered to the tabletop. Her crimson glow underlit SonLara's pale, aged face.

"It is," said SonLara, who pulled aside the bedding resting atop the stump, climbed atop it and knelt. She stroked its smooth surface with her hand until strands of woodflesh unknit themselves and opened a thin vertical maw to reveal a wrapped bundle. She plucked it out before rubbing her thumb along the opening to reseal its top. She laid the bundle and unwrapped it to reveal the bronze sword.

The Dogwood Sword? chimed Ven. *Are you sure?*

"This sword has caused untold suffering in our world," said SonLara. "Millennia of wars fighting over a weapon that should never have existed; so powerful as to make our most monumental mages appear vacant. Had…Seth attempted his worldender with this, it truly could have destroyed nations."

I remember how it responded to the boy, chimed Ven. *I'm glad I didn't know it was the Dogwood Sword until later, or I might have attacked him.*

"Scared me, too," said SonLara. A smile tugged her lips. "When it caught on fire?" She shook her head. "If ever someone with his magic were to use this sword with its full potential…I dare to say even a worldender might look like a spark to the true fire this would create."

And you're giving it to the vacants? asked Ven.

"There's no better place than among those who have no ability to use it," said SonLara. "It's just another sword in Adamar's hands, if at least with an unbreakable edge."

If you say so, chimed Ven.

Holding it for a long moment, SonLara dismissed the endless urge to study it since they arrived more than a decade ago. Instead, she wrapped it and stood. "Coming?"

Ven followed SonLara out the door into the arms of Adamar and Eva.

Eva wrapped her in a fierce hug. "I will miss you so very much, Lara."

The two cried as they embraced.

"Are you sure you won't come with us?" Adamar asked again. "I can't see any reason why you should stay."

"I can't, Adamar," SonLara released Eva before they clutched each other's hands. "I can't. This was all about you going to a place especially for you and your kind. For vacants. My friends, this is…where we say goodbye."

"I don't want to say goodbye!" stammered Rysa.

"I don't wish to say goodbye either," SonLara kissed each child. "But you must go, and where you go, I cannot. This is where I belong."

Adamar took her in a bear hug. "You have done so much for us. You will never be forgotten. Never."

"Thank you, young man," she whispered.

Adamar stepped back.

"Oh dear, what a family," SonLara wiped her tears. "And you with another on the way." SonLara smiled at Eva's belly. "Have you named him, yet?"

"Seth," Adamar smiled. "After your wizard."

Overcome, SonLara could only nod for a moment before she smiled. "I wish I could be there to see the world you will create, Adamar. There's no one better for this mission than you."

Adamar nodded.

"I will miss you all very much," SonLara let the tears flow. "I never thought I could know the love you've offered me. Or to feel the way I have felt here. In all my years, I never had imagined it."

"What will you do?" Adamar asked.

"Like I said before, I will continue growing the island," said SonLara. "It's why I'm here. Why I was born."

"And Ven?" Adamar asked.

"She says she will stay until I am gone, one way or the other," said SonLara. "Then she will try to make her way back to Pangea, if she can."

"We will miss you both. And we must get going," Adamar said. "Before the tide changes."

"Yes, let's go down," said SonLara.

The group headed westward along the shore, through narrows of climbing walls of rock into the cove where the three ships awaited.

She slipped her arms around the children and drew them close as newly minted sailors waited by the ships boat. "May the Great Self keep and watch over you. May He bless your years, your sons and daughters and the generations to come after you. Never forget where you came from, and never forget the Great Self."

The family smiled as Ven encircled them all in her own farewell.

"Adamar, I have a gift and a task for you, if you're willing," said SonLara, who raised her bundle.

"What is it?" Adamar asked.

"Take this with you and teach your children never to use it."

"Is this the sword Haephan used?"

"It is powerful in this old world," said SonLara. "but in the new world it's important it's kept hidden."

"Why?"

"It's best you don't know," said SonLara. "And that your wife never touch it. Ever."

Sharing a long, knowing look, Eva nodded. Adamar accepted the package.

"Come," SonLara smiled and ushered them along the slope to the beach. Once at the boat, she embraced each one in kind one last time before they climbed aboard and the men rowed them out to the waiting sailing ship.

"Bye, Ven!" Rysa waved. "Byyyee!"

Tell her I said goodbye, chimed Ven.

"She says goodbye!" SonLara called after them.

"Byye!" they cried.

Now that they were actually leaving, terrible loneliness crashed into SonLara. She clutched her belly as the family dwindled across the water. They crossed the reef break, climbed aboard the ship, hauled up the boat, weighed anchor and opened sail.

She soaked in every final second as each ship began to move and headed out across open ocean for the new world.

Taking several deep breaths, SonLara headed for her hut with Ven upon her shoulder. Once past the high rock formations, the ships sailed into the distant sunset. Tears drooled down her pale cheeks along her long facial scar.

Standing on the beach under the fading evening light, she remembered the rough first months eking life from the thin layer of soil created by the lightning and the aurora. Not all survived those first few weeks fishing for food and fertilizer.

Within a day of the planting, Ven confirmed Haephan's death somewhere in the direction of the new world. SonLara wept for a week.

A decade here aged SonLara well beyond the time. Intense use of magic and spiritual energy had worn her so that she aged more like the four-century-old Gold Librarian. She helped them survive slavery, death and the ebsa to a barren island straddling their new world.

When the ships disappeared into the murky horizon of approaching night, she headed for her cozy cabin. It did not appear so welcome knowing it would be her final, lonely home.

SonLara plodded along a wave-washed beach as stars twinkled through dusk, struggling against the dread of never hearing a human voice again, when a deep, echoing caw cut the air.

The priestess spun with a pounding heart to a familiar sound, one that haunted her since planting a new La'Du Lira Al'Cular.

Ven bolted from her shoulder into the air. *Someone is here!* chimed Ven.

"Someone? Like who?" SonLara stammered. "Who is it?"

Ven's mouth opened and shut as she struggled to comprehend her feelings. She fired toward the gentle ridge south of them.

SonLara sprinted after her, up the ridge and into a midnight forest. Ven slowed well enough to light the way over steep, rolling terrain to a dark thicket.

Gentle sobbing stilled SonLara with sudden fear. Hesitant, the priestess parted the bushes and gaped.

Facing away from them huddled a tiny girl in a brown dress. Above her loomed a darkness deeper than a moonless night, whose gaping jaws sucked away Ven's ambience. Red eyes locked upon the child as it descended for her.

Without thinking, Ven unleashed bolts of power that repelled the bogey, who screamed in protest and fled.

SonLara snatched the girl from the thicket and retreated to safety. Once out from under the trees in the light of a rising moon, she gasped, "Rysa! What are you doing here? How did you get here? I saw you leave on the ship with your parents!"

"I dunno!" Rysa cried. "I was at the bow on our way out. We passed through a big glowing wall and the world changed, the waves tossed and we were in the big ship, and then there was a bright light and…A shadow came. Across the floor! And snatched me and— I'm here! Where's mommy!? Where's mommy!?"

SonLara watched the starlit ocean knowing the ships would never return.

"Oh dear, my little sweet one!" SonLara rocked the girl on her shoulder.

SonLara, chimed Ven.

"What is it?"

Look! Ven pointed at the little girl.

"You can talk!" Rysa said.

"You can understand her?" asked SonLara.

"Yeah! Say something else!" Rysa pulled her hair aside.

Don't you see it!? Ven exclaimed.

SonLara's breath caught. "Oh Great Self in heaven. Is it?"

Yes it is! Ven swooped in to land on Rysa's shoulder. Where she touched emanated faint golden ripples that faded away.

"What's wrong?" Rysa asked.

"I don't know, Rysa. But…" said SonLara. "Something has happened."

"What?" Rysa asked.

Ven and SonLara shared a look.

"You're like that brave young man, Haephan," said SonLara. "The one I told you about? I don't know how, but you're just like him, now."

"How is that?" Rysa asked.

"You wear his mantle, Rysa," said SonLara as the unmistakable golden lattice shimmered around the girl.

Ven cupped her mouth.

"You're the Pan."

TO BE CONTINUED IN ...

LEGEND OF THE PAN: PETER

AN EXCERPT FROM
LEGEND OF THE PAN: PETER

Richter's Deep

Lord Pan of Eden, William Baley, emerged from the captain's quarters to face the Unionist witch who was ripping apart his mages on The Sumter's bloody deck. Casting lightning bolts and flashes of ice, the Unionist shielded herself from alliance counterattacks and used an air blast to knock an Edenon mage overboard.

You silly ass! chimed a golden fairy as she bolted from the dark room behind William around to his blood-smeared face. *You're already exhausted from the last three attacks. We can't lose you! You need to get back-*

"You'll lose me anyway if this ship goes down," William replied and moved past her and the alliance mages shielding the doorway. He glanced at the Swinnen ship bound to his own with a spiked boarding ramp before facing the witch.

I- can't help you, William! Tinker Belle chimed as he stepped out into the cloud-mottled midday sun. Moist, tepid air reeked of the sharp iron of blood and foul scat from dead men. *William!*

"Finally!" The witch smiled at his approach and gathered her power in a flush of smoky blue light before firing three entwined arcs of lightning. William raised his left hand to catch all three arcs and channeled them out of his right hand upward as a web of energy across the enemy ship. In seconds, every sheet of canvas, rope line, and mast burst into flame. Dozens of sailors dropped from electrical burns.

Those unharmed rushed to put out the fires spreading across the ship. The witch's face faltered when she realized her lightning had set her own ship ablaze.

William drew up his power and fired a spread of yellow-red balls of fire through his open palms. She twisted out of the way as shock painted her yellow-skinned face, angled eyes, and full lips.

"You son of a bitch!" she countered with a powerful blast of wind.

William braced a magical shield with both arms just in time to divert the gusts, then dove aside as she cast a binding spell. A sailor behind him crumpled to the deck when the spell landed on him instead.

"Back!" William barked at the crew.

Dressed in Unionist red and blue, the midnight-haired witch matched him to prevent him flanking her. Arrows fired by marines slowed and fell lifeless to the deck when they struck her magical shields.

The witch unleashed an attack of ice to drive him back. He diverted it off-ship and countered with broiling gusts of air, which she cooled before the wind struck her. Advancing, she cast quick flashes of light to blind him before unleashing more arcs of lightning.

He allowed the energy to land just above his person upon a robe-like mantle, creating a brilliant shimmer of auroric light over a golden lattice. The witch flinched as William's mantle — the magic that defined the pan — flared with the flush of power, giving him the chance to counterstrike, doubled with his own magic.

She hesitated between shielding herself and rechanneling the energy outward as William had. Her hesitation created a notch in her defense. Energy pierced her body. Her trunk ripped open in a muted explosion that flailed out, her two halves connected only by her spine, before slapping to the deck. Her anchored shields flickered out.

William stumbled to a knee and snatched the starboard rail as his energy bottomed.

You can't keep fighting! Tinker Belle flew across the deck. *You're exhausted. You need to be where it's safe!*

"What do you want me to do, Belle?" William glanced at the enemy ship and motioned to one of his surviving mages who rushed to destroy the ramp in an explosion of fire and wood before helping the sailor bound by the witch's spell. Powerless without lines or sails, the enemy ship drifted away as its crew scrambled to save themselves from fire. "Those selfdamn Swinnens are already ripping us apart. Our mages, no matter how skilled, aren't powerful enough to deal with the sheer number of theirs."

You're to lead from the rear so you remain protected, Tinker Belle growled. *You keep stepping out here and you're gonna get killed. Stay behind and safe! We should fall back to Admiral Liston's ship so he can better protect us!*

Sailors around him policed the dead from the blood-smeared deck. Spelled arrows bristled the corpses of alliance mages and had set sections of wood on fire. William ran his fingers through his thick brown hair and forced himself to his feet. A striking man with broad shoulders, straight nose and full chin, William dominated the deck standing akimbo in his hunter green long coat, open over a voluminous white blouse tucked into forest green trousers, belted and booted in amber brown leather. His high, straight collar framed his shaking head as he took in his decimated crew. "If they all die, I will, too."

"Lord Pan!" Captain Larimund Shelley approached with Leftenant Rupert Dennison on his heels. A stout Alderlander with charcoal skin and broad curly hair, Shelley moved across the deck with the grace of his decades of experience at sea. "Well done, my lord. I think we lost fewer of our own than we feared."

"The fleet?"

"Admiral Liston signals to regroup," Shelley said. "We plan to move on their center now that we've split their right flank. Of all nations to denounce our alliance and throw in with the Unionists, why Swinne!? They do not go down easily."

"Among other reasons, Nailata, Tarnia and Gemria forge the strength of the alliance's maritime forces," William growled. "The opportunity to take out their greatest maritime competition is something Swinne would never pass up."

Shelley grimaced. "They may match our numbers, but I have faith in alliance captains. We are the finest in Pangea. The Unionists can be fervent and dead, for all I care."

"Regrouping is wise," William said. "My family?"

"Rupert, here, checked on them personally." Shelley motioned to Dennison, a tall man with pale brown skin and a broad nose under a mop of sun-brightened curly brown hair.

"They are well, my lord," said Leftenant Rupert Dennison.

"Good," William said. "Bring me a-"

"Captain!" the pilot cried. "Ahead!"

William and Shelley raced to the bridge with Tinker Belle in tow for a better view. A forest of inky smoke columns billowed from a field of burning vessels.

"Report." Shelley scanned the battle.

"There!" The pilot pointed just right of the bow.

A lone ship wove among his own fleet with alarming speed as if carried by the water itself.

"What is it?" Shelley asked as William leaned forward. "We need to retreat, Lord Pan, not fight another ship."

"Wait." With his mantle-powered eyes, William watched magic erupt from the lone vessel toward an alliance craft in its path. An ocean wave carrying the enemy ship flushed forward, grew by a mast's height, and crashed into the ship, which buckled under the immense power and twisted onto its side.

The ohna marina, Tinker Belle gasped.

"What is it?" Shelley extended his spyglass. "Oh … no."

When a second alliance ship in the enemy's path sank in two breaths, a cry rose among the crew.

William gripped the railing.

Shelley paled. "Great Self save us."

"What?" Rupert gaped. "Wh- what's happening?"

"Blasphemers!" Shelley snapped. "A first power! An ohna!" Sailors kissed their knuckles and ducked their heads.

As a third alliance ship attempted to block the on-comer's path, a humpback whale exploded from the surface and crashed upon its side. Sailors on William's ship gasped when a second whale appeared and repeated the attack from another point. More whales breached to batter the alliance corvette. A pale beluga managed to fall on the ship's deck, scattering what sailors it didn't crush.

The ohna makara, Tinker Belle growled. She scanned the field of ships and pointed. *There's a second ohna bearer over there by at least a mile. He's got amazing control to push whales this far across the battlefield.*

"How are they doing that?" Rupert asked.

"There's another ohna," William growled.

"*Another* first power?" Shelley asked.

With its path cleared, the enemy ship darted into view with a fresh wave building from beneath its keel.

"So fast," Rupert said.

"Turn toward them." William's level voice cut the tension. "Now."

Shelley barked orders to get the ship moving again, echoed by his officers. Expert crew darted into action as William raced across the deck and out onto the bowsprit with one hand on a forward line to steady himself.

As the gap closed between the Unionist vessel and The Sumter, William locked onto the ohna bearer on their forecastle — a midnight-haired woman with dark khaki skin and a bold, hooked nose, clad in light, crimson armor. From the woman's right fist danced light visible to the pan and the haraven, alone. She raised the ohna.

"Athyka Bonduquoy." William grit his teeth and reassured himself that while he stood at the fore of The Sumter, her powers would fail. A wave of water climbed from under the hull of her ship but disintegrated two ship spans away from his own.

Athyka scowled when the ohna's power failed on approach. She tried again with a different weave. The ohna's power crossed the waters to open the ocean beneath his ship. Again, the power failed and left a faint ripple across the choppy waves.

The Sumter gained speed, but at William's hand signal, the ship's attentive pilot guided the vessel a bit to lee to avoid hitting them head on.

William held out his hand. "Bow."

One of marines behind him offered their bow and quiver.

William took it, plucked an arrow and used one swift pull to loose an arrow at the enemy ship. Athyka screamed a warning too late. William's arrow took the enemy captain through the eye. As the enemy crew erupted in surprise, their mages threw up tardy shields from their positions at the forecastle.

William loosed two more arrows, knowing they would burn up in the enemy's shields. He then signaled The Sumter's pilot, who angled the ship more to lee as William raced atop the starboard rail and prepared to leap across to the passing enemy ship. Once upon the enemy deck, he could rip them apart.

Before he could leap, the water beneath the vessels welled and drove the enemy's ship away from The Sumter and out of his reach. William snatched a line to keep himself from falling into the water. Several alliance sailors cried a momentary victory while Unionist mages unleashed bolts of fire, lightning and spelled arrows that flared on shields raised by alliance mages.

As Athyka used the ohna to speed her ship away, her ship's exposed aft revealed its name — Unity's Light.

"Is they runnin'?" asked a nearby sailor when Unity's Light avoided the next alliance vessel.

"No." William clenched his jaw and the line in his left fist. Unable to match the enemy's speed or maneuverability, he could do nothing but watch Unity's Light dance around his ships with impunity. He rubbed his face. "Selfdamn it. Richter's Deep, Shelley. I should have seen it. The largest pod spawning waters in Pangea. With the ohnas marina and makara, they can master all water and sea life. We-" He exhaled. "Great Self, we don't stand a chance here."

Shelley stiffened.

"Is it really an ohna? A first power? A holy power of creation?" Rupert breathed. "I didn't want to believe."

"How does it look?" William asked.

Counting ships, Shelley sighed. "What we have now will ... we're down by about fifty of our original three hundred, but so are they. Out of their original two hundred and fifty or so, that's a bigger hit on them." Unity's Light avoided ships attempting to block its path as it moved deeper into the alliance fleet. "If they can get out of range of that thing. How far can they wield it?"

"Not far," William growled, "but Athyka can dance out of our reach until she's picked off who she wants. We can't fight all that by ourselves." He grimaced and spat. "It doesn't matter if we have superior numbers and captains if they have the ohnas. It's the same selfdamn tactic they've used since taking those fucking ohnas from their seats. Self damnit."

"What tactic?" Rupert glanced at Shelley.

"The Unionists enticed larger forces into a seemingly easy victory due to the Unionists' small numbers," Shelley offered with a frown. "Then they used the powers of creation to create a bloody rout."

"But … you're the pan," Rupert said. "Can't you do something? We're a fleet of nations! Surely, they cannot hope to stand against our alliance. Not with captains and admirals like Liston, Dubair and Afgunati! Not with you! They say the first powers are as nothing to you! My lord."

"Were I alone…" William looked downward where belowdecks his wife, son, and two guards awaited the battle's end. Fear passed through him at the thought of his family coming to danger before he tamped it to focus on the moment. "But as it stands, even I cannot stop an entire fleet, even a small one. Not when they can do that." He pointed at Unity's Light avoiding alliance efforts to attack and slow it.

"She's going for Admiral Liston," Shelley breathed as Unity's Light turned on the Nailatan flagship. He leaned onto the bannister when Liston's vessel, identifiable by the colors flying above the center mast, sank in moments. Shelley's eyes closed.

"She won't need to take us all out, Shelley," William whispered. "All she needs is to take our finest — the very ones we need most. The rest will crumble."

Moans of alarm died across deck when it became apparent a balance of power had shifted.

"Swinne has made their choice. The Unionists …" William's breath faded as the situation's gravity settled on him. He flexed his hands and let his eyelids sink. "They have won, Shelley."

"But she's only taken a few more of ours!" cried Rupert. "Surely, if we gang up on her …!? We can take her!"

Everyone on the bridge blanched in the following silence.

William hesitated once, then twice. "Signal the fleet."

Hatred and despair fought dominance in his chest. Swinne had sided with the Unionists. Eden, his home, was laid bare before the insurgents. He and his family had no place in the civilized world to retreat. Unionist-whipped mobs raged across the continent — there was no safe place to hide from the sway of angry, ignorant masses, incited by quiet political actors. The world burned in a fire fabricated by opportunistic nobles, corporatist merchants and true-believing sheep.

"The message, my lord?" Shelley straightened.

"Disperse," he said. "No rally point. … Survive."

Shelley relayed orders to the signalman. "How did they know we would be here?" Shelley fisted his thick hands. "Intelligence said they were far to the north. How did they know our route to flank them?"

"Betrayal," Rupert breathed.

"Never!" Shelley snapped.

"No, he's right." William slicked more water from his hair. "We've been betrayed by someone in Eden."

"Eden? Who would betray us in Eden?" Rupert asked.

"Our plans were known only by a few," William said. "I fear my sister has been taken."

"Councilor Baley?" Shelley asked.

William nodded.

"You mean she betrayed us?" Rupert asked.

Shelley stiffened.

Mixed feelings passed over William's face. "She was not part of our planning meetings. We were betrayed in Eden. That is all we need know. And more importantly, it means Eden-" He didn't want to say it. "Eden has fallen. And my sister, regardless of her role, is likely dead. All Baleys are a target to the Unionists."

"Because we were betrayed?" Rupert asked.

"Because if they knew we escaped," Shelley growled, "Eden would be vulnerable. So much for sneaking you out of the city, Lord Pan. I'm so sorry."

"But what will we do?" asked Rupert.

William scowled. "I don't know."

A silence fell on the bridge. William soaked in the tang of salty air, heat of the sun and the gentle rock of deep open waves rolling beneath their hull while the faint cry of sailors on nearby vessels drifted over the sparkling waters.

"Ere it comes, the days long past, we danced across the waters." Shelley's quiet voice drew every eye but William's. "Fight the fight, fulfill our vows, and go to meet our fathers."

"Aye, away to Eden," said the pilot.

"Aye, away to Eden," echoed the bosun.

"Orders, Lord Pan?" Shelley prompted.

Where do we go, Will? Tinker Belle chimed.

Glancing at the pixie, William used the sun to calculate time and distance in his head. With a final glance toward Unity's Light and his own fleet in flight, he sighed. After escaping Eden under the cover of night, racing for weeks across Pangea to meet up with the alliance fleet, and weeks more asea before finding failure, yet again, he felt void of choices.

"We're in the Far West Pangean Sea? Make for south by southeast." He looked across the waves at a point upon the horizon he could find without sun, map, or compass from anywhere in any weather, a place that ever tugged on his soul. "We make for Algueda." He focused on that distant point. "We make for Neverland."

END OF EXCERPT

Commission of the Immortal

FULL TEXT
Anderon Era
High Graelan Period

Here comes the herald, child of forever
Dreamers among the holes
For born from Algueda, replacements none greater
Of the tale Eternity told

The pan is the child, within lives the wild
Returning the Tree to its place
And calls into being, the path into meaning
To bring all of living new grace

Eternity called it, Immortal enthralled it
Seeds for new worlds they had set
The Pan soon befounded, of heraldry grounded
So founded in spirit of Self

Behold of this mantle, the power so handled
By hands of inception's behest
Preserving the powers, maintaining the hours
To leave the long living at rest

Soon comes the founder, the child abounder
Who travels afar and unmoved
The deeper desires igniting the fires
Alighting the first of the new

From out of the suffering, foundations enumering
Worlds of the Alter arise
Advent the exodus, heroes from vestiges
Those under sight of our eyes

The boy who could fly, through eternity's eyes
Dreams of a world in his sight
Rises to challenge, emerges the talent
A mantle forgone from its right

Restoring the balance, that envy unfounded
Righting what once was made broke
Soon so restoring, the Tree to its glory
Origins Immortal awoke

The minder she sees, 'cross distances be
Mother to beasts of the soul
Discovering power in Graela's last hour
To learn what grievances stole

She carries the dreaming of beasts so unseeming
And settles accounts of the heart
Renders asunder, the monster of plunder
The evil within he imparts

Companion to higher, though nothing aspire
Evils of Eden return
Climb from the timid, the tinker soon livid
To face the evil so burned

The darkness unravelled, serpentia gaveled
Judgement so long in the wait
Returned from the darkness, the powers undauntless
The meek overcoming the great

Come priestess of people, alone sees the evil
Obliging the seer's unrest
Daughter of princes, a spirit of lenses
Layers of time on request

The shadow awakened, tormented and plaguing
She sews split spirits entwine
And then for the island, takes chaos so riling
Bring forth the lady of time

Born from the darkness, a monster so harkened
A child of beast in the midst
Destroys all by touching, his terror enclutching
Upon which evil enlists

Return to the taking, revenge then awaking
Predator focused aprey
And forge them together, the source of Forever
A Wind even time will obey

Ere' comes the story, eternity's glory
A mantle of Self's own demand
Wrapped among lovers, from one to another
Across all dimensional lands

She found her forever, arisen the better
In present the moment is found
Immortal so borne in, a tale made of warning
Life from the lips hope abounds

Eternity's tale, began with the whales
Wandering 'mong the worlds
Pan's high beginning, of threatening thinning
Magna to pixie unfurled

So soon come the ending, begun by the lending
Of hoping so higher the young
Planted in arbor, anchor life's ardor
By the Self salvation come

From planting to culling, the great and the lulling
The eras passing us by
Life from beginnings, hopes and their endings
No one borne of Self to die

The Immortal and Eternity

WHAT DID YOU THINK?

LOVE OR HATE IT, PLEASE LEAVE A REVIEW!

Social proofing is an important part of the media industry, today, and your reviews go a long way toward supporting authors like me! Please take a moment to rate and write out an HONEST review of this book on the same site you bought it.

Thanks so much for reading! If you want to track upcoming content, go to www.LegendofthePan.com and sign up for the Panverse! I look forward to getting the next one into your hands!

Author

Christian Michael

I had an epiphany one day while watching the movie "Hook." When Rufio grows jealous of Peter Banning's growing fanfare among the Lost Boys, he cries out: "I've got Pan's sword! I'm the pan, now!"

It struck me: What if Peter wasn't merely "Peter Pan," but "Peter ***the*** Pan?"

What kind of a position would a pan hold? What would be his connection to Neverland? How would a golden pixie, English preteen girl and her brothers, boys lost from Earth and a wandering Native American tribe play into that legend? What else might we find in Peter's grander expanded universe?

Twelve years later, I began to share this incredible story with Peter, a today release its prequel. I hope you fall in love with my version of J.M. Barrie's classic characters as much as I have!

"Aye, away to Eden!"

About

Born in Georgia and raised mostly across the American South, Christian has moved more than sixty times across eleven states and two countries. A twenty-year enlisted Air Force veteran, professional voice actor, visual designer, web developer, data analyst and all-around info nut, he dislikes being bored.

A staunch individualist, Christian believes power resides within arm's reach and that people can live their fullest lives when they draw their eyes from the ambitions of world change to the quiet victory of inner peace.

Christian grew up an "Accelerated Reader" (yeah, buddy) reading the likes of Orson Scott Card, Poul Anderson, Greg Bear, Isaac Asimov, the Hardy Boys and the expanded Star Wars X-Wing series. As an adult, he has delved in Robert Jordan, Terry Goodkind, Brandon Sanderson, Matt Ridley, Ayn Rand, Brent Weeks, Mercedes Lackey, C.S. Lewis, Thomas Sowell and more.

Non-Pan by Christian

The Journey and the Dance (2024)
Last Battle: Dusk of Xanthar (2010)
Stardusk (2015)
Roses & Ravens: Search for Something (2015)

2021

Coming Soon...

PANVERSE
THE FIRST WORLD

www.ingramcontent.com/pod-product-compliance
Lightning Source LLC
Chambersburg PA
CBHW030551310726
48979CB00011B/2111/J

* 9 7 8 1 7 3 7 0 5 3 2 7 9 *